BEOWULF

BY STEPHAN GRUNDY

ISBN13: 978-1-959350-25-5

©The Three Little Sisters
USA/CANADA

I

Wealhtheow awoke to the soft pattering of mist droplets dribbling down from the thick woolen edges of her tent to the wet earth. Although it was dark within the tent, she could smell the damp scent of dawn already, overlaid with the tang of the cooking fires' smoke as the thralls who had come to serve her father's war band began to ready breakfast. Half a day's ride to Hrothgar's hall: then the rites of marriage would be carried out, to seal the truce that had been bought with her betrothal to the Scylding war leader. Wealhtheow did not fear her oaths of marriage, nor what would come several hours later, in the darkness of Hrothgar's bedchamber: the trembling deep in the marrow of her slim bones stemmed from awaiting the feast in between, when men who had slain each other's brothers and sons, fathers and kinsmen, sat on the benches together with swords at their sides, filling themselves with all the ale the wealthy Hrothgar could give, until they grew merry or blood was shed.

A wedding was hardly to be counted worthy of the name if a few fights did not break out at the feast; this time, however, it would not be men bloodying each other's noses and biting off ears, but men bloodying their swords in each other's bodies, with those around them more likely to join the fight than to laugh and place wagers. Frige, frith weaver, Wealhtheow prayed, twisting her hands about each other to stop their shaking. *I have been offered up as geld to end a feud: let that price be enough to hold the frith tonight, when I must bear the ale about between men who have good cause to hate each other.* Calmer, she pushed her loose hair back behind her ears and unfastened the thongs holding her tent flap tight against the mist, bending to creep out into the gray light of dawn. As the chill damp air struck Wealhtheow's face, she shivered, reaching back for a cloak to wrap over her linen shift.

Most of the men of Hadulf's war band were up already, only a few stragglers still crawling out of their tents with eyes squinting against the sudden brightness. Wealhtheow walked briskly through the camp, although the savory smells of frying sausages and porridge brought a keen pang of hunger to her belly and set the waters flowing in her mouth. Hadulf had set up beside a small, swiftly flowing stream that led out of the woods, and Wealhtheow walked along its banks until she was out of the men's sight, though not so far that she could not hear their voices ringing distantly through the bare gray branches of the beech trees growing thickly about her. If an outlaw or foe should come upon her she was a strong woman, with a good dagger on her belt to defend herself against a first attack, and a single scream would bring the whole war band to her aid. But this was her wedding day, and she would not go unwashed to meet a groom she had never seen.

Laying aside her thick dark cloak and stripping her shift from her, Wealhtheow knelt on a thick bed of moss beside the stream, dipping her cupped hands in to pour icy handfuls of water over her shivering body. The water's bite was sharp on her goose pimpled skin, her nipples standing out hard and almost purple from its cold touch. She scrubbed herself as hard as she could to awaken and move the warm blood within her, until her skin tingled with cleanness. She would not come to Hrothgar pale and wan, as though she had spent the night on a grave mound; she would be flushed with health and good color, as if meeting a long awaited love. When her body was clean, Wealhtheow leaned down with her long honey brown hair cast forward, lowering it slowly into the stream until the water's cold stabbed sharply around her skull like a crown of ice, then withdrawing it and wringing out the sodden mass. Putting on her shift and cloak again, Wealhtheow cast her hair back and walked to the camp again, pausing by one of the fires with her hands out over it until the warmth crept slowly back into her frozen fingers.

Though most of Hadulf's men had known her since her girlhood, they were oddly quiet now, looking away from her gaze as though they felt some shame before her. Of course: how could Halga, whose handsome face had been forever scarred to ugliness by the sword stroke that had put out his eye in the same battle in which his brother had fallen, come to her and wish her joy in her marriage with the man who had led his foes that day? Or Hrethbert, who fought with a shield strapped to the stump of his right arm now because of Hrothgar; or Beorn, who had vowed to slay one of Hrothgar's men for each gash he counted in his father's body when the bloodied corpse was borne to the pyre? They had all taken an oath to hold the frith of the wedding holy, else they would have been told to stay behind on this faring, but it was too much to ask them to be joyful about it as well. Wealhtheow ate quickly and silently.

The men were already beginning to take down their tents, to saddle and load the horses. She would have to hurry in readying herself not because any of them, even her father, would say anything if she made them stand for an hour while she combed her hair and arranged her jewelry, but because the less time they had to think and mutter, the less they could brood on all the wrongs Hrothgar had done to them and their kin. And she wanted them to think well of her, today of all days; for kindness to her might hold their rough tongues and hot tempers back that night, when the ale had washed away all considerations of the good that would come from ending the long feud between Hadulf and Hrothgar. When she finally came out of her tent again, however, Wealhtheow was adorned as befitted a drighten's daughter on her bridal day. She wore a dress of bright red linen over a white linen shift, embroidered at neck and cuffs and sleeves with golden thread and shining white horsehair. Her arms were bedecked with twisted rings of gold, gleaming hotly against her white sleeves, and her hair was braided back into a single thick plait.

Upon the full swell of her bosom jingled a gold linked necklace of bracteates thirty thin discs of gold, embossed with the swirling images of gods and men and beasts, bought from the great temple on the island God Home to bring her luck and blessing and her strong fingers were weighted with the gold serpent coils of rings. That jewelry, together with the wedding gifts that Hrothgar would give her, was Wealhtheow's safety and surety in case anything should ever go amiss between herself and her husband: he could not turn her, wretched and poor, onto the wet roads of the wilderness, but if she left, she would go as a wealthy frowe of high birth.

The men were loaded and mounted already. At her nod, three of the thralls set to pulling out her tent stakes, lowering the carven cross pieces and wrapping them in the tent's thick woolen cover. Wealhtheow went to her white mare who stood saddled and ready, the silver pieces adorning her tack gleaming dully through the morning mist, and mounted up. Hadulf flicked his fingers lightly against the reins of his bay gelding, wheeling the horse to ride back to her. Though they were to be going in a feast of frith, he wore full armor nevertheless, well polished chain mail shirt clinking as he moved and the hammered gold of his helm's stylized eyebrows and mustaches glinting bright from the duller sheen of the iron.

"Are you ready, daughter?" He asked.

"I am ready," Wealhtheow said.

"Let us go, then."

The mist thinned slowly as the Sun rose higher, showing faintly through the gray sky like the gleam of a round white shield in the fog. The horses' hooves thudded dull into the damp leaf mold as they skirted the edge of the wood; that, and the jingling of the men's byrnies and the soft dripping of mist from the bare twigs, were the only sounds to be heard as Wealhtheow rode towards Heorot. Though Wealhtheow did not know why, she could feel the hairs prickling up on her neck as though something were watching them from behind the thin gray tatters of mist drifting across the meadows that stretched away from the forest.

Hrothgar's scouts, perhaps? She had often heard her father's men speak of how such a feeling had pricked them to awareness in time to meet a hidden ambush: no one doubted that a man's gaze, for good or ill, held all his might. But as another shiver rippled down her spine, she realized that she was sure though how she could be, she did not know that whatever waited in the darkness where the mist still lay too thickly for sight to pierce was nothing human. Without thinking, Wealhtheow made the sign of Thunar's Hammer, the mighty weapon that warded the Middle Garth against eotens and thurses and trolls, all the kin of the great eoten Yma who ever lurked at the borders of the earth to threaten men and gods.

For now that the edge between summer and winter had been crossed, the dark things grew ever closer to the Middle Garth, and so it would be until Yule, when the Sun had fallen to her lowest ebb and the ways between the world stood open. Wealhtheow would not have chosen a Winter nights wedding for herself, but the truce between Hrothgar and Hadulf had come at the end of a summer of strife, sworn and sealed just in time to stave off the last battle before all their men had to come back to their own fields to get the harvest in. Before departing, Hadulf's folk had slaughtered their beasts and held their own Winter nights feast; Hrothgar would hold his tonight.

But this is the feast of Frea Ing the Frith Giver, and of the alfs and idises, all our ancestors who gather to take their children's offerings for another year of fruitfulness and weal, Wealhtheow reminded herself. What better time for a frith weaver's wedding? Still, she wished with all her heart that the woods they rode past were springing with fresh green leaves, rather than bare and gray with the mist beading upon their last brown leaves; that the earth beneath blossomed with flowers, rather than pale mushrooms and red capped toadstools; and that the Sun could shine down on her in summer's first brightness, instead of glowing dim and half hidden behind the shifting veils of cloud.

Although the mist had faded to a thin haze over the fields by noon, Wealhtheow heard the sea long before she saw it the far off crashing of wave on rock, the hollow booming of water beating against a cliff face. Hadulf lifted his head, and though his helm hid his face, Wealhtheow could see how the muscles of his shoulders tightened beneath his chain mail, like the rippling muscles of a snake suddenly tensing beneath its shining armor of scales.

"Soon," Wealhtheow's father said quietly to her, "we shall be at the barrows of Hrothgar's forebears. It is near enough to mid day; he should be there to meet us, and have the stead made ready to seal your wedding on the spot."

Wealhtheow nodded, following him as he reined his horse about to follow the well trodden track through the sparse grass. They rode on, rounding a low hill. As they came about its curve, Wealhtheow lifted her head in sudden delight. From here, the land sloped down swiftly onto a wide white beach, and beyond lay the sea gray blue waves maned with white froth, glittering in the sudden brightness as a cloud passed from the face of the Sun. There were no boats to be seen on the wide blue field; only the water tossing endlessly, farther than her eyes could see. And beyond that? The lands of the Geats and Swedes lay to the north, those of the Angles and Jutes to the south and south west, but none had sailed farther to the west and come back to tell of it.

A sudden longing seized Wealhtheow's heart, though she did not know for what; it was as if a gleam danced upon the waters, just out of her sight's reach, luring her onward. To ride the wave horse, the ship's deck rocking beneath her and the salt spray in her face, following the mewing of the white gulls and gray terns that circled high above her. Wealhtheow sighed, turning her gaze resolutely to the sandy track before her. There was enough for her to think on this day without chasing alf dreams as if her soul could flee the duties that lay before her. Better to turn her mind to the words that she would have to speak that night to calm the hearts of feasting foemen, the speech runes and soul runes that would weave her web of frith over Hrothgar's hall.

"Look ahead," Hadulf said to his daughter. "You see: Hrothgar's folk are already gathered by the barrows; there, above that great stone on the beach."

Wealhtheow strained her eyes, gazing forward. The low green heaps of the two grave mounds were still half hidden by light mist, but through that grey film, she could see the gleam of metal, and the white flashes of linen dresses, like the half seen shapes of light alfs at summer's beginning.

"His women are with him," she said. "That bodes well."

Hadulf reached over to pat Wealhtheow's shoulder, his heavy ringed hand gentle on her.

"That is well seen, and you are right. Be easy, daughter, for you have nothing to fear."

As they rode closer to the two barrows above the tall gray stone, Wealhtheow could see the throng more clearly. Like her father's men, Hrothgar's also wore their armor, bright byrnies and boar crested helms and shining hilted swords, but by every man's side was a woman, dressed in white or golden linen and holding a basket. Apples and blackberries and red rowan berries; rounds of braided bread and the succulent orange trumpet shapes of mushrooms; green fronds of hwanna and a few sprays of late blooming flowers woven into sheaves of wheat and dried linen blossoms; the folk were clearly gathered with nothing else than a wedding and Winter nights feast in mind, and Wealhtheow began to breathe a little more easily.

Then her heart caught in her chest, for one man stepped forward from between the mounds with a spear in his hand, uplifted as though he meant to cast it over them, and she could see nothing of kindness or rejoicing in his grim thin featured face. He wore no helmet, his silver streaked brown hair flowing thick and free over his shoulders; his graying beard was long, but braided into a single narrow plait. Meeting his gaze, Wealhtheow shuddered. His eyes were deep gray, almost black, shining with the thoughtless cruelty of a raven gazing on the bodies of battle slain men. His blue black cloak billowed behind him in the fresh sea wind, and when he spoke, his voice was harsh as the cry of a carrion bird.

"You come here well arrayed for a feast of frith, with weapons by your sides," he called out to Hadulf's host. "Better that those who come to buy a truce with their own bloodlines should approach more humbly. Lay your swords aside, before you step within the hallowed garth bounded by the barrows of the fathers of the Scyldings!"

"What right have you," Hadulf roared back, "to ask such terms of us? If Hrothgar asks me to set my sword aside, and will do the same himself, I may. But we do not come as beggars, nor cowed, to barter the greater worth for the lesser out of fear. Let Hrothgar meet me as befits the man who wishes to be my son by marriage: I will not bandy words with you longer, Unferth, though you be Hrothgar's thule upon the Scylding howes!"

Unferth stood regarding them, his gaze lingering longest on Wealhtheow. She stared down from her horse at him, unwilling to turn her eyes away while he still watched her. Strangely, the first fear that had come over her faded even as she remembered what she had heard of him. Unferth Brother Bane, Hrothgar's thule, who stood upon the mounds of the Scyldings to speak with the voices of the dead; Unferth Wodensman, harsh and cruel tongued as the god he served, but touched by the god and hence holy and honored within Hrothgar's hall. Suddenly it seemed to Wealhtheow that it was she who Unferth challenged, though he spoke to her father; it was she who sought to come within the ring bounded by the bones of Hrothgar's forebears, and she who should reply. Wealhtheow slipped down from the back of her mare, walking towards Unferth until she stood face to face with him.

"See, I come unarmed," she said, loudly enough for all the gathered folk, both Hrothgar's and Hadulf's, to hear. "I come to my wedding feast, for I am to be the frowe of the Scyldings' hall and your frowe as well. And this I swear to you, Unferth: that when the vows have been spoken and I have taken my place in the high seat beside my husband in Heorot, it is to you that I shall bear the first cup of frith, as a sign of the friendship I wish to hold with you while we live. But do not ask my father and his men to set their weapons aside, for even those hallowed dead who tread beneath Walhall's roof timbers bear their swords with them, following the rede of your own friend god Woden."

Unferth stood looking down at her he was a tall man, though thin. His grip tightened on his carven spear shaft, and the wiry muscles of his arm bulged out like the corded strands of heavy rope beneath the deep blue sleeve of his tunic. Suddenly he smiled, the look transfiguring his narrow face.

"Well answered, Wealhtheow. Come within, and all your kin and thanes with you, for you shall be a worthy frowe for Heorot." He stepped aside, letting Wealhtheow step into the ring of folk.

Although she had never seen Hrothgar before, Wealhtheow knew him at once. He stood above the rest, a little way up the northward barrow with his back to the sea. Though no more than a finger's width taller than Wealhtheow, his shoulders and chest were broad and powerful beneath the glittering rings of his mail, and his thick arms bore nearly a shield's weight of gold rings. Wealhtheow knew that Hrothgar was in his mid forties, only a few years younger than her own father, but the hair and beard whose curls edged his boar crested helm had already gone pure silver. Beside him, a white fleeced ram stood tethered to the ground, calmly cropping the grass of the howe.

To Wealhtheow's surprise, there was a woman waiting by the ram as well, holding a keen bladed knife whose hilt was a large Northern whale's tooth, a dark wooden bowl carved with rune staves and wide eyed faces, and a crown woven of gold leafed birch twigs. The woman wore a plain white dress, but her breasts and shoulders were covered by a mass of amber necklaces, glinting in every shade from peat dark to ale ruddy to the smooth yellow white of butter. Her long reddish gold hair flowed free down her back, and her gilded belt clasp showed the figure of a cat writhing about itself, garnet chip eyes half covered by a paw or was it drawing the paw away to reveal its fearsome gaze?

As she moved, Wealhtheow heard a faint chiming sound: the dress was not so plain as it appeared, for its hem was fringed with a great many thin and finely worked gold plates. Wealhtheow breathed deeply, for now she realized the honor Hrothgar had done her. Honor, and a clever surety against treachery on the part of his bride's family: Hrothgar had brought one of the gudhijas from God Home to hallow and witness their wedding, and in her sight, none would dare to break the frith of the feast, or raise any strife against the vows they spoke. Hrothgar lifted his helmet from his head, handing it to a small, dark haired boy who stepped forward to cradle the weighty helm in his arms. Despite the silver of his curly hair and short beard, Hrothgar's face was only slightly worn, the first creases of forehead and eye corners just beginning to grave themselves deeply into his weathered skin. His features were blunt, heavy of nose and jaw, but not ill made, and Wealhtheow found herself warming to his hearty smile even as she answered it.

"Hail and welcome, Wealhtheow, my bride," Hrothgar said. His voice was strong and pure, its bright resonance ringing between the barrows like the sounding of a brass gong. "Gladly are you met here, in the howe stead of the Scyldings, that war may end with our wedding."

"Hail and welcome, Hrothgar, my husband," Wealhtheow replied. "Gladly I have come, to dwell in happiness in your hall, and bring frith between our folk." She walked up to him. As the sole of her shoe touched the edge of the mound, she felt a strange thrilling through her foot, as though a hive of bees hummed against the thin leather like a great wyrm hissing, deep within the howe. Yet there was no ill in it: whatever might waited within the Scylding barrow, it was no foe to Hrothgar or his bride. The gudhija's blue green eyes met Wealhtheow's a moment, and her lips curved slowly into a secretive smile, as though some thought of her own amused her richly.

She set the gold leafed crown on Wealhtheow's head, then lifted a hand, gesturing to Unferth. The thule came to stand on the other side of the couple as Hadulf walked up before them.

"Hrothgar and Hadulf, you would weave wedding from strife," Unferth said roughly. "The living have made truce and set terms. Say, before the gathered folk and the gods: what are they?"

Hadulf spoke first, then Hrothgar, laying out the details of the peace they had forged between them before sealing Wealhtheow's betrothal to the Scylding drighten. Payments made, each to the other; land given, land taken, and the right of the children of Wealhtheow and Hrothgar to inherit all. Hrothgar paused only for a heartbeat as they spoke of inheritances, his blue eyes flickering down to the boy who still held his helmet, though the child's thin arms were beginning to shake with the weight. A by blow, a thrall's get? Wealhtheow wondered. No, the boy was too well dressed for that, his golden tunic adorned with fine red embroidery and a large gold pin holding his rust brown cloak at his shoulder. Some other kin, or noble fosterling: she would find out as soon as she might, since she, most likely, would have to be mother to the boy before she ever bore her own bairns.

"The living have their geld, and have named it fair enough," Unferth said, wrenching Wealhtheow's mind away from the mystery of Hrothgar's little helm bearer. The thule lifted his spear; behind her, Wealhtheow thought she heard the jingling of armour and sword rings, as though her father's men were putting hands to hilts. "But what of the dead? Eofer and Aelfred, who fell fighting Hadulf what has been offered to them, that their ghosts may not rise in wrath at the foe sitting at the benches where they once drank with their friends?"

"Eofer's blood I avenged myself," Hrothgar replied. "Aelfred died slaying his slayer; a red gold ring I gave to his mother, though little it might soothe her at the loss of her son."

"What of Sigberht and Osfrith? What geld have they gotten, that they may let Hadulf and his thanes pass through Heorot's high timbered door?"

Wealhtheow listened to the litany of names and repayments, half entranced, half horrified. Behind her she heard the rustling and muttering of men, whether Hadulf's or Hrothgar's or both, she did not know. How can I hope to hold the frith tonight, when every word of Unferth's scores both sides with another bitter memory of bloodshed? She wondered. Though the air around the barrow was clear, it seemed to her as though she could almost see the ghosts drawing in to the sound of their names, the droplets of blood still gathering chill as dew upon their byrnies from their death wounds. And yet, for each name Unferth spoke, Hrothgar had the tale of a geld paid, in red blood or red rings of gold.

Slowly the mutterings settled, and Wealhtheow began to understand. With the tally full told, none of Hrothgar's men could arise that night to claim a kinsman unavenged or a weregild outstanding, nor could the ghosts themselves whisper in the drink dazed ears of the living to rouse dead battles to life. The gudhija waited quietly, white fingers stroking over the carvings on the whale tooth hilt of her knife, and Wealhtheow could not read the thoughts in her eyes, though they were as clear and blue green as sunlight through shallow waters.

"So the dead are full paid for their bane," Unferth said at last. "None will stand against this wedding, nor the feast that follows." He lowered his spear, stepping back, and Wealhtheow's breath hissed from her lungs in relief.

Now the gudhija spoke, her low sweet voice thrilling through Wealhtheow's body.

"Before the oaths are spoken, the gods should hear what kin are gathered here. Hadulf, tell the tale of your forebears, that all may know them."

"I, Hadulf, am the son of Hromund…" Hadulf went on for a little while, counting his ancestors and their great deeds. Wealhtheow hardly listened: she knew each name and tale better than she knew the coiled curves of the serpent ring on her smallest finger, which she had worn since she was a girl of ten winters. Hrothgar tilted his head as if in great interest, but his blue eyes sparkled with suppressed impatience, as though he could hardly wait his own turn to speak. That came soon enough: Hadulf finished the tale of his clan, and Hrothgar raised his powerful tenor in turn.

"Often Scyld Scefing took the mead benches of many clans, the hosts of his foes; the earls he awed, since foeship was first found. He offered comfort, grew under the clouds in glory, until all those about him, who heard of him over the whale roads, sent tribute geld to him: that was a

good king! To him came the mighty maid Geofe, she who plowed out
Sealand with her oxen in earliest days; and from their loins came forth
Beaw their son, whose renown sprang widely through all the Scylding
lands. Scyld knew the hour shaped for him, when the mighty one must fare
back to Frea Ing's keeping; his dear kinsmen bore him to the water's edge,
as he bade himself while his words still ruled, the friend of the Scyldings,
beloved land leader. There " Hrothgar gestured to the stone pillar on the
beach, down beyond the barrow "at the shore stood the ring prowed ship,
icy and eager, readied for the atheling.

Wealhtheow drew in her breath sharply, for now it seemed to her that
she could see it in truth, as though she looked through the rippling waters
of a clear well the long curve of the ship with its gracefully curled prow, the
old man propped on embroidered pillows by its tall mast. About him were
heaped great treasures, battle weapons and war garb, swords and byrnies,
and gold glittering everywhere among the steel, rings and chains woven
through it like the gleaming red scales of a dragon twining through the
hoard of weapons and armor.

"No less they let him have of allotted offerings," Hrothgar went on, "of
the folk treasures, than those did who in earliest of days sent him forth as a
child, alone over the waves."

It seemed to Wealhtheow that the dream of the treasure laden death
ship wavered in her sight, so that now she saw the old man drawing his
last gasping breaths beneath his golden standard, and now she saw the
fair haired child in his little boat, sleeping upon his shield with his head
pillowed upon a sheaf of wheat Scyld Scefing, drifting as a babe to shore
to answer the Dane folk's call for a true born king; Scyld Scefing, sent back
over the waves to that unknown realm from which he had come.

"Men cannot say truly neither hall counselors nor heroes under the
heavens who took him up at last," Hrothgar said. He kept speaking,
recounting the generations from Scyld to himself, Beaw and Healfdene,
whose bones lay within the two barrows.

But Wealhtheow was not listening: the sea still drew her gaze, though
she could no longer see Scyld's ship upon it, only the golden haze of
sunlight glittering from the waves. At last Hrothgar was still, and the
gudhija spoke again.

"Men make war, and women weave frith. Frige, bride of Woden, hear;
come thou to bless this wedding! Frowe, necklace adorned and fairest of
all: hear thou, come to bless this wedding! Frea Ing, mighty boar warder,
giver of harvests and fruitful peace: hear thou, come to bless this wedding!

Hrothgar and Wealhtheow, swear your oaths on the back of the white ram whose fleece Frige spins for her weaving in Fen Halls, that he may bear your vows between the worlds, as you have spoken them before gods and alfs and folk."

Hrothgar stooped to lay his hand on the ram's thick wooled back.

"Wealhtheow Hadulf's daughter, I swear to take you as wife and hold you in gladness through your days. Bed and board and hearth I give into your keeping, for you shall be frowe in Heorot henceforth."

Wealhtheow put her hand on the ram beside Hrothgar's. Through the heavy pelt, she could feel the sheep's breaths coming quicker, its heartbeat thrumming deep through its blood paths; though the dirt and muck had been washed from its wool, she could still smell its warm, musty scent.

"Hrothgar Healfdene's son, I swear to be a good wife to you, biding with you in gladness through your days. Bed and board and hearth I shall hold well for you, as frowe in Heorot henceforth."

The gudhija nodded to Hrothgar; he shifted position, taking a firm grip on the sheep's shoulders as she lifted her knife, driving it swiftly in at the point behind the ram's jawbone and slicing outward. The ram's legs kicked, its body twisting as the bright blood gouted out of its throat and into the blessing bowl, but Hrothgar held it fast while the life bubbled from its lungs, lowering it at last to the ground. The gudhija dipped her fingers into the bowl; the blood was already congealing, but she marked the foreheads of bride and groom with it.

Hrothgar's gaze met Wealhtheow's across the limp white body of the ram, his blue eyes utterly bright and clear in his solemn face as he drew the large bunch of iron keys from his gold embroidered belt pouch and lifted them towards her. Wealhtheow's hand trembled as she took them and threaded them onto her belt: by this act, Hrothgar gave and she took up queenship over his hall and lands. It is no little thing, she thought, for him to have chosen marriage as the means of sealing truce.

"So it is seen and witnessed," the gudhija said. She did not pour the blessing blood out on the earth then, as Wealhtheow had thought she would, but instead walked about the barrow, down to the stone on the beach that marked the site of Scyld Scefing's last faring, and tipped it out over stone and sand, where, at high tide, the waves would wash it clean. When she came back, her hands were lifted high, dark bowl and red sheened knife gleaming in the sunlight. "Hrothgar, bear your bride forth to her hall."

Hrothgar's strong shield arm reached around Wealhtheow's back; his sword arm swept down behind her knees, lifting her easily off her feet. A cheer went up from the gathered folk as he carried her out of their ring and along the pathway. Heorot stood within a ringed palisade of sharpened poles, the gilded carvings of its roof beams shining out above the lesser buildings that surrounded it. Upon its gables were mounted the high swept, many tined antlers of red deer from which the hall took its name Heorot, the Hart and the points of the antlers glittered bright with gold. Though her father was not lacking in wealth or lands, Wealhtheow had never seen such a great burg as this. It seemed fit for the very gods to dwell in but was Hrothgar not sprung from the land goddess Geofe, as he had told himself?

The byrnied gate guards lifted their spears in salute as Hrothgar bore his bride in. Though not a small woman, Wealhtheow felt cloud light in her husband's powerful arms: he carried her steadily, without quiver or falter, straight through the doors of Heorot and up to the twin high seats that stood, raised on a dais above the rest, at the end of the great hall. There he set her in her throne, and took his own place beside her as his folk and the men of Hadulf's war band followed them in. There was a second seat on Wealhtheow's other side, but it was empty: she guessed that it must have been set there for the gudhija. By Hrothgar's side was a large chair, which Wealhtheow thought her father would sit in, and a smaller one between the two. At Hrothgar's feet stood a large three legged stool, its thick black legs carven into the shapes of twisting wyrms. Unferth took his place beside the stool, but did not sit yet. Instead, when everyone was inside, he raised his spear and shouted,

"Hail to Hrothgar, drighten of Heorot! Hail to Wealhtheow, frowe of Heorot!"

"Hail!" The cheer shook the rafters, and Wealhtheow felt the blush warming on her cheeks as though she had stood too long in the sunlight.

Yet, though all those gathered there, Hrothgar's men and Hadulf's alike, were smiling, it seemed to her that the glimmer of burning coals was not held to the long fire pits down either side of the hall, but rather that the treacherous writhing of the glow beneath every stirring of the air covered the whole straw strewn floor, a bed of fire only lightly banked, waiting for the first strong wind to stir it into flames that would eat the wooden walls, chewing up the pillars like rising waves of hot brightness to drop the roof and devour the high arched antlers cresting the gables' ends.

Almost against her will, she found her gaze flickering to Unferth's grim face, remembering the words of Woden: *I know that seventh song: if I see high flames in the many seated hall, it does not burn so broadly but that I can still it: I know how to sing that song.* Upon the table before the high seats was a pitcher of fine Southern glass, milky streams trailing through the clear crystal like the draping edges of a misted spiderweb, and it was filled to the brim with golden mead; beside it were two matching goblets.

She took up one of these now, pouring the mead into it, and walked around the table to Unferth as he sat down upon his stool.

"Behold, Unferth, I am able to keep my oath to you already. Thule of Heorot, take this draught from my hands, that there be frith between us for aye. Wise redes in council, and runes of understanding, for the weal of Heorot and the health of Hrothgar: this do I offer, in trust that you will give the same in turn."

Unferth took the goblet from her, turning its stem in his long fingers as he looked into its clear golden depths. His dark eyebrows drew together, furrowing his forehead so deeply that it almost seemed to Wealhtheow that she could see the sharp staves of his thought runes graven upon his face. *Does he see, in that mead, the same thing that I saw in the fire?* She wondered. *But it takes little wisdom to know that two bands of foes, even under oath of frith, are no safer to stir than a nest of sleeping adders. Yet if he stands with me, I think we can hold Heorot this night.* The thule looked up at Wealhtheow, his dark eyes holding her as surely as though he had gripped her with all his warrior's strength.

"We can," Unferth said, so softly that Wealhtheow was sure none but herself could hear his words. Louder, he answered, "Wise redes and wise runes: for long Woden has given Hrothgar his gifts in all battles, and rule over the lands of his forebears. Now that sword and spear may rest for a little time, it is well that Frige's words may be heard within Hrothgar's hall, for even the great drighten of the gods goes often to seek the counsel of fore sighted women. In their names, I drink to frith between us for aye, Wealhtheow Hadulf's daughter." Unferth lifted the goblet; she could see the sharp edged lump of his voice box moving as he drained the mead in a single draught.

Only then did Wealhtheow think how it must look, for a new bride to give the first cup not to her husband, lord of the hall, but to the man who sat at his feet. Suddenly afraid, she glanced guiltily up at Hrothgar, but he only smiled down at her, as though he understood well enough. And when she filled the goblet again to bear it to him, he wrapped his strong warm fingers around her cold ones on the stem of the glass, drawing her closer to him.

"That was well done," he whispered. "My worst fear was of strife between you and Unferth."

Then, before he drank of the mead, Hrothgar pulled Wealhtheow to him with an arm about her waist and kissed her, long and thoroughly. At first her mouth was stiff and clumsy beneath his, for she had never been kissed so, but it was strangely pleasant to feel his lips hot and firm upon hers, the soft curls of his short beard brushing against her cheeks and the strength of his arm holding her fast to him. Wealhtheow's breath was coming more quickly when Hrothgar let her go, lifting up the goblet and saying, "Fair built is Heorot; wide are my lands, and mighty my thanes. Yet none would fulfill all my joy, if it were not for the frowe who rules now by my side."

He drank the goblet half off, giving it back to Wealhtheow so that she might finish the draught. As she drank, the sweet mead flowing warm down her throat, she saw a darker glimmer through the milk trailed clearness of the glass. On the small seat beside Hrothgar and her father sat the child who had borne the drighten's helm through the wedding, his pale blue eyes fixed steadily on hers. For him she filled the goblet half full, cursing herself that she had not been able to ask his name yet.

"Gladly I bear this draught to you, young atheling," Wealhtheow said to the boy. "You bore Hrothgar's helm well and strongly: may you always uphold him so bravely."

"That I shall, while he and I live," the child answered. His voice was strong, a low alto with the promise of future power in its depths. "I am Hrothulf, son of Halga Hrothgar's brother. Though my father was slain, I have found a second father within this hall." He drank quickly, as though he were trying to match a man's draught; Wealhtheow saw his small face tighten with the struggle not to cough, but he mastered himself quickly, swallowing hard and waiting for his throat to clear before he spoke again.

"My thanks for your kindness, frowe Wealhtheow."

"It is always yours," she replied.

Then it was Wealhtheow's duty to bear the pitcher about the hall, with fitting words for each man: to her father, then between his thanes and Hrothgar's alike, taking care that neither side might feel itself scanted. With her mother, she had often poured drink for her father's men in his hall, for it was the honor of an atheling frowe to thus greet thane and guest: even as a drighten dealt out gold rings from his own arms, so a frowe dealt out mead and ale, her touch and her words uplifting those who drank from her pitcher and binding their troth to her. Although here, where she had to ask after the names of more than half the men and the wives and daughters who sat, braided and adorned beside them and try to link them swiftly to faces, one after the other, lest any feel himself slighted afterwards when she could not remember who he was at once she felt that she was treading a dance among half burned coals, yet it was a dance she knew well, and her mother had taught her to perform it with no small skill.

Other maidens hurried behind Wealhtheow, their skirts rustling through the fresh straw on the floor, so that her glass pitcher was never empty for more than a heartbeat, nor did those she had served first find that their horns were dry before she had finished her round of the hall. That done, she could seat herself again, sipping slowly at her own goblet as she looked about herself. Heorot was as splendid within as without, the carvings of the beams and the great pillars upholding the roof picked out with gilding and, here and there, the blood dark glint of a garnet. Upon the roof beams were graven scenes from a tale that every dweller on Sealand knew well.

Here the goddess Geofe, disguised as an old crone, bent before the high seat of the Swedish king Gilpa; Gilpa's wooden mouth was open in laughter at the tale she was telling him. Her reward: as much land as she could plough around in a day and a night the next scene showed Geofe at her plough with the four oxen sons she had gotten with an eoten, the steam of their breath swirling wildly from their nostrils as she whipped them on. Next, Geofe sitting on her high seat with the waves curling at her feet and trees behind: her sons had ploughed so deeply that they had cut Sealand away from the earth, towing it into the ocean where it sat as an island now. The last scene was a wedding, Geofe standing with her hands twined in those of a tall man with a gilded beard Scyld Scefing, before whose feet lay the shield and sheaf of his name, their gold glinting bright where it reflected the shimmering firelight.

Wealhtheow marked then that her own high seat was carved with oxen, their high horned heads upholding its arms, while Hrothgar's was adorned with gilded sheaves. Again, she found herself marveling at the honor Hrothgar had given her, that he should have set her in the place of Sealand's land goddess. But why not? She was born of Sealand's soil, and it was through her that Geofe's blessings would be spread to Hrothgar's folk, if she proved worthy to bear them. Wealhtheow's gaze slipped sideways. Unnoticed, the gudhija had taken her place; now she smiled at the younger woman, as if to agree with Wealhtheow's thoughts. Yet there was a distant look in the gudhija's blue green eyes, as if she were already weighing the new frowe's worth from far away far enough not to be caught up in the excitement of the wedding, or to hear the words that Wealhtheow had spoken. Something in her look stirred Wealhtheow to uneasiness, so that she turned to the other woman and said,

"You do us great honor, to have come to this wedding."

"I came because I was bidden," the gudhija replied.

"Will you…" Wealhtheow gulped, but having begun, she could not stop. "Gudhija, will you fore see for us this night?"

The gudhija looked cooly over the hall, her gaze lingering for a moment on Unferth before she turned back to Wealhtheow.

"You do not wish me to. The threads tremble in Wyrd's web here, for Hrothgar wrought a thing of greater might than he knew in Heorot's building. Best to take them into your own hands, and deal yourself with what is shaped: for what I see and speak may warp them otherwise."

"I thank you," Wealhtheow said, though she did not know what for.

It was not long until the food was brought in maidens carrying plates of wreath braided bread, bowls of berries, and platters heaped high with fat glistening coils of dark and light sausages; men heaving the roasted carcases of sheep and ox. Wealhtheow's head swam as she breathed deeply of the savory odors, and she realized that she was almost faint with hunger, for she had not eaten since her early breakfast. Hrothgar rose to claim the finest cuts from the ox's back for the high table, slicing the thick slabs of meat off with his gold hilted dagger and heaping them onto silver platters as Wealhtheow cut her own portion from the steaming loaf of fresh white wheat bread before her.

The roast was delicious, cooked with strips of leek and spear leak threaded deeply into it so that their flavor spread throughout the meat beneath the brown crackling fat. Mindful that she was being watched, Wealhtheow forced herself to eat slowly, chewing each tender morsel thoroughly and sopping up the rich juices on her platter with her bread. She was careful of her drinking, as well, for she knew that the honey brewed mead was stronger even than festival ale and would mount quickly to her head: she did not think the men in the hall would take such care, for it was only right that a feast should be marked by good drunkenness, but it was her duty to keep her thoughts clear in case her words were suddenly needed.

When she had satisfied her first hunger, Wealhtheow rose with her pitcher of mead to begin another round of the hall. Most of the feasters were too busy at their eating to do more than acknowledge her with a nod and a smile, for which she was much relieved. But as she came towards the far end of one of the long tables, she heard the sound of two men's voices beginning to rise, their undertone of anger ominous as the low humming of a roused swarm of bees. One voice was unmistakably that of her father's man Halga, for the scar running from his ruined eye socket to his chin had twisted his mouth enough to slur his speech a little; the other she did not know.

"My knife was in that slice first," Halga said. "Give over; there is more than enough left for you."

"And I should let a wolf take his plunder even in my drighten's own hall?" The second man replied. "I reached for it first, so it is you who should find another."

The fires were burning lower at this end of the hall: Wealhtheow blinked against the shadows, following the gazes of the other feasters who were beginning to lift their heads and look towards the voices in hopes of a fight? Halga's lean cloaked shape was silhouetted against the glow of the coals; he and a shorter, broader man with a thick braid of red brown hair stood facing each other across the table end, their knives both stabbed deep into a slab of meat on the platter between them. No battle so quick, as when knives are already out, Wealhtheow's mother had told her.

"What marks of battle do you bear?" Halga asked. The rippled pink rivulet of scar tissue down his face was darkening as it always did when he grew angry, until it was red as if new healed. "I have slain more of Hrothgar's men than you of Hadulf's, I will wager: I have never shrunk from the fight, nor shall I draw back from you now, though you know nothing of the manners of host towards guest."

Wealhtheow did not stay to listen longer, but set her pitcher down and ran light footed down the hall to the high table, where she snatched two fine slices of meat and her own platter. Hurrying back, she knew she had moved none too quickly, for she just heard the voice of Hrothgar's man shouting, "...ugly face!" Her hand was on Halga's knife arm as he jerked it back from the platter; a heartbeat later, Wealhtheow knew, and he would have sheathed the blade in the other man's belly. Her strength would have hindered him little, but he checked himself at her touch, turning the violence of his thrust downwards into the heap of meat on the table again. Hrothgar's man had withdrawn his own blade, holding it point out towards his foe; he stared warily at the two of them for a moment, but his blue gaze turned downward under Wealhtheow's steady regard, and he lowered his knife.

"Hrothgar would be most saddened," Wealhtheow said quietly, "to think that, at his own wedding, he had not laden his board well enough for both his trusty thanes and his honored guests. Halga, and you " O Frige, what is his name?

"Wulfstan, my frowe," Hrothgar's man supplied quickly, a sudden shy smile curling beneath his beard for a moment.

"Leave that piece for another, for it is badly tattered now, and I have brought you each a better one myself." Wealhtheow laid one thick slice on each man's plate, smiling at both of them. "If Hrothgar's openhandedness is not to be slighted, surely there is no cause for quarrel between you, and a draught of good mead will wash away the memory of words spoken hastily and lightly." She fetched her pitcher, filling their horns.

"So it is, good frowe," Wulfstan acknowledged, and drank.

The glimmer of anger had not gone out of Halga's eye, but his scarred face softened as he looked at Wealhtheow.

"For your sake, frith," he said, and drank as well.

Wealhtheow laid her hand lightly on his ring mailed shoulder.

"Thank you," she murmured. She stayed there with the two of them, speaking lightly settling a clear layer of words over their quarrel like the winter's first ice thickening gelid on a lake's surface: if it would not bear much weight, at least a sudden wind would not whip the water into storm.

Hrothgar turned from his quiet speech with Unferth when Wealhtheow came back to her seat, raising a silver eyebrow at her.

"All is well," she told him. "It was only a misunderstanding, and the matter is settled now."

"Indeed?" He murmured. "Well, I shall trust in your judgment."

"You place much trust," she could not help saying, "in a woman you have hardly met."

Hrothgar laid a heavy ringed hand upon Wealhtheow's, his clear blue eyes looking straight into her own.

"I know that your mother is said to be one of the wisest of women, and your father's cunning has scathed me on the battlefield as many times as mine has scathed him. How, then, should their daughter not be worthy to bear the burden of Heorot's queenship? And you have already won Unferth's friendship, which is no small undertaking."

"He and I share the same goal," Wealhtheow replied, feeling herself suddenly flustered beneath her husband's gaze.

"And that is?" Hrothgar asked quietly.

"The weal of Heorot and its folk."

Hrothgar laughed, a warm soft sound that Wealhtheow found easing to her heart.

"Then I can place nothing but trust in you, my bride. And you have done very well already, for Wulfstan is a good thane, but hot tempered. He has come within a sword length of being outlawed twice already; nor did the man he was arguing with have the look of one who settles quarrels by quiet words."

You saw, and said nothing? Wealhtheow wondered. But it had been her place to still the strife between thane and guest: Hrothgar, she realized, had been testing her, as surely as he might test a skilled, but unblooded youth by sending him into the thick of battle to live or die by his own strength and luck. And he would not be such a great king if he were afraid of risks for his folk as well as himself.

"A drighten needs thanes of fierce heart about him," Wealhtheow said. "I have heard that hounds with a bit of wolf blood hunt the best, though they need the most skill to train and keep."

As if in answer, Hrothgar snapped his fingers, and a thick furred gray dog padded up between their seats: save for the twisted curl of its plumed tail and the breadth of its solid chest, it might have been a wolf itself. The drighten of Heorot passed down a piece of meat to the hound, which mouthed it from his hand, rolling deep brown eyes adoringly up at its master.

"That is true, for when Ecgtheow the Waegmunding gave Wulfa to me eight years ago a thanks gift, for I had sheltered him during his blood feud with the Wylfings he told me that her father was a wolf, and if I tended her carefully, I would find no hound more clever and eager in hunting the red deer than she. And she is to thank for most of the antlers that adorn this hall: though she is not as strong or swift as she was in her youth, she has grown more cunning with every year, and still leads pack and hunters to their quarry without fail."

Wealhtheow reached down cautiously to scratch behind the wolf dog's velvety ears. The bitch sat obediently, curly tail thumping on the straw strewn floor, and took the meat Wealhtheow offered her with a gentle lick.

"And thus you sleep warm in a fine hall, with good flesh in your belly and no lynx or bear to threaten your pups, hmm?" Wealhtheow said to her. "Is it better to hunt beside men, and be petted and praised by them, than to be hunted by them through the cold winter nights and steal your meat from their pens like a wretched outlaw?" Wulfa wagged her tail, as if to say that it was.

"The other dogs feared her at first," Hrothgar added, "but now half the hounds in the hall are her pups, and they love her dearly: even wolves care for their own kin."

Wealhtheow sat talking with her husband for a little longer. She already felt at home with him, as though they had been wedded for years; but beneath the comfort of Hrothgar's words and the warmth of the fire at her back, an uneasy tingling was creeping along her spine, as if a tendril of the cold night mist had drifted into Heorot. Many of the women and the older children had already left the hall, for the men were drinking in earnest now, and as the ale and mead flowed more swiftly, the tone of the feasters' voices was changing like the purr of a lynx shifting almost imperceptibly into a warning growl. Again she rose with her pitcher, bearing it about; and on her way between the tables she stopped for a few moments to speak with Hadulf's poet Alfric.

"Since you will be going back to my father's hall tomorrow," Wealhtheow said softly, looking down into the fair haired poet's blue eyes, "will you sing tonight? I have heard your harp at all the gladdest of Hadulf's feasts, and it would be a sorrowful thing to me if I had to bid you farewell without hearing it once more for my wedding."

"Of course, my frowe," Alfric replied. He unfastened the straps of his harp's deer hide case and drew the instrument out, brushing his fingers across the six long strings stretched over the carven maple wood sounding board. He winced at the jangling discord, fumbling in his belt pouch for the little tool he used to turn his tuning pegs, then bent close, plucking softly at the strings and adjusting them to suit himself. Wealhtheow waited beside him until he raised his head again, settling the harp into position on his lap, and brought his hand down across the strings to strike a startlingly loud chord that silenced the men around him, his clear baritone ringing out strongly through the stillness.

"Hwaet! You have heard of hoary Eormenric,
Wolf wild drighten, doom filled of mood.
Swanhild he wedded, Sigefrith's maid..."

Wealhtheow, taking up her pitcher again, frowned at the tale her father's poet had chosen: the old and unjust ruler of the Goths married to a young woman, whom he had killed on the advice of an evil counselor, and who was afterwards avenged by her brothers. This hardly seemed fit for a wedding, or Wealhtheow glanced up the hall, to the silvery gleam of Hrothgar's hair in the firelight and the shadowed shape of Unferth at his feet far too fit. But she could not stop Alfric now; the poet's eyes gleamed bright and clear as he stared through the smoky air of the hall into the realm of his song, and the words that flowed effortlessly from his open throat had already won the still hearing of all those around him.

To her relief, however, Alfric's was not the only harp in the hall that night. Two of Hrothgar's men, a tall, dark haired youth with bulging shoulders and scarred forearms and an old, white haired man whose eyes were pale with the dimming frost of age, were tuning their own instruments into readiness. Better a battle of harps than of swords, Wealhtheow said to herself, walking on to pour out more mead. Still, she was glad when she was far enough away to hear Alfric's song only as music and snatches of words, blurred by the speech of those who were not caught up in the poet's performance. Hrothgar was sitting quietly, leaning forward with an elbow braced on the table as he listened to Alfric.

"Your man sings well," he said softly to Wealhtheow when she took her seat again. But his heavy silver eyebrows were drawn together, and she knew that he had not missed the threat glinting in Alfric's song like the gleam of a dagger blade half hidden under a sleeve, even as the poet brought his tale to its end, with the death of Swanhild's brothers.

"Though Guthrun gave them gift of her spell craft, That no iron bite ever her sons, an old man, one eyed, offered Goths counsel: 'Stones will serve you where swords have failed.' Then Sorli fell slain before gable, and at the hindwall, Hamthir was slain."

The ringing of Alfric's last chord had hardly faded into the clamor of renewed speech before another voice rose to still the hall again. The young man who had been tuning his harp was singing now: his voice was harsher than Alfric's, but its high notes cut more clearly through the sounds of talking and drinking, and he was chanting a praise song to Hrothgar.

"Then was Hrothgar host strength given, fame in warring that friends and kinsmen heard of gladly. He fed ravens, strewed the field with feasts for wolves. None could boast in battle e'er to match him..."

Wealhtheow cringed inwardly as Hrothgar's poet went on to relate his drighten's victories: every man there knew that more than one of those battles had been fought against Hadulf, and Hadulf's thanes were beginning to mutter, the sound of their low voices giving the song a dark undertone like the pattering of a deep drum beneath the harp strings.

Wealhtheow could see the gleaming of their eyes in the torchlight, Hadulf's men glaring at Hrothgar's and Hrothgar's staring suspiciously back. She rose again, walking towards Alfric hoping to reach him before the song ended and he began another; but she had not moved quickly enough: she was only halfway to him when he struck a chord from his harp and sang,

"Dark was the dawn on day of the battle,
The hosts were gathered by Hama's Spring..."

Wealhtheow closed her eyes. The fight at Hama's Spring had been one of the last battles between Hadulf and Hrothgar a hard fought strife, in which many had fallen on both sides; neither had won ground, but Alfric, and undoubtedly Hrothgar's poets as well, had sung of it as a victory. The muttering was growing louder now, and she could see knuckles clenching white on the hilts of eating knives. I must put an end to this, she thought, glancing back towards the high seats. Hrothulf and her father sat still as carven god images, but Unferth leaned forward on his stool, and she could see the gleam of his teeth, the shadows gathering around his head like a ghostly hood.

"In Hrothgar's own hall..." someone hissed; another, "How dare he mock us..." and another, "Someone should..."

It seemed to Wealhtheow, standing in the middle of the hall, as though she were suddenly ringed about by wolves in the wood, circling and waiting for the pack leader to leap. She fought down the chill in her guts, the trembling of her hands, as she slowly drew two gold arm rings from her wrist, praying that no one would strike before she had a chance to speak. Alfric's fair cheeks were flushed, whether with mead or the hot bravery before battle Wealhtheow could not tell. But she saw that several of her father's men had moved closer to the poet, their eyes flickering about: one blade drawn, or even a fist lifted near him, and there would be open fighting in the hall. He flung down his last defiant chords, their sound sharp as a spear cast to signal battle's beginning, and in that moment Wealhtheow raised her own voice.

"It is well to sing of battles fought with honor, for the names of those who clashed sword on shield will be remembered forever," she said. "I thank you poets both, who sing the praises of your lords my father and my husband as is fitting." She tossed an arm ring to each of the singers; Alfric caught his neatly, but Hrothgar's poet, his mouth open in amazement, lifted his hand too late and fumbled his catch; the twisted gold circle skittered away from him and under the table, so that he had to duck and scuffle for it. Before he could raise his head again, Wealhtheow walked over to the old man who sat with his harp in his lap, his age dimmed eyes peering feebly towards her. "The young men have had their turn at singing, and raised the hot blood of youth. Will you now bless us with the wise songs of your age will you tell us of the strength of the gods, and the shaping of the worlds, to soothe our hearts and give good redes to our minds?"

"I will sing as you please, queen of Heorot," the old poet answered. Even as he spoke, Wealhtheow knew she had been right in asking him. No age crackled in his deep voice: it was smooth and soft as ermine fur, and though he had seemed to speak quietly, strong enough to ring through every corner of the hall. The dark polished wood of his harp was adorned with gilt mounts, finely wrought images of eagles and boars, and the bridge holding the strings was carven of butter amber. When he set his fingers to it, the music rippled through Heorot's rafters like the shimmering of air above a great fire, and the last drunken voices were silent.

"Yma dwelt in earliest days: No sand nor sea nor salt chill waves, there was no earth nor upper heavens. A gaping chasmn of grass sprang forth..."

Wealhtheow shivered. The harp's low thrumming beneath the poet's deep voice showed her, as if she stood in the depths of a dream the great black abyss, lit only by the flaring sparks that shot from the seething fire on one side to burn and die like falling stars in the darkness, their light gleaming briefly across the void, reflected greenish white from the slopes of the huge glacier across the Gap.

Rime edged rivers mightier than any on earth plunged, muddy with yeast and venom, over that icy edge, seething into the blackness...and from their mists a pale shadow took shape, a great distorted man figure with fire spark eyes. Yma, the eldest of the eoten kind, father of all eotens and thurses and trolls; all the dark nightwalkers, born of the cold fog that whirled over the Gap before Sun ever shone on the green earth. For ages Yma and his kin dwelt between fire and ice, but at last the gods arose, bright, to do battle: Woden in his youth, his two eyes gleaming like the points of twin spears, and his brothers Will and Wih beside him.

Their blades pierced the old eoten's frost rimed hide, his cold salty blood gushing forth in torrents that rose to fill the Gap with storm whipped waves, whelming the great brood of his children as they struggled and swam and sank. Yet two escaped, cast up on the harsh shores of ice: there, bounded by the sea of their father's blood, the eoten Bergelmir and his bride dwelt upon the glacier's edge, and began in the darkness to breed their own kind once more. But the gods, their battle won, turned to their shaping: Yma's bones became stone, his hair grew into trees. They fixed the flaring sparks in the sky as stars, they set greater flames as Sun and Moon. The Sun shone from southward onto the new earth, and green grasses and leeks sprang forth as the ice melted from the crags and crannies of Yma's skin: thus the Middle Garth, the home of men, was made.

"Bright shining fields bounded by water, Sig glorious gods set. Sun and Moon gleaming, to light the land's new dwellers, and adorned the Earth with treasures, Limbs and leaves, all life they shaped, and every kind of living thing."

The poet's voice was bright, the music of his upper strings joyous; but beneath, Wealhtheow could still hear the low thrumming theme of Yma and his children, like the rumble of distant thunder through sunlight. For the eoten kin were not destroyed utterly, only cast out...and through the dark nights of winter, they drew closer to the walls of the Middle Garth. But when the old poet had finished, the rafters of Heorot rang with cheering, Hadulf's men shouting along with Hrothgar's. Wealhtheow, still dazed from his song, reached slowly to draw another ring from her arm, but her husband moved first, rising from his seat with one of his own massive gold armbands in his hand. The poet took his reward gladly; Hrothgar spoke to him a moment, and his fingers touched the strings again, drawing out a lively tune. Hadulf's thane Beorn began to clap along with it; others joined in quickly, clapping their hands or stamping their feet to the rhythm of the song.

'Limbs and leaves, all life they shaped and every kind of living thing.'

The poet's words rang clearly through the misty night around Heorot, bright as the first sparks of a torch setting home thatch alight. Grendel clenched his great fists as he heard the joyful shouting arise within the hall; his teeth grated with anger, harsh as iron spikes within his mouth.

It was insult enough that they, children and fosterlings of his kin's slayers, had raised their stead so close to his own, denying his rule over that wild march land where sea hammered against sand and cliff. Yet he had let Heorot stand, for those laws had been pulled within the depths of Wyrd's Well long ago: that the day walkers, sons and daughters of Ash and Elm, should own the settled bounds of the Middle Garth, while the kin of Yma must settle for the harsh lands without where humans could not dwell. But now they gloated over that first slaying, the murder of Grendel's eldest grandfather by Woden and his brothers, and that was beyond bearing.

"Did you think," Grendel whispered to them, though he knew they would hear nothing but a sharpening howl of the wind over Heorot's wooden shingles if they heard it at all through their own sounds of laughing and stamping and lively music, "that a wolf does not live in a murdered man's young son, or that life could be spilt and homestead stolen without a were gild taken in return, in blood if not in gold? Long before the children of Ash and Elm ever gathered to set laws and deem payments at their Things, eotens and gods alike knew the price of strife and crime. Though the gods had the strength to flout that geld once, the debt for Yma's life remains."

He paused, staring up at Heorot. To Grendel's sight, the mist shimmered clear as day, the gilded carvings of the hall's roof beams glimmering in lines of golden fire and the hallowed stags' antlers gleaming with red might. They were proud, those men, who would struggle to rival the dwarves for skill in their carving and metalwork, who sought, with their craft work and songs and calls to those mighty ones whose blood they bore, to bring the grandeur of the gods' halls forth in the Middle Garth. But their greatness would be their downfall, for Hrothgar had wrought better than he knew: he had uplifted Heorot beyond the bounds of earth, and thus opened his doors to the worlds beyond. Where gods and alfs might tread where Scyld's son and Geofe's daughter might sit together in their high seats, the golden blessings of their hallowed forebears pouring from them onto the land about like mead from a pitcher there, also, Grendel could walk, for there was no warder in Heorot with the strength to withstand him.

"I shall take that hall," murmured Grendel. "Hall and lands: my share of Yma's legacy, for only the sea his blood and the earth his flesh are left as his children's portion. My kin have been slinking in the dark too long, wretched and outlawed; and not for any crime, but because we suffered our grandfather's murder and could not avenge him at once." Grendel stooped down, his clawed fist closing on a stone the size of a man's head. Though it was rimed with early winter frost, cold with Yma's long death, Grendel could still feel the life that had once been within it, feel his kinship to the shard of Yma's bone within his own living body. "A thrall takes his revenge at once," Grendel said slowly. "A coward, never. By my eldest grandfather's bones, I swear vengeance on you who gloat at his death."

He cast the stone hard: it hissed through the mist, blackness trailing behind it like a tattered battle flag in a storm wind, to arch over Heorot's roof. Seated beside her husband again, her limbs still trembling with relief, Wealhtheow suddenly started.

She did not know what had disturbed her; she had heard no sharp noise through the sounds of singing and laughter, nor had anyone touched her unexpectedly. Yet she felt like a hind in the woods hearing a branch crack beneath a hunter's foot: suddenly awake, her muscles tightening to run as she sniffed for any hint of strangeness on the air. Beside her, the gudhija's blue green eyes suddenly widened, and her hand clenched on the ivory hilt of her eating knife.

"What is it?" Wealhtheow asked her softly.

"I do not know," the other woman replied. "Yet I feel..."

Unferth, too, was sitting bolt upright, dark eyes flickering about the hall as though he thought to see a foe stepping out from behind one of the great carven pillars. But the hands of the other men were clapping with the music or lifting drinking horns: none hovered near the hilt of knife or sword, and their faces were flushed with mead and laughter, not anger. If Hrothgar had been touched by the same stirring that had unsettled the three of them, he showed no sign of it. At the same time, Wealhtheow realized that her bladder was achingly full; though she had drunk carefully, she had been in the hall for a long time, and even a queen could no more deny certain needs than could a bondsmaid.

"I must step outside," she said to Hrothgar. He smiled, and began to tell her where the outhouse was. When the gudhija broke in smoothly.

"I will show her the way, since it is dark," she said. "Come, Wealhtheow." The gudhija took an unlit torch from a heap by the wall, thrusting its wrapped end into a fire pit until the pitch and cloth flared up, and led Wealhtheow to the hall's back door.

As the gust of cold air caught her in the face, sweeping back the torch's flame into a long stream so that it shed no light on the blackness outside, Wealhtheow hesitated. Had it not been for the other woman beside her, she did not know if she could have brought herself to step out of the hall's warm safety. But as if she had spoken aloud, the gudhija trod lightly around her and out, and then Wealhtheow was able to follow her to the small building with its smooth wooden seats. By the time the two women had both finished, Wealhtheow was shivering: the damp chill of the icy sea mist seemed to creep into her bones like a black serpent, winding through the warmth of her marrow, and the gold rings about her arms and fingers had turned to bands of frost. The gudhija laid a hand on Wealhtheow's arm, as if to steady her. The light of her torch sheened the smooth curves of her face with ruddy gold, shadowing the hollows from which her eyes gleamed like clear blue green gems.

"I will see for you now for you, and for my friend Unferth."

"But you said..." Unsure of her words, Wealhtheow let her voice trail off.

"When the feast began, I would not. Now the turnings of Wyrd have settled, however it is that they shall come to pass. And as I sat in the hall just then, I heard the howling of a great wolf: I fear that a strong soul is of wolfish mind towards Heorot, and that ill may come of it."

"How so? Hrothgar had no foes who could threaten him, save my father, and that feud is now at end."

"If you would know more, call Unferth out, and he and I shall seek to learn what we may."

"And Hrothgar?"

The gudhija's bright brows lowered, her forehead creasing in thought a moment.

"Yes. Whatever may come to pass, he should know of it but no others."

Wealhtheow slipped quietly back into the hall, laying her hand upon Hrothgar's. He jumped at her touch; against his warm skin, her own seemed cold as frost on iron.

"I hope your feet are not so chilly between the blankets," her husband said, laughing. "If they are, I shall not get much sleep."

"Hrothgar," Wealhtheow said softly, "the gudhija says that she will see for us now."

Looking up at her, Hrothgar sobered at once, a grave look settling on his face.

"Is something amiss?"

"There may be. She wishes for you, and I, and Unferth to be there: no others."

Hrothgar frowned. "I had hoped that she would speak before the hall: it is always well to have a fair spae at a wedding. But if she fears ill...perhaps it is better so."

He leaned down to touch his thule on the shoulder. Unferth rose at once, taking his spear in his hand, and the three of them made their way out of the hall to where the mist dimmed flare of the torch showed the gudhija's shadowy figure. Without speaking, the gudhija led them to one of the smaller houses Wealhtheow guessed that Hrothgar had ordered it made ready to guest her.

It was warm and bright inside, a good fire burning within the stone ringed hearth in the middle of the floor, and the bed was heaped high with thick blankets and furs. By the fire was a three legged stool, much like Unferth's, save that it was made of pale birch wood and the legs were carved with falcons and leaping cats rather than wyrms. Beneath the stool was a leather sack, its worn hide stained with deep red rune staves and signs. The gudhija settled herself upon the stool, gesturing Hrothgar and Wealhtheow to sit on the floor before her. Unferth stood by the door with his spear, still and dark as a yew tree on a howe. From her bag, the gudhija drew a ruddy mottled falcon's wing and a smaller pouch of dried herbs.

She sprinkled the herbs into the fire, fanning the sweet cloud of their smoke over herself, Hrothgar, and Wealhtheow as she began to chant wordlessly. Slowly, a sense of deep ease began to creep through Wealhtheow's body. The air within the hut was rippling like the clear water of a well; it seemed to her that the gudhija's white clad figure shimmered far away, pale as a fair banner against a green field. Though the woman no longer chanted, the last echo of her voice still rang clear around them, as though the wooden walls and earthen floor had become a great bell of gold. Wealhtheow sat transfixed in silence, waiting for her to speak. Yet it was Unferth's deep raven croak that broke the stillness, floating down as if from the top of a high tree.

"Guthhild, dreaming in the depths do you hear me? Spae wife wise, seeker of Wyrd, do you hear and will you answer?

"I hear," the gudhija murmured, her voice a distant whisper. "I will answer."

"Guthhild, spae wife, what do you see? What ripple of Wyrd stirred Heorot this night? What was set; what shall it shape?"

"I see..." For a moment Guthhild was still. Then she spoke again, her soft words casting shadows into Wealhtheow's mind until the young queen was not sure what she heard and what she saw.

"Bones of the earth, the old stones stirring...black with rime, crusted with the salt spray of Yma's blood. I see him moving in the mist, eyes pale lamps of hate. Grendel he is named, foe to the children of Ash and Elm. A boat sailing, bearing seeds between the worlds...Something rising forth from the waters, from the dark pool where the fire snakes swim; whether man or troll, I cannot tell. The bear cub lies in the warmth, with the taste of honey in his mouth, but he is scratched where the children have baited him with sticks: bid well to the gods and bless him, that he not fare to the woods as a foe to men, for help may come of him in time. Heorot is ringed with flames, ringed with feuds; newly kindled, and old as Yma's bones. Let the kin of the high ones beware, for hate is inherited with might, and no blood is spilt without geld. I see, seasons passing, and Heorot yet under darkness, though Scyld's stone burns as a beacon on the shore, a mark for seafarers driven from afar over the flood's dark mists. A king by day, another king by night, and the hall straw soaked with blood and strewn with tatters of flesh. Troll kin alone may meet troll kin's strength, if the gods do not give their help."

Guthhild was silent: Wealhtheow could hear only the gudhija's hard breathing, as though the woman's head had just broken the surface of a pool after a deep dive.

At last she said, "I can see no more."

"Well have we asked, and well been answered," Unferth replied. "Come back to us, Guthhild, from the depths of your dream; come back, spae wife, to the Middle Garth."

Guthhild shuddered, her limbs twitching hard, then slowly unlocking. Unferth stepped forward, taking her hands in his own. She blinked twice, as if trying to clear fog from her eyes.

"That was a dark foretelling," Unferth said softly to her. "Did more come to you?"

"Nothing, save…Hrothgar must be warded, for the sake of his life, and to him alone can I offer safety."

Hrothgar frowned. "What of Wealhtheow?" he demanded. "If there is danger, it is she who should be warded; I have need of nothing save the strength of my sword and my thanes at my back."

"Vengeance seldom strikes at women," the gudhija told him. "Whatever it was that I saw…it is not in Wealhtheow's wyrd to be slain by it."

"And what of young Hrothulf, our fosterling and Hrothgar's brother son?" Wealhtheow asked. "Can you do nothing for him?"

"Brother son," Unferth said, his voice rough and heavy, "and closer yet by blood. Do you not know the tale of his birth?"

"Another time," Hrothgar broke in, but Unferth shook his head.

"Hrothulf's father Halga took to wife the daughter he had fathered as a youth, the maid Yrse. He did not know it, nor did she, but when the truth was told them, Yrse left him. She is wedded now to the Swedish king Ongentheow, though she is young enough to be his granddaughter he slew Halga, though not without cause, and paid a good weregild for him and few know how Hrothulf was born."

Wealhtheow bit at her breath, afraid to let any words out. It was known throughout the Northlands that Hrothgar and Halga had been the closest of brothers while Halga lived; she did not dare to speak, lest Hrothgar take amiss anything she might say. Unferth, however, did not flinch, but went on gravely,

"It is not beyond thought that Hrothulf's birth may have some part in drawing whatever ill it is that may fall upon Heorot."

"No!" Hrothgar said, and Guthhild shook her head at the same moment, sweat darkened strands of copper hair falling away from her face.

"It was nothing to do with Hrothulf: I have seen his wyrd already, when Yrse brought him to God Home as a babe. Much that is dark and strange lies before Hrothulf, but he will not be slain within Heorot's walls, nor did his birth bring your foe upon you remember that, when you sit at speech with your rede givers! But as for you, Hrothgar, if you do not give us leave to ward you, you will lie in your mound before a year has passed: that I know."

Guthhild's eyes were clear and cold as the blue green heart of a glacier; though that gaze was not turned on her, Wealhtheow shivered within. Hrothgar held the gudhija's eyes steadily, not looking away, and at last nodded.

"So be it," he said. "Ward me as you will. Wealhtheow, go back to the hall, lest it be thought that we have cheated our friends of their joy by slipping silently away to our marriage bower."

"No, she shall stay here," Guthhild told him. "Her strength, too, is needed for this. Wealhtheow, stand by Hrothgar and embrace him, that you may lend all your heart and will to this work."

Wealhtheow put her arms around her husband's broad body, holding him tightly. She could feel the powerful beating of his heart beneath his byrnie; his breath was warm and sweet with mead, and it seemed to her that she could feel true love for Hrothgar beginning to quicken in her, like the first kicking of a child beneath her heart. Slowly, steadily, Guthhild and Unferth began to circle them, chanting together. The gudhija's voice wove smoothly in and out through Unferth's harsh drone, echoing through the house and Wealhtheow's skull alike.

"Son of Scyld Scefing, shield wall around you..." Son of Scyld Scefing, shield wall around you; Son of Scyld Scefing. The thin pieces of embossed gold hanging from the hem of the gudhija's dress jingled and glinted in the firelight; it seemed to Wealhtheow as though a swirl of golden sparks rose up from Guthhild's feet as she circled, blurring Wealhtheow's eyes with a brightness that cast no light.

The gudhija's white hand flashed in the firelight like a fish leaping from the sea, dipping into her bag to scatter more dried herbs on the fire, the scent of their smoke musty and sharp with a faint underlying sweetness. Wealhtheow's head swam as she breathed it in; she clung more tightly to Hrothgar, her legs trembling beneath her. Thunar, ward him, she thought dizzily. Frige ward him, Frea Ing and all the gods, ward my husband from whatever woe the spae wife saw. Now Guthhild held a small clay flask in her hand, flicking dark drops onto Hrothgar as she chanted and circled, her words rising high above Unferth's ceaseless refrain.

"The main of the earth, and the rime cold sea; holy boar's blood, dawn water from blessed stream. Linen and leek, to hold the drighten hale; harrow drops of god horse, howe earth of the Scyldings; yew, hold Hrothgar safe from all ill! Son of Scyld Scefing..." As she took up the chant again, Unferth drew a small rod of polished, rune graven wood, no more than half a hand span long, from his belt pouch, and began to trace the shapes of rune staves in the air as he called out their names. Those were not strange to Wealhtheow, though she knew little of using the might that each stave shape was said to hold beyond and above the word strength of the runes they set on wood or stone for those who were able to read.

"Elhaz I bid; Eihwaz I bid; Sowilo I bid: I give auja," Unferth intoned; and it seemed to Wealhtheow that she could see the three staves glowing behind the tip of his wand as though he had scored the air with a burning twig: He chanted that rune thrice, then traced three more staves: "Tiwaz I bid; Ingwaz I bid; Othala I bid: I give auja." Thrice the rune was spoken; thrice the staves were drawn, and once more Unferth chanted and traced:

"Uruz I bid; Raidho I bid; Wunjo I bid: I give auja, I give auja, I give auja. Warding and weal and luck to Hrothgar: I who sit upon the thule's seat, I who speak from the Scylding howes I, Unferth Erulian, have risted this rune in Wyrd's Well. Whether eoten or alf come against Hrothgar, draug from the darkness or daylight foe; whether witch speak cunning words or wizard sing curse runes to do him ill, no hate shall harm him, no woe shall wound him, but all who seek to scathe him be thwarted. So I have rowned; so I have pulled; so have I wrought, by Woden's great staves and galdor craft!"

As Unferth spoke his last word, he touched Hrothgar lightly between the eyes with the tip of his small rod. Wealhtheow felt Hrothgar jerk in her arms as though a lightning bolt had shivered through him, but he made no sound.

"Son of Scyld Scefing," Unferth whispered, his voice slightly out of time with Guthhild's so that the sound seemed to set up an odd quivering within the room, "shield wall around you." He staggered back, sitting down heavily on the bed, as the gudhija moved more gracefully to her stool. Unferth and Guthhild were both white faced, shaking and drenched in sweat like horses who had been run past the bounds of their strength; but Hrothgar stood solid and powerful as a well trained stallion in Wealhtheow's embrace.

He turned towards her, his arms going about her, and suddenly she was kissing him with all her strength, her tongue seeking out the mead warm depths of his mouth. A taste of salt seeped into the kiss: to her surprise, Wealhtheow realized that she was crying. Hrothgar turned his head, leaning his soft bearded cheek against her face.

"All is well, beloved," he murmured to her. "Do not weep."

"I thought; we have not been married a night, but I fear to lose you," Wealhtheow stammered.

"You shall not lose me," he assured her. "Guthhild and Unferth have made sure of it."

Wealhtheow clung to Hrothgar, unwilling to let him go, though the hard iron links of his byrnie crushed painfully against her breasts. She wanted to clutch him more tightly, to take him into herself and hold him. This is our wedding night, she thought.

"We could go to our house now, and be alone," she whispered to him. Hrothgar stroked her hair, straightening her birch leaf crown on her head, and she could see the keen longing in his blue eyes. But he shook his head regretfully.

"The women are waiting for us in the wedding bower, and the men must light our way there with torches and song, that none may say that this marriage was not held and witnessed rightly. We shall be alone together soon enough." He kissed Wealhtheow once more, then let go of her, turning towards the other two. "Is there anything I can do to help you?" Hrothgar asked them. "You have striven hard for my sake this night."

Unferth reached for his spear, using it to push himself up like an old man leaning on his staff.

"A little while to rest, and a horn of mead, and I shall be myself again," he croaked.

He stretched out a hand to Guthhild, helping her to rise as well, and the four of them made their way back through the cold mist to the great hall. Grendel stood staring at Heorot for a little while, waiting to see if anyone would come out. But if anyone within had marked the sound of his stone striking earth, they thought nothing of it; his challenge had gone unheard or unnoticed, as if it were no more than the hooting of an owl through the foggy night. He had watched the warring of men through the long years of his life: he knew that when the foemen had feasted long in their hall, their eyes blurred into sleep with ale, was a good time to strike.

He could bar the doors then, heap sticks and light them until the wooden roof shingles flared up, and burn his enemies in their hall. But there was more than death and destruction in his mind, for he had a fair cause, and would not burn what he sought to gain. He would be lord in Heorot himself: he would claim it as a hall of Eoten Home, and his kin would sit upon the mead benches he had won. And strength alone would not serve that end: he would need wise rede, if he were to achieve it. Unwillingly turning his gaze away from the gold shimmering hall, Grendel plunged through the fog, skirting widely about the barrows in which the bones of the Scyldings lay. The stone pillar upon the beach glowed with rivulets and pools of foxfire in his eyes, little glimmers of blue flame fading above the scattered droplets of offering blood around it.

If he had the might, he would have torn Scyld's stone down and broken it, casting the scattered shards to the waves. But he knew well that the pillar would sear his hand if he reached out to it: though Scyld was long fared away, the stone was still a beacon through the worlds, the crack of a door left ajar which Grendel could not push shut. He breathed more easily as he left the Scylding howes behind, striding out over the sucking mud and weeds of the marshland beyond. Grendel's feet sank ankle deep in the cold slime; tiny things wriggled away beneath his tread. Behind him, the brackish water oozed up from the mud to blur and hide his track. Soon the rising tide would sweep away every trace that he had been there: the folk of Heorot, deaf to his words, would be blind to his passing as well until the night when he strode into the hall to make it his. Beyond the marsh, the shore rose again to low, wind carved cliffs.

Grendel made his way among them, following his familiar pathway through narrow gorge and stone passages until he came to the shore of the mere that was his home. Above, a stream tumbled from the wooded bluffs, churning a spew of froth upon the still dark waters; the twisted trees that grew upon the stony slopes around the small lake stretched their branches out over it, the last dead leaves still trembling on their twigs. Ghost light shimmered upon the water like the echo of fire glittering from the treasures below, but no man had ever been so brave as to dive into the mere to seek its gold. For within the black water, even human sight could see the streaks of cold green flame writhing and twisting, sea wyrms that swam and hunted and bred in the salt currents that flowed in and out with the tide.

They scattered as Grendel plunged in, their lightless fire streaking the blackness like the afterimages of whirled torches. He drew the cold water deep into his lungs as if it were no more than thick mist, tasting its scents the fresh clean ice of the waterfall's stream, the bitter edged saltiness from the ocean, rich with seaweed and dead fish, the lingering flavor of the sea wyrms, faintly acrid like the taste of air after a lightning strike. As always when he had been out striding across the moors and marshlands, it felt good to swim again, the strength of his arms bearing him easily through the heavy currents of the mere, as surely as if he had drawn on an eagle hide to beat his way through the winds on pinioned wings. Down to the depths of the lake, and through the narrow black passage of jagged rock, then a light push upward, and Grendel's head broke the still surface of the pool that covered nearly a quarter of the floor of his mother's hall.

"You come home early, my son," his mother said. Though muted, the powerful resonance of her voice still rang through the great stone cavern until the edges of the tapestries hanging along the stone walls shivered with it. "Winter has just begun, and the dawn is farther each night. Why, then, are you not hunting through the woods or the marshlands?"

Grendel vaulted lightly up over the jagged lip of stone that edged the pool, shaking himself dry.

"There is more in my mind now than hunger or play. Mother, I have come home because I seek your rede."

His mother set down her spinning and rose from her seat, stretching to her full height for a moment before she turned to the low stone ledge behind her where the flickering light of the fire played from the glittering facets of the rime chalices that stood there. She filled one crystal goblet with dark mead, bearing it to her son.

"Sit, Grendel, and tell me what troubles your thoughts."

Though the ice cup seemed dainty as a snowflake in Grendel's large clawed hand, it was carved of clear bright stone: it would not shatter in his grip, nor even if he dropped it carelessly upon the floor. He drained the goblet, welcoming the hot strength of the draught the stinging venom of the bees mingled with their sweet honey, the hint of bitter sea salt from his mother's brewing water, and the coppery taste of blood shed warm and living into the seething wort. His mother filled the chalice for him again, then one for herself, settling back upon her spinning stool. Grendel sat upon his own chair, the last sheen of water on the scaly greenish black hide of his feet hissing up in steam as he stretched out his legs to the fire.

For a moment Grendel sat looking at his mother, considering how best to tell her his plans. The children of Yma were greatly unalike in shape, and the women more so than the men. Among his kin, Grendel counted hundred headed troll wives and stone hewn hags with mossy beards and pelts of shaggy lichen. And yet he was also, though many generations separated them, distant cousin to the shining eoten maid Geard, whom the god Frea Ing had seen from afar and wedded; and to Scatha, the fair daughter of the old thurse Theasa, who had claimed a husband from among the gods as were gild for her father's slaying: often, it was said, the ugliest eotens would sire the fairest maids.

It was that blood which showed most clearly in Grendel's mother. She was tall and straight limbed, with a swimmer's broad shoulders, and though her white skin was beginning to crease with age now, it only drew the more tightly over the fine lines of her high cheekbones and jaw. Her long hair, deep chestnut with glints of gold, was pulled tightly back from her face in a long plait, sharpening the delicate points of her nose and chin. It was easy to see that she had been one of Eoten Home's lovely ones in her youth. Yet her bony hands bore talons the equal of Grendel's own, and he knew well that she had a grip to match his. The teeth within her thin lips were sharp as the spikes of iron nails, and when angered, her blue eyes flamed with an icy green glow that could even chill her son's heart. One of his mother's claws rang softly off the rim of her crystal goblet, the bell like sound tinkling through the cave. As if mirroring back a glint of light, the gold rings and coins strewn about the floor echoed faintly in answer.

"Well, Grendel?"

"In Heorot this night, they sang of the eldest murder; once more, the children of the gods boasted of Yma's death. I would take my part of revenge upon them."

"And has it not long been your way to slay those men who stray foolishly from their path into our marshes and moorlands, or wander lost in the darkness over our lands? What more should you wish to do? What is ours, we hold; when they pass the gates of their garths at night, they are lawful prey, for so the feud between ourselves and the gods ever stretches to their bairns and fosterlings."

"And yet Heorot stands where once I walked at will, before Scyld Scefing came over the sea. Mother, I would overcome Hrothgar and take that hall."

Grendel's mother looked at him for a long time, and he could see the grimness in her face, keen as the edge of an ice shard. Grendel felt a sudden shiver of uneasiness, for there was something cold and remote in her blue eyes something reminding him that the Norns, too, were her distant kin: for even those three maids who tended the Well of Wyrd were sprung from Yma, and Bergelmir after him.

"That is not wise, my son. Though you are strong and brave, and no son of Ash and Elm can match you, nor any three, or ten of them, yet enough could surely pull you down. And I feel I know, as surely as if I read it in carven rune staves that if you keep on with this, your blood will be poured out within Heorot's walls."

Grendel's heart was pounding hard in his breast, its hollow boom loud and echoing as a bass drumbeat ringing off the stone walls of the cavern. Yet he answered steadily,

"I shall not flee from this, even if you know me to be fey: I was not born a coward. Should I let the fear of death hold me from just vengeance, and skulk in the mists of the Middle Garth's borders, when the bones of Yma cry out for revenge?"

"The time is yet far when the hosts of our kind shall gather against the gods," his mother replied. "What do you hope to gain by striking early at the children of men?"

"I shall silence their songs, that our songs may be heard; I shall take their mead benches for our own, and broaden the borders of Eoten Home."

Grendel's mother shook her head, her plait swaying between the sharp points of her shoulder blades. "Live, and gather your strength. Beget more children on the daughters of Ran in the ocean waves, that your nicor bairns may bring down ships to the old sea wife's hall, or seek a bride for yourself among the wild cliffs and bergs train your sons to hunt and do battle, and send your daughters to learn wisdom from me. That is the way of our kind: have you watched men at their warring too long?"

"It may be so. And yet, now that you have named my doom, I may not turn aside from it. What legacy could I give my heirs, if I knew myself to be afraid of the strength of men, and too weak to answer their taunts against my clan? If you wished me to live forever, you should have raised me in your wool basket."

Grendel's mother closed her eyes, and it seemed to Grendel that he could see the sorrow already graving deeper lines into her face, like the scratches of a sea bird's claws in damp sand.

"Wyrd may be turned, if one well knows how," she murmured. "What I can see mayhap I can ward against it."

She set her goblet aside, picking up her spinning again. The pale cloud of wool streaming over her arm shimmered in the firelight like a banner of dawn lit mist; with a deft touch, she set her spindle whirling, drawing out the wool into a long fine thread. Grendel watched his mother's spinning silently, waiting for her to speak again.

At last she said, "By Yule this fleece will all be spun and woven. From that weaving I shall make you a shirt, a byrnie of wool, that shall keep you safe from fire and iron, so that no sword edge or arrow or spear may scathe you. Thus warded, you shall fare as safe as you may be within Heorot's walls, and my fears for you never come to fruit, for no weapon forged by men shall ever pierce your hide." She glanced up at the cave wall where Grendel's great sword hung, an eoten blade whose hilt gleamed with gold work, pulled with runes. "And no man," she added softly, "has the might to wield one of our brands, nor do the Scyldings deal with the dwarves."

The days passed quickly for Wealhtheow after Winter nights. As at home, there were still beasts to be slaughtered, their meat hung over fires to smoke or salted away in brine for the winter. Heorot's storehouses were full of grain; Wealtheow had to oversee the malting of barley for ale and small beer, the grinding of rye and wheat into flour, and the endless rounds of baking soft bread to be eaten at once, holed rounds of hard flat bread to be strung on poles high above the storehouse floors, out of the reach of mice and rats. From the coarse hulled bread for the thralls to the fine wheat bread for Hrothgar's table, seeing to all the provisions in Heorot was Wealhtheow's duty as frowe.

Even with strong and well trained bondsmaids to do most of the work, Wealhtheow had little time to herself; but now and again she would walk down to the Scylding howes, looking past Scyld's stone and out to sea. It seemed to her as if she were waiting for something waiting, perhaps, to see the high ringed prow of a ship, glittering with gold through the gauzy veils of mist that drifted across the water. But no friend or foe was awaited, and as the winds bit colder with the first sharpness of winter snows on their way, whipping the gray waves into leaping torrents of white froth, few would dare a long ship faring by choice. And despite that strange longing that drew her down to the water's edge again and again, Wealhtheow was happy.

For the first time since she had reached womanhood, her courses had not come upon her at the dark of the moon, and she was sure that a child was growing in her womb. She had not spoken of it to Hrothgar yet, for she knew that many misfortunes could unseat a babe from its mother's body in the early months; she would wait until she felt its first movements within her and knew for sure that it was alive and well. The first snows of the year began to fall at the beginning of Yule Month, a sparse scattering of white flakes drifting down to dust the hard trodden earth around Heorot and glitter faintly over the brown stubble of the shorn fields of grain. The days were growing short now, and even Hrothgar spent more time sitting by the fire in the hall and talking or listening to his poets' songs and tales than riding out to hunt in the woods.

Wealhtheow was content to sit beside her husband and spin: she had bought a silver blue fleece which she meant to make into a tunic for Hrothgar, for its color would bring out the startling clear blue of his eyes. She could have given the wool to one of her bondsmaids to spin up, but she wished no other hand to work on her first gift to her husband, for as her spindle turned, she whispered her prayers for Hrothgar's health and safety, as if she could strengthen his warding against whatever danger Guthhild had seen on their wedding night. By the first night of Yule, the snow was ankle deep, trodden into a hard crust within the stockade. Wealhtheow saw to it that Heorot was swept out and fresh straw put down in thick drifts that would serve as bedding for drunken thanes and the unseen guests the alfs and ghosts who came to visit the living through the dark Yule nights alike.

Wreaths of dark needled yew and bright berried holly hung about Heorot's walls; the icy air was laden with the scents of baking bread and seething meat, and Hrothgar's beautiful gray wolf dogs crowded eagerly about the cook houses, filling their bellies with scraps and gnawing happily on bones. Strong thralls had carried kegs of ale and mead in, their squat shapes standing around the hall like so many dwarves waiting in the shadows, and the tables were heaped high with loaves of bread, rounds of cheese, and baskets of apples. Hrothgar's best boar, a great bristly beast, was tethered to one of the hall pillars by the gold ring in his nose, grunting and snuffling softly through the straw in hopes of finding a stray bit of food. Wealhtheow and all the other women had put aside their spinning; the grinding wheels lay idle, and the sound of metal clashing on metal no longer rang from the forge, for the year's work was done, and would not be taken up again until the nights of Yule had ended and the new year begun. Although a gray blanket of cloud hid the sky, Wealhtheow could tell by the gathering gloom that the Sun would be setting soon. She made her way from the hall to her house, drawing her thick cloak of red wool tightly about herself against the icy wind.

Hrothgar was already there, pulling his richly embroidered feasting tunic over his head. He paused for a moment to kiss Wealhtheow before he finished dressing, holding her gently to his warm body.

"Is everything ready for the feast, my love?" he asked.

"It is."

"Hardly three months of marriage," Hrothgar said, "and already I do not know how I was ever able to rule without you by my side, I have come to trust so completely in you." He kissed her again. "Will you wear your morning gift this night?"

"Of course I will," Wealhtheow answered, opening the carven box that held the great gold neck ring and lifting it out.

Her husband's wedding present to her was the finest piece of gold work she had ever seen: seven rings of filigree covered gold layered upon each other, with tiny dragons and mask faces and little beasts soldered in between each ring, hinged at the back and opening in front. With the firelight shining on it, the gold glittered and shimmered as if the filigreed beasts were running about between the rings, their delicate beading rippling with brightness.

When Wealhtheow put it on, the huge collar reached from her throat to her breasts, and, although the rings had been made hollow for lightness, it still weighed as much as an iron sword. It was a treasure whose price Wealhtheow could not so much as guess at; but, much as she loved to look at it and run her fingers over the elaborate figuring of the gold, it was too heavy and cumbersome for her to wear often. But at Yule Wealhtheow must dress in her best, both to honor the gods and ghosts and to give a fine display for her folk, and if the price was a little stiffness of the neck and soreness of the shoulders, it could not be helped. Hrothgar's smile was bright beneath his silver beard as he looked at Wealhtheow, caressing her with his eyes.

"My beautiful bride," he said, reaching out to straighten her gold collar and unpin the plain piece of white linen that covered her braid crowned head. In its place, he helped her to put on her best headdress, of red linen embroidered with gold threads and adorned with ring mounted gold coins from the south; thus dressed, Wealhtheow knew that she looked queenly indeed. Hand in hand, Wealtheow and Hrothgar walked towards the hall.

Hrothulf was outside playing with a few other boys, tossing and catching a ball of wool stuffed leather. Although the others were shouting and laughing, Hrothgar's nephew was strangely quiet, leaping for the ball and throwing it in grim earnest. Dark streaks of wetness on his yellow tunic showed that he had already fallen in the snow more than once; Wealhtheow thought about calling him away from the game and telling him to change clothes before the feast, but then thought better of it. Although polite enough, Hrothulf had made it clear to her that he would have none of her efforts to mother him: they got on well enough, but only so long as Wealhtheow treated him like a grown man.

Given the strange history of his birth, perhaps that was easy enough to understand. Wealhtheow did not know what the boy had been told about his mother, but he must have heard enough sideways whispers in his young life to make him wary. Almost unconsciously, she touched her stomach, as though to give a pat of reassurance to the tiny life sleeping within her. If Frige and the Frowe were kind to her, she would have her own child to mother soon enough.

It would be due at Midsummer, born to warmth and long bright days. A snowflake brushed cold and light over Wealhtheow's face, then another. She and Hrothgar left the boys to their game, hastening into the hall. Unferth was inside already, the gold and silver rings on his arms gleaming from the loose folds of his deep blue tunic as he bent to scratch the boar's dark bristled back. The animal grunted in pleasure, rubbing up alongside the thule's legs, and Unferth tossed him a turnip.

"It's the best night of the year for him," Hrothgar said, looking proudly down at the prize animal of his herd. "Just be careful that no one feeds him too much ale before we have to lead him around the hall. I remember last year…"

Unferth smiled crookedly. "I shall mention it to Hrothulf; I believe it was he who kept filling the boar's bowl. He never thought that a pig could get drunk like a man. Well, it is almost sunset. Shall I blow the horn to call the folk in?"

"I think so."

Unferth's blowing horn was twin to his drinking horn, the long curved head spear of an aurochs, polished to glistening with beeswax and bound at the rim and tip with finely worked silver over its black surface. Standing in the open doorway with the white flakes sifting in about him, the thule raised the instrument and blew three long blasts, their call floating low and hollow over the snow crusted fields. The sound sent a tingle up Wealhtheow's spine, as though she could feel it echoing through the hidden worlds about them: with those three notes, Unferth was bidding in not only the living guests, but also the dead who rode from the howes to feast with their kin at Yule.

"Come, ye wights who come in frith," Wealhtheow murmured softly. "Come who wish to come, stay who wish to stay, fare who wish to fare, bringing weal and without harm to Heorot." A soft chill flowed over her as she spoke, prickling up the little hairs on her arms and the nape of her neck; a sudden gust of wind swirled Unferth's cloak about him in a whirl of snowflakes, whipping back his long silver streaked hair.

The boar grunted loudly, lifting his head to peer about himself for a moment before going back to his snuffling through the straw. As always, Wealhtheow walked about the hall pouring ale for the men and stopping to speak a little with each of them, wishing them a glad Yule. Now that she knew all of Hrothgar's folk, it was hard for her to remember how frightening she had found that first sword edged night in Heorot. Even Unferth seemed to be of good cheer that Yule night, laughing now and again as he spoke with Hrothgar and Wealhtheow.

When the eating was done, the gods' horns were carried about the fires and lifted in blessing: to Woden for battle luck and sig, to Frea Ing and Nerthus for fruitfulness and frith, and to the great alfs and idises who looked after the house of the Scyldings. Then the feasters wrapped their cloaks about them and took up torches, going singing and dancing through the snow to the Scylding howes, where Wealhtheow and Hrothgar left ale and food for those who dwelt within the mounds. At last Unferth led the blessing boar around the hall, so that all those gathered there might have a chance to lay a hand upon his back and speak a boast or an oath before gods and men. He came last to Hrothulf, Wealhtheow, and Hrothgar.

"By the bristles of the boar, I have an oath to swear," Hrothulf said, his low voice clear, with no childish hesitation, and his small square chin set firmly. "Let the gods and all here witness: while I live, I shall never flee from fire or iron."

A shudder ran down Wealhtheow's mind as the boy spoke; it seemed to her that she could hear his words ringing through Heorot's antlered rafters, their echoes shivering farther and farther beyond, like a stone dropped into a still well. For a moment Wealhtheow sat dumb, glancing from the thule's dark eyes to the boar's, and then it flashed into her mind what she must say.

"By the bristles of the boar, I have a great boast to make," she said, her voice carrying high through the hall. "In my womb is growing a child of the Scylding line: may the kind goddesses look well upon it, bringing it to a good birth and a wyrd worthy of its forebears!"

A cheer went up, so loud that Wealhtheow could almost see the hall pillars trembling, and she felt the pleasant warmth of a blush spreading into her cheeks. Hrothgar kissed her soundly, his grin flashing white from his shadowed face.

"By the bristles of the boar, I have this boast to make," he called out. "No man in the Middle Garth's ring has made a better marriage than I this year: in both fairness and wisdom, I have won the finest prize, and I will meet any man with the sword who says these words are not true."

Wealhtheow smiled, her heart warm within her. Although she knew that her child was too small for her to feel it moving yet, nevertheless it seemed to her that she could feel something twitching inside her body, a tiny movement promising that the goddesses had heard her prayer and would send her a good birthing. Wealhtheow awoke with a start, clutching at Hrothgar with shaking arms. The first gray light of dawn was just glimmering through the smoke hole; her ears still rang with the high nightmare scream that had shaken her from sleep. What was I dreaming? She thought. But Hrothgar was sitting up already, looking wildly about himself.

"Did you hear..?" He gasped, even as a second scream tore through the air. "Stay here!" Hrothgar ordered. He leapt from bed, pulling his breeches on hastily and grasping his sword from its sheath before running, barefoot and bare chested, out into the snow.

Even beneath the thick blankets and furs, Wealhtheow was shivering, but she forced herself to climb out of bed and put on shift, dress, and shoes as quickly as she could with trembling hands. If Heorot was under attack... But she heard no war cries, nor any clashing of sword on sword. Her heart pounding in her ears, Wealhtheow crouched beside the firepit, blowing the gray fur of ash off the banked coals and slowly feeding in twigs and sticks. A good blaze was just beginning to flare up when the door opened again and Hrothgar stepped back in, his face grim.

"What was it?" Wealhtheow asked. "Is all well?"

"No. The gods help us..." Hrothgar's voice cracked and broke, as if he were about to weep. Wealhtheow straightened up, going to embrace him. The skin of his chest and back was chill as iced metal to her touch, and she could feel the deep shivers rippling through his body.

"Some thirty men dead or missing," Hrothgar said. "Those who had fallen asleep in the hall they were torn limb from limb, their bodies scattered and..." he gulped, as if to swallow back a wave of vomit... "partly eaten."

"Eaten," Wealhtheow echoed dully: she could not take in what her husband had told her for a few seconds, but then she felt her heart clenching within her, the blood dropping cold from her face. There were no bears on Sealand, and few wolves and she had never heard of wild animals who could storm a hall and overcome a band of men, even men sleeping off their Yule night ale.

"There are tracks in the snow," Hrothgar went on. "Something that walked on two legs like a man, but huge." He held his hands out to show Wealhtheow the length of the prints, twice as big as a man's foot. "And clawed. It carried some of the bodies away with it; there is a blood trail as well."

Wealhtheow could say nothing: the gudhija's words were coming back to her with choking force. A king by day, another king by night, and the hall straw soaked with blood and strewn with tatters of flesh.

"Guthhild foresaw this," Hrothgar said quietly, as if he had heard the words in his wife's mind. "Help me dress, and then I shall go to find Unferth I pray to the gods that he did not sleep within Heorot last night. If you stay away from the hall until we have had time to gather what is left of the bodies and build a pyre..."

"No," Wealhtheow told him firmly. "Whatever has happened in Heorot, it is my affair as much as yours, and I shall do my best to help tend to our dead."

Several men were standing outside the door of the hall, staring down at the tracks. Alfberht and Aeschere, Frithgar and Helmwig, and Wealhtheow almost wept with relief as she recognised Unferth's tall thin figure, swathed in his blue black cloak. The thule's long hair was disheveled, his gray streaked beard half plaited, and he was murmuring something under his breath.

"An ill dawn," he said as Wealhtheow came up to him. "Hrothgar has told you?"

"Yes."

The tracks were clear, just as Hrothgar had said; dark spatters fanned out around them where the hot blood had sunk into the snow as though whatever had attacked Heorot had walked off swinging the bleeding bodies like a child with a doll, scattering blood as it went. Wealhtheow looked at the footprints for a long time, trying to imagine the thing that could have made them. Twice as big as a man's foot, and clawed...again she thought of bears: she had heard tales of great white bears in the ice of the farthest Northlands, bigger and fiercer than any brown woodland bear.

But how could such a beast have come unknown to Sealand? If a trader had brought a white bear south, its tale would be known through the whole island in a week or two, for no news traveled faster than stories of curiosities. Nor could a captive beast have escaped without a hunt: alive or dead and skinned for its pelt, a white bear would be too valuable to be let free. Wealhtheow realized that her mind was wandering, as if to seize upon anything that would keep her from having to go into the hall and see what the night marauder had done. But she had claimed her right and duty, and there was no getting away from it now.

The smell hit her first as she stepped through Heorot's door: the slaughter scent of fresh blood, over the heavier foulness of shit and piss. Wealhtheow stopped to let her eyes grow used to the dimness, breathing heavily through her mouth to keep the smell out of her lungs, but it was no use: she could taste the blood in the air, sharp and coppery. Her stomach heaved, belching up an acrid bubble of the last night's ale to sting the back of her throat. She swallowed hard, forcing herself not to vomit as she looked about.

The fresh straw on the floor was sodden in places, black with damp blood the thing had come not long before dawn. All the food that had been left on the table for the ghosts had been eaten or torn about and scattered; the boar's tether had been broken, and he was snouting happily through the bloody straw after cheese, though the gray hounds were crouching together in a corner, shivering and whining. Why did it not kill them as well? Wealhtheow wondered.

Dogs and a tethered swine: easier prey than men, surely? One body lay stripped and headless on the high table, the white shards of ribs sticking out from its glistening red tatters of flesh; the man's entrails had been scooped from his body like a nutmeat from its shell, leaving a gaping hollow between shattered ribcage and broken pelvis. By Wealhtheow's feet was a leg bone that had been cracked for its marrow, then licked clean and tossed casually aside; and the ruined face of a severed head stared up at her out of its one remaining eye.

She recognized it by the red brown braid: it was the head of Wulfstan, the man who had been willing to let her make peace between himself and Halga at her wedding. Wealhtheow turned aside, closing her eyes as she retched dryly. But when the convulsions of her stomach eased, she made herself look again. Most of these men had wives, women who would have to gaze upon their torn bodies even, Frige help them, to look closely at the limbs that had been wrenched away and flung about the hall, to say,

"I recognize that scar; I know that ring; that is the sleeve of the tunic I wove for my husband." And some would not even have the slight comfort of a body to burn, for the shadow walker had carried away much of his kill. Tears blurring her sight, Wealhtheow reached down to close Wulfstan's eye. His skin had not cooled completely yet, but the eyelid would not stay shut: no matter how she tried to smooth it down, it kept drawing back from the glazed eye beneath, as though, in the last moments of his life, Wulfstan had seen something too horrible for even death to shut out of his gaze.

She was weeping hard now, her tears mercifully blinding her to the ravished hall; but each choking sob drew in a great breath of blood laced air. There is much to be done, Wealhtheow told herself firmly, clenching her hands to stop their shaking and trying to stanch the flow of tears from her eyes. And how can I expect our folk to meet this foe bravely, whatever it is, if I cannot even rule myself when looking upon what it has left? She stood again, forcing herself to walk about Heorot and see which of the bodies could still be easily recognized.

A few had hardly been mutilated aside from their gaping death wounds; but others had been torn to shreds, no more than mangled messes of ripped meat and shards of bone. At last she left the hall, gratefully breathing in deep gulps of the clean air outside. Hrothgar reached out to support her, but she shook his hand off.

"I think it will be best," she said, "to make a single pyre for all. And we will have to hurry, for they should be burned before nightfall: whatever troll did this, I do not wish to see what will happen when darkness touches the bodies of those it slew."

Hrothgar winced at her words, glancing at Unferth. The thule nodded slowly.

"It was no thing of the Middle Garth that came to Heorot last night. I will take a few men and follow these tracks, if you will let me: if we can find the night walker's den, we may be able to bring battle to its home."

Hrothgar stood silent in thought for a few moments, then shook his head.

"Best if you see to the bodies: if you fear that the slain may walk again, you know best how to keep them from it. I shall lead the hunting party, for these men were my thanes and it is mine to avenge them, if there is any way to do so." Alfberht smiled grimly, thumping the butt of his spear into the snow in approval; Aeschere, Frithgar, and Helmwig nodded, and a little colour began to come back into their pale faces.

"As you will," Unferth replied.

"Wealhtheow, will you see to gathering our folk when the hall has been cleaned? Everyone must know what we face, that we may be ready if it should come back but what it has left behind is enough to steal the heart even from a brave man. And your good words will be needed, for there will be much sorrow when these deaths are known."

"Yes. Be careful on your hunt, my husband."

Hrothgar brushed his lips lightly across Wealhtheow's, then turned towards his men.

"You four, put on your byrnies, gather your bows, and come with me. I would bring this to an end as quickly as we may."

The thralls that Wealhtheow had summoned were little willing to touch the mangled bodies in the hall: she had to shout at them and threaten whippings, as she had never done before, and the bravest of them could bring himself to lift the corpse off the high table. Beneath it, the wood was stained with blood; Wealhtheow thought of eating from that table, and her stomach turned within her again.

"When you have carried the bodies out," she ordered, "break up all the tables and benches which have been soiled: we will burn them as part of the funeral pyre. Sweep out the straw for burning, as well, and fetch fresh straw in to cover the floor." There was nothing that could be done about the blood that had soaked into the hard packed earth, but at least it could be hidden from sight. Outside, Unferth had set other thralls to chopping and stacking wood, building up a tall flame house like a tent of logs, as though they meant to make a beacon fire that could be seen from Geatland's far off shore.

The bondsmaids were down at the river gathering clay to caulk the pyre's chinks with so that the fire would burn strongly enough to char the corpses' bones. Wealhtheow had seen pyres with more bodies stacked inside after battles, but she was grateful when the last pieces of flesh were hidden behind the ring of logs.

The news had spread quickly: although Wealhtheow had not blown the horn to summon them, Hrothgar's thanes and their wives were gathering slowly, murmuring in hushed tones as they looked at the great tracks and the blood marks on the snow. Wulfstan's wife Alfrida was weeping, quietly and hopelessly; Thunara, whose husband's body had been taken by the night slayer or torn beyond recognition, was raising a soft keen, her fair hair streaming wild and unbound around her plump shoulders. Wealhtheow knew bitterly what was in the woman's mind, as if she could hear the words; each wife of a dead man would be thinking the same.

If only I had not let him sleep in the hall last night; if I had made him come home with me, however drunk or joyful to be feasting with his friends he was, he would be alive now. If Heorot had been built, as many halls were, with a chamber at the back where Hrothgar and his wife slept would the slayer have burst through to their bedroom early that morning? Wealhtheow shuddered at the thought, making the sign of Thunar's Hammer over herself. Unferth began to walk widdershins about the pyre, spear uplifted in one hand and drinking horn in the other.

"Fare forth, fare forth, to the green worlds of the gods," he called. "Rent from the Middle Garth, now the fire must free you. Hrothgar's thanes, who fought with honor for him, though grim your death, you will not be forgotten. I hail thee, Aethelstan, matchless in strength, who ever warded Hrothgar's side in the shield wall..." As he had done at the wedding, the thule named each of the dead, following every name with a few words about the man's worthy deeds and flicking a spatter of mead over the pyre from his horn. "You good thanes, now fallen, Hrothgar goes to seek out your slayer; the wise minded drighten, open handed breaker of rings, has set his soul to avenge you. The warder of Heorot's folk will see that your blood was not spilt without answer. Hail to Hrothgar!"

But the cheer that went up was ragged and weak, and Wealhtheow knew, to her sorrow, that the trust Hrothgar's folk placed in him had taken a heavy blow. She did not need to hear their thoughts spoken aloud, for the same questions had already run through her mind: had Hrothgar somehow angered the gods, for this curse to fall upon Heorot? Was it something in the being of the great hall itself, its gilded carvings and the antlers which should have warded off all ill, which had instead drawn the murder minded troll and opened the way for it to step in? Had the luck of the Scyldings run out at last, the god sprung line come to its end?

Not to its end yet, Wealhtheow reassured herself. Not if her child lived and then there was Hrothulf, standing small and solemn before the pyre. He, too was a Scylding: if Hrothgar fell, if Wealhtheow's bairn did not come to adulthood, then Hrothulf would be the lord of Heorot and all its lands. Yet there was no comfort in that thought for her. Perhaps Hrothulf was too young now to see what Hrothgar's wedding and her own Yule boast would mean for him, or think of what now stood between himself and Heorot's high seat, but sooner or later, that knowledge would have to come to him. And then? Wealhtheow shivered, hugging her cloak around herself. It is an ill day, she thought, when I must suspect such things of a child. And there are many years yet to win his friendship and trustiness for my bairns. Unferth came to a stop in front of the single gap between the logs of the burning house.

With his spear he traced several staves, murmuring their names: a rune to bind the dead out of their rent bodies and send them forth to the god homes. Wealhtheow quickly went to fetch a torch from the hall. The thralls were still scrubbing hard at walls and roof posts; the smell of blood was fainter now, but still stained the air.

"Burn a load of apple wood in here before darkness," Wealhtheow ordered them. "And anything else with a sweet smell: this hall is still not fit to feast in."

When Unferth thrust the torch into the pyre, it caught slowly at first, flames writhing up through the little tinder sticks and hissing over the blood damp straw like little glowing wyrms. The thule crouched patiently before the narrow doorway, as if he were speaking to the dead in their high peaked house of wood and clay. The heat inside grew fiercer, melting the snow about Unferth's feet and reddening his narrow face. Then, with a sudden roar, the flames leapt up from the pyre's pointed top, casting a long black banner of trailing smoke upon the wind. Thankfully, the fire was too hot for Wealhtheow to see more than shadows through the gap in the logs, but she could hear the sizzling as the slaughter flames chewed at the torn corpses within. Wounds bursting open in the heat, blood springing out to hiss up in steam; skulls melting, the fire devouring all that the shadow walker had left uneaten.

Behind her, Wealhtheow heard the notes of old Athelbeorn's harp, high and plaintive, like the ringing of metal hoof guards on ice. The sound stung in her eyes like smoke, bringing the hot flow of tears down her chilled cheeks. She wept bitterly as he wove his lament around the crackling roar of the fire, for it seemed to her that he was mourning not only the dead, but the hopes of Heorot. As the pyre burned, the gathered folk slipped away by ones and twos, coming back with gifts in their hands. A husband's favorite tunic; a friend's sword to bear with him to the god worlds; a loaf of bread or string of sausages, that the dead not hunger on their faring; all of these, and more, were cast into the raging man oven. Aethelhild knelt before the pyre, her ruddy brown hair hanging over her face like a veil to hide her tears, and Wealhtheow heard her choking out,

"My love, I wove and embroidered this cloak for your Yule gift. May you, may you receive it well for your faring."

The fire was still burning, its beacon flames shooting up high against the darkening sky, when Hrothgar and the four men who had gone out with him rode back. Wealhtheow's heart leapt within her; she ran to his horse's side, but when her husband took off his helm, she could see by the grim paleness of his face that his news was ill.

"We followed the tracks over the marsh," he said heavily. "It was an easy enough trail." He touched one of the bulging bags that hung from his roan stallion's saddle, then gestured towards the pyre. Silently Unferth began unloading the horses, carrying the heavy sacks over to push them in through the fiery gap in the half charred logs. "It led us through a dark and craggy path, down to the mere where the blue howe fire burns at night. No one has ever dared those waters, for we have long known them to be uncanny and dangerous...I believe our grim hall guest dwells at the bottom."

"What can we do?" Wealhtheow asked.

"I had thought of setting an ambush by the mere. But we do not know whether its den has another way out: it would be too easy for it to take us from behind in the night. Whereas Heorot has only two doors, easily guarded. If the troll comes tonight it will find the hall full of wakeful and armed thanes, ready for vengeance."

Wealhtheow let her breath out slowly. She knew well that Hrothgar might be standing to his death that night; and yet she could not speak against it, for if he did not meet the strange attacker boldly, then he would lose his rule and his name.

"Call your men to you as fast as you may, then. There is not much daylight left...Have you eaten this day?" Her own legs were shaky beneath her with hunger and her mouth dry, for she had not broken her own fast with so much as a sip of water.

Hrothgar shook his head. "Not after seeing what was left behind."

"The hall is clean; I shall see to it that food is brought, for you and your thanes will need all your strength this night."

"Do that, and then go to our house and bar the doors. I shall set a guard about you to be sure that you are safe."

"That will not be needful," Wealhtheow replied. "I am Heorot's queen, and I shall stay within it tonight. If this troll is so mighty that you and your strongest men cannot overcome it, then nothing will keep me safe. But at our wedding I swore to bide with you would you have me break my oath so soon? I say now that one wyrd shall befall us both, to live or die together as the Norns have shaped it."

"You are as brave as you are fair, my love," Hrothgar said. "But you bear my child within you: would you risk its life as well as your own? If I am slain..."

"Then what is left for me? I would not live to tell your child that I left your side."

Hrothgar sighed. "There is little time to argue it. Go see to the food, but consider carefully, for I know that none will think the less of you if you do not stay in Heorot tonight."

"Yet they will think better of me if I do for it may be that I shall need to have a name for bravery soon."

"That is so," Hrothgar agreed, then, under his breath, "but I would rather be sure of your safety."

"And I of yours, my love, but Wyrd did not rist it so," Wealhtheow whispered back to him.

The high peak of the death fire suddenly swayed, then caved in with a great crash and a shower of sparks, the flame eaten posts falling in upon each other. A few charred logs rolled free, hissing over the ring of damp earth around the pyre to still their fire in the snows beyond. If any bones were still left unburned, they could not be seen beneath the heap of flaming wood; by the time the fire was burned out, there would be only ashes to gather up and lay in a mound when winter was over and the earth could be dug again. Hrothgar unslung his blowing horn from his shoulder and let out one long blast.

Wealhtheow did not stay to listen as he spoke to the thanes, but hastened on to be sure that the tables would be laid for them. The sweet scent of the burning apple and pine wood within the hall had covered the blood stink; Wealhtheow had smelt worse from men coming to table at the end of a slaughtering day. The gray hounds had gotten over the night terror that had them cringing in the corners at dawn, and were sniffing about for food; wolf born Wulfa nuzzled Wealhtheow's hand and licked it warmly. Wealhtheow cut the end of a loaf and a piece of salty cheese for herself, chewing on them as she ordered the thralls to move the tables and benches over to the walls, that they might not hinder Hrothgar's men in fighting.

Tomorrow she would have to speak to the women who had lost their husbands, and go through the storehouses to see what Heorot could spare for the bereaved families. At least they all had lands and goods of their own, for Hrothgar was open handed with his thanes, and those who slept in his hall were not among the least of his men. The warriors filed in, taking their places. Spearmen stood behind those armed with sword and shield at either side of both doors, ready to strike; the shield wall formed up before the front door.

Hrothgar had clearly ordered the men to eat in shifts, so that a full guard would be standing all the time, but none would be left with empty bellies. He himself gnawed at a length of sausage as he walked about the hall, waving his men into position. Wealhtheow carried about draughts of ale not the powerful dark Yule ale she had brewed for the season's feasting, for that was too strong to give to men before a fight, but a lighter draught that would give Hrothgar's thanes heart while not dulling their skill.

She was glad then that she had chosen to stay, for she could tell by their smiles and words of thanks that having her there eased their minds. When his warriors were arranged to his liking, Hrothgar took his own place in the middle of the shield wall, leaning the wide round of painted linden wood easily on thigh and shoulder as he waited. He drank gratefully of the horn Wealhtheow bore him, dashing a few drops of froth from his silver mustache.

"Feed up the fires, if you will," he said. "We shall need light to do battle and it may be wary of the flames."

The thralls had already left the hall, going, no doubt, to cower and shiver in the huts where they slept. But they had stacked deep piles of wood while there was daylight, and Wealhtheow well knew how to build up a good hall fire. Soon the flames were crackling high, driving out the last chill in Heorot's air. The firelight flickered from gilded sword hilts and helms' golden boar mounts as if from the rings and jewels of feasters, but its red glints shone more coldly along the patterned lengths of swords and the silver edges of spears; and no feast was ever so silent, marked only by the harsh sound of breath beneath helmets and the jingling of chain mail as men shifted restlessly from foot to foot.

Suddenly Wulfa lifted her head, sniffing about and voicing a low, whining howl. Those men who were still eating rose at once, lifting their shields and drawing their swords. Wealhtheow crouched down beside the fire at the rear of the hall, poised to dodge or run. She wished desperately that she had asked Hrothgar for a boar spear anything to fend the night walker off with, to buy herself a few seconds if it came for her. It almost seemed to her that she could see the smoky air of the hall thickening, as if the fen mist were rising within its walls; though she was within arm's reach of the fire, its brightness seemed to flicker without warmth, its flames too weak to fight against the cold crawling over her skin.

Blindingly fast, Heorot's front door burst open, the hall's roof posts shaking from the strength that had cast the door aside. The thing that stood upon the threshold was twice a man's height and width, its talons carving an arc of glittering darkness through the air to sink into one thane's neck, tearing his helmeted head from his body and tossing it lightly away, letting the blood spewing corpse drop. Hrothgar roared, leading the shield wall forward as the men on either side of the door stabbed and struck. It must die! Wealhtheow thought fiercely, grinding her nails into her palms.

Whatever it was almost man shaped, body covered in a pale tufted pelt with a long fingered growth flapping down from its middle and limbs shimmering with wet adder scales, eyes glowing foxfire green in its shadowed face it could not stand against the spears and swords assailing it from all three sides: however strong it might be, those weapons must be finding a home in its flesh. Yet, though she could hear the dull thump of the blows striking home upon it, the troll thing did not falter as it seized another man about the waist, slitting his byrnie with its claws like a hunter making the first skinning cut down a rabbit's belly and biting out his guts as he writhed and screamed, still trying to slash at it until the sword fell from his limp hand. Who?

Not Hrothgar; she could still see his boar crested helm, bright gold before the thing's dark shape. Then the shadow walker struck at him, its big clawed hand blurring in Wealhtheow's sight. Before she could cry out her despair, the blow glanced past Hrothgar, sinking into the shoulder of the man beside him. Unferth? No: Unferth was to the left of the troll, stabbing two handed with his spear a spear whose point bent to the side beneath the strength of his blows as Wealhtheow looked, as though the thule were striking a wall of stone in his full battle madness. Dear gods, Wealhtheow realized in horror, they cannot wound it! The iron does not harm it! It will kill them all, and they can do nothing. She wanted to run, but her legs were frozen beneath her, so that she could only crouch shivering, staring at the battle. The troll thing bent over Hrothgar, snapping and clawing as he stabbed at it. His shield splintered beneath its first hammering blow, the crack echoing through the hall.

He dropped the useless metal boss, holding his sword with both hands and thrusting up at its belly with all his strength. The point seemed to skid upward, harmless as the other men's weapons; but its teeth slid over his helm with a terrible screech, and its claws found no grasp upon his body.

"Son of Scyld Scefing," Wealhtheow gasped, "shield wall around you…"

As if the shadow thing had realized that it could not harm Hrothgar, it straightened up with a howl, grasping for another man. The links of his byrnie parted in its grasp with a shriek of rending metal, blood spraying out as it tore his body asunder, ripping huge gobbets of meat away and stuffing them into its mouth. The battering of sword and spear on its body seemed to trouble it no more than drops of rain as it finished its grisly feast, casting the half gnawed legs and arms aside in the straw like a man tossing a sheep bone to a hound.

Then it leapt forward, its swift rush carrying it past Hrothgar and down the length of the hall towards Wealhtheow. For a second it paused, staring at her. Wealhtheow wanted to close her eyes, but the glimmering green gaze held her, helpless as a rabbit beneath a lynx's paw. Dimly she heard the sound of the men shouting and running behind it, Hrothgar's roar of "Turn! Turn and face me, gods curse you!" But although the troll thing did not seem to speak aloud, nevertheless she heard its voice, hollow as the sound of a river rushing through an echoing cave of stone. As its words came clear in her mind, she realized that it was not hairy as she had thought, but clad in a tunic of tufted wool, and the growth hanging from its waist was a bag shaped like a huge glove.

"I am Grendel, born of Yma's line. Yield Heorot to me, and my feud with you will be ended."

Wealhtheow did not know how she dared to speak, nor how the troll Grendel heard her above the battle shouts of Hrothgar and his thanes around it. But, from some hidden spring of will within her, she managed to choke out the single word, "Why?"

Weregild, for the sake of Yma's blood. And because these were my lands long before Scyld Scefing came.

Grendel turned, gliding past Hrothgar. Casually he reached out for one last victim, tearing the thane's head off and crushing the body in his grip before he stuffed it into the great fingered bag at his waist. Then he was gone into the shadows outside, and though one or two men cast their spears after him, none tried to follow him further. Hrothgar tore off his helm, sinking down on his knees beside Wealhtheow. Although the fight had not lasted long, his hair was deep iron gray with dripping sweat, and his breath was coming in hard gasps.

"What did it do to you? Are you harmed?"

Wealhtheow shook her head.

"No," she stammered. "He only, he only spoke to me."

"What did he say?"

Wealhtheow told him. Hrothgar rocked back on his heels, his eyes wide open.

"I have heard of a wight called Grendel: carles who have wandered out late at night have often seen strange shapes in the fen mists, something like a man and a woman; and Grendel is the name they have given the man troll, for as long as anyone can remember." He stood, slamming his sword back into its sheath. "But whatever sake Grendel has to quarrel with us, he shall not take Heorot from me! Not while I can do battle with him."

"My drighten," the thane Aeschere broke in, "we have seen that we cannot do battle with him, for our weapons will not wound him."

Hrothgar looked at the graying warrior standing firmly beside him, plain helm dangling from the chin strap in his hand. Aeschere's byrnie dripped bright with a spray of blood, though he showed no wounds; he must have been standing beside one of the slain men. Hrothgar's shoulders sagged.

"That is true, strange thing though it is. And yet should I yield hall and honor to a thing that comes from the mist and does murder where it will? The gods gave men the Middle Garth to hold: I will trust in that, and uphold it with what strength I may."

"Better, then, to seek the rede of the gods," Aeschere suggested. "Let us leave Heorot for a little while, that no more good men be killed while we wait to learn more of what we face."

Hrothgar looked towards the door posts: they were drenched with blood, as though the hall had newly been hallowed. The straw below was sodden black, but the mangled limbs and bodies of the slain still glistened freshly red.

"Guthhere, Helmwig, Wihstan, Hildwulf, and Alfberht," he said slowly. "They were brave men, who did not flee when their weapons failed to bite, but faced their deaths unflinching."

"You did not flinch either," Unferth said quietly, coming up on Hrothgar's other side. "And all Grendel's hate could not scathe you, though he strove chiefly to slay you. The luck of the Scyldings is still strong, to ward you against such a wight."

Wealhtheow sighed in soft relief. Unferth's words were more wisely placed than any she could have spoken then, for what he had said would be noised about. If Grendel could not fell Hrothgar, then all would know that the god born might of the Scyldings was still strong. None would be able to creep away from his side, saying,

"Hrothgar's luck has turned against him; why, therefore, should I stay?"

"That is so," Hrothgar answered. "But now, I think, we must gather our dead and go where we may hold counsel in quiet. Unferth, Wealhtheow, Aeschere, Frithgar: come with me to my sleeping house. And someone fetch Athelbeorn to join us as well, for he has seen more winters than any of us, and his redes are most often good."

Grendel waited inside the palisade of pointed stakes that ringed Heorot and all the buildings around it, listening to the murmurs of the men within the hall. He could not make out their words clearly; but after a little time the door opened again, spilling out firelight and the shadows of warriors walking out. None of them went alone; they all bore torches against the night, and their hands were close to their sword hilts as if he needed to spring from the darkness to take them unawares. Hrothgar was last to leave the hall, and Grendel ground his teeth silently as he looked upon the Scylding. He did not know what might it was that had kept Hrothgar from dying beneath his talons like the others, but the Scylding drighten was warded as surely as Grendel himself, so that neither of them could harm the other.

And yet I have harmed you, Grendel thought, for you could not save your men and now you are leaving your hall to me. It crossed his mind, fleetingly, that he could have wreaked a more cruel vengeance by taking Hrothgar's bride. But save when a woman acted in the stead of the male kin she had lost, women had no place in the ring of revenge and feud, and Grendel knew that Wealhtheow had heard his message and given it on to Hrothgar: he had no quarrel with her. When the torches no longer cast their long light over the snow, snuffed out within the dark walls of the houses around Heorot, Grendel arose and strode leisurely towards the hall again.

The fires still burned there; kegs of drink still waited behind the tables that had been set aside to clear the space for battle, and plates of food stood on the board as though a welcome feast had been readied for him. He did not turn aside, however, but went straight to Hrothgar's high seat at the end of the hall. The gilded sheaves of the drighten's gift stool glittered in the firelight: he who sat there had rule over Heorot. And yet, just as he could not bite into Hrothgar's flesh, Grendel found that he could not lay his hand on the carven armrest of Heorot's high seat. The wood seemed to spark and thrum beneath his clawed fingers, a warning certain and deep as the hiss of an adder. Cursing, he understood: though Hrothgar had withdrawn for the night, he had not yielded yet; and until the Scylding gave over his rule, Grendel could not claim it for his own.

"So, Hrothgar, this war is only beginning," Grendel murmured. "But we shall see whose strength fails first: yours or mine." He stretched himself out on the table before the high seats a new one, he marked, with no scent of the blood he had left upon it the night before and reached into the eoten glove at his waist that served as his hunting bag, tearing a deeply gashed leg free of the half crushed body within and beginning to gnaw thoughtfully at it as he considered how his kin would feast in this hall once Hrothgar had given up his last claim.

II

Berki stood up in the wain, clinging to its edge as the wheels bounced over the icy ruts plowed deep into the snow covered road. Stretching to his tiptoes, he could just see beyond the tall mounted figures of his father Ecgtheow and the twenty thanes Ecgtheow had brought with him for the faring to Hrethel's Yule feast. The high peaked roof of the king's hall glittered white as silver in the sunlight, its thatch crusted with a thick layer of ice; beyond the wide cluster of buildings sprawling about Hrethel's hall, the dark branches of pine trees shadowed through the snow that lay heavy upon the woods save on the western side, where the earth swept, clean and white, sharply down through a gap in the reddish granite crags and into the gray edge of the ocean. The wagon hit a rut and bounced. Berki lost his footing, sitting with a heavy thump on the wooden floor. The boy's thick fur lined cloak padded his landing, well enough that Berki was able to swallow his wail of surprise.

Aethelred, the driver, glanced about sharply, then snorted a puff of frozen fog past the red fox fur edging of his hood and turned back to his work. Thus chastened, Berki did not try to stand up again, but sat hugging his knees inside his cloak. The frothing tide of excitement, briefly stemmed by the shock of his fall, was rising in him again. He had never been so far from his father's hall at Hreosnabeorh; but the king's men had been part of his life from the beginning, striding into Ecgtheow's dwelling in their gilded helms and shining ring mail whenever Hrethel had need to summon his thane for rede or war, or coming bedecked with bright tunics and gold arm rings to share in Ecgtheow's feasts. And now that Berki had reached his seventh winter, it was his turn to be taken into the king's hall as a foster son, there to learn all the ways of a man.

The sound of hoof beats thundering through the snow made Berki look up again. From the woods on either side of the trail, a score of riders burst out, their horses' hooves scattering great fans of snow crystals behind them. Berki cried out in fear, for their faces were not human: grim nightmares of gnarled brown flesh and tattered green hair, they shouted as they pounded down towards Ecgtheow's wain and horsemen. Bright flashes of sunlight off metal seared Berki's squinting eyes; he pulled his hood over his head so that he would not have to look, and crouched trembling in the bottom of the wagon, waiting to hear the harsh clashing of swords and the snarling of the wild wights waiting for the claws to hook down into the wain, grasping him and stuffing him into a bag for the trolls' Yule feast. Instead he heard the hoof beats pulling up and slowing to match the slow crunching of Ecgtheow's steeds, and the sound of men's mirth: his father's deep booming laugh, and a lighter chuckle above it.

"That's a fine group of trolls you're leading, Hygelac," Ecgtheow said. "Tell me, did you get them all on the same hollow backed wood wife?"

"Fine trolls, and finer men," the higher voice replied. Berki was still shivering, but he pulled back a corner of his hood cautiously, peering up over the side of the wain.

His father had reined his horse back, and sat talking with a slim, broad shouldered youth of twelve or thirteen winters whose golden hair, now free of the fierce mask he held casually beneath his arm, streamed silkily over the spotted lynx fur of his cloak.

"This is my own troop, which Berki will join as soon as he can ride and fight well enough to be thought one of us. Where is he, anyway? You did not lose him on the road?"

"Berki!" Ecgtheow bellowed. "Stand up, boy!"

Berki scrambled to his feet, but his shaking hands could not keep a firm hold on the wain's edge, and he sat down roughly again. Some of the smaller troll riders laughed, their high pitched giggles scorching Berki's ears with shame.

"We frightened him!" One of them said. "Ha, if he is so weak hearted, he will never be a member of our troop."

Hygelac turned in his saddle, glaring at the distorted mask of the boy who had spoken.

"Hold your tongue, Thunarstan. Berki and his father are our guests this Yule, and insults given them are a shame to my father's hall." Hrethel's son looked down at Berki again. "How old are you, Berki?"

"S s s...seven winters," Berki stuttered, his tongue still frozen with the numbing relief from shock.

"Thunar, but you're a big one I would have taken you for eleven or twelve, at least, and strong built for that. You'll grow to match your father, most likely. But I am forgetting my duties. Ecgtheow and Berki and all your men, I, Hygelac Hrethel's son, give you welcome in my father's name. As ever, you are the most welcome of guests in this steading, and we greet you with joy this Yuletide. The ale stands ready in our hall, and the board bedecked for your coming."

The whole troop, Ecgtheow's men and Hygelac's boys, rode up to the hall, where thralls were already waiting to take over the care of Ecgtheow's horses and lift the bundles from his wain. Aware that the other boys were watching him closely, Berki tried to vault over the wain's edge as Aethelred had done, but misjudged his leap and tumbled heavily into the snow, landing hard on his back and knocking the breath from his body. He lay for a moment with his cloak spread out about him, the mound of his round belly shaking as he gasped air back into his lungs. His father was staring down at him, huge as a bear rearing against the sunlight. Beneath the thick tangle of brown beard that covered Ecgtheow's face and spilled over his massive chest, Berki saw a look he knew well: lips half curled in contempt and pity, jaw muscles twitching as if to hold back harsh words.

Another of the boy troop giggled, then another. Slowly Berki sat up. Hygelac dismounted, swinging easily off his horse, and held out his hand to help him. Berki clasped it firmly, hearing Hygelac's soft grunt of effort as the youth heaved Berki to his feet before helping him to brush the snow off his cloak.

"Come, my father waits within," Hygelac said, leading Ecgtheow and his son through the wyrm carven doorposts.

Hrethel's hall was twice the length of Hrethel's, and already filled with men and women in their feasting day finery. Gold glittered everywhere Berki looked: glinting from arm and finger rings, flashing from the brooches that pinned heavy cloaks at the shoulder and tunics at the neck, glimmering from tiny threads interwoven into the bright designs trimming sleeves and hems. After the long ride in the cold, the warmth and smoke of the crowded hall smote hard against Berki's face, so that his nose began to run and he had to blink and snuffle hard, then quickly wipe his face on his sleeve. Ecgtheow looked down at him and frowned, but said nothing; Berki slumped down, trying to make himself smaller in hopes that no one would notice him. The roar of voices stilled as Ecgtheow, with his men behind him, marched along the hall to Hrethel's high seat. The king was a man from much the same mold as his son: slim, but broad of shoulder and chest, with long golden hair.

It seemed to Berki that he could see already how Hygelac would look when he took his father's place in the raised wooden throne, his boyish features hardened with the first lines of age and a short golden beard covering the clean lines of his jaw. He spoke kindly to me, Berki thought. He will be a good king.

"Welcome, my kinsmen," Hrethel said. "It is a long faring between our halls in winter; it gladdens me to see you here so soon." He paused, waiting. A tall, dark haired woman came forward with a horn in one hand and a silver pitcher in the other. She was adorned more finely than the other women in the hall, the elaborate knot of her braids woven with gold threads and several necklaces of gold pendants nestling between the glowing strands of amber about her neck. The horn she carried was an aurochs horn, its smooth curve gleaming darkly between the bright glitter of gold ringing its lip and decorating its end. This would be Hrethel's queen Wynefrith: Berki's father had said that she had guested with them before, but Berki had been too young to remember her.

"Welcome to our hall, brave Ecgtheow," Wynefrith echoed. Her voice was high and breathy, but carried through the hall like a strongly blown reed pipe.

"For the love we bear you, and the troth you have ever shown to Hrethel in blade play and frith, you are ever a guest to be met with joy." She lifted the horn to Ecgtheow, who drank a deep draught before giving it back to her. "And you, young Berki. We are glad to have you with us, indeed, for much must be looked for from the son of such a mighty father, born from our beloved daughter's womb."

Berki began to tremble with fear, as he always did when older boys sought him out to trade blows with him. Whatever it was Hrethel's queen wanted from him, he knew he was bound to fail: he had never been good enough at anything to please Ecgtheow, and he could see already that it would be the same here. But thankfully, Wynefrith only offered him the horn, and though his hand shook, he was able to drink from it.

The mead within was sweet as honey cakes, and its taste lifted his spirits a little. Ecgtheow gestured his son closer to him, waving his men forward beside them. They came bearing the gifts Ecgtheow had brought for his king: pelts of bear and lynx and seal, lengths of fine cloth and a weighty bag of silver ingots. Hrethel marked each with a quick glance and a murmur of thanks as his queen refilled her horn and greeted each man by name with her guest draught.

"And lastly," Ecgtheow rumbled, "I bring you my own son, that he be raised up with your sons and other youths of good kin and learn all that an atheling should. For all that you have done for my sake, my king, I count as kindest your offer to take Berki as fosterling in your own hall. May he grow into a mighty warrior under your teaching, to uphold you in all things when I am grown too gray and bent to wield a blade."

"That will be a long time yet, my friend," Hrethel said, white teeth glinting in a smile. "And from the looks of your son, he is not too far from manhood. I had thought to see a small boy, not a youth near as tall as my Hygelac. Tell me, is he like to follow you as a berserk?"

"Berki is but seven winters old," Ecgtheow replied, and Berki thought that he could hear a gleam of pride in his father's voice, though it was fleeting as the silver flash of a minnow through a clear stream. "It is too soon to tell if he has gotten the berserk blood."

"Indeed! I had heard it whispered that there was eoten blood in your clan, which has ever bred the largest men of the North. Looking at your son makes it easy to believe that tale."

Ecgtheow drew himself up a little taller, the muscles of his great chest swelling beneath his red tunic.

"It has been rumored so. And his mother Hildebere was not the least of women, although..."

"Aye," Hrethel said gently. "My dear daughter was as tall and strong as any of her brothers have grown to be; she had the strength of a shield maid in her arms. But Wyrd is no kinder to women than to warriors."

His gaze fell upon Berki again, and the boy wanted to hide his face from shame. His mother Hildebere had died only three days after bearing him, for her womb had torn in the birth, and she had lost too much blood to fight the fever that came on after: and whenever Berki angered his father by proving himself clumsy in swordplay or fist fighting, Ecgtheow was not slow in telling him that he was not worth the life his mother had given up for him. The big warrior coughed roughly.

"Well, Berki is here for you, anyway, and ready to take his oath as foster son."

Hrethel looked up. "Herebeald, Hathcyn, Hygelac," he called. "Come forward; there is an oath for you to witness.

Hygelac ran forward lightly, almost dancing, to stand beside his father. The two older youths came more slowly, as if their new dignity as men was something that could be broken with a careless movement. The taller one was as fair as his father; his brother was dark haired and heavier of build, with a grave and thoughtful face already shadowed by a sprinkling of black hairs on jaw and chin.

Hrethel leaned forward, drawing a gold ring from his arm a thick unbroken circle of three strands twisted together and holding it out for Berki to rest his hand upon. The metal was warm and smooth beneath Berki's fingers; the boy thought he could stand holding it for hours, tracing the three wide bands of gold as they wove in and out over each other like wyrms in the water, diving only to surface again.

"Frea Ing and Nerthus hear us, and," he lowered his voice a little, as if in fear of the name, "the all mighty Ase. Berki Ecgtheow's son, I swear before the gods and men, and all good wights, to take you into my hall beside Herebeald and Hathcyn and Hygelac as if you were my own son, to raise you to manhood and do all a father's duties for you."

The sweat broke out in a hot prickle upon Berki's brow. His father had taught him the words that he must say, but now, with Hrethel in front of him and the oath ring in his hand, he could not remember any of them. Frantically he fought for something to say, stammering wildly in his panic.

"Hygelac...I mean Hrethel, I'm sorry...I swear, I swear to be good and..." His mind flailed like a drowning man in high seas, grasping desperately at the nearest piece of flotsam in his memory. "And to uphold you in all things." He glanced up nervously at his father to see if he had spoken well enough. Ecgtheow was scowling slightly, but said nothing to help him. "May the gods witness it," Berki finished.

Hrethel smiled kindly at him.

"A well spoken oath, Berki." He stood, reaching down to embrace the boy. His sons followed; the hugs of Herebeald and Hathcyn were mere touches about Berki's shoulders, but Hygelac grasped him heartily, as though truly pleased by his words.

"Well spoken, indeed," Wynefrith said. For a moment her gray eyes seemed to stare through Berki, as though his plump body were no more than a waver of hall smoke. "And perhaps better than you know." She took Hygelac's slim hand, setting it on the ring between his father's and Berki's. "Hygelac, Berki shall be in your keeping as a brother before all, for he is both oath brother and sister son to you, and you shall look to him, as he to you, for help at need."

"So shall it be!" Hygelac replied. "Come, Berki. If you are not needed any longer here..." Hrethel nodded at his son's questioning look... "then I shall show you about your new home while there is still daylight, before the real trolls come out of the woods."

"Are there truly trolls here?" Berki asked as Hygelac led him away.

"Of course, great fierce ones. I have often heard them roaring and stamping upon the rooftops in the winter, and when summer is drawing nearer, they break the icicles from the eaves as swords and fight with them until they melt; you will see them scattered about after a night of battle."

Hygelac showed Berki all about Hrethel's burg: the houses where his sword thanes slept, ready to rise and fight for their drighten at need; the bath houses with the steam rising from the chinks in their logs; the smithy, still and quiet for the Yule nights, but still smelling of long burning coals and hot iron; the long byres where the cattle, mewed up for the winter, shifted and mooed restlessly; and the stables, now filled near to overflowing with the horses of Hygelac's men and all his Yule guests.

"Beyond the fence, to the north there, is a grave field. You cannot see the mounds from here, but should you be out riding or hunting late in the day, you should be careful not to tread there after sunset. In my father's great grandfather's time, a man named Ansugrimar was buried there. He was a puller of runes, a berserk and a great follower of Woden his mound is marked with a stone carved with a long row of staves. Since he was laid in his howe, that field has been an uncanny place. There are many folk who say they have seen him riding on a gray horse with his hounds behind him whenever there is to be a shedding of blood, and his cloak billows behind him even when there is no wind to blow it. He is often out and about at Yule."

Berki shivered, looking nervously through the narrow gaps between the sharpened logs that formed the wall about Hrethel's burg. He could see nothing but the field beyond, its snow yellowing in the lowering light of the Sun.

"Do not fear, Sunna is still high enough to drive away ghosts," Hygelac said lightly. "And it is well to know all the wights when you come to a new place. Let us get a pitcher of ale and a bowl, and I will show you where to make offering so that our home ghosts will know who you are."

When Berki, guided by Hygelac, had poured out ale on the rough boulder near the hall door and the flat topped stone by the stables, Hrethel's youngest son clapped him on the shoulder.

"That is well done. Now, is there any one god you call friend, Berki? Our harrow grove is just outside to the northeast, next to the barrow field. I shall take you to it, if you wish to go there before the sun is down."

"My father worships the Lord of the Hanged," Berki whispered, "but I am afraid of him."

Hygelac nodded, his sharp features sober.

"There is no shame in that, for many men grown do not have the heart to look the One Eyed in the face. Perhaps you find Thunar more to your liking, for his size and strength?"

"I do not know," Berki murmured. "I have not thought about it."

"Ah well, you are young yet, and I have heard that the gods make themselves known in their own time, if they wish it. For myself, my heart is good towards all of them, but I must say that I have a special warmth for Thunar and for his travel friend Loca, for there should be laughter among the gods as well as among men. But it will not be long before sundown; is there anything else you wish to do while we still have light?"

"Will it be long before we eat?" Berki answered wistfully. The bread and sausage he had enjoyed in the wain seemed a long time ago, and he could smell the scent of roasting meat drifting from the cook houses.

Hygelac laughed. "Come, there will be some food set out in the hall. It would be ill done of us to starve you on your first day with us."

Berki sat at the high table between Hygelac and his father. The food was good: chunks of elk meat floating in a thick savory sauce, sausages with golden drops of fat bursting through their brown skins, and succulent pink slices of ham, together with braided loaves of white bread and sweet nutty tasting goat cheese, all washed down with draughts of a warm honeyed ale that soon had Berki yawning a little and rubbing at his eyes. The talk of the older folk at the high table was boring, all about men whom Berki did not know and battles of which he had never heard. Busy filling his stomach and wondering if he dared ask if there would be honey cakes, Berki heard almost missed his father saying,

"...Had thought to give Berki a puppy of that line."

Berki straightened up hopefully, wiping a smear of crumbs and grease from his face with the corner of his sleeve. Ecgtheow did not even seem to notice as he went on.

"She did not come on heat this year, alas. I have often wondered how her litter mate fares, the one I gave to Hrothgar those years ago. News of him does not reach me as often as I would like."

"It will be no trouble finding a good hunting hound for your son, if he wishes a puppy," Hrethel replied. "As for Hrothgar himself I have heard nothing of his hounds, but I know that he was wedded at Winter nights, to the daughter of that drighten Hadulf with whom he was at war for so long. It is said to have been a fine wedding, with a gudhija from God Home to bless it, and I have heard nothing but good of Hrothgar's wife Wealhtheow, while it is also said that his new hall, Heorot, is finer than any other standing in Middle Earth, save perhaps only the great hofs at Upsala and God Home. From all accounts, the line of the Scyldings fares better than it has since Halga's death."

"Then that is well," Ecgtheow said cheerfully, lifting his silver bound drinking horn. "I drink to Hrothgar's health and joy, and trust that the gods may ever keep and bless his line."

"May it be so," Hrethel replied. "Hrothgar has ever been a friend to the Geats." The others at the high table all raised their horns as well, drinking deeply.

"And without the Scyldings in the south," Hathcyn cut in, "we should have to look for more trouble from the Swedes."

Hrethel frowned. "That is true. We have had little trouble with Ongentheow in the last year, but the Swedes are ever greedy for land, and I fear that this time of frith will not last."

At last Ecgtheow emptied his horn and rose from the table, looking over at the small group of warriors who stood speaking quietly in the corner. Three of them wore gray wolf cloaks; the others bore heavy bear hames draped over their shoulders, so that their shadows in the flickering firelight seemed more like those of beasts than men.

"I must go now to join my brethren, to ready ourselves for this Yule night's dancing."

Ecgtheow's voice was beginning to slur with the thickness of strong mead, and the gaze he turned on his king was no longer mild with friendship: Berki could see the wildness kindling in his father's dark eyes, like the glare of a bear creeping from its shadowy den his fetch looking out from within the human skull and he shrank back as if to hide himself behind the table.

"Go quickly, then, for I see that the berserk's wod is coming upon you," Hrethel said.

Berki watched as his father joined the others, the nine of them slipping quietly out of the hall. He could not move or turn his eyes away until Hygelac slapped him lightly on the shoulder.

"Ha, perhaps you will join the berserk band someday. It is often that a son will follow his father in that."

Mutely Berki shook his head. He could not put his thoughts into words: he only knew that Ecgtheow's fierceness frightened him, for when that look came into his father's eyes, there was no telling how he would strike out, or at whom: thus Ecgtheow had started his blood feud many years ago. And, although Hygelac's face was bright with excitement, Berki could tell that Hrethel was uneasy, as though the king shared a little of Berki's own fear.

Yet Hrethel held himself calmly, not starting even when he heard the unearthly wolf howls and deep snarling cutting through the singing and laughter of the feasters. The king rose to his feet.

"Back!" He shouted. "Woden's men will soon be among us, filled with all the might of the god's host. Beware, for the wod is upon them, and they know neither kin nor friends; greet them well, that they bring Woden's blessing to this hall."

The thralls hastened to pull the tables aside, Hrethel's thanes and their wives crowding back. Several of the women, Wynefrith among them, filled horns to the brim with mead, golden droplets splashing over the rims and falling glimmering to the straw as the holders' hands shook. The howling was growing louder; though the door was still closed, it seemed to Berki that he could feel the cold storm wind blowing through, shaking the hall pillars. He shut his eyes, then squinted them open again, afraid not to see what would come. The door thundered open, and the berserks burst in. Their shapes twisted into their shadows until they seemed to fill the hall: huge men, naked except for the sword belts over their shoulders and the bear and wolf fells they wore or had they sprouted thick pelts of hair, dark pricked or pointed ears?

Their eyes caught the firelight, casting it back like golden mirrors as their howls and snarls echoed through the hall. Swiftly Wynefrith stepped forward, offering her greeting horn to the grim gray wolf coat who led them with upraised spear. He snatched the horn from her, emptying it in a single draught and tossing it away in a high glittering arc as those behind him did the same with the horns of Wynefrith's women. Hrethel let out a deep sigh of relief as the women moved back to shelter behind the tables. The berserks tossed their shaggy heads back, barking together in a fierce deep chorus like hunting hounds on a trail.

"Wod! Wod!" The leader lifted his spear, whirling its blade in a flashing circle; the others drew their swords, iron clashing on iron with the sharp ring of breaking ice as they wheeled and stamped, their foot beats drumming harshly through the hall.

Berki stared in horror at the snarling masks of their faces, the froth flying from their mouths as their dance grew wilder. Now and again, he thought he saw a blow strike hard against flesh, but no blood sprang out beneath the keen edges. His head was beginning to spin with watching them, and he thought that he might be sick. The berserks broke apart, then wheeled together again.

One bear coat's arm flashed across a table, tearing a horn from the hand of the man who held it; the berserk emptied it down his throat while parrying his fellows' blows, never missing a movement of the whirling sword dance. Other folk, perhaps braver, offered up their drink willingly, reaching over the tables towards the maddened beast men. At the end of the hall, a woman screamed: a berserk's uncaring grasp had caught her hand as well as her horn, dragging her halfway across the table and twisting her arm out of its socket. Berki did not know how long they danced: it seemed a single endless moment of terror to him. But suddenly, as if called by a single word that only they could hear, the berserks turned at once, racing from the hall.

The door banged shut behind them, the silence broken only by the sobs of the injured woman as her kinsmen wrenched her arm back into place. Hrethel stood, the beads of sweat on his fair brow gleaming red in the firelight like gems on ivory.

"Hail to Woden!" He said. "His men have come among us as friends, doing little harm they have drunk our mead, they have brought their blessing. May the One Eyed cast his spear over our foes; may we be blessed with sig in all our battles this year!"

"Hail!" The cry went up, full throated with relief.

"A fine sight, was that not?" Hygelac said to Berki. "I have often wished that I could be one of the berserk band, but that blood does not run in my line. They did not," he added in a lower voice, "even bother to test me, as they do with the young men whose fetches are bears or wolves."

"How do they know?" Berki asked around another honey cake.

"Ansuwulf he is the oldest of them, the one in the wolf pelt with the spear is a spae man, who can see what is hidden from others, and which animal runs unseen before your footsteps. It is he who chooses the youths for testing and takes them away into the woods. They do not always come back," Hygelac went on, an ominous tone in his voice, but then added hastily, "yet you will have nothing to fear if he chooses you, for you are Ecgtheow's son."

"What happens?"

"Only those of the berserk band know, and they will not speak to others about it."

It was very late when Hygelac at last rose, yawning and stumbling, from the bench.

"Come, Berki. You shall share a house with Haethcyn and myself, for that you are our brother now."

Although Berki was almost asleep himself, the crisp bite of the frosty air woke him from the hall's drowsy warmth at once as they stepped outside. The moon was down, the stars glittering like spear points between the ragged banners of black cloud sweeping over the sky. Hygelac paused, looking upward.

"No sign of the old man," he said, a hollow echo of disappointment sounding in his slurred voice. "It must be that we will have a year of frith to come."

"Is that so bad?" Berki asked. He did not like the look of the streaming clouds against the stars; it seemed to him that he could see their misty blackness swirling and stretching like great troll fingers, reaching out to snuff the glimmering points of light.

"Not for you, since you are too young to ride out with a warrior troop yet. But if there is fighting this year, it will be my first chance to measure myself on the field. Well, Wyrd pulls as she will, and if there are no battles for me this year, there will surely be next. Come along, before our noses freeze off."

Berki followed Hygelac's unsteady steps, stopping in the shadow of the palisade to relieve himself when the older boy did. A bed had already been laid out for him in the house Hrethel's younger sons shared; against the wall, Haethcyn was snoring lightly beneath his blankets.

"Sleep well, Berki, and glad Yule," Hygelac said as the two of them climbed quickly into their beds. "And remember your dreams as best you may: there is always truth in the first dream you dream within a new house."

The fur lined blankets were warmer and thicker than those Berki had slept in at home. Bundling himself up so that the cold air could only reach the tip of his nose, Berki was soon asleep in their soft comfort. It seemed to Berki as though he woke in a strange hall a hall higher than any he had seen, whose carven roof pillars and antler adorned rafters glimmered with gold, its brightness clear even in the low light of the red coals glowing along the bottoms of the fire trenches. About him men were sleeping: strange men, their long braided hair and beards disheveled from a night's heavy feasting.

Only he was awake; only he saw the door swinging open, the dark shape gliding through on a curl of mist. He tried to shout a warning, but his voice was soundless as a flake of snow whispering through still air. The shadow walker he could not see it clearly reached out; Berki saw a glimmer of dark talons as it seized upon the first sleeper, tearing his head from his body with a single twist. The blood spurted out over the face of another, who turned, sitting up and brushing at the wetness. He lifted his hand to look, dazed, at the blood; the dark thing grasped his arm, pulling until it ripped loose from his shoulder. His cry awoke the others, who turned and cursed or reached at once for their weapons.

Then the night terror seemed to be everywhere, slashing and biting; Berki saw swords bouncing harmlessly from its hide as it rent the bodies of the men around it with gaping wounds, tearing and chewing at their flesh until nothing stood in the hall save the mist blurred shape of the troll and Berki himself, peering out from behind the shadow of the high seat. He froze, hoping it would not see him, and perhaps it did not, for it bent to the grisly work of pulling the dead limb from limb, stuffing their bodies into the great five fingered bag that hung from its belt like a huge glove.

At last it loped off, black droplets of blood fanning out in a spray from the headless corpse swinging in its hand. And now the silence that had frozen Berki's voice melted in a moment, like a handful of snow cast into a bonfire, and the high nightmare scream burst from his throat, echoing through his skull like a horn blast reverberating through a stone cave. Berki's eyes were open, staring into the darkness; his throat felt ragged from his scream, the harsh sound of his panting almost drowning out the voice shouting,

"Berki! Berki, what is wrong with you?"

For a moment, he did not know where he was or who was speaking to him. Only when his breathing began to ease, the thunder of his heart to slow, did Berki remember that he was at Hrethel's hall, in Hygelac's house, and know that the strong lithe hands gripping his own must be those of his foster brother.

"What is wrong? Speak to me, Berki. Has the Wod Host stolen you away?"

Berki coughed, swallowing hard. "I dreamed, I dreamed something terrible."

"What was it?"

But Berki could only shake his head, shivering. Beside the bed, he heard other footsteps, and a lower voice spoke.

"I have no doubt that he dreamed something terrible, if you poured as much mead into him last night as you downed yourself, Hygelac. Boys should know better than to try to drink like grown men, and you, my brother, should know better than to egg them on. I shall be surprised if as many as half of your troop are able to stand this morning and tell me, how is your own head?"

Berki felt Hygelac's slight wince through his hands, but Hrethel's youngest son answered boldly enough.

"And I suppose that you went to bed sober? You were snoring like a bull in rut when we came in, and I would wager a gold ring that if I followed your tracks back to the hall, they would hardly run in a straight line."

"Straighter than yours, at any rate, for that I had the sense to leave the feasting when I felt the mead beginning to mount too high in me. 'Ale is not so good as is thought for the sons of men.'"

"And you are too young to speak like a man with a hoary beard," Hygelac replied.

"As may be." Berki heard the sound of Haethcyn walking away; then the door opened to gray light, a swirling of snowflakes scattering into the house. "See, Berki," the older youth said, his voice more gentle, "dawn has come, and you have nothing to fear from night terrors. Rise, if you are able after an evening of my brother's guest friendliness, and make yourself ready for a day of games and enjoyment, at least as far as the weather will allow. As for me, I am going to the hall to break my fast, and I think you would be best to do the same." Haethcyn wrapped a thick cloak of brindled reindeer hide about his shoulders, heedless of the way the loose hairs scattered behind him, and strode out into the snow.

There had been a heavy fall late in the night, for his feet sank halfway to the knee in the fresh whiteness, and, looking out the door, Berki could see the drifts heaped high beneath the eaves on the northern sides of the other houses.

Hygelac shrugged, reaching down to a small chest and taking out a silver comb to tidy his disheveled mess of fair hair.

"Haethcyn thinks that because his beard is beginning to grow, he must be as wise and cautious as the oldest of rede givers at least when speaking with those who lack a few of his own winters. You need pay him little mind."

"Still," Berki said cautiously, "breaking fast sounds good to me.

Hygelac tied a woven band of patterned red and gold about his head to hold his hair back.

"Well enough. If we hurry to the baking house, it may be that old Amma will have made some honey cakes."

A curl of gray smoke drifted from the roof of the baking house, swirling warm through the snowflakes. Hygelac and Berki crowded in quickly, stamping the caked snow from their boots. As Hygelac had promised, the sweet scent of honey filled the small house; a young, lank thrall maid was just lifting a flat baking shovel from the fireplace while a fat old woman kneaded dough, calling orders to her helper.

"Amma, what can you spare for myself and my sister son Berki?" Hygelac asked. The old woman cackled, shaking her head to toss a few wispy locks of white hair from her face. The hanging flesh of her wide arms and sagging bosom quivered as she turned and pounded the dough, never missing a beat as she replied, "Take what you will, although the cakes will burn your mouth if you eat them too quickly. Berki, hmm? A proper little bear he is, too; I guess he must eat like a bear cub in summer. Go on, Berki, have a honey cake. Your mother always loved them: I made them for her from the time she was a small girl, when her little fingers could hardly hold a spindle, and served them to her at her wedding feast."

The sticky roll was almost too hot for Berki's chilled fingers to hold. He juggled it from hand to hand, biting into it quickly and then blowing over his tongue to cool the hot honey scorch. With the first sweet bite, his hunger awoke fully: he finished that cake in a few bites, then reached for another. Hygelac nibbled more fastidiously, talking with Amma as he ate.

"Aye, the weather grew wild before dawn," the old woman said. "The snow was so fierce, I could not see my way here: if I had not been walking that path since before you were born, I would have wandered lost for a time, I tell you. But it has stilled now, so you will have a good enough day for your Yule games."

"Did you see anything strange? Or hear anything?" Hygelac asked eagerly.

Amma laughed, her plump wrinkled cheeks and jowls wobbling. "Nothing at all, young fro. No ghosts or draugs or even blue lights flying through the clouds nothing save the snow and wind. But there are eleven more nights in Yule, so maybe something will happen for you before the holy days are done. And what of you, little bear? Are you looking for a Yule omen, too? A dream of mighty battle, or perhaps of the girl you shall marry?"

Although it was warm in the baking house and he was still wrapped in his heavy cloak, Berki felt a chill come over him as though he had plunged suddenly into icy water. Not daring to speak, he shook his head hard and bit into a fifth honey cake warm and sweet and solid, the taste of summer flowers and ripe wheat driving away the terror of his dream as surely as the sign of Thunar's Hammer.

He had just finished the last cake when two other boys burst into the hut, a tall, thin youth with his red hair bound into a single thick braid down the back and a shorter, broader one whose round face was framed in a tangle of gold brown curls. "Ha, Amma, what have you got for us?" The redhead demanded.

"You will have to wait a while, Widuhund," the old woman said. "If you had been earlier to rise, you might have gotten a honey cake before the little bear here ate them all."

The boy looked down his long nose at Berki. "Little bear, indeed," he muttered scornfully. "No wonder you are so fat, if you do nothing but eat and sleep through the winter."

"Hold your tongue, Widuhund!" Hygelac told him sharply. "This is my sister son and oath brother: did you not hear his oath taking? No doubt he will show you how wrong you are to make fun of him when we fight with wooden swords later."

"Bravely spoken, but we shall see what he can do then," the shorter youth said. "I did not think him such a threat when he cowered from us in the wain."

"Enough, Agilar. Berki is my close kinsman, and I will hear no words against him," Hygelac answered, his voice low and menacing. The other boy looked away, abashed.

When they came out again, Berki could hear the cracking of wooden swords and high cries of encouragement, like the squawking of a flock of magpies. He rubbed the smoke of the baking house from his eyes, looking around through the light veil of snowflakes still whispering down. In front of the hall, the snow had been swept out of a rough circle, and two youths were sparring inside it, their friends calling to them from outside the circle. Standing a little way from the boys was a short, sharp faced man with a closely trimmed red beard, whose gray streaked blond hair was pulled back into a narrow braid. He stood barefoot in the snow as if he did not feel the cold, his gray wolfskin cloak hanging carelessly over a short sleeved tunic of deep blue. Hygelac poked Berki in the side.

"See, that is Ansuwulf watching there his name is Wulf, but he is called Ansuwulf for that he is given to the Grim One. He often helps with our training, in order that he may learn our measure. Be sure you do your best before him! He is the brother of Eofor, one of my father's thanes who guards our northeastern marches, and sometimes he will choose the best among the youths to fight in Eofor's war band for a season, for there are always small battles and raids there."

Berki stared at Ansuwulf, open mouthed. Last night in the hall, the berserk had seemed the size of an eoten, towering above other men like a shadow cast on a mountain by the setting sun. Now, in the light of day, Berki could see that Ansuwulf was no more than a finger width or two above his own height, though his shoulders and chest would have been broad even for a man a head taller. There was no sign of the berserk wildness in his deep gray eyes this morning, but there was something wolf like in the keen set of his face as he stared at the boys, sharp nose tilted forward as though to sniff out their weaknesses.

"You need not fear him, though," Hygelac added softly. "They say when he was younger, few men would sit at drink with him, for that he was so quick to fight when the ale rose in him: he was nearly outlawed once, but his mood has grown calmer with the years, and now he is a welcome hall thane."

The bout ended with a thud of wood against flesh; the two youths who had been fighting walked out of the circle and pulled off their helmets, the smaller of them rubbing his bruised ribs ruefully.

"Well done, Thunarstan. Herebrand, you will never live through your first battle if you do not learn to move your shield faster," Ansuwulf said mildly. "With a real sword and a man's strength behind it, that blow might well have cut your lungs half through."

The boy he had reproved looked down, a flush suffusing his sweaty face and darkening the splotchy red birthmark on his left cheek to purple. "You often cast your shield away in battle, and you are still alive," he muttered.

"Few berserks reach my years, and that is by Woden's will alone," Ansuwulf answered. "But that is a matter that you will never need to think on for yourself, Herebrand. No, put your helm back on and stay in the circle: I would see how you prove yourself against young Berki, for his first fight among us."

Berki stopped in his tracks, the snow gathering on his shoulders. Even back at Hroesnabeorh, he had only been matched against boys two or three years older than himself, not against youths who were nearly grown men. He wanted to refuse, to say that he had but seven winters; but Ecgtheow beat him if he ever tried to turn from a fight, and he knew that Hygelac would think ill of him if he did now.

"Go on," Hygelac whispered encouragingly, taking the helm from the youth who had won the bout and helping Berki to strap it on. "Ansuwulf has given you an easy match for your first one, and you have the weight and, I daresay, the strength over Herebrand. Go on, I shall hold your cloak for you."

Berki scuffed through the snow as if he were wading through knee deep surf. His hands seemed too cold to close tightly about wooden hilt and shield strap. Awkwardly he climbed over the mound of snow ringing the circle, taking up his guard and trying to remember what his father had told him. Shield high; you can drop faster than raise, and live easier with a sword through your leg than through your head. Sword ready to strike. At least the training shield and sword were lighter than those Ecgtheow had given him was it the other's eyes he was supposed to watch, or his shoulders?

"Begin," Ansuwulf ordered.

Herebrand circled Berki slowly, warily, as though he were waiting for a sudden lunge, and Berki's breathing slowly began to ease. It was as if he could hear Ecgtheow shouting at him, If you're too Hel rotted slow to make a good attack, then wait for him to come to you! A man's always easiest to hit when he's just struck out. The other boy swung: his blow was fast, but with little strength behind it, and Berki was just able to get his shield across for the wooden sword to glance lightly from it. As hard and swiftly as he could, Berki struck at Herebrand.

His blow landed squarely in the middle of the other's shield with a loud crack; Herebrand stumbled back a step, but recovered at once, lunging in; and before Berki could counter, he had received a stunning blow to his right thigh and a thump that rang off his helmet.

"Still a little slow on the attack, Herebrand, but at least you have learned not to trust that a single stroke will kill at once. Berki..." Ansuwulf leapt lightly over the mounded snow into the circle, taking the shield from Herebrand's arm and looking closely at it. "I thought so: you have cracked the wood. It is as well for Herebrand that you are slow as a snake in winter." He tossed the shield spinning away, gestured to Hygelac to throw him another, which he caught neatly by the strap.

The berserk's gray eyes stared dizzyingly into Berki's for a moment. Berki could not turn away, but there was something in the dark depths of Ansuwulf's gaze that terrified him like looking into the empty eyes of a hanged man dangling from his noose, or glancing into the blackness within an open barrow. Ansuwulfar smiled slightly, nodding.

"The two of you will fight again, and you will try to move faster, but not hit so hard. I do not wish to spend the rest of my Yule coaxing a boy's broken bones to heal. And remember that strength will do you no good if a faster man has already split your head, nor will it help you if you do not have the skill to use it, as you do not yet. Learn what you are doing first, before you try to put your might into a stroke."

Limping slightly on his bruised leg, Berki lifted his sword and shield again."Bend your knees deeper, Berki, and widen your stance," Ansuwulf called. "You will never be able to move your feet properly if you start like that."

This time, Herebrand did not bother to circle him; he came straight in, his sword flickering out faster than Berki could counter. His first blow bounced off the rim of Berki's shield, but the second clanged hard on the younger boy's helm again, dropping Berki to his knees in the snow. Berki looked up, dazed and foolish, expecting to be hit again, but Herebrand had already stepped back, lowering his sword. Through the ringing in his ears, Berki could hear the murmuring and the soft snickers.

"You two, out," Ansuwulf ordered. "Agilar and Widuhund, I shall see you fight now."

"Are you hurt?" Hygelac asked Berki when he had given over his helm and weapons. "Those were good blows you took."

"My leg hurts. So does my head." Berki was trying not to snuffle, but his thigh was beginning to throb fiercely and his skull felt bruised. Though he had hardly begun to sweat, his skin felt chilled and clammy, and he knew the older boys were laughing at him.

Hygelac felt quickly through his hair, pausing at the two sore spots. "You are only banged a little, and will take no harm from it. When you have rested a little, Ansuwulf will call you in again and you will have a chance to get your revenge. Perhaps you would like to practice a litle with me first, to keep your muscles warm?"

Berki wanted only to go back to the baking house, to sweet honey cakes and a warm fire and the kind words of old Amma. But he could not disappoint his new brother so early, so he forced himself to nod his head. They started slowly, Hygelac bringing his wooden sword around in carefully controlled arcs to tap gently against Berki's shield. Even so, Berki could not block more than half of the older boy's blows, and he was greatly relieved when he heard Haethcyn's low voice saying, "Ha, Hygelac, leave off that and come with me; our father wants you."

Hygelac laid down his practice weapons and patted Berki on the shoulder.

"You stay here for now, brother. If anyone gives you any trouble, just you give them a good thumping."

Forlorn and desolate, Berki watched Hygelac go. He had almost made his mind up to creep away before he was called back into the sparring circle again when a hard blow struck the back of his shoulder. Agilar stood behind him, a red bruise already beginning to darken along his cheek. He smiled at Berki, an unpleasant, lopsided smile.

"Not ready for more fighting?" He asked. "Suppose you practice a little with me."

Uncomfortably, Berki shrugged his shield back onto his arm and squared up with the other boy. Agilar was on him at once, in a flurry of blows that ended up with Berki on his back in the snow, trying to hide beneath his shield as the wooden sword landed again and again. Finally Agilar stepped back, sneering at him as he got up painfully and put down his weapons.

"See, Berki has no business being here," Agilar said to the others who had moved away from the sparring circle to watch. "He is only Hygelac's tame bear cub."

"Berki?" Said one of the other youths, a boy whose white blond hair hung about his shoulders. "A bear that has grown fat and slow from honey and berries, I should say. He is surely no danger to anyone but the bees."

"Aye, he is a mighty hunter of honey, a true wolf to the bees," Agilar laughed. "And that is a good kenning for Berki: Beowulf, the honey eater, since he is good for nothing save eating and sleeping. What of it, Beowulf? Ward yourself, here come the stings." He began to make a buzzing noise with his lips, dancing in and jabbing hard at Berki with his forefingers. Berki flailed at him, but the other boy was far too fast, his sharp pokes landing with bruising force. The blond youth snickered, waving his own arms around. "See, Beowulf, the swarm is coming after you!" He said, poking Berki in the stomach.

Already hurt and angry, Berki rushed at him, waving his fists wildly. The blond sidestepped with ease, stabbing the younger youth with his forefingers as Berki skidded in the snow. The other boys were buzzing as well, surrounding him. Beyond them, Berki could see Ansuwulf watching, a slight smile on his sharp face, but the man neither spoke or moved to stop the game. One of Agilar's pokes landed hard between Berki's bruised ribs, the hurt sharp as the blow of a knife, and Berki put his head down, starting to run.

"Look, Beowulf is afraid of the swarm!" One of the boys said. "Where is he going to hide?"

They were keeping up with his lumbering steps easily, buzzing and jabbing at him between cutting remarks. Berki did not know where he was going, only that he wanted to get away from them. He hardly noticed when he had passed through the western gate, but the ground sloped down smoothly and it was easier for him to run, trying to break free until his feet crunched through the frosty rim of ice over smooth sand and the first shock of cold water soaked through his shoes.

"Bzzz, bzzz, bzzz," Agilar chanted. "You cannot escape the swarm."

Breathing hard through his mouth, Berki turned and ran straight into the ocean, his legs kicking up a spume of icy spray. The water was so cold that his legs went numb at once, chilling the pain of his bruises away. He kept going, floundering deeper until the water was up to his chest, flailing his arms hard against the waves. One comber, stronger than the rest, swelled beneath him and then he was swimming, the ocean bearing his body up more lightly than the lake at his father's stead ever had. The first shock over, he could feel the blood singing through his limbs as he swam, like the tingle of snow after sweating in the bath house.

"Hey!" Someone shouted. "You Beowulf! Come back, you witling, you'll be drowned."

Berki glanced back, to see the other boys standing dumbfounded on the shore. He did not care, he decided: if he were drowned, it would be they who had to tell his father, and he would never have to go back to the bruising shame of the practice ring, nor listen to their taunts again. He turned away, ducking his head beneath a curling gray crest and bringing himself up again with a powerful stroke of his arms. The tide had caught him now, bearing him swiftly along the beach; he was already more than an hundred yards down from his tormentors.

As he swam along the shore, the waves grew stronger, each one sweeping his head beneath the surface; and each time it grew harder for Berki to pull himself up. The cold was beginning to seep deeply into him as well, and when he gasped air into his lungs, the breath came hard between his chattering teeth. Another wave tumbled Berki under, whirling him so that he did not know if he was swimming up or down. I will drown out here, he thought suddenly. But strangely, he felt no fear, though his ribs ached with the struggle of holding air in his lungs, like barrel staves straining to keep the frothing new ale from bursting their bonds.

He was floating freely in the water, moving more easily than on land it seemed to him as if he were flying, swooping through the sea like an eagle in the air, and he could not fall as long as he held his breath. His head was pounding, a scattering of red lights flashing giddily behind his closed eyelids, and yet he did not want it to end. But as the swirling darkness rose around Berki, his right foot found smooth sand beneath, his leg kicking out hard without thought to drive him upward again. The harsh wind scoured his face as his head broke out into air; he gasped, panting in breaths of searing ice as the waves pushed him closer to shore.

He had rounded the point of Hrethel's harbor, and now he could fight the sea no longer, but only let it carry him in towards the beach like a piece of shivering driftwood. When the sand scraped against his knees, Berki stood, hugging his arms tightly around himself, and waded from the water onto the snowy beach. His hands and feet were numb, his fingers blue white and stiff as the fingers of a corpse; but worse was the hollow gnawing in his stomach, as though he had been starved for a week. Faint with cold and hunger, he began to stumble back through the snow. Black spots still whirled before his eyes, so that he almost missed the scuffle of tracks at the beginning of the track up to Hrethel's hall, but he managed to trudge back through the gates, along to the baking house, where Amma stood kneading dough.

"Frige help us!" The old woman cried when she turned around. "Little bear, did you fall through the ice? Stand near the fire, and take those wet clothes off at once; it is a wonder you are still alive. I have seen grown men die of the same cold."

Berki was shivering too hard to speak, and his frozen fingers could not tighten on his tunic clasp. Amma was quick to help him, stripping his clothes from his body and wrapping him in her own cloak, then sitting him on a stool before the fire and chafing his hands and feet between her own warm hands. At first he could feel nothing, then a sudden rush of sharp pain stabbing up through his fingers and toes made him cry out.

"Ah, may the gods be thanked," Amma sighed. "You will not lose any part of yourself that you can feel now what of your ears?" She grabbed the sides of his head, rubbing hard until Berki shrieked at the hot needles of agony boring through his earlobes.

"Truly you have strong luck," she declared, satisfied at last. "Here, eat this. I have tended shipwrecked sailors before, and a man who has been in the cold water must always have something sweet when he comes out." She pushed a small pot of honey into Berki's hands. Although his fingers were still too stiff to grasp the horn spoon, he was able to close his fist weakly about its handle, lifting the sweet honey to his mouth. At the first taste of it, it seemed to him that he could feel a rush of strength pouring back into his body, and he ate greedily until he had scooped the last sticky drop from the clay and licked the spoon clean.

"Now, tell me what happened to you. Where did you fall in? Were you fool enough to walk upon ice without asking where it was thin?"

"They chased me," Berki stammered. "The other boys, they chased me to the beach, but I got away. I swam."

"You swam?" Amma repeated, watery blue eyes wide in disbelief. She placed her fists on her broad hips, staring angrily down at him. "You should have died out there, you witless creature! The tides are treacherous enough by Whales' Ness in summer when the sea is calm. Now you will swear to me that you will not do such a thing again, else you shall never see another honey cake of my baking."

Berki looked mutely up at her, beginning to snuffle, and in a moment she had bent down to wrap her heavy arms about him, her wrinkled cheek soft against his.

"Ah, stop crying, little bear," she murmured into his ear. "You have had a good fright, and no less than you should, but you are alive and safe now, thanks only to the blessing of the gods, I am sure. Now what did those young wretches do to you, that you should do such a foolish thing as plunge into the winter sea?"

"They were playing at bees, and they stung me," Berki sniffled. "They called me Beowulf, and said I was only good for eating and sleeping. They said I should not be among them. They beat me badly at sword play, and laughed at me. And Hygelac had gone away, and Ansuwulf did not stop them." He began to cry in earnest then, and Amma held him, stroking his hair.

"They are rough and foolish young creatures," the old woman said. "That is the way of boys, that they see nothing but what they think is before them. Do not let them take the heart from you, little bear, for a cub is always fat and clumsy, but I daresay they shall laugh from the other side of their mouths when you are grown. Now, you shall stay by the warm fire and eat honey cakes for a little while I send that useless girl where has she gone? to fetch dry clothes for you, and then you shall go to let everyone know you are safe, before they begin searching the shore for your body. If those young trolls have had the bravery to tell anyone where you went, that is. And if not, I shall have some things to say to them the next time they come skulking around here after food, you may believe that."

Amma said many things more, of much the same sort, before the bondsmaid came back with dry clothes for Berki. Behind her was Hygelac, his golden hair disheveled and his eyes wild, with Berki's cast off cloak in his hand. Berki shrank away from the fierce look of anger on his foster brother's face.

"Be easy, Berki," Hygelac said. "No one will hurt you now although, Thunar witness it, there are some who need to have brains knocked into their skulls. Are you well?"

Berki nodded.

"Who was it that drove you into the sea?"

"Agilar...He started it, and the others followed him."

"I see. Well, put your clothes on and we shall go have some words with him."

Berki took the clothes from the bondsmaid, turning away and hiding himself as much as he could with Amma's cloak to put them on. More than he ever had before, he felt the shame of his body the round sag of his belly, the thick rolls of fat layered upon his chest and back, his broad, waddling legs. He was happier when he was shrouded completely in his own cloak, so that no one could see him too clearly. The boys were still practicing with wooden swords and long poles for spears, but they were all paired off now, with Ansuwulf wandering about between them, pausing here and there to speak a few words of praise or correction. Hygelac did not wait for Agilar to finish his match, but grabbed him by the back of the cloak at once, spinning him around so that the shorter boy lost his footing in the snow and nearly fell. Hygelac's right fist was cocked up, ready to drive into Agilar's wide mouth.

"What do you want?" Agilar sputtered, trying futilely to free himself. "What did I do?"

"You know full well what you did. You bullied my kinsman, guest friend, and fosterling on his second day with us, and you might well have been Berki's death, if not for the good will of the gods and, I am sure, his own strength at swimming. And did you seek to pull him from the water, or even to find someone to help him? You did not, and for that, had he died, you would have been named murderer and outlawed from the lands of the Geats and I should have spoken for that sentence at the Thing, if you survived the berserk Ecgtheow's vengeance for his only son, and Hrethel's revenge for the son of his daughter."

Agilar's broad face was white as bleached linen, a scattering of faded summer freckles standing out on his cheeks like flecks of dried blood. He had stopped struggling, and it seemed to Berki that only Hygelac's grip was holding him upright. Hygelac looked closely into the other youth's eyes.

"Now, I see, you understand," he said softly. "What geld do you think you owe Berki, for the harm you have done him?"

"But, but, he is not harmed," Agilar stammered, his green eyes flickering sideways to Berki.

"And that is no thanks to you, who drove him into the sea and left him to die. Now I, as Berki's mother's brother and Hrethel's son, shall judge this matter here, and if you find fault with my doom, then we can take it up before my father where he sits on his high seat this night."

Agilar gulped and nodded. "Since you set the others on Berki, it is only meet and fitting that you should become his shield against them, and against whatever may befall him. You will go with us to the grove, and there you will swear on the holy white stone that you will ever stand by Berki, whatever befall, and that never by your will shall he suffer any harm or shame, but that you will die to keep it from him. Is that a fair geld? I do not think my father will give you an easier one, and Ecgtheow will be sitting beside him to help in his deeming."

Agilar's glance slid sideways again, then he looked back up at the youth who held him. Hygelac's clean features were hard and angry, a silver brightness glinting from his blue eyes: the look of a king's son, keen as an adder's gaze. Berki did not know what the other boy saw in Hygelac's face, but Agilar lowered his eyes, nodding slowly.

"I will go with you, and swear as you say."

"He will not. Agilar, go back to your weapon work." The deep voice came from behind their backs. Hygelac whirled with his fists half up as though to challenge the one who had gainsaid him, but lowered them when he saw who had spoken.

Ansuwulf stood with his bare feet hidden beneath the snow, looking at all of them with the same calm, dark regard that had frightened Berki so the first time.

"A man fights his own battles, Hygelac, and must earn such oaths for himself. You may mean to help Beowulf with this, but you will only bring him shame."

"Beowulf?" Hygelac enquired.

Ansuwulf smiled. "Beowulf, the honey eater. That name has already clung to him, and you may as well get used to hearing it for the ruler who tries to silence what is in every mouth will not stay ruler long. If he wishes a better name, he will have to win it by his deeds."

An angry flush of red warmed Hygelac's high cheekbones, the muscles of his shoulders and neck tightening beneath his cloak as Ecgtheow's did when he was about to start shouting. But Ansusulf stared into his eyes, and Hygelac's lips clamped into a tight white line like a rivulet of silvery solder sealing the edges of a metal box: whatever was in his mind, he would not say it to the berserk.

"And think, too," Ansuwulf added. "Beowulf is a slow and clumsy fighter still, but he has swum in the winter sea and come home through the snow without taking hurt from it. If you, or any of these others, had done the same, we would now be looking for your corpse along the shore." A bare smile, no more than the twitch of a wolf's tail, touched the berserk's lips.

"Bees may try to sting a bear, or flies bite at his eyes and nose until he grows restless, but no bear was ever slain by bees or flies, however much they annoyed him. But a bear kept as a pet will never learn to do battle."

He turned his back on the two of them, walking over to Widuhund and Thunarstan. Berki looked at Hygelac, bewildered.

"What did he mean by all that?"

"He meant," Hygelac said fiercely, "that he thinks the others are likely to keep tormenting you until you have thrashed them for it, and that I should not order them not to do it. And…" Hygelac paused, a smile suddenly breaking through his grimness like a shaft of sunlight through shifting veils of rain. "I believe he thinks that you are a berserk born, for that you must have a bear as fetch and you bear the cold so well, even as he can stand bare footed in the snow. And if that is so, you need fear no one, for there are few men who dare to meet a berserk face to face, and fewer who can stand against one. Just wait: when Woden's band has taken you into the wood and brought you out again as one of themselves, all those fools who tease you now will be afraid of you."

Berki looked at Hygelac, then at the other boys, fighting or laughing and joking among themselves as they paused to rest with their sweat steaming from their skins in the cold air. Suddenly he began to cry, deep gut wrenching, blubbering sobs. Turning away from Hygelac, he began to run again.

"Berki! What is wrong?" Hygelac called from behind him. "Come back!"

But Berki ran out the gate, following the pathway around the palisade and into the woods. He was winded early, but he kept on, the icy air aching in his lungs with each breath, until he broke out into a clearing where a great white boulder stood beneath a towering yew. There he collapsed in front of the stone, weeping with hitching breaths. At last no more tears would come from his eyes, though the wind bit sharply against his swollen cheeks. The snow had begun to fall again, and Berki leaned against the pale stone to push himself to his feet, shaking a scattering of flakes from his hair and shoulders.

He knew where he must be: in the hallowed grove that Hygelac had offered to show him yesterday. A deep trembling shuddered through his bones, for he knew that there were many holy places where certain rites had to be followed by all who stepped within their bounds, lest the gods be angered.

"I am sorry," he whispered. "I didn't mean to come here now I will bring an offering next time, I swear it."

A breath of wind rustled through the dark needles of the yew, dusting a fall of snow from its heavy laden branches. Something trembled above his head, in the depths of the tree; Berki glanced upward, and saw the rope crusted with crystals like tiny thorns of ice, its noose end half rotted away from weather and damp. He covered his eyes with his hands, for he knew what must have hung there once: Woden's most favored gift was the offering of human life.

"I do not mean to make you angry, Grim One," Berki murmured. "But I do not want to be a berserk I do not want everyone to be afraid of me. I just want them to stop hurting me, and be my friends."

Then, though he did not know why he was doing it, Berki scraped at the thick cap of snow on top of the holy stone until he could touch the white rock beneath. He felt that he ought to be praying to someone else, but he did not know who. He tried to think of the gods and goddesses he knew. There was Thunar, of course Thunar, with his red beard and his mighty Hammer, who warded gods and men against their old foes, the eoten kind. There was Woden's wife Frige, who his nurse Ansudis had always called upon: Ansudis said she was a mother to all, kind to children and those in need of help.

There was Loca, but few prayed to him, though he was Thunar's dear travel friend. Berki remembered when he was two or three, he had reached into the hearth to play with the pretty flames and burnt his fingers; when Ansudis was done scolding him, she had told him that Loca was like that, bright and light hearted, but as likely to harm as to help if he were approached by one who did not well know how to deal with him. Scatha, the fair eoten maid she was a huntress, hard of soul, and Berki was afraid to pray to her. Then he thought of the gods of the Wan tribe, of Frea Ing and his twin sister the Frowe. Berki had heard less of them, for his father spoke mostly of Woden and Thunar.

Though Ecgtheow made his offerings to the Wan gods at ploughing and harvest time, Berki had once heard him say something scornful about godmen of Frea Ing who lacked manhood. Berki had sometimes wondered what he could have meant, for the wooden image of the god who was carried about the field for the first sowing had a great upright manhood, enough to put Ecgtheow's big hairy leek to shame, let alone Berki's little dribbler. But Frea Ing was supposed to be a god of frith, of clear skies and good harvests and laughter, and Berki was sure that he had no berserks in his hall.

Of the Frowe Berki knew less, save that she was the fairest of women, with a fine necklace, and she wept tears of pure gold. But he remembered the carven face of Ing's image: roughly shaped, and yet seeming to smile beneath the grooves of his beard, with wide wise eyes that looked kindly out over the damp earth of the furrowed field and the folk who laid flowers and poured ale and, if the year boded fair, the blood of a suckling pig out before him. Frea Ing was a loved and trusted god and that, more than anything else, Berki longed for.

"Will you help me?" Berki asked, looking down at the white stone. "Will you be my friend?"

For a heartbeat, it seemed to Berki that he could see the stone rooted deep in the earth, shooting up from the greater rocks below like a spear leek's leaf pricking up from the buried bulb, its shining strength rising high above the snow capped boulder under his hand. A flush of warmth flowed into his icy cheeks, and there was a taste of honey in his mouth. Then the feeling was gone: he was alone before the holy rock, shaking with the cold and tiredness leeching deep into his bones.

The white snow was blushing now beneath the reddening light of the setting Sun, the shadows of the ice crusted trees woven long and black over the clearing. The night's feasting would begin soon, if it had not already, and Berki thought that it would not go well with him if his father could not find him, should he want him. And Hygelac had said that the hallowed grove was close by the barrow fields...

"I will come back tomorrow with my offering," Berki swore, and hurried from the holy place, back to Hrethel's hall.

The feasting had already begun, but Berki was able to slip into his place without any word from his father, who was deep in talk with Hrethel. Now and again Ecgtheow would bang the gilded tip of his horn on the table, sending a wave of foam slopping up to drip over the rim.

"...Been your march warder at Hroesnabeorh all these years," Ecgtheow said loudly. "Who better than I should know the signs when the Swedes are gathering for war? Do not many of my own Waegmunding kin still fight under the golden boar banner? I tell you that Ongentheow does not have riding to battle on his mind this year, though I am sure he would be quick enough to change his thoughts if we showed him weakness. My king, you have my oath, but do not ask me for foolish things: those men you would like me to lend you will serve better where they are, tilling their home fields in the spring and showing Ongentheow our strength there on his eastern march, than they would here.

I do not doubt that they would learn well and that you could send them out more swiftly in case of need if you had them, but you can hardly ask men to leave their homes unguarded while they battle to save those of strangers. In any case, it is through our lands that Ongentheow would be likely to ride first: they would only have to hasten back home to fight."

Hrethel sighed. "Seventy five good men for three years you could easily spare them, and I would send them back to you as strong thanes, well worthy of fighting before a king's hall."

"But that many, at the right time, could mean the difference between a battle won and a battle lost. Now, if you wish to lure Ongentheow to attack us, I have thought of several ways..."

Bored, Berki looked at Hygelac, but he and his brothers were leaning eagerly forward, listening to their father's speech with Ecgtheow. Now and again, Herebeald would drop in a remark, which the older men seemed to consider with full weight; Haethcyn did not speak, but thought quietly, while Hygelac was almost quivering with eagerness. He wants to fight this year, Berki thought. I wish I could be of some use to him.

But the deep ache of the bruises along his legs and ribs reminded him shamefully, like a cold and constant whisper in his ear, of how hopeless he was at weapon play alongside the rest of Hygelac's boy troop. A deep horn blast sounded from the door. Hrethel rose from his place as those men and women still milling about in the hall hurried to find seats on the long benches.

"What is happening?" Berki whispered to Hygelac.

"That was the signal that the Sun is fully down. Now Father will lead the boar about for oath swearing best think of a good one now, before you have to speak it."

Hrethel's boar was a large and fair beast, his bristles honey gold with mottled dark splotches like splashes of ale on the polished birch wood of a god image. Though Hrethel held the lead that went through the gold ring in the boar's nose, Berki could see that the swine was really following the thin, neatly dressed thrall lad who walked before him with a basket of turnips, their scent luring the beast on. When he dropped one, the boar stopped, rooting through the rushes on the floor and munching happily. Hrethel raised his hands and head towards the sky, his golden hair streaming down his back and the short curls of his golden beard gleaming in the firelight above the ruddy glint of his twisted neck ring.

"Hail, you gods and goddesses who feast with us through these holy Yule nights!" He called. "You who walk among us, seen and unseen, when the hallowed kettle is lifted from the fire hear our oaths upon the bristles of the boar, as though they were spoken and sworn within the waters of Wyrd's well. Frea Ing and Frowe, mighty riders of Gold Bristle and Battle Swine, on your own beast we swear: givers of frith and wisdom, see that our word seeds come to good harvest!"

There were many oaths to be sworn, but Berki only listened to them scantly. It was more fun to watch the boar snuffling and chomping his turnips, happy to have his back rubbed while he ate. Berki wondered whether the ring through the swine's nose would really serve to lead the large beast, if he didn't want to go. Pigs were very strong, and they could be stubborn as well. Last Yule, Ecgtheow's oath boar had tried to run away halfway through the swearing, and it had taken Ecgtheow and two others to hold it still so that everyone in the hall could make their vows.

One of the men had gotten his arm bitten to the bone, too, though he had borne it bravely, holding up the dripping limb and making a joke about the Fenrir Swine. Berki tugged his thoughts back. He would have to swear an oath himself this year, and he did not know what he could say. He had already spoken his troth to Hrethel and Hygelac. I could swear to make the other boys stop calling me Beowulf, he thought. But he did not know how he would keep such an oath, and it was the worst of luck to swear and fail: if he had not managed it, he would have to die, he thought vaguely. And besides, if his father had not heard the shameful name, Berki would not be the first to speak it. Hygelac was standing now, laying his hand upon the boar's bristly back.

"By the bristles of the boar," he said, his high tenor voice ringing through the hall like the pure ring of gold on gold, "I swear that I will do a man's work in war for my father the king this year!

Berki heard a couple of muffled gasps, and though Hrethel was smiling, Berki could see the muscles of his jaw tightening beneath his short golden beard. Haethcyn stood, walking slowly over to the swine in his turn.

"By the bristles of the boar, I swear that I will give my brother wise rede this year, that the play of his mind may do good and not ill."

Herebeald swore next, vowing to uphold Hrethel in war and frith so that whatever befell, none could say that he was not the truest of his father's thanes; and then Ecgtheow shoved Berki in the small of his back, so hard that he nearly fell off the bench.

"Go on," his father hissed at him. "Make a worthy oath, if you have it in you."

Berki slowly walked over to the boar. As he came near, the swine lifted his head, looking up at the boy. The boar's eyes were a strange colour: dark enough to be black, yet the gleam the firelight caught from them was not red, but clear blue, like a glint of sunlight reflected from something bright within deep water.

"By the bristles of the boar," Berki said slowly, his boy's voice sounding very weak and thin after the others, "I swear..."

Now that he stood there, with the rough warm bristles beneath his hand and the sound of the boar's snuffling close in his ears, the hot moist stink of the swine's breath against his leg as it sniffed to see whether he had brought food, he found that he could not speak the words that were in his heart. I swear, that if I am ever bigger and stronger or a better fighter than other men, that I will not harm those who are weaker than I, but help and ward them against whatever would do them ill, so far as I have the strength.

Berki knew that he would be laughed at if he said that; but Ecgtheow's urgent whisper buzzed in his ears like a swarm of bees, "Speak now, Berki!" Yet he could not bring himself to name another oath.

"Let him be," Ansuwulf's deep voice said suddenly. The wolf berserk had come up silently behind the high table, as if to listen more closely to the vows spoken there. Ecgtheow whirled in his seat, a deep scowl on his thick bearded face, but the smaller man faced him without moving. "Often the truest and strongest oaths are those which none hear save the speaker and the gods. What Beowulf has vowed in silence, let him hold in silence: there will come a time when all know its truth." He waved Berki back to his seat. Berki gave the boar a last scratch behind the ears, curiously unwilling to leave the beast's company, and the pig nuzzled against his leg in a friendly manner before the young swineherd tossed down another turnip from his basket for it.

"Beowulf?" Ecgtheow growled, a low, threatening rumble in his chest. At home, Berki would have run when he heard his father snarling so, but Ansuwulf did not so much as flinch from the fearful sound.

"The honey eater so the other lads call him, and that is as good a kenning for a young bear as any other," Ansuwulf replied. "If he dislikes the name, he may learn the means to teach them better manners. And it is usually the fattest cub in a litter that grows into the largest beast, as you should remember yourself."

The look of rage dropped from Ecgtheow's broad face like a mask falling off, and he smiled ruefully.

"Aye, you were always the quicker of us with sword and foot, but you could never beat me wrestling, or lift a stone more than half the weight of the ones I cast could you?"

"Not then, and not now," Ansuwulf agreed. "For the wolf, speed and guile; for the bear, strength; and Woden's mead for both."

Watching the berserks link arms and raise their horns to drink together, a small cold shiver ran through Berki's bowels. I will not be like my father when I am grown, he thought, and the thought seemed to rush into his unspoken vow like a small river flowing in to swell the flood of a greater. Ecgtheow stayed through the twelve nights of Yule, then took his leave, embracing Hrethel and draining his last draught from Wynefrith's horn at the door of Hrethel's hall. His farewells to king and queen spoken, the berserk turned to his son.

"You have not begun as well here as I had hoped," Ecgtheow's deep voice rumbled softly. "But a day is not to be praised until evening, nor ice until it is crossed, and it may be that your oath kin and Ansuwulf can make more out of you than I have been able to. Do not shame me before them, Berki."

"I will try not to," Berki answered, biting back his tears. He knew that he was glad to see his father go, glad that at least, when the other boys beat him in sword play, he would not have to look about himself in fear of seeing Ecgtheow's hulking shape looming above him, looking down and shaking his head grimly. And yet with Ecgtheow gone, there would be nothing of home left to him, nothing save the tunics Ansudis had embroidered for him and they were already growing tight across his shoulders and belly, for the food was good here and Amma always had a few honey cakes or sweet buns for him when he stopped by the bake house.

Ecgtheow patted Berki clumsily on the shoulder, his strength enough to rock the boy back on his heels as no blow from any of Hygelac's boy troop could do.

"Be brave, and keep your shield up. When I guest here again at Hrethel's summer Thing, I shall expect to see you knocking whoever comes against you arse over head in the dirt."

He took the reins of his horse from the thrall who stood waiting beside him, heaving his great bulk up and into the saddle. Both relieved and forlorn, Berki stood watching until Ecgtheow and his men had ridden out the gates of Hrethel's settlement.

"Come, do not be so sad," Hygelac said merrily to him. "The hearts of young men should ever be lighter when they are out from under the eyes of the old. Will you wrestle with me, Berki? I know it is cold for taking off cloak and tunic, but the struggle will warm you, and I know that the bath house is hot for afterwards."

All Berki wanted to do was go back to the bakehouse, where he could eat something warm and sweet and listen to old Amma's comforting grumbles while he sat by the fire. But he did not want to disappoint Hygelac, so he took off his cloak. He was less willing to shed his tunic, to show Hygelac and the world how much flab swelled over his breeches band or give the other youths cause to start mocking the two rounded slabs of fat that quivered on his chest like a maiden's breasts. Yet Hygelac had already stripped to the waist, the thin ridges of muscle on his chest and belly stippled with goose bumps in the cold, and Berki had to follow his lead. Hygelac circled him slowly, then pounced like a lynx for Berki's wrists, shoving at the same time.

To Berki, it seemed that his friend was hardly trying at all to hold or unbalance him; he shook Hygelac off easily, waiting for the real attack. Hygelac closed again, catching Berki's hands in his own and crouching to twist sideways with legs and hips. Berki did not shift his ground, for he was sure that Hygelac was only playing, letting him hold his own for a little while so that he would not be too humiliated when he was finally dumped in the snow. But Hygelac put his shoulder against Berki's, straining as if he were trying to get a bull through a stuck gate, and at last Berki pushed back. To his own amazement, Berki's shove lifted Hygelac from his feet, tossing him backwards he seemed light as a straw doll.

If Hygelac had not held tightly to Berki's hands, he would have fallen; instead, he twisted to right himself, eyes wide open, and swept a foot out behind Berki's legs, crooking it into the hollow of his knee and pushing again. Berki stumbled slightly, but Hygelac was not strong or heavy enough to knock him off balance, though he tugged this way and that. Berki realized, surprised, that if he could get a good grip on the other youth, he could easily fling him down; and for the first time, he went on the attack. But Hygelac was too agile and swift, twisting easily out of Berki's clumsier holds and dodging away whenever Berki tried to grapple him. At last, their gasping breaths puffing out in white clouds and their strain reddened faces steaming in the icy air, the two of them stopped, staring at each other. Hygelac grinned as if he had won every bout, pushing a sweat darkened lock of golden hair from his forehead.

"Now I have found your skill!" He said. "I should have tested you at wrestling earlier, for your father is much famed as a wrestler and Hildebere," he added, a faint shadow of sadness touching his struggle reddened face, "could always outwrestle any of us, even when Herebeald had gotten big enough to give her a good fight. By Thunar and Loca, you are already as strong as a man full grown; and since I cannot topple you, I am ready to wager gold that none of my other young men can either we shall win an arm ring or two tomorrow, before they find that out. But come, let us go to the bath house, for I have a few wrenched muscles that will need hot steam to soothe them."

"Are you all right? I did not hurt you?" Berki panted anxiously. He was still out of breath, but he had not gotten so much as a bruise no worse than a couple of scrapes from Hygelac's nails on his wrist, where the other youth had sought to hold him.

Hygelac laughed. "No, nothing of any great matter. Though I daresay if you had been able to clutch me tight and throw me down as you were trying to, I would have sore ribs for a week. Before the gods, Berki, I have never heard of anyone like you: if you are so strong at seven winters, when you are grown and have learned more speed and skill, you will be ready to wrestle Thunar's son Modi, and allow him the first fall out of three into the bargain! It must be true, as my father says, that there is eoten blood in your line. This will make fools like Agilar laugh out of the other side of their mouths, you just wait and see."

Even as Berki pulled his tunic hastily over his head so that no one would look at his body as they walked, he could not help smiling with pride. He almost wished that Ecgtheow had been there to watch...but he knew what his father would have said: he had heard the same words before when he wrestled with other youths at home. So he could not throw you down what of it? You could not put him on his back either. Victory is more than not being beaten: it is beating your foe. And Berki knew, as well, that no matter how well he showed his strength at wrestling, it would be easy enough for the other boys to keep taunting him from a little distance.

Yet Hygelac was pleased with him, and that was good enough for now and when he needed to flee, there was always the ocean. Even now, with the chill of the wind already freezing the sweat in his hair to salty little crystals, the thought of the water's cold freedom beckoned to him, as if the pounding of his heart echoed the deep beating of the waves on the shore, and for a moment a fierce longing seized him. The desire to break away from Hygelac's friendly arm over his shoulder, to run down to the water's edge and plunge in again to feel his heavy body suddenly weightless, his clumsy limbs moving with ease and speed, skimming through the waves like a tern through the winter winds for a moment he could think of nothing else. But Hygelac was still talking cheerfully, and Berki could not turn away from him. Later, when Hygelac was busy with other things and had no time for him, then he could slip away to the sea.

The first thaws came early that year, icicles dripping longer and longer
from the roof of Hrethel's hall like spears of clear rime and the goat willows
putting out their first silvery gray catkins above the bare patches of mud
between the grimy swathes of melting snow. Berki had settled himself, if
not into happiness, at least into a kind of stable and quiet misery, relieved
often enough by Hygelac's friendship and Amma's honey cakes. With
the thaw came wilder weather, the waves leaping high and frothing like a
horde of white byrnied warriors storming the beach, but it did not keep
Berki from swimming whenever he could steal away unnoticed.

Even as the sea's strength had grown with the shifting of the seasons, so
had his own: he could swim out farther and stay out longer before cold and
tiredness drove him back to the beach, and he had learned the ways of the
tides there, which would seek to sweep him away and which would cast
him up on the shore. It was after such a long swim one day when Berki,
coming up the path from the beach with his cloak's hood up to hide his wet
hair, saw the stranger riding towards Hrethel's western gate with two laden
horses behind him. The man's gray cloak was shabby and patched, but a
glint of metal shone from the byrnie beneath it, and his sparse strands of
yellow hair straggled out from beneath the rim of an iron cap.

Bold from winning his day's struggle with the ocean, Berki ran up to the
stranger. "Who are you, and what do you wish here?" he asked. He had
hoped to sound like a man, but try as he might, his voice still piped and
fluted in a boyish alto.

The stranger looked down at him with a smile, showing wide gaps
between his broken and stained teeth. He had clearly seen his share of
fights: a white scar slanted across his forehead from the dark metal rim of
his cap to the eyebrow on the other side; another, twice as thick as Berki's
thumb, ran along the back of his left hand and disappeared into his plain
gray sleeve; and his nose had been badly broken once, splaying out and
skewing far to the left.

"I am Guthlaf the Peddler, young man. King Hrethel knows me well, for I
have often brought amber and other fine goods to sell to him for the delight
of his queen. And who are you? I have not seen you here before.

"I am Berki Ecgtheow's son," Berki answered. Guthlaf nodded, lifting a
scarred hand from his horse's rein's to smooth his windblown yellow beard
back into a long point.

"Ah, I should have guessed. You have something of your father's
look about you, saving his beard, of course. It is sure that you are a
Waegmunding, and Ecgtheow said that you were uncommonly large and
well fleshed, though I thought you were younger..." He broke off suddenly,
as if realizing that his words might give offense.

"Have you been to my father's home? Have you news?" Berki asked
eagerly.

"All in good time, my young friend. Perhaps you will do me the honor of letting King Hrethel know that I am here, with goods and...other things about which he may want to know."

Berki hurried ahead of him, up to the hall. Hrethel was not there, but Herebeald was, sitting at his ease with several of his friends.

"I still say," said one of them, a young man with a massive brush of red beard and curly red hair that flared out around his head like a brushfire, "that if you had not frightened that stag by coughing at the wrong moment, he would have kept on towards me, and the killing shot would have been mine. You owe me the first place when we go after boar tomorrow, so you do." He drank a deep draught from his horn, thumping its pointed end firmly on the table.

"He had already caught your scent, and you know it," Herebeald replied. "You saw how he raised his head when the wind shifted, ready to flee; it would have made no difference to him whether I was silent or stood up banging on a drum yes, Beowulf? What is it?"

"There is a man outside who calls himself Guthlaf the Peddler," Berki reported dutifully, though Herebeald's unthinking use of the hated nickname had stung him. "He says that King Hrethel wants to see him."

Herebeald drew in his breath, rubbing his knuckles thoughtfully along the scanty growth of close cropped golden beard on his jaw. It was a gesture Berki had often seen Hrethel make: daily, Herebeald seemed to be growing more and more like his father.

"Father rode out early today, and will not be back before sunset, I think," Herebeald mused. "But Mother is down at the malting. Go bring her the news, that she may make our guest welcome. She can keep him busy enough showing her his wares until Father comes home, I think."

A plume of smoke rose pale from the roof of the malting house, and when Berki stepped in, the warmth and the smell of damp barley was enough to make him dizzy. Wynefrith was overseeing several of the thrall women as they turned the grain spread out over the floor. Although she wore a simple dress of brown wool for her work, a large amber necklace glowed upon her breasts, and gold pins gleamed from the long dark braid coiled about her head: even at work that any farm wife might do for her family, she was queenly, Berki thought. "More evenly, Raudhilde," she scolded one of her thralls.

"This is all for one batch of ale; if it is heaped thick or spread thin, the grain will not sprout at the same rate. Move that which was near the fires farther, that which was faraway nearer." She bent down, picking up a few grains and rolling them between her long fingers before she crushed them, considering carefully what she saw.

"Another two days, and we will be ready to roast. Frea Ing and Nerthus be praised, we have enough grain left that we shall be able to toast summer's beginning in strong ale this year."

Berki coughed softly, and Wynefrith turned to him.

"Ah, Berki. I see by your face that you have some tidings for me?"

"Guthlaf the Peddler is here. Herebeald sent me to call you so you could make him welcome."

Wynefrith smiled at him, and Berki felt a warm glow in his heart, as if she had already poured him a cup of the strong ale she was making ready to brew.

"That is welcome news, and the bearer of welcome news often finds a gift in his hand. Come to the hall with me, Berki, and perhaps we shall find something to suit you in Guthlaf's packs."

Willingly Berki followed Wynefrith out. They stopped by one of the storehouses on the way, where Wynefrith considered several kegs.

"We shall give him mead, though our stock of that is running short," she said at last. "If he has ridden long, his stomach will be empty, and it will go to his head more quickly and loosen his tongue. You will be a drighten someday, and you will need to think on such tricks."

Berki thought about that a moment. It seemed to him somehow unfair to try to fuddle a man with mead, like handing another a shield with a faulty strap before challenging him to fight. But he knew it would be rude and silly of him to say that, so instead he asked,

"Why do we need to loosen his tongue?"

"You see, Berki," Wynefrith explained, "Guthlaf does not only buy and sell fine goods. He also trades in knowledge and messages, and though we always greet him as a friend, it is by no means sure that he is a friend to us. He is of Swedish birth on his mother's side, and though he travels everywhere, he often lingers longest with Ongentheow, and sometimes rides away from the Swedes with his packs fuller than when he came."

"Why do we let him in, then?"

"Firstly, because it would give us an ill name to turn a traveler away without good reason. Men who wander, peddlers and singers, they bear the news of both good and bad from land to land: for that, as for the sake of the gods, they must be welcomed and guested well. And we cannot say that he has ever done us harm what we may guess and wonder is not fit to speak at the Thing. Secondly, what Guthlaf says or does not say tells us something of Ongentheow. At the very least, we know what the king of the Swedes wants us to hear, and there is some worth in that; and likewise, we can send our messages back to him. And...when there is an adder in your house, even if you cannot kill it, you are best off knowing where it is. Remember: if there is one whom you trust ill but may get good from, you should speak fair words, though your thoughts are dark; you should laugh with him and speak contrary to your heart, and pay lies back for lies."

Berki nodded soberly. "Does my father know about Guthlaf?"

The smile that touched Wynefrith's lips brightened her face like the glitter of a gold coin from deep water.

"Of course he does, though Guthlaf's road does not lead past Hroesnabeorh Ecgtheow is no buyer of fine jewels, nor does he often wish to hear tales of his kinsmen among the Swedes but that is well thought for you to ask. You will make a good rede giver to Hygelac when you are grown. What did the peddler say to you of himself?"

"He said that he had goods and other things about which Hrethel might want to know."

"Ah. News of some weight, indeed: he is seldom so forthcoming about his second line of trade. Berki, can you help me with that keg? It is heavy, but you are strong and I think the two of us can manage it. We have whiled a little longer than we should, and I am in no mind to wait for a thrall."

The keg Wynefrith wanted was a small one, standing no taller than the mid point of Berki's thigh. He crouched down to pick it up, then heaved it up to his shoulder.

"You need not trouble," he said proudly. "I can do it."

Wynefrith stared at him for a moment. "That will give Guthlaf something to talk about, indeed," she murmured, as if to herself. "He will think that Sigemund the Walsing is born once more."

Berki shivered violently, almost dropping the keg. His father had often frightened him with stories of Sigemund Sigemund the werewolf, Sigemund who had killed his sister's two sons when they proved too fearful to knead an adder into the meal for the evening's bread, then, at her behest, had gotten another son on her of full Walsing blood, fierce and cruel enough to aid them in their vengeance. Though Ecgtheow had never threatened him with the fate of Sigemund's sister sons, Berki had dreamed several times that his father had put him to the same test and woken screaming, his bedlinens soaked with the hot urine that had gushed from his bladder at the dream touch of Ecgtheow's big hands about his neck.

"That is too heavy for you alone!" Wynefrith said, reaching to steady the keg. "Let me help."

"No, I have it," Berki insisted stubbornly, leading the way out of the storehouse towards the hall.

Guthlaf had already unloaded his horses and sat inside by Herebeald, who had sent his friends away. The peddler had taken off his iron cap as well as his cloak, showing a half bald pate crossed by long scattered strands of thin yellow hair; the scar across his face ended in a huge patch of withered white at the crown of his head where a flap of skin must have been sliced away. When Berki and Wynefrith walked in, Guthlaf looked up, raising a bushy eyebrow as Berki let the keg easily down onto the table.

"Hail to you, Wynefrith," he said. "Surely you do not mean to taunt a weary peddler's dry throat with a keg so empty a boy can lift it?"

"It is full to the brim," Wynefrith replied. Along the way she had stopped to get her greeting horn, and now she deftly tapped the keg, sending a golden stream of mead gushing into the vessel. "Berki has gotten a full share of his father's strength."

"Indeed, there must be the makings of a mighty man under all the lad's flesh." Berki nodded at the praise, though it stung like a sharp blow from a wooden sword: he knew he had gotten fatter since Yule, for he had needed new tunics and breeches made. "And your nose is the ugliest I have ever seen, he thought spitefully at the peddler, but I am not rude enough to speak of it to your face when we have just met. No longer looking at Berki, as though the boy were a dog he had patted from politeness, Guthlaf went on, "I am as grateful as ever for your kindness, Wynefrith " he took the horn from her hands, raising it to her and drinking deeply "and, perhaps, you will find some of my trinkets enough to your liking that you will think it worthwhile to have given such a fine greeting to a poor man. I whiled the early part of the winter in Jutland, and the storms were strong, so that Ran's daughters grew careless and tossed many of their finest jewels ashore. I have kept the best of those pieces back for you, for I well remember how you are gladdened by the sight of fine amber. And perhaps Herebeald will wish to fetch his brothers as well, for now they should be all of an age to think on buying trinkets for maidens."

"That is so," Herebeald said, rising to his feet.

They talked for a little while more before Hrethel's sons came in and Guthlaf got down to opening his packs and spreading out his treasures. As he had promised, he had a great store of amber, in colors ranging from solid white streaked yellow that looked like butter with cream swirling through it to the clear deep red of the strongest and finest ale. Some of his pieces were still rough as stones Berki reached out to heft one in his hand, wondering at the lightness of something that looked so like rock but most were polished, drilled through for hanging on a necklace or carven into the shapes of beasts and men. There was one piece that drew his eye again and again: a narrow, rounded oval with a pointed cap of silver at each end, its clear ruddy gold glow spangled through with round bright flecks that shimmered as Berki picked it up and turned it over in his fingers. The amber pendant nestled into his palm as comfortably as the hilt of his eating knife, smooth and warm as his hand closed around it. Guthlaf grinned at him again.

"Ah, you have a good eye for amber, son of Ecgtheow. The sun spangled pieces are not found so often; that is one of the finest I have seen, and I doubt you'll find its like again. It could hardly be better, not unless it had a bee trapped in it for luck as well. Buy it for yourself, and it will bring you happiness and good luck, and when you are old enough to go courting, it may bring you more pleasure yet, for there was never a woman born who could turn her eyes away from the gleam of the Frowe's sea tears. Aye, the fair goddess' tears fall as red gold on land, and that is dear enough, but her tears that fall in the waves as amber burn more brightly, and call more sweetly to maidens' hearts."

"Do you want it, Berki?" Wynefrith asked softly, cutting the peddler off in mid speech.

Berki did not dare to answer, but he kept his hand clutched tight around the pendant and nodded his head as hard as he could.

"Then we shall have that one, and a stout thong to keep it safe about his neck," Wynefrith said. "As for the rest I do not doubt that we can come to some agreement on a few of these other pieces, for you have a long way to go this year yet, and silver rings are easier to barter for food and lodgings along the way than is amber meant to sell in a kingly hall."

"Silver?" Guthlaf gasped. He grasped a handful of his yellow beard in each hand, tugging as though he meant to tear it out. When he let go, it stood out from his chin in a crooked fork, one tine pointing up and one back towards his throat. "Fair queen, I know it is often the way of athelings to jest with simple folk..."

Berki hardly noticed as Wynefrith and the peddler began their bargaining. It was enough for him to feel the light warm firmness of the amber in his hand, realizing, though he could hardly believe it, that it was his. A jewel from the sea, the plaything of Ran's daughters: he would keep it tied tightly about his neck so that it could not be lost when he swam, wrap it in warm furs and leave it beneath his pillow when he went to fight with wooden swords so that it could not be broken.

The fleeting thought came to him that it might be dangerous to go into the ocean with a treasure that one of Ran's daughters had lost, lest she take it back and him with it, but there was no fear of the water in his heart: he thought that the sea maid would see it, and know that she had a friend. It was almost dark outside when Hrethel came in, casting aside his heavy mantle as his wife rose to meet him with her horn. Mindful of what Wynefrith had said, Berki noticed that, although Hrethel held the mead to his mouth for a long time, his throat was not moving: the king was barely wetting his lips in greeting.

"Hail to you, Guthlaf," Hrethel said heartily. "I see that you are at your yearly business of trying to beggar me by offering my wife half again the worth of all I have. At a price that she would be a fool to turn down, of course."

Guthlaf made an exaggerated wince, as though Hrethel had run him through with a sword.

"Such unkind words for a great king to speak! Though your queen is the fairest woman in the Northlands, surely she must have a wolverine as a fetch, for her shrewd bargaining is merrily stripping the very flesh from my limbs and leaving me to bleed upon your straw. Beggar you? As clever as your bride is, if you were not thrice as openhanded as any king from the Franks' lands to those of the Finns, you would have no room in your hall to move for the stacks of gold."

Berki watched, keeping his thoughts to himself. If it had not been for what Wynefrith had told him, he would have staked his right hand that she and Hrethel were the best of friends with the peddler. It was past anything he could have guessed at, how the three of them laughed and bantered like siblings born, and yet all of them knew that he was Ongentheow's man, who had not come to Hrethel's hall to do the king any good. Wynefrith called for food, and the thralls were soon carrying in platters of bread and steaming bowls of rich sealmeat stew.

Though it was still too early in the year for cow milk, there was plenty of soft white sheep cheese and the brown nutty tasting goat cheese, which Berki liked best for its sweetness. Wynefrith and Guthlaf kept up their bargaining as they ate, and by the time Berki's belly was full, they had struck their deal. Wynefrith layered three of her prizes a short string of round beads, pale golden as the first light of dawn; a long strand of deep ruddy brown, whose center piece was nearly the size of a gull's egg; and one of middle length on which square cut dark beads were interspersed with butter pieces as creamy pale as old bone around the glowing strand that already hung about her neck, sweeping the rest into a pile before herself.

Herebeald had chosen a fine red gold necklace a gift for a maiden, surely, but he only smiled when asked for whom he meant it. Haethcyn had taken a small raven carven out of the darkest amber, almost black until it was held up so that the light could catch a bloody gleam from its deep red depths; and Hygelac had a gilded brooch set with smooth cut rounds that glittered with the same sun spangles as Berki's pendant. Berki tied his own piece about his neck himself, knotting it again and again until he was sure that nothing could shake it loose. When his goods were packed away again, Guthlaf let Wynefrith fill his horn once more and leaned back, covering a soft belch with his hand.

"As always, I am leaving poorer than when I came here," he sighed. "But such is the price for dealing with friends. And others, I hear, have suffered far worse ravages this winter than I have this night."

"What do you mean?" Hrethel asked. The king's fine features were open and friendly, nothing but curiosity sparking in his blue eyes.

Whether on purpose or not, Herebeald was mirroring his father's look almost without flaw; Haethcyn sat still as a day struck troll, but even without looking at Hygelac, Berki could feel the trembling running through his friend's body as a deaf man might feel the shivering of a beaten drum skin beneath his fingertips.

"Do you not know? I would have thought such news would spread as if Woden's ravens were bearing it, but of course, few ships sail when the sea is still bound by ice. You know Hrothgar the Scylding, and have heard of the wonders of his hall Heorot?"

"Most have," Hrethel replied. "Has his old feud with Hadulf flared up again? I would have thought the wedding would have put an end to that."

"Aye, it did, but now Hrothgar must struggle in a far worse feud, and one that he has less chance of bringing to a good end. As for Heorot, its fires are dark and cold in the evenings now, and the joy of its thanes has turned to mourning, grim need wretchedness and night evil come to its folk."

"What could that be?" Herebeald asked. "What man is so mighty that he could assail the Scylding drighten so?"

Guthlaf stroked his disheveled beard into a smooth single point again, then pushed back the thin strands of hair straggling across his scarred skull like tatters of half spun flax. Though his ugly face was fittingly sober, Berki could tell that the peddler was enjoying the spinning out of his tale, tasting each word in his mouth like a man chewing slowly to make a fine piece of meat last: his voice slipped into a half chant, as if speaking the words of a song.

"No man at all, so it is said. That grim guest is hight Grendel, well known treader of the borderlands, who holds the marshlands, fen and fell. He is of the kin of Ymir, father of eotens and elves and orcs, who have long warred against the gods. When the first night of Yule had fallen, he came seeking in the high house where the Ring Danes were sleeping after ale: there he found the athelings in their symbol deep slumber, unwitting of sorrow. That unhallowed wight, grim and greedy, was at once ready, fierce and furious. He took thirty thanes from their sleep, and glad of his catch, turned homeward with his slain booty. Then the first dawn light revealed Grendel's battle craft to men, and after the feasting weeping was raised up, a great morning cry. Nor was it long again: after nightfall the mighty murder bale came once more, and did not shrink from his cruel deeds, for they were too fast in his mind. Now it is easy to find those who seek quieter resting places, beds in the outer buildings; but Grendel, against all right, rules alone in Heorot from sunset to sunrise."

As Guthlaf spoke, Berki closed his eyes, shivering. He remembered his Yule night dream: the dark death shadow, the welter of blood and limbs, the corpses rent asunder and stuffed into the bag. When he opened his eyes again, he saw that Hrethel and his family had gone very pale. Herebeald made the sign of Thunar's Hammer; Haethcyn stared into the darkness between the hall fires.

"That is strange and ill news," Wynefrith said quietly. "What has Hrothgar done?"

"He sought to stand against the wight, but no blade forged by men could harm Grendel. Yet, men say, Hrothgar has not lost the favor of the gods, for Grendel could not scathe him either, though he reaped a mighty harvest of man death among the Scylding's thanes. Yet now Hrothgar can only wait: he has offered great reward to anyone who can free him of his foe, but he has lost many of his best men, and there are few who would dare to match themselves against Ymir's kinsman."

"What manner of wight is this Grendel?" Hygelac asked eagerly, leaning forward. "How does he fight?" Berki saw the gleam in his eyes, like sunlight glinting blue silver from the hilt of a sword, and again he shivered. But Hrethel would never let him go, nor Hrothgar set a youth against a man killing thurse.

"They say he is like a man, but twice a man's size, with ripping talons like a lynx and the skull crushing bite of a bear. No one has seen him clearly, for he comes in darkness and is shaped of darkness, a gliding shadow walker. He bears no weapons save his strength, claws, and teeth, but he needs no more why should he, when he can tear a man's head from his shoulders as easily as you might pull off a sparrow's, and none can harm him in turn? If Sigefrith the Walsing were not dead and burned some eighty years ago, then he, with his dragon blooded hide and god crafted sword, might have stood against Grendel, but no such hero is living now."

"That is a cruel Wyrd for Hrothgar to thole," Hrethel said. "Has he sent to the wise folk at God Home or Upsala for rede? I know of no others who could speak on such matters."

"I do not know where he has sought," Guthlaf replied. "It would be strange if he had not, though, when Unferth his thule once dwelt at God Home and learned his lore and skills there. But we may safely guess that Grendel cannot be driven out by rowan berries and the sign of the Hammer, nor have fat oxen been enough to buy the gods' aid."

"And what of his men?" Haethcyn inquired. "Do Hrothgar's thanes stand by their troth?"

"The best of them do, for they will not leave their drighten in his need, and take his safety as a sure sign that the luck of the Scyldings dwells in him yet. Others have fled: some southward to the Franks, some westward to the war band of Cerdic in Britain they would rather battle Artorius, who is but a man, than lie wakeful to fear Grendel's whispering footfalls in the night." Guthlaf paused, scratching at the side of his misshapen nose, and his eyes hooded briefly in thought.

"I have heard it said," he added, "that Hrothgar could be easily overcome in war now, save that none dare attack him, lest they draw Grendel's ire on themselves. It is not a little ironic that Hrothgar's foe has become his warder, as well as his destroyer."

"Not a little," Hrethel agreed heavily.

They spoke until late into the night, Wynefrith pouring out generous measures of mead. However, when Guthlaf began to yawn and his speech to slur, instead of staying to talk, he rose from the table.

"I have ridden far this day, and I will need my wits about me tomorrow, when your thanes and their wives come to fleece me of the last of my stock," he said. "Of your kindness, if you will show me a corner where I may lay my weary head..."

Haethcyn rose as well. "There is a guest house made ready for you. Come, I shall show you the way." He shouldered two of the peddler's packs and lit a torch from one of the hall fires, leading Guthlaf out.

No word was spoken until Haethcyn came back alone. "He is resting quiet," Hrethel's middle son reported. "I think we may talk freely now."

"Yes." Hrethel stroked his close cropped beard. "These are most grievous tidings Guthlaf has brought. If Hrothgar can neither check the Swedes nor draw their attention, then Ongentheow will have no one save us to turn his mind towards. At least Ecgtheow is not here, for if he had heard what we have heard tonight, it would be no easy task to keep him from riding straight southward, to repay the debt of life he still owes to Hrothgar it is well for us that Guthlaf's road never takes him through Ecgtheow's burg."

"But it did!" Berki blurted. Horrified at his own boldness, he clapped his hands over his mouth, but the words were out. They were all staring at him, Hrethel's face growing terribly grim. Berki tried to brace himself against flinching, sure that Hrethel was going to strike him now as his father would, but he could not keep the wince from rippling through his flesh as Hrethel raised a hand.

"Calm yourself, Berki," Hrethel said. "Why do you say that?"

Berki found himself stammering, barely able to force the words out. "I met him at the gate. When he was just riding up, and I said who are you, and he said who are you, and I told him, and he said my father spoke to him of me, but he wouldn't tell me any news from my father's home."

Hrethel drew in his breath, hissing deep through his teeth. "Luck alone that you were here, and first to meet him; luck, or perhaps the good will of the gods, that Guthlaf did not guard his tongue as carefully as he might in a child's hearing. If Ecgtheow has heard the tale of Hrothgar's woe already, there is no time to waste." He looked at his sons carefully, as if weighing each of them in his mind, then gave a sharp nod.

"Hygelac, you have often boasted of how swiftly and surely you can ride, even at night. Go saddle your horse at once, and make all the speed you can to Hroesnabeorh. Tell Ecgtheow that, for the sake of the oaths he swore me, he may not leave his stead. It was clever of the Swedes to seize this chance to get him out of the way so quickly, with his love for Hrothgar the chief weapon in their hand, but they shall not succeed as easily as they think. Though Ecgtheow's heart may bleed for it, he is our strongest bulwark against Ongentheow, and if he leaves his post now, I shall count it oath breaking and betrayal. And, Hygelac..."

The youth's hands were clenched into fists with excitement, his body quivering slightly like the nose of an eager hound about to be loosed on a blood track. He looked up at his father, saying breathlessly,

"Yes?"

"Do not think that I have forgotten the Yule vow you made. If you can reach Ecgtheow before he has gone too far, and if your words can rein him in and hold him to his duty to the Geats, then I shall say indeed that you have done a man's work in war for me this year. For this is war, as surely as if Ongentheow's first cast spears had already struck against our shields; and if you succeed, you shall have warded our folk from a mighty blow."

"I shall do it, Father. Have no doubt."

Hrethel pulled a coiled gold ring from his finger and handed it to Hygelac.

"My luck go with you, my son. Hurry now, for there is no time to waste. Berki, gather some food and help Hygelac saddle his steed."

Berki stopped by a storehouse to quickly gather a bag of hard cheese and dried fish for the road, then followed Hygelac out to the stables, his heart beating hard in his chest. Hrethel had not quite told him to go on the ride, but he was sure that Hygelac would not deny him: it was his right. The night had grown cold not sharp and keen with the taste of snow, but heavy with the chill mist creeping in from the sea. Hygelac's roan stallion stamped and shifted restlessly in his stall as he saw the flickering torch flames, but quieted as Hygelac stroked his flank, talking to him in a low voice.

"Soft, soft, my brave one, my strong Guthlac. Gather your strength and your wits, my joy, for we have a mighty ride ahead of us."

Berki fetched Hygelac's saddle, but when he brought out the reins and bridle with their gilded plates, Hygelac waved them away.

"The plain ones are more supple, and will draw fewer eyes on the road."

"And which shall I take?" Berki asked.

Hygelac looked at him in astonishment, his eyes wide and dark in the dim light of the torches. "You? Berki, you are not going."

"But, but..." Ecgtheow is my father, Berki wanted to say, and I was the one who warned Hrethel. I deserve to go along.

But his thoughts, toppled by the sudden rush of disappointment, were tumbling through his head too quickly for him to shape them into clear words.

"You have done well this night, but you ride too slowly and clumsily for all your size and strength, you are still far too young, and more of a burden to a horse than I am at that. It would take thrice the time if you went with me, and Ecgtheow would be long gone by the time we got there. No: rest glad in knowing that you have helped to thwart the plans of the Swedes, and another time, when you are older, it will be your turn to ride out. Give me a leg up, now."

Berki cupped his hands, boosting Hygelac to the saddle, then opening the stable door for him. Hygelac's teeth flashed once in the torchlight; he turned Guthlac around, touching his heels lightly to the stallion's sides, and within moments he was lost in the dark sea mist. Berki stood staring into the blackness after his foster brother, too stunned even to cry. Now it struck home to him: for all Hygelac's kindness, even he, when it came down to a real matter of need, knew Berki was useless. He was fit for thrall work, that was all: good only for lifting kegs and packing food and saddling horses; able to wrestle like a farmer, but not to fight with sword and shield like an atheling. Slowly he trudged back to the hall, but paused at the door. The firelight glowed warm through the cracks, shining ruddy about the smoke holes on the roof; he could hear speaking within, Wynefrith's soft breathy murmurs above the deeper voices of the men.

He did not want to go in and say that Hygelac was on his way to Ecgtheow's hall while Ecgtheow's own son was left behind, standing in the mud like a beggar. Instead he turned, his feet finding their way along the path to the sea. Berki had never swum at night before, and he knew that it was madness to go out on a fog thick night when he would never be able to see the shore or the marks along it that told him where he was. Yet, even in the darkness, his body remembered the way to the boulder where he always laid his clothes to keep them from getting wet. He stripped down, welcoming the mist chill against his naked skin no one could see him out here, there was no one to mock him save the barking seals, who were fatter than he. He ran down the beach, his feet skidding in the soft sand at first, then thumping down harder as he crossed the tide line.

A rush of icy froth swirled up around Berki's calves, catching a laugh of surprise from his mouth. He ran faster, the water not slowing him at all, even when it had risen to his waist. Then he fell forward like an eagle launching itself from a high tree top, letting the water catch him and lift him upwards. The waves were strong that night, tossing him about like a piece of driftwood, but Berki did not care: sometimes he let them fling him up and cast him down, sometimes he faced them head on, wrestling the grip of the water with all his strength. Once or twice it seemed to him that he could feel fingers gently tugging at the piece of amber about his neck, but when he reached to touch it, he found he had only felt the rushing of the waves around him. Dark as it was, the feeling of the currents told him when he had swum past Whales' Ness; lithe and agile as Hygelac on horseback, Berki twisted about to slip back into the swells pushing towards the beach.

At that moment, something stroked against the length of his body. Berki choked down a yelp of surprise, sputtering and coughing bitter salt water, and began to thrash wildly towards shore. Sharks, killer whales, sea nicors: the thoughts flashed quickly through his mind, but were gone at once as it brushed past him again, slithering over the backs of his legs. Whatever it was, it was sleek and soft, its touch both playful and caressing a seal? Seals could bite fiercely if they were angered, but Berki meant it no ill.

He paused, treading water as the wave swells lifted him up and down, waiting for it to come back. At last the water shivering began to overwhelm Berki, and the seal had not touched him again. Perhaps it had thought at first that he was kin, then guessed its mistake; he did not know. Cold and weary, but steadier in heart than he had been, Berki swam back towards land. When Berki came back to the house he shared with Hrethel's two younger sons, the fire was burning brightly in the middle of the floor and Haethcyn, still fully dressed, was sitting on his bed.

"Where have you been?" He asked quietly.

"I helped Hygelac to get ready."

"That did not take you so long. And I can hear your teeth chattering from here, and…" Haethcyn raised his dark head, sniffing at the air. "You smell of the sea." He stood up, his hand flicking out to toss back Berki's hood and brush against his hair. "You have been in the ocean, haven't you, Beowulf? If Father knew, he would forbid you to go there again."

Berki nodded. He suddenly felt that he wanted to cry again, though he was not sure why. Perhaps it was only that he was so hungry, as he always was after swimming, and he knew that he could not get anything to eat until morning.

"Don't call me that," he said, his voice shaking. "My name is Berki."

Haethcyn sighed, sitting back down on his bed and resting his chin in his hands.

"If you don't like being called Beowulf," he said reasonably, "why don't you do something about it?"

"What? They all call me that, even Ansuwulf, and I hate it. What can I do? I can't beat any of them in a fight, and when Hygelac is away, they won't leave me alone."

"Why do they call you Beowulf?" Haethcyn persisted.

"Because…because I'm always eating honey, and I'm fat." Berki's voice broke into a sniffle.

"If you didn't eat so much all the time, and ran and rode all day instead of sitting in the bake hut with old Amma, you wouldn't be fat."

"But I like Amma!" Berki protested. "She's the only one, except for Hygelac, who's nice to me."

Haethcyn sighed again. "Old women are usually nice to little boys. And perhaps if you weren't so big, no one would think anything of it. But you are the size of one of Hygelac's youth troop, and of course everyone expects that you should act like one of them. Instead you sit and eat by the fire and get fatter: it is no wonder that the other lads look down on you for a coal biter. I know you are not a lackwit, but ofttimes you look like one, because you are large and speak little; and when you are pressed too hard, you cry or you run away into the water. The one is cowardly, the other is strange; and you cannot expect to be liked for being cowardly or strange."

This was too much for Berki, and, though he tried to fight the sobs back, he could hear them choking in his throat as the tears rose hot to his eyes.

"There, you see," Haethcyn said, his voice still very calm. "I am not telling you this because I hate you, I am telling it to you because you are my foster brother and you need to hear it for your own good. You do not have to store up fat for a long winter's sleep, so leave the honey and the sweet fruit cakes alone. If you fight back when you're bullied instead of running away, you may get a few more bruises, but in time the others will learn to respect you: put your head down and swing hard, and they will find that it is not wise to ask for your blows. And stop creeping off to swim in the ocean alone, for that seems more than odd, when there is no other, boy or grown man, who can do that at this time of year. If you were not otherwise such a butt of mockery, there would already be strange whisperings about you for it: folk would wonder if you were a hide shifter or seith worker, and that is not the best of things to have rumored. Men despise that which is weak, but hate that which they fear; and worst of all is to seem both weak and uncanny. It may be, perhaps, that when you are old enough, you will join a berserk band: Hygelac thinks that Ansuwulf and your father have such hopes for you. Then you would have your wod brothers beside you, and a berserk may be as strange as he likes, for few dare to rouse his wrath. But you have six winters to get through until then, and if you do not learn to get along with others, you may not last that long." He paused for a little while, as if waiting for Berki to answer him, but Berki made no reply. "Well, think on those things for a while. If you are unhappy or feel that no one likes you here, you have the means to deal with it, if you only have the bravery and strength to carry them out."

Berki turned away to strip the chill clothing from his body, slipping into his bed as quickly as he could. Lying in the dark, shivering until his blankets warmed up and trying not to heed the aching pangs of hunger in his belly, he felt miserably alone, worse than he ever had been. I wish I were a hide shifter, he thought. If I were, I could put on a sealskin and turn into a seal, and go off with the seal that played with me in the water tonight. Haethcyn's redes are always cold; I wish Hygelac were here to talk to I wish he hadn't left me behind.

And Haethcyn's words about the berserk band troubled him worst of all, for they echoed the question that had been haunting Berki since Hygelac first said that he might be a berserk: is there no choice but that others either despise me, or fear me? He clutched at the amber pendant about his neck, closing his hand around it. It was warm from his body, and he could feel his blood beating in his tight grasp as though the amber itself were pulsing like a heart in his palm. The Frowe gave her tear to the ocean, and Ran's daughter gave it to the land, and Wynefrith gave it to me, Berki said to himself, and the thought made him feel less lonely. Hygelac came back by night, tired but gleeful.

"Father, I have Ecgtheow's word that he will stay as long as you need him. It was not easy to talk him out of faring to Heorot, for he is still mindful of the debt he owes to Hrothgar but he agreed that he cannot break the oaths he swore to you."

"That is well done, my son!" Hrethel said. "And thus is your own Yule oath fulfilled." He clapped Hygelac on the back, then drew a thick ring of gold from his arm and gave it to his son. "A man's deed for me, and a man's reward: henceforth you shall stand beside your brothers in council or battle, as may befall, and leave your boy troop to those who have not proven themselves yet."

Hygelac beamed, but Berki felt smaller and more lost. With Hygelac among the men, he would have no one to watch out for him, or shield him from the older boys. He had tried to follow Haethcyn's advice about eating less and not swimming by himself, but there was no other refuge or comfort for him when Agilar and Thunarstan and the rest began to mock him: staying away from the things Haethcyn had warned him against only made it easier for the others to seek him out and torment him.

A hard frost followed the first thaws, but soon gave way to milder weather again, and then planting season took everyone out to the fields for weeks of hard work. Even Hrethel, though he did not drive a plough and scattered only the first seeds as he asked the blessing of the gods, was busy, for he had to order which grain should be planted in which site, how much should be planted and how much should be saved for next year, in case the harvest was bad the king spent a long time closeted with Ansuwulf and Wynefrith for that, and Hygelac told Berki that they were reading runes to see whether the weather would be good or ill, so that they would know how much of their stock it was worth risking in hopes of gaining more.

"But they have to be very careful with it, for such things are hard to tell." Hygelac said.

"We are lucky that we have Ansuwulf, and that Mother is wise. Other kings have to go to spae women, and I heard once Father told me as a warning that such asking can be chancy. There was one king who went to Upsala and asked, just as we are asking now, how the harvest would be. He had been having ill dreams, you see, and feared a blight. The spae wife could not believe that he had come all the way to Upsala for such an earthly matter: she thought he meant the fate of his deeds, and told him that he should make friends with a neighboring drighten with whom he had quarreled. Perhaps she was not seeing too clearly, for his neighbor replied with insults to both the king and the spae wife, and then decided to go try his luck at battle raids in the South before any more could come of it; but the harvest was blighted, just as the king had feared, and many folk went hungry for years afterwards, because the spae wife thought so well of her deep soul that she did not understand a question asked in plain words."

Hrethel's Midsummer Thing was a great gathering. The weather was fair and warm, the Sun shining brightly through the day and barely dipping beneath the rim of the earth at night. Berki was not the only one swimming in the ocean now: Hrethel's thanes and the men of the drightens who came to his Thing gleefully raced and wrestled in the waves, while the other children played close to shore. To be alone, Berki had to wander farther and farther along the beach before he went in, otherwise the boy troop would chase him through the shallows with pointed wooden sticks, shouting,

"A whale! A whale by the shore! Who can harpoon the whale?" And once they had stolen his clothes so that he had to run naked through the settlement, hands over his privates, as they pointed and laughed at him.

Yet the Thing was not all bad: there were merchants there from all over, selling fine furs and walrus ivory from the North, amber though none so fine as Guthlaf had carried from Jutland and Sealand, and even a few rare pieces of glassware from farther south. The weapon smiths did a brisk business, as did the brewers, selling their jars of strong fruit and herb flavored mead.

Other stalls offered smoked reindeer meat and large rounds of cheese, leather shoes and pouches, bolts of weaving in dazzling colors and finely dyed wool; smooth bowls and lamps of soapstone or clay...whatever anyone might need, they could buy at the Midsummer Thing. Hrethel and his sons were sitting in judgement much of the time, considering cases or witnessing betrothals and contracts: for the first time, Berki saw Haethcyn's betrothed Garhild, a short, dark haired girl whose delicate hands were always fluttering like a butterfly's wings, whether turning the spindle that always hung from her waist or deftly stitching on some piece of embroidery. When Haethcyn was not sitting beside his father in court, he was walking about with her, and the amber raven he had bought from Guthlaf now hung about her slender neck.

As well as the merchants, there were plenty of contests: horse and foot racing, horse fighting, wrestling, stone casting, ball games and fighting with wooden swords and spears. Ecgtheow took part only in the wrestling and stone casting, but there no one could beat him: Berki watched in awe, munching on a honey cake, as his father tossed the bodies of those who came to wrestle with him about like a bear playing with salmon in the river, then lifted a rock that two other men together could not raise and cast it a good spear length past the farthest that anyone else could throw.

"Are you next at the stone casting?" a sweet high voice asked beside Berki when the thunderous cheering for Ecgtheow's feat had faded.

Berki looked down to see who had spoken to him. It was a girl of his own age a head and a half shorter than himself wearing a richly embroidered red apron over a white linen dress. Her fair hair, shining white as the Sun, hung down in a shimmering sheet past her waist, and her violet blue eyes looked up into his face. She was slender and delicately built, her skin as fine as spider silk and her waist small enough for Berki's hands to span. He dropped his head, feeling hulking and clumsy beside her.

"No," he admitted. "I am too young for the men's contest but that is my father who just won it," he added, more cheerfully.

The girl considered him carefully. "How old are you? I thought you were full grown, but if Ecgtheow is your father, you must be going to get much bigger."

"I am seven winters. How old are you?"

"Seven winters, as well. If Ecgtheow is your father and you are seven winters old and the size of a man, you must be Berki of the Waegmundings, and grandson to Hrethel. My father has spoken of you."

"Yes. Who are you?"

"I am Hygd. My father was Haereth of the Brondings, who fell battling the North Swedes in a raid around the northern shore of Lake Wener two years ago. Afterwards my mother wedded his cousin Beanstan, the Bronding drighten. Beanstan is a father to me now, and he rules wide lands at Hrethel's northern march. It was my adopted brother Breca he is three winters older than I who won the young boys' foot race and wrestling prizes. I have a real brother as well, Hereric, but he is fostered with a drighten in the northwest. Why weren't you in any of the contests?"

"Because I wasn't," Berki answered shortly. At once he regretted it, for Hygd's dainty lips turned down into a frown and she lowered her eyes. "Would you like a honey cake?" he said. "Our thrall is a good baker."

Hygd smiled at him again, taking the last cake from his sticky fingers and delicately nibbling at its edge.

"These are nice. That is a pretty piece of amber you are wearing. May I touch it?"

Berki bent down so that Hygd could stroke his pendant. The touch of her fingers against the amber set his heart beating hard, and he held his breath as if she were a wild bird that he feared to frighten.

"It is lovely," Hygd said. "I like the amber Queen Wynefrith wears, too. When I am frowe of my own hall, I shall have amber to drape about my neck as she does."

A shadow fell across Berki, and he looked up to see his father bearing down upon him. He cringed, thinking that Ecgtheow would speak sharply to him for standing and talking with a girl instead of running off with the other boys, but the big man was smiling, his bearded cheeks still flushed from the strain of his last great stone cast.

"Berki, did you mark that throw well?" He demanded. "You should strive to match it someday. Ah young frowe Hygd, I see you have found my son. Are you two getting on well?"

"We are, thank you," Hygd replied. "He has given me a honey cake already."

Ecgtheow laughed, then fished about in his belt pouch and came up with four southern silver pieces, which he handed to Berki.

"Why don't you show Hygd about the market, Berki? Perhaps you will find a trinket fit to adorn such a pretty young maid. She seems to like amber. Be careful that you are not cheated, now: when you are told the first price for a piece, offer half of that, and do not raise your offer too quickly."

"Thank you, Father!" Berki said.

Hygd smiled. "You are very kind, fro Ecgtheow. My father said that you were open handed as well as mighty in battle."

Ecgtheow grinned at her. "Your father is a well spoken man, and a great drighten. Run along and enjoy yourselves, you two."

The two of them made their way through the crowd to the market stalls. Berki was still stunned by his father's show of good temper. It must be for Hygd's sake, he thought. She is fair enough to make a troll eat from her hand. That reminded him of stories he had heard: how men of the eoten kind, great clumsy louts, were always seeking the Frowe in marriage and here he was, walking with Hygd's small fingers wrapped around his own big sticky paw. But such tales always turned out ill for the eotens: Thunar's Hammer always bashed their skulls in at the end, to save the fair goddess from such unwelcome bridegrooms. The thought saddened Berki, even as Hygd's chatter cheered him. Hygd looked carefully through all the stalls that were selling amber, at last settling on a pale gold piece cut in the shape of an apple, with a silver stem and leaf. Like Berki's pendant, it had a few shimmering sun spangles in it, though not as many or as bright. When the merchant, a short untidy man with light brown hair straggling from his braid, told them the price, Berki was truly shocked, for it was nearly twice what Ecgtheow had given him, and Hygd reeled back as if in horror.

"You cannot mean it!" Hygd exclaimed. "Surely you are jesting my mother paid half that last year, for a piece of amber twice the size."

"But look, young frowe, at the clearness of it and the skill of its shaping, and the sun spangles are so rare! But aye, raw amber is cheap if you have a craftsman of your own, I can sell you rough pieces at a price you will like better. Perhaps your friend there can cut and polish them for you?"

Hygd drew herself up, tilting her face so that she could look down her dainty nose at the merchant.

"Berki is the son of a drighten and grandson of a king, whose hands are fit for sword work, not carving. If you have nothing better to do than insult us, we can go elsewhere. Come, Berki."

Bewildered, Berki let her tug him away, but before they had gone three steps, the merchant called,

"Ah, come back, I meant no insult. Surely, for a maid so lovely and well born, I can lower the price a little not too much, mind, for my children must eat this winter, but somewhat."

Hygd turned back, picking up the amber apple and turning it over in her fingers.

"How much is 'somewhat'? Think carefully before you speak, for though I am but a child, I know the worth of the rings my mother's husband Beanstan gives."

Berki watched as Hygd argued with the merchant. It seemed to him that, though she was no older than he, she bargained as well as Wynefrith had with Guthlaf, tossing her long shining hair back and clutching at her heart. He could tell that the merchant was struggling to keep a smile from his face as he dealt with her, and when at last she told Berki to show what he had in his pouch, the amber seller broke into a broad grin.

"It is well for me that you are no older, else I would find myself giving my whole stock away for two copper pins and a single glance from your bright eyes," he said to Hygd. "The apple for those four silver pieces, then. And to show that I bear no ill will even though you have rooked me shamefully, maid of the Brondings, I shall give you a little silver chain to hang it on as well. In turn, perhaps you will speak kindly of me to the frowe your mother, should she be seeking more golden sea tears to adorn herself with, and do not forget that I shall be here next year with many more things for your delight."

Hygd bent her head, holding her hair back so that Berki could fasten the apple about her neck. She stroked the sleek amber, centering the pendant perfectly between her collarbones.

"It is just what I wanted," she said, well satisfied as a mother lynx curled about her furry kittens. "Now let us go to see if anyone has milk or sweet ale to offer us, for my throat is dry with talking."

"You did that very well," Berki said. "I could not have."

Hygd smiled up at him. "A woman must know how to do these things. I have what I wanted at a good price, and the merchant is happy enough, for he has fine southern silver and has found a new customer, which is the way things should be. My mother is teaching me everything about ruling a hall, for I shall marry a great drighten someday. And she says that a girl of seven winters is nearly a woman already, while a man of eighteen is still a boy."

They were almost at the food stalls when Berki heard the shout, "Hey! Beowulf!" He cringed, for he had been hoping that Hygd would not hear the shameful nickname. But when another boy's sharper voice called, "Hygd, what are you doing with him?" he had to turn and face them.

Agilar, Widuhund, and Thunarstan stood together with a smaller boy, whose white blond braid and dark blue eyes were the double of Hygd's. Though Berki had not watched the contests, he guessed that this must be Hygd's brother Breca: he was long legged, broad shouldered, and muscular for his size, bouncing on his toes like one who could not wait for a fight to start. He came forward now, looking Berki straight in the eye even as he spoke to Hygd.

"Come away, and do not waste your time with that fat coal biter. There are better men here, whom I would have you meet."

"I am happy to be with Berki," Hygd answered cooly. "And we are on our way somewhere else. Go away and leave us alone, Breca."

Breca laughed scornfully. "My friends here have told me what a shame this fattened ox is to Ecgtheow's line. They call him Beowulf, the honey eater, because he is good for nothing else not for fighting, nor to do the work of a man. A maid of the Brondings should look for something better. Come along, now." He grabbed Hygd by the arm, pulling her away. She let out a little breathless shriek, looking up at Berki as if for help.

"Let go of her!" Berki said. He had cringed back at Breca's words, but he could not bear to see him manhandling Hygd so.

Breca laughed again. "She is my sister, and I was told to look after her. Get out of the way, sea pig, or I'll render your carcase down for oil." He tugged at Hygd's arm again.

Berki grasped Breca's wrist, tearing his hand away from Hygd. The other boy's knee came up at once, but missed Berki's groin, thumping painfully into the meat of his thigh. Berki yanked harder and suddenly there was a loud cracking noise, and Breca yelped, going down to his knees and clutching at the arm Berki still held.

"You've broken it, the trolls take you," Breca gasped through gritted teeth.

His face had gone very white, and beads of sweat were beginning to roll down from the hairline.

"Let go now, or I swear by Woden that my father will chop your arm off as were gild."

Horrified by what he had done, Berki let go. "I did not mean to, I did not want to hurt you," he stammered. "I only, I swear I only wanted to get you off her.

Hygd was staring round eyed down at her adopted brother, but then she smoothed down the rumpled linen of her sleeve where he had grabbed her and said,

"You will not handle me like that again when Berki is beside me. And I think he has paid you back for your words well enough. I saw that you were trying to strike him a low blow, too."

"You only say that," Breca grated, wincing as he rose to his feet, "because you have your eye on Ecgtheow's hall already. And I see you have a new necklace, too did you promise the dwarves four nights of bed for it? I think you are a cuckoo in the Bronding nest."

Hygd's bright face flushed, and she was about to reply angrily when Agilar and his comrades began a slow clapping.

"Well done, Beowulf!" Agilar mocked. "You have broken the arm of a boy half your size. Are you proud of yourself now? You have broken the frith of the Thing as well, and I doubt the geld for that will come cheap."

If it had not been for Hygd beside him, Berki would have run off in shame then. He knew that he had already broken his Yule oath, by harming someone weaker. But I only did it to keep him off Hygd, he pleaded to himself; yet he could not still the sucking sense of guilt that dragged at him like thick bog mud.

"Give them no heed," Hygd said, taking Berki's hand in hers. "Come, we shall tell our fathers how matters fell out before anyone has a chance to lie to them. Breca, go find someone to tend to your arm."

"You cannot tell me what to do!" Breca answered. "I shall come with you so that you cannot lie about how Beowulf attacked me. And my father will believe his blood kin first."

"A maid of the Brondings does not lie, and Beanstan knows it," Hygd told him proudly. "But you may come, if you must."

The three of them found Ecgtheow first, standing in the meadow where horses were being offered for sale. He was running his hands carefully over the hocks of a tall dapple gray mare, his bushy eyebrows drawing together as he probed the lump of an old scar.

"She has been injured, and I am not sure that she would have the strength to bear me for any long way," he said. "I think this leg would quickly become sore beneath my weight."

The horse trader shook his head so that his black braids whipped about, waving his hands to protest, but before he could launch into a speech, Berki stepped forward.

"Father, we must speak to you."

Ecgtheow frowned down at his son, then smiled as he saw Hygd beside him.

"What is it?"

"Your son Beowulf Berki," Breca corrected hastily, "attacked me and broke my arm in the middle of the market. Unless you give me self judgement, my father will be bringing my case before the Thing."

"Breca attacked him first," Hygd broke in. "He tried to knee him in the balls."

Ecgtheow looked at the three children, and Berki could see he was almost revolted at the thought the corners of his father's mouth turning up beneath his thick brown beard. He is pleased that I hurt Breca, although it was not fair.

"Be calm, now. Berki, tell me what happened."

"Breca tried to drag Hygd away, and she didn't want to go. I pulled him off her, and his arm broke. I didn't mean to do it."

"Such things will happen, when weaker men argue with stronger ones," Ecgtheow rumbled. "Well, I shall go speak to the Bronding drighten, and I am sure we can sort things out." He clapped Berki hard on the shoulder. "As for you, my son, perhaps you should save your strength for wrestling matches, where no one can fault you if the other man's bones do not stand up to your throws."

He strode off, leaving the children to look after him. "My father will sort him out," said Breca confidently, and followed. Hygd sighed. "I suppose I should go with them, too. Thank you for the amber, and for looking after me." She gave Berki's hand a last squeeze and hurried away, the embroidered hem of her red apron fluttering behind her.

At the feast that night, nothing was said of bringing a case before the Thing, but Breca was wearing a bright new gold ring on his good arm, and looked smug in spite of the splint on the other one. Berki did not have a chance to speak to Hygd, but Hygelac saw him looking at her, sitting small and calm between Beanstan and his plump, fair haired wife, and murmured,

"I hear you have made a good start at a betrothal."

"What do you mean?" Berki asked.

"There is hardly a marriage where one of the bride's kin does not object to the bridegroom, and he must fight father or brother to prove his right to her. And Hygd is a very pretty little girl of good family; Haethcyn says he is sure that Ecgtheow wants to see you wedded to her. It would be a fine match, when you are old enough to be married."

"Do you think so?" Berki said hopefully.

"Of course. Did I not just say so? Keep speaking sweetly to her, and giving her presents, and when you are both grown, she will have no one else. That is how Haethcyn got Garhild, after all."

Berki glanced over at Hygd again. She giggled and looked away, as though she were embarrassed to have been caught staring at him. "She knows it, too," Hygelac went on softly.

"I have heard that, young as she is, Hygd can set her mind on a thing and not stop until she gets it. Hildebere was like that: as long as I could remember, my sister never failed to get anything that she wanted, from a pretty gold ring to a great hairy berserk who would follow her about like a tame bear no shame to Ecgtheow, but his manners were better while Hildebere was alive. But do not forget, my friend, that there are a great many maidens out there, and you have plenty of time before you have to settle on one. I would not tie myself down so quickly; indeed, my parents have spoken of seeking a wife for me, but I am of somewhat the same mind in the matter as Herebeald claims to be though he is also waiting, I think, until Father has yielded the high seat to him. But as for me, I am too young yet to let myself be bound, while there are so many lovely maids who might be eager to walk out in the woods with me. And Hygd is pretty now, but who knows what she will become? Her hair may darken, or she may stay thin with no breasts all her life, though I will grant her mother is a fine looking woman and one can often see from the mother how the daughter will turn out."

Berki was sad when he had to bid farewell to Hygd at the end of the Thing, but she promised that she would come back next year. Though Breca glowered at him as Beanstan's family and thanes rode away, Berki stayed and waved to Hygd until she was out of sight. After the Thing, Berki did not dare to wrestle with the other boys: he could not forget the sickening feeling of Breca's arm snapping in his grip, nor could he stave off the guilt of it for long. He spent more time away in the ocean, and did not heed anyone who mocked him for it.

The summer passed by quickly, and soon it was time for harvest. Because of his strength, Berki was not set to a child's work of cutting and gleaning. At first he was put to help with the threshing, but he pounded the grain too hard, so that he beat the corn to powder together with the chaff; after that, he was sent to carry heavy bales and bags. He did not complain at the work, but he liked being called an ox and prodded with makeshift oxgoads little better than he liked being called a whale and having sticks cast at him for harpoons. With the turning of the seasons, Berki went out to Whales' Ness more often, either to swim or to sit on the high headland and watch the whales go by.

The small ones, the dark blunt headed grind, the swift and deadly spekheawer whales with their white splotched black hides, and the high warbling white whales would swim quite close to the point; father out, Berki often saw the wide backs of the blue whales and cachalots, and sometimes a humpback would breach for him, leaping free of the ocean to crash down in a huge torrent of spray. He did not dare to go into the water when the spekheawer whales were about, for fear they should mistake him for a seal, but he loved to watch their black fins cutting through the waves like proud prowed ships, and hear their low musical groans as they blew puffs of mist above the surface of the ocean.

As Berki had thought would be the case, Hygelac had less and less time for him as the king's son spent more time with his father's thanes, riding out now and then on raids and coming back to share proud tales of his fights with other blooded warriors, so that Berki had none save old Amma and the sea to talk to. Ecgtheow came to see him at every Yule feast and Midsummer Thing, but Berki's father grew no more satisfied with his son as time went on. By the age of ten, Berki was bigger than many grown men, and Ansuwulf at last had to forbid him to practice sword work with the youths, for though his strokes were still slow and clumsy, he was breaking both shields and wooden swords in every fight, and the berserk told him sharply that,

"If you should ever by chance land a good blow with one of those sticks, you would kill someone."

It seemed to Berki that he lived only for the Midsummer gatherings when Hygd came to Hrethel's hall with her kin: she alone seemed to look kindly on him, or treat him as if he were not a useless witling and, much as Berki hated to think on it, and seemed that the other youths had learned from Breca's broken arm, for when Hygd was walking with him, they left him alone. Ecgtheow always gave Berki silver to buy presents for Hygd, and for her sake, though he would not wrestle, he was even willing to show his strength in the stone casting. He took her to see Whales' Ness, and the holy grove; and in his fourteenth summer, in a strange burst of bravery, he even took her walking in the barrow field. She showed no signs of fear, even peering carefully at the long rune carven on Ansugrimar's stone.

"I can read those," Hygd declared. "The staves are clear, though the rune is strange. It says, "I the Erulian risted this rune. No man may bare it when the waning moon runs; bale workers may not lay the stone aside. The ash of Grim sprinkled it with the corpse sea, he rubbed the dwarf's boat thole with ravens' mead. I bid the high gods, I bid the holy ones, I bid the oath kinsman of Hel..."

"I would hear no more," said Berki shuddering. "Are you not afraid to read it?"

"Not while you stand here by me," Hygd answered, looking up at him.

She was a full two heads shorter than he now, and still dainty of build, though her breasts and hips were rounding out the sky blue linen of her dress. About her neck she wore all the amber Berki had given her over the last six years, from the apple pendant of their first meeting to the large strand of deep red beads they had bought that morning. Her shimmering flaxen hair had never been cut, and now it flowed more than halfway down the backs of her thighs.

"You are bigger and stronger than any man I know of, save your father, and you came within a hand span of beating him in the stone cast this year: my mother says that you are likely to outmatch him easily by the time you are full grown.

I have not forgotten how you handled Breca when we first met, and I know that you would do the same to anyone, living or dead, who threatened me."

"So I would," Berki said, standing a little taller. Amma had told him often enough to stand up straight, but when he was around others, he was in the habit of hunching down with his shoulders rounded so that he would not seem to hulk over them so dreadfully.

"You see, I have nothing to fear here," Hygd said. She laid her hand upon his forearm for a moment; her delicate white fingers would not go halfway around it. "And I have heard, also, that most folk think it likely that you will be taken into Ansuwulf's berserk band this year, and there are few, within or without the Middle Garth's ring, who can match might with a berserk."

"And few men who will sit with them at ale drinking, and few women who wish to be wedded to them," Berki replied. "It does not seem such a fine thing to me."

He remembered his first Yule feast at Hrethel's hall, how the poor woman with the horn had screamed when one of the berserk band had wrenched her arm out of its socket even as he had carelessly broken Breca's arm. Hygd laughed, giving his arm a little squeeze.

"Weak women may fear many things, but Woden is the father of berserks, and I have not heard that the Frowe ever barred him from her chamber on that account. You may be sure that I will never be afraid of you, Berki."

But I fear myself, Berki thought. And I would rather lop off my own limbs than let my clumsiness do you harm. Yet he could not say that. Instead he brushed his fingertips across the back of her white hand, and said,

"You shall never have reason to." His voice cracked on the last word, dropping from its boyish alto to a surprisingly deep note. He blushed, bringing his hand to his mouth as if he could call the sound back. Hygd laughed.

"You will be a man soon, Berki. And I shall remind my mother of that, lest she forget though she says I am too young to be betrothed yet."

Berki thought on what Hygd had said often after she had gone, letting them warm his heart when others spoke unkindly to him. If she wished a betrothal, then they would be betrothed: he could think of nothing better. And yet there had been a warning in her words as well: thereafter, he was even more wary of Ansuwulf than before, dodging behind houses when he saw the broad shouldered figure of the berserk walking about his business and being very careful not to catch Ansuwulf's eyes in the hall. The summer passed, and harvest after: it had been a good year, and Hrethel's Winter nights feast was rich with heaped apples, fresh meat, and free flowing mead.

Berki did not linger too late in the hall, for when the men who had been in Hygelac's boy troop when he came there grew drunk, they were more likely than usual to taunt him, even throwing bones at him when Hygelac had gone out to piss and Hrethel and Wynefrith were looking elsewhere. The night was very clear, the milky path of the Winter Way glittering faintly beyond the stars like a dusting of moonlight mirrored on the dark sea. The full Moon cast a chill brightness over the frosted ground, silvering dead grass stalks and thatched roofs against their black shadows. Berki barely noticed the bite of ice in the air, nor the glimmering white puffs of his breath, except as the cold stillness came as welcome relief after the smoky heat and noise of the hall.

Although he had not wanted to stay and drink, Berki was not yet sleepy. After a little while, it came to him that the holy grove had been well blessed in the last day with the blood of all the cattle and swine of the winter slaughtering, and, if he went to ask something of the gods now, they might look kindly upon him. Hygd had spoken of betrothal: would it not be well to ask the blessing of Fro and Frowe, and of Frige, who looked after marriages and tended the home? For the more Berki thought upon being wedded to Hygd, the gladder he became; and yet it gave him much to trouble his mind as well. She thought that he would be a great drighten after his father, but how could he? He was a figure of fun here, and he did not think that matters would be any better when he went home to dwell with Ecgtheow.

He was too slow to fight well, and he doubted that anyone would be willing to follow him in battle or in frith. In his years here, he had watched the sons of Hrethel, and seen in them what he lacked himself: Herebeald was loved by all, bright of face and mood; Haethcyn was wise, so that even his father listened to his redes with more than half an ear; and Hygelac was brave, willing to risk himself at the least chance in battle or any deeds that called for daring, so that there were as many songs about him as about the other two together. And none of them was without bravery or wisdom, and all three of them were loved and trusted by Hrethel's men: a drighten needed to be thus. And Berki was sure that Hygd's kin had heard the bad about him as well as the good: whatever her will in the matter, they might not give their consent in the marriage if he had not somehow managed to prove himself worthy of her.

For that matter, it would be foolish of Hrethel to give him Ecgtheow's march stead to hold after his father, when what that place needed was a man mighty enough to hold back the Swedes by his fame as much as his strength and skill. Berki had also seen, at the Yule feasts and Midsummer Things, that Ecgtheow's thanes were rougher than Hrethel's, big scarred men who were quick to fight or take anger at a word men much like Ecgtheow himself, fittest to ward a march in times of battle and least at ease when smooth words were called for in times of frith: they would be less patient with Berki than Hrethel and his kin were, and swift to try their wills in struggle against his if he were set over them. Though Hygd trusted in him, he knew that she was not a woman who would be glad as the wife of a simple hall thane, and Berki did not know if he could hope for any better, though his blood and Hygelac's friendship should assure him of that much, at least.

There was no man with whom he could share such thoughts, for fear of what they might bring, but the gods kept the words that were trusted to them, and it seemed to Berki that they alone could help him. So thinking, he went out the gate and started along the path that wound around the southern side of Hrethel's keep. The leaves had already fallen from the birches, only a few withered scraps, now white with frost, hanging from their pale branches. Beyond them, the pines loomed dark under the shimmering film of crystals on their needles, and Berki quickened his steps: from Winter nights on, the world outside the garth walls of men was given over to the wild things, wolves and trolls and those who rode unseen through the night. A wolf howled, and another answered it. They sounded very near, and Berki began to wonder if it had been wise of him to step out of Hrethel's hold into the woods. He had not been given a sword yet, only the long bladed knife that hung at his belt; and he had heard that a pack of wolves, if they were desperate enough, might even bring down a bear. But wolves were seldom dangerous to men until deep into the winter, Berki reminded himself: now they should still be well fed from the summer's young elk and deer.

A third wolf howled; it sounded as though it were only a few feet from the path. Berki drew his knife and backed up to a tree, looking about himself. Wolves could have the frothing wod, and there was no leeching for such bites, he remembered, nor did beasts maddened by it have any fear of men. For a moment he thought of running, but he might as well lie on the ground and offer his throat up as run away from a wolf pack they would attack more quickly if he showed his fear, though there was nothing he could do to keep them from smelling it. And he was no longer a child, to flee from every threat: had not Hygd said that she was afraid of nothing while he was beside her? *If her trust is rightly placed, I should prove it now.* Suddenly, before Berki could think or act, wild yells sounded on either side of him, and something black blotted out the moonlight. Harsh ropes tightened on his wrists and ankles, and a powerful blow struck his shoulder, though it did not push him away from the tree at his back. The ropes yanked hard enough to cut into his flesh; shocked by the pain, Berki yanked back, and the bonds at his wrists snapped, freeing his arms. He flailed about himself wildly; one blow landed, and he heard a man's yelp, cut off quickly.

"Come with us," a voice said a deep voice, hardly more than a snarl. "Little bear, I call you by the name your father gave you when he sprinkled you with water Berki Ecgtheow's son, child of the Waegmundings and Geat rulers, I bid you by the might of Woden, drighten of wolves; I bid the mighty bear who runs before you to follow us, that we may test his birthright in your soul."

A prickly loop of hemp fell over Berki's head, tightening on his throat; and though the tugging at its end was gentle, Berki could not help following. His limbs were shaking with fright, for he knew now that he was in the hands of the berserk band he would have to face Woden in his full madness that night, as he had hoped that he never would; for the words that had been spoken bound him more firmly than the frail rope at his neck. Berki did not know how long they led him, but when they stopped at last, taking the blindfold from his eyes, he was in a clearing that he had never seen before.

Around it were nine yew trees, no more than thrice a man's height not young saplings, for they grew more slowly than any trees in the wood, but slimmer trunked than the span of Berki's hands and by each was a flat hewn stump with a keg resting upon it. In the middle of the clearing was a fire with an iron cauldron hanging from a tripod over it. A wide horned elk lay dead by the fire, his neck and belly gashed and torn as though he had been set upon by wolves. His blood was still glistening fresh, and steam rose from his wounds; and beside him lay the brown skin of a great bear, head raised and eyes empty as though a mask had been set in place of its skull.

There were twelve men in the clearing with Berki, and all of them were naked save for sword belts and the hides of wolves or bears. Only Ansuwulf did not wear his gray fell over his head, but bore a helm with two wide bronze curves arching up from it, the flattened horn shapes ending not in points, but in the heads of two ravens whose beaks were almost touching. He lifted his spear, whirling it overhead so that its tip traced red glittering swirls against the stars, then lowering it to point straight at Berki's heart. Then he threw back his head and howled, the high eerie sound stabbing through Berki's spine like an icicle, and the other berserks howled and snarled in answer.

"Bear, awaken!" Ansuwulf growled. "Beowulf, honey eater, fat and strong from the summer: long have you slept, and the winds grow cold, but the time has not come for you to turn to your den. Now Woden shall have you for his own, or you shall not tread living for this place; for you are come among his berserks, and if you cannot bear his wod, you shall be rent asunder by it. Fetters you have broken already: now take off the clothes of a man!"

Slowly Berki stripped, letting his cloak, tunic, and breeches fall to the ground before him. He was ashamed to show his body before these men, though a few of the others were wide in the belly, but none of them spoke. At Ansuwulf's gesture, he fumbled at the knot in the thong holding his amber pendant tightly about his neck. But his fingers were too clumsy; it would not give, and at last the berserk leader signed to him to leave it. Kicking the shed clothes aside, Ansuwulf picked up the great aurochs horn that lay before the cauldron, dipping it into the steaming brew and signing the threefold knot of Woden over it.

"Grim One, Awesome, Wanderer, Bear! High One, Hoar Beard, Spear God, Bale Eye! Yule God, Slayer, Gallows Swinger, Host God, Wod! Hallow this draught to break through the soul walls; hallow this draught to open the way. Wod Stirrer it hight, with heart blood it is brewed: words to the skald, to the berserk, wod! Rouse the sleeper to wild waking, rouse the bear from his deep den, rouse the cub to his grown strength."

He held the horn out to Berki. It trembled in Berki's hand, smooth as polished amber and warm as the blood of a living thing. Berki did not want to drink, yet he was afraid that if he turned it down, the berserks would rend his living flesh as they had rent the elk; and though the top of Ansuwulf's head came only to the middle of his chest, the shorter man's dark eyes bored into his with a deathly gaze that Berki could not overcome. The draught was sweet with honey, but there was a foul taste beneath it, musty as rotting tree bark and thick with slimy clots of blood.

Berki managed to swallow one gulp, then he knew he could not get any more down. But Ansuwulf took the horn back, drinking and handing it on to the bear berserk at his side, and so it went around the circle. The last of them, a tall grim man in a wolf hame Berki could not recognise him, or any of them except Ansuwulf, though he knew he had seen them in the hall a thousand times filled it again from one of the kegs, and Ansuwulf gave it to Berki again.

"Drain the horn," he ordered. Berki did not need to sniff at it as he raised it: the powerful honey scent of mead nearly overwhelmed his nose, its heat searing down his throat as though he had never tasted strong drink before. The berserks drank in turn, each draining a horn full at a draught. Berki's head was already beginning to spin, but there was a strange clearness to his sight, as though the moonlight were growing brighter, gleaming off the eyes behind the beast masks and the gold ringed hilts of the swords.

One of the bear men had a drum in his hands, though Berki had not seen him pick it up. He began to beat it, the low thumping echoing through the clearing. Slowly the others began to move, the bears' feet shuffling and the wolves' feet moving more lightly and quickly. Berki blinked. The sound of the drum was echoing through his skull, drowning out his thoughts, but he still felt sick to his stomach and afraid. The shapes of the dancers seemed to shift as he watched, now lowering to all fours, now rising to both feet and waving huge shaggy paws in the air.

Only Ansuwulf, standing a little to the side, still seemed human and had he grown taller, one eye glowing brighter from beneath his bird helm even as the other darkened? The steps of the dance quickened, the dancers snarling and swiping at each other with claw and blade; the trees at the side of the clearing stretched higher, great hall posts holding up the dark arched roof of the sky. It seemed to Berki that a wind was blowing through between the trees, chill and dank with the scent of rotting gallows fruit, and the swords in the paws of the beasts caught the light of the fire to burn like flickering red torches. He crouched down, hugging himself with both arms against the cold as the dance grew wilder.

One of the wolves suddenly broke from the whirling ring of dancers, bending over the dead elk to tear away a piece of dripping meat with claws and teeth before he spun back in among the others. A bear followed him, growling and snapping ravenously, then another. Ansuwulf watched silently, waiting until all of them had fed before reaching down to rip off a piece, which he carried over to Berki. Berki took the wet meat from him nervously. It was still warm, its stink of fear sharp blood burning in his nostrils. He thought that if he tried to eat it, he would throw it back up. Ansuwulf waited, his one bright eye staring fiercely down at Berki.

"I cannot," Berki whispered.

"You must." Ansuwulf's voice had changed, no more than a deep sigh of wind rustling through yew needles. The sound of it froze Berki's bones with terror, and unwillingly he raised the bloody flesh to his mouth, worrying a small bite away with his teeth.

The smile that touched Ansuwulf's lean face was no more than dead lips pulling back from the teeth of a skull, but he turned away, letting Berki cough out the raw lump and toss the meat away unnoticed. When Ansuwulf came back, the horn in his hand was brimming full; the drops that spilled over the rim to trickle down off its point glowed like sparks as they fell.

"Drink," he said, and Berki did. As Berki lowered the horn, something heavy and warm fell across his shoulders hairy sleeves molding to his arms, clawed gloves to his hands.

He tried to cry out, but heard only the growl of a bear. Frightened, he shambled forward, the smaller beasts whirling about him. A sword sang past his face, missing his snout by a hairsbreadth; the cold wind of another stirred the fur of his shoulder. The thumping of the drum was louder now, but he could not catch its rhythm; his feet came down unevenly, his paws swinging uncertainly. He was very hungry: he could smell the elk's rich blood, but above it was the strong sweet scent of honey in the kegs. Falling to all fours, he walked over to butt his head against one. Then there was a horn in his paws: he sat back on his haunches, raising it and spilling the honey drink into his mouth.

He could hear the sounds of anger growing in the other bears' growls, the snarling of the wolves, but he did not care: his belly was filled with warmth, and his ears were humming with the soft song of the bees. A claw scraped against his side, and he reached back, lazily tossing away the little wolf that had leapt at him. The man was speaking: even in his daze, he could feel the words buzzing about him, but they were not enough to rouse him from his place. But the other animals were circling him, ears back and mouths open to show their fangs. He rose up, stretching to his full height and snarling briefly; they backed away, and he settled down again. The honey scent was still rising from the keg, and he could not get at it, which was beginning to anger him, so he whacked at it with his paw. One of the staves cracked in, spilling out the sweet drink; he put his mouth to it, eagerly lapping it up. A powerful blow knocked the keg away, and a smaller bear was there before him, snarling in his face before it lunged in to bite at his neck. He swung a paw, striking the other bear to the ground before its teeth could close on him.

It lay dazed before him, and he lumbered over to the next keg, prying at its top with his strong claws. Now the man was speaking more urgently, his voice rising and falling like a storm wind through the trees. He paid the chant no heed, grunting with satisfaction as the wooden circle sprang loose and lowering his snout into the honeyed sweetness. As his long tongue licked the last drops from inside the keg, a deep growl startled him into looking up. The man was gone, but before him stood a great grim wolf, the ruff around its neck bristling and ears laid flat against its head.

He dropped the little barrel, but could not move swiftly enough to fend off the jaws that fastened high on his left leg. With a snarl of pain, he tore the wolf from him, flinging it halfway across the clearing. It landed heavily, rolling, and rose to face him again. Though the bite was sore, there was no anger in him: he did not feel like killing, he only wanted to be left alone with the sweet kegs of honey and the pleasant warmth in his belly. But when the wolf sprang again, he was ready for it, cuffing it away to keep it from biting him. Again and again the wolf attacked leaping full on, circling about to slash at his hamstrings with its jaws, feinting and whirling to snap at him. Each time, he was able to fend it off; and at last it crept away into the darkness outside the clearing.

He waited a little while, looking around, until he was sure the wolf was gone. Then he was quite alone, but the other honey kegs had vanished as well, as had the elk carcase: there was only a dark patch of melted frost, stained with dribbles of blood, to show where it had lain. Disappointed, he lay down with his snout on his paws. He was very sleepy now, his eyes drooping closed, he was warm in his hide, as if he were curled up in a winter den, warm, it seemed to him that he saw the meadows in full summer bloom, white daisies and blue toad flax and golden buttercups. A fair haired maiden walked beside him, ruffling his fur with fingers gentle as a warm breeze, and fed him honeyed berries from her basket; amber and gold glowed about her neck, and though she smiled, now and then a tear would drop from her eye, gleaming fiery gold in the sunlight.

"My bear, my own bear," she crooned. "Salmon fisher, honey eater, mighty folk warder; eat and grow strong, for summer comes after winter, and grim morning may brighten to a glad day, and golden sunset."

Berki awoke shivering, blinking against the painfully bright light. Cold dribbles of rain were running down his face, and something heavy and stinking lay on top of him. He rolled over, pushing at it, and his fingers met the coarse damp fur of a fresh tanned bearskin. With a groan he sat up, rubbing his aching head, then turned his face to the side and threw up. His vomit was sweet, but left a foul taste in the back of his mouth, and the night came rushing back to him. The berserks had taken him away Ansuwulf had given him something strange to drink, that was the nasty taste and then? The head of the bearskin had been carefully stitched onto a mask that could be pulled over the head, like the furred hames the berserks wore.

But Berki was sure that he had not gone berserk, or they would not have left him here alone like this. They would have been around him, welcoming him as a brother even as they groaned over their hangovers with him he had seen his father with the other berserks often enough to know that. And yet he was alive, when everyone had said that youths who failed the berserk testing were never seen again. Although his eyes kept blurring out of focus and everything he looked at seemed to have a shimmering ring of brightness about it, Berki could see the clear trail leading back along the pathway he had walked last night, men's bare feet and the claw marked tracks of bears and wolves mingled together. Unless they had led him greatly astray, he should have no trouble getting back to Hrethel's hall.

Berki pushed himself up, stifling a moan as pain stabbed through his left thigh. It was marked with a neat red pattern in the pointed shape of a wolf's jaws, as though the wood hound's teeth had closed on him but not pierced the skin. He rubbed it, wondering, but could remember nothing of how he might have taken the wound. His clothes were where Ansuwulf had kicked them, though they were trampled and stained, and stank as if someone had pissed on them. Slowly he put them on, fastening his breeches and belt with stiff fingers.

Berki had never been so sick after mead before, but he had seen Hygelac in a worse state a few times, and he knew that Amma could make a brew that would ease the worst of his pain. For a moment he thought about bringing the bearskin with him, but he did not want it. Instead, he left it hanging on a low branch of one of the yew trees: the berserks could keep it for someone better suited to their hidden ways. Although it was nearly midday, there was hardly anyone around when Berki came into the keep. His head was pounding harder, and he had thrown up twice along the way, but his eyes had cleared and the worst of the shaking in his limbs had passed. He decided that he would put on fresh clothes before going to Amma for her brew. Hygelac was in the house they shared, rummaging through his clothes chest. He did not look up as Berki came in, but said sadly,

"Herebeald, have you seen my deep blue tunic? It is not fitting for us to wear bright clothes when our sister's only son is dead."

"Hygelac?" Berki said. "I am not dead."

Hygelac whirled, a wide grin spreading across his short bearded face. He ran to Berki, embracing him hard and pounding him on the back.

"You are not dead!" he shouted joyfully. "The berserks came into the hall without you, and I was sure..."

"Do not shout at me, my head cannot bear it. They left me in the wood. It was not hard to find my way back, but I drank something last night and I am very sick."

Hygelac's nose wrinkled, catching the stink of Berki's clothes, and he stood back.

"You smell as though you fell into a barrel of sour mead, all right. But are you a berserk, then? They should have brought you before us with them."

"I am not. I do not know what happened, but I must have failed their test somehow. But they did not kill me."

"Put on clean clothes quickly, and we will go to the hall. It will ease everyone's heart to know that we have not lost you."

As they walked up to the hall, Ansuwulf strode out, spear in hand. Seeing them, he stopped where he stood.

"Hygelac, go on," he said quietly. "I must speak with Berki a moment."

Hygelac hurried light footed through the carven doorposts. Ansuwulf peered up into Berki's face, squinting as though he, too, were struggling against the painful brightness of sight that had troubled Berki that morning. He was very pale, his eyes red rimmed, and his breath had the same reek of stale mead with a foul under taste that was still in Berki's mouth; Berki was afraid he would cast his stomach up again from smelling it.

"You are not a berserk," Ansuwulf said. "What do you remember?"

"Only…"

Ansuwulf put his hand up to silence Berki.

"You will never speak of it. You have seen what no one who is not of our band should see and live; and yet, though you are not one of us, you are truly a bear with strength to meet the berserk might. Someday you may yet fall to tooth and claw, but your wyrd was not risted to come upon you then. Since Woden would not claim you, either as thane or as offering, it may be that the troth of your soul is pledged to another: I do not know. In any case, it is no longer a matter for me to deal with save that, if you tell anything of what took place last night, I will seek you out and slay you myself. Do you understand?"

"Yes."

"That is well." He walked past Berki without another word. After a moment, Berki took a deep breath and stepped through into the hall.

It was easy for him to see the relief on Hrethel's face: his grandfather must have been dreading the tidings he thought he would have to send to Ecgtheow, as well as sorrowing for the loss of his daughter's only child.

But Hrethel said only, "Sit down, Berki, and break your fast. You look as though you were long at feasting last night."

The smoke and the smell of spilt ale and grease stains from the feast, were soon too much for Berki to bear, and he left the hall as early as he could, seeking out fresh air. As he was used to doing, he made his way down to the ocean, thinking that a long swim would clear out the last of the dizziness in his head and get the blood flowing cleanly through his limbs again. The sea was rough with the first winter winds, waves rising in caps of froth to beat hard against the shore. Berki stripped down and waded into the water, welcoming the icy chill against his overheated skin.

The waves' pounding against him thrilled through his body, thrumming deep in his bones as he walked deeper, stopping when the water was up to his chest. He felt a strange tingling in his loins, such as he had never felt before, at once pleasant and wildly urgent. Curious, his hand went to his groin, feeling the swelling and the pulsing heat, like an iron bar burning too fiercely to be quenched even by the rime cold sea. The powerful ebb and flow of the ocean tugged at him, stroking against him in a rhythm he could not deny and did not want to stop; the waves broke hard against his chest and face like slapping caresses, stirring his need unbearably, and it seemed to him that he could hear a deep sighing through the crashing of the water against the shore. Caught in the grasp of the sea, Berki moved his hand faster, his moans lost in the sounds of the ocean and the mewing of the gulls above, until at last he had to cast his head back and cry out, his groin bursting with a pleasure so strong it was almost pain as his white seed spurted out to mingle with the white foam.

Berki stood panting in the water until the last spasms had faded from his flesh, then turned and waded back to shore. Only when he had dressed himself did his hand go to his throat, where his amber pendant had hung. Though he knew it had been about his neck when he changed clothes and he had not taken it off, there was nothing there now. It was gone, lost in the sea which had once cast it to shore. Though he knew that he should be heartbroken at his loss that later, by habit, he would reach for it and feel the emptiness at his neck like a sleeve dangling over a missing arm now he felt only a strange sure quietness.

Ran's daughter has taken back her plaything, he thought, and was content enough with that. After his failed berserk testing, Berki found that he was more of an outcast than before. Men who had stayed their tongues for fear that they would suddenly rouse a berserk wod in him had nothing to hold them back now, and the young women, thrall maids and the daughters of thanes alike, turned their faces from him and tittered when he walked by. That year, for the first time, Ecgtheow did not come to Hrethel's Yule feast, and Berki knew in his heart that it was because he had disappointed his father's last hopes for him. At Midsummer, Ecgtheow rode in a few days before the Thing began. After he had drunk the welcome draught in Hrethel's hall and spoken for a little time with Hrethel and Wynefrith, he took Berki aside.

"Ansuwulf sent me word that you are not a berserk," he said, the sullen bear gleam glowing balefully in his eyes.

Struggling not to turn away from his gaze, Berki realized that he was actually looking down at his father: where he had been half a hands breadth shorter than Ecgtheow at the last summer Thing, now he was almost half a head taller, and wider as well, though Ecgtheow's shoulders bulged with muscle above the swell of his belly and Berki's body was layered thickly with fat all over. Ecgtheow seemed to realize it too, for he stepped back a pace, looking his son over.

"It is a waste," he went on angrily. "You are a king's grandson and as big as a son of mine should be, but there is nothing but fat heaped upon your limbs; you are not a man, but a mist calf made of clay, with a timid mare's heart beating in your breast. You never fight, not though every man makes mock of you, and you are good for nothing but carrying loads like an ox and splashing about in the ocean. Your time of fostering should be over at Yule but I am not sure I want you back, for I cannot feed a boy who eats the food of five men and cannot take the place of one in my shield wall."

"Does Hrethel speak so ill of me?" Berki asked, deeply hurt if not surprised at his father's words. But at least, he thought to himself, I am not a berserk, who cannot tell friend from foe, nor times of fighting from times of frith, when the wod is upon him; and perhaps that is worth the cost of your scorn, Father.

"He does not," Ecgtheow admitted grudgingly. "Only because he is too well mannered to speak ill of a child he has taken as foster son, even when it is deserved. But others are not so careful of their tongues, and though my hearing is not what it was in my youth, I am not so deaf as you seem to think I am. Ansuwulf has washed his hands of you, and there is no other war leader who would choose to take you on."

Stung, Berki answered him proudly, "Hygelac has told me that I will always have a place beside him when I am old enough to bear a sword in battle."

Ecgtheow frowned, and his voice deepened to a growl as he replied, "Hygelac is a young fool. He lives up to his name, for his soul is ever at play, without a grown man's wisdom to steady it. Still, I wish that you were more like him: he has won fame for bravery, while you are known only as Beowulf, the honey eater. When you broke Breca's arm as a child, I thought you might amount to something, but Breca, too, has become a fine young warrior, blooded in battle and first among the young men of the Bronding household in all skills, and you are still a coal biter." He paused, heavy brows furrowing. "Yet Hygd, I am told, is still of a mind to be betrothed to you. Her kin have pleaded with her to choose a better match, but she is proud of soul and stubborn: it may be that she thinks she can make a man of you where everyone else has failed. And I have hoped for this wedding almost from the time of your birth, since the Brondings are as strong a clan as we could hope to be allied with. Still, the dealings for such a betrothal will not be easy, for I must try to tell them that they are not giving the fairest gem of their house to adorn a fatted pig and I am not sure that I believe it myself: I can hardly swear before the gods that you are worthy of Hygd. What shall I say to them, Beowulf?"

Berki held his breath as his father spoke, his heart thudding hard in his breast. For Ecgtheow to speak of his betrothal, even as he cursed Berki's unworthiness it seemed unreal to him, glimmering like a pearl cast ashore in the sea foam. He let the name go by, for it was a little thing, and answered,

"Say that Hygd shall never suffer any harm while I am beside her, and that if she loves me as I love her, we shall be happy together. If you do not want me, I shall stand beside Hygelac while I live and trust in him for land and rings; and if you cannot speak well of me to the Brondings, then let Hygelac speak for you." To Berki's pride, his voice stayed deep and steady through his speech, without cracking or wavering; he knew that, at least, he sounded like a man.

Ecgtheow thought on that a moment, his blunt fingers twining through the graying mass of his bushy beard.

"At least you have learned the worth of fellowship with a drighten. I hope that Hygelac does not suffer for his kindness to you but I shall do as you suggest. Still, you should not think that you have gotten out of your duties to your clan: if there is need in battle this year, I shall call upon you, and then, by Woden's spear, you will either prove yourself worthy of wedding the bride you have chosen, or you will lie slain on the field." He reached below the curve of his wide belly, unbuckling his sword belt and handing it, sword and all, to Berki.

"Ansuwulf should have given you a blade to wield if you had shown yourself fit to stand among the berserks, but I suppose this can be denied you no longer. Do not shame me when you come to use it! We must have a coat of mail made for you as well, or the first edge that meets your flesh will go through all that fat like a spekheawer's teeth through whale blubber until then, hardened leather with rings set in will have to do for you. I brought a byrnie of my own for you, but you have grown bigger than I thought you would. You will need a larger shield than other men carry, too, for that there is more of you to strike at and you should find the weight of a big shield not too hard to carry. And I will find a helm for you shortly so that you look better at the Thing, as a man of your birth ought."

"Thank you, Father!" Berki said, overwhelmed.

Hygelac had gotten his sword at a high feast in the hall before the eyes of all the thanes, swearing his troth to Hrethel on the gold ring of the king' own sword pommel. Berki had never thought that he would be given a man's weapon thus, its honor cast at him between reproaches with no one to witness or lift a horn to toast the deed; but here it was, solid and weighty in his hand, not lessened a bit by the brusque manner of its giving. He wrapped the belt around his waist big as Ecgtheow was, the buckle barely reached the last hole on Berki and closed his hand on the ridged horn of the hilt.

"I shall bear it well, and stand by your side whenever you have need of me."

"See that you do," Ecgtheow answered roughly. "If you have not the skill to strike with the edge, at least you should have the weight behind your blows to crush a man's head with the flat. I am going to speak with Hygelac now. Try to keep out of the way while we are talking over the betrothal, and do nothing that the Brondings can take amiss." He drew two gold rings off his fingers, wide heavy coils, and dropped them into Berki's palm. "Since you have bought Hygd amber every year from the time you met, I see no reason why you should not get her something fine this year as well. At least, for all your faults, you have not managed to fail in your wooing yet."

Ecgtheow made good on his words: by the time Hrethel lifted the heavy gold oath ring in his hand on the Thing meadow and called the gods to witness its opening, cutting the throat of a white fleeced ram and sprinkling its blood on the oath ring and the earth, Berki was decked out in a boar crested helm and heavy leather armor with metal rings sewn in over his chest and belly, and he had a broad linden shield to clash his sheathed sword against as he cheered the king. He was the tallest man in the throng, and it was easy for him to look over the heads of the others to where the Bronding clan stood and see Hygd's flowing wealth of shimmering flaxen hair and the sunlit amber upon her breasts.

She looked up; their eyes met for a moment, and Berki's heart swelled with joy, knowing that Hygd had not forgotten him nor changed her mind in the long year since they had walked in the barrow field together. But Breca showed his teeth beneath his helm, and there was something in the fierce way he glared at Berki as he clashed sword on shield that let Berki know that the young Bronding had not forgotten his injury, nor had his thoughts grown any kinder towards Berki with the passing seasons. After the rite was done and the throng began to break up into smaller groups, Berki saw Hygd arguing with her parents. He waited, not daring to push in where he might not be wanted, but at last she broke away, coming over to him. She was almost skipping as she made her way across the meadow, her violet blue eyes glimmering with joy.

"Berki!" She called when she was close to him. "I have the best of news for us."

"What is it?" He asked, his heart racing, though he was sure he knew the answer.

"Beanstan has agreed to speak with your father about our betrothal!" Hygd plunged heedlessly forward to fling her arms about as much of Berki as she could reach. He returned the embrace very carefully: he could feel the delicacy of her bones beneath her blue linen dress and pale green apron, light as the body of a sparrow in his hands. Her breasts were warm against his leather corselet, and Berki was grateful that the armor hid the stirring of his groin at her touch.

"That is the best of news, indeed," he replied, smiling down at her as he let go. "Nothing could make me more joyful."

Remembering her modesty, Hygd stepped back, straightening her dress and smoothing her long hair.

"He said that I was too young, but my mother was a year younger when she was first betrothed to Haereth. And you are armed and armored as a grown man now, so none can say that you are not of an age to wed, either. Tell me, do you think you will stay at Hrethel's hall for a while longer, or will you go back to Hroesnabeorh and fight beside Ecgtheow this summer?"

"My father has said that he will call on me if there are battles to be fought this year," Berki answered. "But until he has need of me, I shall stand beside Hygelac."

Hygd nodded, satisfied. "It is well to be close friends with a king, or the sons of a king," she declared. "The man who begins in a high place gains fame most quickly. But tell me, what has happened to you since last we saw each other? If you were taken up by Hrethel's berserk band, surely I would have heard did they not test you?"

"They tested me," Berki admitted. "I am not a berserk."

Hygd's dark eyes opened very wide. Berki could not help admiring the brightness of her long eyelashes, glittering as though she had dusted them with ground gold.

"Then how is it that you live yet?"

"They did not kill me I cannot speak of it."

"Of course," she murmured. "I shall not ask, for such things are not for women to know of. And yet you must have shown some great strength, if you saw their rite as an outsider and they could not slay you for it."

Berki thought of Ansuwulf's strange words after the testing. *Someday you may yet fall to tooth and claw, but your wyrd was not pulled to come upon you then. It may be that the troth of your soul is pledged to another: I do not know.* They filled him with a strange uneasiness, and he cast about for ways to change the subject.

"What of you?" He asked. "I have heard only a little news from your hall in the past year."

Hygd shrugged, the round gold pins that held her linen apron straps glittering as her breasts shifted beneath them.

"There has been little to tell. Breca went out with the men to fight: he chanced to kill a strong warrior of the North Swedes, one Hnaef Shaggy Hair, in the first battle after planting time this year, and he has been unbearable ever since. As for me, I have been spinning and weaving, and embroidering tapestries that shall hang in our hall one day, for I hoped that Beanstan and my mother would be willing to draw up a betrothal contract this year, and if one is ready to meet one's hopes, it is all the likelier that they will come about."

Berki nodded, though he could hardly say if her words were true or not. But he could easily see Hygd at her handwork, talking pointedly of how she was readying her house goods for her wedding until she had shifted the matter from doubtful consideration to certainty in the thoughts of everyone around her he did not know how anyone could deny Hygd whatever she had set her mind to. He only wondered why she had chosen him, rather than Haethcyn or Hygelac. But he could hardly ask her such a thing, even if her talking ever paused long enough for him to get the words in not that he minded, for it was a great relief to listen to her and not be expected to speak in turn. If what Hygd wanted was a quiet man in whom she could trust, he would be that man, so long as there was blood in his body.

"And my mother," Hygd was going on, "has given me the wherewithal to buy the fine stuffs I need for bridal clothes. I have been hoping that someone will have southern silk to offer this year: few other women can boast dresses of that. Even silk thread for embroidering and weaving trim with will be good perhaps I shall weave a headband of it for you, to keep those long brown curls out of your eyes, though I must say your helm does that very finely now." Still talking, Hygd took Berki by the hand, leading him towards the market stalls, and he followed her willingly.

To her disappointment, Hygd did not find any large pieces of silk for dressmaking. But there were several merchants with spools of silk thread as well as fine drawn gold and silver for weaving, and after some searching, she chose several colors, including a bright green which, she said, was just the colour to bring out the green of Berki's eyes. After they had wandered about the stalls for a while, Hygd bought a small bottle of sweet mead.

"Now I would like you to walk me to Hrethel's holy grove, for I think it is time to make an offering to Frige and the Frowe, that all may go well in our betrothal dealings."

Berki took her hand, leading her along the pathway through the woods. Although the birches were in full green leaf now, when he reached the spot where the berserks had taken him, he could still see the faint marks that his struggle had scuffed into the earth. Perhaps it was the memory of that which gave him the bravery to ask,

"Hygd, why have you chosen me? Not that it does not give me the greatest joy," he added hastily, "but you could as easily have one of Hrethel's sons. And Hygelac is handsome and bold, and Haethcyn is deep minded, and they are both well famed, as well as being the sons of the king. Whereas I I am fat, and many folk think I am lacking in wit, and none save Hygelac and you speak well of me."

Hygd stopped, catching his hand in both of hers and gazing up into his eyes.

"Berki, you must not think so poorly of yourself. I chose you years ago because I wanted you: is that not enough?"

"Of course it is! And yet, I cannot help wondering..." Hygd chewed at her lower lip, looking down, and a little furrow appeared between her pale brows, like a crease in white linen. "It is not only because you are the son of a great drighten, which my brother has cast in my face many times though I will own that I spoke to you first at my mother's bidding when we were children. But as I have said before, I feel that no ill will come to me when I am with you, whatever should befall. And...I am no seith wise woman or spae wife, but maybe at times the Frowe whispers some of her wisdom to all women, even little maidens before their breasts are grown. For there was once a time, years ago, when I watched Hygelac riding about on horseback, skilled and bright, and I wondered if I might be wiser to turn my thoughts towards him. But then it seemed to me that a shadow came over him, and I thought that his luck flared high now, but it would be quicker than I thought to burn out. And I looked at you, and it seemed to me that I could see a steady flame burning within you, that would grow with the years and cast its light over all the land, from the Scylding lands southward to the great lakes in the north of Beanstan's holding, and that dark trolls and thurses howled and threatened outside the edges of that light, but within it all was safe. Therefore I pay no heed to what anyone else might say: whoever thinks you are lacking in wit has not spoken to you, and whoever does not speak well of you is lacking in wisdom themselves. And besides, you are not only strong but kind very unlike Breca, who cannot win a finger ring's worth of praise without at once using it to shame and belittle others...and I know as well as you what it is like to come to a strange hall as a child and not always be met with kindness by everyone there, for Breca has never let me forget that I was not born Beanstan's daughter. And that, Berki, is why I love you and want you for my husband, and have no doubt that you shall be a man of great renown someday."

"Thank you," Berki murmured, both deeply warmed and abashed by her words. "I hope I shall prove worthy of your trust."

"I have no doubt that you will," Hygd replied staunchly. "But we must hurry to make our offering now we should not be away from the Thing too long together, lest Breca notice and start saying that we have been doing what we should not yet do. He has an ill mind and a sharp tongue, and he has not yet forgiven you for the injury you dealt him at our first meeting, nor has his love for me grown since my mother wedded his father."

Fleet of foot and skilled with a sword, Breca easily won most of the young men's contests, foot racing and sword play and shooting, and barely nudged Hygelac out of the way by a nose length in the horse race.

"Will you not wrestle this year?" Hygd asked Berki as they stood watching the first contenders. "I should hate to see Breca unbeaten at anything, for he is already too proud, and I am sure you could throw him easily."

Berki shook his head. The memory of Breca's arm snapping beneath his hands was too stark in his mind, and he did not trust himself to hold back if Breca were to taunt him as they fought, as Berki was sure he would.

"I have harmed him once already," Berki said. "I would not wish to do it again."

Hygd tilted her head, her fair hair brushing his leather clad shoulder for a heartbeat.

"I suppose you hardly need to test yourself against him, when it is so clear who would win. But you will show yourself at the stone casting? Beanstan would be most pleased to see you do well before the folk."

"Of course," Berki answered, for it seemed to him that he could hear what she was not saying: Beanstan's words to her must not have been too unlike Ecgtheow's words to him. He was more amazed than ever that Hygd should be seeking their betrothal, when it was clear that her kin thought little of it, but he would not gainsay her in anything.

To Berki's surprise, Ecgtheow was not among those men lined up to show their strength at casting stones: instead, he stood beside Hygd and grinned broadly at Berki.

"Come on, my son!" he shouted, his deep voice carrying over the field.

Since Berki had come in second the year before, he was last to throw. The stone Ecgtheow had cast last year still stood where it had landed; none of the others had even fallen near it. Berki walked out to heave the rock from the earth where it had sunk, carrying it easily back to the starting line and lifting it over his head. Though it had seemed heavy to him last year, it was light in his hands now. Glancing at Hygd, he flung it forth with all his strength, and the cheers as it landed told him that he had outstripped his father's mark.

"Well done!" Hygelac shouted, running forward to clap Berki on the shoulder. "A spear's length and a half farther than it fell last year, or I am quite blind."

Berki looked over at his father, thinking that now he would hear words of praise, but Ecgtheow barely grunted,

"Well done," before he turned away. Bewildered, Berki stared after him.

"It is not easy for a man to be outdone so greatly by his son," Hygd said softly, patting Berki on the arm. "He knew that you would win, but not that you would beat his best cast so widely."

"Stone casting!" Breca sneered. "What good would that be in battle?" He had come up unseen, and now stood right in front of Berki, as if to block his way.

Berki looked down at the smaller man, trying to think of words that would still him. Breca had grown well in the last year. His head came almost to Berki's chin; his shoulders were broad, and Berki could see their muscles rippling beneath the shining links of his mail shirt as he clenched and unclenched his fists. Although Hygd's father Haereth had only been a cousin to Beanstan, the Bronding blood ran thick: Breca was as handsome as Hygd was fair, and the delicate lines of her face were firm and strong in his, as though they were brother and sister by birth.

Only the small tuft of golden beard on Breca's chin spoiled his looks, for he was still too young to grow more than a rabbit tail pinch of fuzz.

"It is not the stones themselves, but the strength that casts them," Hygd told her brother. "Have you not learned already that Berki is too strong for you to dare safely?"

"Ha," Breca replied. "If strength is all you want, you should buy yourself an ox; you would save much trouble by it. Everyone says that Beowulf the honey eater will never amount to anything, whereas I have proven myself more than well in battle, and am skilled in all the things a young atheling should know. I can play tables and read rune staves, I can shoot a bow better than anyone here; I can run, ski, and row with great speed, and I know a bit of smithing as well; and besides that, I can play the harp and make verses that would not shame a poet. Can he do any of those things? I doubt it. I did not even see him on the field when the other young thanes were striving to measure their manhood."

Hygd's fingers clenched on the hem of her apron, crumpling its brightly woven trim.

"If you think so well of yourself, why don't you measure yourself against Berki now and stop your whining? Choose some contest, and I shall be the judge of it."

Breca gestured broadly towards Berki. "Well, Beowulf, what shall it be? Do you know how to do anything that is fitting to the sons of great drightens?" His gold tufted chin jutted out arrogantly as he looked up at Berki, resting his fists on his mailed hips.

Berki thought hard. To his shame, he had to admit that he had none of the skills of which Breca had boasted: he had tried to learn to shoot a bow once, but the bow had broken asunder beneath his hands. He was not swift enough to challenge the other youth to a race, and he was loath to do anything in which Breca might come to harm, for he was sure that the Bronding clan would not overlook a second injury to their son when they were speaking of sealing a betrothal. Then it came to him: he could do one thing better than anyone, and in the calm summer weather, there would be little risk to Breca in striving against him.

"Can you swim?"

"I can, and better than you, for I do not think you can move that hulk you call a body swiftly through the waves. I will go faster and farther than you, and stay out longer, for none of my father's men can match me in the sea."

Hygd clapped her hands together. "I shall stand on Whales' Ness and watch. I shall not be surprised, Breca, if Berki has to carry you sputtering and puking to shore."

"Aye," Hygelac agreed. "I shall wager this gold ring on my arm against anything you care to name that Berki is the winner of this contest. What of it, Breca?"

Breca tapped one of his own gold arm rings, his neatly trimmed fingernails clinking softly from the metal.

"You may as well give it over now. I am as skilled in swimming as I am in all a man's other accomplishments, and I have proven those against all the young men of your household even yourself, Hygelac, for though your words may be bold now, you lagged behind me in the horse racing."

"Many would say that such a close finish was won by luck as much as skill," Hygelac answered, still smiling. "Another time I shall outstrip you but now I shall be glad to see Berki have his day. How shall the matter be judged? By speed, or by length of the swim?"

"Let it be both," Breca replied boldly. "Standing on shore, you shall see which of us is first out of your sight; and he who is furthest along when we must come to land shall be called the winner. And this I will say, as well: let us swim in leather armour with our swords belted about us, for I mean to go through deep waters, and it may be that we must fend sharks or spekheawers from us that shall be named a true test of manhood! Have you the heart for that, Beowulf?"

"I do. We will have to grease our weapons so that the salt water does not rust them; but whatever you dare, I shall dare as well." For however badly he had fared at the things that were put to him on land, Berki knew that he could not fail in the ocean.

"Done!"

By the time Breca had changed his mail byrnie for one of leather and the two swimmers had coated their weapons with goose grease, a crowd had gathered upon Whales' Ness to watch. Looking up from the beach below the cliff, Berki could make out the figures of his old tormentors, Agilar, Thunarstan, Widuhund, and the others; but now they were shouting for him, their voices clear through the still summer air.

"Make him eat your wake, Beowulf! Show the Bronding puppy what the men of Hrethel's house are made of!"

Their acclaim startled Berki, for he had expected them to jeer at him but there was not one of them who had not been beaten in a contest by Breca that year or at the Midsummer Things before, and after hearing how scornfully Breca had spoken to Hygelac, Berki knew that the Bronding's sharp tongue could have won him few friends among the sons of Hrethel's thanes. There are worse things, after all, than being fat and clumsy, he thought wonderingly. Among the taller young men, Hygd looked very small, but she held herself so straight, with her white shimmering hair blowing out in a long stream like a war banner behind her, that there was not the least danger that Berki would miss her in the throng. Her high voice cut through the deeper calls of the others like a bright sword glimmering through the mist, "Go on, Berki, my betrothed! Let everyone see the worth of your pledge!" Berki raised his arm to salute her, and she fumbled at her neck a moment, then held up one of her necklaces, the amber beads gleaming in the sunlight like a strand of tiny sparks.

"Are you ready?" Hygelac called from the top of Whales' Ness, his arm upraised.

"Yes!" Breca shouted, and Berki echoed him.

"Then go!" Hygelac's arm dropped, and the two of them plunged into the sea.

From the first moment of matching Breca's pace, Berki knew that he could out swim the Bronding. Although Breca moved smoothly and swiftly through the waves, he was still a stranger in the water; its weight slowed his arms, and he did not feel the stirrings of the currents beneath the surface as Berki did. Berki pulled ahead easily, not hampered in the least by the ring strengthened leather on his body.

He could no longer hear the shouting from the cliff, but when he glanced back, he could still see the sunlight shining on Hygd's hair, and the sight spurred him to swim faster. Only when they were well out of sight of Whales' Ness did Berki slow, the swells gently lifting and dropping him as he trod water and waited for Breca to catch up with him. He did not want to leave the other alone on their swim, for the dangers of the ocean would be more than twice as great for one alone: if one of them began to cramp without the other nearby to bear him up until it eased, or tangled his feet in drifting weed, he would drown without hope of help.

"The test of speed is over," Berki said when Breca's water darkened head surfaced beside him at last. "Now we have a long swim ahead of us, if you still wish it."

Breca's handsome face twisted, and he spat into the sea. "Do you think that I am so weak as to turn back now, or own myself beaten so easily? You may have had the advantage of knowing the currents by the shore here, but that will not help you in the end." He stroked strongly away, turning from the path that had led them into the open ocean; if he kept on as he was going, they would be following the shoreline.

"As you will." Berki murmured and swam after him, pacing himself to Breca's speed.

Breca was a fine swimmer, Berki had to admit, and had Hygd's adopted brother taken up such a challenge with anyone else, he might have won by the time the sun was beginning to lower red over the sea. But though Berki was hungry and thirsty, he was not yet beginning to tire; and Breca's strokes were becoming less even, his moments of floating on the surface drawn out longer. Berki slowed to match him, and after a while Breca rolled his head to the side, panting,

"Have you had enough yet? It must be past time for your dinner." "We brought no food with us, and if we made shore now, we would hardly be back at Hrethel's hall in time for the feasting to start. Do you wish to give over?"

Berki had meant the offer as a kindness, but Breca seemed to take it as a taunt, for he swam a little faster, kicking up spray to splash into Berki's eyes. Berki quickly overtook him, holding his place beside the Bronding. Through the dim purple of the evening, Berki kept a close watch on his fellow swimmer to make sure that Breca did not fall asleep and swallow water, for he was beginning to move like a man in the dream, his limbs stirring just enough to keep him afloat.

By morning, Berki's arms and legs felt very heavy, the water dragging against them; his lips were cracking with the salt, and there was little wetness on his tongue when he ran it around his mouth. Yet Breca was in a worse state, for he had begun to shiver and Berki could hear his teeth chattering when he swam close. Berki knew that the other should go up to shore until his shaking stopped, or he would fall asleep and die; but worn as he was by the long swimming, Breca's eyes still glared bright from their salt reddened rims, and Berki was sure that he was too proud to admit how close to failure he was. And a limb that is broken once may never heal as strongly: in fairness, I owe Breca a better chance because of the harm I did him.

"It would be an ill thing," Berki forced out, the words rasping in his dry throat, "if one of us were to lose this contest through thirst or hunger, and the salt has dried our mouths greatly. Now I suggest, to keep our swimming trial fair, that we go to shore for a little time, to find water and such food as we may, and then keep on from the mark where we left off."

Breca nodded. Already he seemed thinner, the flesh hollowing beneath his strong cheekbones, but the thought of dry land and fresh water seemed to spur him on as he struck for shore. It was not long before they made land, walking up over a stony beach until they had passed the high tide point. Breca dug one water wrinkled toe into the ground, scoring a short line.

"Here we came ashore; we shall go forth from here," he croaked.

They did not have so much as a piece of twine to make a snare, but wild strawberries grew thickly near the banks of the little stream they found trickling down to the sea; and if Berki was not able to fill his belly, at least the sweet fruit fueled him and gave him new heart for more swimming. He wondered if he had been wise to suggest coming ashore, for it would only lengthen their swim and strengthen Breca's stubbornness.

Yet it was better than going on until Breca's head slipped beneath the swells, for if Berki were worn enough himself by the time the other could swim no longer, he might not be able to bring Breca safely to land. Sooner or later, Breca would have to admit that he was over matched, and then it would come to an end without either of them taking harm from it. After they had drunk and eaten, Berki and Breca slept for a little while, each watching over the other in turn. They made their way back to the line Breca had scratched among the rocks, pacing carefully down to the surf.

"You should know," Breca said as they waded into the frothing waves, "that I shall not be the first to give in not if we must swim all the way northward to the Heathoreamas' coast."

"The Heathoreamas have ever been friends to King Hrethel and his kin," Berki said. "Should we go that far, they will welcome me there."

"Still," Breca went on, his mouth twisting as though he already tasted the bitter sea salt, "I must say that you have done better than I thought you would. Perhaps you may even have proven yourself worthy to offer betrothal to my kinswoman, though I do not know why you would want a maid who is only eager for your father's hall and lands." He dropped forward, leather clad arms arching over his head, and began to swim.

Berki swam hard after him, the hot bile taste of rage in his mouth as he reached out towards Breca. His hands had almost closed on the other when he stopped in shame: for a moment, he had been ready to drag Breca beneath the waves until the salt water cleaned the unworthy words from his mouth. *He will be shamed enough to know himself beaten,* Berki reminded himself, *and Hygd has borne with his taunts these many years: I should not make matters worse, for I know the truth of how things stand with her, and it is Breca's own fault if he is too ill minded to see it.*

They went on for four more nights like that, and however grudgingly, Berki's respect for Breca had to grow: though his tongue might be sharp, at least he was a man to live up to his boasts. No matter how badly Breca shivered in the water, or how harsh a toll hunger and thirst were taking on him, he would never be the first to suggest that they go ashore, and when they had rested a little, he always insisted steadfastly that he was fit to swim on. Still, Berki knew that Hygd's adopted brother could not last too much longer: the bones of his skull showed clearly through his face, and even on land, his movements were growing slow, as though the cold water were daily leeching more strength from him than the small amounts of food and rest they found on shore could replace.

As for Berki himself, the leather that had been tight on him when they began was growing loose, but he did not feel greatly weakened; if anything, he felt lighter and lither than he had been, not so badly cumbered by his own weight. The clear weather held until the evening of the sixth day, when a black bank of cloud rose swiftly above the sea to the north, rolling towards them with a deep rumble of thunder. The swells were lifting higher, and more than once Berki lost sight of Breca's head as the hills of dark water pushed them apart.

"Should we take shelter on land?" Berki asked. "That looks as though it will be a mighty storm."

"If you are afraid, go on to shore," Breca rasped. "But I will swim farther than you do before I turn towards the beach. We came here to test ourselves against each other: let the storm prove who is the better swimmer."

The wind blew harder, ruffling up the swells into whitecaps and casting sprays of foam into the two swimmers' eyes. Whenever Berki lifted his head to breathe, chill wind and water slapped against his face, as if it were winter instead of the height of summer. He could not tell when the rain began, but soon the sleet harsh drops were lashing into the waves like a fall of icy arrows, and it grew harder and harder for him to stay by Breca. One swell, greater than the others, caught Berki by surprise, lifting him and flinging him away. He raised his face to shout a warning to Breca, but the strength of the wave dragged him flailing under, twisting about in the airless darkness to fight his way back to the surface. When his head broke water again, Berki stared desperately through the deepening night, but he could see nothing of his companion.

"Breca!" He shouted, the cry rasping harshly through his salt bitten throat. "Breca, where are you!" Berki heard no answer, nothing but the thundering of the sea around him; and then he must struggle with all his strength to keep afloat in the violent tossing of the water.

Though he called out for Breca whenever he could draw a good breath, there was no sign of the Bronding anywhere in the storm whipped sea. He is likely dead already, and I may soon be, Berki thought. But he was swimming too hard for fear to overcome him. There was something that felt good beyond understanding in battering his way through the mast high swells, taking the ocean's blows full against his body, such as he had only known when daring the sea in the height of winter, when each wave struck hard enough to sway him from his feet, or cast his swimming body here and there like a leaf of bladder wrack.

"Come on!" Berki gasped, slapping his palm against the churning water. He did not know whom he was challenging, but a rush of warmth swept through his body, lifting him up and strengthening his limbs. "Try your best you will not overcome me!"

A black wave reared up before him, white foam glimmering against its darkness like fangs in gaping jaws. Then it plunged forward at his head; Berki twisted sideways, feeling the scrape of teeth against his leather clad shoulder, and as he struck out, his hand met a wall of cold scales. He grabbed swiftly for the sword at his side, tugging it from the sheath. The sticky grease made it hard to draw, but he pulled desperately with both hands, forcing it free and treading water.

In the dark of storm and night, he could barely make out the looping black coil rising and sinking through the waves, but a glint of green from an eye and the sound of a hiss through the pounding waters warned him, and he turned to see the sea wight's head darting at him again. He met it full on, his muscles humming as he struck downward with all his might, as he had never dared to strike at any human. The sword rang in his hands, cleaving through scales and bone; the fronded black head split in two, and the next swell sucked it out of his sight. Breathing hard, his sword still in his hand, Berki began to swim as fast as he could towards shore towards where he thought the shore was, for he had lost his bearings. Something slimy brushed against his leg; he yelped in surprise, bitter salt splashing into his mouth.

Then the pain shocked fiery up from his foot, grinding deeper as he kicked out. He coiled about himself, stabbing blindly downward, and felt his sword sinking into something that writhed and snatched at him, its slick arms pulling him beneath the water. Again he stabbed, and again, and then the dread grip loosened, letting him fight his way to the surface again. But the pain in his foot was not easing, and when he tried to kick, he felt the weight still dragging at his leg. Frightened, he reached down to push away the thing that had hold of him. His hand met a tangle of weed slimy hair, a broad, rock hard head twice the size of a man's its teeth still fastened in his foot, though it did not flinch or blink when he jabbed a thumb hard into a wide flat eye.

Shaking with horror, Berki sucked in a deep breath and let himself sink down as he set the point of his sword into one eye socket and pushed with both hands until he felt the dead nicor's shark teeth ripping out through his flesh, the agonizing sting of salt rushing through the wound in its wake. Berki struck for the surface again, swinging his sword in wide arcs about his body and beneath his feet: the movements that had seemed so slow and clumsy on land came easily and swiftly to him in the ocean. Father, he thought, half hysterically, you never thought that your blade would get its first use in my hands thus, did you? The cold seawater filled his mouth again, stopping the mad laughter before it could begin; choking and spluttering, he pushed upward to cough his lungs free. Then his sword stuck in something, jolting to a stop. As Berki tried to yank it free, a mighty blow struck his chest, knocking him backward in the water.

Teeth grated against the metal rings set into his leather corselet, and more teeth fastened in the heavy leather at the back of his thigh, jerking his body from side to side as they worried in towards his flesh. Kicking hard against the thing in which his sword had lodged fast, Berki managed to shove it off his blade. He could feel the gruesome cold of the nicors' scaly flesh through his armor even as he attacked them, tearing them away from his body with powerful thrusts of his sword. Even through terror and pain, a strange joy surged up in Berki's heart as he fought, as if he were swimming in wilder waters than the winter ocean, where he could at last call on all his strength without fear.

The nicors' teeth and claws tore at his armor, raking his arms and legs below it, but he felt no pain, only the urgency of his sword whipping through the swells and striking, hard and solid, into the dark bodies of his foes. Berki did not know how long he fought, beating against the nicors as they clawed and bit at him. After a time, there were no more slick scaled arms wrapping about his body, no more snarling, weed haired faces springing up from the water in front of him, but he kept mindlessly swinging his sword around himself, striking at the battering waves and the draw of the deep undertow beneath him. When something else tightened about Berki's chest, pulling him downward, he sucked in a deep gulp of air before the water closed over his head and tried to twist in its grasp to strike out again, but it seemed to him that he felt the sword plucked lightly from his hand.

Now I shall die, he thought but he had no more strength to struggle: between the long swimming, the desperate battle, and the blood draining from all the lesser and greater scratches on his limbs, he was suddenly light headed and weak, helpless as a puppy in the soft grip that held him. But he held his breath as long as he could, until the darkness before his eyes burst into swirls of red, and the mounting pressure of air in his lungs began to bubble up from his mouth. Then, as Berki's aching chest swelled unwillingly to suck in water, he found himself breathing freely again. Dumbfounded, he opened his eyes.

He stood on his feet within a great hall, timbered with the barnacle crusted beams of ships and adorned with old wind weathered figureheads. At the far end loomed two shadowy thrones of bleached whale bone, carved with the twining shapes of maned sea wyrms, and beside them were nine smaller chairs wrought in the same manner. For a moment Berki thought the hall was ablaze, for fires burned everywhere about the floor, the warm red flames leaping up from piles of gold rings and necklaces that had been scattered carelessly about. Shimmering ripples eddied and whirled above the gold fires like the writhing of unseen snakes, and Berki realized that, though he could hear the sound of his own quick breaths, his long hair was floating freely in the water around him like brown sea grass.

He was naked: his armor had dropped from him, lying in a heap upon the sandy floor beneath his sword. Even the gilding on the leather and sword hilt glowed, tiny flames licking up from the thin gold.

"Be welcome in my father's hall, most beloved guest," a woman's voice said beside him harsh as the mewing of a gull, yet ringing clear and wild as the wind whipping over the waves. Berki turned to see who had greeted him.

The woman who stood before him was taller than he by almost a hand span, naked and sleek as a porpoise, with wide shoulders, plump broad hips and powerful thighs, and great full breasts that swayed gently in the little ripples running through the hall, their swollen nipples standing out ripe and rich as plums. The hair swirling behind her was long as Hygd's, but its gold glimmered with the greenish cast of sunlight through the shallows; the triangle beneath the curve of her belly was green gold as well, sleek and short as a seal's fur.

In her right hand she held a goblet carved of clear ice, filled with amber dark mead. Its facets glinted back red flashes of firelight, dazzling Berki's eyes; and as he blinked, he saw that around her neck she wore a long pendant of sun spangled amber, capped with two hoarfrost silver tips the pendant he had lost in the sea some eight months ago. Dazed, Berki took the rime chalice she offered him. Its stem was smooth and hard, heavy as stone in his hand when he lifted it to his mouth.

The taste of the mead was beyond anything he could have dreamed, its rich sweetness bursting upon his tongue in a storm of subtly mingled delights and its heat rising at once to his head and glowing through his body in kraken tendrils of warmth. The sea maid stretched like a seal sunning itself on a rock, her breasts shifting in the water, and Berki, embarrassed, dropped his free hand in hopes of covering himself. She laughed and reached to pull his hand away, looking unashamed at the hard thick length rising between his legs.

"Do not be shy, my beloved," she crooned. "I have seen, and touched that before do you not remember when you gave me this?" Her fingers brushed over the amber pendant at her neck. "You must be proud, for weaker men shrivel and shrink in the sea, but a great toothed whale would not be shamed by your stand."

Berki flushed, but he could not tear his gaze from her. "Who are you?" he asked, his tongue thick in his mouth.

"Where am I?"

"I am Heofenglowe, the daughter of Eagor and Ran, and it is my parents' hall where you stand now. O my sea bear, I have watched you since you were a little cub, running gladly into my arms my sisters and I fought long over who should get the joy of playing with you and stroking your warm hair, but I would not let them take you from me. Let them have all the lost sailors they please, those little men who struggle fearfully in the wave maidens' grasp and break when they are held too tightly; let them cavort with sharks, and bear sons to water thurses! I am the ninth wave, who goes farthest up the beach, and my sisters cannot overcome me; but you alone, of all those who dwell on the shore, are mighty enough to bear my embraces, to warm my sea cold heart, and now you have come to me. You need not fear that I will seek geld for my playmates, the nine nicors you slew though I only wanted them to bring you down to me. They breed wherever the weeds grow thick upon the rocks, but there is no one else like you in all the Nine Worlds."

She took Berki's hand in her cold fingers, pulling him swiftly through the water like a small boat racing on the line of a harpooned whale. Soon they were at the whalebone thrones, and Heofenglowe lifted Berki up to seat him in the greater of the two, wriggling in beside him so that her breast and thigh pressed tightly against him. Twining her fingers in his hair, she pulled his head back to kiss him. Her chill lips were gentle on his, her tongue snaking softly between his lips as she reached to stroke roughly between his legs, then tilted the ice stone goblet to his mouth again. "Do you like the mead?" she asked. "My father Eagor is the best of brewers: he makes the ale for the feasts of the gods in his great cauldron, but his mead is only for us, and the most honored of our guests."

"It is very good," Berki managed to say. It was hard for him to think of anything save the brushing of Heofenglowe's large tight nipples against his chest and her clutching hand urging on his pulsing need, but he managed to ask, before the thought could flee from his mind, "What has become of Breca? Is he drowned?"

"The little man you swam beside? What of him? Perhaps my sisters have had their sport with him; perhaps they have tossed him up on shore already. I do not know, or care but you, my love, you are ready for me."

Heofenglowe threw a leg over Berki's lap, wrapping her powerful arms about him so tightly he could hardly breathe and heaving herself down onto him. He gasped, clutching her back with all his might and thrusting upwards with his hips, sinking as deeply as he could into her chill slippery recesses. The sea maid's body was sleek and yielding, but his ribs creaked beneath her strength as she wrapped her legs about his waist tightly enough to splinter the bones of a lesser man. Crushing her to him as if in a deadly wrestling match, Berki growled in wordless exultation as they strove, Heofenglowe's claws raking along his back and the amber at her throat gleaming as she tossed her head back.

"Oh, yes, my love!" She cried out. "Kindle your fires in me yes, harder!"

At last Berki could hold back no longer, the pleasure of his release shattering through him as he drove one last mighty thrust into her. Heofengleowe clenched her fists hard on his arms, her thighs and buttocks spasming, and shrieked high and shrill as a sea mew. The heavy muscles of the eoten maid's legs trembled beneath their sleek padding as her body eased around him, and she nuzzled against Berki's neck, her pointed teeth nibbling sharp little kisses along his jaw.

"I have never had such a man as you," she murmured, her lips cold against Berki's ear. "Once Loca, that godly liar, boasted that he had enough fire to warm me and all my sisters, but he never did more than tease us and dart away. But you are steadfast and mighty, and you will stay with me."

She pushed herself off him, a thin pearly strand drifting up between her legs, then lowered her head to his lap and stretched out full length in the water before him, her white feet kicking gently to keep her in place as she kissed and sucked at Berki's manhood until he began to harden once more. Enchanted by the endless delights of Heofonglowe's body, Berki did not know how time might be passing above the ocean. He and the sea maiden chased each other through the waters of Ran's hall; they fed each other upon the firm sweet meat of lobsters and licked the soft flesh of oysters from the polished shells, passing sips of Eagor's mead between their mouths. Berki hardly noticed when the water of the hall began to chill and the currents to flow more strongly with it; but at last Heofonglowe said,

"Now you shall help me to bring out the benches. The winter is coming swiftly, and we may expect guests my mother is swimming about with her silver net, for the storm waves will soon be breaching the hulls of stout ships, and she must catch the souls of the drowned sailors and bring them here to feast."

Berki drew back, staring at her their eyes were level now: how long had it taken him to grow to her height? Heofonglowe's blue green eyes glittered with excitement; her pale tongue licked the corner of her lips, and he could see the white points of her teeth between them. In his dazed delight, he had forgotten what manner of wight she was, but now a shiver of ice ran through his blood as he looked upon her. He could see the cold black greediness of a conger eel behind Heofonglowe's eyes as she spoke of Ran's booty, and she and her wave sisters would play games with the bodies of the dead before tossing them up, swollen and fish eaten, on the storm swept beach.

Even as his mouth opened in horror, Berki remembered what had been far from his mind since she brought him to Eagor's sunken hall. He was to have been betrothed to Hygd how could he have forgotten her, even in the sea maid's embrace? She must think him dead by now: how could he have left her to mourn him? Now a great longing seized Berki, to walk upon the green earth once more with Hygd by his side, her small hand warm in his and the sun bright upon her gleaming hair. And he had sworn his troth to Hygelac and Hrethel, and said that he would bear his sword at his father's side whenever Ecgtheow needed him what had become of those oaths?

"Heofonglowe," he said, "I must go. I have been away too long."

"Oh, no, my love!" She cried, leaping at Berki and locking her arms and legs about him. "I have you, and you are mine, you shall not flee me!" Heofonglowe's teeth gleamed like a shark's in her mouth, her clawed fingertips digging into his shoulders, and suddenly Berki was afraid: if she could not hold him, he knew, she would rend him to pieces. Once he had been too weak to break her grip; but then he was exhausted from long swimming and battling, and now he was stronger.

Violently he strove to wrench her limbs from him, twisting and tossing in the water until he had freed himself for a moment, and dove down to snatch up the sword that still lay, unsheathed and gleaming beneath its thin film of grease, on his half forgotten armor. Heofonglowe followed Berki, clutching at him. He could not strike at her with his blade, but fled towards the arched whale ribs that shaped the hall's doorposts as swiftly as he could, blood trailing black from the wounds her claws had left on him. The rime cold currents caught Berki as he passed through the door, whirling him helplessly away. Tossed about by the deep waters, he could not breathe; he could only hope that he was swimming up, rather than down. As he struggled there in the dark sea, Heofonglowe's forsaken cries of anger echoed in his ears, howling all about him like the wailing of a wounded whale in the depths.

"If I have as much might over you as I think, I lay this on you: may you have no joy from that woman whom you await on the land, nor shall you have your delight with any woman within the Middle Garth's ring! And you have done good to neither of us: you did not keep your trust in me."

Lungs swelling with pain and ears ringing, Berki stroked desperately through the water. His heart hammered against his aching ribs; with no air to drive it, the strength was fading swiftly from his arms. Then, just as he must breathe or die, his head burst from the water, and he gasped in air mingled with wave spray. A great breaker lifted him up, and he saw a faint yellow glimmer of light through dark clouds above, shining through the blowing snow onto the storm hammered walls of high sea cliffs. Berki could not tell where he was, but he could see the water beating and whirling about the black rocks that jutted out near the shore. One wave caught him, flinging him sideways against a boulder and driving the breath from his body; before he could catch hold of it, another tore him free.

At last, battered and bruised, Berki managed to get his footing, staggering ashore. He was too tired to hold his head up; the wounds the water nicors had given him were breaking open again, so that blood spattered about him as he walked. He was sleepy, as if he had walked too long through deep snow, his limbs growing too heavy to move, until finally he collapsed at the foot of a great crevassed boulder. Berki did not think he slept, but his eyes kept closing, the white snow gathering around him dimming to black, shot through with flashes of pale blue lightning. The wind and waves gibbered around him, speaking in a singsong tongue that he could not understand. Then a warm hand touched his cheek, and it seemed to him that he was home.

"Amma," he moaned. "Will you give me honey? I have been long in the water, and I am hungry and cold."

"Honey?" A man's voice, strangely accented, said, and then more words that Berki could not recognize. The hands propped his head up, and a dripping spoon forced its way into his mouth. He sucked greedily, like a babe at the breast, and the sweetness gave him the strength to look about himself.

He was surrounded by a band of little dark haired men dressed in hide tunics, with furry cloaks, leggings, and shoes of reindeer skin. Their broad slant eyed faces shone with grease beneath their pointed skin caps, and they carried long sturdy spears and bows. The one who was tending him had a pack upon his back; four of the others were dragging a trellis of branches lashed together with sinews.

"Who are you?" Said the man who knelt beside him, an old man whose face was cracked and weathered like leather used for many years. "Are you saajvoe?"

"I am..." His mind was slow with cold, dizzy and confused. Perhaps that was why he answered as he did, or perhaps it was because he knew that no one would ever speak the name in mockery again. For it was his name alone, and whatever came after, he knew that he had already done such things as to fill it with worth, and cast it in the faces of those who had shamed him with it. "Beowulf. Beowulf, the honey eater."

The old man drew back, hissing through his teeth. He spoke quickly to the others, and they hurried forward with the trellis, heaving onto it and covering him with their cloaks.

"Who are you?" Beowulf pleaded as they began to drag him away, raising their voices in a sonorous song. The old man walked beside him, spooning honey into his mouth and brushing the light snowflakes away from his face.

"Honey eater, apple of the woodland," his tender chanted half a beat after the others, as though he were clumsily translating their words, "Fair one with the paws of honey, be not filled with causeless anger. We ourselves have not o'erthrown you. You yourself have left the woodlands, wandered from your pine tree covert. You have torn away your clothing, ripped your brown cloak in the thicket: slippery is the winter weather, cloudy are the days and misty. Golden apple of the forest, shaggy haired and lovely creature, for your food we'll give you honey, and the freshest mead for drinking. Do not show your anger to us, raise no storm or tempest at us, for we smote you not with spear heads, and we shot no arrows at you."

Beowulf closed his eyes, welcoming the familiar hot prickling of the blood in his fingers and toes. He had heard of men in the North who were small and dark and dressed in animal skins: they were the Finns, the hunters of reindeer, who bartered the high horned deers' thick hides southward for grain and milk and cheese. But if he were among the Finns how far were they? More than two months' journeying overland from Hrethel's hall, at the least, and those who dwelt by any coast known to men were farther yet, around the Heathoreamas' coast and down to the North. When Beowulf opened his eyes again, the old man had stopped chanting and was peering intently down into his face.

"Honey eater, the drum foretold a good hunt, and so we came to the siejdde with offerings, that we might find you old man of the woods, shaggy forest walker, salmon gulper. And here you are, though you speak in the tongue of southern men, that none among us but myself knows. You have walked long, for your feet are tattered; we shall give you new shoes of the finest leather, from the whitest reindeer hides, and a new skin to wrap yourself in, for your pelt has grown scanty through summer rubbing."

"Thank you," Beowulf murmured, for he did not know what else to say. "And...can you tell me where I am? How far am I from King Hrethel's hall?"

The Finn rubbed at his sparse growing beard. "I know not King Hrethel. In the summer some of us go south to trade with men who speak your tongue: they bring us sweet milk and iron knives and many other good things, and we give them walrus ivory and the furs that grow thickest in our winter's cold. But you are among the Merak Sabme now, the best of fishers and hunters, and you may have heard of me. For I am Paanja the naaejtie, and well known to many in the wide worlds, from jaemiehaajmoe and saavjoeaajmoe to the southern lands from whence the traders come." He looked down at Beowulf hopefully, then shrugged when he got no answer.

They went on a little way, until they came to an encampment of small dwellings made from birch trunks arranged in conical rings like burning houses, the chinks between the trees caulked with moss and earth. A couple of tame reindeer wandered between the houses, nibbling at the moss in the wall cracks. The naaejtie chanted a few lines loudly; Beowulf heard a rustling within the houses, and the soft sound of female murmuring, but none of the women came out. The hunters carried him to the largest of the dwellings, knocking loudly upon the peeling barked trunks, but they did not bear him in through the hide hung front door.

Instead they dragged the sledge around the back, and Paanja leapt through a smaller door with a sharp cry. At once the men lifted Beowulf up, easing him carefully through the opening where Paanja had gone in. The dwelling was as simple inside as outside: a small fire burned in the middle of the hut, with a large clay pot hanging from the inner tent poles above it. To the side was a mound of reindeer skins heaped above a bed of soft pine twigs, and several bulging bags were tucked against the curve of the birch trunk wall.

Paanja was running around the hearth, circling it three times as he let out soft growls and whistling cries. The women flocked in through the front door then, bearing strips of smoked meat and pots of dried berries in honey. They gathered about Beowulf, putting food into his mouth and stroking wonderingly at his face and hair his beard, he realized, had begun to grow while he was underwater, and it was strange to feel the women's little fingers running through the short damp curls. One of them, an older woman with silvery ornaments woven through her dark braids, bore a stone mug forward. Paanja drew a plaited twig from his belt pouch, giving it to her and taking the mug, which he ceremoniously carried over to Beowulf. It smelled like mead, though with some sharp scented fruit that Beowulf could not recognize.

Still, he lifted it towards his host and the lady who had brought it, saying, "May all the gods and goddesses bless you for your kindness to a weary wayfarer." He drained it off at a single draught, for he was very thirsty.

As he swallowed, he felt something tight at his throat, and lifted his hand to touch it. His fingers met the well known smoothness of amber, the warmth of the long oval with the cooler points of silver at either end: Ran's daughter had given back his gift. The feast went on for three days, during which Beowulf learned little more than he had known before. He gathered from Paanja that the boulder against which he had fallen was a siejdde, a holy stone, and that the Finns thought he was a bear who had changed into a man, or perhaps a man who would change into a bear: in any case, they believed that his coming would bring them the greatest good luck. Paanja was not quite a chieftain that distinction seemed to belong to a younger man, tall and keen featured for one of his folk, who kept bringing his spears and arrows for Beowulf to touch before he went out hunting.

Rather, the old man seemed more like the godfolk of Upsala or Godhome, or a spae man, who spoke to the wights of the land and could tell, by placing a piece of copper upon the picture marked head of his drum and beating it, where and when the hunting or fishing would be good. By the time Beowulf's wounds had all healed and he was ready to start finding his way home, the snows were falling hard and thick, the drifts outside the door of Paanja's little birch house often rising as high as his chest, above the heads of any of the Finns; the sun no longer rose even to the horizon's edge, and the naaejtie insisted that there was no hope of him making a winter faring by himself. It was so cold that when Beowulf stepped outside to relieve himself, the yellow stream froze to ice as fast as it splashed down; Paanja, with some delight, told him of winters when men had found themselves frozen to the earth in the act of pissing.

"And there was one winter," he said, "when my uncle, a great naaejtie, went out to sing a joik by the siejdde. It was so cold that the words froze as they came from his mouth and did not sound until the first summer thaw."

The Finns did not let Beowulf come with them when they went out to hunt walrus and foxes or chop holes in the ice for fish: Paanja said that he was holy, and his power might overcome or confuse the saajvoe of the land if he were there with them. But Beowulf also noticed the speed with which the Finns moved on their skis and wide snowshoes, and thought that perhaps the naaejtie had a more sensible reason for telling him to stay behind. So he had nothing to do save sit by the fire in Paanja's house he was not even allowed to tend it and think, and worry. He did not greatly fear what might happen in the course of his long walk home, even if he had to pass through the lands of the Swedes on the way; after his battle with the water nicors, Beowulf thought, he hardly had reason to be afraid of men.

The thought that gnawed more dreadfully at his mind, like rats gnawing on a coil of sealskin rope at the bottom of a storehouse, was that he did not know how long he had been in Ran's undersea hall long enough for him to grow almost a hand span in height, long enough for the scattered hairs on his face to thicken into a beard and his chest to sprout the beginnings of a curly pelt. He had thought that beneath the waves, he had gained back much of the weight he had lost in his long swim, but when he had come from the water, the skin had hung in loose folds over his muscles again, as though he had burned his flesh away in escaping from Heofonglowe's home. And everyone knew that time in the Otherworld ran differently than it did in the Middle Garth; there were an hundred stories of brides or grooms who had been alf taken at their wedding feasts and thought that a single night had passed within the alfs' howe, only to come forth and find that everyone they knew was long dead of old age. But there was nothing Beowulf could do about it, and no one he could ask whether King Hrethel still ruled or was laid in his mound. So he waited until the days grew long again, the snows beginning to melt and the first leaves budding out on the birch trees.

Then Paanja and a band of young men gathered their hides into bundles, filling their sledges and harnessing their tamed reindeer for the trek southward to their trading point; and Beowulf laced a pair of broad snowshoes onto his feet and set out with them. The men who traded with the Finns were dwellers in Halogaland, far down the northwestern coast beyond the Heathoreamas' lands. They had never heard of King Hrethel their own king was a young man called Godhagastir, who had just taken rule the year before but they were able to tell Beowulf the way southwards to the Geat lands, past the territories of the Heathoreamas and Swedes.

They did not go so far themselves, but they were glad to take him along as far as they could, for the sake of his sword and his strength, and even willing to pay a little for his help. Paanja's trading went well: his tribe had been lucky in hunting all winter, and had a good store of glistening blue and white fox pelts, white furred ermine and thick haired reindeer, to trade, as well as the tusks of many walruses three times as many as they had caught in any year before.

For this the naaejtie praised Beowulf greatly, as the bringer of all their blessings, and when the young Geat said his farewells to the Finns and began his journey south with the traders, he was dressed in the best clothes the Finns could make for him: tunic, breeches, and pointed cap of soft pale leather, warm reindeer hide leggings and sturdy shoes on his feet; a cloak of bearskin, and a blanket made from the pelts of six of the choicest reindeer, white with only the faintest of lavender brown markings. He had a new sheath for his sword, as well, and a long knife fashioned in the Finnish style, a southern forged iron blade for the Finns worked no iron whose hilt and sheath were made out of a single large piece of reindeer antler, curved sharply at the end and decorated with red dyed engravings of bears and six petaled stars.

"Bring these gifts to your own land, and remember us well when you are at home in the saavjmoeaajmoe," Paanja said to Beowulf. "The knife will stand you in good stead in that world, should your other weapons ever fail you. We have fed you on honey, given you new shoes and clothed you in your hide again; bid your kinsmen to come to us at the turning of the seasons, for we shall treat them as well." Beowulf bent down so that the Finn could hug him about the neck and kiss both his bristled cheeks before turning abruptly and setting off towards his younger companions.

The Geat thought that he would miss the old man: Paanja had been kind, and his tales and songs had made the endless night of winter lively.

"It is sad to part from friends," he murmured to himself, watching the Finns go.

Beowulf worked his way down towards the land of the Geats, often chopping wood, baling hay, or moving cattle and sheep from field to field to pay for his lodging and food. When his Finnish garb began to draw too many questions, he got himself simpler clothing, carrying his fine gift clothes in a pack. Still, wherever he went, folk looked strangely at him, for however carefully he moved, the tunics of smaller men would split along his back and arms in the course of a day, their trousers opening at the seams when he flexed his legs; and his forearms and calves showed hairy beneath the straining cuffs of his clothes; as for his shoes, he had to go barefoot, and his soles swiftly thickened to hard horny layers of leather that even the sharpest rock edges could not pierce. Though Beowulf tried to keep his hair and beard tidy, small children would run from him, screaming,

"Mama, a troll! A troll from the woods! It has come to eat me!" And even grown men would make the sign of Thunar's Hammer towards him when they thought he was not looking, glancing sideways beneath their eyelids to see if he would howl and flee back to the mountains. None were stingy with their food, however: often when farm folk saw Beowulf's great shape looming at their door, they would hastily proffer sausages and bowls of ale for his friendship; and in return he cleared fields of rocks that no one else could lift and carried loads that would have made many days' hard work for smaller men.

As he made his way southward, Beowulf found that his time beneath the ocean had changed something in him: having dwelt with Ran's daughter, he could see things that had been hidden from him before. There was a certain shimmering about stones and waterfalls where wights dwelt, might coiling around them like the water eddying through Ran's hall; and sometimes, as he perched uneasily on a farmer's little chair or squatted beside his hearth, a moment of foresight would come upon him, so that he would find himself saying,

"You should bring your cows in from the north field, for it is grazed by the cattle of the alf folk and no cows belonging to men will ever thrive there," or, "If Disa marries Frodhmar, their children will be sickly and short lived, but if she marries Gudhbrandar, their children will have strong luck for nine generations." Beowulf often felt embarrassed to have spoken so, for as soon the words passed from his mouth the moment of blinding clear surety would fall from him and leave him bewildered at what he had said; but the folk he spoke to listened, and, loath though he was to take any reward for his speaking, would try to give him such things as simple carles could afford, a copper brooch or ragged edged piece of a southern coin.

In time he reached lands where men knew that King Hrethel still ruled the Geats, that Hrethel and Ongentheow still watched each other warily as hound and wolf, each waiting for a moment of weakness that would give him the chance to attack. Beowulf walked all through the summer, as the red brightness of the rowan berries gave way to the golden brightness of the turning birch leaves and the nights grew longer and colder. He was grateful for the reindeer blanket Paanja had given him, for though, as reindeer hides did, it continually shed a snowfall of coarse hairs over whatever it touched, it kept out the chill rain and gave him a warm place to sleep on nights when there was no farmstead nearby.

As Beowulf passed into the territory of the Geats, he became shyer of men: he did not wish to show himself first among the Brondings, lest, finding him alone, they should seek vengeance for Breca's death. He kept to the damp woodland ways, eating berries and mushrooms when he ran out of hard bread and dried meat. Though he often saw the tracks of wolves, or heard their howling in the distance, they did not bother him. The great bull elk who stalked lordly through the woods, their bellows and the sounds of antlers clashing ringing out at dawn and dusk, were more dangerous to men, for the rut was upon them and they were ready to fight whatever crossed their paths; yet even they turned aside from Beowulf. He did not hunt, for he had no weapons save sword and knife, but once he found an elk carcase that the wolves had left a little flesh upon, its meat still fresh enough for him to eat when he had roasted the chunks well on green twigs over a small fire.

The first winter moon was rising full in the night sky, the pine branches casting stark black patterns through its golden light, as Beowulf neared Hrethel's burg at last. Everyone would be at feast in the hall: the Winter nights slaughtering would have ended that afternoon, and the time had come to make offerings to the alfs and idises, to Frea Ing and the Frowe, for a good year's harvest. Reaching the edge of the barrow field, Beowulf wavered for a moment, but then stepped firmly forward: he knew that he no longer had any cause for fear there. The shadows of the mounds patched the field with black against the moonlight, and a chill wind rustled through the long grass that grew over them, moaning softly beneath the rings of stones between the barrows. A hound barked, its voice deep and clear in the frosty night. Beowulf strode through the howe meadow without faltering, stopping only when he heard the sound of hoof beats behind him. The mounted man reined his horse in, looking down at Beowulf; the two gray hounds by his side sat down on their haunches, long tongues lolling out between their white fangs. The man was gray bearded, clad all in black, and his cloak billowed behind him in the wind; the dappling of his gray horse glimmered like silver moonlight through shifting leaf shadows.

"Where are you going?" The rider asked, the words hissing through his teeth.

"I am going to my grandfather's Winter nights feast, for I have come a long way to get here."

The mounted man stared at Beowulf a moment. The dark overhang of his shaggy brow ridges shaded his eyes, so that Beowulf could only see two black wells above the moon white arch of his cheekbones, like the eye holes of a skull. He spoke again, chanting,

"Late are hall fires lighted
Life is e'er with strife fraught
Ride I on the roads dark,
Round the Hel oak's mound fare.
Spear God's choice shall spare one,
Spill one, his bane willed not.
One gnaw flames of Wind God,
Woe for Hrethel grow soon,
Woe for Hrethel grow soon."

Before Beowulf could speak or move, the gray bearded rider spurred his horse hard, racing past with his hounds running behind, until they were lost in the darkness of the barrows. Beowulf made the sign of Thunar's Hammer to turn the ill foretelling away, but he could feel the chill of its truth in his bones. He remembered what Hygd had said of Hygelac: A shadow came over him, and I thought that his luck flared high now, but it would be quicker than I thought to burn out. It is well that I came back now, Beowulf said to himself. No man may stand between another and his Wyrd; but whatever befalls, Hygelac shall know that I am by his side, as he stood by me for so long. He hastened his steps towards Hrethel's burg. As Beowulf stepped into the hall, a hush fell over it, and he heard the murmurings and rustling as the folk on the benches nearest the door tried to move away from him. But Hrethel rose from the gift seat at the end of the hall, treading boldly forward: his sword was still sheathed, but his hand was on the hilt.

"Who are you, strange wight, to come unbidden to my Winter nights feast?" He asked, staring steadily up at Beowulf. "If you come in frith, bringing harm to none, be welcome here. If not, go forth at once, for this is a stead of men, warded by Thunar's Hammer and hallowed this night by the blood of offerings to the gods: my hall shall not suffer as Heorot has."

Several folk were already making the sign of the Hammer, touching the amulets about their necks as they stared at Beowulf. Shocked into silence, the words dried in his mouth. He could see the fear even in Hrethel's wide blue eyes and the trembling of the king's hand on his sword hilt, and it seemed to him that he could hear the thoughts in Hrethel's mind, as surely as if the ruler spoke aloud: Men say that Grendel has ravaged Heorot for eleven winters now has he chosen to come here for the twelfth? I shall die fighting him before I share Hrothgar's long sorrow.

Beowulf's heart ached with a sudden pang: it had hurt to see carles and their children fleeing from him, thinking that he was a berg troll, but it was far worse to hear the words of his grandfather, to see Hrethel standing small and bold before him, thinking that he dared his own death in speaking to Beowulf. He should not have been surprised that the king did not recognize him at once, for his beard hid much of his face now and he was no longer the ox fat youth who had swum out from Whales' Ness, but he took it ill that his own grandfather should have mistaken him for the night thurse ravening in the Scylding lands.

"Do you not know me?" Beowulf asked plaintively. He pulled back a flap of his bearskin cloak, lifting up the amber pendant at his neck. "I am Beowulf Berki, your grandson. The sea parted me from Breca, casting me up in the land of the Finns, and I had to overwinter there and walk home, else I would have been back sooner."

Hrethel peered at him closely, then his bearded face broke into a broad smile and he ran forward, flinging his arms about Beowulf. "Berki! We mourned you as dead, and cast grave offerings into the sea, that you might not dwell as a beggar within Ran's hall Breca said he was sure of your death, for he had seen you go beneath the waves in the storm that cast him ashore, and could not reach you to help."

"Does Breca still live?" Beowulf asked, astonished. He did not blame the Bronding for thinking him dead, since he had been as sure of Breca's end.

"The sea cast him up on the Heathoreamas' shore. No one has ever made such a swim before, and he has boasted greatly of it but you may say that you won your foolish challenge now."

"And what of Hygd?" Beowulf questioned eagerly. "She will be gladdest of all to hear that I live."

The joy dropped from Hrethel's face all at once, like a mask cast aside, and he glanced over his shoulder. Beowulf, too, looked towards the end of the hall where the king's kin were seated. Wynefrith was there, her coiled dark braids showing more gray even in the light of the fires; Haethcyn, sharing a horn with Garhild, her maiden's flow of hair now demurely pinned up to show that she was wedded; Herebeald, Sitting to the right of Hrethel's high seat, and Hygelac and beside Hygelac sat Hygd, her long hair braided up, like Garhild's, beneath the gold decked linen headdress of a married woman, and the slight swell of her belly already pressing against her wheat golden linen gown.

Hygd stood up, coming slowly towards Beowulf. She no longer moved with the light grace he remembered, but walked with care, though her womb had not rounded enough to unbalance her yet; but her tread was the stately tread of a queen. The firelight glimmered in the pools of her violet eyes, glowing deep from the amber layered about her neck and glittering off the gilded rim and eagle head tip of the white horn she held out to him yet it seemed dim against the memory of the gold flames of Ran's hall, dulled by his lingering mind sight of the eoten maid's crystal cup shining bright through the water.

"Hail and welcome," Hygd said sadly. "I wore deep blue for a year after Breca brought the news of your death may his tongue fall from his mouth! But Beanstan would let me wait no longer, for many men sought me as their bride. Hygelac was among them, and I thought that if I could not wed you, it would be best to be given to your kinsman and friend, even as my mother came to Haereth's cousin after my father died. Hygelac and I were married at the Midsummer Thing this year."

Beowulf wanted to curse Breca, but he knew that he could not even blame his loss on the Bronding's malice: it was Beowulf himself who had tarried too long away, first with Ran's daughter, and then among the Finns. *Two years gone, and I felt only one passing,* he thought. *But if I had known this, I would have set out alone, even in the worst winter cold, to reach you before your wedding vows could be spoken.*

"Breca spoke from the best of his knowledge," Beowulf answered heavily. "He is not at fault, nor are you or Hygelac: Wyrd pulls as she will." He reached out, very slowly and carefully, to take the horn from Hygd's hand.

Beside him, she seemed tinier and more fragile than ever; he was afraid that any careless touch from him would harm her. Beowulf remembered how tightly his arms had clenched about Heofonglowe, the strength with which her heavy hips had met his thrusts: what woman of the Middle Garth could he embrace thus? *Heofenglowe,* Beowulf said silently, *your curse has bitten deep. I should not have stayed with you so long but once staying, I should not have left.*

III

The stag's body was a light burden over Grendel's shoulder as he bore it into Heorot. No torches still burned there, but the fresh straw was already stained with the ale that Hrothgar's men had spilt in their daytime feasting and the coals glowed in the long fire trenches. He pulled back his lips in a snarling laugh: only at Heorot, through all the Northlands, did the bairns of Ash and Elm begin their offerings at dawn and drink while the sun was up, creeping away to their houses when the sky began to redden in the west.

"For Heorot is mine by night," Grendel said, dropping his prey heavily upon the table before the high seat. He had crept up on the stag in its bed, his scent and sound hidden by wind and rain; he had broken its neck with a single swift blow, that he too might feast. Slung over his other shoulder was a skin bag full of his mother's ale. He lifted it off, raising it high. "Eleven winters; and this is the beginning of the twelfth. Hrothgar will not live forever, and when he is gone, there will be none to bar me from Heorot's high seat."

Grendel drank a deep draught of the ale, its heat stinging down his throat. A few drops ran from the corner of his mouth, sizzling in the straw eoten brews were too strong for the things of men to easily bear.

And yet, he thought, settling himself upon the table, I have not won. While Hrothgar still held to his right, Grendel could not take the high seat and claim his rule; and till then, he could not call his kindred in to feast with him. Angrily, Grendel slit the stag's belly open with his claws, slicing through the great vessels to catch the cooling blood in his hands.

"Yma, eldest father!" he called. "Give me your blessing, as I seek your were gild. Bergelmir, who brought us to land through the great flood, before the foes of our folk raised the Middle Garth and walled us out give me your blessing, as I seek to claim what is ours by right; help me to win this hall, that I may take a bride, and fill this realm with our clan as you filled the Out Garth that we win our war at last against the kin slaying tribe of Woden and his brothers." Grendel sipped of the dark pool in his hands, its taste salt sweet in his mouth, then cast it about the hall, the droplets spattering like blood from a hard struck wound. But none fell upon the high seat, its gilding still untouched.

How long must I wait? Grendel wondered. He tore at the body before him, clawing off pieces to bring to his mouth; he could taste the musk of the stag's rut in the flesh.

"At least you did not die without furthering your line, high horned one," Grendel said softly, as if the antlered head dangling loose over the edge of the table could hear him.

"From the size of your crown, you must have run in the wood many winters, and fathered many young stags and does, a mighty atheling aeht to live after you."

And Hrothgar, too, had his bride and his sons, Grendel could have killed the boys or Wealhtheow at any time, breaking into the drighten's house at night as he had broken into his hall. But his war was not with women or children; when Hrethric and Hromund had come of an age to stand against him, then they would choose whether to face him or flee and leave him Heorot as his own.

"Then I shall no longer be alone," Grendel whispered. He looked along the benches still, to his sight, glowing slightly warm where Hrothgar's men had sat on them in the daytime. It seemed to him that he could see how it would be: the heads of the greater eotens rising shadowy to the rafters where they sat stooped over their mead; his mother at his left hand, with the crystal cup raised up, and Heofonglowe the daughter of Ran to his right, with strings of amber gleaming soft over her creamy breasts. The craggy rock trolls, the weed dripping water trolls all of his kindred, gathered to hail him in the stead he had won back from the children of the gods, as none of Yma's sons had been able to do before. And in time, the sons and daughters of Grendel would grow so many and fierce that no man would dare set foot within leagues of Heorot, and the shores of Sealand would be feared by all seafarers, the barrows of Scyld Scefing's sons standing as a warning for all ships to turn aside.

"I need only wait, and hold my place here," Grendel said to himself. Still, though he could hear the howling of the storm over the roof, its voice singing in his ears with the wailing of the troubled ghosts and those of his lesser kin who rode through the winter winds, a heaviness was beginning to settle upon him.

Eleven years was nothing to the eoten kind but he had come to Heorot every night, and felt the daily round of the Sun as he never had in his mother's cave beneath the waters. Eleven years of night watches by himself, apart from the friendship of his own kind, of the sea nicors who hunted and drank with him like brothers, the white armed daughters of Ran who gave their favors freely and joyfully...and Heofonglowe, the ninth wave, fairest and strongest of all Eagor's maids: once she had smiled upon Grendel, her pale body gleaming like ivory as she darted through the water before him; he had felt the cool strength of her legs clasped about his waist, and tasted the sweetness of Eagor's mead in her sharp toothed mouth.

Grendel drank deep again, the burning draft of ale washing the taste of blood from his lips. He remembered the words of Thrum, that mighty thurse drighten...sitting upon a howe, his hounds collared with gold and his horses with adorned manes, yet longing for the love all his riches could not buy...Here in my garth walk the gold horned cows, black oxen to gladden the eoten. Many are my treasures, I have much wealth; I think that I am only lacking the Frowe.

Water wore down stone, and long loneliness could wear down even the hearts of Yma's children; more than one great eoten had died for that soul sickness, when thoughts of the Frowe's fairness overcame him in the end, and he sought to win her from the gods. But I do not wish so much: only a woman of my own breed, and the friendship of my kin. Yet if I turn from what I have begun, then I will be rightly scorned for ages: the eoten kind do not forget. Eleven winters, and this the twelfth, Wealhtheow thought, looking down bitterly at the tracks of clawed feet leading away from Heorot's door. Last night, when the storm raged, Grendel's weight had sunk deep into the mud, his trail crushing out the lesser marks of men's shoes; now the sky was scoured to icy blue, and glittering rime crusted the edges of the troll's footprints.

"Why do you stare at those tracks, Mother?" Hrethric asked, coming up beside her. "Grendel comes to the hall every night; is there something new here?"

Wealhtheow gazed at her son, her heart sinking within her. At eleven years, Hrethric already showed promise of his grandfather's height and his father's strength, his young shoulders beginning to broaden even as he grew taller. His long hair was the colour of dark honey, still streaked with gold from the long days of summer; his blue eyes were almost as bright as Hrothgar's, and he wore the gilded dagger on his belt with great pride. It tore at Wealhtheow within to hear him speak so. And there is the sorrow of it, she thought. If Hrethric were vowing to slay the troll who seeks to take his place as Hrothgar's heir, I should be overcome with fear for him; and yet I can hardly bear it, that he has grown so used to Grendel's night rule of Heorot. But how not, when he has known nothing else in his life?

"Nothing new," Wealhtheow answered heavily. "Let us go in; sooner or later we must see what the eoten's son has left of his Winter nights feast." Hrothgar's folk had made their offering by the barrows at the sea's edge, and feasted during the day before night drove them back to their own homes so it had been, since Grendel first came.

The heavy stink of clotting blood and torn entrails lay thick inside Heorot. Wealhtheow braced herself, looking about but the head dangling over the edge of the high table was the antlered head of a stag, and when Wealhtheow looked more closely at the ruined body, she saw the hoofed legs wrenched aside and the ruddy tatters of hair hanging from it. Grendel had slain a deer and brought it in to devour in the hall, feasting at his ease on its flesh and entrails; he had spattered its blood about, as if in mockery of the Winter nights blessing to the gods. But at least no man's blood stained Heorot, unless Grendel had hidden a grisly gift somewhere in the hall.

Wealhtheow shouted for the thralls, telling them to clean the hall and burn what was left of the stag: there might be meat left on it, but no one had ever been so hungry as to eat Grendel's leavings, not even at the end of winter when bellies were tightest. The stag's head rolled loosely as one of the thralls lifted it from the table, and Wealhtheow's belly tightened with nausea. It is only a beast, killed and butchered as men do, often enough, she thought: have I not seen enough men slain? Is this not a little thing? But a glazed dark eye looked blindly at her from the stag's dead face; her hands were shaking, her knees trembling, and she knew that she could not stay in the hall any longer. The clean icy wind from the sea cut at Wealhtheow's cheeks as she stepped back out; she breathed deeply, washing the scents of blood and death from her lungs.

She did not know which she feared more: to be so worn down by the long horrors of Grendel's reign that, at last, she might break and beg Hrothgar to leave his fathers' land or at least let her go, or to become so used to the troll's night visits that she no longer cared that she and Hrothgar could not sit in their hall after sunset, nor give it in time to their sons, nor hold Freawaru's wedding feast by firelight beneath Heorot's gilded antlers, and lead her with torches through the night to her bridal bower. Slowly Wealhtheow walked out of the palisade, following the sandy track down to the barrows of Beaw and Halfdan beneath the gray stone.

Cold as the wind was, the frost was already melting from the dead grass beneath the Sun's bright light; only where shadows fell did the white rime still lie thickly. When Wealhtheow reached the Scylding howes, she saw that she was not alone. Unferth sat with his back to the gray stone, his deep blue hood drawn down over his face and his spear in his hand. She stood still for a moment, wondering if she should turn and go: if the thule were seeking wisdom from his god friend Woden, it would not be well to break his thoughts. But Unferth must have heard the sound of her shoes on the sand, for he pulled his hood back, rising to his feet.

"What brings you here, Scylding queen?" The thule asked harshly. The whites of Unferth's eyes were tracked with red, and his voice was raw throated, as though he had drunk deep the day before though, in truth, he had hardly done more than sip at the feasting ale. "What gift did Grendel leave us last night?"

"Only a stag. The gods be thanked that it was not worse," Wealhtheow answered. "And you, Unferth have you won any better wisdom this Winter nights?" She had learned over the years, that when Unferth was in an ill mood, it was better to answer him with rough words than soft ones, and she could tell from the grim look on his thin face that his thoughts had not been good.

"We have gathered often to chew over runes of rede, and considered how brave men might best win in sudden onslaught; we have tended the harrows and holy steads, and given offerings, asking the gods' help against this land's curse; and yet none of it has brought us any good. Why, then, should Woden suddenly aid us now, if we cannot win through ourselves?"

Wealhtheow could hear the pain beneath the jagged sarcasm of Unferth's voice, like black water dropping deep beneath uneven ice. She knew that he had often fasted for days, seeking help from the gods; that beneath his dark tunic, his chest was scored with long scars from the edge of his spear where he had gashed himself to let his blood stream onto the tall gray stone, embracing its roughness with his wounds on every Yule eve in hopes that Woden would answer his offering.

"I do not know," Wealhtheow answered truthfully. "Save, perhaps, that all ill must come to an end someday, and it is usually the way of the gods to repay the trust that their children put in them."

"Aye, and Sigemund the Walsing whiled twelve winters in the woods while his son Sinfjotli grew to manhood, and Wayland forged without sleep on the island Sea Stead; and Thioderik, so men say, was forty years an exile before he came to the kingdom he rules now. All of that is well enough, but I do not think Grendel is going away, and no young heroes of Walsing blood are growing up here to put an end to him."

Wealhtheow was glad for the wind's sting then, for it hid the flush of anger and shame on her cheeks she might have been thinking much the same about her sons, but it was another matter to hear Unferth speak the words.

"Wyrd set this wight to be the Scyldings' foe but for all that, I have not seen you seeking out a wolf's heart to feed to Hrethric or Hromund, if it is strengthening that they need."

Unferth's dark eyes closed a moment, as if in thought or pain too deep to cry out.

"If either of them is to take his father's place, you would not wish them to have wolfish hearts. Nor are the bravery and strength of men enough to bring Grendel his bane: we have lost enough lives in proving that. Troll kin alone must meet troll kin's strength, if the gods do not give their help."

A chill ran icy as an adder down Wealhtheow's spine: she had not forgotten the words of the spae wife from God Home in the eleven years past.

"And I am no wiser as to what that may mean," Unferth added. "I have cut and cast the runes each year, seeking to learn but they have given me no rede: my lore all seems as useless as our swords against Grendel's hide."

His deep gray gaze slipped past Wealhtheow as he spoke, staring up at the tall pillar of stone; such words did not come easily from the proud Woden's man. Wealhtheow looked out past him, over the sun glittering sea to the blue horizon fading into mist. Scyld Scefing, it was said, had come over the waves in answer to grievous need; but how could that need have been worse than the sorrows that were upon them now?

"If your lore is not enough," Wealhtheow said quietly, "should we not seek out others, who may know more? Guthhild the spae wife does she dwell yet at God Home?"

"When last I heard, she did."

"What, then, if we go to ask her rede? Eleven years have passed since she spoke for us: might she not be able to see more now?"

Unferth's shoulders shrugged beneath his heavy dark cloak. "Who can tell? I had thought of this before...yet what if the answer is ill? Little heart remains in our war band; only those thanes who are strongest and truest have stayed, but we are all worn down with these long years. And Hrothgar himself..." Unferth shrugged again.

"He has grown old," Wealhthow admitted, wrenching the words from the depths of her heart. She had watched her husband's belly swelling and his shoulders sagging over the years, his hair fading from bright thick silver to thinning white; she had sat too many nights with him as he stared into the fire of their sleeping house, knowing that Grendel sat at his ease within the hall, Hrothgar's pride and hope turned to his curse. "If the wise folk of God Home can foretell only ill..."

"That could well be his death."

"Yet I see no other thing that we can do."

Unferth tugged thoughtfully on the long gray braid of his beard. There was little brown left in his hair now, and the faint creases that had lined his face when Wealhtheow first saw him had deepened to harsh crevasses.

"If it is to be done," he said, "then best it were done in secret, with none knowing it save we ourselves. I know the way to God Home, though it has been many years since I last walked Fyn's shores. If the weather holds clear, I can row there and back."

"How long will we be gone? I would not put Hrothgar in fear: if we vanish suddenly, he is likeliest to think that Grendel now walks by day." For with winter's beginning, the mists lingered longer after dawn, and rose earlier as the shortening days darkened: Grendel had been seen stalking the moors by twilight on such foggy evenings, though he never set foot in Heorot before sundown.

"Or else that you and I have fled together to another land," Unferth said dryly. "For though you are no maiden, you are hardly old enough for age to wither your womb yet, while Hrothgar, I think, is unlikely to set another child there."

Wealhtheow flushed fiercely, her face burning as though she stood too close to a great bonfire. She would have shouted at the thule then, save for the hard lump of tears choking her throat: Grendel's ravages had stolen more joys from Hrothgar than it was fitting for anyone to name.

"I hope you would not speak so," Wealhtheow choked, "if there were any other to hear it."

"Many things have been spoken of me, and some of them true, but you know that I have never betrayed Hrothgar's trust in me. Yet between you and I, if we are to go to God Home and ask for rede in our land's sorrows, there can be no lies and nothing hidden and think further, as you wish to do, of Hrothgar."

That rede, too, was good, Wealhtheow thought as she blinked back water from her eyes. Only she had heard Hrothgar's weeping not the soft tears of weakness, but the dry racking sobs of a man torn beyond his strength to bear in the night when all her caresses could not rouse him, or when, worse, his man's leek leapt up in false promise, only to wither when he came to seat himself within her. He had fathered Hromund not long after Hrethric's birth, strengthened by the hope of Grendel's death that came with the new heir to the Scylding line; but Grendel had held his place, and there was no easing of sorrows.

After Hromund came Freawaru and by the time Hrothgar lifted his daughter to the light and gave her name to her, sprinkling droplets of water to gleam in the little fair wisps on her tiny head like a headdress of berg crystal set in gold, the strength that had driven his seed to spring forth from its hoarding bag had sunken and did not rise again. Though Wealhtheow's sturdy hips had carried her children proudly and with ease, and borne them with little suffering, and though she often wept as her womb bled when the Moon hid his face each month, for she longed dearly for more bairns, the richest of earth could grow no grain when seeds were never sown in it.

"Then what shall we tell him, that his mind be no more troubled than it is now?"

Unferth's graying beard braid coiled like a serpent between his twisting fingers, and he looked up at the tall pillar of stone again, as if waiting for some wisdom to issue forth from it.

"Freawaru is yet young, and unbetrothed," he mused. "And Ingeld the Heathobard is but four years older than she he whose father Froda was slain by the Danes years back: were it not for your wedding and our alliance with your father, and Ingeld's youth, the Heathobards might have come seeking revenge long since. Now it is not unknown that the folk of Godhome have aided in such cases, where a messenger from a late foe's hall might be slain out of hand. If your daughter is to follow in your footsteps as frith weaver, we have good cause to go to that hallowed holm. Nor may Hrothgar come with us, for I have long guessed that if he should leave his lands, then the blessing that holds his high seat safe from all Grendel may do would fail, and Heorot belong to the troll utterly."

"Freawaru is young for such a betrothal," Wealhtheow said carefully. "A maid of but nine winters..."

"Old enough to be sworn to wed, and by that to keep us safe from without, when Ingeld begins to feel his manhood: do you think he has not heard the songs of his father's death at Danish hands, a hundred and a hundred times and more? Young men are ever eager for battle and revenge, and sniff like wolves for weakness in the old and though the fear of Grendel and ill luck has kept any foes from storming Heorot these eleven winters past, that cannot last forever: there will always be someone willing to dare what others do not."

Wealhtheow could not gainsay the thule's words. Though but a youth two years older than Hrethric, Ingeld the Heathobard was said to have slain his first man that summer, and to be quick of temper with little forethought, though as yet his father's rede givers still hedged him about with older men's sense.

"Would a boy coming into manhood accept betrothal to a maid so young?" Wealhtheow asked doubtfully.

"If it is put to him rightly, and if he must. A wedding is as good a were gild as a slaying, as you know yourself. Freawaru is a maiden of great loveliness, and any eyes can see that she will rival any woman in the Northlands when she is grown. I do not think Ingeld will believe himself scanted. And at least Starcath, that old strife stirrer, has gone from Ingeld's side and no news has been heard of where he wanders now: the young atheling will get wiser redes without him, and be likelier to accept our offer."

"If that must be, then so it must," Wealhtheow agreed. A trickle of deep unease ran through her mind, like a dark spring dribbling cold round the base of a rock, but she pushed it aside: there, too, the folk of God Home might give rede. "Let us go to Hrothgar, then, and speak of this with him."

The thralls had scrubbed away all of the deer's blood and strewn the floor with new straw, but an echo of the slaughter scent still hung heavy in Heorot's cold air like deep blue mourning curtains arraying the walls. Hrothgar sat in his high seat, staring into the long fires where the little flames were beginning to eat their way up along the fresh logs. Beside him stood Hrothulf, gazing earnestly into his uncle's face. Though the young man's madder red tunic was richly decorated with bands of woven silk and gold about the hem and cuffs and neck, it hung upon him as if upon a stick of wood: Hrothulf ate as much as any youth his age, but little flesh would cling to his bones, though he was no longer shooting upwards in height.

"Hrothulf..." Wealhthow said, then hesitated. She had thought to ask him to call Freawaru; but even when he was younger, he had taken it ill to be sent upon any errand, and seen slights where there were none.

"What do you wish?" Hrothulf asked, turning to look up at her he was short as well as small of build, though Halga was said to have been a hand span taller than his brother Hrothgar. "I am here."

"I would speak to my husband alone," Wealhtheow replied.

Hrothulf's gray eyes flickered past her to Unferth, and he lifted a dark eyebrow. Halga, it was said, had been a man of fine looks, and his daughter wife Yrse had captivated two kings. Their son was not what Wealhtheow would have called handsome, but his features were striking in their strength: high cheekbones planed straight to the square corners of his jaw, which tapered sharply to a strong squared off chin.

Hrothulf's nose was long and very pointed, jutting from his face like the proud prow of a ship; his brows were thick and straight, low over narrow, slightly slanted eyes that were pale gray and light filled as the winter sky. Though he shaved his face clean, his jaws were dark with the shadow of stubble. A few spots of youth still marked his skin, but the intensity of his gaze already gave him the look of a man who could not be easily set aside, or reckoned with without care. He would be fit to rule in any hall save Heorot, which should belong to Hrethric and Hromund.

"Alone, or with Unferth?" He asked. His pure low boy's voice had deepened to a clear baritone that would have graced the throat of any poet; though he plinked the harp with but indifferent skill, he was asked to sing almost as often as Eadmund, the young man who had taken old Aethelred's place when the aged word smith had slipped quietly into death. "And if with Unferth, what words would you speak that it would not be seemly for me to hear?"

"Stay, then, if you will," Wealhtheow said. "Perhaps it were more seemly that you had a voice in this, for it touches on the good of your cousin Freawaru and her brothers through her, and they are yet too young to deem such matters for themselves."

Hrothulf regarded Wealhtheow seriously. She could not tell what thoughts might be turning behind his steady gaze, but at last he nodded.

"It is indeed fit that I should be here."

Hrothgar blinked his wrinkled lids, looking up at his wife with reddened eyes. He had not slept well: twice in the night Wealhtheow had awakened to find her bed cold, and seen the shadow of her husband looming before the fire coals, wrapped in a heavy cloak brooding, she knew, over the feasting that had not rung from Heorot's gables in the night, waiting in fear to see whether the day of blessings would spur Grendel past his usual bounds.

"What is in your mind, beloved?" He creaked.

Swiftly Wealhtheow and Unferth outlined the plan they had decided upon: to go to God Home, to seek aid in making a wedding alliance with the young lord of the Heathobards. Hrothulf leaned forward as they spoke, like a raven pecking at unknown food, but Hrothgar sat silent until the end of it, when at last his heavy head moved in slow assent.

"Freawaru is young, aye," he said. "And many things might yet come to pass before she is of an age to be wedded but such a betrothal may help to keep her brothers safe while they grow to manhood."

He did not speak further of what might befall Hrethric and Hromund; but Wealhtheow knew the many staves in that heavy bundle bowing her husband's broad shoulders, and this not the least: the time would come, and perhaps not too slowly, when Hrothgar, by death or age, could no longer hold Heorot's high seat. Then Hrethric or Hromund must stand against Grendel for the Scylding's right or betake themselves elsewhere to win new lands; and then the foeship or friendship of the Heathobard aeht would weigh heavily in what might become of them.

"And what do you say, Hrothulf?" Wealhtheow asked. "Would you have Freawaru given to young Ingeld, as payment for his father Froda's death?"

"If the wedding were with another man, or an older one, I should say yes. But who can tell what Ingeld may become, or whether holding one piece of the Scylding treasure might whet him to gain more? From all I have heard, Ingeld is greedy and unmeasured in his deeds, though he may learn better with age: but a wolf often lurks in a young son, though he be glad of geld, and it is not often well to trust the kinsmen of a man you have slain. And Ingeld was fostered in his childhood by Starchath, of whom, for all his strength and deeds, I have heard more ill than of any other living man."

"Starchath is very old," Hrothgar began, but Unferth broke in.

"Aye, and he was very old when I was a lad, some forty winters past. It is said that Woden gave him thrice a man's span, and Thunar ever a foe to his line, for that Starchath was born of eoten blood deemed that he should do one great deed of betrayal in each lifetime. And indeed he slew his own drighten, who should have been beloved by him above all men: who knows what rede such a man might give to an atheling youth? Yet Starchath is gone now: by the gods' will, may he never wander back to Ingeld's hall! And if he does, better to have Ingeld bound to us by oath and blood than ready to be heated to war."

"True enough," Hrothgar rumbled. "So be it, then: go you to God Home, Unferth, and see how matters may be arranged there."

"I shall go as well," Wealhtheow said. She saw the sagging of Hrothgar's face as she spoke, his flesh slackening beneath his white beard, and quickly laid a hand upon his forearm still thick, but softer than when she had wedded him. "No, it is not that I wish to leave you, my husband. But weddings are a matter for women, and I would no more pledge my young daughter without more knowledge than you would send our sons untried to fight in an unknown war band. If all goes well, we shall not be long."

"The seas can be harsh in winter," Hrothgar murmured.

"Unferth knows the way well, and I do not fear to trust me to his sea skill."

"And I shall also go," Hrothulf broke in. "As well as her mother, Freawaru should have a man of her blood to speak for the Scyldings. While you hold your stead, Uncle, would you not have me standing for our kin outside it by my father Halga's memory? If I am not Heorot's heir, at least I can hold the place of those who are until they come to the age of men."

"It is true, you have that right," Hrothgar acknowledged. "So did Halga and I ever uphold each other, so that his words might have come from my mouth or mine from his. Go well, beloved brother son, and ward my wife with all your care. When do you three mean to fare forth?"

Hrothulf looked at Wealhtheow; she, in turn, glanced at Unferth.

"As soon as we may. Nor would I have it spoken about where we have gone: tales can often grow easily in idle minds. But it should not take long for us to ready ourselves, and the sooner we fare, the sooner we shall be gone."

"Take what you need, and go as you will," Hrothgar murmured. "Hale in going, hale in faring, hale in coming back: may the gods bless your way."

Wealhtheow bent to kiss her husband, his mouth warm beneath the soft rasp of his white beard.

"Be blessed in your staying, beloved. We shall be gone no longer than is needed."

Far beneath the waves, there was no night nor day: even in the upper reaches of the sea, the water cooled the burning sunlight to a soft green glow, no worse to Grendel's eyes than the cold green flames of the sea wyrms that coiled and darted through his mere. He stroked through the strong underwater currents as though they were no more than hangings of silk fluttering about his body, the dark salt sea scents filling his nostrils. The seals fled from him, scattering in their fear.

For a moment the thought stirred in him, to chase one down and feed on its rich fatty flesh, his mouth drinking the hot gush of its blood but he had eaten well enough last night, and hunger was the least of his needs. A school of herring darted beneath him, flashing like a flood of southern silver coins spilled glittering over the side of a ship. Farther above, the sound echoing wavery and distorted through the water, he heard the deep moaning breaths of a pod of spekheawer whales lifting their black and white heads to spout again and again, filling their great lungs before they dived; and further yet, out in the deep ocean, sounded the slow notes of a great whale singing, her voice thrilling plaintive and beautiful through the sea.

The song strengthened the longing in Grendel's heart: the singer was a maiden cow on the brink of full growth, calling out her desire in the manner of her kind hoping that another voice would take up her song in the distance, answering her in a resounding duet as they swam to each other across long leagues of water. May luck be with you, sister, Grendel thought. He would feed on whale flesh when he found a carcass that had not been full stripped by spekheawers and sharks, but they were too large for him to seek out as prey, and their songs were akin to the songs of his own kind.

Grendel swam deeper down, his sight clearing as the brightness through the water faded to deep twilight. When the winter storms swept up, tossing the waves to gray wildness, then the daughters of Ran would be found above, tearing at the planks of ships and sundering the little vessels of men to broken driftwood in their rough play. But though Winter nights had passed, Eagor was still in mild mood; the great sea eoten was as like to still be drinking ale in his hall as doing any other thing, while his daughters strewed the floor with fresh seaweed and poured beer for drowned sailors, awaiting the new guests that winter shipwrecks would bring them. A dark shape ghosted through the water towards Grendel, moving with the same ease as himself; behind it trailed the sleek shapes of two sharks, their bellies pale through the shadowy water. Grendel paused a moment, his clawed feet treading softly, as he waited for the other to draw near.

"Hail, Grendel," the nicor hissed. The sharks circled slowly; Grendel watched them from a corner of his eye, for Ran's sharp toothed hounds scarcely had the wit to obey their masters' orders, and would often forget themselves and assail guests as well as foes. "It has been a few winters since you came to feast with us." He grinned, showing teeth layered like a shark's, and a green glimmer of good fellowship sparked in his flat dark eyes.

"Hail, Sceathsecg. So it has, but I hope that I am not so quickly forgotten in Eagor's hall."

"O, you may be sure of that," Sceathsecg replied. "You are ever welcome here though I hear that these nights you sit in a hall above the waters, and have little time to drink or hunt with your old friends. Tell me, Grendel, have you fallen in love with some maid of the Middle Garth, that you would take the Scyldings' hall for your own?" The nicor laughed, a crackling hiss of bubbles through the water.

"Far from it," said Grendel. "It is no daughter of Ash and Elm that I mean to seat beside me when Hrothgar yields to me his share of Yma's were gild. Rather, I have thought long in Heorot on whom I would have with me when that day comes that our kin can claim our lands again forever, and therefore have I come here now."

"And not to see me and lift a horn of old Eagor's brewing together? Grendel, I am ashamed!" Sceathsecg's laughter was gone as quickly as it had sprung up, his thin lips closing tight over his teeth again. "But you are a welcome guest here all the same, if you have come to see Heofonglowe again. Two summers pasts, she drew a land dweller down to Ran's hall alive, if you can believe it. But he was a mighty man: nine of my brothers he slew before she took him."

"Who?"

Sceathsecg named the dead with little change in his hissing voice. Grendel had known them all, hunting fellows and drink friends beneath the wave, with whom he had often wrestled in sport; it nearly passed belief that one of the children of Ash and Elm, however strong, could have killed them in the water.

"Death comes to all," Sceathsecg said, shrugging, "and none can flee his wyrd. Yet the Middle Garth man left Heofonglowe at summers end, and she has not been the same. She takes little joy in the bright amber, and none in her play. Though she is fiercer than before in rending the bodies of lost sailors, she clasps none of them in her white arms any longer, and weeps when she hears the songs of the whales."

"Who is that man?" Grendel asked fiercely. "Tell me his name and dwelling place, and when I have fulfilled my vow to take Heorot, then I shall see Heofonglowe's hurt avenged. If a son of Ash and Elm was fool enough to leave her, he does not deserve to live, and for that he caused her sadness, I shall gladly rend the heart from his breathing body and give it to my mother to brew into our wedding mead."

"I do not know his name," Sceathsecg replied. "Yet you shall speak to Heofenglowe, and maybe her heart will be gladdened to find a better love than the one she lost."

Sceathsecg clapped his black scaled palms together and the two sharks turned, their long gray blue bodies rippling graceful curves through the dark water, to follow the nicor as he led Grendel down towards Eagor's hall. Grendel knew the great sea hall well, for he had often sat feasting at its long benches where the dead sailors thronged with water wights sitting at their ease between them in Eagor's frith drowned men had no more to fear from the scaled nicors, when the last air had bubbled stale from their lungs and the crabs and eels stripped the bloated flesh from their bodies. Those who had sunken to their deaths with gold rings on their arms and fingers sat high in the hall, warmed by the fires that blazed from the heaps of ruddy glistening metal; those who had been snared as paupers by Ran's silver net held places near to the doorway, for the great eoten wife of the sea did not look kindly upon those who brought no gold to her hall.

Eagor and his bride sat on their thrones of carven whale bone, their long gray hair drifting about them like strands of seaweed. Ran's soul catching net dangled from her hand, its silver glinting as it swayed in the water; she wore a silvered diadem of shark teeth, and her pale green eyes were cold and flat as those of the huge blue gray shark that hovered near her chair, its fins barely stirring as it waited for its mistress to toss it a gobbet of meat. But Eagor grinned deep in his greenish beard, drinking amber mead from a huge cup of polished berg crystal that one of his daughters kept topped up; his keen deep blue eyes met Grendel's across the hall, and the sea king lifted his shining vessel towards his young cousin in friendly welcome. Even for Grendel, it was a long swim beneath the weathered ship timbers that arched over the sea hall's roof, seeking the green gold glimmer of Heofonglowe's hair above the richer glow of her amber: she would be pouring out the drink for the eotens' guests, as befitted an atheling frowe at feast. It was not she whom he spied first, though, but one of her sisters, Blodugheafod, who delighted most in battles at sea and whose long fair hair was streaked with shining red.

"Hai, Blodugheafod," Grendel called to her. Eagor's daughter paused and looked up, then snatched up a long straight horn of fine grained ivory, filling it from her green glass pitcher as she swam over to him.

"Be welcome here, as ever, Grendel," Blodugheafod said, giving him the horn. Grendel lifted it and drained it in a single draught: so far beneath the roof of the sea, even he found the rich warmth of Eagor's ale welcome. As Blodugheafod filled the vessel again, Grendel's clawed fingers delicately tracing the spiraled whorl: it had been fashioned from the wide end of a northern narwhale's tusk, and the fire of the gold gleamed warmly from its polished white surface.

"It is well to see you here once more," Eagor's daughter said, tossing her long ruddy streaked hair to float about her in a cloud and arching her back so that her heavy breasts jutted out sleekly. "Have you finished with Heorot, that you come back to us now? I hear the land folk have proved more stubborn than you thought."

"I am not yet done with Heorot," Grendel admitted. He fought down the dark rush of anger and shame that her words roused in him how was it that Hrothgar had held against him so long; and did all those beneath the sea know it, and laugh at him? "But it came to me that I would see your sister Heofonglowe again, and speak with her."

Blodugheafod laughed, thoughtlessly as the crashing of waves. "She is here if you want her, though no man has gotten any good of her since that land dweller left her. But if you have a mind to warm one of us, I might not say no."

She stroked her hands lightly down across her dark nippled breasts and the creamy swell of her hips, turning her body in a graceful curve to circle Grendel. He nearly reached out for her then, for it had been long since he had sported with a water maid. But Blodugheafod was changeable as the rest of her sisters: she would tumble with him in the currents and forget him, nor would she ever be willing to sit in the hall as his wife. Only Heofonglowe had a spark of constancy in her; she was the ninth of them, the one who ever came farthest up the beach, and it was she whom Grendel would have beside him when Heorot was his.

"Further along there, you see her?" Blodugheafod laughed, pointing through the gold lit ripples that swirled through the hall. "Go on, and good luck."

Heofonglowe swam slowly and steadily above the benches, the stream of ale from her pitcher dark against the clear water as she filled the horns and cups that drowned hands held up for her. She did not look at any of the dead men, though once she had stopped to flirt with any drowned sailor that caught her eye, choosing ever those who were largest and strongest for her delights. Only a single strand of amber, as dark as jet save when a bright flare of gold fire kindled an answering red spark from within the large smooth beads, hung between her round breasts; she wore no flaming girdle of amber set gold about her powerful hips, nor did any burning rings encircle her white arms.

"Hail, Heofonglowe," Grendel said, swimming up beside her.

"Grendel," the sea maid answered. Wearily she lifted her pitcher, pouring a few drops more into the brimming whale tusk. "What brings you here?"

Face to face with Heofonglowe, Grendel found his tongue halting. So that he would not stammer like a fool before her, he took a deep gulp of the ale, the sea rich malt flowing almost untasted down his throat, and felt a little bolder.

"I came to see you, for that we have been apart so long."

"Long?" Heofonglowe said. She set her pitcher down on the table below her, pushing back the greenish fair hair that floated like a veil before her face. "It is scarce twelve winters; that is hardly long. I had not marked that you were missing though you used to come here more often, that is true enough, and lately I heard a rumor that you had been creeping about some hall on land."

"For the sake of our grandfather Yma, I have driven out the Scyldings from their hall. It will not be long now before Scyld's great grandson yields his seat utterly to me and I hold it as my own. I slew Hrothgar's warriors, and cast his realm into fear, so that no man there now dares to step from his doors between sunset and sunrise, nor to pass Heorot's threshold in the hours of dark."

"Few eotens can make such a boast but what are the dwellings of the Middle Garth to us? Of all the land folk, one only..." Heofonglowe bit her lip, a tiny dark trail of blood rising from her sharp teeth to spread and fade in the water, and turned her face from Grendel.

"Your sister said something of a land dweller," Grendel murmured carefully.

Heofonglowe turned back, her strong hands wrenching at the dark smooth rope of amber that lay over her broad white shoulders. The thin silver wire that held the beads parted with a sound like the chiming of a tiny bell; the pieces of amber scattered, slowly drifting upwards.

"Aye, it is a matter of mirth to them, and they mock me for it. But I had found a man of the Middle Garth who was strong enough to bear my embraces without breaking, warm and soft skinned as a seal and brave as a bull whale and he forsook me, all for the thought of a little human maid whom I could shatter with my least finger, if only she ever stepped into the sea. I loved him dearly, and would have clung to him forever, but he left me, he left me!" Heofonglowe's lovely face contorted with angry weeping, her tears floating from her face in streaks of brightness. Grendel tried to take her in his arms, but she pushed him away; he could have held her by sheer strength, yet he let her go.

"Tell me his name and where he dwells. Then, when I have won Heorot, I shall seek him out, and he shall pay with a broken bone for each tear you have shed over him."

Heofonglowe looked up at him, her blue green eyes bright with fury. "I do not know his name, for I did not need to ask it. He was my sea bear, and there was only one of him."

"Then tell me where I might find him."

"He came to land far in the North, and I have not seen him since. Yet he used to play off the shores of Geat land, by Whale's Ness: that was where I saw him first, and where he first gave me his love."

"When I have won Heorot," Grendel said again, "I shall seek him out. I shall slay him, and that will be an end of it: you may forget him, and then..."

"And then..., I do not care. Go back to your land dweller's hall; you may as well take a daughter of Elm for your wife, too, for I shall not have you!" Heofonglowe snatched a floating piece of her amber from the water, flinging it at Grendel's face.

Even a heavy stone would have bounced without scathe from his hide; he barely felt the light graze of the gleaming sea resin, but the shock of the words she hurled with it seemed to strike him like a dwarf forged hammer. Heofonglowe cast herself backwards, swimming swiftly away from him. For all Grendel's speed in the water, he knew he could not catch her, and the giggles of her sisters were already sounding through the hall, sharp as the shriek of ship planks ripping upon the rocks. He turned, diving low to the gold strewn sand of the hall's floor, and made his way from there as swiftly as he might hot with rage and cold with sorrow, as though he had taken a wyrm's bite whose venom both fevered and chilled. *How did I anger her so?* Grendel wondered as he swam up from the depths. *What did I say, that she should answer it with such bitter runes?*

But his resolve was firm: Heorot should be his, and then he would slay the land dweller who had given Heofonglowe such pain. Years were short to the eoten kind, and life long and someday Eagor's fairest daughter would smile on him again. The little boat Unferth steered rose and fell easily on the smooth blue swells; the sea wind that bit through Wealhtheow's thick woolen cloak was icy, but clean, bearing no breath of coming storms. Such a fair day following the Winter nights offerings should have been cause for gladness and indeed, though Wealhtheow felt disloyal at the thought, she could not keep her heart from rising as the green barrows of the Scyldings shrank behind them. Unferth pulled steadily on the oars, sculling along; Hrothulf sat in the stern of the boat, watching the shore carefully, as though he were learning the way for himself. *He will be a good rede giver for my sons, even as Unferth is for their father,* Wealhtheow told herself. For all Hrothulf's thoughtful quietness, though, he was still young, and he could not hide the quiver of eagerness in his voice as he leaned forward to speak to Unferth.

"Tell me of God Home, Unferth. What may we await on those shores?"

"I have been long away," Unferth answered. "But there are those things that have not changed since the earliest days. As long as our folk have dwelt in the Northlands, Nerthus' lake, and the grove about it have been holy: only those chosen by the gods may look upon the waters of that mere and live. The hof God Home stood long before the days of Sigimund the Walsing, and there the gudhes and gudhijas have tended the tree gods without ceasing for more than three hundred years. Before the hof is a market where many folk bring goods to sell, and where glass and silk from the South may be found, or even weighted southern coins traded for amber. The holy folk mostly dwell by the hof, though there are some who keep to themselves. And on Hawk's Height is the place where the gudhes craft small holy things of gold, bracteates and little plates with god images that may be worn or given in the hof for blessing. Behind it lies the mound of one of the great gudhes of elder days, Woden's Karl, who first made those signs known to men. I often went to that barrow when I dwelt on God Home, for though Woden's Karl died an hundred years ago, his wisdom may still be found by those who seek it from him. But as for ourselves, we shall be speaking chiefly with Guthhild and her sisters, and mayhap with the gudhe Brycghelm, for he is the leader of those who do Tiw's work, and as mighty in the battles of law and oath as any hero wielding a sword though he is no mean man of his hands, either, when matters come to fighting.""Now," Unferth went on, his strong lean shoulders never pausing a moment in the rhythm of the oars he pulled, "there are these things the two of you should have in mind. The gate of the hof will be warded by a man named Wihstan his fathers have held that stead since the hof was raised. We must leave our weapons with him, for only those blades given to the gods may be brought within the hof's frith garth. He will let me through without doubt, for that I was given to Woden years ago, but even the kin of kings must wait outside if Wihstan says they must. Do not try to gainsay him! It may be that we must while a day or two before we are able to speak of our business, for I do not know whether the Winter nights feasting began or ended at the full moon this year sometimes it is one, sometimes the other, according to how the signs are read. If it began yesterday, then we shall do well, for we shall be bidden to take part, and that is a time of much gladness and great holiness. But if it ended yesterday, many of the holy folk will be yet abed; it may even be that we shall be bidden to help in such work as cleaning and sausage making. If that is so, then turn your hands to it with a good will, and do not think it beneath you, for the greatest of gudhes must eat as surely as the least of thralls, and the very offal of the beasts given in blessing is hallowed. It will not be held against you if you are unskilled, but it will be seen whether you work with a good heart or scornfully and the wages you get for your trouble will be more than worth it." He turned his head for a moment, smiling grimly at them. "And do not fear: if you are asked to do messy work, the hof folk will give you more fitting clothes for it."

I will gladly carry wood and turn a quern stone like a bondsmaid, if it means that there may be a little more hope for Heorot, Wealhtheow thought. Looking back at Hrothulf, she saw that his lean face was thoughtful, but he said nothing; and she wondered if he had guessed that she and Unferth had more in their minds than arranging a betrothal for Freawaru. The island Fyn rose low and green from the sea, its shores sloping invitingly up from the water. A wooden pier jutted out from the beach, but there were only a few boats tied up to it, and only one of those was much larger than Unferth's little vessel. The thule sighed.

"We have come too late for the feast, after all: yester evening, pier and beach would have been full, but most of those who fared here to make blessing will have left this morning." Unferth rowed close to the pier, casting out the rope to loop about one of the wooden pillars that held it and making it fast, then tossing their bags up and laying his spear more carefully beside them. The boat rocked perilously as he hauled himself up onto the flat planks of the landing. "Come, Hrothulf, help Wealhtheow up."

The thule crouched, holding his hands out. Wealhtheow gripped his hard palms, and Hrothulf braced himself against the sides of the boat, making a cradle of his hands for her to step into. The little craft tilted, nearly overbalancing, as Wealhtheow put her full weight on Hrothulf, but the young man pushed hard, and with Unferth's help, she managed to step up onto the pier. Hrothulf followed at once, boosting his thin body over the edge with little trouble.

"Now tidy yourselves," Unferth ordered. "Whatever the hof folk may ask of you, you must come to them looking your best, and the sea wind has disheveled you into a couple of trolls."

Wealhtheow paid the roughness of his speech little mind, but she felt through her belt pouch for the hard smoothness of her silver comb. She had only to straighten her gold adorned headdress of white linen and tuck a few straggling locks back under it, but the band of deep red silk around Hrothulf's dark head had not been enough to keep his hair from being whipped into violent tangles.

"It will go more quickly if I do it," Wealhtheow said to the young man. Hrothulf's scowl showed that he liked the thought little, but he nodded, letting her work the comb over his head. His hair was clean and, even though Hrothulf seldom let another comb his hair, few lice showed white against its darkness, for in the summer he swam often, and as the days grew colder, he went more often to the hot steam baths than most men, as befitted a youth of good family.

That done, Wealhtheow let her cloak fall back, adjusting her huge gold neck ring slightly to be sure that it was not askew. Her shoulders were sore with its weight, but Unferth had given her rede to wear it, for it was yet the finest thing she owned. Beneath the thick dark wool of the cloak, Wealhtheow wore a dress of bright sky blue pinned with arched brooches of garnet set gold just above the points of her shoulders, and a shift of pale green linen below. The soft gleam of black silk interwove with the harder gleam of white silver in a pattern of cross armed whirls along the armholes of her overdress; a band of the same swirling silk and silver weave ran down the front of her skirt.

Her girdle was made of many linked plates of gilded silver, deeply chip carved with images of round eyed horses with their heads arched over their backs, and from it hung an eating knife with an ivory hilt and a sheath of tooled and gilded leather, and a silver spoon with a silver set ball of crystal nestling in its bowl: with the great gold collar shining above her breasts, though Wealhtheow had left her keys behind, there would be no doubt that she was a queen. Hrothulf had wanted to wear his best helm, the one crowned with a gilded ridge ending in a swan's beaked head above his brow and adorned with silvered squares of pressed metal showing riders with spears flanked by birds of prey; but Unferth had told him sternly that it would be best to go unarmored to the hof. Still, Hrothgar's brother son bore a fine sword with gleaming beads of amber and crystal on its sheath and a gold ring through its silvered hilt.

The aurochs horn slung across his thin chest was rimmed with filigreed gold and tipped with a gilded eagle head, and his deep red feast day tunic was fit for a man of the kin of kings. Unferth was less splendid to look upon, for his over tunic was plain deep blue and he was adorned only with a silver spear pendant at his throat and a thick twisted coil of silver tipped with wolf heads around his wiry forearm but the over tunic, dark dyed as it yet was, did not hang with the stiffness of new linen, and when Wealhtheow looked more closely, she saw that its threads had the soft sheen of woven silk. No sword hung from his leather belt, but the shaft of his spear was carved with many red stained signs: eagles and ravens with the faces of men hidden in their feathers; the threefold triangle of the walknot; a twisted wyrm at its base, and runes running along its length. Unferth in the lead, the three of them walked towards the hill where the hof stood, the gilded horse heads at its gables shining brightly in the sunlight.

The plain below was trampled and muddy, with many post holes to show where tents had stood until lately; the fence itself was hedged off with heaped stones and carven posts marking the bounds of the frith garth, and gray smoke rose from the far side of the hill, as though large fires were burning there. Before the gates, the fresh hide of a white horse was draped high on a frame of poles, hooves dangling down on empty legs and flies blackening the eyes and muzzle of its heavy hanging head. The man who stood before the two great pillars marking the way in was both tall and broad almost a full head taller than Unferth, his huge bare arms gnarled with muscle like the limbs of an old oak. The thick brown curls of his beard hid most of his face, tangling into a wild array of thick brown hair. He was bare foot and clad all in white; his only weapon was a staff of black wood, but Wealhtheow had watched warriors all her life, and she could see from the big man's light stance and easy movements that he would need no more than his staff to defend against any who might challenge him, however they were armed.

"Hail, Wihstan," Unferth called to the hof's warder when they were close enough. "How is it with the Ases; how is it with the alfs; how is it with the holy folk?"

"It is well with the Ases, and well with the alfs," Wihstan's bass voice boomed in reply. "As for the holy folk, you may ask for yourself within. Though the feast is eaten and the ale drunk, there is still welcome for our old friend Unferth and for the Scylding queen, and Hrothulf Halga's son. Come in, if you will; but Hrothulf must leave his sword here, for the sake of the gods' frith. You may be sure, young Scylding, that it will be well warded. You may leave your baggage here as well, if you will: a house in the village will be made ready for you before the day is over."

Hrothulf silently unbuckled his sword belt, giving it over to the hof man, and Wihstan stepped aside to let them in. As she passed between the pillars, Wealhtheow drew in a deep breath. It seemed to her that she could feel the seething might beneath the soles of her feet, that the air within the garth of the gods was thick like thunder air, but instead of weighing heavily against her, it seemed to tingle through her skin like standing under an icy waterfall, save that its chill was not bitter, but thrilling. Tilting her head back to gaze up at the hof, it seemed to her that she could almost see flames playing about the gold covering the horses' heads, the gilded roof shingles and carven eaves, and the keen silver edges of Unferth's black iron spearhead burned blue in the clear light.

The doors of the hof were wide open. Some folk were bearing joints of meat or butchered animals out and around to the back of the hill, and others carrying buckets of water in: as Unferth had said, there would be much work to be done after a Winter nights slaughtering in such a holy stead. Wealhtheow and Hrothulf followed Unferth up the hill and into the hof. Stepping in through the carven door pillars, Wealhtheow had to pause a moment to gather herself. It seemed to her as though she had just stepped into an unimaginably great bell of bronze; the sound of its ringing had died away, but its walls still vibrated with the last echoes, too deep to hear, but mighty enough to make her unsteady on her feet. The hof was lined with tree gods, images of all the dwellers in the Ase Garth. One was wholly veiled in dark linen that would surely be Nerthus, on whose face it was not meet for the children of Ash and Elm to look, save if they were given to her as husbands or offerings.

By Nerthus were placed her children: Frea Ing, garlanded with a fresh woven necklace of braided leeks adorned with the gleaming white knobs of spear leeks, his mighty phallus jutting up from between his legs, and the Frowe, shaped of a tall slim forked tree, with her narrow shoulders bedecked with a four ringed gold collar much like the one Wealhtheow wore and the cleft between her branching legs carved to mark it more strongly. Woden's image was helmed and byrnied for war, a spear resting in his hand; Thunar held his Hammer, a short handled iron weapon that only the strongest of men might lift. The grooves of his beard and hair had been carefully stained with red, his round staring eyes gilded and the haft of his Hammer wrapped with gold wire.

Frige was clad in blue and white linens, a distaff wound full with fine wool thrust through her belt and a great bunch of keys by her side; the headdress covering her wooden hair was adorned with silver and shining rounds of berg crystal. By Geofe's feet rested a plough, and in her hand was an ox goad; Hamdeall bore an ur old horn of gleaming bronze that coiled about his shoulders like a serpent, the patterned disk of its bell rising high above his head; and the other gods and goddesses were likewise made clear in wood to the sight of men. The wood of all the tree gods was dark from age and countless offerings of blood and ale, but freshly polished and shining with well rubbed beeswax. In the middle of the hof was a harrow of heaped stones, with a wide flat boulder on top, flanked by two shield shaped rounds of figured bronze. Upon the harrow rested a wooden bowl that Wealhtheow could hardly have spanned with both arms, carved with the faces and signs of the gods and goddesses, and written about with blood reddened staves.

The harrow itself was crusted with streams of dried blood, ringed with horned heads that had been heaped up about it the night before, for the heads were still fresh enough. Long tables ran the length of the hof, and the bodies of cattle and swine and sheep lay upon them, tended by men in dark clothes with cleavers and knives and saws. Other folk heaped apple wood and dried herbs upon the two long fires, the sweet scent driving out the smells of spilt blood and ale, and still others were scrubbing blood splatters from the walls.

Wealhtheow could not help but shudder, for the leavings of the holy offerings were too like what she had seen in Heorot after Grendel's night guesting: in her sight, the dull dark eyes of the ox heads piled about the harrow shifted to the glazed blue eyes of men, and the drops of blood that the blessing twigs of the gudhes had flung about looked far too like the sprays of red that fountained forth when men's limbs were wrenched from their bodies; she had seen, too often, women washing that blood from Heorot's hall pillars, and smelled the scented wood and worts sweet above the stink of slaughter.

One of the women who was busy there with buckets and cloths looked up, and to Wealhtheow's surprise, she recognized Guthhild's blue green eyes, though the gudhija's ruddy gold hair was tied up into a tight knot and she wore a plain brown apron dress with the gray woolen sleeves of her under shift pushed up past her elbows. Guthhild wrung a stream of dirty brown water out of her rag and came over to the three guests.

"Hail and welcome, Unferth, Wealhtheow, and Hrothulf," she said. "What brings you here after Winter nights? Have you come to help us clean the hof?"

Unferth looked down at Wealhtheow, clearing his throat meaningfully.

"If there is work that I may help with, I will be glad to do it, for the sake of the gods and the aid the dwellers in God Home have ever given," Wealhtheow answered.

"And I," Hrothulf agreed.

Guthhild's lips curved in the secretive smile Wealhtheow remembered. She has aged better than I, Wealhtheow thought. The years of Grendel's reign had furrowed the Scylding queen's forehead and drawn her eyes tight at the corners; but, at least in the shadows of the hof, no such marks scarred the gudhija's pale skin.

"That is well," Guthhild said.

It was not long before Wealhtheow, all her festival finery put aside, was shown the way down the hill to the large bare field within the frith garth where the sausage making and smoking were going on. Guthhild pointed her to a group of young men and women who squatted on the ground, taking washed entrails from wooden buckets and carefully turning them inside out over smooth sticks, then scraping off the slimy inner membranes. Wealhtheow had overseen such work often, for sausages were often served at Hrothgar's table, but she had never done it herself.

Still, she told herself, I can surely do whatever a bondsmaid can, nor must I scorn to turn my hands to a task that the folk of God Home will take on. It was not long, however, before Wealhtheow discovered that making fresh entrails into sausage casings was not so easy a task as she had thought. They tore when she tried to stretch them over her stick; her knife's edge either passed over the slimy surface without scraping it clean, or, despite its dullness, went too deep and opened holes in the skins.

Although she sat in full sunlight, her wet fingers quickly went numb in the icy breeze, and the smooth wooden knife hilt, smeared with the mucus from the entrails she was trying to clean, was frighteningly slippery in her hand, so that now and again she nicked herself slightly. Hrothulf seemed to be doing a little better: he was going among the fires where the high drying racks rose, layering up poles hung with thin cut strips of meat. His gray work tunic was soaked with sweat and his face was red from the heat, for often he had to lean over the fire and risk singeing himself, but he did not so much as pause in his work to ask for a cup of water.

"Hai, it has been long since you last did such work, if ever you had to turn your hand to it," a fair haired young man said, squatting down beside Wealhtheow and looking at the pathetic pile of ruined entrails beside her. "Perhaps you were best put to something else, for we have enough scraps for the hounds already."

"I am sorry," Wealhtheow said. She reached up to wipe the stray wisps of hair from her face, then looked at her mucky hands and thought better of it.

"No, do not be so downcast. There is no shame in not knowing how to do a task, but this work takes more skill than it would seem. Come, the hides that were salted down on the first day of the feast are ready for scraping, and that is more easily done, but goes quicker with two pairs of hands. I would be pleased if you would do it with me." He smiled kindly at Wealhtheow, and she found herself smiling back. Like the other hof folk, he wore a simple brown tunic for his work, so that there was no way to guess his kin or the place he might hold in God Home, but he was a handsome man, his face clean featured and lively with long yellow hair tied back in a tail and a neatly cropped yellow beard. His skin was still tanned golden, as though he had spent much time in the sunlight through the summer, and his body was lithe and broad shouldered, the muscles of his strong forearms deeply defined. His eyes were summer blue, bright with happiness and good health. Now I would wager a gold ring that he is a sworn husband of Nerthus or the Frowe, Wealhtheow thought. For even a goddess might have an eye for such a fine looking man!

Leaping to his feet, he reached out a hand to help Wealhtheow rise, lifting her up with easy strength, and led her to the wooden frames where the salted hides had been stretched.

"Where are you from?" The handsome hof man asked Wealhtheow as he showed her how to scrape the inner surface of the taut cowskin clean with the outer edge of a crescent knife. "I do not think you live on Fyn, and nearly all our Winter nights guests are gone home."

"I am from Sealand," Wealhtheow answered. She was shy of telling him her rank, lest he misunderstand why, and think that she was trying to get out of the messier work. "I could not come here before, and I was told that sometimes the Winter nights feast here was held before the full Moon, and sometimes after."

The young man laughed brightly. "And for greetings, instead of a horn of hof ale, you were set to cleaning sheep's bowels! I hope you are not thinking ill of us now. But it is the custom here at God Home for all who come to the hof in times of work to take part: for all of the Middle Garth's men, thrall and carle and king alike, are the children of Hamdeall, and we give worship to the gods by making full use of their gifts. And when Sunna sets and the day's work is done, then we shall have joy enough for welcoming our guests who are the more welcome when they come to offer their strength in helping us, rather than simply to join in feasting and blessing."

Although the salt from the hide stung fiercely in the little cuts on Wealhtheow's hands, she was able to smile back at him a smile that barely hid the tears of relief flooding to her eyes. Perhaps it was the simple work, however bad she was at it, that lightened her heart by freeing her from the unseen burdens of being a queen. No: it was the easy way in which he had spoken of the Sun's setting, without the chill of dread on his words and without glancing up at the sky to guess how much longer they could safely stay out. Eleven winters of terror, Wealhtheow thought. Eleven winters, since I last heard sunset hailed as the joyful sign for work to end.

"What is wrong?" The young man asked. "Such a fair face should not be so clouded with sorrow; have I spoken amiss?" He put his hand over hers, and though his skin, like hers, was chilled from wet work in the cold, Wealhtheow could feel the warmth beneath it.

"You have not," she reassured him. She thought that she should pull her hand away, but she did not, and after a moment he lifted it himself and went back to scraping the remnants of fat and flesh from the stretched hide.

"What is your name?" He asked her. "I am Wihbrand."

Wealhtheow did not want to answer him, for he would surely know her name; it was not a common one. And that, she feared, would change the easiness between them, for he would know of Heorot and its curse, and guess at once why she had come Hrothgar, I am not betraying you, she thought. Yet it has been so long, and to be, if only for a little while, with someone who does not know me as the queen of the troll blighted Scylding hall. But hiding her name would not change her wyrd, nor all that it had brought her: she might have left Heorot, but while Hrothgar still dwelt there, and she was still wedded to him, she could not flee Grendel's shadow.

"I am Wealhtheow," she said reluctantly.

Wihbrand drew in his breath, the smooth planes of his face standing out sharply.

"Wealhtheow of Heorot?"

"Aye."

"I had thought you would have been older, for all I had heard that Hrothgar had wedded a young bride. But you can scarce be twenty winters."

Wealhthow felt the warm blush coming to her cheeks, though she knew he could only be speaking such to cheer her: she had eight more years than he had counted, and they had not been easy ones. Still, unbidden, she thought of tales she had heard of God Home: how a gudhe or gudhija might, at times, bring the blessing of a god or goddess with the gifts of their bodies, and none thought it shameful or unwholesome. Now it seemed to her that the emptiness of her womb ached within her, for the long years she had gone without the joys of wedding. If he were to offer me blessing thus, could I turn it down? Should I?

"You speak too kindly to me," she said. "I am the mother of three children, and if it is not too soon for me to speak of my business here..."

"Speak as you will: are you not working for it?" Wihbrand's fingers touched hers again, brushing lightly over the back of her hand.

"I have come for aid in the betrothal of my daughter. So you see that I am by no means a young woman."

"If you are not a silly maiden, you are far from old," Wihbrand answered warmly. "And your years do not show on your face, though you do not hide your sorrows. But I am surprised to hear that you have come here to see to the betrothal of a girl of nine winters, when Heorot's harm is known to all."

The scraping knife dropped from Wealhtheow's numb fingers, and without warning, she found that she was sitting on the cold earth, weeping with great loud retching sobs. Wihbrand knelt beside her, his strong arm warm about her shoulders, and without shame Wealhtheow buried her face in his stained tunic, crying against him.

He wiped his free hand clean on his trousers and stroked her head gently as she wept, whispering to her, "There, there, fair frowe. You have been hurt long, but tears are the beginning of healing, and the gods do not scorn the weeping of a broken heart."

Slowly Wealhtheow's shuddering spasms ebbed and she sat up, sniffling and wiping her flushed wet face on her tunic sleeve. She was so close to Wihbrand that she could smell the sweetness of hwanna root and mint on his breath, and see the tiny flecks of gold about the irises of his blue eyes. He did not let her go from his embrace, but pulled him closer, and she could not help wondering if he were going to kiss her.

"It was not truly for Freawaru's betrothal that you came here, was it?" Wihbrand murmured, his breath soft in her ear.

Mutely Wealhtheow shook her head. "Guthhild thought that you might have come long before though, she said, folk are often fearful of seeking out their last hope, lest that too be lost. Was that so?"

Wealhtheow nodded. "Who else knows why you are really here?"

"Only Unferth. Hrothulf has come to speak for Hrothgar over Freawaru, but he does not know. Even Hrothgar, we did not even tell him..." Wealhtheow felt the tears rising hard in her throat again, but she managed to choke them back.

"I shall speak to Guthhild," Wihbrand said kindly. "And it may be that we can give you some help. I hope that I may be of help myself, for I have been learning spae craft from her for six years, first as a singer and then as a seer."

Though Wealhtheow had learned to hide her thoughts from her face, she was still leaning against Wihbrand with his arm circling her shoulders, and he must have felt her twitch of surprise, for he laughed.

"Aye, I came here as soon as I knew that my choices in life were three: to become one of Frea Ing's dancers, or to suffer nith and scorn in my father's war band or, worst of all, to be wedded to a woman. Be sure, you are as safe as a sister in my arms, fair Wealhtheow! But such men as I are often as gifted at spae sight as women, for we walk between the worlds and can open our souls to the sight of the gods. And I shall be your friend for I think that you have much need of friendship now: sorrow eats the heart of the one who cannot speak all his soul to one other."

Wealhtheow sighed, for she had learned the truth of that well in the last eleven years. Had it not been for Unferth, who would hear her darkest doubts and answer them in his own way, she did not know how she could have borne the length of Grendel's reign; for she loved Hrothgar too much to add the weight of her sorrows to his own.

"Should we not get back to work?" She asked. "My thoughts are far too long to tell in a few words, and it seems to me that there is much yet to be done."

As before, Wihbrand helped Wealhtheow to her feet, lifting her up as though she weighed no more than a little girl. She was grateful for his steadying, for her knees ached already from sitting on the ground and her right foot had gone numb, the blood flowing back into it with sharp nettle prickles. But instead of turning back to the hide they were scraping, he put his arm around her shoulders again, guiding her with gentle strength to the small gate at the rear of the hof's garth.

"You bear the burden of a queen, whose hardest work is done while others feast at their ease, and who has not nearly so much time as a bondsmaid to think of herself," the gudhe said to Wealhtheow. "When was it that you last walked in the woods without some duty calling you away?"

Wealhtheow looked past the brown field to the holy grove the smooth gray trunks of the beeches, a few withered leaves still clinging to their wide spread twigs; the gnarled dark oaks, a ruddy bright leaf hanging here and there from their crowns like tatters of long wrecked battle flags, and one or two bare white birches slim and small beneath them. She thought back to her wedding day, when she had slipped away from her father's war band to bathe but even then, her mind had been full of how matters might go between her blood kin and her oath kin, and what she must do to weave her web of frith.

"I do not know," she answered.

"Then come with me. I shall guide you safely through the grove, for you may not yet look upon Nerthus' lake. But it may be that you will find the words you need there or at least the easing of your soul that must come, if you are to aid us in finding healing for Heorot's sorrows."

No hedge marked the border of the hallowed grove, but as they walked beneath the high branches of the trees, Wealhtheow felt her heartbeat slowing, her breaths coming more deeply and easily. If it had not been for Wihbrand beside her, she would have been frightened, for it seemed to her that she could feel the might of that stead not as the thrumming tingle of the hof, but rather as a deep still lake, so deep beneath her feet that she could not guess at its spring, and rising drowning high above her head.

Though the drifts of dead leaves rustled about her ankles, twigs breaking sharply beneath her soft leather shoes; though a thrush twittered above her head, speckled brown upon a gray beech branch, the sounds all seemed hushed, whelmed by the pooled holiness of the grove. Once they came upon a great fallen log lying across the path: it had lain there long, for it had half fallen into black ruin, with orange horn mushrooms and pallid shelf mushrooms growing thickly from its rotting bark. Wihbrand said nothing, only put his hands about Wealhtheow's waist to lift her easily over it, then vaulting lightly over himself.

A few late blackberries still hung on their thorny shoots along the edge of the path, glistening like tiny polished clumps of jet beads, and now and again they passed a sloe tree whose deep purple berries bore the misty blue bloom of ripeness, or a crab apple with its small fruits hanging golden among brown leaves and scattered over the ground below its branches, but Wihbrand did not touch any of them: what grew in the hallowed grove, Wealhtheow understood, must be left for the gods.

At one point Wealhtheow could not see any mark, but Wihbrand seemed to know where he was the gudhe bent to untie his shoes, carrying them by the laces in his hands, and Wealhtheow did likewise. Her first barefooted steps were faltering, fearful of sharp stones and thorns, but the woods mold was soft beneath her soles, the new fallen leaves crackling pleasantly under her touch. When Wihbrand unbound the yellow tail of his hair to let it fall about his shoulders, Wealhtheow also untied her braid, running her fingers through the plaited strands to free them.

As her long hair flowed free, it seemed to her that she felt all her muscles easing as well, as if a heavy yoke had been lifted from her shoulders, so that she walked lithely as a maiden beside the young spae man. With the loosing of her bonds, Wealhtheow did not know whether she wanted to laugh or cry; but Wihbrand moved more swiftly, almost dancing along the path, and she had to follow him. The shadows of the trees had grown long, the Sun's light showing red through the branches, when Wihbrand led Wealhtheow into a small clearing. Out of old habit, Wealhtheow glanced up fearfully we are far from any dwelling; can we get back safely before night? But Wihbrand rested his hand on her shoulder, smiling at her.

"No harm can come to you here, Wealhtheow," he said softly. "No thurse or troll can pass the bounds of God Home's grove, and those ghosts and alfs who walk among these trees are friends to their younger kin." Standing there, tall and straight and fair with the sunset light shining golden from his face, Wihbrand might almost have been one of the alf kind himself; Wealhtheow felt the water standing in her eyes as she looked upon him.

"I have been afraid so long," she said, the words choking in her throat. "And we called on the gods, and they gave us no help: there were only the bodies of more good men dead. My husband has lost his hope, and my womb has gone empty for nine years; thanes creep from his lands, and no strong boughs of battle grow to take their places. And I did not truly know, until I came here, how I have longed to leave Heorot. With words and cups of ale, I wove frith to still the hate of men, but what draught could I pour out for Grendel to end this strife?" Wealhtheow's voice was steady as she spoke, but the silent tears rand down her face.

"Yma's kin differ even as men do or gods," Wihbrand answered. "Frea Ing gave his sword to take an eoten maid to wife; but her brother's hate could not be stilled, so that Frea Ing even he, the warder of frith had to slay him bare handed. There are men, too, who cannot be calmed by women's wise runes and will do battle, whatever gifts may be offered them. And though Grendel may not be scathed by sword, the Scyldings and you among them have fought a mighty battle by keeping to Heorot, and held the door to the Middle Garth safe while others feasted within, blind to the nearness of their foes. It is little to be wondered that you have all taken mighty wounds. And though wounds of the soul cannot be measured by spilt blood and long scars, they are often as grievous: men have died of such hurts to the heart before."

"I fear for my sons, for they have not their father's strength, and I do not know what will become of them when Hrothgar is dead. And Hrothulf is wise and strong, and true to Hrothgar in all things. But I fear that his heart will change when the time comes for Hrethric to sit in his father's seat, for it is ever hard for the greater to be ruled by the lesser and I do not think Hrethric or Hromund will grow to be Hrothulf's match."

"Time will show the worth of all. It is well to look with care to what may come, but do not seek sorrow before it is needed, for that will rob you of joy all your days."

"And...I do not know what will become of me. I am not the woman I was when I wedded Hrothgar. I swiftly learned to love him, but I do not think I could bear to be sent again to a strange drighten's hall as his wife and I fear that rumors of the ill luck that drew Grendel will cling to me where ever I might try to go, so that none would have me even if I were willing. When my days as the Scylding queen are done and another woman sits in Geofe's seat, shall I then have to labour in the kitchens like a bondsmaid, or end my days wandering the wet road?"

"That, at least, shall not happen," Wihbrand answered. "For in your long battle, you have won strength and holiness, and I believe that you have more gifts of the gods than you know. If you will not stay at Heorot when Hrothgar's days are done, then ask Unferth to bring you back to God Home with him. Just as his seat here will still be ready for him, there will be a seat made ready for you as well."

"And what of Grendel?" Wealhtheow asked. "Do you yet see an end to his rule?"

"This is not the time for me, or any other, to look so deeply. Stay with us, Wealhtheow: these next three days while the hof is cleaned and the flesh of the offering beasts made ready for the winter, you shall spend in thought and in cleansing yourself, and then Guthhild and I will aid you in looking for the answer you need."

"Then it is well enough." Wealhtheow's knees sagged beneath her, and Wihbrand stepped forward swiftly to catch her, lifting her to cradle and rock her in his strong arms as if she were a babe.

As Wihbrand had decreed, Wealhtheow was not set to work again: instead, he took her to a small house in the woods on the far side of the holy grove, where she might sit or sleep or wander as she chose, listening to the voices of the birds, the wind in the trees, and the gentle rippling of the little brook that ran by the house.

Though the sky had grayed, an occasional shower of snow drifting down, Wealhtheow's cloak was warm and there was plenty of wood for her fire, and even the icy cut of the wind felt clean and good upon her face when she stepped outdoors. At dawn and sunset, Wihbrand brought her to a steam bath by a deep pool, sitting naked on the wooden bench beside her and chanting songs and runes of cleansing as he sprinkled water on the glowing stones, the clear drops of sweat running down his fine muscled body like crystal beads reddened by the stones' low light, or scourging her gently with bunches of dried birch twigs whose leaves had been softened in water, that their stroke might tingle and clean, but not sting: after such cleansing, the pool's cold did not chill, but soothed and wakened.

Wealhtheow did not see Unferth and Hrothulf during those three days, nor any other save Wihbrand, who brought her fresh meat and bread and cheese, light golden ale and goat's milk still warm from the udder, and often brewed teas for her from a bag of dried herbs that he bore at his belt they tasted a little odd, and Wealhtheow could not recognize any of them, but the teas were not unpleasant. By the evening of the third day, Wealhtheow felt that she could stay in the little forest hut forever.

The driving urgency, all the fears and strains that had gnawed at her for years, had faded into a deep inner silence: she no longer watched the course of the sun as if it were measuring out her hours of life, but when the clouded eastern sky began to grow dark, she greeted the sunset with calm joy, as the sign that Wihbrand would soon come to take her to the birch scented heat of the bath house. When they came dripping from the pool, Wihbrand carefully dried Wealhtheow's body with soft linen cloths. At first she had been loath to let him see her so, for that her belly bore the white lines of childbirth and her breasts, thrice suckled, were no longer as firm as they had been when she was a maid, yet he tended her as he would polish the wooden shape of one of the hof goddesses, with love and admiration, but no sense of lust drawn by her womanhood or quelled in disgust by the first signs of her aging, such as another man might have felt.

Wihbrand dressed her in white linen, wrapping a warm cloak of white wool about her shoulders, and rubbed and combed her long hair until it was free of tangles and only slightly damp to the touch. By the time the gudhe pulled on his own white breeches and tunic, the last light had almost faded from the sky, but he took Wealhtheow by the hand, leading her safely through the darkness to the gods' garth, and up the hill to the hof. The two fires that ran the length of the hof behind its pillars were lit, casting a ruddy glow upon the shining bronze shield rounds that hung by the harrow and bringing the tree gods' gilded eyes to gleaming life.

The tables had been carried out, leaving the hof empty save for the high seat at the far end, carved and gilded and hung with finely woven cloths of deep blue and red. Unferth and Guthhild stood by the high seat; the Woden's man wore his dark blue cloak and held his spear, but the spae wife was dressed as she had been at Wealhtheow's wedding, in her white dress fringed with thin plates of worked gold and her shoulders and breasts covered with masses of amber. Wihbrand led Wealhtheow straight to them, and Guthhild looked up at her, blue green eyes bright in her shadowed face.

"Are you ready?" She asked. Though her voice was soft, Wealhtheow had heard little of human speech in her three days in the woods, and the gudhija's words seemed to ring off the bronze shields by the harrow, echoing up to the high rafters.

"I am."

"Wihbrand tells me that he believes you have the gift of sight. Now if you are willing, you shall mount the high seat, and we shall prove whether you can learn more of this matter than we."

Wealhtheow wet her dry lips, swallowing hard and looking at Wihbrand. The gudhe's beautiful face was very still in the firelight as he met her eyes: no flicker of his light blue eyes or curve of his finely modeled mouth gave her any hint of what she could say. He had brought her to this, she realized; but her own will alone could bear her onwards.

"I am willing," Wealhtheow whispered.

The seat of the spae throne was as high as Wealhtheow's head, with a footrest jutting out below. Together, Unferth and Wihbrand boosted her up, and she settled herself upon the feather stuffed silken cushion. As a girl, she had climbed trees, but never felt the dizziness of height as she did now: it seemed to her almost as if she sat, not on a heavy oaken chair, but on a platform of birch branches swaying in the wind.

She gripped the smooth carven coils of the armrests, breathing deeply. Unferth looked up at her, his dark gray eyes barely a gleam beneath the shadow of his hood. Though she did not lean down to grasp his hand, it still seemed to Wealhtheow that she could feel his strength steadying her, a single well known touch amid the strangeness, and for that she was grateful.

Silently Wihbrand picked up a bag from the foot of the high seat and walked the length of the hall, casting handfuls of dried herbs into the fire on either side like a carl sowing grain into glowing furrows. The smoke rose up in gray streams, coiling into the dark air and spreading like a veil of thin linen before Wealhtheow's eyes. When he had trodden the length of the hall, Wihbrand turned and came back. There was a rod in his hand now, its end tipped with a golden eagle head. He stopped before the harrow, reaching out to tap on one of the hanging bronze rounds.

Though he barely seemed to brush it, its tone rang deep and powerful through the hof, shivering through the rafters and the hall pillars, trembling in the wood of the throne where Wealhtheow sat. As the echoes began to die away, Wihbrand touched the other round; its note was higher, sounding a bone chilling harmony to the first. A third pure note joined the other two as the voice of the deeper gong swelled again, rising high above them, then a fourth, low and raspy as the note of a great reed pipe. Wealhtheow saw that Guthhild and Unferth had both opened their mouths, chanting a single toned wordless drone in harmony above and below the gongs; and as they paused to draw breath, Wihbrand began to sing, his tenor voice high and pure.

"I call afar, to kin of old,
From world the horn to world rings out,
Roots 'neath mold run through nine worlds,
Mist rises high from mountain peak,
Mist rises high from mountain peak.
Now saddle up the steeds all gray,
From world the horn to world rings out,
Ride on to well of Wyrd the old,
Mist rises high from mountain peak...

Wealtheow's head was spinning, the sound of the song and the ringing of the gongs echoing within her skull; the thickening smoke mist was beginning to sparkle before her eyes, as though she had held her breath too long. She could see her hands resting pale on the dark carven wood of the spae throne, but she could no longer feel it solid beneath her touch.

"A woman weaves where waters run,
From world the horn to world rings out,
Her shuttle runs to runes unknown,
Mist rises high from mountain peak,
Mist rises high from mountain peak.
Her spindle draws the skein of thread,
From world the horn to world rings out,
Though she speaks little, sees she all,
Mist rises high from mountain peak...

It seemed to Wealhtheow now that the mists surrounded her: she could not see the glow of the long fires, nor the bright glitter of the bronze gongs, and their ringing was fading from her ears as though a ship bore her swiftly from the shore where the hof folk sang. Yet, though she could not see Unferth through the grayness, it seemed to her that she could still feel him standing dark and solid by her; and but for that, she would have given way to fear.

Though Wealtheow knew she was not moving, she felt as though she were rushing swiftly through the dark mists swift as falling, save that she was going forward. She could hear the sound of running waters beneath her now, rippling and murmuring quietly, like the waters of a fen stirred by soft winds; and it almost seemed to her that beyond that she heard the low sound of a woman weeping, and the hollow little splashes of teardrops dripping into a pool.

Wealhtheow felt herself slowing, then stopping, as the mist began to lift from her sight. Before her feet was a wide stretch of water, black as the darkest pools of a peat bog, but shining, though there was no moon above to light it, only grayness. She did not know how to name the strangeness of her feeling, for she knew that she still sat in the high seat in the hof, yet here she was standing, and could see nothing but the dark water and gray fog. When at last she heard Unferth's rough croak, it was as though from very far away, and she could not have sworn that she really heard it, or only dreamed it.

"Wealhtheow, dreaming in the depths do you hear me? Spae wife wise, seeker of Wyrd do you hear, and will you answer?"

"I hear," Wealhtheow murmured through numb lips. "I will answer."

"Wealhtheow, spae wife, what do you see? What do you hear?"

"I see black water before me, and the mists are all around. I hear the fen waters rippling, and the sound of a woman's tears."

"Wealhtheow, spae wife, gaze into the waters. Watch, and tell me what you see."

Wealhtheow looked into the black waters, her eyes drawn to the slow ripples of brightness over their depths. It seemed to her then that she saw a ship, ring prow rising high over the waves and bright shields hanging along its sides. A flock of swans swept before it, and above it towered great cliffs; the breakers foamed away from its fore stem. Men in shining mail coats, with golden boars wrought at the crests of their helmets, moving upon the deck with the rise and fall of the waves. Yet the one who towered at the tiller, standing apart from the others, was no human man. Though he, too, wore a byrnie of tight knit iron links, he stood a head and a half above the tallest of the warriors. His shoulders were broader than a man's; his face was that of a bear, but tinged sea green, and his hair dripped with water weed as though he had just risen from the depths of the ocean. He reached out a great clawed paw, lifting it palm upwards as if to touch Wealhtheow. Grendel! Wealhtheow thought, shivering in the cold of terror.

Does he lead a band to destroy us now? Yet the vision melted, all save the figure of the bear eoten from the waters. His byrnie shimmered into sea spray, and through that blurred mist she saw that he was fighting with another unearthly wight of like size, wet scaled and fanged: the two of them strove against each other with the strength of their limbs alone, and it seemed to her that they were evenly matched.

The mist was thickening again, though she strained her eyes; she thought that one of them was gaining the upper hand, but she could not tell which...Then she blinked, and the seeing was gone: there was only dark water before her, and gray cloud around.

"Well have we asked," Unferth's far off rasp floated to her, "and well been answered. Come back to us, Wealhtheow, from the depths of your dream; come back, spae wife, to the Middle Garth.

It seemed to Wealhtheow as though her bones had frozen into long staves of ice, her flesh no more than rime mist rising from them. She did not know how to move, how to come back... but she could hear the bright sound of singing like a golden thread stretching out to her through the fog, the words growing clearer and the swift beat pounding like a horse's hooves beneath her.

"Far you have flown, now fare you home,
Swiftly the falcon wings sweep you along,
Ride back the path as rode you out,
Far you have flown, now fare you home..."

Slowly Wealhtheow's sight cleared: the white clad figures of Guthhild and Wihbrand, the long glowing trenches of coals, Unferth dark beside her. She was shivering hard, as though she had stood long in the snow without cloak or shoes, and her numb hands were clenched too tightly on the wood of the spae seat for her to loose them by herself. Wihbrand reached up from one side and Unferth from the other, prying her fingers loose; the two men lifted her down as they had lifted her up, half carrying her over to one of the fires where Guthhild wrapped a thick fur lined cloak about her and thrust a piece of honey dripping bread into her hand.

"You have done very well," the gudhija said warmly. "Eat now, for you need it."

With the first few bites, Wealtheow's shivering began to ease and she could feel the strength flowing back into her chilled body. She looked up at the three of them, meeting Guthhild's blue green eyes, Wihbrand's light blue, and Unferth's deep gray in turn. "What did it mean?" Wealhtheow asked through chattering teeth. Wihbrand glanced questioningly at Guthhild, who bit her lip.

"I do not know," Guthhild admitted softly. "There is no doubt that you saw truly, looking into Frige's mere. But it is beyond me to know its meaning, or say whether Heorot's sorrow fetters will be loosened soon."

"You must not be too downcast," Wihbrand added. "Often it is so with spae sight: the gods show us truth, but that does not mean that we know all we must in order to read it rightly. But you have done well, Wealhtheow: do not give up hope."

IV

The morning after Hrethel's Winter nights feast dawned clear and fair, but freezing cold. A thick fur of frost layered the dead grass, its white tinged pink as the petals of a dog rose from the red light of the rising sun, and the muddy paths around the king's stead were hard as stone beneath the foot. Beowulf had slept the night on the floor of the house that once he had shared with Hygelac and Haethcyn. The king's two younger sons had better dwellings with their wives now, and Beowulf had the house to himself, but no bed could be found that he could stretch his length in; so he had wrapped himself in his reindeer hide blanket, and slept as if he were still making the long faring home.

Though the feasting and drinking had lasted until well after the moon was down, a group of men was already gathered outside the king's hall, carrying hunting arrows and spears, with bows slung over their backs and curved blowing horns hanging at their sides. Hrethel's three sons were there, and Ansuwulf and his brother Eofor, as well as Agilar and a few other warriors. By their feet sat three hounds, pointed gray ears pricked up and thick curly tails thumping against the ground. For a moment Beowulf hesitated, remembering how scornfully Agilar had spoken to him when there was hunting to be done before. But now, though his old tormentor had become a well grown young man, his curly gold brown head did not reach as high as the middle of Beowulf's chest, and his wide mouth twitched in a grimace that might have been fear as he saw Beowulf approaching.

He can do me no harm, and he never could have, Beowulf thought a thought tinged with sadness, like the first bluish gray bloom of mold on a loaf's brown crust: if he himself had not been so fearful of Agilar's cutting words, he would not have plunged into the rime cold sea, and in the end never have passed beyond the bounds of the Middle Garth. The other men drew back a step as well as Beowulf came up to them, save for Ansuwulf, barefooted on the frozen ground as always, who looked searchingly up into his eyes. It came to Beowulf then that he was wearing the bearskin cloak Paanja had given him over his tattered farmhand rags: Ansuwulf was seeking for a sign that the berserk wod had come late upon him. For a moment they stood so, the cold air clear and still as a great berg crystal about them.

Beowulf could not even hear the breathing of the other men or the rustle of their woolen cloaks, and though the short berserk seemed small as a child beside him now, Beowulf could see the might that shimmered around him like waves of heat rising from a bonfire. Of all the men about them, Ansuwulf seemed to have changed the least, save that he had grown more wolfish with the years, his close cropped red beard brindled with gray and the pupils of his gray eyes ringed with golden amber or perhaps it was only that Beowulf saw more clearly, so that the berserk's sharp nose was shadowed in his sight with the long point of the wolf's muzzle, his square palms blurring into clawed paws at the ends of his wolf narrow wrists.

"No," Beowulf said softly and it seemed to him that no other, save Ansuwulf, could hear his words. "I am a bear, yes; but not the Grim One's bear."

The berserk nodded, a quick jerk of his gray streaked blond head, and sound and movement came back to Beowulf's ears.

"Berki, will you hunt with us this day?" Hygelac asked. "If you have not had enough of wandering in the woods for a while, that is?"

Beowulf felt the prickling of the other men's nervous gazes along his skin, but when he glanced back at them, they dropped their eyes. Still, it was as if he could hear their thoughts: beyond Ansuwulf, there was not one of them who would choose to walk in the woods with him. But Hygelac's voice was anxious, its high clearness straining, and Beowulf could see the stress on his old friend's fine featured face. He fears that I no longer love him, for that he wedded Hygd when I was thought to be dead.

"I would gladly hunt with you," Beowulf answered. "I have no bow, nor did I learn to shoot one while I was away; but if someone will lend me a spear, I will wield that."

"Throwing or thrusting? We mean to go after elk, but there are no hounds like to these when running loose to bring an elk to stand eh, Thunarheall, Sceadhangrieg, Trolle?" Hygelac bent to pat the gray hounds, who wagged their tails more furiously, tilting their muzzles up to lick his hand. "We should easily come in close enough for a thrusting spear to be used. The rut may be nearly over, but we should be able to find a fierce bull who will give us some sport with horn and hoof though my prudent brother here says that he would rather down a young cow or a yearling who will give us tender meat."

"I have no taste for a tough old bull stinking of rut," Haethcyn said. "And as for a fight, I shall get better when the spring planting is done; I should rather clash my sword against another man's shield than the antlers of a beast." Hrethel's second son had a bow in his hand and a quiver of white feathered arrows slung over his shoulder. His deep green cloak, like those of the other men, was carefully pinned at the right shoulder to leave that arm free with a simple pin of black iron, though he was a king's son, for gold or silver would flash a warning to the great deer they hunted.

"As for myself," Herebeald broke in, "I shall take whatever the wood ruler maid sends my way." He smiled brightly, his white teeth gleaming in the bright cold air. "And if we wish to hunt, it were best if we were on our way soon. But here, Beowulf, you may take my spear, and I will be content with my bow."

Though the thrusting spear was broad shafted and broad headed, it felt like a twig in Beowulf's hand. He wondered if it would break beneath his grip when he used it but, after all, he was only going on the hunt to ease Hygelac's worried heart. Hygelac snapped his fingers, and the hounds sprang up, running forward in short bursts to cast about with their noses to the ground, then back to the path in front of the hunters as they walked to the wood.

Beowulf could not help but notice that, except for Hygelac, the other men kept a careful distance between themselves and him, and that weighted upon him, it seemed, more heavily than the scorn he had gotten from them in his youth. Agilar, in particular, stayed on the other side of the group, glancing sideways at Beowulf every so often like a farmer's dog awaiting a blow. This is not what I wanted, Beowulf thought this is not how I wished my homecoming to be. He remembered Agilar cheering him on in the swimming match, the first friendliness he had ever gotten from the other boy.

If he had only beaten Breca in the sea, then he would have come home to glad greetings and a place, at last, as a man among men... but now? Winter had come swiftly this year: only a few birches still glimmered like golden torches against the dark background of the night black pines, the frozen mushrooms were already sinking to black slime in the thick forest bed of brown needles and fallen birch leaves, and the icy air cut deep and clean into Beowulf's lungs with each breath.

Small birds twittered back and forth from the pine branches; it seemed to Beowulf that a note of warning sharpened their high voices, as if they were reminding each other that the leaves were dropping and the snows nearly upon them. When the hunters were well into the woods, Herebeald stopped by a shadowed outcropping of ruddy pink granite, laying a hand upon the rough stone where little crystals of rime still glittered. The hounds sat back on their haunches, mouths open and tongues hanging out: they were as thick coated as wolves, and a day that was cold to men was still summer warm to them.

"Hail to you, wood ruler, hallowed maid," Herebeald said, his voice soft beneath the rustling pine branches. "Here we give you our gifts, that you may give us yours in turn." He laid a finger ring of silver on the stone, uncorking the flask of birch wood that hung at his waist and pouring a stream of dark ale over it.

"Lend us one or two of your cattle, I bid you; for the Weather Geats have ever been your friends, and never fail to make you offerings when we come to hunt in your realm." A shaft of sunlight through the dark branches above lay full upon Herebeald, gleaming like a golden crown upon the blond braids knotted close to his head; its brightness seemed to lift him beyond himself, as though a god had stepped for a moment into his hide. But beside him, his dark haired brother Haethcyn was shadowed; and as Haethcyn stepped forward to lay his own gift upon the wood ruler's stone, Beowulf caught his breath, for it seemed to him that he could see the shadow moving with Haethcyn, like a carrion crow following so close that the shade of its wings covered its prey; the gray fletchings of his arrows were darkened as if with blood, and the words of the barrow rider came back to his mind.. "Spear god's choice shall spare one Spill one, his bane willed not. One gnaw flames of Wind God Woe for Hrethel grow then…"

"Haethcyn," Beowulf said, the words coming from his cold numbed lips without thought. "It were better if you did not go on this hunt, for there is ill luck about you, and I fear that you will come to harm this day."

Haethcyn turned swiftly to look up at him, blue eyes narrowed and mouth set firm beneath his neatly trimmed dark beard.

"You have been long away from the land of the Weather Geats," Hrethel's second son said calmly. "Have you then learned spae sight in your wanderings?"

Beowulf did not know what to say. As always, once the words had left his mouth, his sureness had gone with them. He did not wish to boast where he was not full certain, nor did he want to say anything more of it, for that it would set him even farther apart from the other men there.

Haethcyn watched Beowulf thoughtfully for a few moments, then said, "Well, if ill luck is upon me for this hunt, it matters little, for there is plenty of meat left from the Winter nights slaughter. And if men hid from every shadow, we should all be as fearful as the Danes of Heorot, who must be inside with their doors closed and latched every night before the last light of the Sun is gone from the sky." He stepped forward and put a round piece of Southern silver upon the wood ruler's stone next to the finger ring Herebeald had laid there, murmuring something that Beowulf could not hear.

When Hygelac, too, had made his offering, Herebeald said, "Now let us scatter on the woodland paths. It is likeliest that our hounds will flush an elk from its daytime bed, and there is no telling which way it will run. Let him who first hears their barking blow his horn; blow again if you see or hear the elk nearing you, twice if it is brought to stand and thrice if you have brought it down. Good hunting and good luck, all." He clapped three times, whistling sharply to the dogs. The largest of the three raised his head, casting about, then set off at a steady trot, followed by the two bitches.

The men broke off by ones and twos, Beowulf going with Hygelac. Though the smaller man was yet more graceful, Beowulf had learned a few things about moving in the woods, and his hard soled bare feet whispered more softly over the twigs and rotting needles than Hygelac's shoes. Hygelac led Beowulf up a narrow ridge of cracked rock and over a small hill, down again through a brook that swirled icy below Beowulf's knees. He hardly noticed the cold biting deep into his bare feet and calves, for he had forded deeper and wider streams on his way down from the North, many of them swollen with snow melt and bitter chill from the mountains.

They crossed a wide clearing, rustling loudly through the dry yellow grass; now and again, Hygelac would stop to point to a track and whisper, "These were made by a cow with two calves, but one of them was limping badly. A wolf or bear may have gotten it by now," or, "Here went a large bull he would be a fine quarry, if the hounds can sniff him out." From his long wandering, Beowulf had learned the spoor of beasts as well as Hygelac, but he said nothing: this hunt was too much like their old friendship for him to risk anything that might spoil it.

The Sun was nearly at her midday height when they first heard the low note of a horn floating through the woods. Both Beowulf and Hygelac froze at once; Hygelac cocked his head, then pointed.

"That way," he murmured. The two of them set off at a steady trot with spears angled down in front of them so as not to tangle in the trees, Hygelac leaping over rocks and fallen branches that Beowulf took in his stride. As they came to a small clearing, a higher toned horn sounded, closer to them the elk was running towards them. Hygelac grinned, taking a firmer grip on his weapon as the deep belling of the hounds came to their ears. "A little further onward! If that elk can be made to stand, Thunarheall, Scadhangrieg, and Trolle will do it, and with a bit of luck, we two will be the first in."

"No, halt here," a low voice said. Haethcyn stepped out, an arrow nocked and his bow ready to draw: standing stock still in his deep green and brown, neither Beowulf nor Hygelac had seen him behind the tree. "Halt, and hide, for it is coming straight this way. If it runs, I shall shoot; if it stands, you shall spear it."

"Fair enough," Hygelac nodded. Haethcyn went back behind his tree; Beowulf and Hygelac crouched behind a low thicket, ready to leap forward. Now they could hear the crashing of hooves and the barking of the hounds, coming straight towards them.

The elk burst into the clearing, running hard, its long ungainly legs almost a blur beneath its dark body. Beowulf had just time to see the three tined spread of its antlers, the rolling dark eyes and the greenish froth at its lips before he heard the thrumming twang of Haethcyn's bow. The young bull swerved. For half a heartbeat, Beowulf thought Haethcyn's arrow had found its mark, but then he heard the sharp cry from the thickets on the other side of the clearing, and the elk was leaping out of sight.

Hunting forgotten, Haethcyn dropped his bow and sprang forward, running through the sunlight to see what he had done. Hygelac was half a step behind him, and Beowulf followed, his heart filled with sick dread. Behind the tangle of bushes, Herebeald slumped face down on the ground, his bow broken beneath him and the foul stench of death already rising from his stained clothes.

Haethcyn drew a mighty bow, for his arrow had passed all the way through his brother's body; it lay on the brown needles a little way beyond Herebeald, the thin sharp silver edges of the black iron tip streaked with red and the gray fletching dark with blood. Haethcyn cried out, a great grieving shriek that shuddered through the pines like a sudden gust of sleet laden wind, and fell to his knees beside his brother's body.

"Herebeald! Herebeald! All the gods help me, what have I done?"

Haethcyn grasped Herebeald's shoulders, lifting him up; Herebeald's fair head rolled to the side, a little blood dribbling from the corner of his slack mouth. His blue eyes were still open, shifting like glass beads in their sockets as his head moved.

"My brother, my brother," Haethcyn mourned. "Trolls take that ill wight that guided my aim; I should have turned back at the wood ruler's stone, but I thought it was only myself I risked." He laid Herebeald's body carefully down, then looked up at Beowulf, eyes wide and wild. "Why did you not warn him?" Haethcyn shouted suddenly. "Thunar curse your sight, he was the one in danger!"

Beowulf stepped back a pace, stunned by the sight before him. He could not speak, for the guilt Haethcyn had flung at him cut at his throat like a splintered bone. Farther on, another horn blew, its deep call ringing mournful through the trees. Haethcyn half raised his hands, as if to shut the sound from his ears. Slowly his face untwisted, settling into a grim mask that was the more frightening for its calmness.

"Blow the horn thrice," he said to Hygelac. "Let them know that the hunt is ended."

Slow tears dribbled down Hygelac's cheeks and into his short golden beard, but he made no sound as he fumbled the strap of his hunting horn over his head and lifted it up. The three notes shivered through the sharp winter air, their sound dying slowly away. The way back through the woods was slow, for Haethcyn bore his brother's body on his shoulders, and even though he soon grew so tired that he stumbled upon every stick and stone in his way, he would not suffer any other to take his burden.

Nor did anyone speak, though often Beowulf caught the dark sideways glances of the other men flicking away as soon as his eyes met theirs. Even the hounds slunk along with their tails straight down, rather than curled proudly over their backs, and now and again one of them would let out a small whine. The Sun was setting by the time the hunters made their weary way up the slope to Hrethel's garth, the buildings and wooden palisade poles casting long shadows over the brown ground. Those folk who were still tending the smoking fires and butcher cauldrons outside stopped to stare, but no one dared to speak. The king of the Weather Geats sat in his high seat with a horn in his hand, talking with Wynefrith, Garhild, and Hygd. Their voices fell silent at once, taking in the dreadful sight as Haethcyn staggered in, the last light through the open hall door falling full upon Herebeald's body.

"My son..." Wynefrith murmured. With the last of his strength, Haethcyn tottered up to stand in front of his father, easing his brother's stiffened corpse down before Hrethel's feet. Then, as though he had spent the last of his own life in the effort, he slumped down to his knees, his arms trailing over Herebeald's pierced chest in a strengthless embrace.

"Father," he croaked. "I have slain my brother. I did not see him, there behind the thicket..." Haethcyn's voice trailed off into a choked sob.

Hrethel's face shattered like glass striking a stone. The gold bound aurochs horn dropped from his hand, a dark flood of ale pouring into the straw like blood from a severed limb. His shoulders shook, but no tears flowed from his eyes. Beowulf had heard tales of men who guested with the alfs, and stepping back to the Middle Garth, aged and crumbled to dust with their first footfall on the earth, for that hundreds of years had passed in the seeming of a single night.

Just so swiftly, Hrethel seemed to grow old as he looked down on his two sons, the slain and the slayer. Wynefrith crossed her arms over her breast as though she were holding her pain to her like a babe, rocking slightly forward and back in her chair. Hygd's face was white in the fire lit gloom of the hall, her violet eyes black with horror as they flickered fearfully from Haethcyn to Hygelac to Beowulf.

"Haethcyn, Haethcyn," Garhild sobbed. Heedless of her fine sea green linen dress with its silken embroidery, she dropped forward from her chair to kneel in the ale soaked straw beside her husband. Her linen headdress fell off as her head dropped, dark braids hanging forward to hide her face like a mourning veil; but Haethcyn shook off her embrace with a twitch of his shoulders. Desperately Garhild looked up at Hrethel. "King Hrethel, spare your son! He could not have done this deed from ill will, for he loved his brother dearly."

"No," Haethcyn said, his voice bleak with despair. "I did not do it knowingly. I would rather that his arrow had pierced my heart. And yet I did it and what were gild can I pay that would be worth my brother's blood? I must die, that Herebeald not fare alone and unavenged to the green worlds of the gods. If you will not wield the blade, let Hygelac do it, that brother be avenged by brother, as is fitting."

For a long moment Hrethel stared down at them. He coughed painfully, as though his throat were full of bitter dust and ashes.

"Am I Woden, that I should raise up one son to take vengeance on a second for a third slain?" He asked. "A fight without repayment cruelly ill done, heart and soul wearying; yet so the atheling must part from life unavenged." Hrethel raised his eyes as if he lifted a great weight, staring down the hall at the fading daylight beyond the door. He spoke slowly, his voice dragging like the stumbling of weary feet. "Thus sadly an old man must bide, when his bairn rides young on the gallows: so he utters a sorrow song, when his son hangs to joy the ravens, and he, though old and wise, may do nothing to help him. Ever is remembered, every morning, his son's far faring; he awaits eagerly no other heir in his burg, when the one, forced by his deeds, has sought out death. Now I shall see, sorrowful and careworn, my son's chambers, the wasted wine hall and the wind swept bed, bereaved of joy. The rider sleeps, the warrior in his grave; there is no sound of harp, no games in the garth, as once there were." Hrethel looked down again. "Haethcyn, you must sit in the high seat of the Weather Geats' hall now, though it bring you no gladness. See that a mound is raised for your brother by Swerting's barrow, and that he is buried with all those things he loved, horse and hound, sword and spear, shield and bow; set a mail coat about his shoulders, and adorn his arms with bright rings, that he go to the gods as befits the son of a king. As for me, I shall go to my bed, croaking a sorrow song after my son: wide fields and dwelling steads, they all seem too roomy to me now. But Herebeald's chamber shall be of a fit size to hold two."

Hrethel stood, walking away with the rigidly straight tread of a man who had drunk too deeply to see his hand before his face. Wynefrith gazed after her husband, then rose herself.

"Beowulf," she commanded, "we have one matter to see to here, and then you shall bring Herebeald's body to his house. Garhild and Hygd, you shall come with me, for we must wash my son and dress him for his last faring. But now, Haethcyn..."

"What am I to do?" Haethcyn asked. "I have lost brother and father at once: if Hrethel does not will it that I be slain for my deed, should I not fare afar as a wretched man or run to the woods as a warg, and leave the king's seat to Hygelac, who is stained by no ill?"

"You heard your father's words," Wynefrith replied. "It was to you he yielded the high seat, and there you shall sit, with all of us to witness. For I know, all too well, what is in Hrethel's soul, and that it shall not be long before we drink his burial arvel together with Herebeald's. Woe to the house of Swerting, and to the Weather Geats, that ever such ill came upon us! But if we do not gather our strength soon, our ills shall grow worse, for these tidings cannot be kept from Ongentheow's ears, and he will not hold back from striking if he thinks our armies are weakened by this." She reached down to grasp Garhild's thin hands in her own, raising Haethcyn's wife from the floor. "Go you back to our bedchamber and fetch a pitcher of the fine mead from the small keg by the door it is yours to pour it, for you shall be queen over the Weather Geats now."

Mutely Garhild did as Wynefrith had commanded, though when she came back, she had to hold the silver pitcher in both hands and, even so, she was shaking so badly that several little streams of mead dripped down from its glittering rim like trails of gilding. Wynefrith picked up Hrethel's horn, holding it out for the younger woman to fill. Much of the mead slopped over the side, but Wynefrith paid no mind to the sticky wetness running over her fingers.

"Rise, Haethcyn, and take your seat," Wynefrith said. "As for your wyrd from this day, the gods may deem as they will; but while you live, you must be king in the land of the Geats. Thus shall you pay your brother's geld: by warding his folk, by lessening their woes, and bettering their weal."

Bracing himself on the high seat, Haethcyn pushed himself up, stepping carefully around Herebeald's body.

"May Tiw and Thunar, Woden and Frea Ing, witness that I did not will this, and do not wish it," he said hoarsely. "Yet for my father's sake, I shall take this seat and hold it as best I may."

He sat down, staring out past them into the hall as though he thought to see a gallows rope dangling from the rafters. The stains from Herebeald's death voiding had soaked through the left shoulder of his cloak, and the dark rings beneath his eyes stood out like soot stains against his gray skin: in his fouled hunting clothes, he did not look like a king, but like an outlaw dragged in from the woods. Wynefrith lifted the horn to him.

"Drink the heir's mead, Haethcyn, king of the Weather Geats. We all stand as witnesses, ready to speak for your right and uphold your rule."

Though Beowulf knew how sweet Wynefrith's best mead was, Haethcyn's mouth twisted as though it had been laced with wormwood when he had choked a swallow of it down. He passed the horn to Hygelac, who raised it up.

"My brother, I was with you and I know that you did not seek to kill Herebeald, nor to hide your blame when the deed was done. Until men can strike at Wyrd's heart with swords, there is no vengeance to be taken for our brother, nor shall I ever seek to spill your blood, but shall stand by you in every way. Hail to you, Haethcyn, king of the Weather Geats." Hygelac drank, and gave the horn to Beowulf.

"As Hygelac spoke, so he spoke for me as well," Beowulf said slowly. "I swore to uphold your father in all things when I came first to this hall; I swear the same to you now. Hail to you, Haethcyn, king of the Weather Geats."

Hygd took the horn from Beowulf's hand. Her chill small fingers touched his on its sticky curve, and Beowulf felt a great sorrow welling up within him. He wanted to take her hand in his own as he had done when they were children, to warm it in his and hold her tightly to him and yet he feared that his touch would crush her, for her fingers felt frail as a dew glistening spiderweb in the sunlight beneath his grasp. But Hygd did not meet his gaze, though he could see the tears pooling deep in her violet eyes.

"Hail to you, Haethcyn, king of the Weather Geats," she repeated. "May no sorrow ever darken your reign again, for it has begun with enough sorrow to sate the heart of the harshest troll."

"My son," Wynefrith said when Hygd had sipped from the horn and given it on to her. "It is a cruel burden you bear, but know this: though your hand loosed Herebeald's bane shot, there are none who think your heart guided it. Rule well these lands your father has left you, as I said before, and may all the gods and goddesses bless your reign hail to you, Haethcyn, king of the Weather Geats."

Garhild stood with her lower lip clenched white between her teeth, staring down at Herebeald's body. With her headdress lying in the straw and braids disheveled, her dress stained dark with ale where she had knelt beside her husband, the small slim woman looked like nothing so much as a maiden of twelve winters being harshly rebuked for spoiling her feast clothes. But Wynefrith took her by the wrist, guiding her firmly to the seat beside Haethcyn, and pushed the horn into her hands.

"Hail to you, Haethcyn, king of the Weather Geats, my husband," Garhild whispered. Then, as though she could not keep herself from looking, her eyes turned back downward to where Herebeald lay, still and white save for the trickle of dried blood crusted at the corner of his mouth, before the high seat that would have been his. "May the gods and goddesses help us all."

Haethcyn reached out to clasp his wife's hand in his own, his sleeve quivering with the fine tremors running along the muscles of his arms. As he looked at Garhild, the grim clench of his dark bearded jaw eased a little, and he took the horn from her before her shaking hand could spill it.

"Hail to you, Garhild, my wife, queen of the Weather Geats," he answered her. "Thanks be to Frige for bringing you to me, for without you, my reign would truly be bereft of all joy."

By the time the folk of Hrethel's garth had gathered in the hall, the king's kin were all dressed in mourning garb of black and deep blue save for Beowulf, for whom no clothes big enough had been found: he had to hide his travel worn rags beneath a dark blanket pinned up as a square cloak for him. There was no sound of laughter; no poet struck ringing chords from his harp, and no voice was raised until Ansuwulf stepped forward into the middle of the hall. For once, the berserk was not wearing his gray fell, but had changed it for a hooded blue black that shadowed his wolfish face. He did not speak; instead he began to sing at once, his rough dark voice resonating through the hall with a might that sent shivers down Beowulf's back.

"Hwaet! I shall sing a sorrow tale,
of awesome born athelings, oaks of the sword,
of Wyrd's skeins cruelly winding about them,
of brother, though blameless, to brother the death..."

Beowulf listened in awe: for in that time between Herebeald's death and the serving of the hall meal, Ansuwulf had put the tale into song, winding it about with words like a jeweler winding an arm ring about with gold wires; and yet everything the berserk sang was true, down to the whining of the hounds about Herebeald's corpse. Beneath Ansuwulf's voice, Beowulf could hear the soft sobbing about the hall. Haethcyn did not weep, but even in the low firelight, Beowulf could see his knuckles whitening as he gripped the arm rests of the high seat. Hygelac, though, wept without hindrance, the tracks of tears shining fire red down his face. Hrethel's youngest son had drunk deep already that night, but none would hold it to his shame.

"And no ease comes to kin of the Geats,
our eye dew drops till ice rimes the fields.
Our weeping draws the wolves to our gates,
the Swedes, who would swing their swords to our bane,
boldened and laughing at losses we mourn.
In Herebeald's memory, hold then to his kin,
that no higher Hrethel's harms may yet wax.
Hold fast, and hail the heir in the king's seat,
Hail you, Haethcyn, hail, Weather Geats' king!"

In the ringing silence when Ansuwulf's song was done, Haethcyn sat straighter, pushing back a dark sleeve and pulling a gold ring from his arm as Garhild bore the eagle tipped aurochs horn to the berserk. Ansuwulf lifted it high, chanting more loudly again, "Hail you, Haethcyn, hail, Weather Geats' king!" He drank, then walked deliberately over to Eofor, who sat at the head of one of the long benches, and handed the horn to his brother. Slowly Eofor rose, and Beowulf held his breath.

If Eofor spoke against Haethcyn now, Beowulf had no doubt, there would be slaughter in the hall. The warrior turned the horn this way and that, looking into its depths as though he sought an answer in the frothing ale. Ansuwulf's gaze never left the face of his taller brother; and Beowulf was struck for the first time by how much alike they looked. Eofor's features were heavier, his bones broader, his hair ruddy instead of gray blond and his red beard bushy rather than close trimmed Wonred's sight had been keen, to name his elder son Boar and his younger son Wolf, as though he had looked upon the fetch beasts who ran before them to show the shapes of their souls. But for all the brothers' sameness was blurred, they still bore the mark of a single stamp, even as Hygelac and Haethcyn and dead Herebeald did. At last Eofor lifted the horn, his thick ringed fingers clutching it tightly. His voice was dull with sorrow; there was no doubt that he took no joy in the words that he must speak.

"Hail to you, Haethcyn, king of the Weather Geats," Eofor said, and drank deeply from the horn. Beowulf felt his own breath sigh out of him, matched by the softer breath of Hygd and Hygelac's gusty pant of relief.

After that, each of the free folk of the king's garth, from the heroes of Hrethel's guard down to the girl little better than a bondsmaid who helped old Amma knead her loaves, drank and hailed their new ruler. The horn only went about the hall once: until Hrethel had died in his chamber or chosen to come forth again, he could not be hailed, and none had the heart to speak of Herebeald, not so soon, not with Haethcyn sitting gray faced and silent in the high seat and his brother's body still stiff and cold above ground.

The women of the kingly household left early, for Wynefrith said they still had matters to tend to that night; nor did many other folk linger over their feast. It was not long before Beowulf and Hygelac were alone in the hall save for the gray hounds crunching meaty bones and other leavings in the rustling straw beneath the table. Hygelac reached for the silver pitcher that Garhild had left on the table, nearly overbalancing from his seat as he did so. Beowulf steadied him, grasping the pitcher and filling both of their drinking horns. Hygelac lifted his vessel, drinking deep; thin streams of ale spattered out at the corners of his mouth, streaking his short golden beard with ruddy brown. He thunked the silvered end of the horn down on the table, resting it upright in his fist.

"Berki, my friend, my oath brother," Hygelac said. His tongue stumbled thickly over the words, and the dim firelight could not hide the network of red cracks already searing the whites of his eyes. "What a shitty homecoming for you, ai? Firsht...first finding Hygd married, and now this." He banged the end of the horn on the table and lost his grip; it toppled over, pouring a wave of ale across the scarred dark wood. "And married to me, of all men." He gripped Beowulf's shoulder, tightening his hand until the corded muscles stood up sharply from his forearm. "Berki, you should hate me." Hygelac began to weep again, the tears flowing painfully from his reddened eyes.

"Never say that, Hygelac!" Beowulf answered, a pang of worry running unseen and painful as alf shot through his body. He had seen his oath brother so drunk before, but not like this: ale usually made Hygelac merrier, so that he laughed even after he had had to cast it up.

"All men thought me dead, and for good cause. And had I died in the waves, as Breca thought, I could have wished no better husband for her than yourself."

And had you not married Hygd could I have husbanded her now? Beowulf wondered. For the words of Ran's daughter still rang clear in his soul, their echoes rising louder within the well of his skull:

"If I have as much might over you as I think, I lay this on you: may you have no joy from that woman whom you await on the land, nor shall you have your delight with any woman within the Middle Garth's ring!"

"I should have waited longer," Hygelac slurred. "It was only a little over two years, and I should have known that Breca would never outshwim… outswim you." Hygelac shook his head, as if to clear a little of the ale fumes from it, then reached for Beowulf's horn. Beowulf let him drink, taking a deep draught himself when Hygelac gave it back. His own head was starting to whirl a little, for he had not tasted the strong ales of a king's feasting since he was cast up on the Finn shores, but the feeling was welcome: it did not cure the gnawing pain of his sorrows, but it dulled them a little, like unspun wool wrapped about the cutting edge of a blade.

"What curse is upon Hrethel's house now," Hygelac went on, "that brother must wrong brother so grievously? Ai, poor Haethcyn: if it had been my hand that fired that shot, I should not have the strength to live. It is bad enough knowing how I betrayed you in love, Berki." He paused, swallowing hard, and said again, "What curse is upon Hrethel's house?"

The curse the barrow rider spoke: the words tingled at the end of Beowulf's tongue. But even with the ale working in him, and though Hygelac might be too drunk to remember what he said in the morning, he knew better than to speak them aloud. For, if he had heard the night farer's verse and understood it rightly, one more of Hrethel's sons had yet to be slain and there was no saying whether it might be Hygelac or Haethcyn. At the same time, a more grievous thought came to Beowulf, so that the half full horn tilted in his hand, sloshing another dark ripple over the wet table. Did I bear that curse into this hall, when I entered it last night? If I had gone on, taking the tracks of my feet elsewhere, would Herebeald still live, and Hrethel still hold his kingship in frith and joy? With the sureness of ale, he knew now that there was some tie between the black cloaked rider on his gray horse and the shadow he had seen behind Haethcyn that morning the unseen hand that had guided Herebeald's bane shot to its mark more surely than any living archer could have aimed.

"Don't...don't washte that, Berki. Waste it. Whatever." Hygelac grabbed the horn from Beowulf's hand again and drank. "If the Swedes strike before the snow falls too thickly to march, our hall could be without ale a long time. For I think our luck has already left us, and the gods have turned their fashes...faces from us."

Beowulf shook his head. He could see it now, the glimmer about the Geats' great hall, the brightness around Hygelac himself, like the rays struck from polished gold by the Sun.

"Not now, and not for a lengthy while yet," he said. He took the ale horn back. It was light in his hand, nearly empty. He poured the rest of the pitcher's contents into it.

"And Father, my dear father, how could he give up like that? I never thought I'd live to shee...see the day I called Father a coward. Trollsh take him, isn't it bad enough for Herebeald to fall, without him crawling off to die like a sick dog in the straw? What manner of inheritance is that for him to leave us?" Hygelac pounded his fists bruising hard on the table.

"He was right, that there should be no more slaying of kin by kin," Beowulf answered gently. "Because he will not revenge himself upon his own blood, and there can be no bettering for the harm that was done what man could live with that? If there were fighting now, he could run to the forefront and hope to fall thus, but it is not time for us to strike against the Swedes. Instead Hrethel has turned the blade of his sorrows inward. Be sure, that by taking that woe upon himself, he seeks to spare both Haethcyn and you from what must otherwise follow, and offers his death in Haethcyn's place! That is not cowardice, but the last act of a man who loves his sons." Beowulf drank deeply from the horn, and passed it back to Hygelac, who drained it. Taking the empty vessel from Hygelac, Beowulf laid it carefully down on the table and clasped Hygelac's icy hand in his own. The fires were burning low now, the hall growing swiftly cold, and through their grip, Beowulf could feel Hygelac beginning to shiver: he would have to take him to his house soon.

"And what about you?" Hygelac asked, looking up sharply. "Are you going to stay here? No one would blame you for going back to your father's hall at Hroesnabeorh, not now, not after..." His voice trailed off, and he blew his nose hard on a corner of his cloak.

"I do not know," Beowulf said slowly. "In truth, I had not thought about it."

"I can't ashk...can't ask you to stay, to watch my child growing in Hygd's womb where yours should be. I know your father was rough of words to you before, but he will speak with the other edge of his tongue now that he sees what you have become. Berki, do you want to go home?"

Beowulf thought on it. To stay, as Hygelac had said; to see Hygd's belly swelling with Hygelac's babe yet that he might learn to bear, for that Hygelac was doing well by Hygd and they seemed glad enough together. But to live among men who had scorned him and now feared him, when he might go to a hall where they would know him only by his lineage and whatever deeds he might do now; that was another matter. At Hroesnabeorh, what Beowulf had been would not wind about to trip him, nor what he had become overshadow him so darkly.

Yet he had sworn to uphold Haethcyn, whose grasp upon the Weather Geats was still by no means firm, for all Ansuwulf had brought the folk of Hrethel's garth to witness his taking of the high seat. And more, Hygelac had taken Beowulf as his man when no one else, not even Beowulf's own father, would have him; and if the barrow rider's stave threatened Hygelac's life, then should Beowulf not stay beside his friend and drighten until that dark spae had been averted or fulfilled, if it was beyond Beowulf's strength to shift it? But, deep within, Beowulf wondered: if he had borne the dark farer's curse to Hrethel's hall, would it be loosed if he left?

"I do not know," Beowulf said again. "I must stay at least until Herebeald is laid in his mound, for I think my strength shall be needed in raising it. And then my father shall surely come for the burial arvel, and we shall speak then of whether my sword shall serve better in Ecgtheow's shield wall at the eastern marches, or beside you, whatever may betide."

"As for myself, I would have you by me in frith and battle." Hygelac's words were growing slower now, yawns swallowing one in three of them. When the ale reached the point of putting him to sleep, it often came on quickly, and his heart had been grievously wearied that day. "But I cannot ask you to stay, not with Hygd...Hygd bearing my bairn..."

Hygelac's head drooped, his clenched fist on the table falling open like that of a child drifting into sleep. He mumbled something more, but Beowulf could not make out the words. Then Hrethel's youngest son put his head down on the table and began to snore in earnest, the sigh of his breath rising and falling like wind through tall rocks. Beowulf sat for some time, watching Hygelac. Even in his drunken slumber, his golden braid and beard half soaked through with spilled ale, he had the look of a man of atheling blood not only in his strong clean features, but in the way his open heart and lively mind had already shaped the lines of his young face, as surely as years of salt spray and squinting into the sun would mark the face of a sailor.

Herebeald had been much the same, but more thoughtful: no surprise, in one who had known from his youngest years that he was likely to inherit his father's rule, and been raised for that task with Wynefrith's careful attentions. Haethcyn he was wiser still than his elder brother had been, but Beowulf remembered the coldness of his redes with aching clarity. Men might follow him for Hrethel's sake, and in time because he had proven himself well, but he would not gain their love as easily as Herebeald had, as Hygelac might. And if one of them, Hygelac or Haethcyn, had to fall, which would Beowulf choose?

For himself, he would have Hygelac living, even if Haethcyn's death were the price of it. But Ongentheow was a cunning foe, and Hygelac's boldness often overstepped the mark to rashness: better, for the Weather Geats, to have a drighten who was careful of thought and not easily lured to foolish deeds by a wily opponent? For Wynefrith's redes could guide either son well in times of frith, but she could not order Hygelac's warriors on the battlefield, nor be there in the thick of fighting to warn him when the old Swede was beguiling him into a trap. As all a youth of kingly kin should be, Hygelac could not be matched but even Beowulf, dearly as he loved his oath brother, was not sure that Hygelac would be the best ruler for his folk. Wyrd works as she will, Beowulf said to himself. But, the gods be thanked, that is not my choice to make!

He stood, bending over to lift Hygelac's limp body in his arms. Hrethel's son stirred and muttered something in his sleep, but did not waken as Beowulf carried him easily out of the hall and through to Hygelac's new house, shifting him to one arm and tapping lightly on the door. Perhaps Hygd would still be tending to Herebeald's body; then Beowulf could simply take her husband back to the house where they had slept before, which at least was warmer than the hall, and with plenty of blankets. The door opened, and Hygd, a small shadow in the dimness, looked up at Beowulf. Seeing her husband draped over his arm, she made a little noise, her mouth opening as if to gasp.

"He is merely drunk," Beowulf told her. "And that is hardly strange, after what he has witnessed today."

Hygd's delicate lips twisted into a reluctant smile. "Best for him, I think, to sleep and forget for a little time, though he will be the worse for it when he wakes tomorrow. Come, bring him in here."

The house Hygelac and Hygd shared was large and fine, its walls plastered within and hung with tapestries. The fires must have been burning all day, for in spite of the freezing night air, it was very warm inside. Beowulf carried Hygelac through the main room to the smaller sleeping chamber, holding him while Hygd pulled back the furs and blankets, then laying him gently down so that she could cover him. When they went back into the larger room, Beowulf would have taken his leave then, but Hygd took two silver cups and a silver pitcher with a golden rim from one of the chests along the walls, filling the pitcher from a small keg.

"Sit here with me for a little while, if you will," she said, pouring the two cups full.

Beowulf settled himself awkwardly on a bench. Finely smoothed and carved as the pale birch planks were, he was no more comfortable on it than he had been in any farmer's hut, his long legs bending awkwardly and the wood creaking beneath his weight. He held the silver cup carefully in his fingers, turning it about to look at the raised design of deep lobed leaves and strange bunches of fruit.

"From the south?" he asked.

"Aye. We got it from the same trader that brought us the wine what do you think of it?"

Beowulf sipped carefully from the cup. The deep red southern drink was something like fruit beer, strong as good mead at least, he could taste the fruit, but no honey sweetened its dryness. He was not sure if he liked it, but Hygd was looking up at him nervously, her fingers twisting in her lap as if she were turning an unseen spindle, so he smiled and told her that it was good. They sat in uncomfortable silence for a few moments, neither daring to look straight at the other. It was Hygd who broke the stillness at last.

"Berki...you were there, and saw what happened. Is there any chance that Haethcyn might have...?" She did not speak the words, as though the thought was too awful to taste in her mouth.

Beowulf shook his head firmly. "None. Haethcyn could not have seen his brother through the thicket: Hygelac and I did not." He paused: why had Herebeald not hailed them when they joined Haethcyn? Unless Haethcyn and Herebeald had already taken their places. "Even if Haethcyn had known Herebeald was there, and wished him ill, no living man could have made that blinded shot. But I think we were all following the sounds of the horns. Herebeald must have seen Haethcyn and Hygelac and I, yes. But I think he wished to surprise his brothers by felling the elk unexpectedly from his hiding place: he would have laughed greatly over that, when Haethcyn saw that the arrow piercing it had gone in from the wrong side."

"That is good to know. I did not truly think that the slaying was murder, but, deep in my heart, I feared for Hygelac, for there is no question but that there are men among the thanes of the Geats who would follow him rather than Haethcyn, if the choice were granted them."

"Yet it shall not be while Haethcyn lives," Beowulf stated. "For I know that Hygelac loves his brother, and holds no hate against him for Herebeald's fall."

"At least that is well," Hygd sighed. She tilted her head back, looking up into Beowulf's face, and he wanted to close his eyes against her beauty white skin, velvety as an untouched rose petal; the golden glitter of her brows, finer than the most delicately worked filigree over her violet eyes; the soft curve of her cheek and the straight short line of her nose, and the flawless molding of her lips, that would have been so warm against his own.

The thick coils and looping braids of her white gold hair it must be long enough to reach her knees when she brushed it out now glimmered bright, shadowed but not hidden by the fine linen of her dark blue mourning headdress. She had taken off the ropes of amber about her neck, but still bore a single piece: the glowing golden apple that Beowulf had first given her when they were children, on the same dainty silver chain that she had worn for eleven years.

"Berki, I am sorry," Hygd said. "If I had any hope that you were yet alive, if Breca had not sworn on the holy stone that he saw you dragged beneath the waves, I should never have thought of marrying another, not even Hygelac."

"Breca did not lie, and you did no wrong," Beowulf answered heavily. "As for Hygelac do you love him?"

"Not as I love you," Hygd said. "But he loves me, and is good to me, and the father of my child...that is to say, yes."

"It is well enough, then," Beowulf sighed.

No tear dropped from Hygd's dark eyes, but they glistened the more brightly in the light from the fire burning in the middle of the floor, like gold rimmed cups filled to brimming.

"Berki, marriages have been broken without shame before. If you would have me, Hygelac and I may yet be parted."

Her words struck Beowulf like a hard blow in the pit of his stomach, so that he must struggle to gasp air back into his lungs. He opened his mouth to answer her yes, but no sound came out, as if a cord had been drawn tight about his throat. Instead, he took Hygd's hand in his. Carefully as he held her, and her slender fingers felt like brittle sticks beneath his own: the least touch of his strength would shatter them, he knew. Nor could he help thinking again of how he had wrestled with Heofonglowe in play, how he had clenched her eoten strong body to him in the spasms of lovemaking, so tightly that the staves of their ribs creaked. And Hygd was small even for a daughter of Ash and Elm: if Beowulf were once to forget himself in bed, then she might as well have been shaped from flowers and glass for what his grasp would do to her and Heofonglowe's curse hung upon him like a weighty coat of ring mail that he could not shake from his shoulders.

He had just seen how such a shadow could turn a man's deeds to ill; how, then, could he risk Hygd's life in his grip, when he had promised years ago that she should never have reason to be afraid of him? Besides that, there was Hygelac, whose soft snores murmured wordless pleas through the door to the sleeping chamber, and the whole clan of the Weather Geats' kings to think of. If Hygd left Hygelac now, it would seem to many that she feared what ill luck might come of Haethcyn's unwilling brother slaying, and that would weaken the kingdom as surely as if a wyrm gnawed at its living roots beneath the earth. As well, Hygelac loved Hygd, and his child was growing in her womb: how could Beowulf heap further sorrows upon him? Nor do you know, a thought whispered in his skull like a traitor murmuring in a darkened hall, which of Hrethel's remaining sons shall be spared and which is doomed to die.

"I love you, Hygd," Beowulf said sadly. "And while I live, I shall desire no other woman within the Middle Garth, but you must stay at Hygelac's side, for he has great need of you now. I wish with all my heart that our threads had been woven otherwise, yet not even the gods can scratch away the staves that Wyrd has risted."

Hygd's hand tightened on Beowulf; her knuckles whitened with her grip, but to him, her desperate clutching felt like the bare flicker of a butterfly's wings.

"You are right, as you must be," she said, her high voice clear and steady, as befitted the bride of a king's son. "Yet o Berki, how I wish that we had been wedded!"

She turned on the bench to embrace him with all her strength, pressing her face into the swell of his chest. Carefully as a jeweler touching a thread thin piece of gold wire with solder, Beowulf put his arms around Hygd, making sure that their full weight did not rest upon her slender shoulders. They sat like that for a little time without speaking.

Beowulf knew, as he was sure she did, that they would not have another such moment: hereafter, they could not risk so much as a whisper that their old betrothal had, after all, borne fruit. Perhaps it would be best, after all, if he left the king's garth to go back to his father's home, where at least he and Hygd would not have to look upon each other's faces every day, or speak of the many matters concerning war band and realm. After a time, Hygd straightened herself, pulling away from Beowulf and sipping from the silver wine cup that had rested forgotten on the bench beside her.

"Tomorrow," she said briskly, "I shall send the women to you, for you must have fitting clothes by the time that Herebeald is laid in his mound and his funeral feast held. It will not do for one of the heirs to the rule of the Weather Geats to look as though he traded trousers and tunic with a peasant and one half his size, at that."

"Heirs?" Beowulf said, startled. "But I am not." Then he thought on it a moment: he was the son of Hrethel's daughter and the king's fosterling as well; and should Haethcyn and Hygelac both fall with no grown children of their own to follow them, he was in truth the nearest kinsman of the kingly line. Before, he had never thought of such things, but now, with one of Hrethel's sons fallen and a second death doomed... "May Frea Ing and the Frowe ward Hygelac and the child in your womb for many years! Whatever I may have been born for, it was not to be king."

Hygd's pale brows drew down, as though her sight were turning within.

"None can surely know what Wyrd has shaped for their day until night has fallen. But be that as it may, you still need new clothes. Now I think it were best for you to go to your house, for there is much work yet to do: Herebeald's mound must be raised while his body is still fit to bear to it, and the drightens of the Weather Geats must hear that they have a new king." She rose, and Beowulf stood with her, looking down at her dark veiled crown of braids that glimmered like gold beneath deep waters. "Goodnight, my bear, and may your dreams bring tidings of better hope than we have had this day."

The digging began in the morning, out in the field where the long dry grass rustled over the low barrow mounds and against the feet of the boulders ringing the hidden earth graves. The rune stone on Ansugrimar's barrow stood out dark against the gray sky; now and again a gust of wind spattered a sprinkling of sleet into the faces of the diggers. Though Hygelac's greenish white face showed how ill he was from the last night's drinking, and once or twice he leaned on the haft of his shovel as though he would be sick, he worked as grimly as any man there. Beside him, Beowulf heaved away great shovel fulls of earth without ceasing, chewing deep into the ground. The sound of axes rang out from the wood like dull bells: those men who were not digging were hewing trees for building the underground burial chamber in which Haethcyn and his father would be laid. Towards midday, the women came out bringing food and drink for the men, fresh sausages and bread and small beer. Wynefrith carried Beowulf's platter to him herself, squatting down beside him as he ate.

"Berki," she said, "if you wish to be the one to bring the tidings to your father, you have that right."

"I shall be needed to carry stones for the cairn, and the digging shall go more quickly with me here." Beowulf answered. "And if there is nothing else I can do for Herebeald or Hrethel, I can at least give them this one last help." That was true enough, but not all the truth, nor even the core of it. It was, rather, that he did not want to come to Ecgtheow as the bearer of such an ill message. His father must still think him dead, for there had hardly been time to send to Ecgtheow with news that his son still lived, and Beowulf still held some hope in his heart that his father would greet him with gladness when they met again.

"If you are sure, then I cannot sway you," Wynefrith said. "Let it be so, then: Haethcyn will ask Ansuwulf to go in your place, for that Ecgtheow may take word of his new sorrows less hard if it comes from the mouth of his old friend."

The weather worsened towards nightfall, a glazing of icy snow whitening the barrow field. By morning, the snowfall was ankle high, more flakes drifting slowly down from the gray sky, so that the men sweated while they worked, but shivered the worse when they paused to rest weary muscles or wrap cloths around blistered hands: save for Beowulf, who had done such work all year on his long faring, they were more used to holding sword hilts than shovels. Yet though the grave digging might be thought thrall work, there was not one of Hrethel's thanes who was not of Beowulf's mind in the matter. And the work was harder in the snow but no fire burned in the house where Herebeald lay, and any man who had ever hunted or butchered an animal knew well what space of mercy the cold brought to spare the bodies of the slain.

No word was spoken of Hrethel through the long hours of digging and building and hauling stones to the great heap from which the cairn would be raised: none, save Wynefrith, stepped into the chamber behind the hall where he had shut himself in, and when she came forth from that room she was silent. Still, in his mind, Beowulf could see it all too clearly: his grandfather lying in bed with his wanhope shrouded face turned to the wall, blue eyes open and unseeing, staring still at the sight of Haethcyn bearing Herebeald's corpse to him and his life guttering down like a torch dropped in the snow, grief gnawing his flesh more swiftly and painfully than any crab rot.

Two days later, the burial chamber was almost finished, its roof already whitened by swirls of snow, when Beowulf heard the three horn blasts before the eastern gate. Carefully he set down the boulder he was bearing to the cairn building pile, making his way towards the road. Even through the shifting veils of snow, he could recognize Ecgtheow's bulky figure upon his sturdy black horse, followed by twelve riders in thick muffling cloaks and hoods pulled low against the weather. But the gate was already opening, his father riding in, and though Beowulf hurried to meet them, Ecgtheow spurred his horse up the hill more swiftly than his offspring could run.

Hastening into the hall behind the guests, Beowulf was just in time to hear Ecgtheow shouting, "Where is Hrethel? I will see him now, and none shall turn me away, by the oath ring on which Hildebere and I swore our wedding vows."

"Ecgtheow!" Wynefrith cried, her hand still outstretched with the untasted greeting horn. "Ecgtheow, you must not..."

From the end of the hall, Beowulf watched in shock as his father whirled away from Wynefrith, running full tilt at the door that led into the chamber where Hrethel lay. The hinges shrieked, bursting away, and the door fell free. "Hrethel!" Ecgtheow bellowed.

"Hrethel, rise from your bed: this is no fit death for a king to die!"

There was silence, then a deep, wordless cry of pain from Hrethel's death room. Beowulf came up beside Wynefrith, and together they cautiously walked to the shattered door. Ecgtheow knelt beside the bed, his arms about Hrethel. The covers had been thrown off, and for a moment Beowulf thought that Hrethel might be sitting up in the arms of his friend; but then he saw how limply the old king's head hung down, arms dangling loosely and bone knobs showing sharp through his wasted flesh.

"Still warm," Ecgtheow said brokenly. "If I had not taken such care in fording the river on the way from Hroesnabeorh, I might have come in time."

"You could not have swayed him," Wynefrith told him bleakly. "You would only have brought him more pain."

Ecgtheow looked up at her, snarling in his grizzled beard. His eyes were drowning black with the bear wod, and without thought Beowulf stepped forward to put himself between Wynefrith and his father. Staring at him, Ecgtheow checked himself.

"Beowulf?"

"It is I, father."

Ecgtheow laid Hrethel's withered corpse down, rising to his feet. Beowulf over topped his father by almost a head and a half now; Ecgtheow stared at him open mouthed in what might have been wonder, but swiftly twisted into anger again.

"Ansuwulf told me that you lived yet and for what?" He growled. "Though you have grown to the size of an eoten, and mighty of thew, you could not wrest Hrethel back from his death faring. I suppose you wear tattered brown wool because you are worthy of no better, and have given no aid in this time of need save for digging earth and carrying rocks: I can see the stains of thrall work upon your clothes and hands."

Beowulf bit his lip, angry at the unfairness of his father's words. No strength could have moved Hrethel's heart; Beowulf still wore his peasant clothes because the fine garb the women had made for him was not fit for hard labor, and none of Hrethel's thanes had scorned that work any more than he.

"As well you did not come back to me," Ecgtheow said roughly. "Hildebere was ever true to me, but I think now that you were laid in our cradle by some troll before name and soul were given you. You have been ill luck to the Swertings from your birth, as surely as Grendel is the curse of my troth friend Hrothgar I would far sooner have Hrethel and Herebeald alive again than you." He shoved his way out past his son; even his great strength could not have moved Beowulf, but his words had knocked the young man off balance more surely than any wrestler's hold, so that Beowulf staggered back from the blow and might have fallen had he not reached out to steady himself on one of the splintered door posts.

"Father," he whispered, his voice no stronger than that of the boy he had once been in Ecgtheow's hall.

Wynefrith reached up to rest a hand on Beowulf's shoulder.

"Berki. Men will often say things they do not mean when their grief is great, more surely than ever they will when strong ale is poured out in the hall. The time will come when your father wishes he had not spoken those words, though he be too proud to say so: you were best to forget them, and keep your heart towards him as if this had never happened."

Beowulf would gladly have believed her, if it had not been for the years of scorn he had gotten from Ecgtheow before and the knowledge of how men looked at him now, as though he had come shaggy and rime crusted from the bergs of Eotenhome. He did not trust himself to speak, but he gently lifted her hand away and walked out of the hall, following the snow hidden path around the icy palisade towards the harrow grove.

The snow was falling thicker now, so that the men at their labors in the barrow field were no more than gray shadows beyond its wind ruffled white shroud. Beowulf knew that he should go to aid them, but the aching in his heart was stronger, and he did not want to see how their eyes would stare when he did not seem to be looking but turn quickly from his glance, nor mark hands making the sign of Thunar's Hammer beneath their cloaks. The leafless tree limbs of the harrow grove were thickly furred with ice crystals already, the dark needled branches of the pine and yew that grew among the other trees layered thickly with snow. If others had trodden into the clearing since Winter nights, the snow had hidden it already.

Beowulf's cold numbed feet sank calf deep into the unbroken whiteness at every step, marking a heavy trail to the snow covered holy stone. The rope that had hung from the yew tree when he first saw the grove was barely a rotted shell; soon, surely, it would be gone as wholly as the green birch leaves that had rustled above when he had made his summertime blessing with Hygd. Grim One, Beowulf thought, were you then so greedy for offerings that you had to choose Herebeald's blood, since no man has been hanged and speared in this stead for long years? Or is it only that I am lacking in knowledge? Though I would not drink the bitter draught of your wisdom if I could.

As he had almost twelve winters past, Beowulf scraped the thick cap of snow away from the white boulder, his hardened palms tingling with its touch as if he had plunged his arms through thin ice into freezing water. He had to bend over to lay his hands on the top of the pale stone now.

"Frea Ing, warder of frith," Beowulf murmured. "Help me now, for there is no frith in my thoughts, but only strife and sorrow. I would have friends among men; I would be welcome in their garth, but my own father has turned away from me. Surely I was not shaped as I am to no purpose: Frea Ing, whom no man hates, and who is thought finest among the gods you who have never made maiden nor man's wife to weep, and who looses every captive from fetters show me how to win friendship, and prove my father's words wrongly spoken, for I have striven to keep that oath I swore upon the boar's bristles when first I came to this hall."

The snowflakes swirled down, catching in Beowulf's long wavy hair and curling beard, gathering upon his cloak like the first froth of yeast thickening on dark ale. They brushed his face lightly as a woman's cold fingertips; he was not sure what moved him, but he stretched out his hand, palm upward, as if reaching to clasp the hand of another. Yet no answer came: no whisper in his soul, no warmth in his veins, not even the easing of his heart. As Beowulf had come in sadness to the harrow grove, thus he left it, and he could not help wondering if his tarrying with Ran's daughter had made him unfit even for the friendship of the gods.

Frea Ing himself wedded an eoten maid, Beowulf reminded himself, but that brought him no comfort, for it turned his mind to thoughts of those eoten carles who sought the Frowe in marriage sitting outside the Ases' Garth, hearing the songs and laughter within, yet forever barred from the love of the goddess who could welcome them to that joy, though the eotens were kin to the gods, not only by blood from the eldest days, but by oaths and marriages since. It was little wonder, Beowulf thought, that some of Ymir's kin nursed such dark grudges against men and gods; did he not himself sometimes wish to grasp one of the men who had taunted him as a boy and sidled nervously out of his path now, lifting up Agilar or Herebrand or Widuhund and shaking him until his bones shattered? He silenced such thoughts as soon as they rose, but he could not always keep them from his mind.

"Frea Ing ward me from all ill," Beowulf whispered beneath his breath. "I am a man of the Middle Garth, no more; and it is no strange thing that Ecgtheow should have sired a large son." Yet he was not sure he believed his own words, for now his father and grandfather both had cast them into doubt.

The snow fell thickly into the night, and even the blazing fires that
ran the length of the hall were not enough to warm it: everyone, from
Haethcyn in his high seat to the thralls and bondsmaids who bore the food
about the tables, was muffled in their thickest cloaks. Ecgtheow had been
given the place of honor at Haethcyn's right hand, but he sat with his hood
about his ears, drinking deeply and not speaking to any, the broken door
behind him standing as a mute witness to his furious grief. No light burned
within the bedchamber, so Beowulf did not know whether Hrethel's body
still lay there, or whether he had been taken away to sleep in the cold house
beside his eldest son as they would sleep in their mound tomorrow.

A few of Hrethel's other thanes and their retinues had made their way to
the Swertings' hall over the last three days, but with the snowfall, no others
could be awaited for a while. They would come in their own time, to make
their offerings at Hrethel's barrow and to swear their oaths to Haethcyn
if they would: Ecgtheow the Waegmunding was not the first drighten to
make his own choice of troth between the Geats and the Swedes. By dawn,
the snow was nearly up to Beowulf's knees, and Hygelac called him out
early to help widen the path from the hall to the barrow field and clear
away the heavy drifts from the open end of the sunken burial chamber.

Four men bore the bed on which Hrethel and Herebeald lay, carrying
it down into the earthen hollow and pushing it carefully into the log built
room. The two Swertings were both clad in byrnies and helms above their
bright feast clothes and gold armrings, with sword belts slung across
their chests. The cold had already crystallized a fine mist of gray ice over
the polished iron of their war gear, like the pale blue bloom on ripe sloe
berries; the same mist seemed to tinge their faces with gray, dulling the
shine of the gold that weighted their eyelids and the golden boar crests of
their helms.

Ansuwulf and Eofor walked behind the bed bearers, their arms laden
with red shields on which the gilded shapes of eagles and fish glittered,
thrusting spears and casting spears with their iron tips adorned by inlaid
rings of silver, and strong bows and arrows, that Hrethel and Herebeald be
ready for battle or hunting, whichever came to their hands in the worlds
beyond the Middle Garth. Hygelac led two finely saddled bay horses,
their bridles bright with silver mounts and steam rising from their proud
nostrils as they stamped their feet in the snow. He stroked their winter
shaggy necks, speaking to them in a soft voice: the Swertings would not
go to the gods on foot, but riding like athelings. After him came Wynefrith
and Garhild and Hygd with pitchers of mead, gilded horns and cups; other
women brought wide platters heaped with meat and cheese and bread. By
the time all the things that Herebeald and Hrethel would need had been
laid within the burial chamber, the folk of the garth and those guests who
had made their way to Haethcyn's hall in time were gathered on the cold
white barrow field.

Most of them huddled close together, as if a deeper chill than the snow laden wind were upon them; but Ecgtheow stood off by himself, and Beowulf could see his hands and the heavy muscles of his shoulders working even beneath the thick fur of his bear cloak. Haethcyn came forward, standing on the hard trodden snow at the rim of the pit where the chamber had been built. Somber in his dark garb, he nevertheless stood straight and dignified, as though he had slowly strengthened himself in the last days to bear up beneath the weight of his sorrow and shame.

"Hail, you gods and goddesses all: be you welcome to this hallowed stead, come to greet and guide your sons." The whining of the wind through the grave field stones was growing louder, so that the young Geat king had to strain his low voice to be heard above it. "Hail, you folk of the Weather Geats, whom Hrethel ruled for twenty six winters: be you welcome to this hallowed stead, come to bid farewell to your king and his beloved son."

Haethcyn spoke then of Hrethel's victories, and of how his father had held the Weather Geats' realm safe against the Swedes. He told how Hrethel had made his offerings to the gods, how Woden had blessed him with victory, and Frea Ing with fruitful harvests, for that Hrethel was a true king, and the Ases and Wans had shown him their favor open handedly. Haethcyn praised the bravery of his brother, whom all men had loved; and at last he called Ansuwulf forth, to sing again the lament he had made for Herebeald. The berserk stepped lightly, barefooted in the snow; his song did not struggle against the rising and fading cry of the wind, but wove through it as though he sang to the music of a deep droning pipe. By the time the last stave had flowed from Ansuwulf's mouth, Beowulf could feel the tears chilling swiftly to ice on his face. The women were wailing openly, their high voices keening above the wind's moan, and more than one man rubbed hard at his eyes with the backs of his gloved fists.

"Hrethel and Herebeald," Haethcyn called out, "take you now our offerings, and call blessings for us from the gods and goddesses who gave you their gifts while you lived."

Hygelac led the horses to his brother. Haethcyn's sword gleamed dull through the snow; the horses' blood shone bright red against the trampled whiteness, clouds of steam rising from the spreading pools to melt the flakes that fell there into nothingness. When the hooves of the two steeds no longer kicked at the air, other men dragged their bodies down into the burial chamber. Then Garhild gave Haethcyn the gold bound aurochs horn from which his father had drunk, that he might drink the draught of farewell to his kinsmen. At last the wide door was closed and latched, and Beowulf could start lifting free the snowbound stones for the cairn as most of the other folk began to drift back towards the hall. To his surprise, Ecgtheow was among the men who joined him, locking brawny arms about the largest of the boulders and grunting as he tried to heave it up.

But that stone had taxed Beowulf's might, and Ecgtheow could raise it no more than a couple of inches above the ground before he had to let it fall again. Beowulf stepped in quickly surely my father must feel some pride in my strength! And raised the great rock from the ground, his feet sinking deep with each step as he carried it down to lay before the door of the Swertings' chamber. Yet when he looked at Ecgtheow, thinking that now he must hear some word of approval, his father had turned his back and was stumping along the path to the hall.

The raising of the mound went faster than the digging and building had done. Heavy and low as the clouds hung, it was not yet fully dark by the time the last shovelful of icy earth was stamped down into the rounded top of the Swertings' howe. The weary laborers hastened past the rime crusted garth gate and up the hill, eager for warmth and food and drink. Within, the ale of the burial arvel was already flowing freely. Beowulf did not stop to warm his frozen feet and hands by the fire, as most of the other men who had hauled stones and earth with him were doing, but took the horn Hygd handed him and drank deeply before one of the bondsmaids set a platter of food and a bowl of steaming stew down in front of him.

Heedless of his manners, for he had not eaten yet that day and his stomach was cramping with hunger, Beowulf spooned the hot meat and broth into his mouth as quickly as he could, taking large bites of the white wheaten bread and the rich dark blood sausage between spoonfuls and washing them down with good draughts of the thick ale. Now and again, a man would rise to tell a tale of some deed Hrethel or Herebeald had done, and everyone would lift their horns to the dead man. Much to the easing of Beowulf's thoughts, a few folk also made toasts to their new king Haethcyn; if the shouting for him was not as loud as it might have been, Beowulf could hear no murmurs of discontent.

Beowulf's hunger was not yet sated when he felt the tapping on his back. Turning around, to his surprise, he saw Amma standing by him with a large platter of honey cakes. Though the old woman was a thrall, she was valued for her skill so that she was never called upon to serve; and indeed, she had grown so fat that it was not easy for her to be on her feet for long. Yet here she was in a gray gown with only a few smudges of flour upon it, a dark scarf tied over her wispy white hair.

"My little bear has grown," Amma said proudly, beaming at him. "But you are not too old to eat honey cakes, are you? I thought sure you would have come to see me before this never mind, eat, you have been working hard in the cold." She set the whole platter down before him. "Come to the bake house tomorrow, and I shall have more for you, and you can tell me all your tales then, for I could do with a good story to lighten my heart."

Beowulf leaned back to give the aged baker a quick gentle hug, and she giggled like a girl before waddling off again. The taste of Amma's cakes was as summer sweet in his mouth as he remembered; yet he could not keep from flinching under his father's glare, and he knew that if Ecgtheow spoke to him again, there would be sharp words about his care for the kindness of a thrall woman. Unthinkingly, Beowulf hunched his shoulders, looking down the hall until Ecgtheow turned away to speak to Haethcyn. He tried not to listen, fearing what he would hear, but his father's roar was hard to shut from his ears.

"...Eleven winters, and this the twelfth," Ecgtheow was saying, his voice harsh and loud above the noise of the hall, and Beowulf flinched again. Was he to hear, once more, how ill his father's thoughts towards him were? At least Ecgtheow could have kept from upbraiding Haethcyn about it. It had not been Hrethel's second son who had Beowulf in his keeping. "Now I have sworn my troth to you, as to your father before you, and I shall keep it as I did with him. But I would ask that you loose me in this one thing, as he never would."

"I cannot say until you have told me what the matter is," Haethcyn answered. "For though my father is with his forebears, I must be guided as best I may by the wisdom he left me."

Ecgtheow grunted low in his chest. Beowulf thought that perhaps he should rise as if he were going out to piss, but sharp edged dread, mingled with a thin bright strand of hope, bound him silent to his place.

"Well then. Near to twenty winters ago, when I had slain Heatholaf the Wylfing, I fled to Sealand a wretched man, without drighten or kin who would stand for me. It was Hrothgar the Scylding who offered me his friendship then, and but for him I should have fallen beneath the blades of Heatholaf's kin. You were only seven winters of age then, so you may remember but little of this. There were several among the Waegmundings my father Ecgwela in chief, may the trolls gnaw his mouldy bones! Who would not have me back after. But Hrethel took me in and gave me your sister Hildebere to wife, and the lands to the east, that I might guard them against the Swedes who had once been my shoulder companions; aye, my kin called me a nithling many times for that, but they turned from me when I had need of them, and Hrethel gave me honor and trust, for all that I had once raised my sword against his men. Then Grendel came to Heorot the winter that I brought my son here for fostering: I first heard of it after the spring thaws, and hoped to repay my old life debt by slaying Hrothgar's foe: you may remember your brother's wild night ride, to reach me before I could take ship southward."

"I remember it well."

"Your father sent word to me then that I could not leave my lands on that errand, for he was sure that the Swede king had meant for me to do that, and leave Hrethel's northeastern flank weakened. But now the snows are upon us, so that it would be hard marching for Ongentheow to attack; and I would go to measure myself against Grendel, that my old troth friend may spend this twelfth Yule feasting without fear in his own hall."

Even through the din of voices, Beowulf heard Haethcyn's sharp sigh. "Hard marching for Ongentheow now, aye but men may make hard marches, if they believe there will be victory at the end, and if this weather holds, it will not be long before they find easy passage across Lake Wener. More than half of my father's drightens have not yet come to swear their troth to me: there is no doubt but that Ongentheow will think the Weather Geats weakened, and if you fare from Hroesnabeorh now, he will believe that few men indeed stand with me."

"That is not so!" Ecgtheow roared. "If there were any who truly thought you had chosen to slay Herebeald, you would not live now: a blade would have drunk your blood before ever I had the chance to avenge him. True, Hrethel's death was bitter, and I shall ever curse myself that I came too late to help. But you are not to blame for it, and if there is any who swore him troth and will not keep it with his son in time of need, they shall answer to my sword!"

"Yet my need now is for you more than any man, just as my father's was in these years past. Ecgtheow, sister husband, if you ask me anything, I shall bind myself to grant it save only my blessing in leaving the march between the lakes that you ward against Ongentheow. For now, of all times, the Weather Geats cannot afford to lose our strongest shield."

Ecgtheow sat quiet, as in a rare moment of thought. Beowulf bit his lip hard, waiting to hear what would spring from the well of his father's heart words that would show that there was love for his son beneath his angry roughness, like a sweet nut hidden under a prickly haulm, or words that would prove the bond of sire and bairn unloosed forever?

"There is nothing else in my mind now," Ecgtheow said. "Save that I would drink more of this mourning ale after my dear friend and Hildebere's little brother. I had never awaited anything but that it would be they who drank my burial arvel, for berserks do not often live long, and Ansuwulf and I are the last of our old band left within the Middle Garth."

V

The snow was still falling hard the next day when Ecgtheow and his troop rode out of the eastern gate, heading back towards Hroesnabeorh. Soon the horses would have to be shod with ice spikes to cross the frozen rivers; sledges would run on the roads in place of wains, and Haethcyn's messengers would have to be shod with skis, sliding swiftly over the snow drifts. Already there was no telling the mound where Hrethel and Herebeald lay from any other: they all stood alike, featureless white hillocks beneath the drifting gray clouds save for the one rune carved stone rising from Ansugrimar's barrow, that Beowulf could not look upon without shuddering and wondering how the next line of the night rider's stave would be fulfilled.

There was no easing of the weather by the time the Winter nights moon had waned to a thin nail paring behind the fast scudding clouds. The snow lay knee deep, and the rivers ran silent beneath their thickening crusts of ice. Yet for all that, Haethcyn's drightens and under kings made their way one by one to swear troth to him, pouring out horns of ale to mark Hrethel's mound with stains that were swiftly hidden by the blowing snow. Though Haethcyn spent much time alone in silent thought, he did not seem to be faltering in his duties.

He greeted his men, giving out rings and weapons and goodly words as needed. The last did not come easily to him, but he strove the harder for it: whether he had learned that part of rule from watching his father and elder brother, or whether Wynefrith had given him rede to do so, there was no telling. Beowulf had sword and helm from his father already, but the leather armor with its inset iron rings had been lost in the sea, so Haethcyn ordered a byrnie of link mail made to his measure.

"That will take twice the time as for any other man, and more," the black bearded smith grumbled, looking up and down the length of Beowulf's body. Sweat ran down his forehead into his thick dark brows, for they stood in the smithy and his son had been pumping the bellows hard; a half beaten spearhead lay on the anvil, its ruddy glow slowly fading.

"Then you had best set your sons to drawing wire and riveting it at once, for Beowulf must be full geared by the time next year's plowing begins," Haethcyn told him.

"The weapons may wait a little longer: I think that having Beowulf by my side in battle shall be worth a score of spears and swords."

Haethcyn did not waste a smile on that praise, as he might have done with a man whose friendship he wished to gain, but only spoke in the flat cold voice he more often used for unpleasant truths; that made Beowulf the more sure that the Weather Geats' king meant what he said.

The heat of the smithy seemed to glow more hotly on Beowulf's face, and he murmured in embarrassment, "I shall do my best to be worthy of that trust."

Haethcyn acknowledged him with a nod, and turned back to the smith. "Make the rings thicker and heavier than is the usual way, as well, for they shall not be a burden on a man of Beowulf's thews. And be sure that the byrnie is not tight on him, but loose, for he is yet thin from his long wandering, and I think that he will eat well this winter, now that he dwells in a king's hall again. Be sure, you shall not think yourself scanted when you have gotten your pay for this but it must be done in time for next year's fighting!"

"Do you plan war for next summer, then?" Beowulf asked Haethcyn when they had stepped out of the smithy, the icy blast of the wind freezing the sweat on their forge warmed faces. "Before the plowing has even begun?"

"Speak not of it to any save our kin," Haethcyn replied quietly. "I have thought of a means by which we may bind Ongentheow in oaths, and be sure of our safety in years to come. All men may not think well of it, and there is more than a little risk to it I myself am not wholly easy about it in my mind."

"What, then?" A worm of unease twitched in Beowulf's belly as Haethcyn spoke, though he did not know why.

"That I shall not tell you yet, for it is by no means sure that things shall come to pass as I guess, and if they do not, there shall be no good in thinking on it. But it were best for you if you spent the winter working with sword and shield, if you can find any willing to stand against you even with blunted or wooden blades. Now I have much to do yet. Why do you not seek out Hygelac, and see if he will trade a few light blows with you?" Haethcyn turned sharply, marching away towards his house.

Though Beowulf had not drawn his sword from its sheath since he battled the water nicors, save to make sure that no rust marked its wyrm rippled length, when he and Hygelac faced off with the wooden training weapons, he soon found that matters were much different than they had been when the youths of the boy troop had left their bruises upon his legs and shoulders. The largest of shields was light as a leaf in his hand; he still could not match Hygelac's speed with the blade, but that made little matter, for his shield moved quickly enough to guard him well. The strokes he swung in return might have been easily blocked if another man had dealt them, but neither Hygelac's sword nor his shield was strong enough to withstand Beowulf's blows.

He was careful to hold back from using his full might, lest he do his friend some harm; but when Hygelac braced his shield hard to keep from being knocked sprawling in the snow, its wood and the wooden sword Beowulf swung cracked to pieces in a single stroke, and Hygelac backed off, rubbing his shoulder and grinning beneath his helm.

"Hai, that answers one question warriors have been arguing about over their ale since before my grandfather's great grandfather's time," Hygelac laughed. "Skill and speed are good, no doubt about it, but enough strength may yet be better though I hope your sword does not shatter like that in a real battle."

"I think iron will cleave before it breaks," Beowulf answered.

"That is likely so, but I have seen the blades of weaker men bend in fighting. And you must work yet harder with your shield, and learn to parry blows better with your sword as well, for in a battle, you will have more than one blade to worry about at once: there may be a spear thrusting at your head even as another man is cutting at your legs. But I always knew that you would grow to be a great warrior, and now I am seeing that fulfilled. Come, we shall get Ansuwulf and Eofor, and see what they can do for you."

Beowulf worked with a will at his training, but when Ansuwulf and Eofor and Hygelac had other things to do, he found himself at a loss. Often he went down to Whales' Ness, staring out at the ice slowly settling around the white rim of the shore and the snow falling into the slate gray waves beyond. He longed to strip off his clothes and fling himself into the water as he had once done, but he feared what might follow. Beowulf guessed in his heart that Heofonglowe's anger at him had not dimmed and he did not know what he would do if he felt her white arms wrapping about his body again.

He had been without the touch of a woman for a year, save in his dreams; and often enough in those he was back in Eagor's sea hall, with Heofonglowe's legs clenched around his waist and her bright hair floating about him like shafts of sunlight glimmering green gold in the water. The sea mews cried above, their harsh voices like the wordless calls of drowning men. There was one large gull that would often fly down to perch on a snow covered boulder, its cruel dark eyes darting about as if it hoped to se the body of a lost sailor bloating upon the shore to sate its hunger. I should have eaten your eyes from your head, the gull's raucous shrieks seemed to say to him, and maybe someday I shall yet.

Beowulf disliked it more as time went on, and sometimes he would throw a snowball at it to make it fly up, but it always settled quickly in its place again. Beowulf's byrnie was done before the first day of Yule. Haethcyn praised the smith greatly, and said that he and his helpers must have worked sleepless like Wayland to have it finished so quickly. Though, as Haethcyn had guessed, Beowulf had put on more flesh with the good food at the Swertings' burg, the mail coat fit well and comfortably, nor was it likely to grow tight upon him by the end of the winter. Ecgtheow did not come to Haethcyn's Yule feast, though he sent a sledge bearing gifts of furs and good ale so that none could mistake his absence for meaning that he bore ill will towards the new Geat king.

Beowulf could not help wondering if it was for his sake that his father had stayed away could Ecgtheow no longer bear to look upon his son? Or was it merely that he no longer had the heart to come feast in the hall where before he had sat and drunk in friendship with Hrethel? Once Beowulf might have spoken with Hygd on the matter, but now he could hardly bear to look at her; not for the way Hygelac's child, six months along, was swelling in her womb, but for the sorrow that shadowed her eyes like the dark mourning cloths that still hung the walls of Haethcyn's hall whenever she met his gaze. I have betrayed her, Beowulf thought sadly. I wished never to harm her: how did this come about, that I could make no choice that would not bring ill? It was on the last day of the Yule feasting that Ecgtheow's messenger came skiing up to Haethcyn's hall. Beowulf recognized the man's broad broken nose and the ruddy tail of hair hanging out beneath his marten fur hat, but could not call his name to mind.

"Well, Beowulf," Ecgtheow's thane said, unbuckling his skis and brushing the snow from his shoulders before stepping into the hall. "Is the king within? I have tidings that he must hear."

"Is all well with my father?" Beowulf asked. It was then he noticed the bandage tied about beneath the dark fur of the thane's cap, and the edge of crusted blood upon it.

"Aye, he is well, though there was dire and ill willing slaughter about Hreosnabeorh. The Swedes came skating across Lake Weter, but this is news for Haethcyn's ears before any other."

Beowulf led him up to Haethcyn's high seat, where the king nodded in greeting.

"Hail to you, Oslaf. How stand matters with my friend Ecgtheow?"

"The Swedes came in the night, when we were drinking the Yule ale, glad and fearing no onslaught. The snow put out their torches so that they could not fire the hall, but they ringed it about and we were hard put to beat them back. By day we pursued them, and found a village burned and the bodies of men and women hewed deeply by the sword and cast about like carrion, with the ravens scratching the snow from them. The Swedes had stolen their horses and slaughtered their other beasts, cattle and sheep and swine and even hounds, so that nothing lived there. We caught up with them upon the lake, and battled there upon the ice; we spilled much hot blood above the water, but more of them escaped us than we slew, and when Ecgtheow came back to himself from his berserk fit, he commanded that we follow no farther, lest they had set an ambush for our host."

"Ecgtheow has grown wise in his age," Haethcyn said with the graveness of an older man.

"But this is surely a call to war. It was ill done of Ongentheow to strike during the Yule nights, and for that, as for the lives of my good folk, he shall pay a full geld when the year has turned. He meant, I think, that Ecgtheow would have come to feast here and he would be able to slay freely in the Waegmunding's land, but he did not reckon with your hardiness. Now I shall send out the word to the other drightens who uphold me, that they may be warned; and an half hundred men shall go back with you to Ecgtheow's hall, lest it come to Ongentheow's mind that this battle has weakened you." He raised his voice, shouting, "Eofor! Come you here."

Eofor rose from his bench, stepping lightly up onto the raised dais where the king and his kin sat.

"Is there fighting in midwinter?" He asked, taking in the grimness of Haethcyn's dark bearded face and the bandage on Oslaf's head in a single glance. "The summer will be a bloody one, then."

Quickly Haethcyn recounted the news from Hreosnabeorh, and Eofor nodded thoughtfully.

"Aye, it shall be well to send men to strengthen Ecgtheow. Do you wish me to lead them, or merely choose them?"

"You shall lead them, though under Ecgtheow's will, and choose as well."

"Shall I be among them?" Beowulf asked. If his father saw him in battle, then, perhaps...

"I would have you, for you are learning well now and it is right that son should stand by his father in times of strife," Eofor said.

But Haethcyn shook his head. "No, Beowulf shall stay here beside me, for I have other things in mind for him. My thoughts are set now as to what we shall do to Ongentheow, and that I shall make known when the time is come."

Eofor shrugged his heavy shoulders. "As you wish, though it is usually better for a young man to take rede from those who have done battle through a lifetime."

Beowulf watched the next day as Eofor rode out with his troop, iron bridle rattles jingling dully through the snowy air. Hygelac stood beside him, reaching up to put a friendly arm about his shoulders. "Do not be so downcast, Berki. I am sure that there will be plenty of fighting for all of us when the spring planting is done." His lynx fur cap had slipped askew; he grinned up beneath it, his cheeks pink with cold above the edge of his golden beard. Beowulf paused; but Haethcyn had told him only that he should not speak of whatever hidden plan he was considering to those outside their kin.

"It will be before that, I think, for your brother was firmly set in his mind that I should have my byrnie before the plowing began, though he wished that only we ourselves know of it. Have you any better guess about that than I? He cannot mean to take men from their fields, lest we all go hungry next winter."

Hygelac frowned, an unaccustomedly serious look on his face. "Haethcyn told me that I should take you out riding every day that I could in the next months, to be sure that you could travel swiftly and skillfully on the back of a horse and that there were horses who had grown used to bearing your weight. I do not know what he could have in mind, but I am sure that this is tied to it in some way." Then he grinned again. "Still, this is good weather to ride swiftly in, for the rime thurses have spread their softest blankets down to cushion your bones when you fall. And you will not fall far, anyway, since the shoulders of our tallest steed are little higher than your waist. Hardest for you, I think, will be keeping your feet from dragging the ground but it is well that we have always bred from the largest and sturdiest lines, for our horses should learn to carry you without too much toil, even with the weight of your byrnie added to your own."

Sharply as the winter had come on, it broke almost as sharply, as though the rime thurses had worn out their grip by tightening it too swiftly. The Moon had waxed and waned no more than twice after Yule by the time the icicles began to drip from the eaves of Haethcyn's burg, the snow within the settlement softening to foot churned mud by day and freezing into ripples of ice again at night.

Haethcyn went about to the smithies every day, followed by a thrall who gathered spearheads and arrowheads to bring them back to his hall where other men sat shaping shafts and fletching arrows. When the first bare patches of dark earth began to show through the melting snow like mange through thinning fur and the silver buds of the goat willows pricked pale through their dark hoods, then Haethcyn took Hygelac and Beowulf aside.

"Let us walk outside our garth for a little time," the Weather Geats' king said to his kinsmen. "The time has come for me to spill out what I have kept hoarded in my mind this winter."

The three of them did not turn northwards to the barrow mead or the holy grove, as Beowulf had thought they might, but southward, walking along the road where the last sledge tracks in the snow were slowly melting into mud. Bare fields stretched to either side; the brown earth was still frozen, but the ice was slowly fading from it like mist beneath the Sun's cool brightness.

"It will soon be time for plowing to begin," Haethcyn said, and something in his low voice tingled along Beowulf's spine.

"Aye, it will, and my byrnie is long since done. As for Feola and Hrime, they have learned well to bear my weight, and I to ride them, though I may never match Hygelac for speed and skill on horseback."

"Since you have guessed so much, do you know what I plan?" Haethcyn asked. Though the weather was still cold enough for him to wear a long fur lined cloak that hid his body and hands, Beowulf could see the muscles at the corners of his jaw twitching beneath his dark beard like snakes under seared grass and he almost thought that he heard a brittle edge of fear in the young king's voice.

"Hygelac and I guessed that you plan to make some manner of raid into the lands of the Swedes but as to what, we have no way of knowing until you tell us."

The cloud of Haethcyn's breath sighed out pale in the sunlight. "You know that every year at plowing time, Ongentheow goes about his realm in a wain, with Frea Ing and the gudhija who is the god's wife riding before: that has ever been the way of the Ingling kings, to bring the god's fruitfulness to their land."

"So it has," Hygelac said. "But what...brother, you cannot mean to attack Frea Ing's frith ride!" Hygelac and Beowulf both stared aghast at Haethcyn. There could be few deeds worse than breaking the frith of the god and Beowulf was sure that, whatever his oath to Haethcyn, he himself could not lift his sword against Frea Ing.

"Calm yourselves, my kinsmen. That is not in my mind; I have no wish to call Frea Ing's wrath against us, neither in hunger nor in plague. But while Ongentheow is away, his wife Yrse shall yet while in Upsala. If we fare quickly and strike suddenly, we may take her; and with her as frith pledge, we shall be able to bind Ongentheow to pay the were gild for the men he slew. And it was he who broke the Yule holiness this year: I do not think that the gods will raise their hands to ward his hall after that, however many swine he slays by holy stone or men he hoists on the gallows tree."

Although Haethcyn stood in full sun, his shadow short on the ground beside him, it seemed to Beowulf again that he could see the darkness behind the king like a man high patch of murky mist. Warm as it was inside his bearskin cloak, he could not keep from shuddering.

"This plan is doomed to fare ill," Beowulf found himself saying. "The frith you find from it will not be that which you seek, though Yrse be taken from Upsala. Yet Woden is not the only god who may claim his offerings in blood, and I think the tusk of the boar will tear old Ongentheow in the dark holt before the game is full played."

Haethcyn stepped back a pace; even Hygelac's blue eyes were wide with fear, staring up at Beowulf as though he had never looked upon him before.

"Can you speak clearer?" Haethcyn asked. "You warned me once, and sorrow came of it; what do you want now?"

Beowulf shook his head like a bear shaking away a cloud of midges: the knowledge had gone, leaving only a faint buzzing in his ears, as though he had stood up too quickly after draining a horn of strong ale. When Haethcyn spoke again, his voice was bitter as mold tainted bread.

"Your sight is of little worth, if it only offers shadows without shape and hints whose truth may not be learned until all has come to pass."

Beowulf did not know what to say to that. When he had whiled with farmers and woodcutters, his redes had come out clearly. But it seemed to him that the wyrds of kings were more tangled and clouded than those of simple folk, and that the wights who aided or troubled the rulers of wide realms worked in ways more deep and subtle than the alfs who grazed their cattle in the mountains beside those of men or the ghosts that brought or stole the luck of farmsteads. Then Hygelac grinned.

"What I heard is that this raid is likely to be Ongentheow's bane. That is clear enough for me; and if he is fool enough to stop for a boar hunt in the middle of a war, then he is no longer fit to be king over the Swedes."

"Aye, that is so," Haethcyn agreed, his face clearing. "Well then, it is a long faring to Upsala, and we must set forth within a few days, for, as we have said, ploughing time shall soon be upon us, and though Ongentheow's realm is wide, he is not likely to tarry too long on his way in the wain. I shall take with me Ansuwulf, and you, Beowulf, and ten others for the raid: one third of our war band shall come with us, but halt along the way, so that we shall be able to turn and fight such part of Ongentheow's host as he can gather most quickly to him, if need be. As for you, Hygelac, you shall stay here with the other two thirds, that the Weather Geats' hall not be left unwarded."

"I would rather fare with you: am I not the swiftest rider in all your host?"

"You are that, but should you and I and Beowulf all fall, there shall be none of our blood left save the babe soon to come forth from Hygd's womb. Then our sister husband Ecgtheow would be next to rule, but he is better known for his fierceness than his deep redes: a strong march warden and battle drighten, but no folk king in times of frith, I think. And one man of kingly kin must stay behind here, to cut the first three furrows in Folde's brown breast, to make the blessings for the Weather Geats and share the cakes that Garhild brings out for plow man and earth."

Hygelac grimaced as though he liked his brother's words ill, but he nodded all the same. "Yet if matters go badly for you, I shall come to your aid, and nothing shall stay me. Better for the house of the Swertings to fall all together than for one to hold back as a craven."

"True enough. Beowulf, sister son, I have given you a byrnie of ring mail and you have sworn your troth to me. Will you fare and fight beside me as a thane now, and not complain of any misgivings you may have to others, lest their hearts be weakened by it?"

"As I have sworn, so I shall do," Beowulf answered.

No more snowstorms broke the warming weather, and it was not long before Haethcyn and his host set out on the northeastern road that would bear them between the two great lakes, Wener and Weter. They rode at a careful pace, so as not to tax the horses, for it was a long way to Upsala; they would walk for a time, then tölt that smooth gait that bore the rider along as fast as a good trot, but did not batter his bones or threaten to shake him from the saddle. Beowulf's horse Feola, a sturdy golden gelding with flaxen mane and tail, carried him along with a will, in spite of the weight of man and byrnie; but Beowulf had two more horses where the other riders had only one each, for if it came to hard riding, his steeds would likely be the first to founder.

Ahead of him, Haethcyn's saddle bags bulged weightily from the gray sides of his own horse, bearing the most beautiful and valuable rings and necklaces that could be found in the Geat king's burg the king and his men would enter the land of the Swedes as a wealthy merchant and his guard, bringing rich ornaments of gold and amber for Yrse's delight and their own profit. Beowulf's own were weighted likewise, though less heavily since his horse bore more of a burden, and so were Ansuwulf's. If they did not have the ill luck to be recognized along the way, they should be easily able to reach the queen. Escaping with her would be another matter, but Haethcyn seemed sure of it, and, as the king had asked, Beowulf spoke to no one of his own misgivings about Haethcyn's plan.

The first part of the way, while they still rode through the lands of the Geats, was easy going. Each night Haethcyn and his men came to a burg that was glad to give them shelter and food and drink for the night, and by day they could stay upon the road and cross rivers at the main fords without fear of challenge. But at last they came to Ecgtheow's hall, perched to overlook Lake Weter from the summit of Hroesnabeorh as a warning and a watch post against the Swedes, and Beowulf knew that it would be the last night of light going. The gables of Ecgtheow's hall were carved with horse heads, still bearded with shrinking icicles that glinted red in the light of the setting sun.

As a child, Beowulf had heard men making jests about those horse heads turned towards the Swedes, but never understood them. Now he knew that they stood as nithing posts to show his father's scorn towards the kin and drighten who had not stood by him in his feud with the Wylfings and perhaps as wards as well, for the soul main of the kings who dwelt in Upsala and the gudhes and gudhijas who slew the offerings at the hof there were well known. Though the settlement was small, the palisade about it was larger and stouter than that ringing Haethcyn's hall, its broad oaken posts sunk deep in an encircling mound of stones and earth. Godric, one of Haethcyn's chosen twelve, bore the gilded ring standard of the Weather Geats aloft, and Ecgtheow's gate warders must have seen it, but all the same, they called out,

"Who would come to the burg of Ecgtheow the Waegmunding?"

"Tell Ecgtheow that his king has come to guest a night with him, and to call upon his aid as may be needed!" Haethcyn cried back to them. "And go quickly, for we have had a long faring already and the sun is lowering fast."

Beowulf heard the sound of heavy feet running swiftly away. It was not long before the threefold blast of Ecgtheow's horn sounded from the top of the hill, followed by the creak of the great gate being unbarred. A score of armed men stood about the gate inside. Though the tips of their spears pointed towards the sky, Beowulf felt their gazes pricking at him as he rode in with the others. When he had left Hreosnabeorh, he had been too young to mark the differences between that burg and the seat of the Swertings or perhaps Ecgtheow's rule had grown harsher in later years, as the Swedes grew in might and boldness. Thralls took the bridles of their horses to lead the tired beasts away to fodder, and Haethcyn marched up the hill with Beowulf at his right side and Ansuwulf at his left, Godric following close behind with the king's standard upraised.

Ecgtheow stood in front of his door posts: he, too, was clad in mail and held a thick thrusting spear, though he leaned it against the wall as soon as the guests were close enough for him to see their faces.

"Hail to you, my king," Ecgtheow boomed out. "And greetings, Ansuwulf, my old friend. Had I gotten word of your coming, I should have readied a better welcome for you: it looks as though my son will be able to eat the meals cooked for half the men in the hall by himself. At least there is plenty of smoked meat left from the Swedes' raid gods curse them, who killed what they could not steal!"

Beowulf flushed angrily, looking at the muddy ground. It was true that his belly was bigger than it had been at the end of his long walk, but it was not yet so wide as his father's, and Ecgtheow had no cause to speak so of him.

"We travel fast, and must travel more swiftly and be known by fewer tomorrow," Haethcyn answered. "I see that your burg is readied well for battle: have the Swedes crossed the march posts of late?"

"They have not yet, but after they attacked at Yule, I hold nothing sure. Well, come in, and I will feast you as best as I can."

When he had ducked his head to pass beneath the low door lintel, Beowulf could not help staring about himself. He had remembered rafters that vaulted nearly to the sky and roof pillars taller and thicker than old oaks; he had remembered his father sitting in splendor, and a din of feasting that rang deafeningly in the ears. But Ecgtheow's hall seemed small to him now, low roofed and dingy; after a day of riding in the clean sunlit air, the smells of smoke and stale straw and men's sweat almost choked him.

Beowulf did not recognize the young brown haired woman who filled their horns with ale, though from her red bordered linen dress and the silver ring upon her slender arm, he guessed that she must be the daughter or wife of one of Ecgtheow's thanes. She smiled prettily at Haethcyn and Ansuwulf, but when she came round to pour for Beowulf, her green eyes widened as she looked up at him. Then her gaze dropped, and she would come no closer than an arm's length to him, as though she feared that he would grasp her and devour her. They sat and drank while Haethcyn told Ecgtheow of his plans. The old berserk listened carefully, thick fingers knotted in his broad beard. When Haethcyn reached the stealing of Yrse, though, he let out a deep bellow of laughter.

"That's the place to hit the Inglings, sure enough! Whether Ongentheow loves her or keeps her chained like a snapping bitch, the luck of the Inglings' rule is in their queens. Yrse never bore any child but young Hrothulf that I heard of, but all the same, Ongentheow has to go to her at the end of every planting time wain round to keep the Swedes' grain growing: without her, he won't hold his high seat long. And he has earned that fully, for that he struck at us during the holy nights of Yule. I'll go with you on this faring, for it sounds well to me."

Haethcyn shook his head. "I shall need you here. We will be fleeing fast with Yrse, and few men move swifter than many. But I mean to leave that part of my host I have brought here in your burg, and ask you to be ready, for when we come here again we are likely to have many Swedes at our backs. Then we shall turn and fight, and they shall find that the rabbit has led the wolf into a trap."

"Well done!" Ecgtheow applauded, as though the deed were already behind them where they sat drinking ale in safety.

While the older men spoke, Beowulf looked carefully about the hall. Even had he not known the faces of the men who had come to Hreosnabeorh with Eofor, it would have been an easy thing to tell Ecgtheow's men from Haethcyn's. The warriors Haethcyn had sent were better dressed and wore more gold than silver on their arms, for though Ecgtheow was open handed enough, a king had more to give than a march drighten. Though the two bands did not hold themselves apart from each other, Haethcyn's men mostly sat together. Yet there was more to it than that: though Haethcyn's thanes were guests, they sat at their ease, whereas Ecgtheow's thanes had a look of wariness about them, like outlaws in a wood fastness.

It was hard to say where the difference in their faces lay: both groups were hard muscled and well armed, their faces and arms seamed alike with the scars of battle, beards and hair hanging loose or braided as the man might choose. But it seemed to Beowulf that he could feel the restlessness seething in his father's followers; their voices sounded more often harsh with anger than uplifted with laughter. And there was that about them a flicking of the eyes, perhaps, or a twitching of hand towards sword hilt that made Beowulf think if he saw one or a few of them on the road, his mind would go more quickly to an outlaw band than to the thanes of a drighten who was well loved by his king.

Their manners were rougher as well; Beowulf marked one black bearded man seizing a passing thrall by the wrist and swinging him brutally in so that he could slice a hunk of sausage from the lengths piled on the boy's platter. When Beowulf looked more closely, he could see the unevenness in the armor of Ecgtheow's band mostly, Beowulf guessed, looted from slain bodies in battle, with the war weeds of the best armored being given out in pieces. One man might wear a fine byrnie, but had only an iron bound leather cap on his head, while another lifted a proudly gilded helm above a plain leather jerkin with iron rings sewn clumsily over his breast. Beowulf remembered Haethcyn mentioning that many of Ecgtheow's warriors were wanderers, wretched from their kin for hard tempers and slayings even as Ecgtheow himself had been.

"If a man is strong and can fight well," Haethcyn had said, "Ecgtheow will take him on without asking why he left his home. It serves him well, there by the Swedish march posts, though his hands have snapped the neck of a man he thought might be a spy more than once." And from Beowulf's own meager hoard of memories came those of hiding behind upturned benches as his father matched bellows with one of his men, an argument ending in a roar of pain when Ecgtheow struck out to belly and face with heavy fists, breaking the other man's nose and leaving him doubled over, bleeding and gasping.

There would be none of that this night, with the king sitting in Ecgtheow's hall but it seemed to Beowulf, looking upon his father's rough horde, that perhaps there were more reasons than one why first Hrethel, and then Haethcyn, had refused Ecgtheow's plea to be allowed to leave his stead to go after Grendel. Perhaps, Beowulf thought, it is as well for me that I did not try to come home. Though Ecgtheow's belly was broadening, his great tangle of brown hair and beard grizzled thickly with streaks of gray and his blue eyes set deeply in nests of wrinkles, with the frown lines of his brow graven in like axe marks, age did not seem to have weakened the berserk: if he were not slain, he could hold his strong armed rule at Hreosnabeorh for many years yet. Beowulf's thoughts shied away from what would happen when the devouring flames finally took his father's cold body would Haethcyn give that hall to another man like Ecgtheow, one well suited to the harsh life of the march warders?

Beowulf had no stomach to rule in the way his father did, by being the strongest and most brutal of the fierce men he had gathered about him. For *I am not like Ecgtheow; I would be loved, not feared.* Though they would be faring away at dawn, Ecgtheow gave orders that the best ale be poured out for the honor of the king and his men, and soon the voices of the warriors in the hall grew louder and harsher. After two horns of ale, Beowulf soon had to go out to piss in the mud.

On his way back, he heard one of Ecgtheow's thanes saying loudly to one of Haethcyn's, "Your sword? Ha! You may boast of your weapon all you like, but it is the hand that wields it that matters."

The speaker, a broad shouldered man with dark golden hair tied back in a simple tail, picked up a sheep's gnawed rib from his plate, holding it lightly in the middle.

"I know where to strike so hard and well, that I could slay you in an eye blink with this bone if I chose." Beowulf paused, afraid that those words would lead to their proving, but Haethcyn's man only snorted, turning his attention back to the pile of smoked meat on his plate, and Beowulf went back to his place.

Haethcyn and his band were weary from their long faring, and Beowulf thought that the king would soon be going to bed, when one of his father's men came up to the dais. The warrior was near as big as Ecgtheow himself, but younger, with little fat overlaying the play of the knotted shoulder muscles pressing against his tunic. Beneath the stained bands of embroidery at the cuffs of his sleeves, he wore gloves of soft leather that had once been fine, but were splotched and scuffed and ragged now, as though he had worn them through many fights.

His black beard and hair were plaited into many small braids, and his left cheek was deeply marked with a livid pink scar: the tip of a blade had dug in deep beneath his cheekbone and torn out along the skin. His over tunic was of fine make, and as richly adorned as that of any king's thane, though his left cuff was missing one of its silver clasp buttons and a small seam in the pale red linen over his chest showed where it had been mended. Many washings had not gotten rid of the faint brownish splotch around the rip: a man had been slain in that garment, and Beowulf wondered if it had been the same man who gave Ecgtheow's thane the scar on his face.

"So you are Beowulf, who came back from two years among the trolls," the braid bearded warrior said, looking at him fiercely. His voice was accented slightly, with something of the same rise and fall that Beowulf heard in his father's speech when Ecgtheow had drunk a few horns of ale though he spoke more clumsily, more like a farmer than a man of high kin: another wanderer from the lands of the Swedes, Beowulf guessed. "I am called Hondscioh. Now there is frith in this hall, and it is foolish for men to test themselves at swords when there are foes outside the gates. But nothing stops us from a friendly wrestling match, and I have always wanted to try myself against a troll for strength."

Beowulf gazed at Hondscioh for a moment. Ecgtheow's man was large and powerful, yes; he was likely as strong as his drighten, or stronger, for that he was in his prime and Ecgtheow growing old. But next to Beowulf, Hondscioh might have been a half grown youth for size and breadth and Beowulf mistrusted the glint in his squinted blue eyes: it was not the look of a man who meant his offer of a test of strength in friendship. He feared that Hondscioh would seek to do him some harm if they wrestled, and that, in warding himself, Beowulf would do more harm to the other; the memory of Breca's arm bone snapping in his grip was still sickeningly clear after eleven years.

"Would that not be better done at another time, when we have shown our strength against our foe together?" Beowulf suggested. "For we must be faring early tomorrow, and when one of us has thrown the other down, there will surely be more men who want to prove themselves against the winner."

"There are but two of this hall's men who I have not cast to the earth time and again: I do not think there will be many who call for another match with me," Hondscioh boasted. "Come now: for all your size, are you a craven good only, as I have heard, for lifting stones and carrying sacks of grain? Is that why trolls are so easily driven to hide in their berg fastnesses, snatching lost children up to eat, but fearful to come and do battle with men of bravery and thews? You are not so brave and strong as your cousin Grendel, then but you need not be too afraid," he added mockingly. "I shall not do you any great hurt in our match."

Beowulf was beginning to grow angry now, but he reined his temper in with a harder grip than he would use against any horse's bit: he had seen what happened when his father let his rage run free. Hondscioh leaned forward, but then Haethcyn spoke.

"Hold, Hondscioh. For myself, I would to see the match between you when we gather to toast our victory: that would be a feast worthy of such a sight. As Beowulf has said, this is no time for the games of frith and joy, and it is not well done to call a man craven because he will not celebrate at dawn as if the day were already won. Thus I would ask you to wait until we have come back: then it will be time for shoulder companions to test their thews against each other in friendship."

Hondscioh nodded to the king with ill grace, the lines of his scowl seaming his scarred face deeply.

"There is still this matter between us, Beowulf but since Haethcyn king asks it, I shall leave it be until the battles are over." He turned abruptly and went back to his place; despite his size, his tread was the light springy walk of a skilled and ready fighter.

"Thank you," Beowulf said to Haethcyn. "I did not wish to wrestle with him."

"And I would have been a fool to let you, for that would have been one man less in our lines, and a strong one lost at that," Haethcyn replied softly. "I think he will not be quite so eager when he has seen how shields and their bearers shatter before your strokes."

His king's trust in his strength should have cheered Beowulf, but instead he felt his heart sinking a little more, for behind Hacthcyn's flat voice, he could hear the certainty that Beowulf would have maimed or killed Hondscioh. The king had turned the other warrior away as he would have turned a drunken man away from a chained bear, or a child from a captive wolf and am I, then, Haethcyn's tame troll? Beowulf wondered. But he had little time to think on it, for the king was already rising, and Ecgtheow standing with him to lead Haethcyn and his chosen band to the sleeping houses that had been warmed and readied for them.

Haethcyn, Beowulf, Ansuwulf, and the other men Haethcyn had chosen set off as soon as the sky began to gray with dawn, saddling their horses with cold stiffened fingers and riding on at a slow walk to start the blood flowing warm through the steeds' muscles. To Beowulf's surprise, they did not turn off the road in hopes of passing into Swedish lands unseen, but stayed upon it, their horses' hooves squelching in the sticky mud. A gray stone on either side of the road marked the end of Geatish land and the beginning of the Swedes' kingdom. Not far behind it were two-score guards, mailed and helmed: several were mounted, and others had war bows strung in their hands. One of the mounted men rode forward.

"Who are you, and why do you ride along this road?" He called.

Haethcyn nudged his horse into a swifter walk to meet him. "I am Ælfred the merchant, and these men are my guards," he answered. "I came from Jutland with a load of gold and amber, meaning to make my way here more swiftly; but winter caught us unawares, so that we must while with the Geats until the snow was melted enough for easy travel. Still, that did me little good, for there was much sorrow among them since Hrethel's death, and few of them were minded to buy precious adornments for arms and breasts."

"Aye, the Geats have ever been close handed," the leader of the march guard agreed. "But show me your wares, that I may know you tell the truth. It is not often that I see merchants with fine swords and byrnies."

"When you see what I have to sell, you will know why my men are armed as if they were the thanes of kings. Even an honest man may be easily tempted, and we have more than once had to make our own way out of a burg when its ruler thought that taking might be cheaper than paying."

Haethcyn opened one of his saddle bags, letting the man look in. His mouth fell open beneath the iron nose piece of his helm, but he shut it again quickly.

"Now it is little wonder to me why you travel so heavily armed, and how you can give your men ring mail and swords. Where do you mean to sell such goods? I'd guess there are not many who can afford what you will ask for them."

"We are going to Upsala, for I have heard that Yrse has an eye for fine things. If they please her well, we can make back thrice the cost of coming here, for all our long winter's wait."

"Pass on, and good luck to you," the guard said. Beowulf could feel the stares on him as they rode through; he tried to hunch down in the saddle to make himself look a little smaller, but it was no use. If he had won any fame beyond the scorn he had heard from Ecgtheow's man, there would have been no chance of passing unknown there; as it was, no one would look for the march drighten's coal biting son in such a troop.

Soon the sun was high in the sky, and even with the cool breeze rustling through the alders that ringed the shore of Lake Weter, the air was warming almost to mildness. One of Haethcyn's men moved as if to shrug off his cloak, but Ansuwulf shook his head. The gleam of ring mail in the sunlight would catch Swedish eyes from far away, and the next folk they passed might be less easily gulled than a guard whose duty was to watch for war hosts on the move.

The first tiny leaves of the birch trees were unfurling now, pale green veiling the white trees' thin twigs. Following the road around by the shores of the lake, the noise of the Geats' riding startled a flock of geese, who rose gray winged from the shallows in a rush of wind, their cries a barking din like a host of hounds suddenly loosed. Sihtric tilted his dark head back to watch their flight, sighing.

"Ah, if only I'd had my bow strung then," he said, cracking thin red knuckled fingers. "Roast goose wouldn't make a bad dinner tonight, not at all. And they fly so close when they're rising, the right arrow from my bow could pass straight through one and into a second," he added boastfully though the boast was not idle: he was the best hunter in Haethcyn's hall, and had made such shots before, which few other men could say.

"You couldn't hit a goose with your arrows if it were hobbled two paces in front of you," one of the other men, Domhere, answered him lightly. "Smoked meat and hard bread will do us well enough for now, and they don't have to be plucked and roasted, either."

Now and again they would pass a farmer out in his fields, prodding at the mud with a stick to see if the chill earth beneath had thawed enough for him to begin plowing. The cows were still in their byres, but the sheep had already left their folds, wandering about in flocks mottled iron gray and white and black, their long shaggy winter fleeces dangling almost to the ground as they dropped their curly horned heads to chew at last year's muddy dead grass and bite off the first sprouting weeds.

Once the Geats had to rein up their horses and wait as a young swineherd drove his bristly brown charges across the road to the woods on the other side, whacking the pigs across their flanks with a sturdy stick, swearing and dodging back whenever one would turn and try to bite him. Farther on, a billy goat with his mouth full of house leeks stared at them balefully from the turfed roof of a small sunken hut, then lowered his head as if he would charge them before he went back to snorting over his meal.

The sight reminded Beowulf of the farmers' houses where he had once worked for his food on his long walk; he thought back to the warm fires with grandmothers and babes and grown folk gathered tightly around, telling stories in the night, the easy talk and once they had made sure that he meant them no ill the friendliness to their strange large guest, even when the best they had to offer was thin sour ale and curds spread on husk filled bread.

Those farmers' families might have thought him a troll as well, but they did not shy away from him as Haethcyn's men did. Even now, save for the king and Ansuwulf, those thanes kept a good space between their own steeds and Beowulf's, as though at any moment he might transform into something fearsome as quickly as a water horse hearing the word "nicor" and plunging into the lake to drown and devour the rider who had spoken its true name. The weather held warm, and though the Geats were riding northeast, they soon began to see men in the fields walking beside their plough oxen, their wooden ards cutting deep furrows in the wet earth, and the first winter thin cattle grazing on the new grass.

At Haethcyn's command, they avoided the wooden walled burgs, for there was always the chance that someone in a drighten's household would recognize them, or even have heard word that the king of the Geats had left his hall. Too, there was truth in Haethcyn's lie about the dangers of traveling with a large pack full of treasures meant to tempt a queen, and Loca, that eoten born faring friend of Thunar's whose tricks brought both weal and ill to the gods, would laugh greatly if the Geat king were caught so in his own net. But at last the Geats came to the shores of the river Sal, rushing hard in its spring swiftness. They followed along the wooded bank for a time, riding beneath the shifting sunlit patterns of the branches. The black buds of the ash trees, sharp as spears, were just beginning to unfurl, the beeches' first leaves already whispered cool and green above their great grey trunks, and Beowulf heard the twittering and rustling of small birds, lively in the new sunlight.

Had they been riding out for the joy of it Beowulf could not yet think of hunting with pleasure again it would have been a fair day. But already his belly was beginning to tighten with nervousness, and more, with the queasy sense that they would be doing some ill. It was such weather for which men praised Frea Ing, and the Swedes would surely be rejoicing that the god was bringing such blessing with his wain as he traveled about their lands. That the Geats planned to strike now, beneath the brightness and warmth the god had given so early and free handedly that year, made Beowulf feel as though they were drinking good guest ale in a hall even as they planned harm to its host.

He wished to say to Haethcyn, "It is not too late: we can still turn back, and leave Frea Ing's frith untouched".

A rustle in the woods startled them. Haethcyn reined up fast enough to make his grey horse dance to the side; Ansuwulf had his sword half drawn and so did several other men. They paused, breathing open mouthed and silent, until the twigs crackled again. Then, suddenly, there was a tall stag standing between the trees to their left. The nubs of his sprouting antlers were wet and soft with velvet, and his ruddy coat gleamed over sturdy muscles, as though he had managed to feed well even in the deepest snow. He looked at them a moment, then dashed on.

It seemed to Beowulf that he had seen a look of reproach in the stag's dark eyes, and, more than ever, he wished to warn Haethcyn to turn back. Still, he had given his word, and so he kept his silence; but he vowed in his heart that at least he would try not to break the frith by shedding any blood on their way out, if there were any way he could keep from it. It was stranger that no one else spoke; even Sihtric, who had spoken of shooting and eating almost every bird and hare they had seen on the way, did not say,

"If I only had my hunting bow out..." Beowulf wondered if they, too, had felt anything in the stag's gaze or if it was only that none would remind the king of his ill doomed arrow. After some time, the Geats reached a ford where a wolfskin was mounted upon a pole like a banner, its paws and tail flapping in the wind.

"We are not too far now," Haethcyn said softly. Guiding his horse down to the steep drop leading into the river." Ecgtheow told me of this place where the wolves often come down to drink or cross the river: such skins are often put up to frighten them away, though it does little good. Here we shall change horses, and leave the ones we have been riding to rest, for we shall have need of fresh horses when we come galloping back. Ægmund, you shall wait here and guard them, for if any ill befalls them while we are in Upsala, we shall surely be caught and slain."

The riders dismounted, leaving the steeds they had been riding saddled and tied loosely. Beowulf patted Feola on his golden neck, and the horse nickered and nuzzled him before dropping his head to chew at the sprouting weeds about his feet. The white mare Hrime rolled her dark eyes at Beowulf she was, Hygelac had said, a little more fiery and strong willed than he would have wanted for Ecgtheow's son; but she was one of the few horses with the strength to bear him at a gallop for any distance, and he could count on her to carry him swiftly away from the burg of the Swedes.

Mounting up again, Haethcyn guided his horse down to the steep drop leading into the river, and the others followed him. Their horses splashed down into the water, the river foaming about their flanks and soaking the riders' legs as they picked their way among the rounded stones slipping beneath their hooves. It was not long before the Geats came out of the woods, riding along between furrowed fields already misted lightly with the pricking green shoots of grain. After a little while, they saw a high green mound with a broken line of smaller ones rising ahead of it, and beyond those the sharp gabled roofs of a pair of great halls, surrounded by lesser dwellings.

"That large one," Haethcyn murmured to Beowulf, "is the mound of Eadwine, father of Ongentheow." Beowulf nodded. He had heard the tales of Eadwine the Old, who gave nine of his ten sons to Woden for long life, and won thereby a span as long as that of three old men, though by the end of it, he could no longer walk or eat, but lay in bed and drank milk from the end of a cow's horn like a suckling babe. Then his folk would not suffer him to slay his last son, and Ongentheow had held the rule, though he was already aging when he took his place upon his father's high seat. "Past them are Ongentheow's hall and the Inglings' hof the hof is that one built closer to the howes, with the gilded carvings upon the roof."

When they got closer, Beowulf could see that the Upsala hof stood outside the wooden palisade that ringed Ongentheow's burg. Only stones marked the borders of the frith garth about it: it needed no walls, for no one would shed blood, save for that of the holy offerings, upon that hallowed land. Before the hof, planted in a deep hollow before one of the mounds, was a huge ash tree, its budding branches spreading wide over a well. Frayed nooses hung from several of the sturdier limbs, and sleek black crows and ravens wandered over the ground beneath the tree; but the offerings themselves had fallen from their places and someone either the gudhes and gudhijas themselves, or birds and other creatures had cleaned away the remains.

The gates of the palisade around Ongentheow's burg were wide open, as Haethcyn's most often were, for what had the kings to fear, each dwelling so far from the stronghold of his foe? The Geats were greeted by a tall, long faced man with light brown hair braided into a knot at the back of his head and his ruddy beard knotted similarly below his chin. He wore a coat of deep blue wool with wide borders of pale blue silk that hung below his knees, wrapped so that the right edge overlapped the left and held at the waist by a broad belt from which his sword hung. The coat's narrow sleeves bore clasp buttons of filigreed gold; beneath its silk edged hem, his close fitting red trousers were fastened up his calves with matching gold clasps. The bone grip of his sword was studded with silver; its pommel gleamed silver as well, and was pierced with a heavy ring of gold.

"Hail, you wanderers," the Swede said, holding up a gold ringed hand. "Who are you, and what brings you to the hall of Ongentheow, ruler of the kingdom of the Swedes?"

Haethcyn repeated the tale he had told the march warder. The Swedish thane cocked his head to the side like a crow looking down brightly from the height of a mound, and grinned.

"Then you shall bring gladness to Yrse's heart, and I think your faring shall not have been made for nothing. The idis of the Ynglings sits in her high seat; I shall take you to her myself. And that is not without honor for you, for I myself am Othere son of Ongentheow."

The Geats dismounted, leading their horses towards the hall. Ongentheow's dwelling was as large and fine as Haethcyn's, its door pillars carved with the shapes of men, some with men meeting their deaths, Beowulf realized at his first glance. One was drowning in a frothing vat; one stood in front of a stone with a long bearded dwarf by his side; another lay on his bed with a woman treading upon his body and a slant eyed Finn wife watching, and yet another was bound upon a harrow stone with a spear wielding gudhe in a long robe about to pierce him through. A moment's thought, remembering tales he had heard, told Beowulf who these were: the earlier kings of the Ingling clan, who had dwelt at Upsala many generations before Ongentheow.

"Regenold, Hror, Guthmund, you stay out to see to the horses," Haethcyn ordered, gesturing at the men he wanted, lest any had forgotten the false names they had taken for the faring. "As for the rest of you. You may help carry in my wares."

Beowulf lifted his own packs with ease, but Ansuwulf had warned him to carry none of the others, lest he draw more attention than he must. Sihtric bent slightly under Haethcyn's saddlebags, for the lightness of the amber he bore was more than counter weighted by the heaviness of the gold; Domhere came to his side quickly, helping him along, and Ansuwulf heaved the third set of saddlebags onto his own broad shoulders. Though it was hardly cold enough for the long fires to be fed high in the daytime, their flames leaped brightly in the dimness of Ongentheow's hall, flickering off the woven tapestries that hung the walls so that they seemed to move.

Among the scenes of battle, Beowulf recognized other Ingling kings of whom he had heard: one man mounted in the middle of his host held a sparrow in his hand, and there was a hay fork flying towards him like a spear. Another dangled from a tree like a god offering, hanged by a rope tied to his gold neck ring, and beside him with the other end of the rope in her hand was a woman his wife Scealfe, from whom the Inglings were also known as the Scylfings. Two rode together, one on a golden horse and one on a gray, and they were striking at each others' heads with the bridles: seeing that, Beowulf remembered how it was said that a doom had lain on that house for eleven generations, since the days of the king Wisbyre, that slaughter of kin by kin should ever be with the race of the Inglings.

With an effort, he pulled his gaze away from the tapestries, glancing about the hall. There were four thanes there, three playing at dice and one up by the high seat where the queen sat. None of them wore byrnie or helm, but they all had swords by their sides, and a few spears and shields leaned against the benches, as though their bearers had only gone out for a few moments, as likely they had. Yrse sat still as Othere not her son, Beowulf remembered: Ongentheow had sired Othere and Onela long before wedding Halga's daughter, and they were older than she led the supposed merchants before her. As Haethcyn bowed and began his tale again, Beowulf tried to look at her without seeming to stare. It was not easy to do, for Yrse drew his gaze like a whirling maelstrom sucking a ship down.

She was of middle height for a woman, so far as Beowulf could guess, wearing a deep blue shift beneath a purple red overdress which was pinned at the shoulders by two gold fibulae, the squares above the arches and the flaring lozenges below them decorated with filigree. Yrse's fine straight hair was a shade that Beowulf could not put a name to, somewhere between brown and gold and red; it was knotted at the back of her head, falling free down her back. Her eyes were gray, but flecked with large splotches of deep green like islands in a stormy sea, set off by sharp arched black eyebrows against skin whiter than birch bark.

Her pale neck was ringed by a thick layered collar of gold wrought all over with fine wire work; gold rings shone butter soft against the dark blue linen of her close fitting sleeves and upon her slight fingers, and garnets glimmered deep red from the ruddy gold of her earrings. The Swedish queen's wrists were very slender underneath the woven cuff bands of her under dress, her feet narrow as a fox's in their gold clasped shoes and her features high boned and delicate. Yet she seemed strongly built: though her hips were slim, her wide belted waist was little narrower, her shoulders quite broad and her breasts full. More: there was something about her that made Beowulf feel that, even should he seize her with all his might, she would not break in his grip, as if her bones were made of dwarf forged steel.

"Be welcome here, you and your men, Ælfred," Yrse said. Her voice was deep, with an unnerving rasp to it, as though it were not meant to be used for ordinary speech. She rose to her feet, gesturing with one thin fingered hand. "Spread out your wares, if you will, on the table by the door. I do not mean to slight you by this, but if you have brought amber, I would see it in sunlight before I think to buy it."

Haethcyn's dark lashes did not so much as flutter, nor his eyes flicker, in surprise at the luck of the queen's command: they could grab her and be out the door before any of Ongentheow's men could so much as draw sword from sheath. But he bowed again, hastening to the table and opening his pack as Yrse filled a golden cup from a cask nearby.

"Be welcome," the Swedish queen said again. She lifted the cup to Haethcyn: it was a fair vessel, beaten from pure thin gold, with a ringed handle that ended in a horse's head.

If Beowulf had not been watching Ansuwulf carefully, he would not have seen the berserk's slight nod. But Haethcyn's hand blurred out, seizing Yrse's slim wrist and whirling her close in to him as he clapped his other hand over her mouth. His men wheeled in front of him, drawing their swords and standing shoulder to shoulder to form a human shield wall before their king as Othere and the other Swedes drew their own blades and ran shouting at them. Behind his back, Beowulf heard Haethcyn gasp as if in pain and Yrse shriek,

"Out the back and call for help, you fools! Can't you see you're outnumbered?"

Two of the Swedes broke off at once, but Othere and the other two kept coming. Ongentheow's son was heading straight for Beowulf, a keening shriek rising from his mouth and his blue eyes wide with fury.

Beowulf froze for half a heartbeat: it seemed unreal to him that a man was running at him to kill him if he could and he was loath to shed the blood of Frea Ing's kinsmen in this time of frith. He barely managed to raise his blade in time to deflect Othere's. Sword edge scraped off sword with a grating shriek of metal; then Othere's weapon was flipping bright through the air like a leaping salmon. The Swedish king's son shrieked again, drawing the long sax at his belt and lunging once more.

Its point stuck in Beowulf's byrnie, wedging tight in the heavy iron rings. Beowulf grabbed Othere's knife wrist, twisting it. He meant only to make the other man drop his weapon, but he had moved too fast: Othere's arm sprang free of its shoulder socket even as his wrist bone snapped in Beowulf's grip. The Swede screamed in pain, yet his free hand was reaching for the hilt of the knife dangling from Beowulf's byrnie. Beowulf picked him up, tossing him lightly away. Othere struck the floor hard, his head thumping back, and did not rise again. Have I killed him? Beowulf thought, horrified. The other two Swedes lay in spreading dark pools, one's head hanging back over the gaping red wound of his open throat and the other writhing in a great shudder that ended with a gout of blood bursting from his mouth and nose.

Behind his men, Haethcyn was still wrestling with Yrse. The queen had gotten one hand free and was struggling like a wild thing; she was trying to knee Haethcyn in the groin and gouge his eyes out at the same time, while he fought to hold her without hurting her. His nose was swelling fast, blood running from it to soak his dark beard, as if Yrse had managed to butt him in the face with her head, and a flap of bloodied gray cloth hung loose from one of his sleeves. Without thought, Beowulf grasped her from behind, pinning her arms to her body and lifting her from the floor. Held thus, Yrse was still trying to kick behind her, but her feet could only strike the heavy muscle of Beowulf's thighs, and he noticed that no more than he would have the tapping of a child's fists.

"Well done," Haethcyn gasped. "Now go!"

The Geats burst out the door, leaping onto their horses and spurring the beasts into a gallop. Behind them, the Swedes were shouting, but Beowulf did not look back to see how close they were: he held to Hrime with his knees, fighting to keep her pointed straight at the open gate and not to tighten his legs enough to crush her ribs. Beowulf held Yrse under one arm as he rode. To his relief, for Hrime was racing hard to keep up with the others and he could barely keep the horse under his control, the Swedish queen had stopped struggling she knew, most likely, that a fall now would go ill for her. As they pounded down the road, Beowulf tried to slow Hrime a little, but she was beyond heeding the bit: even with Yrse's weight added to his own, she was passing the other horses one by one.

"Beowulf!" Haethcyn shouted as they galloped past him, but there was nothing Beowulf could do, save hold on and hope that Hrime would slow of her own will before he fell off or she dropped.

To Beowulf's great relief, Hrime slowed to a painfully bouncy trot, then to a walk, as they neared the ford. Her head was hanging low and she was blowing hard, foam spraying from her nostrils with each breath; the saddle skirting and the inner thighs of Beowulf's trousers were soaked with the horse's sweat. Haethcyn and the others were out of sight behind them, and after a moment's thought, Beowulf dismounted, taking Hrime's reins in one hand and setting Yrse on her feet with the other though he kept tight hold of her arm, lest she try to break away. A quick glance showed him that the gold mounted knife sheath on her belt was empty: Haethcyn must have disarmed her in their struggle. Yrse's hair had come loose, falling wild and disheveled around her face, and her green flecked gray eyes stared balefully up at him.

"Come with me," Beowulf said gruffly, leading horse and woman down into the river. The current swirled around them, and Yrse stumbled as its strength caught her; it might have knocked her from her feet if Beowulf had not been holding onto her.

Ægmund's boyish grin of delight dropped from his face as he saw they were alone. "What of Haethcyn?" He asked in alarm. "Where are the rest of them?"

"You need not fear, I hope," Beowulf answered. "Hrime outran all the others, and if she had not grown tired, we would be halfway to the Geats' land by now."

Yrse's eyes widened in surprise. "Haethcyn you are Geats! And was that Haethcyn himself who laid such hands upon me?"

"I think you did more harm to him than he did to you," Beowulf replied. "But I hope that you took no hurt from our ride."

"You are a fool, to ride a horse that is so far beyond your skill," Yrse stated bluntly. "No, I am not hurt, though that is no thanks to you. I should rather call it a blessing of the gods that we did not both fall from her back and break our necks. What do you mean to do with me now?" Her lips were set in a thin pale line, her white knuckled fists clenched tight upon her slim hips, and Beowulf could not tell whether she was shaking with anger or with fear.

"We shall treat you with the honor that is fitting for a queen, and give you back to Ongentheow in due course," Beowulf answered. Then he breathed out in relief, for he heard the sound of galloping hooves growing closer. "But now you must make a choice quickly. Will you ride before me, and give your word that you will not try to get away, or must I carry you under my arm again?"

Yrse barked a short unkind laugh. "I will not ride with you again if I have any choice. And I doubt," she added, looking pointedly at the high arch of the front saddle bow on Feola's back and the thickly padded rear bow, "that both of us could ride on that saddle. If Haethcyn can handle a horse any better than you can, let him take me before him if he dares. I swear by the Frowe's necklace that I will not try to get away, at least not until we are within sight of my husband's men. And you may let go of my arm now!"

The rest of the Geats were splashing down through the ford; Beowulf handed Hrime's reins over to Ægmund and quickly untied and mounted Feola.

"Are you followed?" He asked Haethcyn.

"They cannot be too far behind," the king panted. "Here we split up; they can follow our trails easily enough yet, but if we go by threes, we will go faster and they will not know who to chase. We shall meet again at Ecgtheow's burg, those who are still alive. Ansuwulf and Beowulf, you two shall come with Yrse and I; the rest of you may go with whom you choose. Beowulf, take Yrse up before you."

"I have sworn to come without trouble," the Swedish queen said, holding her head up proudly. "Haethcyn, do you dare to let me ride with you?" The flesh around Haethcyn's eyes was beginning to darken, his nose swelling across his face Beowulf thought Yrse might have broken it and his dark mustache and beard were clotted stiffly with blood.

"I trust the honor of your oath," Haethcyn replied, mounting up and lifting Yrse to sit in his lap. Though the front bow of his saddle was padded well with plaited oat straw under the leather, it would be an uncomfortable ride for her; she had spoken wisely when she doubted that she could ride double with Beowulf. Then he looked back at Hrime, taking in her lowered head, sweat grayed hide, and frothing muzzle. "The other horses can go with us, but I think she would founder on the way. We must leave her behind."

Beowulf thought of the beasts the Swedes had slaughtered in the village near Hroesnabeorh, and of Hrime's brave gallop under his weight.

"The Swedes are likely to slay her if they find her," he said.

Yrse nodded. "She will be given as an offering, that Frea Ing not be too greatly angered at the breaking of his frith faring."

"Still, we can neither take her nor tarry," Haethcyn told him.

Yrse looked at the horse, her delicate features drawn in thought. "I may be able to help her. Let me down."

"A few moments, no more," said Haethcyn curtly.

But he lifted Yrse to the ground. The Swedish queen walked over to the white horse, running her hands over Hrime's wet hide and whispering in the mare's ear. The hairs along Beowulf's spine stood up: he could not see what Yrse was doing, but he could feel the might coiling up from the earth like an adder wakening in the summer sun. Hrime lifted her head, tossing her pale mane and pawing the ground with one fore hoof.

"Now she has the strength to run again," Yrse said.

They set off at a good pace, though the woods were too thick to let them gallop. The king and his captive headed northwest, since that was the least likely of the ways they might go. They would ride for a day, then circle southward again. Yrse did not speak, but clutched the heavy bronze rings on either side of the fore bow tightly: she might be a good rider when sitting alone in the saddle, and the tölt a smooth gait, but when they could, they broke into a canter, and then Beowulf could see that the Swedish queen was having a hard time in her uncomfortable perch before Haethcyn.

Though often the riders had to slow to a walk or even pause for short whiles, lest their horses founder beneath them, Haethcyn did not let them stop for longer than it took for the steeds to get their breath back until the sun had set and the twilight was fading into full dark. Only then did he dismount, fumbling in the dimness to unsaddle and tie the horses. Ansuwulf, meanwhile, hurried to gather sticks and clear a space on the ground for a fire. Tinder he carried in his small buckled belt pouch, but he had to take the strip of leather off to start it, for his oval striking stone was attached to the back of the belt by bronze eagle headed mounts and the iron headed stick hung in its own sheath beside it.

The berserk was skilled at lighting fires: it was only a short while before one of the sparks caught, smoldering gently beneath his breath, and he began to blow and feed the flame up into life. Although they had nothing better than smoked meat and hard bread, Yrse ate as neatly as if she were sitting in her own high seat.

Though the light score she had left on Haethcyn's arm had soaked his torn sleeve with blood in the course of their ride before he bandaged it during one of their brief stops, the Geat king lent her his knife, and now haggled at the tough meat with his teeth while she sliced off little strips one by one from her own portion, chewing them carefully and thoroughly. The trust and the honor which Haethcyn was showing her seemed to have warmed the Swede queen's mood; at least, she was no longer glaring at her captors, though she spoke little.

"Thank you for giving Hrime strength," Beowulf said at last. "I would have liked it little if we had needed to leave her behind."

Yrse looked into his face, and he felt the same prickling shiver over his skin that he had felt before. The firelight cast her cheekbones into stark relief above the dark shadows of her face, hollowing the sockets about her gray green eyes; and where she had looked younger than her years in the light of day, now she might have been old as corpse white Hell herself.

"I did not do it for you," Yrse said. "But she would have made a fair offering and now, I think, Frea Ing will choose his gift for himself." Her deep voice seemed to grate through Beowulf's bones, and his nettle prickling skin felt almost as though it would slip from his body like the scales of a snake.

Haethcyn paled in the firelight, but Ansuwulf leapt to his feet. "Be silent!" He commanded. "It is not well for you to speak such things not for us, nor yet for you, for you do not know whether that choice will be to your own liking or not."

Yrse rose slowly to her own feet, facing the berserk across the fire. They were almost of a height, for Ansuwulf was a short man: both wiry bodied and broad shouldered, they might nearly have been brother and sister. It seemed to Beowulf that shadow and brightness flickered between them, back and forth, now burning as a ring of sparks around Yrse's layered gold necklace, now glittering from Ansuwulf's pale hair as though he wore a gilded helm. In the light of the flames, her purple red dress and his black cloak melted into the same darkness; and when she answered his words, her rough voice echoed above his in a chilling harmony.

"What do you know of my liking?" Yrse asked. "It may be that Ongentheow still owes me geld for my father Halga's death, and for my husband's as well: the two were slain in a single blow. And it may also be that I have been handed from king to king with little choice in the matter, and have no mind to be a gaming piece, however gilded, in your battles. Then again, I may have plans of my own, for I have seen certain things that shall surely come to pass, and this has its place among them."

Ansuwulf snarled a laugh. "I think you mean to frighten us, for if you had foreseen this day and willed what may come of it, you would not have struggled so hard in Haethcyn's arms."

Yrse's lips curled into a smile, and though she did not break her gaze by looking at the Geat king, her slender hand gestured towards him, her red gold rings flashing as though the fire had leapt up to coil about her fingers.

"Would I not? No man lays hand on me without my leave, unless he pay the price for it and that price, I can swear to you, is not any necklace, though it be forged by the hands of the dwarves. Even you, Beowulf, strong though you be; even you shall find that you have paid more than you would wish to give before this turning of Wyrd is done, and shall pay more when she rises from her Well again, though the price shall be far less than it might, for that you strove to keep Frea Ing's frith, and shed no blood in the Inglings' hall. Though neither of you drank from the guest cup I bore you, yet you must still drink your draught from Wyrd's vessel." She paused, still staring at Ansuwulf.

"And as for you, Woden's wolf you have done me no ill, so I shall do you good in turn. Though your gray hame cloaks you in a byrnie no iron can pierce, be warned: you shall soon be struck by a sword that is more than iron. If you do not bear a helm upon your head in the battles that are coming, then you shall surely die; if you do, you may live."

Ansuwulf watched Yrse warily, but she said no more. Instead she lowered herself carefully as an old woman, squatting in the mud again, and began to tear greedily at her meat with her teeth as though she had been starved for days. When she moved closer to the fire, the men could see that she was shivering. Haethcyn took off his cloak.

"Wear this, if you will," he offered. "It is the least I can do since I gave you no chance to take whatever clothes you had ready for this journey."

Beowulf could not tell from Haethcyn's voice whether he was mocking Yrse or seriously agreeing that she had foreseen what they would do; nor, with the Geat king's face swollen from her head blow and the shadows of the fire hiding his mouth completely in the darkness of his beard, could Beowulf guess at his meaning from any twitch of his features. Yrse seemed as confused as Beowulf, but she took the cloak from Haethcyn's hand, wrapping it tightly around her shoulders.

"I thank you," she said. "Though you took me with no thought for my will in the matter, if you go on as you have begun, none shall say that you have not dealt as well with me as you could."

VI

Haethcyn and his companions traveled hard, but not as swiftly as the Geats would have liked, for they did not dare to ride along the roads now. They picked their way through green springing woodlands and around the edges of bogs, and when they came to streams or rivers that were shallow enough, they rode through the water as far as they could so that their tracks could not be traced. For all their care, though, they had to stop at small farmhouses now and then, first to get plain clothes for Yrse, then to trade the odd snippet broken from thin silver arm rings for food. Guessing their way by the course of the sun, at last they came to the shore of a broad lake whose far side was past their sight, its waters rippling gray beneath low clouds and rising mists.

"Lake Weter?" Beowulf said. "We must be almost to my father's burg."

Haethcyn reined in his horse, staring out over the inland sea. His face had healed in the course of their ride, but his nose had mended flattened and askew, leaving him with a grimmer look than he had borne before.

"No. We bore too far to the west: this is Lake Wener. Another day's riding should have us past the Swedish march posts but we are in our greatest danger now, for Ongentheow is likely to have his marches heavily guarded, if indeed his host is not already awaiting us there."

"Still," Ansuwulf mused, "it is no little way between Wener and Weter, and Ongentheow cannot watch that whole stretch of land. If the gods are with us, we shall slip through his net. If not well, no man can flee his Wyrd, and we may bargain Yrse for our lives at need."

Beowulf glanced at the Swedish queen to see if she would take those words ill. Clad now in plain gray wool, with her gold all hidden away, it was still clear that Yrse was no farmer's maid. She sat straight backed on the saddle before Haethcyn, her long loose hair bright as winter touched leaves over her dark gray cloak and a look of unearthly calm on her high boned face: had she borne a spear in her hand, she might easily have been taken for a waelcyrige, one of Woden's daughters horsed before the hero she had chosen for Waelhall.

"So be it, then," Haethcyn said, tightening his knees to urge his horse onwards and towards the east.

Beowulf slept ill that night: the soft damp chill of the lake mist did not bother him, though they had not dared to light a fire, but even after the day's riding and his turn on guard, he found that he was turning restlessly, his muscles tightening with every rustle of breeze or crackling twig. At last he gave up on sleep, standing up and going over to Ansuwulf. The berserk was barely a black shadow in the clouded darkness. Without moon or stars to light them, Beowulf thought, there had been little need to set a watch. No man could travel through the woods on such a night, nor had Yrse any hope of escaping, even had she chosen to break her word.

"So you feel it too," Ansuwulf murmured to him.

"Feel what?" Beowulf asked cautiously.

"There are many wights abroad this night, both lesser and greater," the berserk answered. "Some are drawn by the scents of the battlefield that shall be, circling above us like ravens and eagles thirsty for their red mead. That is no strange thing, but the wights of Swede land and Geat land are also stirring, as though they await some great change. The dwarves groan before their stone doors, and the alfs ride about their howes. And when I slept, while you watched..." Ansuwulf was silent for a long moment, his breathing soft and ragged in the darkness.

Then he drew a deep breath, as though steeling himself for a hard burst of strength, but when he spoke again, his words were so soft that Beowulf could barely make them out. "Far though we are from Whale's Ness, and the great howe on Eagles' Ness beyond it ...I saw the glimmering eyes of the wyrm."

"The wyrm?"

"Do you not know of it?"

Again there was silence in the dark, broken only by the whispering of wind over wet leaves and the quiet lapping of ripples against the shore of the lake.

"But Geatland did not always belong to the Geats. More than two hundred winters ago, many years before Sigemund the Walsing was born or Swerting raised his hall by Whale's Ness, another folk dwelt there a wealthy folk, who gathered many treasures. Death took them all in that early age. But there was one, a man of that host, who lingered the longest, mourning his friends: he, likewise, might enjoy that wealth for but a little time. The barrow was readied, dwelt on the plain by the sea waves new by the headland, made fast where none might easily go. There within he, the ring warder, bore ruler's treasures worthy of being hoarded, ornamented gold, and spoke a few words." Ansuwulf began to chant softly, his voice rippling low through Beowulf's bones.

"Hold you now, earth, what heroes now may not,
athelings' treasures in earlier times,
brought from you by good men; battle death took them,
greedy life bale bore off each of them,
of my folk, from their given lives,
beholding hall joy. Who are the sword bearers,
or polishers of gold goblets adorned,
dear drink vessels? vanished, that host.
Those hardened helms hand wrought with gold,
are bereft of ornaments bondsmen are sleeping,
who should make bright the battle masks.

This coat of war likewise that in clash of arms knew
biting of iron over breaking shields,
moulders with men. Nor may byrnie's rings
widely with battle's wielders fare,
by heroes' side. No harp sound's joy,
the glee wood singing, nor good hawk any
flies through hall, nor horse swift running
tramples through burg yard. Baleful death
so very many sent forth of my kin.

"Thus, in mourning mood, and mindful of youth years," Ansuwulf went on, "alone, last of all of them, he wended unblithe day and night until death's flood touched his heart. And there he lay, the fallen warder of that gold, among the treasures and bones of his kin and then the wyrm coiled about the hoard in the howe's darkness, where it lies yet. The hot fire of the gold burns in its breath, and the cold barrow fire in its eyes: but long it sleeps, and stirs only when great things ripple in the well of Wyrd."

"What does this betide?" Beowulf asked. "And is this stirring good or ill?"

"Who can say? The wyrm lurks at the roots of the mound, and its gold is hulled in stone and earth like a seed in its shell; it is from such roots and seeds that the might of the land springs, and from the bones lying white and gray within the home hills. Yet, were it ever to come forth from the howe in wrath, its fire would scorch all that lay before it, for though the wyrm lies within the Middle Garth, it is a wight of the worlds beyond, and such things are too strong for the sunlit lands of Ash and Elm's children to bear." The berserk sighed. "And this, too, you must remember, Beowulf. Though you fear the spear and noose and storm of the One Eyed, and turn towards the Wan gods' sunlight, Frea Ing is also the king of the mound, and the Frowe a stirrer of strife between men. The gold fire that sets brother against brother comes from their hands as surely as the ripening grain, and they are no strangers to the wyrm that sleeps in the barrow's depths."

Ansuwulf fell silent, and Beowulf could bring himself to ask nothing more. Yet it seemed to him that, straining his eyes into the night's blackness, he could see a faint gleam: cold howe fire burning blue, its chilly spark mirrored pale from the coils of gold rings and cups, brooches and helm crests and bridle mounts. The glow brightened into twin hoarfrost flames, steady as if they burned in a place where no wind had stirred within man's memory. Beowulf felt himself drawing closer; a hint of rot and mold, like a far off whisper on the wind, tainted each breath he took. Though fear slicked his bowels with ice, he could not turn his gaze away from those two ghastly lights: pale and faint as they were, they seemed to burn through his eyes, glimmering within the darkness of his skull as within the stone ringed darkness of the mound. Something closed on Beowulf's shoulder, and he leapt up, flailing madly about himself.

"Hold, Beowulf," Ansuwulf's deep voice said. "It is only I the dawn is nearly upon us, and we must be going.

As Beowulf's sight cleared, he saw the graying sky through the night dark branches, and Ansuwulf balanced lightly on the balls of his feet before him, a little beyond his reach. Beowulf drew a deep ragged breath, as though he had just come up out of deep water.

"I saw...Ansuwulf, I saw..."

"Speak not of it!" Ansuwulf hissed to him. "There are some things best kept in silence."

"But last night you said..."

Ansuwulf only shook his head. "Eat quickly, if you hunger, and then help us to saddle the horses. You have more things to worry about today, for if the sword's edge is doomed to be your bane, then thinking upon the lore of shadows and ghosts will give you no help in staying your death day."

That brought to Beowulf's mind what Yrse had said to Ansuwulf.

"If there is to be fighting today, then will you take my helm?" Beowulf asked.

The berserk laughed. "Aye if I had the fleece of a whole sheep to pad it with, for so much larger is your skull than mine. But death is a little matter to one who is given to Woden, after all. Should I fall, make as sure as you can that Eofor gets all my goods, and ask Haethcyn to see that he marries again soon, that the line of Wonred's sons not be lost forever."

Ansuwulf's tone as he spoke those words was lighter than Beowulf had ever heard it, as though the threat of death in battle actually eased the berserk's mind. Perhaps he is fey, Beowulf thought, but the thought did not unnerve him as it might have: that was a matter between Ansuwulf and the god to whom he had given himself long ago. But as for me, Frea Ing, I would ask for life, if you will grant it, and frith at the end of all this.

Take your offerings as you will, but let there be no more suffering than need be, for that you are a kindly god, and friend to the children of men. They turned away from the shores of Lake Wener, picking their way carefully through the woods; Haethcyn said they had been lucky that Ongentheow had not set men riding about the lake, but he would likely think of that soon enough. Haethcyn and Beowulf wore their boar crested helms now, for there would be no way for any disguise to hide them if the Swedes caught sight of Yrse, and the paws of Ansuwulf's wolf fell were draped over his chest, the gray ears pricking up above his head and the muzzle drooping over his brow.

Riding along, they tried to move like elk or deer going a little way, then pausing to listen carefully for any sound of men on the wind; it was a hunter's trick, done so that prey would not be alerted by the unnatural sound of a creature that moved straight forward without stopping or looking about itself, but now it was they themselves who were prey. And yet they were also hunters, for they had to watch the ground carefully for any spoor that would show men or horses had passed lately, and guess the age and path of the tracks as if they wished to seek out the ones who had made them.

The next night was silent and chill as the one before, but Haethcyn and Ansuwulf guessed that they were not far from the march stones now, and if they could cross that straggling line of boulders unseen, then they were likely to make it safely to Ecgtheow's hall. They were coming upon tracks more often now, however; and not the clear marks of a single horse's hooves or pair of shod feet, but the churned blurs left behind by bands of riders and marchers, with only a few sharp edges left stamped in the mud to prove that it had not been long since the men had passed.

Whenever they found such spoor, the Geats changed their path quickly, getting a safe distance away and then halting to listen once more for voices or hoof beats or the muted sound of jingling byrnies. That day, they did not pause long enough to eat, only drinking a few sips of water from wide stoppered flasks of birch wood as they rode. By afternoon, Beowulf was beginning to feel faint from hunger, though he said nothing. He had gone longer without eating on the way back from the land of the Finns, but a winter of good food had stolen some of that hardiness from him. Suddenly, during one of their short halts, the wind shifted and the Geats heard the deep murmur of human speech, though they could not make out the voices.

Beowulf, Haethcyn, and Ansuwulf looked at each other, and Beowulf could guess what his companions were thinking: were those Swedes on their trail, or had they already passed between the far flung border markers without knowing it? Haethcyn put a finger to his lips, and they froze, but there was no way to keep their horses from snuffling at the curly green fern fronds or biting off mouthfuls of leaves. The Geats could only hope that whoever was nearby, they would not recognize the faint sounds for what they were. Yrse's scream shattered the silence, ringing through Beowulf's head like a hard sword blow to the skull. Ansuwulf's horse reared, and Haethcyn's spare mount tore its lead reins from the king's hand, plunging away through the underbrush with a loud crash; even stolid Feola crab leapt sideways, so that Beowulf was hard put to stay on his back.

"Trolls take you!" Haethcyn raged at Yrse, his dark face reddening. "Ride, all of you drop your lead ropes and ride!" He touched his spurs hard to his horse's flanks; the gray whirled so fast that Yrse would have flown from the saddle if Haethcyn had not been gripping her tight to him, and they charged off, Ansuwulf's bay following closely and the loose steeds racing beside them. Feola broke into a trot, but there was a mouthful of fern fronds sticking out about his bit, and he seemed little minded to go faster while he was still eating.

Though Beowulf had never spurred a horse before, he had dutifully strapped the heel plates with their pointed studs onto his feet when he shod himself. Now, in desperation, he dug them hard into Feola's golden sides. Feola gathered himself and shot forward in a bound that was almost a leap. The front saddle bow jolted painfully against Beowulf's belly, but without it, he would have gone straight over the horse's neck. Haethcyn and Ansuwulf were out of sight already, but Beowulf could hear them crashing through the woods, and the sound of men shouting and other horses galloping close to them. He crouched down in the saddle, holding tight; but though Feola was not so fast as Hrime, at least he answered to his reins. Still, when they came to a stream, Beowulf could not check him. For a sickening moment the horse was airborne, then he landed with a lurch that nearly tore Beowulf from the saddle and pounded on.

"Halt or die!" a man's voice shouted shrilly ahead; the challenge was answered by a curse that rose from a snarl into a wordless howl. If I turn now, I could go for help, Beowulf thought but he could not leave Haethcyn and Ansuwulf to the Swedes.

Then, in a blurred flash, Beowulf was upon the others: Haethcyn alone on his horse, sweeping about with his sword at the four Swedes around him; Ansuwulf on foot, his face fixed in the grimace of a wolf dying from the howling wod and droplets of froth spewing from his angrily gaping mouth as he hewed at the foes that ringed him; and Yrse standing to the side with three men guarding her, watching calmly through half lidded eyes. Feola would not stop. Desperately Beowulf hauled on the reins to turn him, and got his head about, but the horse kept going forward.

Too late, Beowulf saw the gray beech trunk and tried to wrench Feola away from it. His steed's shoulder banged hard into the tree; frightened and hurt, Feola leapt up, bucking hard. Beowulf's sight spun as he hurtled sickeningly through the air. The ground struck him harder than the blow of any mighty wave, his head snapping back into blackness. Beowulf awoke lying on his back with a fierce pounding pain at the back of his skull, his body aching and his head swimming. Dizzily he tried to reach behind himself and push himself up, but his hands would not move. He blinked the worst of the blur from his eyes, and saw that a pale snake wound around his wrists no, it was many coils of rope that bound him, both hand and foot. The sky was dark above, but a gray light lay over him and after a few moments, he realized that he was near the doorway of a large tent.

"The gods all be blessed, you wake," Haethcyn croaked. The Geat king sat bound on the other side of the tent. His byrnie, helm, and sword had been stripped from him, and a rough blood soaked bandage was wrapped about his shield shoulder. "It is not going so well for us as I had hoped."

Beowulf managed a faint cough of a laugh, but the effort made his entrails lurch in his belly. He turned his head to the side, waiting for a few moments to see if he would cast up the little water he had drunk that day. When his stomach had settled again, he rolled his head back to look at Haethcyn.

"Where is Ansuwulf? Is he dead?"

Haethcyn tried to smile, a twisted grimace beneath his crooked nose.

"As best I know, he got away. He slew four of the men he fought, but the fifth broke in fear and ran from him. With the berserk wod upon him, he gave chase if he did not drop to lie weak and helpless in the woods from the strain of the fit afterwards, and if no more Swedes came upon him, he may yet have made it to Ecgtheow. If we have any hope left to us, it is that, though that is little enough."

Beowulf closed his eyes in pain, thinking on the last moments he remembered. He had struck no blow, nor even drawn his sword...

"Haethcyn, my king," he whispered. "I am sorry. I failed you."

"You did not fail me at Upsala, which was why I brought you. It is true that I should have chosen a better rider to come with Ansuwulf and myself on the way back. But then, we might as easily have found ourselves standing to fight as running. I chose you on those grounds, and it was my own choice that failed me, for I knew the bounds of your skill on horseback. And had you set your feet safely on the ground before they were upon you, there were still twelve of them, a king's chosen thanes all, and three of us.

Doughty as you may be, few could win with such odds." Haethcyn's voice was flat and unyielding as always, yet for once, Beowulf found himself taking some comfort from it. He is growing to be a good king, Beowulf thought and then, because he could not help it: Or will be, if Ongentheow lets him live.

Beowulf yawned, his jaws stretching and cracking with the depth of it. He was suddenly very sleepy. Closing his eyes, he readied himself to drift off.

"Beowulf!" Haethcyn snapped. "You must not sleep."

"Why?" Beowulf asked.

"Because you struck your head on a stone when you fell. If you had not been wearing a helm, I think your brains would be leaking into the leaves now. But when a man is hit on the head and knocked out like that, then he must not sleep too soon afterwards, or else he may never awake."

Beowulf lay like that for a long time, with Haethcyn's voice calling him back whenever he seemed near to fading into sleep. Each time he opened his eyes, his sight seemed a little blurrier, and when he finally forced himself to sit up, he had to turn his head to the side again as his stomach threatened to spew. The light through the open tent door was dimming when a shadow fell across it. The man who stooped to enter was tall and thin, his long gray hair braided back from a balding head. He wore a golden cloak trimmed with gleaming dark fur, pinned at the shoulder with a gold fibula that might have weighed a full mark.

His knee length kirtle was bright red, hemmed with a woven band that showed the figures of boars and horses wrought in yellow silk thread upon a green background; its long sleeves, fastened along their whole length with gold clasps, were tight enough on his arms to show every shift of his stringy muscles, and the garment's belt was decorated with a line of gold plates showing boar crested warriors and men battling with beasts. His ring hilted sword was slung on a shoulder belt, mounted likewise with gold adornment. The aged atheling's nose was sharp and thin as a knife blade, and though his face was lined deeply with age, his beard and eyebrows nearly white, his cheeks did not have the sunken look of a toothless oldster's.

His blue eyes were pale as a winter sky, quietly piercing as wind whispering over a field of glistening rime. There was something in the hoarfrost light of their steadiness that disturbed Beowulf, for it seemed to him in his head wounded daze that he could see the glimmer of the wyrm's eyes there. Beowulf might have known Ongentheow by his bearing, let alone the richness of his garb and adornments: but if he had any cause to wonder, the heavy gold ring below the corded bulge of the Swede king's left bicep marked him beyond doubt.

A boar's head with curled tusks and garnet eyes gleamed at either end of that ring, and its curved arc was as thick as a woman's wrist, wrought around its full length with the smaller figures of swine and bearded faces shaped in beaded gold wire: that was Sweogris, the holy ring which was drenched in the blood of a boar and a man and set upon the arm of each new king of the Swedes when he stepped up to take his father's high seat. None save the Swede king might bear it, and upon that ring the Inglings swore their mightiest oaths, with Frea Ing their line father to witness.

A younger warrior, with byrnie hanging from his wiry shoulders and gold crested helm upon his head, followed Ongentheow. At first Beowulf thought that he was looking upon Othere again, and his heart was gladdened to think that he had not slain the young Ingling at Upsala. But then he saw that this man was a little shorter than Othere, his silk plaited beard longer and his eyes pale green instead of blue: this would be the Swede king's other son, Onela.

"Haethcyn Geat king," Ongentheow said mildly. His voice was high and nasal, but it did not crack or waver. "This is not the meeting with me you awaited, I think. But when king sets his strength and wit against king, then the Norns alone know who shall win the day."

"That is so," Haethcyn allowed. "Ongentheow Swede king, it seems that you have me for now. But since you have bound my hands and feet, I see little good in dancing about matters. What do you mean to do with me?"

"What did you mean to do with Yrse?" Ongentheow countered, looking down at his fellow king.

"To hold her until we had come to terms of frith, as proof that you would keep to them. It was you who struck at my lands first, burning and slaying about Hroesnabeorh; for that, I would have a full geld, and the sure knowledge that it shall not happen again. As for Yrse, you may ask her how I treated her. She had the best of our food and the warmest cloaks, nor did any man do anything to her which would not be seemly for brother to do to sister."

"Yrse has told me as much," Ongentheow said. Then his thin pale lips spread in a slow smile. "Though that man would be unlucky whose sister handled him as Yrse dealt with you when you took her from my hall. But as for bartering Yrse's freedom for terms of frith and geld for a few farmers slain for the son of a king, Haethcyn, you seem to lack the will to take and hold what you may get. I await far more from your capture, by the time I have fully done with you and yours."

"Speak plainly, then. He who awaits much should not fear to face the means of his gain."

"And he who is bound should not speak so to those who stand free and armed," Onela broke in. His father frowned at him, making a small gesture with his hand, and the younger Ingling quieted at once.

"It is not well for a man to boast too highly of what he has not done, nor wise to tell his thoughts to a foe," Ongentheow mused. "Yet your theft of Yrse was both bold and cunning, though it did not turn as you wished. Nor did you slay Othere in my hall, though you shed blood in that garth during a time of frith: I think you might have taken my son's life easily there. And thus I am minded to answer you in full."

Onela tugged hard at one of the plaits of his brown beard, until the red silken thread braided into it slipped its knot and began to ravel loose.

"Father, what is the need of that? They are doomed already, and there is nothing to be gained by speech with them."

"Be still, Onela, or you shall learn that the old boar has a tusk or two left to slash with!" Ongentheow glared at his son until Onela dropped his eyes, an angry flush spreading across his thin cheeks like redness swelling around a fevered wound. The Swede king turned his gaze back to Haethcyn. "As for you: I shall take you and your thane back to Uppsala, and there your lives shall be spilt by the holy harrow, as geld for Frea Ing's sake. You, Haethcyn, broke his frith faring, and the god is angry for that. As for Beowulf, I can see the shade of Ecgtheow in his face, and I have an old score to settle with the Waegmunding who was once my sworn and stout warrior: the death of Ecgtheow's son will pay that scot. Then there is no doubt but that Hygelac will raise his host to war, and come forth to do battle with me. But Hygelac is young, while I have seen more years of fighting than most men have years of life. Thus the Geats shall fall, and the Swede realm reach through all this land north of Scania. As for Scania in the south Hrothgar grows old, and fails daily beneath Grendel's blows, even as my wife's son Hrothulf waxes to manhood: his claim on the Dane kingdom is as good as that of Hrothgar's sons. Now this knowledge may give you little cheerfulness, but I believe that a brave man would rather go open eyed to his doom than stumble to it blindly."

Haethcyn nodded gravely. "I thank you for that. Should you yourself come into my hands, I shall do the same for you."

Ongentheow looked at Beowulf, his cold pale eyes thoughtful. "How fare you? My thanes tell me that you fell from your horse and struck your head. You are pale as a dead man, and your eyes are darkened as if you had drunk a draught of ale. Is there aught that you need save your freedom, which I shall not give you?"

Beowulf did not dare shake his head, for he was still dizzy and pain burst from the back of his skull each time he moved. The bitter taste of bile burned at the back of his throat, a thin sharp trickle rising from his stomach. He swallowed hard, trying to gulp it back down so that the Inglings would not think it was Ongentheow's promise of death that had sickened him.

"No? Still, I shall send Yrse in to you, in hopes that she can aid you. Tomorrow you must set yourself upon the road of a long faring, and you are too great a burden to be slung over the back of a horse like a set of saddlebags, while I will not put you in a wain where you might have more chance of getting free. Until tomorrow then, Haethcyn Geat king, Beowulf son of Ecgtheow." The old king nodded again to them and left the tent. Onela trailed a little behind his father, the sound of his footfalls sharp and angry.

"It shall not go so well for the Swedes when Ongentheow is dead," Haethcyn said, his voice cool as if he were speaking of the matter over ale in his own hall. "I think that Onela and Othere shall not find it easy to share the rule of their realm, and for all Frea Ing is a god of frith, the brothers of his line have often been at each others' throats before. Nor do I believe that I am the only man of kingly kin in this camp who wonders whose arm Sweogris shall rest upon when Ongentheow bears it no more."

Haethcyn is a brave man, Beowulf thought. Why is it that his rule has been blighted by such ill? And yet, unfair as it might be, Beowulf found that he was nursing a tiny spark of gladness in his heart, like a single coal glowing beneath the chill gray ash of a winter morning. If Haethcyn died, Hygelac would live: thus the stave of the Swertings' doom had promised. He sighed, easing himself down to lie on his side, for the pounding in his head was growing worse, lines of pain radiating out from the lump on his skull like a web around a great baleful spider. His eyes were closing again, and each time he dragged them open, it seemed that Haethcyn's urgent voice called from a little farther away.

Someone was kindling a fire just outside the door of the tent; Beowulf heard the sound of an iron stick tip striking sparks against a stone that rang softly beneath its blows. It was not long before the flames sprang up, bright against the deepening twilight gloom that cloaked Haethcyn's shape darkly and hid his face in the tent's shadows. A little while passed, and Yrse stepped in, a small leather bag in her hand. She had put off the simple gray wool that the Geats had gotten her; the purple red dress in which she had been stolen away would never be fit for an atheling bride to wear again, but Ongentheow must have brought other clothes for her.

The Swede queen wore an overdress of fine diamond woven twill, pale green with deep green threads patterned through it, above a white linen under dress with a band of shiny black horsehair embroidery running up the seams of the sleeves. Yrse's layered gold collar was back around her neck, but below it drooped several long strands of fire glowing amber, and about her waist was a belt mounted, like her husband's, with figured gold plates. Beowulf thought he knew the amber and the belt: the queen must have taken them out of the Geats' saddlebags. But while he and Haethcyn lay bound in the Inglings' tent, who was to say that the treasures with which they had tricked Yrse were not her rightful plunder?

"Greetings again, Haethcyn and Beowulf," Yrse said. "I told you that you would get a fitting return for taking me."

"You also swore not to try to escape unless your husband's men were in sight," Haethcyn replied.

"And so I did not. But I never gave oath that I would not do my best to make it easy for them to find us! Now, Beowulf, I saw you fall, and Ongentheow tells me that you are ill from the blow to your head. Lie still."

Yrse knelt down beside Beowulf and undid his braid, her slender fingers searching carefully through his thick hair to probe at his skull. He bit his lip to silence his gasps, for every touch of her fingertips sent a bright flash of pain through his head, and gentle as she was with him, she was very thorough. Standing, she brought a burning stick from the fire and held it close enough to Beowulf's face that he could feel the warmth scorching his cheeks.

"Open your eyes."

He tried to, but could not. Her fingers pulled his lids open and she nodded, murmuring to herself as she tossed the brand out through the open flap.

"It is harder to give strength to a man than to a horse," Yrse said. "For a horse does not question or doubt, but a man's mind will not always believe what he feels, and thus shuts the door through which blessing might flow. Be still, Beowulf, and calm your thoughts: you are not a man to be overcome easily, if you will not freely take what I give you."

She rocked back on her heels, humming softly, though if there were a tune in her deep throat, Beowulf could not follow it. His head was wheeling as if he had tried to sit up again, his thoughts melting like a child's sand burg beneath the lapping of the waves. The gleaming of Yrse's figured necklace caught his eyes, drawing his gaze along the whorled and beaded patterns of the gold layered ring on ring. It seemed to Beowulf that he could see the stars above, the Wain swinging along its heaven road, white sparks against the blackness. He lay on the cold naked earth, his limbs numb with its chill.

Though he could not turn his head nor move, from the corners of his sight he could see the sprawled bodies about him, shields shattered and blood dark on their byrnies. But Yrse towered above him, tall as a birch, her white body gleaming through its thin green veil. Though it was night, her long unbound hair shone like amber in the sunlight, her gold wrought girdle sparking like sap rich pinewood bursting in the heart of a bonfire and her necklace flaming upon her breast. Her green splotched eyes were huge and gleaming as a lynx's in the darkness.

In her right hand, Yrse held a small yellowish white bone, thin and pointed. She leaned over Beowulf with it, and it seemed to him that he could see her white breasts swinging free beneath the mist of green that cloaked her, and her ruddy brown nipples standing out like hazelnuts. Her breath wafted over him as a soft wind, warm and sweet with summer flowers and the faint scent of honey mead; for a moment, her face blurred into Hygd's, framed in white blond hair, and he wanted to reach up and take her hand in his, but still he could not move.

"Waken," Yrse sang, her growl low as a she bear's. She touched Beowulf's groin with the end of the bone, and a tingling fire began to spread there, his blood pulsing hot into his rising man leek. "Waken, and live. Meredeall calls you; Sugu calls you; Geofe calls you: live!" Yrse drew the pointed bone slowly up his body; it felt as though she were slicing into him with a flame heated knife, but there was no pain. She paused over Beowulf's heart, tracing some sign upon him, then went on until the tip of the bone touched the middle of his forehead.

"Hard the blow to helm berg," the Swede queen chanted. Her mouth gaped wide; Beowulf could not see her lips move, but the words spilled out of her throat in a rush of air. "Wound sea pools in the thought coffer, dark water hides the gold in the bone howe. Let the stream be stanched, let the blood mere sink! The leek grows shining, deep in the earth; bright waters spring from under berg, and from hidden roots rises might. Rise and wake, rise and live! I walk among the fallen, and no wound can withstand my might.

Flesh knits beneath my touch, blood warms in the chilly veins; the slain rise and grasp their swords to win the new day. Waken, Beowulf, waken and live!"

Yrse tapped him thrice upon the head with her bone wand. It seemed to Beowulf that he could feel the pain in his skull fading, sinking back like a puddle melting into the earth. All his limbs tingled with warmth, his stones tightening in their sack and his leek throbbing; he felt that he would spurt if she touched him there once more. But she only stayed kneeling beside him, one burning hand upon his head and the other over his heart. Slowly the rush of need faded from Beowulf's body, his sight clearing. He blinked hard, staring up at Yrse. The flaring brightness of her necklace and girdle had dimmed, only a few small glints catching the light of the fire outside the tent door. But the fire had burned down to a few tiny flames snaking over charred logs, and it was too dark inside to see her face clearly.

"Lie still and rest this night," Yrse told him. Her voice was huskier and more grating than usual, as though she had strained it grievously. "I shall send food and drink to you, for you need it, but no matter how strong you feel, do not try to rise."

"I thank you," Beowulf mumbled. "And I thank the Frowe for her might."

Yrse smiled, a brief flash of white teeth in the shadows. "

You see and hear more than most and you were closer to the shores of your long faring than you may have known. Now, Haethcyn, you may safely let him sleep. If he does not waken, it is only because Frea Ing has chosen him early as an offering but I do not think that is so."

"What did you see?" Beowulf asked Haethcyn when Yrse had left the tent.

"Only that she sat beside you for a very long time and mumbled something I could not hear. She drew a small wand from her bag, but her back was to me and I could not see what she did with it." Haethcyn sat silent for a while, then stretched out upon the ground. When he spoke again, Beowulf could barely make out his words. "Perhaps, after all, it was foolish of me to set my will against such a witch."

A guard of four warriors came in the morning, unbinding the feet of the captives and leading them out into the woods to relieve themselves. The swollen lump on the back of Beowulf's head had shrunken to a bruise, mildly painful when he touched it, but no worse. As soon as he stood, he felt that all his strength had come back to him. The ropes around his wrists seemed frail as loose spun woolen threads, and he knew that he could break free in less than a heartbeat. But two of the guards had arrows nocked in their bows, ready to draw and loose; the other two bore naked blades in their hands, and when Beowulf's eyes met Haethcyn's for a second, the young king twitched his head in a quick sideways jerk.

Not now: there may come a better chance Beowulf heard the words as clearly as if Haethcyn had spoken them aloud. The Swedes had not been slow in gathering their men for the march southward: more than half an hundred riders surrounded Ongentheow, his family, and his captives, with four times that number of warriors on foot. Yet, if the Geats had made their way more swiftly towards Ongentheow's hall, they would have had to go on the roads, and likely been captured all the same, Beowulf told himself. The Geats were given horses to ride, but their hands were still bound: two of Ongentheow's men held their lead ropes. Beowulf recognized Feola and Hrime and Haethcyn's gray, but the Swedes had chosen not to put their captives on the backs of horses that were known to them, lest a sudden press of the knee should guide the steed to its rider's freedom a wise choice in Haethcyn's case, Beowulf thought ruefully.

As for himself, he could not ride at all without the reins in one hand, and he was glad that his hands were bound so that no one could see them shaking as his guards heaved him to the saddle. Now he understood why Hygelac had always said, "If you fall from a horse's back, get back on at once: otherwise, you may never ride again." It might be that the Swedes were doing him a kindness by setting him on a steed here, whether willed or not. As they started off, the first drops of chill rain began to fall from the gray sky, spattering the bright helmets of Ongentheow's thanes and soaking dark into the iron bound leather caps of his lesser warriors: even the golden boar standard raised proudly beside the Swede king's horse dripped dully beneath the low clouds. The sparse heavy drops gave way to scatters of driving mist rain, enough to chill the skin and dampen woolen cloaks, but not to slow the Swedes' pace. More and more men joined them as the day went on, scattered bands of searchers who had just gotten the news that the hunt was over.

For reasons of which Beowulf was not quite sure, Ongentheow rode beside Haethcyn and spoke with him through most of the day. Onela would have little to do with the captives, but Othere, though his right wrist still bore a splint bound tightly to it by crisscrossing leather wrappings, seemed to hold no grudge against Beowulf for besting him.

"That is a good byrnie you were wearing," the Swede king's son said. "So close, with a strong thrust, my knife would have broken most other rings. I thought to wear it when we had taken it from you, but its weight was too great for me to move easily in but no, that is ill of me to say, for it is grievous of a warrior to be stripped of the gifts of his drighten, and the work of the worst of thralls to gloat on it. Was that byrnie made just for you?"

"It was," Beowulf answered shortly.

"If you were to see the smith again, you could tell him of the worth of his work. Was he the same man who made the knife you had at your belt? I thought the sheath and hilt looked like Finnish work, but I know they smith no iron."

"The knife...was a gift from a friend." With a sudden pang of longing, Beowulf thought of old Paanja again, the Finn's slanted eyes bright as jet beads as he looked up through his gray fringe of hair, his high voice half chanting, The knife will stand you in good stead in that world, should your other weapons ever fail you. "And if I am to be slain as an offering, this one thing I ask: that it go with me, and lie upon my body when I am dead."

Othere frowned, biting his lower lip. "It is not mine to speak on such things, not while my father is the living ruler of the Ingling house and hof; and giving a Finnish weapon to a death doomed man seems to me a chancy thing, but you spared my life when I would have slain you, though I think you could as easily have torn my arm off my body as wrenched it from its socket. There is surely the strength of thirty men in your hand grip, and, as living man or drow, you will be no more dangerous with the blade than without it. So I will do my best to see to it, but I can say no more than that."

The second day was much the same as the first, save that the weather had grown worse, low clouds drifting swift and dark as a ghostly army marching across the gray sky and cold rain blowing straight against the Swedish host. Beowulf and Haethcyn suffered worst, for they could not even wipe the icy wetness from their faces, let alone pulling hoods over their heads again when the wind had tossed them back. Through the sounds of hooves and feet sloshing through the road's thickening mud and the marching songs that this lot of men or that would strike up to cheer themselves, Beowulf often thought he heard mutters such as;

"...Frea Ing frowning on us...think the fields will be frosted?...Fighting in holy times, ill must come of it...if only this foul rain would slacken!...Best to be back in Upsala soon..."

The Swedes stopped to pitch their tents well before sunset, cursing as they tried to pound the wooden stakes fast in the mud. Though the road wound around the edge of a great forest, and the rain had let up for the time being, it would be hard work to find dry wood for fires that night, and there was only so much even thick shaggy wadmal and oiled hides laid down as tent floors could do to keep those who slept on them dry and warm.

The tent in which Beowulf and Haethcyn were put that evening was in the middle of the camp, its door flap facing away from the wood, as though Ongentheow were wary of their slightest chance to break free. Still, if the heavy clouds and weather held, then in the utter blackness of a rainy night...Even if their guards sat inside the tent with them, it would not be easy for them to swing their swords in that narrow lightless space without being as likely to hit each other as their captives. Beowulf would be better favored in the darkness, for he had only to lay hands on his foe, and whoever wore a byrnie or helm was not Haethcyn. Nor could the archers shoot at them as they fled, for there would not be moon or stars to show where they ran, and the campfires would be few and low.

"Where are we now?" Beowulf whispered to the Geat king.

"At the edge of Ravenwood," Haethcyn murmured back. "Should we have the chance tonight, we shall run into the woods, going as far and fast as we may. And if we lose each other in the dark, or if they find and slay us by daylight tomorrow, that is still better than being brought to Upsala's offering grove like fettered kine."

Beowulf nodded. They said nothing more then, for a young man who wore a plain helm and a byrnie made of iron rings sewn onto boiled leather, armed with a simple sheath knife and an axe hung in a leather loop on his belt, was coming in with salt herring and hard bread for them.

It was a poor meal, but no worse, Beowulf thought, than the Swedes themselves were eating that dreary evening. Ongentheow's man had just lifted the first piece of fish and bread to Beowulf's mouth when the shout went up outside,

"Arm yourselves! To arms, men of the Swede folk! The Geats are upon us!"

Beowulf did not hesitate so much as an eye blink: he snapped the ropes that bound his wrists and ankles, clamping a hand upon the guard's weapon arm before he could get his axe more than halfway out of its loop. He tightened his grip; the warrior's fingers dropped numb from the haft, and Beowulf snatched the axe and knife from his belt.

"Not a sound, or you die!" Haethcyn ordered.

The youth's wide green eyes stared up into Beowulf's face in terror, his lips trembling. He was younger than Beowulf, his beard no more than a downy froth about his mouth and chin. Then, swifter than Beowulf could think to slash at him with the axe, he leaped out of reach in a single bound and shouted from the tent door,

"Aid me! The Geats are breaking free! Aid…"

The young thane gasped sharply, his body stiffening, and dropped with a low moan of pain, curling up in the doorway. To Beowulf's surprise, the next thing he saw was Ecgtheow's bushy beard spreading out beneath the gilded cheek pieces of his helm and the dark mask of the bear fell draped above as his father pushed his way in over the Swede's twitching body with a bloody sword in his hand. Ecgtheow wasted no words there. Beowulf could see the bear snarl pulling his father's lips back and the way his hands shook so that he could hardly cut Haethcyn's bonds: Ecgtheow must have been struggling to hold back his berserk wod, perhaps harder than he had ever struggled with any man.

The moment the last rope fell free from Haethcyn's ankles, the darkness in the berserk's eyes swelled drowning deep, and a stream of spittle welled frothing from his lips. Ecgtheow roared, and for a moment Beowulf froze in fear: a berserk might not know against whom he lifted his sword until his killing fit was sated with blood. But the old warrior turned, his foot coming down heavily on the moaning body of the dying man in the tent door as he burst out to do battle. Haethcyn closed the space between the two of them in a single stride, taking the axe from Beowulf's hand.

He paused long enough to snatch the helm from the head of the fallen Swede, pushing it down hard over his own skull, then ran out behind Ecgtheow. Though Beowulf's only weapon was the slain man's knife, he followed his king. The fighting raged all through the camp, men's hoarse shouting mingled with the clashing of blades and booming of shields. The clouds to the west had broken, the sun's red light streaming over the dark wood and flashing from the edges of swords and spears like fire burning from blood.

"To me!" Haethcyn shouted, running forward. "Men of the Geats, to me!"

"Haethcyn!" The ragged cry went up in return, spreading throughout the camp, and was answered by shouts of "Ongentheow!"

Beowulf ran after Haethcyn, slowing only once when he stooped to grab a fallen sword. A fully armed warrior stepped into his path, crying,

"Ongentheow!"

Still running, Beowulf slashed hard at him. He felt the crash of a shattering shield beneath his blade, but did not stop to see if he had done his foe any harm. The Inglings' gold boar was raised high at the edge of the camp, shining red in the sunset light; the battle was thickest around it, and that was where Haethcyn was heading. As Beowulf had done, the Geat king stooped a moment, tearing a shield free from a fallen arm. A man bore in towards Haethcyn's side, shouting the Swedish battle cry; Beowulf swerved, charging to meet him.

At the last second, the Swede braced his sword against his shield to take the shock of Beowulf's blow; but Beowulf's weapon drove straight through, splitting the man's painted shield planks like a heavy axe blow and cleaving through byrnie and collarbone down into his chest. Beowulf wrenched the sword free its blade was bent a little, but it would still serve and ran on.

"Geats, to me!" Haethcyn shouted again. Now Beowulf could see that some two-score of Ongentheow's men had formed a shield burg ringing the king's standard, and there the Geats were attacking most fiercely.

Ongentheow himself stood in the middle, his long arms and keen eyes giving him a deadly advantage; as Beowulf watched, he beat aside the thrust of a Geat's blade with the flat of his own sword, stabbing in quickly to send a gout of bright blood spurting from just below the other man's armpit. A little beyond Ongentheow, Ansuwulf and Ecgtheow attacked the shield wall side by side beneath gray wolf hame and grizzled bear fell, howling and snarling in their battle madness: there, the Swedes had to leap again and again to close their rank over the bodies of their fallen, lest the berserks break through.

Eofor traded strokes with a Swede who over topped him by almost a head, their blades licking about each other more swiftly than any flames and the gilded adornments on Eofor's shield flashing bright as he tilted and swung it to meet the blows from the man who stood at the tall warrior's side. Onela was on the other side of the shield ring but Yrse stood in the middle holding the boar standard, her eyes flaring with a fierce brightness that almost froze Beowulf in his tracks; and though Othere could not wield a sword with his broken arm, he held his place beside his stepmother, his shield lifted to ward her against any stray stroke.

Gathering himself, Beowulf ran faster, fixing his gaze on Ongentheow. Still, Haethcyn was faster; his axe edge met the Swede king's sword, and Beowulf swerved to the right, crashing full strength into the man whose shield guarded Ongentheow's sword flank. That shield gave way before him, its bearer flying off his feet; Beowulf's rush took him across the ring, his sword ramming deep into the body of a man on the other side. Then Beowulf was battling two men at once, one cutting at his legs from the left and one swinging up towards his head from the right.

Without a shield, he could only leap in too close for his left hand foe to swing at him, grasping the man's neck and feeling the windpipe crumble like rotten wood beneath his fingers even as he struck the other Swede's sword aside with his own. The might of Beowulf's blow knocked the Swede's weapon out of his hand. Bladeless, the man backed off before Beowulf could strike again, but a Geatish axe head rang down on his helmet and he dropped like a hammer stunned ox.

"Men of the Geats, to me!" Eofor's voice cried sharply, carrying across the din of battle. "Our king has fallen! Gather to me!"

In the little space his slaying had won him, Beowulf moved in beside the axe wielder, each guarding the other as they fought their way through to Eofor. The shield ring had crumbled, swords flying fast where the Swedish shields had held their small garth; in the middle of the fighting, Yrse clung to the standard, blood spattered across her white headdress and her lips pulled back in a wild grin. The Swedes surrounded the knot of Geats now, Eofor leading them as they grimly battled their way towards the edge of the woods.

"To me, or fly to the holt!" Eofor screamed. "Our battle is lost!"

Almost threescore Swedes stood between the Geat band and the long shadows of the trees, the black shade web knotting fainter as the twilight darkened. Eofor's eyes, their whites shining through the brow rings of his helm, flickered towards Beowulf.

"Now!" he said, and began to run, Beowulf at his right and his berserk howling brother to his left.

The three of them struck the Swedes like a great wave slapping a boat full broadside; the solid ranks of men caved in before them, and then they were into the woods. Eofor glanced back but once, to be sure that the others had followed tight behind him; but the Swedes were coming after them, more men than they could ever stand against, and there was nothing to do but run deeper among the trees, crashing through thornbushes and thickets and hoping that their strength would hold until full darkness, when their foes could pursue them no longer.

The Geats ran, panting in ragged despair, until they could no longer see to leap over stones and fallen logs. Eofor slowed to a stop, his shape a dark blur in the shadows. Halting beside him, Beowulf bent over clutching at the searing cramp in his side and gulping air in great greedy gasps. Sweat streamed from his forehead, stinging his eyes painfully, and he was not sure that he would not cast up his stomach. But he was not the worst off: behind himself, Beowulf heard the solid thud of a body hitting the ground.

"Who was that?" Someone asked.

The little twigs cracked between Eofor's feet as he moved back to see who had fallen.

"My brother," he answered. "The berserk wod has left him, and he is worn out. Can somebody light a fire?"

"Maybe," Sighere's voice replied. "But what of the Swedes?"

"They turned back a little time ago. I think they mean to gather their strength again and seek us out in the morning. We shall deal with that later; but as for now, we must have a fire to see to our wounds, warm those who are hurt and mayhap, if luck is with us, to let any other Geats who made it to the wood know where we are, for every sword arm shall be needed here tomorrow."

Beowulf heard the sound of scuffling, then saw the bright sparks flying from the oval fire stone in Sighere's hand. While he had run, he had not thought, but now a dark worry crawled over him like a horde of black ants swarming a fallen scrap of meat. Ansuwulf was here, though he had dropped from the aftermath of his berserk fit what of Ecgtheow? He had been at the Swedes' shield ring with Ansuwulf and Eofor. Beowulf looked about him, straining his eyes through the gloom. It was hard enough to make out faces now, the more so when eyes and noses were hidden by helm steel, but he could not see any shape that loomed large enough to be Ecgtheow.

"Eofor," Beowulf said, "is my father with us?" His breath had not come back to him yet, and he could not keep the trembling out of his voice.

Eofor rose from beside his brother. His warm hand touched Beowulf's shoulder: he was close enough for Beowulf to smell the stink of fighting that hung about him, and the faint staleness of his breath.

"Beowulf. Your father fell beside his king."

"No. Oh, no."

Beowulf felt the great howl of despair building up within him a sorrow lake mounting swiftly to burst its earthen bounds, a mighty wyrm rising from the depths to sear away the world. His heavy limbs shook like trees trembling beneath a rising storm wind: he could think only, I failed Haethcyn, and now. A heartbeat before Beowulf's cry would have burst free, Ansuwulf spoke from the ground, his voice soft and wavering, but clear.

"He was long lived, for a berserk.. And it is not the worst of deaths for one of Woden's men to fall to the god's keen edged hall fires: his sword will burn the more brightly among Walhall's torches for that."

"One gnaw flames of Wind God..."

The barrow rider's second death was fulfilled now, Beowulf thought numbly: the sword had bitten Haethcyn, though Beowulf had not been skilled enough in skald craft to read that rune. And then, My father was right: I bore the curse to the Swertings. It would have been better had I never come back to their hall still, I am likely to die tomorrow, and perhaps that shall be an end to it. A tiny flame crawled up from the glowing tinder on the stone in front of Sighere, hissing about the twigs and flaring to crackling in the half dry pine needles with which the Geat was steadily feeding it. Further off in the woods, they heard the trample of feet, and those men who were standing drew their swords and turned to face the sound.

"Geat or Swede?" a cracking voice called from the darkness.

"Geats!" Eofor shouted back. "Come and be welcome but if you are Swedes, your welcome may be more lively than you like."

"We are Geats!"

Still, Eofor's men did not sheath their weapons until the men were close enough for Sighere's growing fire to cast a little light on their faces, grim and pale beneath battered helms. There were about fifteen of them, three leaning upon others to hold themselves up, with blood crusted byrnies and makeshift bandages hastily wrapped around arms and legs.

Beowulf thought he recognized their leader from Ecgtheow's hall: it was the man who had boasted of being able to kill his table fellow with a sheep's rib bone if he chose. His blocky shoulders slumped with tiredness now; his mail coat was spattered with blood, but there was no sign of a wound upon him, though the nose piece of his helmet was broken off jaggedly and a long bright groove scored its front. If that had happened in the day's fighting, then he could be counted among the luckiest of men.

"It is well that you have found us," Eofor said. "Our band is small enough together we do not make a full threescore while the Swedes have a goodly host left. But we shall fight the better by each others' sides."

Ecgtheow's man nodded, taking off his helmet. His hair was dark with sweat and had come half out of its braid, sodden rat tails spiking out wildly from his head.

"Aye, that is so. Can you guess how many others…"

The deep sound of an aurochs horn winding, a little towards the east, silenced him. Sighere took off his battle torn cloak, holding it to hide the small fire's light.

"Geats!" a man shouted in the distance, his cry ringing through the forest like a horn of bronze. Eofor opened his mouth to answer, but Beowulf grasped his shoulder, gesturing him to silence: he knew Ongentheow's voice. "Geats, come out if there are any of you still living, wretched leavings of the sword! Your king is dead, and you will be soon, for I have you hemmed in here in the wood. At dawn you will feel the edges of swords; some of you will hang on the gallows tree for the joy of birds, but none shall come from this holt alive, though you fled like deer running in terror when I cut your leader down."

In the faint glow of the cloaked fire, Beowulf could just see the shine of men's eyes turning to one another, and the chill that went over him was not wholly that of the night's cold creeping through his sweat sodden cloak. Frea Ing was the Inglings' father, but the Swedish kings gave worship to all the gods and goddesses in their turn. By speaking those words, Ongentheow offered their lives to Woden warriors slain on the field or battle captives hanged on the tree, the dead were of like worth to the grim god, as to the ravens that plucked out their staring eyes.

"There is a long way between words and swords," Eofor whispered grimly, loud enough that all the men there could hear, but not so loudly that it might carry to the ears of the Swedes. "Ongentheow may shout as he likes, but while there are still blades in our hands, he shall not have as much joy of our king's death as he thinks to await."

After a time it began to rain again, droplets spattering cold on the new leaves and gathering on the branches to drip down the Geats' necks. The wounded had been tended to: they were the least hurt of Haethcyn's host, who had been able to flee into the woods and stay on their feet. As for the others Beowulf did not like to think on it, whether they were bound with their deaths clear before their eyes as he and Haethcyn had been, or whether Ongentheow had already carried out his grisly threat on their bodies.

He was thirsty, parched from fighting, and his belly rumbled painfully with hunger, but there was nothing to be done about that, for if one man left the others to look for water now, whether he ran into the Swedes or not, he would have little hope of finding his way back. Beowulf's clothes hung clammy on him, and the Geats did not dare build their fire high enough to give more than a little warmth for the men who were worst hurt, while the others sat around them. Ansuwulf, too, lay close to the little flames, shivering and twitching in the violent aftermath of his fit, and sometimes a little froth would dribble from his mouth, as though he had been poisoned.

Beowulf had heard it said that a berserk who did not fall by the sword was likeliest to die from the strain of bearing his wod might too long, for that men's flesh was not strong enough to feed that fire forever; looking at Ansuwulf now, he wondered if the wolf would live a night longer than his bear friend. Father, Beowulf thought. Though I failed Haethcyn once, I fought well today. If you had lived to hear of it, would your mood then have turned more kindly towards your son? It seemed to him a great betrayal, that Ecgtheow should have fallen in Beowulf's first battle and whelmed with berserk wod, at that: he would not even have had the memory of seeing his son wielding blade bravely to warm his heart when the waelcyrige came to lift him up on her wind cold horse.

Your god did not do as well by you as he might have, to leave you bereft of that one last joy. And how has Frea Ing answered me? Beowulf shivered, clutching his chill wet cloak about himself. The rain was falling harder now, its icy rivulets soaking through his thick mane of sweat damp hair and running over his face; the fire hissed like an adder, and the small flames were sinking down. Soon Sighere and the others who were taking it in turns to feed and cloak the fire would have no wood dry enough to burn, and Beowulf knew that the wounded would likely be burning with fever by morning. Has the god, then, forsaken me? Is this where it all ends for me? Yet the Frowe's might had healed him when he would have died: Yrse's spell craft had given her a pathway, but Beowulf had lain with Ran's daughter, and he knew that it had been no earthly woman who brought him back from the shore of death.

If Frea Ing's sister had blessed him with life, then perhaps the Wans were not so angry with him as he feared, though he had not turned Haethcyn back from his ill fated deed. Frea Ing, may it be so! Lord of fruitfulness, lord of frith, giver of warm summers and joy once I asked you to be my friend, and have tried to be friend to you in turn. Are you with me still? Beowulf heard nothing save the dripping of the rain and the soft curses of the men who were trying to keep the fire alight.

Far off, a wolf howled, and another answered it, their high eerie calls echoing through the wood. Again the Geats glanced sideways at each other, as they had when Ongentheow spoke. All men knew that Woden's gray hounds, like their allies the ravens, could tell when a feast would soon be spread out on the earth men's bodies robbed of their byrnies by those who had slain them, left ready for the wolves' snouts to snuffle among their entrails, and teeth to tear their sword hacked limbs.

Beowulf did not know just when he first felt the kernel of warmth glowing within his chest staves: it seemed to sprout like a seed at summer's beginning, too slow to mark its unfolding, yet stretching forth its leaves and roots swiftly and surely, fastening its strength in his flesh as in rich earth. He was no longer shivering, neither from cold nor fear nor sorrow. For what has fallen, he thought, must rise again, and green grass grow long on the barrows of the slain: evening's reddening is morning's wakening, and life harvests what death has sown. He did not know from whence those words came to him, but they soothed his trembling heart: his hands were steadying, and the tight knot of unshed tears loosening in his throat.

The warmth within Beowulf was growing stronger, until it seemed to him strange that he could not see its brightness streaming from his body like firelight through the open door of a hall at night. But after a little while he rose, moving closer to the wounded men who huddled about the last traces of heat left in the black hissing sticks of the drowned fire. He felt strange, as though his body were not his own flesh, but a shape carved of wood and draped in a man's clothes that yet could move to his will if it were his own will that moved him: he did not know. And yet it seemed to him as well that he could feel some part of himself reaching deep into the ground, drawing up might from the hidden depths like a tree drawing up water through its roots.

One by one Beowulf touched the wounded, his big hands moving to loose or tighten their bandages slightly. With the fire out, he could not see who he was tending or what he was doing, but it seemed to him that each of the men's bodies shimmered with its own unseen light, as though he were looking upon the bright shadows of alfs flitting at the edges of a high mountain pasture in the mists of dawn and he could see that light brightening beneath his touch, and feel their shivering ease in the warmth that flowed from him. Last of all he came to Ansuwulf. There he stopped; but the berserk reached up to him, grasping his wrist with small wiry fingers and pulling him down close.

"Do you know?" Ansuwulf whispered.

"Yes."

"Then bless me as well for to love one god is not to scorn the gifts of the others."

Beowulf laid his hands upon Ansuwulf's cold chest. The berserk's life light seemed dimmer than that of the other men, a mere spark in the blackness of his body, like the fire's last ember struggling against the rain. Beowulf breathed deeply, and as the air sighed out of him, it seemed to him that he saw that ember glowing more brightly even as Ansuwulf's shaking lessened.

"Sleep," a man's voice said, low and gentle. Beowulf wondered who had spoken...but then he realized that it was his own lips moving, his own chest thrumming with the words. "Sleep, and rest: it is unknown of knowledge, what the dawn may bring."

Ansuwulf sighed, but did not answer, though the rise and fall of his chest grew deeper and slower. A soft noise came from the berserk's lips: he was snoring already, a quiet snuffle like that of a sleeping hound. Suddenly Beowulf yawned himself, his ribs stretching with the depth of it.

Though the cold was not stealing back through his clothes yet, he felt the warmth that had lifted him and moved him sinking back, like coals banked for the night beneath a blanket of ash. He could no longer think on anything that had happened that day: it was too much for his sinking head to take in, or his heart to hold; and heedless of damp and stones and the sharp poking of sticks beneath him, he found that he was measuring his length on the ground, his eyes closing tight against his will. Beowulf slept deep, without dreams, and woke to a hand shaking his shoulder.

"Rise now, Beowulf," Eofor said. "I smell the dawn coming hard upon us: soon we shall need your sword."

Beowulf raised himself to his feet, his nose wrinkling as yesterday's stench wafted to his nostrils from his rumpled clothes. It made little matter: if he were to die this morning, he would soon smell far worse. The clouds had blown away in the night, leaving the stars to glimmer through the leaves. Around Beowulf, the others were also standing up, stretching themselves and yawning. To his relief, none of the wounded lay moaning and fevered on the ground, and Ansuwulf's eyes were bright in the darkness beneath his helmet.

"So you took Yrse's rede, after all," Beowulf said softly to the berserk
Ansuwulf laughed silently.

"What harm can it do? If I am doomed to fall, a thrust shall take me elsewhere, and if not well, Woden shall have the choice." He turned to Eofor. "Tell me, brother, how shall we array ourselves to sell our lives most dearly?"

"A shield wall must be another thing in thick woods than on the open meadow," said Eofor slowly. "But the trees shall ward our backs and be our shields as well let each man choose another, so that half of us stand with a tree trunk to his left and a shield friend to his right, while we are arrayed in the thickness of the wood so that the man on the right also has a tree beside him to guard his far flank."

Beowulf turned to Ansuwulf. "Will you fight with me?"

"A berserk holds no such order. I will run and fight as I always do, and may it be confusion to the Swedes!"

"I will fight with you," said another man. It was the leader of Ecgtheow's scattered men, his skin pale gray in the starlight. "I was always first at your father's side, and I will be first beside his son, whether you be a changeling or not. My wife would have something to say to me if you fell here too! And big and strong as you are, you still have a few things to learn about fighting, and you have no shield of your own. You need a good man to stand beside you, if you will have me."

"Most gladly," Beowulf answered, for he knew the man spoke the truth: he was lucky to have lived the day before without his shield. "But tell me, what is your name?"

"I am Sweartwulf, called Sweartwulf the Wrestler, for not even Ecgtheow could best me without weapons, and for all his pride, I have put Hondscioh on his back often enough. As for my skill with the sword, I slew three of Ongentheow's guard yesterday, and there is not so much as a scratch on my hide."

"There is little time to talk," Eofor broke in. "You may boast when the ale is served in the hall or when we sit with the gods together this night, as it may be. Take your places, each man!"

Arraying themselves among the trees was not as simple as Eofor had said, for sometimes three or four men were needed to bridge a gap, and sometimes one could stand by himself with wide trunks to left and right, where no one could come at him easily. But at last the Geats stood in a loose ring, ready to meet their foes, though their swords were still in their sheaths and the weight of their shields rested upon their thighs. Though none of the men could see the gray light of morning yet, the chill in the air told Beowulf that it was not far off, and above the Geats' heads a raucous crowing sounded suddenly, dark wings flapping heavily into the air.

"The ravens are greeting the day," Sweartwulf murmured. "They know it will not be long before the slain bodies of Swedes are laid out for their feasting: may they enjoy a good meal of our foes! Today we shall avenge Ecgtheow and our king."

Beowulf wished that he could share in his shield friend's sureness. But since he could not, he did not speak: if death were to come, anyway, it were better to meet it with a brave heart. Slowly the woods lightened, the black branches of the trees against the starlight fading to shadows in the gray dawning, then clearing again beneath the brightening blue of the eastern sky. The calls of small birds sang out to match the ravens, a high pure twittering above the low croaks like song above the beating of the waves.

Beowulf felt each of his nerves tingling beneath his chill skin: the dark shape of Sweartwulf's shield rim, the patterns of moss on a smooth gray beech tree in front of him, the cold damp scent of dawn they all seemed sharper and stronger to him, as though, knowing that he must soon leave the Middle Garth, he struggled deep within himself to grasp everything about it, loading his soul boat for his long faring. A deeper call joined the ravens' voices, the winding of the Swedes' aurochs horn. Thrice it blew, shaking through the trembling leaves.

"They come now," Sweartwulf whispered.

He drew his sword, though his shield still rested against his left thigh. Beowulf's sword was already in his hand, for it had no sheath. At least the weapon was not shaking, though his gut tightened with readiness and his breath was coming faster. Now Beowulf heard the sound of many men's feet marching through the woods, a steady tread that gave no heed to the snapping of twigs underfoot.

His hand shifted slightly on his sword grip it had been made for a smaller man, and the edge of his fist overlapped the pommel uncomfortably. The first gleam of byrnies and helms showed through the bushes ahead of them, and Sweartwulf lifted his shield at last, holding it so that it would ward both Beowulf and himself. Beneath the broken nose piece of his battered helm, his lips pulled back, showing a fierce grin. Ansuwulf, standing by himself, was snarling low in his throat, his teeth gnashing; his head snapped forward, teeth biting down on the hide edged rim of his shield and froth darkening the leather about his mouth as he worried at it.

The Swedes' horn sounded again: the crashing footfalls began to pick up speed, armored men breaking their way through the underbrush. Then, high in answer and farther away, came a second blast, clear and pure as the sound of a great flute.

"Hygelac!" Eofor gasped. "I know the Swertings' horn: Hygelac is come!"

"Hygelac!" The Geats shouted in answer, bracing with new heart to meet the onslaught of the Swedes. But the sound of Hygelac's horn had given their foes pause. The Swedes did not charge onward at once, but hesitated, and Beowulf heard Ongentheow shouting orders.

"First hundred forwards you can take these wood skulkers easily. The rest of you, turn about with me!"

More stamping and crackling through the bushes; then the Swedes burst into view, running hard at the Geatish ring. Beowulf braced his sword hard point forward, trusting in Sweartwulf to shield him. The first Swede who ran at him fell because he thought he could knock Beowulf's blade to the side before he closed near enough to get his own blow in, and instead spitted himself in his own rush. Beowulf swung and swung again as others followed: often a stroke came too swift for him to meet, but Sweartwulf's shield was always there to block it, chips of red painted wood flying from beneath the hacked leather rim. Beowulf's own blows sent men flying, and often enough, they did not rise again. Sweartwulf was shouting something, but at first Beowulf, his ears dazed with the din of battle, did not hear it. "Hell eat you, get down!" Sweartwulf cried.

"Grab another sword now!"

Beowulf swept up his own blade to knock another strike; for a heartbeat, he stared numbly at the shattered metal splinters sticking from the hilt in his hand, and that would have been his death if Sweartwulf had not been shielding him. He dropped, lunging for a sword that lay on the ground. Coming up beneath Sweartwulf's shield, he drove the new blade up beneath the byrnie of the man who was hacking downward at him, lifting him from his feet and casting him backward with his bowels streaming in a bloody trail behind him. Then there were no foes before him: only the cries and moans of the wounded strewn about the ground, and blood soaking deep into the forest mold from tattered flesh.

"Move!" Eofor shouted. "Your king is fighting hear the sounds of battle?" Those Geats who were still on their feet Beowulf had no time to count them sprang forward, halting only to grasp shields from the fallen in place of those that had been hacked to pieces.

Farther on, the fighting was wilder. The lines of men broken by trees and bushes, there was no thought of shield walls or swine arrays, but every fighter took on whoever he could reach as best he might, each warrior bawling out the names of his king hoarse throatedly as the sweat streamed down beneath his helmet, lest he be cut down by a friend who thought him a foe.

Beowulf could see neither Ongentheow's gilded boar nor the golden ring standard of the Hrethlings, but there was no time to look when blades flashed towards his face or cut sharply downwards at his legs: it was all he could do to stay alive, shouting;

"Hygelac!" As blood and sweat spattered salt across his face.

The battle pressed onwards. It seemed to Beowulf, in those heartbeats of thought when no one stood facing him, that the Geats were pushing the Swedes slowly back, but it was hard to tell with the two hosts whirling among the trees like herrings in a maelstrom. At last he glanced up for a second to see the glistening boar ahead of him yes, it was moving, backing steadily farther away.

"Hygelac!" Beowulf cried, the call rasping harsh through his throat as he leapt forward again.

He thought he caught the gleam of Hygelac's standard in the corner of his eye, but he did not dare turn his head to be sure, for now he was facing two men at once. He thrust his shield hard to catch one's blade; the edge of his sword skidded off the other's leaping weapon, so that it ripped along his tunic sleeve instead of plunging deep into his bowels. Beowulf cut at his right hand attacker hard, his sword biting in through the man's neck to his collarbone.

The other's weapon had stuck in Beowulf's shield just long enough; the Swede wrenched it free of the splintered wood, but Beowulf swung his sword over in a powerful arc, slamming it down on his foe's forearm. Though the blade was already blunted with fighting, the man's hand dangled broken, blood spurting from the deep gash that had cut halfway through his wrist joint. Save for a few knots of men struggling on, the Swedes were all moving back through the trees now. The Geats followed them, baying,

"Hygelac!" Like hounds after an elk.

Beowulf ran after, his long legs letting him catch up quickly. The land rose sharply ahead of them, a high wooded ridge like the edge of an eoten's palisade. Most of the Geats hurried up it, thighs burning and lungs struggling hard for air. Beowulf was one of the first to the top; but when he looked down, he saw why Ongentheow had chosen that place to fall back to. The earthen ridge did not slope gently down: instead it crested in a small stone cliff, plunging more than an hundred feet beneath the overhanging shelf. From above, the Geats could not get in a clean bow shot or spear cast, for the jutting rocks shielded those below; the ground beneath was a deep gully walled on the other side by great boulders.

Ongentheow's boar stood high from behind one of those huge rocks. Beowulf saw no white linen beneath it, but the flash of a man's helm and byrnie: the Swede king had not chosen to risk his queen's life in battle again that day. The Swedes had formed into ranks, guarding both ends of that narrow pass they would not be taken easily. But those Geats who had turned to run around the ridge were boiling in, their duped fellows running downward to meet Hygelac's standard, now rounding the left hand edge of the steep earth wall. Beowulf followed, leaping over boulders and fallen branches, but he could not keep from glancing down when he heard Ansuwulf's wolf howl rising high.

The berserk had reached Ongentheow, battering his way beneath the Swede king's longer reach with sheer wod strength. A slash of Ansuwulf's sword, and blood spurted under the long gray mane hanging loose beneath Ongentheow's helmet. The aged Scylfing answered the blow swiftly, hewing down between the gray wolf ears of the berserk's fell so hard that sparks flew and Beowulf heard the crack of metal breaking beneath metal. Ansuwulf dropped loose jointed, but before his body hit the ground, Eofor was standing over him.

The Geatish thane had lost his shield, wielding his great longsword in both hands. He swung inward towards Ongentheow's hip; the Ingling dropped his shield, and in that moment, Eofor twisted his stroke upwards, striking at Ongentheow's head. Beowulf saw the Swede king's nasal caving in under that crashing blow, the blood spurting out bright over the darkening stains clotted on Eofor's byrnie. Ongentheow fell. By the time Beowulf, his limbs shaking with tiredness and each breath burning fiercely in his lungs, had reached the fighting below the cliff, it was all over.

Ongentheow's boar was down, its pole bloody where the standard bearer, now sprawled beside it, had clung to his trust till the last. Onela sat on a stone, glaring at the three men who held him at sword point; his left hand grasped his right forearm hard, stanching the wound that had left his narrow red sleeve sodden and dripping blood; a few other Swedes were held captive as well. Eofor knelt over his brother's body, and Beowulf quickened his steps to crouch down beside them.

"Is he..?" Beowulf could not finish the sentence, but Eofor looked up at him, a quick grin splitting his red beard.

"His helm is broken and his head bleeds a little, but he lives yet. The gods be blessed, he lives! And it was my sword that tore Ongentheow in repayment: my brother may rise again, but Ongentheow never shall."

Beowulf's whole body shuddered so hard that he almost dropped the hilt in his hand. The tusk of the boar shall tear old Ongentheow in the dark holt he had failed to read his own rune until too late, but Ongentheow had fallen as he said: Eofor, the Boar, had slain the Swede in the wood. And Frea Ing has taken his offering by his own beast. The sun blazed bright on Beowulf's sweat damp head, and he swayed, thinking for a moment that he would fall.

"Berki!" Hygelac cried, clapping him hard on the shoulder. Beowulf blinked, looking down at his king. A thin splatter of dry blood splashes freckled Hygelac's cheek and stained a streak down his short golden beard, but Beowulf could see no wound on him. Hygelac was grinning, and in the next moment he flung his arms around his kinsman, hugging Beowulf as hard as he could. "Berki, I thought you dead. I came as fast as I could, but I feared I would be too late to save you as I was for Haethcyn," he added, his voice lower and his face suddenly grave. "But hurry with me now, for the Swedes who guard their wains and queen back on the road must learn that Ongentheow is dead and that we have Onela."

Eofor rose to his feet, gold glittering in his hand. "My king, this is for you to take for it may be that Othere puts more trust in Sweogris than in his brother." He handed Hygelac the huge boar headed arm ring that Ongentheow had worn.

Hygelac turned the ring over in his hands, looking at it in quiet wonder.

"The very luck of the Swedes' realm lies in this," he mused. "And if there is to be frith now, it shall be on our terms, as my brother dreamed." He raised his eyes again, the fine cut lines of his mouth hardening. "Come now! Back to the road, my men. And bring the captives with us but stand ready to cut them down on my word."

He is becoming a king after all, Beowulf thought, amazed at Hygelac's sudden harshness. But then, he has a brother to avenge and no kinsmen left alive to stand with him, save myself. And he was never a fool, or weak: perhaps he was wiser than any of us, to joy in his freedom while he had it.

VII

Hygelac and Othere met between their two armies on the road. Beowulf stood at Hygelac's side, and Yrse beside Othere. The Geatish captives from the night before were bound in the middle of the Swedes; the Swedish corpses had been laid out ready for burning, but the Geatish bodies were strewn in an untidy heap, and the ravens, sleek and black, were already wandering over them, their feathers glistening with a bluish sheen in the sunlight. My father is there, and Haethcyn, Beowulf thought: if he could have, he would have run forward with his arms waving to drive the black fowl flapping away from the dead men. Since he could not, he tried to turn his gaze away, but he could not keep his eyes from flickering back at each jerk of a raven's long beaked head.

"A life for a life," Othere was saying. "My father paid for your brother's death with his own: I think there is no weregild owed on either side here, and I am willing to own that yours is the sigright in this battle."

The Ingling's long thin face was calm, with no sign of sorrow or fear in his blue eyes: the brown knot of hair at the side of his head and the ruddy plait of his beard were neatly tied up with threads of yellow silk, and his blue coat and gold clasped trousers were clean and neat as if there had been no battle that day, nor any cause for him to worry or grieve, but his smile only touched his narrow lips. Yrse showed no sign of grief either, her features smooth and calm as if they had been carved in pale birch wood. She watched Hygelac and Beowulf with the unblinking gaze of a lynx, but did not speak. Hygelac stared coldly at Othere from beneath the gilded eye rings of his helmet.

"You say that now, but what will you say to your men when you are back in Upsala? And what will your brother say, he who saw Ongentheow fall and could not save him, but was taken captive himself? Will he not seek some bettering for that harm?"

"Keep Onela as a frith bond, if you wish," Othere replied. "With my brother in your hands, you may be sure of your safety."

The new Geat king looked over his shoulder at Onela, his hands bound and two men with drawn swords standing beside him. Onela's light green eyes glared back at him, and Beowulf thought, Othere will keep his oath, but I do not trust his brother.

Too, he remembered how differently Othere and Onela had spoken when the Swedes had held himself and Hygelac, and he was glad that it was Othere who would be claiming Sweogris back from the Geats' hands. Though Hygelac knew nothing of that, he must have judged the hate on Onela's face swiftly, for he said, "It is not meet to keep a man of kingly kin chained, and I would sooner let a wolf run free in my hall than Onela now. I shall take your oath on Sweogris instead. Then we shall burn our slain here by Ravenswood, and feast to our frith as best we may.

But you must give back our captives, together with their weapons and armor, while we shall give yours to you, but keep their war gear. As well, there were the treasures which Haethcyn and Berki and Ansuwulf bore in their packs, which I see bedeck your queen mother here. Those must come back to us too, and likewise the helms and byrnies and swords that my brother and Berki wore when you took them. I think you will not count that too great a price to pay in order to wear Sweogris on your arm, rather than see it borne back to the Geats' burg on mine. Othere frowned.

"And what geld will you pay for your brother's scorn of the gods? His men shed blood in our hall, in a time of Frea Ing's frith: there must be some offering made for that."

"Haethcyn has paid for that with his life as well, for the gods know well how to send their wights to shield in battle those they would have live. As for breaking holy frith, it was your father's men who attacked Hroesnabeorh during the Yule nights. But we shall seal our oath with feast offerings: I will give a fair price to any of your folk who have oxen and swine to sell, and you will no doubt do the same. Together we shall slay them, and together swear, that the gods may be content with what we have done."

The Ingling gave a tired nod. "So be it. Lift up Sweogris, that we may swear."

Hygelac lifted the huge boar headed arm ring, the swines' garnet eyes glittering brightly in the sunlight.

"Let the gods and goddesses all witness this! I, Hygelac Hrethling, do swear to hold frith between myself and Othere of the Swedes, and to do all that I have said here that I shall, so long as he keeps to his own oath to me."

Othere put his own knobby knuckled hand on the thick gold ring.

"Let the gods and goddesses witness it," he echoed. "I, Othere Ingling, do swear to hold frith between myself and Hygelac of the Geats; to trade captives for captives, and give back all that which we took by strength, and to let the frith be kept between us so long as Hygelac holds to his oath to me. Should one of us break this vow knowingly or by ill will, may the ship not glide that bears him, though the wind be fair; nor steed run beneath him, though he would flee his slayers; may the sword he wields not bite, save when it sings about his own head."

"May it be so," Hygelac finished. He let his arm drop, leaving Sweogris in Othere's grasp.

The Ingling's dark eyebrows lifted, surprise on his face for the first time.

"You are not slow in the keeping of your vows."

"Why should I be? If you mean to play me false, I would rather know it now than later."

Othere smiled full heartedly for the first time, reaching into the overlapping fold of his coat and bringing out a long knife. Beowulf's hand was on his sword before he realized that the blade was not drawn that it was his own knife, with grip and sheath of red graven reindeer horn, and that the Swede was holding it hilt first towards him.

"Beowulf, I believe this is yours. Oath or no, I had meant to give it to you this day, whether you came living through the battle or not."

"I thank you," Beowulf replied, taking the knife from Othere's hand.

"I wish that we had met otherwise than we did, but as there is frith between our folks now, I would offer you my friendship. And let there be friendship between your line and my own for my sons Eanmund and Eadgils are yet too young to join battle, but none save Wyrd knows what may betide when they are old enough to lift swords, and I think it shall be well for them to know that there are those among the Geats in whom they may put their trust."

Beowulf wavered there a moment, for this was no little thing Othere was asking of him. But the ridge of gold cresting Hygelac's helmet flashed a glimmer into his eyes as the king's head nodded slightly, and so he said,

"It shall be so. May no ill ever come between us!"

The Swedes and Geats stayed in that place for three more days, tending their wounded and building great funeral pyres for their slain save for Ongentheow, whose corpse Othere had sent back to Upsala. Beowulf learned that Hygelac had gathered his men and ridden out when Garhild came to him weeping one morning.

"She said that she had dreamed that she saw the Swertings' hall bedecked as if for a wedding, with fresh straw on the floor and shining mead in the pitchers," Hygelac said. He sat cross legged on the ground, resting the tip of his horn on the earth before him; it was night, but the huge bale fires were still burning, casting their ruddy light over the two encampments that flanked them.

"But all the flowers and garlands and hangings were black, and the long fires on the floor flared from the blades of swords. And then she saw Haethcyn enter, and a troop of dark clad women came forth to fill his horn and welcome him; but one stood before the others, and she embraced him and greeted him as a husband. The women of our household spoke of this together, and they were sure that Garhild had seen the idises beckoning Haethcyn to death. You had then been gone long enough, and so I did not wait for any news of sig or loss to reach me, but got to Ecgtheow's hall only a day after he and Eofor had left. There I learned what had happened, and we hastened as swiftly as we might but you know the rest."

He lifted his horn, sipping lightly at his ale, then looking over at the pyre where the Geatish bodies sizzled dark in the center of the flames, and the firelight showed a single shining track down his cheek.

"O my brother, your kingship began in woe, but you ended it well and bravely."

The pyres had been burning for almost a day, filling the air with the uncomfortably savory smells of pine smoke and roasting flesh, and there was no way now to tell which corpse was which: byrnies had melted into the bodies of those who had worn them, and helms fallen from heat burst skulls, hair and beards long gone in hot flares of stinking smoke. Still, Beowulf found himself staring into the fire as if he might pick out Haethcyn's shape from the blackened and twisted bodies, or recognize Ecgtheow's heavy limbs there, though the thick pelt of the bear hide that Beowulf had laid carefully over his body had burned swiftly to hide him beneath a charred blanket of soot.

"It was my father who freed Haethcyn and I from our bonds," Beowulf said suddenly. "He held back his berserk wod just long enough…"

"Eofor has told me how well he died," answered Hygelac. "And I think he would be joyed to know that you fought like a hero, and that you yet live to be lord at Hroesnabeorh."

"Are you sending me away, then?" Beowulf asked. He could not keep the raw note of pain from his voice, and Hygelac looked up in surprise.

"Who else should have Ecgtheow's burg and lands? Yes, I would keep you by my side but though Othere has sworn his oaths, I do not fully trust any of the Inglings, and his brother Onela least of all, for I saw how he spat at me with his eyes. So now you must hold the march hall as my bulwark, and wed and beget sons to keep that troth after you. I could almost wish," Hygelac added, "that we were not such close kin, so that I could betroth my daughter to you."

"Your daughter?"

"Aye, she was born two weeks after you went away a strong and fair little maiden, whom I sprinkled with water and gave the name Hildegeard. But since you cannot wed her, I have offered her to Eofor when she is old enough, to himself, or any man of his kin that he chooses as a fit husband for her, if he is well wedded by then or thinks her too young for him."

"Is it not early to betroth your daughter to a man of Eofor's age?" Beowulf asked numbly. He thought of Hygd, crying out in childbirth without him, of her holding the living babe to her breast, her white gold hair tumbling about her pale face; little Hildegeard's hair would be golden as well, with blue eyes that might darken to her mother's violet in time and she could have been his own bairn.

"Early, yes, but what more could I give him? He will not rule over more land than he owns already, for then he must turn his mind to fields and farms, and could no longer train men and lead troops as he does. I mean to shower him, and his brother as well, with gold rings and treasures, but that is not enough for his deed. Only Hildegeard, our dearest home ornament, is a fitting reward for Ongentheow's Bane."

Hygelac has become a king indeed, Beowulf thought. Where did he come by such cold redes, to weigh his daughter's happiness so lightly against a hero's reward?

"Though I think it likelier," Hygelac went on, smiling slightly beneath his fire reddened beard, "that Eofor will marry a full grown woman soon, in place of the wife he lost last winter, and it shall be his son Ingemund who is wedded to Hildegeard in the end. Still, it shall be a good thing that we can call the line of Wonred kinsmen. So the strength of the Swerting house grows even as you befriended Othere: that was well done!"

"He seems to me a man worthy of friendship, and I am glad that it was Othere and not Onela who had the luck to take Sweogris in the sight of his own thanes."

"Indeed so. And that was your doing as well, was it not? Ansuwulf has told me of all that took place at Upsala."

Beowulf wondered if the berserk had also spoken of Yrse's foreboding words to them, but he thought it as well not to ask. Instead he mused,

"What do you think Yrse will do now? Will she go south to join her son in Heorot?"

"It would be foolish of her to go willingly to that hall, and none have ever spoken of Yrse as a foolish woman. There is something uncanny about her: I think it likelier that she will stay at Upsala, making offerings to the gods in the hof there and perhaps doing such other things as it is said the Swedes are skilled in."

"Aye, she has great might," Beowulf agreed. He was on the edge of telling Hygelac of how she had healed him, but there was something about it that he could not name, at once too holy to speak and almost shameful, as if he had lain with Yrse there in the captives' tent. "And what of us now what shall we do?"

"When the ashes of our friends and kin have been buried in the earth here, and our feast of frith done, then we shall ride to Hroesnabeorh, where you shall take your father's high seat before all, and drink his burial arvel. After that, we shall go to my hall where I shall do the same after my brother. Then, I suppose, you shall come back to Hroesnabeorh and take up your rule there. Though the gods know how I shall miss you! I have often heard old men mourning that their kin and friends set forth on their long faring before them; I never guessed that, so young, you and I would be the last men of our aeht living..." Hygelac swallowed hard, the tears gleaming fire reddened in his eyes. "Berki, do not take it ill of me that I ask you this. I know you have had little time to think of such matters between mourning and the work of tending to the slain but now that Ecgtheow has fallen, do you mean to take a wife to be hall frowe in Hroesnabeorh soon?"

"I had not thought on it," Beowulf lied.

"Hygd spoke to me of the matter. She said that it grieves her heart to think of you alone and sorrowful."

Beowulf's heart clenched within him, as though it would twist loose of the blood reeds from which it hung in his chest. So much she loves me, that she would see me with another woman in my arms, rather than letting the knowledge of what might have been and what is gnaw at me.

"And Mother also says that you would do well to wed soon enough. There is time," Hygelac went on. "But if you are willing, I shall do my best to help you find a fine bride of good kin." He paused, a line of thought appearing between his golden brows. "Berki, do you find Yrse fair? Or is she too old for you? That would be a well made match, if she were to your taste. I do not think Othere would refuse you, and the Scyldings have ever been our friends."

Beowulf laughed, though it rang hollow as waves in a sea cave. "And have Onela as a stepson?" He said, to make a jest of it.

Hygelac laughed as well. "I think he would come to guest with you but seldom."

"Anyway, I do not think that a woman who has been queen in Upsala, and idis of the mighty Yngling aeht, would take well to being the house frowe of a march drighten."

The thought lingered, teasing at Beowulf's mind: he hardly needed to fear harming Yrse and Heofonglowe's curse fell only within the Middle Garth's ring. If she were willing. Yet, fair and strong though Yrse was, Beowulf could not see himself wedded to her. He did not want a woman of such a hard heart and grim mood; he did not think that Yrse would go laughing with him beneath green leaves, or share honey cakes with him and lick the stickiness from her fingers. And Hygelac had spoken truly of Yrse's uncanniness: perhaps it was that Beowulf feared what she would make of him, or what she would call forth from his own depths.

"Perhaps you may be right, at that," admitted Hygelac. "Still, there is no shortage of good wives in the world. If you like..."

"Not yet," Beowulf said. "Give me time to mourn, and think and to learn the ways of life at Hroesnabeorh, for I have seen that matters there may be different than in your hall, and it is long since I dwelt there last."

At last the bale fires burned down though the bones of the slain could still be seen, brittle blackened sticks among the flame eaten logs; and sometimes a gust of wind would stir the ashes so that the byrnies and helms and swords gleamed among the sooty heaps in strange ruddy dark rainbows. The Swedish drighten who dwelt nearest to Ravenwood, a cheerful broad faced man named Oswald, sent for his thralls and farmhands, and two great mounds were raised over the black ash rings of the dead. The skies stayed clear, arching warm and blue, so that the diggers stripped to the waist, sweat streaming down backs that were first winter white and then scorched painfully red.

Beowulf would gladly have lent his strength to that work, but his hand
was stayed by the memory of Ecgtheow's scornful speech at the mound
of Hrethel and Herebeald and, as Hygelac had said, he was now the Geat
king's nearest kinsman: it would not do for the Swedes to see him flinging
dirt about with a shovel. Hygelac made good on his word by buying an ox,
a swine, and a sheep from Oswald, and when the mounds were built, each
king went up onto the roof of his cindered dead and slew the beasts as his
offering to the gods and the ghosts of those who slept in the earth houses
beneath, though when Beowulf chanced to overhear men talking of the
matter, most seemed to be of the mind that the good weather showed that
the deaths of Haethcyn and Ongentheow had soothed Frea Ing's anger at
the breaches of holy frith.

More large fires were built to roast the animals, and Oswald had casks
of ale brought from his burg, together with all the tables and benches
he owned, so that at least the kings, their drightens, and their favorite
thanes might sit at their ease beneath the stars, while the other warriors
lounged about on the grass, drinking and sinking their teeth into dripping
hunks of savory roast meat. Ansuwulf had recovered well from the wound
Ongentheow had dealt to his head; the dark scab still showed through his
fine gray blond hair, but he was healing swiftly. He and Eofor sat at the
high table between the fires together with Hygelac, Beowulf, Othere, Onela,
and Yrse, though Hygelac had taken care to make sure that the sons of
Wonred were seated as far from Onela as they could be.

Beowulf sat next to Yrse, and he did not know what to say to her. It
seemed ill to him to speak of Ongentheow's death, not least because he
did not know whether she mourned her second husband, or felt herself
revenged for Halga's death at last. Nor could he ask about her son
Hrothulf, lest that bring up dark reminders of how the child had been
gotten on her and for all the time they had traveled together, Beowulf
realized that he truly knew very little about Yrse. But she has kept it so by
choice, I think, Beowulf thought, looking sideways at her.

As always, Yrse ate very neatly, with no drop of meat juices staining her
silk woven cuffs or dripping upon the fine sky blue linen of her gown; her
knife flashed red in the firelight as she sliced the beef before her into small
strips. Silhouetted against the flames, her profile was sharp and fine as an
alf maid's, and Beowulf remembered that the father of the Scyldings had
come over the sea from unknown lands, and was whispered to bear the
blood of gods in him. With her husband slain, Yrse had let her hair down
like a maiden's, rich glimmers of red and gold shining about her head like
a metal woven band. Again Beowulf remembered Hygelac's suggestion that
he might ask for Yrse to be gifted to him in wedding. My father might have
liked such a match: she is the brother's daughter of his old friend Hrothgar.

Yrse glanced up at Beowulf, and for a disturbing moment, he almost thought he saw the Scylding woman's eyes gleam green as a lynx's at night. His thoughts shriveled at once, as though he had leapt into icy water.

"Why do you stare at me so, Beowulf?" She rasped. "You did not look at me like that while we were faring together."

Beowulf felt the warm blush rising to his face as if he had trodden close to the fire.

"I did not mean to stare," he stammered. "I only thought..."

Yrse laughed, a surprisingly rich sound from her rough throat. "You thought it odd, perhaps, that I should wear blue after Ongentheow, and yet have my hair down as if I sought a husband already?"

"Even so."

"Well, Othere's wife must be queen over the Swedes now, and so I may do as I please. Perhaps when you have reigned over your own lands for a little while, you shall come to long for such freedom as well."

Beowulf could not say anything to that, for he was already beginning to feel the burden of Hroesnabeorh weighting his thoughts.

"I am told that your father was slain in this battle, and that you shall be Hygelac's march warder hereafter," Yrse said suddenly. "That is a fitting stead for you."

"What do you mean?" Beowulf asked, puzzled.

"We understand one another, you and I: we both know what it is to cross past the march stones of the Middle Garth and back again. There is much strength within you, if you did not fear so to loose it."

The hot meat Beowulf had eaten seemed to chill in his belly, his blood moving cold and slow as winter sluggish snakes through his veins. He knew that Yrse was not mad, no more than he himself, and he had felt the might of the Frowe breathing through her body yet the words of the eoten woman Hundle, speaking to the goddess as she rode on that lover whose shape she had shifted into the likeness of a golden boar, came to his mind:

"You are false, Frowe, thus to try me. Your eyes show this to me: that you have your man on his slain faring."

"That is as it may be," Beowulf said. "But why are you telling me this?"

"Because it has come to me that you and I might be well matched, though I am fourteen winters older than you."

Beowulf's heart jolted as though a shield rim had rammed into the pit of his belly. Has Hygelac been speaking to her, after all? He wondered dizzily. But as sure as he had been before that he did not want to wed Yrse, those thoughts were as a dead leaf clinging wavering to a tree branch when measured against his rock sureness of it now.

"I do not think so," Beowulf answered.

He could hear himself breathing hard, the way he had as a child when he could not get away from facing his tormentors. Yrse was so small beside him how could she fill him with such fear, when her words were of friendship? The Scylding woman's laugh rumbled low in her chest.

"Then there is little good in speaking further on the matter, is there? But let me offer you another choice. My Hrothulf has a half sister named Scyld " Beowulf started at the name: as a man's name, it meant shield, but as a woman's, it meant guilt or debt; and it was the name men gave to Wyrd's youngest sister. "She is the daughter of Halga, fostered with a highborn family in Scania; she is a fair and accomplished maid, two years younger than yourself. Though she was not born within wedding bonds, she is still acknowledged as an heir of true Scylding blood, and is growing into a mighty hall idis.

She would make a fine bride for you, if you would have her and it would gladden my heart, more than you know, to see you take her safely to wife."

Hrothgar's brother had no shyness in spreading his seed, did he? Beowulf thought, though it would have been cruel of him to speak so to Halga's daughter wife. Instead he declared,

"I am of no mind to be wedded now, not with my father's ashes barely cooled in the mound."

"What better time to set your seed within a womb?" Yrse asked, the rasp of her voice sinking almost to a purr. She was smiling at him now, her teeth glistening white as bare bone beneath her parted lips. "Men are born and die, even as grain is sown and reaped, but the aeht soul springs ever new from the barrow's dark hull so long as kinsmen are born that it may live on. Surely you do not mean for your line to die with you?"

"You know better than I how the Waegmunding line fares," Beowulf answered, though he could not wash the thin trail of bitter gall from his tongue as he spoke. "My father spoke seldom of his kin, and when he did he seldom had good to say; but he never said that his Swedish aeht had dwindled to a few."

"That is true enough," said Yrse lightly, and somehow Beowulf knew that she had set the matter aside; it seemed to him as though the heaviness that had ridden the air since she began to speak had gone on, like lightning sheeted summer storm clouds blowing darkly past without dropping their threatened rain. "There are Waegmundings even here at this feast though I know not how they would greet the son of Ecgtheow."

Beowulf closed his eyes, struck by a sudden pain. There had been times when his father looked scornfully at him, that he had wondered if he could seek out his Swedish kin, and if they would greet him as a lost grandson or scorn him the more cruelly, because he was Ecgtheow's bairn. And yet it was but a few days past that Beowulf had straightened his father's clenched limbs and brushed away as much as he could of the clotted blood that matted his bearskin's pelt into black spikes, trying not to look at the great wound where Ecgtheow's throat had been sliced so deeply that his neck bone showed white through the butcher red of his severed flesh.

Ecgtheow's face had been grim in death, his bearded mouth frozen into the berserk's snarl and his eyes gaping in blind fury at the flies that walked over their dulling blueness it could even have been, Beowulf thought, one of the Waegmunding's own bittered kinsmen who cut him down, for that aeht had ever stood close to Ongentheow. Beowulf did not wish to weep before Yrse, and so he said gruffly, "My father had little love for those he left behind. He would not take it well, did I seek them out at his burial arvel."

To thrust his point harder home, Beowulf lifted his horn and drank. Oswald's ale was a little thin, and sharply flavored with rowan berries, but it was strong enough to wash down the choking in his throat.

"It may be that you shall have more joy of them another time," Yrse agreed solemnly.

Beowulf rode beside Sweartwulf for most of the way back to Hroesnabeorh, listening carefully as the warrior told him of how matters stood there, pointing out one man or another and telling Beowulf what he knew of them. Sweartwulf himself, it came out as they talked, was a half Finn from the far North, son of the daughter of a tribal headman and a Norwegian who made a yearly journey to the Finns to trade for pelts.

"I have a place there yet, should I choose to take it," he said. "But none of my mother's blood shows in my face, and so I was always made to feel a stranger among the Saame."

Beowulf could see that easily. Not only was Sweartwulf's hair dark gold, but his features were that of a Northman, blunt and straight lined; he was burly and heavily muscled, and of middle height among the Geats, more than half a hand span taller than most Finns: only the slight slant to his blue eyes betrayed any hint of his mixed birth.

"Then I thought that I should get a better welcome among my father's folk. Yet to them I was a Finn, who might tie winds up in knots or put on a wolf skin to eat their cattle though I never had much to do with the naaeijte crafts. I was always a hunter and a warrior: I learned the art of swordplay swiftly among my father's people, but when I put their best wrestlers on their backs, they said it was through Finnish witchcraft, and looked askance at me. So, in time, I came to Hroesnabeorh, where no man asks too closely after the past of another if he is able to hold his place well in a shield wall. There I married Frithugeard the Gudhija and fathered my son Hraefn; you shall see them at Hroesnabeorh. As for the ways of my mother's folk, I hold little by them. Woden is my drighten, as he was my father's: he has dealt well with me in war and frith, and no doubt he shall take me in turn, as he did my father. But I see by your knife that you, too, have dealt with the Saame if you came by it through fair means," Sweartwulf added, his face suddenly grim. Beowulf told him briefly of how Paanja and his tribe had found him cast up on shore, and tended him through the winter.

He did not mention that the Merak Sabme had thought him a wight from beyond the world; but Sweartwulf recognized Paanja's name and tribe, and looked long and thoughtfully at Beowulf after he had heard them.

"You do well to have the friendship of such a naaeijte," the half Finn mused. "Few white men are given such a blessing, though it is the way of the Saame to be friendly with their guests."

"I would surely have died without their aid," Beowulf said, eager now to turn the talk elsewhere. "But tell me more of how matters stand at Hroesnabeorh. When I rode through with Haethcyn, I was challenged by a man named Hondscioh, who wore leather gloves and boasted that he could out wrestle all but two of the men in that hall."

Sweartwulf grinned wickedly, his hard set face suddenly looking much younger.

"Hondscioh is not the worst of men, though he is somewhat rough and rude of speech, and thinks over well of himself. He will be boasting now that he can out wrestle all but one, until you show him differently you do know somewhat of wrestling, do you not? I heard that it was you who broke Othere's arm."

Ashamed, Beowulf admitted, "I know little of it, because there were none in the Swertings' burg who could match my strength well enough to teach me."

The half Finn laughed. "There is more to wrestling and fighting bare handed than strength. The Saame know this well: a small folk without iron swords must learn other ways to stand up for themselves. This evening when we have camped, you and I shall go off a little way, and there I shall begin to teach you what you need to know a wise reded man will not trust too much to his strength, for he will find when he comes among the bold that no one is always strongest. Even you, though I have never seen your like, you may find your match in might someday, and then you will be glad to have learned some skill as well."

True to his word, Sweartwulf led Beowulf away from the tents that evening, coming to a small clearing among the trees where no other could watch them. They began slowly, to get each other's measure. To Beowulf's surprise, he found that it was hard to get a firm grip on Sweartwulf, who seemed to have mastered the art of slipping like a fish beneath his opponent's fingers, and could often twist free even when Beowulf simply lifted him off his feet to lay him down in the grass.

Sweartwulf, in turn, found that Beowulf was not so easy to trip up as he thought, and holds that would bring another to his knees in pain were hard to fix on arms as thick and strong as the Geat's though he often pointed out where, if they were not wrestling in friendship, a hard blow to the side of a joint or in such places as the throat and the pit of the belly would bring a man of Beowulf's size and thews down as surely as anybody.

"And you must learn how to deal and ward yourself from such blows, for when a man finds himself mastered by strength, he may fall into an ill mood and strike to hurt or if you must ever fight without a sword for your life, you could easily kill a man thus."

By the time the sky grew too dark for them to go on, both men were bruised a little, but Sweartwulf declared himself pleased with how quickly Beowulf was learning.

"Still, you must learn to wield your strength: it will never serve you well if you cannot rule it so that you never strike or grasp harder than you mean to, but can use your might to its fullest when you have need." And when Beowulf wrapped himself in his cloak to sleep that night, he was thinking, It may be that life in Hroesnabeorh will not be so hard, with such a friend beside me.

There were only four men on guard at the wall ringing Hroesnabeorh when Hygelac's troops came back, but the gates were still barred shut, and the challenge called out was the same:

"Who comes to the burg of Ecgtheow the Waegmunding?"

Beowulf looked to Hygelac to answer, but Hygelac shook his golden head. "This is your hall now, and it is for the host to lead his guests within."

Clearing his throat, his hands tightening on Feola's reins, Beowulf shouted back.

"Ecgtheow the Waegmunding has fallen; his ashes lie in a howe by Ravenwood. It is I, Beowulf Ecgtheow's son, who come to this burg, to claim my right and inheritance, and beside me rides Hygelac, now the folk leader of the Geats."

The gate swung slowly open. The man who stepped forward was tall and slim, with two coppery braids hanging down beneath his iron cap and a beard plaited into a fork.

"Hail and welcome, Beowulf. You bring sorrowful tidings; but so it often must be, when a son comes to take his father's seat and lands."

Beowulf sat on his horse's back for a moment, unsure of what to say. But he had dwelt ten winters in a king's hall, and listened often enough to the redes Hrethel and Wynefrith gave their sons. Now he spoke firmly, hoping that his face was not too pale from nervousness.

"Call you all my folk together, for I would have them witness when I sit in Ecgtheow's high seat this night. And see to it that there is a feast worthy of my father laid out."

The fork bearded man's arched brows tightened. "There is little enough left in our storehouses, for we have had to feed Haethcyn's thanes as well as our own folk these past weeks."

"Then send to our herdsmen and see which beasts are fit for slaughter. I shall not begin my rule here, nor flyte my father's ghost, by being close handed with food at this feast."

Ecgtheow's man soon his own, Beowulf realized: it would be he to whom the toasts were raised and oaths sworn that night nodded, a grudging smile stretching the corner of his mouth, and turned to go.

"And you," Beowulf said to another of the guards, "find someone to see to the stabling of these steeds and unloading such wains as may be needed." Where would Hygelac and his troops sleep this night? Most of Haethcyn's thanes had slept in the hall, but there were guest houses as well... "Tell the thralls to be sure that the guest houses are clean and fit for the king and his men."

The square bodied guard pushed his helm back on his head, little blue eyes squinting up into Beowulf's face. His thick jaw muscles worked under his light brown beard as though he were thinking of spitting, though he did not go so far.

"It is not my work to be an overseer of thralls," he said slowly, his voice slightly slurred by missing teeth. "Tell them yourself."

Beowulf knew what his father would have done if he were flouted so rudely: Ecgtheow would have leaned down from his horse and, at best, shaken his man until what was left of his broken teeth rattled in his mouth. Beowulf would not begin thus, for there was no way to know where it might end.

"Do you wish to shame us before our folk ruler?" Beowulf asked him. "If you have so little care for the fame of this hall, it may be that you would be gladder elsewhere. What is your name?"

"Unswifor," the guardsman answered sullenly.

"Ho, Unswifor!" Sweartwulf shouted from behind Beowulf. "Be still and do as our drighten asks, or you shall surely feel my fists. What would Ecgtheow have done if you had spoken to him thus?"

"Not so fast," Unswifor grumbled. "I shall see to the matter, though I think it well beneath me."

Relieved that he had not had to go any further with the guard, but unquiet of mind that he should have been met thus at the beginning, Beowulf led Hygelac and their men up the hill to the horse gabled hall. As they walked up the path, the full weight of what the first thane had said began to sink in. Not only must Beowulf learn to know and lead the rough men who had followed his father and that would be no easy task, as Unswifor's rudeness promised but he would have to keep a count of what was in the storehouses, lest his own folk starve.

He would have to look to the numbers of beasts in his herds and the depth of ale in his casks, ordering breeding and brewing and planting he would have to take up many of the burdens that Wynefrith had always kept from the backs of her husband and sons. Hygelac had given good rede when he said that Beowulf should have a hall frowe; how had Ecgtheow managed alone, those last eighteen winters of his reign after Hildebere's death? For a moment, Beowulf wished that he could turn away and run as he had at the Swertings' burg, fling himself forward to be borne up by the cold ocean waves and leave all his land troubles behind as he matched his strength against the sea.

But Hroesnabeorh was far from the shore, and Beowulf was not a child now, but for good or ill the drighten who must hold the march between the lakes for his king. No fires burned in the long trenches behind the hall pillars, for the day was warm; but there was a musty smell of damp and stale straw in the cool air. It seemed to Beowulf that he could feel his father's dark scowl on him, as though Ecgtheow still haunted his hall and looked upon his son with little welcome would he have given it over to Beowulf, if he had been asked his will before his death came upon him?

It is only, Beowulf said to himself, that the folk here did not know when to await our coming, or whether it would be the Swedes marching down the road instead: they have had more things to do than see that fresh straw was strewn and fires lit. Yet there was not even firewood stacked along the walls. There should have been thralls and bondsmaids about, cleaning or ready to run errands; instead the hall was empty, save for the wolf dogs who lay in the filthy straw with pointed muzzles resting on gray paws. The burnt down rush lights and torches were black in their holders, their dead soot already filmed with a light gray rime of damp mold.

"Seat yourselves as is fitting," Beowulf said, trying to hide the shame rushing warm into his face. "Though we gave no word of our coming, I shall see to it that a welcome draught is brought before you soon, and that the steam bath is heated so that we may wash ourselves before this night's feast." He turned to tap Sweartwulf on the shoulder. "Sweartwulf," he whispered out of the side of his mouth, "help me now."

The half Finn nodded, leading him from the hall. His face was set hard in its customary frown.

"Leave these thralls a day, and they will forget that their backs ever felt stripes," he muttered, then brightened. "But come, now you shall meet Frithugeard, and she shall soon have matters arranged as they ought to be."

Sweartwulf's house was not large, but it was neatly kept, with a well thatched roof and beautifully carved doorposts. Some of the designs Beowulf recognized, for they were close kin to the petaled stars decorating his knife sheath and the beast shapes he had seen on the polished horn jewelry of the Merak Sabme: as well as warrior and wrestler, it seemed that Sweartwulf was a skilled and keen eyed crafter.

The woman who unlatched the door at Sweartwulf's knock bore a stunning wealth of dark hair looped about her head in heavy braids: it was so long, thick, and shining that, had it been gold, she could almost have been taken for Thunar's wife Sibbe. She was shorter than her husband, generously built, with full breasts and well rounded hips; her heart shaped face was very pretty, bright blue eyes set beneath rounded dark brows and skin the rich deep white of fresh cream. In her arms she held a large babe, who stared up at the two men in lively wonder without the least sign of fear at the huge stranger beside his father.

"Sweartwulf!" She said joyously. "Blessed be Frige and the Frowe, for bringing you home safe!" Frithugeard hurried out to embrace her husband, and he folded both her and their son gently in his thick arms, kissing her deeply and stroking the soft golden down on the child's head.

"How is it with you, my Hraefn?" Sweartwulf asked the boy, taking him from his mother and lifting him up as the child chuckled, reaching out to grasp at his ridged helm crest. "You have grown again, haven't you, little warrior? It won't be long before you are ready for a helm and byrnie of your own. Have you been good?"

"He has been very good," Frithugeard asserted.

Watching them, Beowulf could not help but smile at their delight, though the loneliness banged against the hunger hollow beneath his ribs: *Hygd could have greeted me so...I shall never know this joy with her.* For a fleeting eye blink, it seemed to him as though Frithugeard, Sweartwulf, and Hraefn stood within their own garth of brightness, while he, but half a pace away, was in cold shadow. Then Sweartwulf turned to him, and the feeling vanished like a mouse flickering past the corner of his eye.

"This boy will be the doughtiest of your thanes someday," the half Finn said. "Here, you may hold him."

Awkwardly Beowulf took Hraefn from his father's arms. He had not held a babe like this before: he was surprised at the solid weight of such a small creature, and how comfortable the child's warmth felt nestled against his chest. Hraefn stared seriously up into his face, his blue eyes unbelievably wise and bright, like those of an all knowing and good hearted old man. Suddenly Beowulf thought of what might have happened to the boy and his mother at Yule, when the Swedes came to burn the burg at Hroesnabeorh, and he had to struggle to keep the rage from showing on his face.

This, then, was what it meant to be a march warder: to stand between Hraefn and Frithugeard and those who would do them harm and now Beowulf knew why Ecgtheow had gathered such a hard bitten troop of men about himself. Not solely because his father could speak in no tongue but harshness and fist blows; but because, there at the edge between two warring realms, it was the strongest and fiercest of warriors who must hold fast.

"He is a fine bairn," Beowulf said, handing Hraefn back to Frithugeard, who smiled lovingly down at her son. He felt awkward now, for he could not bring himself to ask her to put the child down and come to help her with greeting the guests in his hall, but Sweartwulf saved him again.

"Now, Frithugeard, the king and his men are here, and we must welcome them. Beowulf, since you have no wife yet, will you let Frithugeard pour out the draught of greeting? Ecgtheow often did that, and left the hall keys with her before we rode out to battle, for that she is gudhija here and always led the blessings together with him."

"That would be well," answered Beowulf.

"As for me, I shall roust out the thralls and see that they get to work. You go back to the hall with Frithugeard now, for you should be there when your guests are greeted."

Frithugeard went back into the house to lay Hraefn in his cradle and take out a large pitcher of black glazed clay, then hastened to the brewing house with Beowulf. The thane who had met him at the gate had spoken truly: Beowulf lifted up one keg, then another, only to find them empty.

"There are still full ones at that end," Frithugeard told him. "But a drighten should not be carrying barrels of drink; that is thrall work!"

"I would have my guests wait no longer than they must," Beowulf argued. Frithugeard pursed her small bowed lips, stepping outside and putting two fingers into her mouth to let out three piercing whistles.

After a little time, two bondsmaids came slouching into the brew house. Beowulf frowned, for Hrethel's thralls had never been so slow to answer; but he also marked the pinched look of the women's faces beneath the smears of soot and dust on their skins, and the way their iron collars hung heavy from their skinny necks. The small bones of the bondsmaids' shoulders stood out sharp against their grubby brown wool, and they cringed away with fear in their eyes as soon as they saw him standing beside Frithugeard, as though they thought he would strike them or perhaps do worse.

"Take that keg to the hall, now," Sweartwulf's wife ordered soft voiced. Again their pale eyes went to Beowulf; he could guess that Frithugeard, mild and good tempered as she seemed, did not find it easy to get obedience out of the thralls in such a steading. He nodded curtly, but when he saw how the two scrawny girls struggled to lift the keg between them, he could bear no more.

"You have not the strength for such work," said Beowulf, stepping between them and lifting the keg to his shoulder one handed.

"It were better if you set yourselves to sweeping and fetching fresh straw and torches for the hall and find some food for yourselves: I do not know how matters have been here before, but I am not minded to see starving maids in my burg. And when Frithugeard tells you what to do, it were best for you to listen to her."

The bondsmaids scuttled out, running before Beowulf and Frithugeard to the hall. Beowulf did not mark whether or not the men stared at him as he set the barrel down on the end of a table, but went up to take his place beside Hygelac, next to the high seat he would not sit there until all the folk were gathered to witness his claiming of his father's place. Then it would be his part to hold that great carven chair, with the bear heads arching over its back and wrestling bears entwined with wyrms and other beasts along its sides, and to give out rings and war weeds to his men...

The thought stunned Beowulf so that he hardly heard Frithugeard speaking her words of welcome as she filled Hygelac's horn: his high seat taking, after a hard fought battle, should be the time for him to give gifts to his thanes, but he did not know what he had beyond the silver capped amber tied closely beneath his beard. Had Ecgtheow had a coffer where gold and silver arm rings coiled like a nest of glistening adders in the darkness and if he had, where had he kept it, and how much might there be?

There would be no hoard of war gear, for Ecgtheow would not have stored away good byrnies and helms and swords if his men could use them. It might be that Hygelac would give Beowulf some of the weapons and armor the Geats had stripped from the Swedes, but there was no way of telling how much, save to ask him, and Beowulf felt uneasy about that: it seemed greedy, to speak of such things with his friend. Frithugeard was standing before him with the pitcher in her hand now, and Beowulf was sure she had just spoken to him. Quickly he unslung the horn that curled around his side, holding it out for her to fill.

"I thank you, frowe," Beowulf said that was a safe enough answer, whatever she had said. She smiled and went on to Eofor, who sat beside Beowulf with his brother.

The thralls were beginning to come in, men bearing loads of firewood and women carrying brooms. They all seemed thin and furtive, and even in the gloom of the hall, Beowulf could see the purple marks of fading bruises about the eyes and jaws of a few. He would put an end to that, if he could: it was seldom that a bondsman or serving maid had to be beaten in the Swertings' hall.

The stirring brooms raised clouds of dust, and it was not long before Beowulf began to wonder if it might have been better to leave the old straw down for the night, rather than draw every eye to the slovenliness with which the hall had been kept.

"Come, Hygelac," Beowulf said to his kinsmen when he could bear it no more. "There is still much of the day left: why then should we linger inside like this? And," he added, his voice lower, "there is a matter on which I would speak to you. Frithugeard, I shall need your help as well."

When they were outside, Beowulf asked, "Frithugeard, your husband said that Ecgtheow left the hall keys with you. Do you know where he kept his wealth?"

Frithugeard sighed, thin lines creasing her white forehead. "I believe that it must be in his house, though I have never gone in there. I do not know which locks all his keys fit."

"Shall I take a short walk elsewhere while you see to the matter?" Hygelac asked. "Or would you rather have me by you?"

"I would far rather have you with me as I do this."

The house in which Ecgtheow had slept was set apart from the others. Though it was larger than Sweartwulf's, it was not as well kept. Crows nested on the roof, their white droppings staining the thatch. They flew up with a raucous cawing as the three opened the door, as though to warn of thievery, and did not quiet: even muffled by the roof, their ceaseless croaking began swiftly to annoy Beowulf. Ecgtheow's house was dark, lighted only by the open door and the slits of light showing through the smoke hole, and the crumbling wooden walls stank of decay.

Layers of dust covered the shelves; on the walls hung old shields, battered and hacked, and they were so thickly dusted that Beowulf could hardly see the colors they had been painted. A mouse skittered along the floor in fright; when Beowulf took another step, the sole of his sealskin shoe crunched on a fragment of a broken pot. Tunics and trousers, some of them torn, lay in grimy heaps on the floor. A couple of throwing spears and a boars pear leaned in the corner here; there were a bow and a quiver of arrows. The weapons alone seemed to have been cared for, their edges gleaming sharp and bright through the gloom.

The second chamber was largely filled by Ecgtheow's bed, a tangle of blankets and furs. His smell still lay thickly there, the heavy musty scent of a man who fought often and bathed more seldom, like the smell in a winter den from which the bear was not long gone. Halfway under the bed stood a plain pot in which something dark rotted beneath a fur of gray mold. Ecgtheow's headboard was carved with the same pattern as his high seat, bears entwined with wyrms; a bears head sprouted from one upper corner, but the matching one had been hacked off long ago, the deep splintery scars of fierce sword blows darkened and worn almost to match the rest of it. Beowulf almost gagged, looking at the mess his father had left behind. From the look of the house, Ecgtheow had not lived like a man for the years since his wife had died, but like a wounded beast: again, he was ashamed to have Hygelac witnessing this.

If need had not driven him, Beowulf would have gone out and fetched a torch to burn his father's house to the ground, sending whatever Ecgtheow might wish to have from his wild den after him to Waelhall. There were three chests beside the bed, the smaller two carved to match the headboard and the larger one figured with images that were almost too dusty to make out in the darkness. Bending to brush his finger over them, Beowulf saw the shapes of men and women embracing, of women lifting horns to men, of dancing pairs with their arms locked about each other.

My mother's wedding chest, he thought, dazed. Silently Frithugeard unbuckled her belt bag to hand him a heavy iron ring of keys. One was smaller than the others, half eaten with rust as though it had not been touched for years. Beowulf set it into the lock: it did not turn easily, so he pressed harder, fearing that it would snap. But at last he heard the clicking within, and lifted the lid in a scattering of dust and pale little moths flying upward. Once the red woolen cloak that lay folded on top had been brightly embroidered with silk and trimmed with fine fur.

Now the moths had eaten it to shreds, small dry maggot casings lying like empty grain husks among the last tufts of crumbling dark hair and the untouched silken threads jumbled in the dust that faded and blurred the colors of the linen beneath. Beowulf wanted to close the chest, but he could not help lifting the garments up one by one to stare numbly at them gowns and headdresses such as befitted a king's daughter, touched here and there with threads of gold or silver clasp buttons.

Among the clothes were girdles adorned with gilded plates; a gold finger ring rolled from the folds of one dress, and an arm ring whose coils ended in two snake heads dropped heavily from another. At the very bottom was a head piece wrought of fine gold wire, with filigreed beads hanging all about it, and a red linen veil embroidered all over with silk the wedding crown that Ecgtheow had lifted from Hildebere's head when he brought her to the bridal bower: Hrethel and Wynefrith would have looked on to witness, and perhaps Eofor and Ansuwulf, and Ecgtheow's other friends, most of them long dead... Beowulf's eyes stung with dust as he laid his mother's garments carefully back into their places.

"Not in here, at least," he said.

The second and third chest held Ecgtheow's clothes and such things. These, at least, were not chewed by moths, and many of them seemed to have been washed that winter. Beowulf did not think that he would ever wish to wear them, even if any of them would fit him; but some, when they were clean, were fine enough to make fitting gifts.

"Look under the bed," Hygelac suggested. "If Ecgtheow hid his treasures away, that is the likeliest place."

Beowulf squatted down, squinting into the shadows. Something gleamed two beady black eyes staring back at him; then he saw the flicker of a long naked tail, and they were gone. He bit back a cry of disgust. With his thane's wife watching, Beowulf could not bring himself to ask for something to prod under the bed with, but he groped very cautiously, lest he find sharp teeth fastening in his fingers. At the very edge of his reach, his fingertips met whorl carved wood and the cold bite of iron.

He dragged the little chest out from the other side, and by its weight, he knew that he had found what he sought. But none of the keys opened the lock.

"My father must have taken that key with him," Beowulf said, almost to himself, "and I am not minded to dig up the mound and search for it in his ashes." He should, he thought, have looked in Ecgtheow's belt pouch as he was laying his father out but he could not have brought himself to do that, even if it had come to his mind: it would have been too much like robbing the dead.

Making up his mind swiftly, Beowulf struck the top of the iron bound chest with his fist. The thick wood splintered beneath the blow; two more, and the top caved in. Ecgtheow's hoard was not as large as Beowulf had hoped, nor as small as he had feared: there were enough long coils of gold and silver to bend out until they would slip over his arms and take off to break as gifts to his thanes, together with a little heap of southern coins, and a few finger rings and gold pendants. Beowulf looked up and saw Hygelac smiling through the gloom.

"A drighten rules with more than gold, but gold is always well to have," he said. "Still, no matter how open handed you are, it would not be well to give out all your store in one night especially since we stand in frith with the Swedes, and there will be no raiding of their steads while Othere keeps to his oath. But there are many good swords and byrnies and gilded helms in our wains: a few I have in mind to give out myself, but the rest I give to you, that your men may learn quickly to whom they owe war sarks and blades."

"That is kind of you," Beowulf stammered.

Hygelac laughed, shaking his head so that his golden braids swung from side to side.

"How should I be stingy with my kinsman, who has been so true to me?" He asked. Then, more soberly, he added, "And I can see that holding the rule of Hroesnabeorh will not be the easiest of tasks for you. But though men's troth is not bought with gifts, it is often seen in the giving and taking: those whose arms are adorned with your rings and weighted with your swords will lift those arms for you when you call them. And it is also true that thanes will more quickly follow an open handed drighten, if he has proven himself in other ways as well."

By the time the sun had set, the hall atop Hroesnabeorh was crowded full of folk, and there was some pushing and shouting on the benches. Beowulf looked upon that uneasily, wondering if he ought to step in before it came to more; but Sweartwulf paid it no mind, so he did no more than watch. Frithugeard and a few other women wives and daughters of the thanes, Beowulf guessed bore drink about, though they did not pour it out so lavishly as the women of the king's household had, and the brew was thin and weak for feast ale. For himself, Beowulf was not bothered by that, save as it meant that the plenty of his hall was bounded more tightly than he would have liked, but he wished that he could offer something better to Hygelac, whose gift of the Swedish war gear was now heaped behind their bench.

"I think all who mean to come are here now," said Sweartwulf across the empty high seat.

Beowulf rose. Hygelac and his men fell still at once, but Ecgtheow's folk still talked and laughed and shouted, paying him no mind.

"Hear me!" Sweartwulf shouted from his seat, his voice cutting sharp edged across the hall's din. "Be still you as well, Guthlaf! Our drighten will speak!"

Slowly the noise died down, leaving the hall quiet. Beowulf drew breath to speak, but found that his tongue had cloven to the roof of his mouth. He stood there for a moment, huge and silent, his brown hair still curling damp about his face from the steam bath he could not guess what the gathered folk thought of him, nor could he think of what to say. Ansuwulf had sung for Haethcyn, but Sweartwulf had already done as much as he should have to. Then Beowulf caught a flash of whiteness from the corner of his eye: Frithugeard was just pinning the shoulder of her dress back over her ample breast, her child's meal done, but she still held Hraefn in the crook of her arm. The sight seemed to loosen his heart like the strings of a grain bag loosening, letting his words flow out like a stream of golden wheat.

"My father Ecgtheow fell at Ravenwood; Woden took his man to himself, where the blood of kings flowed onto the earth. Long had he warded this march, lifting his sword against the foes that threatened our folk; and even in his falling, the Geats won the sig in battle through aid of his might. Now the flame sea has borne Ecgtheow onwards, and he has forsaken the Middle Garth for Woden's halls. But I am Ecgtheow's son, born to his own wife Hildebere; with his own hands he gave me a man's sword and helm, and I fought in the battle where he fell. Here I swear, before Frea Ing and the Frowe, Woden and Thunar and Tiw, with all of you to witness, that I shall hold Ecgtheow's seat well warding his folk with all my might and main, cutting down what harms them and furthering what helps them, in battle and frith as the gods shall send."

Beowulf sat down in Ecgtheow's high seat. Big as his father had been, the wood creaked beneath Beowulf's weight, and he filled it tightly from side to side. But it did not break under him, which would have been the worst of ill signs. Frithugeard had given Hraefn to another woman to hold; now she came forward with her pitcher to take his horn from him and pour it full. Her voice was low and sweet, and the murmurings that had run beneath Beowulf's words stilled as she spoke.

"Hail to you, Beowulf, drighten at Hroesnabeorh, march warder of the Geats. May you hold this land well in frith and joy; may you ward it well in Woden's red weather. I call the blessing of Frea Ing and the Frowe upon you " as she spoke, she traced a sun wheel above the horn; and Beowulf had to blink, for in that moment it seemed to him that he saw a glimmer of gold spiralling down into the ale from the fire lit air. "I call upon you the blessings of Thunar and Sibbe " Frithugeard made the sign of Thunar's Hammer, and it seemed to Beowulf that a red flash of lightning sheeted from her plump white fist. "I call upon you the blessings of Woden and Frige, and all the high gods and goddesses. May their might uphold you, and the alfs and idises look upon you with friendly eyes; may the wights of this land ever be of good heart towards you, Beowulf Ecgtheow's son."

Beowulf took the horn from Frithugeard's hand and drank. Though the thin ale tasted no better, it seemed to him that he could feel the might that the gudhija had called into it tingling down his throat in a rush of strength.

"Hail to you, Frithugeard Gudhija," Beowulf answered. "I have heard that my father put his trust in you; I shall do likewise, while you and I dwell both in this steading, and may this ring be the sign of our troth." He drew one of the gold coils from his right arm, giving it unbroken to her, though in pieces it would have been a good reward for three thanes. "Sweartwulf next," he whispered to her.

Frithugeard carried the horn to her husband, who leapt to his feet.

"Hail to you, Beowulf son of Ecgtheow, drighten at Hroesnabeorh!"

Sweartwulf shouted, flashing a grin at Beowulf before he looked sternly out at the other folk. A few cheers followed, though they sounded a little half hearted but most of those there knew little of him, Beowulf reminded himself; he could hardly await their love on sight.

"And to you, Sweartwulf," Beowulf answered. "You warded me with your shield at Ravenwood when I was shieldless, and were a true shoulder friend to me when the battle wands flashed about us." He reached down for the pieces of war gear he had set aside for the half Finn: a gilded helm, the finest of the ones Hygelac had given him, and a sword in a tooled and silver studded sheath with wyrm patterns rippling light and dark down the blade, at least the match of the one Beowulf had gotten from his father's hands. "My thane, I saw that your own war mask was broken in fight you hold great luck, to have taken no hurt from it! May this helm keep you from harm as well as you kept me, and may you always wield this sword as well as you did the one you held that day when we fought side by side."

"May it be so!" Sweartwulf shouted, grinning widely now. "I hail thee again, Beowulf, my drighten!" More cheers went up, and Beowulf thought on Hygelac's rede to him: it seemed that even the most heedless of the young Swertings had learned much of rule from Hrethel and Wynefrith.

All went well until Frithugeard bore the horn to Hondscioh. Instead of taking it from her hands, the big man rose to his feet, scowling as he stalked up before the high seat. He was dressed as he had been before, though he was wearing a cleaner pair of leather gloves.

"Well, Beowulf," Hondscioh sneered, dragging that name out like the insult it had once been. "Do you remember what I said when we last met? Now the Geats have won the battle, and you cannot hide behind Haethcyn to get away from me."

Beowulf heard the hiss of Hygelac's breath through his teeth, and the Geat king's mouth tightened, but though he leaned forward as though he wished to take Hondscioh on himself, he said nothing. The eyes of Ecgtheow's folk glittered in the firelight, staring eagerly at Beowulf.

There was no getting out of this, indeed; but if he showed his strength now, it might save him from more trouble later.

"If you wish to wrestle with me, then this is the time for it," Beowulf answered as lightly as he could. He unclasped his cloak, stepping out of it and down to the floor before the high seat table.

Hondscioh did not waste more words. He crouched, leather cased hands open before him, and began to circle Beowulf slowly. Beowulf moved with him, watching, not for his rush, but for one of the kicks that Sweartwulf had warned him about. The black bearded warrior shot out a foot, hooking it towards the tendon at the back of Beowulf's ankle as he moved in to grasp and push. Beowulf dodged the kick; he tried to grab both Hondscioh's hands at once, but clamped down only on his right wrist. Turning to the left as he pulled, he swung the thane around and off his feet as if Hondscioh were a harvest doll made of dry wheat stalks, whipping his arm over and sharply down as Sweartwulf had taught him to. Hondscioh cried out as his heels flew high and he went down flat on his back with a rib shattering thump, his head striking the hard earthen floor beneath the straw and flopping back. He did not rise. Have I killed him? Beowulf thought, horror struck. That would be an ill beginning to his rule indeed, to have slain one of the very folk he had just promised to guard. Frea Ing, may he yet live! Beowulf crouched down beside Hondscioh. A wheeze of air gasped from the thane's lungs, and Beowulf felt all his limbs sagging in relief; he very nearly collapsed on the floor himself.

"Well done, Beowulf!" Hygelac called out, echoed by Sweartwulf's "Well done, my drighten!"

Many of Hygelac's men were stamping and shouting as well but, Beowulf marked, few of his own. Instead the folk of Hroesnabeorh were staring wide eyed, and Beowulf was sure he heard the words troll kin, changeling muttered, like a night wind whispering over gnarled roots and through dead leaves. But surely, he thought numbly, they have seen Sweartwulf wrestle before, and know the look of his skill.

Is it that strange for a bout to end swiftly, when one man is so much smaller and the other the friend of the hall's best wrestler? Yet Beowulf knew that the tales of his years away had gone before him, and that they had grown in the telling as such things must: why else should Hondscioh have named him a troll when they first met? Two of Hondscioh's fellow warriors ran out and dragged him away as Beowulf went back to the high seat. Sweartwulf stood to clap him heartily on the shoulder.

"You could hardly have done that better," he praised. "The fall was a bit rougher than it might have been: had you flung him against a bench or table thus, it would have broken his back. But then, you could easily have snapped his arm or torn it from the shoulder, and Hondscioh tried hard to earn his sore head and bruised arse if," Sweartwulf laughed, "he ever knew the difference between them, which is no sure thing. He will not speak so boldly to your face again, you may be sure of that!"

Still, when Frithugeard carried the horn to the next man that he might toast Beowulf, the thane's words were slow in coming, with little life to them; as if he spoke not because he had seen his new drighten's worth for himself, nor even from duty to Hygelac or Ecgtheow's memory, but rather with the point of a knife in his back or from fear that, if he did not, Beowulf would serve him as he had Hondscioh. A sudden gloom shrouded Beowulf's mood like heavy fog rolling out of the ocean.

In trying to stave off trouble, he had done that very thing that he had least wanted to do. He had proven himself like his father, but worse for Ecgtheow could not have whirled Hondscioh's body, near as heavy as his own, so lightly from his feet, nor overcome him with such ease. Though the food was borne in when the last man had hailed Beowulf as his drighten, and it was good and plentiful enough, the feast was rather sombre after that, with more folk murmuring in corners and drawing together in tight little knots than Beowulf would have liked to see. And when at last Beowulf and Hygelac had eaten and drunk their fill, and were making their way to the guest houses for Beowulf would sooner have slept on the naked earth than in his father's dreary dwelling with the mice and rats scuttling about him

Hygelac said, "I should rather have you as witness when I take the Geat king's high seat than any other man living. But tell me, Berki, is it really in your mind to ride away from Hroesnabeorh so soon after you have come to it, while the folk here have had so little time yet to mourn Ecgtheow's death?"

It had always been Hygelac's way to be sparing of his younger friend's feelings in his words, but Beowulf knew what he meant: If you leave so soon after this night, I fear you will never be able to hold the rule here. And if Beowulf had not already sworn his oath before the gods and goddesses that night, he would have answered in words that meant, Then let it be so: I would gladly leave this hall behind me again.

Instead he said, "I would not stay away from your homecoming by choice, nor would I be missed by Wynefrith and Garhild and Hygd, if by being there I could ease some part of their grief over Haethcyn. And I greatly wish to see your daughter Hildegeard. But you are right: this is no time to leave my folk, with my father's ashes hardly chill in his mound, and not even laid where they may make offerings upon his howe." Although if Ecgtheow dwelt in the barrow after death, thought Beowulf feeling little kindness towards his father's memory at that moment he would be no kindly alf, but a drow, greater of strength and fiercer of mood than he was as a living man. "And our frith with the Swedes is so new that it hardly seems real to me yet: how then, to those who have warded our marches against them these many years? It is best, I think, if I stay here for now and come later to hail you as king."

"That is a wise choice. And though it shall sadden us both to part so soon, I think that you and your folk shall be the better for it."

Beowulf stood and watched the next morning as Hygelac rode away with his troops, their bronze bridle rattles jingling and flashing in the sunlight. The Geats' folk leader wore no helm now that he was in his own lands, and his golden hair gleamed above the deep copper sheen of his red steed, his gilded bridle mounts glittering fiery about the horse's head. With each swift prancing movement of hooves, Beowulf felt as though he himself were sinking a step deeper into soft bog: though he knew Hygelac had done all he could to help his friend, and must go on, he could not help the sense of betrayal that shivered deep in his bowels.

"It is not easy to part from a friend," said Frithugeard, coming up beside him. Beowulf looked down at her. Today her great mass of shining dark hair was caught up in a single braid that wrapped once about her head beneath a thin yellowish veil, then trailed free down her back almost to the richly rounded curve of her buttocks. Large bronze pin heads, polished nearly to the brightness of gold, fastened her head covering and braid in place, studding the fallow linen with a knobbly crown ring that sparkled with beads of light as she moved. The arm ring Beowulf had given her shone over the tight green linen of her under dress, its deep butter red sheen shaming the harder glitter of the simple brass clasps that held her long sleeves at the wrists.

"It is not," Beowulf agreed, sighing silently with relief at the chance she had given him to lay his deeper thoughts aside, "and Hygelac was ever my friend, even when I had no other: he kept the other youths from bullying me, as much as he might, and stood beside me when I had need of him."

Frithugeard raised the dark curves of her brows in surprise. "It is hard to think that you could ever have been bullied, or needed another's aid to stand up for yourself."

"I wish that I had come here while my father yet lived," Beowulf said for he found that he had little wish to speak more of his childhood. "It is a strange thing, to suddenly be drighten in a hall I do not know if not for you and Sweartwulf, I should be wholly lost here. But I am glad that my father put so much trust in you, for I think that you will be able to help me with the things I must know."

"Of course!" Frithugeard answered warmly.

Through the course of that day, she took Beowulf about the garth that had been his father's, showing him all his inheritance. The storehouses were not quite as empty as he had feared: there were plenty of dried fish, for the lakes Wener and Weter were fruitful; the cows were coming into their heaviest milk time, so there was no lack of cheese and butter, and Frithugeard said there was enough grain to get them through the hungry gap of Hay Month, if they were sparing with it. Beowulf told off three thralls to gather the bent and broken weapons, ring shattered byrnies, and dented helms that had been brought back from the battlefield among the whole gear but in the end he had to sort through them himself, for the thralls gave little care to their work.

When Beowulf bent his head to pass the door of the smithy, the smith, tall and brawny, but somewhat stoop backed, moved behind the anvil and lifted an ingot of red hot iron as if to hold it between them, and his eyes, pale in his soot smudged face, flickered to the side as if he thought to flee. Beowulf had not been the first to think of bringing broken war gear to him for repair: a pile of byrnies lay over a bench, and next to it were stacked bent swords and chipped axes, with battered helms set in a neat line along the floor like empty skulls in the stone chamber of an ancient mound.

"Is all well with you?" Beowulf asked, more sharply than he meant to.

"Yes...yes, all is well," the smith stammered.

"That is good to hear, for you have much work ahead of you. Come," he called to the thralls, who staggered in beneath their bundles of hacked iron, dropping them with a loud clatter. The sweat was already springing out on Beowulf's forehead from the heat of the forge.

"I...I shall, I shall get to it at once," said the smith, and Beowulf saw that the ingot cooling dull red in his tongs was shaking so badly that he was in danger of dropping it.

"First deal with the ones that my men brought to you themselves," Beowulf said, trying to make his voice quiet and kind. "When those are mended, you may start on these. Be sure," he added, remembering Haethcyn, "you shall not feel yourself scanted when you have gotten your pay for this work."

"As you wish," the smith said, his eyes dropping like a whipped hound's. Beowulf would have clenched his fists then, for the seething anger at the legacy Ecgtheow had left him, but that would only have made the man sure that his drighten meant to strike him. And besides a few droplets of sweat suddenly beaded together to run warm down his forehead, stinging into his eyes Beowulf could not truly know how much of the smith's unmanly cringing was because of Ecgtheow's hot moods, and how much stemmed from what he had seen of Beowulf himself.

When he was outside again, the mild breeze cooling his heat flushed face, Beowulf asked Frithugeard the question he had been fearing to hear the answer to all day,

"How goes it with Hondscioh?"

"I looked at him earlier this morning. He will be abed for a day or two yet, until his head has stopped aching so badly, and walk stiffly for a few weeks; I think three of his ribs are cracked. But he cannot complain that you served him ill, for it was he who wished to fight, and his mouth that would have loudly shamed you if you had held your hand."

"And what does he say now?"

"Chiefly, that it were best if no one laughed at him who is not brave enough to stand against you himself." Frithugeard's mouth closed tightly, and Beowulf guessed that Hondscioh had said other things as well, but he did not press her.

In the lengthening days, it was most often Sweartwulf who took his drighten outside the garth, riding with him over the lands he ruled. The green shoots of grain rose knee high now, the light warm winds rippling over their rows in silvery waves; the flax was beginning to bloom, a cloak of pale blue blossoms laid lightly over the fields. The cows were fattening quickly on the rich grass, their iron bells clanking dull around their necks and their little calves bawling across the fields, while the sheep, their thick curling horns ridiculously heavy above their little fresh shorn bodies, drifted over the meadows.

The reeds grew tall around the shores of the two great lakes Wener and Weter: often, as Sweartwulf and Beowulf rode by, they would rustle as a duck paddled out to open water with her little brown ducklings trailing after her, or hiss beneath the flapping wings of a startled flock of geese taking to the air in a great honking cloud. As the twilights lengthened and brightened, Beowulf often saw elk in the lakes, long nosed cows standing by the shore with their little red furred calves half hidden by the reeds, or the dark heads of bulls with their knobbly sprouting horns and deep dewlaps breaking the shining water.

Sometimes a family of wild swine would come down to drink, the grown pigs trotting black and grim tusked before the tawny brown striped piglets. The cuckoo called in the woods, his deep hollow chuckling going on and on

"He must have two full meals of cherries before he changes his song," said Frithugeard once.

Remembering Herebeald's death, Beowulf still could not bring himself to go hunting; and, in truth, it was only Sweartwulf who ever asked him to. But he and Sweartwulf went out often to wrestle or fight with wooden swords together, for Sweartwulf would not do it where others could see.

"It would not be fitting for your men to see you overcome," Sweartwulf said staunchly. "Your father never forgot that I had stained the back of his tunic with earth in front of his thanes he always looked well upon Frithugeard, but after that, I was never one of his favourites among his warriors."

Beowulf stared bleakly at him. "I am not such a man as my father."

"I know that well!" Agreed the half Finn. "But we need no other eyes upon us while you learn your fighting skills."

And it was well for him that he could go out with Sweartwulf, Beowulf thought sometimes. Else, had it been his way to ride off alone in the evenings, his folk would have looked even more askance on him than they did already. None dared speak against him to his face, but he marked how there was little jostling on the benches to sit nearest his high seat. At his order, his thralls were fed better than they had been, and he never saw the marks of fists on their faces any more.

But once in a while far too often for his liking, for he would that it never happened he would see a bondsmaid walking stiffly, or a thrall carle wincing as he pissed a stream that was redder than it should have been. Then, when he asked if any had done them harm without his leave, they would always shake their heads, their eyes dropping from his face or slithering slyly to the side beneath his gaze. And, worst of all, Beowulf did not know whether their silence came from fear of whoever had beaten them...or from fear of him.

Yet there was nothing he could do about it, short of trying to pry and set spies among his own folk; and that would have led to worse feeling among them yet. The nights shortened until men went to their beds at twilight and woke with the sun full up, and Midsummer Eve came more swiftly than Beowulf, always busy and worried about his duties to a folk who seemed to take his rule so ill, had time to think of readying his garth for that holy day. But Frithugeard sent the women out into the wood to gather flowers and greenery for garlands, while the men chopped down a tall straight tree and lopped the branches from it, leaving only stubs from which the leafy rings of braided twigs, brightened with flowers and the pearly roots of small leeks, might hang.

Others heaped up wood for a bonfire before the Midsummer tree; the tables and benches were carried down from the hall and baskets of little wild strawberries laid upon them by children coming in from the woods, and the scent of browning bread wafted softly over the burg from the bakehouses. The herdsmen had tethered a white ox near the Midsummer tree, so close that every so often, when the great beast lifted its head from the grain sprinkled grass at its feet, it could stretch out its black velvet nose and lip a few of the green leaves and white frothing hwanna blossoms from the garland nearest to it, rolling huge mild brown eyes in contentment as it chewed and chewed. The voices of the women and children floated high over the fields, rising up where they sat in rings around baskets of birch twigs and rowan twigs with their little berries swelling green, pink white dog roses and blue flax flowers and sprays of small leaved Sunne wort, their nimble fingers weaving the long stems together as they sang.

"Sunne shines and sings above,
in holy height, all hail, fair maid!
We weave her worts in winding ring,
to drive hence woe wights, witches, trolls."

Frithugeard walked by one of those circles, taking two wreaths of flowers to hang around the ox's blunted horns. She stroked its white neck a few moments, speaking softly into its ear, before she went on. Others passed and took single wreaths to put upon the Midsummer tree it was said that those whose garlands withered quickly would die soon, while those whose greenery stayed fresh would have long life. Beowulf himself stooped to take a ring of leaves and leeks from one of the maidens, stepping back before she could flinch away from him. Beside the green wreathed pole, he leapt up as high as he could to loop his wreath on a stub far above his head, just below the very crown of the Midsummer tree, where no one else could reach by themselves.

For once, Beowulf felt almost at ease among his folk. Though few of them stopped to hail him as he strode among them, the uneasy mood that had hung over Hroesnabeorh since he took the high seat seemed to have lifted, and even the thralls lifted their voices in snatches of song as they bore wood to the fire and the bake house's ovens, or hauled buckets of water from the spring behind the hill. Some men were up near the roof of the hall on rough ladders of tree trunks with evenly lopped branches for footholds, draping wreaths and braided ropes of greenery over the necks of the horse heads glaring balefully towards Sweden; others were out in the fields, tying red strings and sprigs of Sunne wort around the horns of the cattle and sheep so that no witch or alf could enchant them that night.

One youth played on a little sheep bone pipe while another drummed, and maidens whirled in the arms of young men to the song on the greensward:

"Sunne shines and sings above,
her horses run in round of year.
We dance in weal, woe, dance out!
Dance gladness for the gods all high."

As that bright day wore on, the wind grew stronger, gusting and eddying about the swinging garlands. It seemed to Beowulf as though he could feel the holy day's might growing in the land, the stirring air tingling about him and the ground thrumming silently beneath his feet as though the alf horses chomped and stamped in their stables beneath the mounds, eager to ride out.

Beowulf, too, was eager: when he stood beside Frithugeard, offering the ox up to the gods with the blood that spilled from its throat to overflow the blessing bowl and richen the earth, when he called their holy gifts forth for his folk then they could see that he was no troll carle after all, nor a bringer of ill luck, for he was sure that he felt the warm breath of the Wan gods in the rising wind, and that Frea Ing would stand with him as he made his blessing for his father's lands.

Sunne was just sinking down, the western sky slowly brightening from blue to reddish gold like fine polished steel heating in the forge and the sky to the east beginning to deepen towards purple, when Frithugeard came hurrying up to Beowulf. Deep creases of worry furrowed her white brow, and her small mouth was set angrily.

"What is wrong?" Beowulf asked, suddenly alarmed.

"Beowulf, we must speak alone."

Beowulf let the gudhija lead him around behind the hill, away from the folk gathered laughing and talking beneath the Midsummer tree. They stopped by the wide pool where the waters of the stream that sprang forth from Hroesnabeorh's roots gathered deep, spilling over at the far side to run swiftly out through the boulder built passage beneath the palisade's earthen wall. The doors of the two bath houses were closed, their log walls still warm, but Beowulf heard no sounds from within, neither the murmur of speech nor the hissing of water from red glowing stones. He thought most of those who wished to bathe had done so earlier, as he himself had. Now the baths were left hot, as they would be at Yule, for the alfs and the ghosts and those young men and women who might go in after sunset with whisks made of nine kinds of twig bound together, hoping to learn something of whom they would marry. The waters of the pool were dark now, save for the froth where the stream tumbled into it and the faint gleam of the reddening sky, rippled by the rising wind.

"What is wrong?" He asked again.

Frithugeard's eyes half closed, as if in pain, and her smooth plump hands tightened on the yellow embroidered bands running up the seams of her green overdress.

"It is ill that I must be the one to tell you this, for it is none of my will. When the first folk said it to me, I tried to gainsay them, and to tell them that I knew there was great luck for blessing and the good will of the gods in you, but..." Her face crumpled as though she would give way to tears.

"Beowulf, I am sorry. There are too many in this burg who still think you half a troll, or more, and they have all told me through this day that they would not have you making the offering to the gods, lest ill come of it for Hroesnabeorh."

I shall kill Hondscioh, was Beowulf's first shocked thought. I shall break his neck with my hands. Frithugeard stumbled back a step, her eyes wide with terror and her mouth opening as if to beg for her life. The air grunted from Beowulf's lungs with effort, as if he were striving to lift a boulder beyond his strength, but he forced his fists to unclench, the snarl to smooth from his face. He would not slay Hondscioh, or any of his other men. Now Beowulf understood the sideways glances, the way folk were silent to his face and murmured when he passed.

He could not even blame Hondscioh too harshly: for how could a proud man, whose standing among others was built wholly on his strength, keep his easy defeat from dropping him from their ranks, save that he had been beaten by one who was beyond human might? Beowulf wished now that Sweartwulf had not been so careful of his fame, for if his men had seen him struggling and sometimes overcome, they might have looked upon him with less fear yet Sweartwulf was half Finn: who, among Hroesnabeorh's thanes, knew but that he worked spell craft of his own? And without their awe of Beowulf, who could say but that matters might not have gone worse yet with him here?

"That is woeful to hear," Beowulf said heavily. "But I do not blame you that you have told me. Ecgtheow trusted the luck of his folk to your keeping, and those who fear that luck has left them will soon find it has slipped through their fingers, whether there was good reason at first for their fear or not. Do not sorrow over what is not your doing!"

Frithugeard took his hands in hers, a firm sisterly clasp. "Yet I have hurt you, to whom I would not by my will cause any pain. And I know that you are a good man, and friend to the gods: it is unwise of the folk of Hroesnabeorh to scorn the gift that they have been given, for that will win them no love in the holy steads." She bit her lip, looking up into Beowulf's face again. "And so because I am gudhija here I would still ask your blessing for this land, in spite of the foolishness of its dwellers. Whether they know that I bear it to them or not, I think that matters will go ill here without it."

Beowulf knew what Ecgtheow would have done: he would have raged and shouted: If they are so unmanly as to fear anyone stronger than themselves, and too blind to see my worth, then let them fall: I would give my blessing to the worms and carrion crows first!

His heart ached to cry that out, to get on Feola's back and turn the horse's golden head towards Hygelac's burg and be done with the rough and ungrateful men of Hroesnabeorh forever. When Beowulf had given his oath to his father's folk, he had not hedged it around with stingy murmurs, nor said that he would do his best for them only so long as they loved him. And they all stood together for good or ill: if summer hail flattened the fields and broke the green grain stalks, little Hraefn would go short of porridge next year as surely as Hondscioh would; if sickness broke out within the garth, Frithugeard would be the one who had to closet herself in the fetid air breathed out by the dying, tending to them with her herb craft and bidding Frige and Are aid. And there is more to it than that.

These same men who name me a troll set their lives at risk whenever sword beats on shield, to ward the land or die in trying: whatever my strength or skill, I could do no better. Do the gods, Beowulf wondered then, look so upon us as though we were children, often foolish and ungrateful, yet bound by the same skeins of Wyrd that weave their lives, and sometimes showing troth and bravery to match even their own measure, in heart if not in might? Beowulf's voice was steady and calm as he spoke, looking straight into Frithugeard's clear blue eyes.

"By the oath I swore before my father's high seat, I give you my blessing for Hroesnabeorh and all its folk and lands. May Sunne shine upon them in gladness, here at her Midsummer height, and the holy fires burn for a year of good luck. I bid Frea Ing, the mighty World Lord, to pour out his blessings free handedly here, in harvest and frith. Let there be joy within and about this garth, the cattle growing strong in the fields, the storehouses waxing full with grain, the kegs filled with amber brown ale. May the ruler of Alfhame lead his bright folk here in friendship; may the idises shining turn loving eyes on us, and the land wights bear to us weal. I bid this with a whole heart and a good mind I, Beowulf, Ecgtheow's son."

Frithugeard stood there for a little time, still as a deep rooted tree. It seemed to Beowulf that he could feel the warm might of the blessing he had called streaming through him, pooling in her like ale filling a pitcher, ready for her to pour out again, as she offered his drink to his thanes in the feast hall.

"Thank you," said Frithugeard, so quietly that Beowulf could hardly hear her words. "That was the deed of an atheling. Will you come, at least…"

Beowulf shook his head before she could finish. "Let Sweartwulf strike the blow to stun the ox: I shall hold it no lessening of my honor if he takes my place there. As for me better if I am elsewhere altogether, rather than being seen to stand back while my folk are blessed."

In truth, he thought he could not bear it, to stand as if he were a warg in his own garth; and he would not spoil the blessing he had given with ill thoughts while Frithugeard spoke it on. He smiled ruefully.

"If there is talk about where I have gone, say that I am sitting on an earth fast stone this night in hopes of gaining some rede about whatever maiden I should take as my wife."

Frithugeard smiled back at him, her eyes lighting for the first time since she had led him away.

"May you have luck in that, and Frige and the Frowe show you the way to a good bride!"

Beowulf said nothing, for half a lie was more than enough. But as he walked around the hill and towards the gate open this night, with only two armed guards on it, and adorned like all doors and windows in the burg with trails of red wool wrapped around bunches of Sunne wort and rowan he heard the song still ringing from the gathering by the Midsummer tree.

"Sunne sets and sings in joy,
　Linger her steeds not long till day.
　Now alfs are riding, all are singing,
　from hallowed howes they hail their kin."

As Beowulf stepped out of the garth, the warm wind blew more strongly about him, whipping his wavy brown hair and beard around his face. A few old leaves tumbled by, caught up from their graves in the mold to fly through the air as they had at winter's beginning. The new Moon was already bright in the sky, a pearl sliver against the darkening blue silver of the heavens; and downcast as Beowulf was, a thrill still whispered over his skin as he looked up to see the Moon's shining paleness set against the red fire wheel of his sister the Sun and felt the wind ruffling through his hair.

There was an earth fast boulder in the woods nearest to Hroesnabeorh where folk often went to make offerings, but Beowulf did not wish to go there that night: there would be too many coming out to set flowers or cups of ale or bits of the blessing ox's flesh upon it, as well as young men creeping into the woods with their maids. Instead he walked down the road until the Sun had sunk to a bare glowing ember in the west, following by habit the path along which he and Sweartwulf often rode out to Lake Wener.

The Sun was down altogether, the evening deepening to purple twilight and the first stars glimmering like a casting of berg crystals over the sky, when Beowulf stopped. He had not thought on where he was going: but here at the edge of the wood, near to the shore of the lake, stood a great earth fast stone a jutting gray boulder, ridged behind and sloping a little towards the water, like an eoten's half hewn chair. Above it towered an old elder tree, covered with masses of white blossoms that gleamed pale in the darkness, tossing like a maiden's fair hair in the wind. Beowulf seated himself upon the stone. His feet barely touched the earth, brushing over the long grasses and tiny star petaled white flowers that rustled about the rock's base.

The shore was dark as far as Beowulf could see, until it dwindled to nothingness behind the vast stretch of water; but the lake itself still shone blue, as though it had gathered in all the heavens' brightness to give back now as the sky darkened, like a rippled gleaming gem set in black iron. The little wind driven waves lapped against the shore, Beowulf's heartbeat settling softly to their rhythm. Another leaf swirled before him, dancing butterfly light on the air; he watched it go, leaping up and spiraling down, until he could see it no longer.

The lake's light faded slowly, but it seemed to Beowulf that he could see it shining faintly yet against the star scattered water, like the echo of an echo. Above his head, the elder branches whispered softly, leaves brushing against leaves, and tiny white blossoms scattered down over him like a host of pale moths in the darkness. Beowulf felt as though his tingling limbs had grown too heavy to move, and yet as though he were hardly there, as if his flesh had burned to a whirling of live sparks around bones of rock.

The waves' soft crashing clanged inside his stony skull, its sound rising higher and higher until it seemed to Beowulf as though he heard the jingling of metal bridle rattles, ringing with the pure sweet note of silver bells; and beneath that, the quick splashing of horses' hooves running light through the water. The sound grew swifter and louder, thrumming through him as if his body were a single harpstring singing unplucked beneath the wind; it seemed to Beowulf that it could lift him aloft, swirling him away on the wild ride of the long fallen leaves.

Then Beowulf did not know if he dreamed or woke, for he thought he could feel his eyelids shutting, and yet everything before him the starlit ripples on the dark lake, the cattails bending before the wind, the clear blackness of the heavens was clearer than it had been before. And now he saw the riders, galloping over the reeds as if they were no more than a cloud of mist under the horses' hooves. Their steeds shone white and dappled gray, with silver glittering from their bridle mounts; their fine sarks and cloaks gleamed silken blue, and the brightness of the crescent Moon pooled glowing in the smooth rounds of berg crystal at their fingers and throats, running in droplets down their silver mounted sword sheaths.

The riders' long hair streamed dark and silver behind them, and their fair faces were pale as the faces of the dead, shrouded by the night; yet they laughed merrily as they touched their horses' flanks with spurs whose points glinted in the starlight. But Beowulf's gaze lit on the one who led them, and could not leave him. The white moonlight could not chill the warm gold of his hair and beard, nor the summer brightness of his blue eyes; his long tunic was the pale green of new leaves, his belt fastened with a garnet eyed golden boar, and the hooves of his steed gleamed red as fresh blood. He wore no sword, but held a gilded stag's antler aloft in his hand, scattering beads of glistening water from its bright tips, while his leek speared mightily up beneath his green linen sark. Then, as they passed the stone, the leader's eyes met Beowulf's.

He smiled, flicking a spray of shining drops towards the elder tree with his antler tines. As the water touched his forehead, Beowulf felt himself utterly whelmed, a joy greater than he had ever known sweeping through him in a sunlit wave that drowned all his thought. Beowulf awoke with the dew chilling on his hair and skin, a spider's web glistening like a pattern of thin beaded gold wire between the elder branches drooping before his face. His buttocks and thighs ached to the bone, the stone's cold striking through his flesh like an icy sword. Careful not to break the spider's weaving, he slid off the rock, staggering back to the pathway through the woods. The sun was well up by the time he met the challenge at Hroesnabeorh's gate, stepping past the wilting spray of red bound leaves. He breathed deeply, the smell of roasting meat that filled the air awakening a rumble of hunger in his belly.

The Midsummer fire still burned low, the flayed and gutted carcass of the offering ox hanging on a spit above it. The ox's white head had been hoisted to the top of the Midsummer tree, a few trails of blood darkening the cracked brown bark below it. Some of the wreaths hanging from the tree's lopped limbs had withered in the blast of the bonfire's heat, but Beowulf's, though splattered by the offering blood from the ox's head, still swung green and bright in its place.

"Ho, Beowulf!" Said Sweartwulf cheerfully. His dark gold hair was disheveled, his eyelids hanging sleepy, but his usual grimness had faded to a mild look of sated comfort: Beowulf guessed that he and Frithugeard had welcomed Midsummer's Eve together all through the night and well into the early day's brightness. "We missed you at the blessing last night but did you win some foresight of your bride?"

Beowulf smiled, but said nothing. Sweartwulf chuckled. "Good enough for you not to talk about her, lest you break the spell? You're a wise man. Come, Frithugeard is making honey cakes for breakfast, and she said there'd be none for me if I didn't bring you back with me. I thought I'd have to go out into the woods to search for you."

Though a shadow of yesterday's bleakness had settled over Beowulf as he looked at the leavings of the offering, it was no more than a faint mist against the memory of what he had seen beneath the elder tree. I have won a better blessing than I gave, he thought. And he knew now, as he had doubted it before, that he would have the strength to sit in his place at the Midsummer feast that night, and wish no ill to those who had turned him away. Beowulf smiled again, letting Sweartwulf lead him back to his friends' house. The weather stayed fair through haying time, the Sun beating down warmly to dry the heaps spread upon the meadows.

Still, there were mumbles and complaints, for Hroesnabeorh had run out of grain before the harvest, so there was no ale left, and what flour there was had to be ground from dried peas, making the meager portions of bread hard and gritty, with a sickly green gray cast, while the stores of salted and smoked meat were gone as well, and they had to make do with fish from the lakes, the occasional waterfowl or deer, and summer plentiful cheese, with sour skyr and water as their only drinks.

Beowulf might have spent the last of his father's gold and silver on grain or ale, but he was loath to do that: there was no telling whether the harvest would be good enough that Hroesnabeorh could be sellers rather than buyers the next summer, and the Swedish frith meant that there would be no chance of winning more treasures in battle. Beowulf watched the weather with a careful eye, for a single hailstorm beating down the grain would bring more hunger than the usual short meals of the month after Midsummer.

But dawn after dawn rose with no worse than a faint mist from the lakes pearling the bright sky, and the silver green waves of grain ripened to pale gold, then to a rich golden brown as the sky blue lakes of flax flowers withered to leave their stalks standing tall. The rowan berries swelled brilliant red, shining like little coals among the graceful sprays of green leaves. Save for the shortage of food, it was as fair a summer as Beowulf could remember.

Yet he often felt the weight of sadness pressing against his limbs, for the Midsummer's offering seemed to have sealed his apartness from his thanes: whether cutting hay in the fields for Hroesnabeorh was not so great a burg that even the drighten's hands could be spared from that work or swimming in the cool lake water in the evening, no one save Sweartwulf and Frithugeard greeted him with any joy. Field work did not end when the hay was all cut and stacked: the men sat about in the hall that night, whetstones singing off the edges of scythes as though they were readying themselves for battle, while the women spun and wound the cords for binding the sheaves.

"Who is to cut the first sheaf?" Beowulf asked Frithugeard softly.

The gudhija looked up at him in surprise, bouncing Hraefn gently on her knee as the boy giggled and reached out to wind little fists in her pale linen headdress.

"Why, you are, of course. Was it not the way in the Swertings' hall for the land fro to begin the harvesting?"

"It was, but I thought..." Beowulf could not finish.

Frithugeard's curved brows drew together in understanding. "Ah. Yet you are drighten here none will stand up to deny that and these are your lands that you hold by right of blood and gift. He that owns the lands must start the harvest: that is how it has always been, and shall still be."

Beowulf rose at dawn the next day, dressing in a white tunic and setting gold rings upon his arms: Hrethel had always worn such clothes at harvest's beginning, that the gods and alfs might know that he came to the work with fitting awe. Frithugeard was also dressed in white, with her bronze pins flashing bright around her shining headdress, and even the thrall maids wore white kerchiefs upon their heads. Taking up his scythe, Beowulf led his folk out to the first field if there were uneasy murmurs behind him, he blocked his ears from them.

The grain had grown thick and richly that year, answering the promise that the alfs' leader had seemed to give Beowulf at Midsummer's, and it warmed his heart to look out over the heavy golden burden swaying upon the stalks. Perhaps now, Beowulf thought, my folk will see that I have brought them weal and no ill luck. Beowulf tilted his head back, looking up into the clear bowl of the sky above the Sun's pale rising light.

The wood of his scythe's handle nestled smooth and polished into his palms, its freshly honed edge glittering a silver new moon sliver along the curve of the black iron blade. In his light dazed sight, it seemed to him that the ripe grain stood rustling over the earth as the long bristles rising on the crest of a great golden boar or was it a woman's long gold hair waving beneath the soft cool wind from Lake Wener?

"Frea Ing, be with us!" Beowulf cried, caught up in a sudden rush of gladness. His scythe swished through the air, grain stalks tumbling down behind its clean swath.

Frithugeard stepped forward at once, sweeping up the heavy laden armful and whisking a gleaming white cord nine times about it before lifting it high above her head so that all could see.

"The harvest is begun!" She called out. "May the gods and goddesses, alfs and idises bless it; thanks be to the open handed wights of this land and the all giving earth."

She tied the ends of her cord into a loop, knotting the first sheaf swiftly to Beowulf's belt. He swung his scythe back again, and the line of reapers moved forward with him. Through the reaping and the flax harvest, the weather held good, though by the time the folk of Hroesnabeorh had reached the last field of grain, the clear air had cooled enough to bring a chill to the reapers' sweaty brows when they stopped for their mid morning meals. The flax had all been pulled, some laid out in the grass to rett in the morning dew and some tied in bundles in the stream where it flowed forth from Hroesnabeorh's palisade wall, its rotting vegetable reek wafting on the cold wind.

Beowulf's early blisters had long since hardened to callouses, and the ache in his back had faded away altogether: none of the other reapers could match his pace, and it seemed to him that showing his strength thus was winning him better will among his folk. Too, there was fresh bread in the morning and evening, and the ale was almost ready to be poured out in the hall; that, and the thought of fresh meat coming soon with the winter slaughtering, had raised the hearts in Hroesnabeorh. The Sun was reddening in the west when the reapers neared the end of the field. Beowulf, growing tired from his day's work and eager to see the last of the reaping done, did not mark how the other scythe swingers were drawing away from him a little and falling back. One great sweep, and the last stalks fell away before him and there was a sudden hush over the field.

"Beowulf has cut the Last Sheaf!" a man's voice cried out behind him.

Beowulf stood with the scythe in his hands, looking at the golden stalks scattered thickly above the stubble. Great good luck, or great ill the Last Sheaf might betide either, for it marked its reaper out in the sight of the gods. At the Swertings' hall, the maidens had always jostled each other towards the sheaf, for it was said that the girl who must bind it would bear a babe before she was wedded. Here, Frithugeard came forward swiftly, a threefold braid of black and red and white in her hand, gathering the stalks together and tying them into a thick bundle. On Beowulf's other side, Sweartwulf came forward with a wooden stake. Taking the Last Sheath from Frithugeard, Beowulf rammed the stake deep into the ground and tied the bundle of grain tightly to it.

"Now the harvest work is done: thanks be to the gods and goddesses, alfs and idises and wights," he said. "Let them bless it in our barns, that it take no harm from worm and mouse. But this sheaf we leave beneath the open sky, that Frea Ing's steed may have fodder when he leads his alf troop through the fields to sow his gifts again on these lands for good harvest and frith I give it!"

Only stillness met his words, and Beowulf wondered if he had somehow misspoken or was it awe that bound the tongues of the men and women standing in the shorn field?

But then, shyly, one of the maidens came up with her wreath of blue cornflowers and red poppies and white dog roses to set upon the Last Sheaf, and the others followed, until the pole and its golden burden were almost hidden beneath the garlands of flowers, while the men bent to gathering the bound sheaves that lay in neat rows upon the stubble, carrying them to the ox cart waiting at the field's edge. As the women, their wreaths given, went to join the men in gathering the sheaves, Beowulf marked that Frithugeard was holding back, and he dropped back to join her.

"Did I speak wrongly?" He murmured.

Frithugeard shook her head. "Not wrongly, but the folk here, I think, are all used to Ecgtheow's blessing, and to the Last Sheaf being given to Woden and his wild host."

Beowulf thought of the night rider who had spoken to him among the Swerting barrows, and a trickle of sweat ran chill down his spine.

"I know whom I would more gladly bid to ride over my lands. Though," he added quickly, "I would not have the God of the Slain as my foe: have I wronged him thus? And if I have, is there aught I can do to make amends?"

Frithugeard looked past him, her brown eyes hooded as she stared at the Last Sheaf upon its pole. "I do not think that Woden is wroth with you," she said, the words wafting slowly from her throat like notes breathing through a deep reed pipe. "It is seldom said that one god begrudges the gifts given to another, and you never swore to keep your troth with our elder kin in just the same way as your father did. So long as the Father of Battles gets his due share at the Winter nights offering, I think you need not fear angering him."

Beowulf caught his breath in relief, but Frithugeard went on, "Still, it seems to me that there is something I know not what. But it were well if we spoke together before Winter nights, so that none may feel that the ways at Hroesnabeorh have changed too greatly since you took your father's high seat. Most of all, we must be sure to put out offerings for Woden's host then, otherwise there are many folk here who will go in fear of the night storms all winter: for that Ecgtheow was a berserk, and filled himself with the god's wod, it was always his way to make a special gift for the wild riders, that the ghosts might bring fruitfulness to his land."

"And will I be allowed to make this blessing?" Asked Beowulf. He could not dull the edge of bitterness cutting into his throat, but when he saw the pain sheening Frithugeard's dark eyes, he wished he had not spoken.

"I do not know how matters will stand...I do not know. The harvest was so good this year that no one can say you have brought ill luck, and you did the work of nine men in bringing it in. Yet there are those who will look ill upon the best..."

"Who will say that the harvest was good because I did not take part in the Midsummer's offering, and who think no better of my strength in the fields than in battle."

"Yes, that is so."

"Still," Beowulf said angrily, "I shall not be driven from my own garth a second time. I shall make the blessing at Winter nights before my folk; and as for those that take it ill they are not thralls, and no collar or chain holds them to this garth."

Frithugeard's heart shaped face was very calm as she listened to him, as though she would veil her thoughts until she had chosen what to say. At last she nodded.

"It is well that you would act, for you have the right there: we cannot go on as we have been. You know that Sweartwulf and I will stand up for you, whatever betide, and there are also a good share of thanes who have marked your open handedness and the fair weather we have had since you took Ecgtheow's seat."

Those words eased Beowulf's heart, but he could not help marking how quiet the feast that night was. Though Frithugeard went about with her blessing bowl to spill out the first brown ale by hearth and high seat, and poured many frothing streams into the horns and mugs of Beowulf's men, there was little of the singing and merriment that had always rung through Hrethel's hall when the reaping was done. At the Swertings' burg, the reaper who had cut the Last Sheaf would be hung with garlands, the women all vying to fill his horn, and toasts raised to him half mocking, half honoring all night; and when the tables were carried away, the folk would dance in a ring about him.

Instead, no one save his friends spoke to Beowulf, and the hall seemed hushed, as though the folk within were awaiting a knock on the door and a bearer of dark tidings or worse: Beowulf could not help wondering if it had been thus in Heorot after Grendel first came, such an anxious waiting to see if the troll would tread over the threshold again. But it was I who cut the Last Sheaf, he thought. What have they to fear? When Sweartwulf rose to toast Beowulf for the harvest luck he had brought them, there were only a few quiet cheers. The firelight shadowed the half Finn's blunt face, so that he might have been staring into the ghost world in the way of his folk, and Ecgtheow's high seat seemed strangely unreal beneath Beowulf. I sit in the drighten's stead, but I might as well not be here at all, save for Sweartwulf and Frithugeard, thought Beowulf dolefully.

Does my father grudge me his place, that matters are yet so uneasy for me here? And when at last Beowulf went to sleep that night. his dreams were uneasy, and he awoke shivering with a cold that his wool blanket could not ease. The coals of his fire had died down, and the air was bitterly chill; his naked skin ridging up into goosebumps, Beowulf rummaged about until he had found his bearskin cloak by touch and pulled it over himself. Warming up at last, he tried to remember what he had dreamed, but could not save that he seemed to be reaching for a seat that he could not touch, and the hall was dark and empty about him, leaving him deep in sorrowful loneliness. After the reaping came a number of tasks: some folk threshed the grain, while others went out to gather in the flocks of cattle and sheep, or herd the swine where the acorns and beechnuts fell thickest.

Still others pounded the flax to break it into fibers for spinning, while the children and some of the women went out to gather crab apples and plums, wild pears and hazelnuts. The first storms were already rolling in, heavy raindrops beating cold over the shorn fields, so that those who had to go outside pulled cloak folds or hoods tight over their heads and wrapped their feet and calves in many layers of wool.

Beowulf himself was more often outside than in, for it was his part to look over the beasts and decide which should be slaughtered and which tended through the winter not an easy choice: there was enough hay this year to feed more animals than in years past, but he had the larders to think of as well, for he had seen how easily his folk grew discontented when there was no meat to be served in his hall. Yet whenever he stepped outside the garth, he felt a nervous prickle run along his spine, as though someone watched him through the drifting gray veils of rain.

Still, Beowulf did not let that stay him: he clambered through the hills calling the cattle and listening for the mournful clank of their bells, and searched muddy footed through the mists for the sheep. Once or twice it almost seemed to him that he had heard someone speak his name: his head jerked up and he looked about himself, but he could see nothing save rain and dark pines and ruddy gray boulders. The feeling of being watched grew stronger as the first day of the Winter nights slaughtering drew nearer. Though all was as it should be the cattle grazing on the stubble in the fields, the sheep driven down from the hills, the wood for the great fires of scalding and smoking and rendering stacked beneath heavy woolen covers to dry Beowulf could not shake off the sense that something ill was hovering about like a crow flapping just out of arrow shot.

Everyone arose early on the day of the Winter nights feast, for there was much to be done. The night before, a strong two year old bull had been tethered on the green before the hill he had served his share of cows, but shown a fierce mood, trying to gore the thralls who herded him from field to field, and Beowulf thought that it were best to slaughter him before he became more dangerous. Though the bull grazed quietly now, water running in rivulets down the sleek curves of his gray hide, the rain lent a wicked sheen to his black horns even in the dull storm light, and Beowulf mistrusted the black brightness of his eyes.

It had been battle enough to get him to the offering stead without letting him harm any of the men leading him there: a tamer beast might have been garlanded with grain and berries, but the women did not dare come close enough to slip a wreath over his horns. Great kettles of water were already beginning to steam slowly over the fires, the raindrops pattering down into them and hissing in the flames.

Sweartwulf waited by the bull's side, sledgehammer and long sax in his hand though even he, Beowulf marked, stood a respectful length from the fierce beast. By his feet was a huge wooden bowl, hollowed from a length of a broad tree trunk, and carved with a ring of images...a dancing couple, a stave bearing woman, a robed man with an apple in his hand, and another cloaked in a wolf skin. A gray hood, already darkened by the rain, covered Sweartwulf's gold brown hair, but he grinned at Beowulf.

"Frithugeard will be here soon. She has gone to get Hraefn and call the folk together."

For the Winter nights feast, Hroesnabeorh's gudhija wore her white kerchief, but her overdress was moss red and her cloak the blackish brown of a sheep out in the sun all summer. She carried her son comfortably upon her hip, and held a long leek in her free hand, its spray of green sword leaves dripping rainwater.

"Make your blessing as best you know how, Beowulf," Frithugeard murmured as she came close. "But do not forget to ask the blessings of Woden's host! It seems to me that this weather may betide their eagerness to ride about, and it would not be well to have them come unbidden to this stead."

Beowulf looked up at the sky. The heavy clouds drifted low and ragged above, darker wisps of mist moving more swiftly before them. A gust of wind cast raindrops into his face, stinging his eyes until he blinked his sight clear again. I would as soon not have them here at all, bidden or unbidden, he thought. His folk were slowly gathering about, hooded and cloaked against the rain. One or two glanced upward; more turned their gazes nervously away when Beowulf met their eyes. It seemed to Beowulf that he could feel the same hushed dread that he had felt in the hall the night the reaping was done, and the unnerving sense of being watched was growing stronger, tingling at the back of his neck.

"Sweartwulf, Osric, Adhalberht, and you, Hondscioh. You four shall hold the bull's ropes for me." Sweartwulf's eyebrows rose as Beowulf spoke Hondscioh's name, and Beowulf could almost hear him thinking, Why did you not choose a man in whom you could put more trust?

Because Hondscioh is too proud to let himself fail at a strong man's task, Beowulf answered silently and if I treat him as a foe, I shall never win his troth. The four men Beowulf had named came forward, Sweartwulf giving Beowulf the hammer and sax.

"Kin in the Ases' Garth and Wan Home, kin in Alf Home and in the holy howes, and mighty wights of the land about us; we bid you here to our feast at the year's winter turning," Beowulf said, raising his voice to carry over the rain to the folk who were tending the crackling fires. "Gods and goddesses, alfs and idises and wights all givers of fruitfulness, givers of blessing, givers of victory, who ward us against all ill we hail you here, who have been friends to men since the eldest days. With glad hearts we give you this bull: may the gods take the offering." He nodded to the four ox holders, and they took their places, grasping the ropes and bracing themselves hard.

Lifting the hammer aloft, Beowulf called out, "Thunar hallow!" As he swung it above the bull's head.

He was already bringing the hammer down when the bull lurched suddenly to the side, the heavy iron head only catching a glancing blow to his nose. The bull bellowed in fury, and had Sweartwulf not thrown his body desperately against the rope he held, the horn that ripped the sleeve of Beowulf's tunic open would have sunk deep into his side. Maddened by pain and anger, the gray bull turned, flinging Sweartwulf and Hondscioh to the ground. The rope had flown from Osric's hands, and it was at him that the bull charged now, twisting his lowered head viciously to the side.

The thane cried out as the horn plunged into his body, lifting him from the ground but stopping to gore Osric had slowed the beast's rush for a moment, just long enough for Beowulf to fling himself at the bull and bring the hammer down with all his strength behind the horned head. A single sharp crack, and the gray bull dropped to the ground, jagged white splinters of bone glimmering around the shattered edge of his skull. Osric rolled free, an arm flopping loose to the ground and blood flowing sluggishly from the great gaping wound beneath his ribs. A little more bright blood dribbled over the thane's slack lips; he twitched convulsively once, and did not move again. Shaken, Beowulf lifted Osric's body, trying not to look at the shifting of the shiny dark and pale masses in his wound. Sweartwulf was at his side at once, taking the limp burden from his arms.

"Go on," he whispered. "Finish it."

Frithugeard walked towards him, straining to carry the huge blessing bowl. Her tread was steady, but all the blood had drained from her face, and Beowulf marked distantly that she had given Hraefn into another woman's arms. Kneeling beside the fallen bull, Beowulf drew his sax, cutting quickly down from jawbone to breastbone, then thrusting it down to slice the large blood vessels. The bull's great heart was still beating faintly, pumping out waves of blood to fill Frithugeard's wooden cauldron. The gudhija stirred hard with her leek to keep the blood from clotting at once, until the flow had slowed to a dark red trickle.

"Frea Ing's blessing be upon you," Frithugeard said, wide eyes almost black against her white face and her voice trembling.

With a shaking hand, she lifted the bloody leek, spattering a few red drops over Beowulf. "May the gods always give you such luck as you have had this day: it can be seen now that your life is dear to them." She went to bless the men who had held the ropes next. For a time she stopped to speak softly over Osric's body, though Beowulf could not hear what she was saying; then she went on to fling droplets of blood over the gathered folk, weaving through the throng, out and back to dip her leek into the great blessing bowl again and again.

Beowulf found that his own hands were shaking, that he could feel the might rushing through him, bearing him up like the strongest ocean current. Thus the giver of offerings became himself the offering; thus the gods had turned the blessing beyond what men's hands would wreak. Frea Ing, Beowulf thought, did you choose to spare me for some reason? Do you mean to take me later? Or was it only that my Wyrd was not written that I should die thus?

Beowulf was still standing there, looking down at the bloody horned body of the beast that had slain his thane and nearly taken his own life, when Frithugeard came back to him. She had to tap his shoulder, as if to rouse him from sleep, so that he would lift up the heavy bowl of blood and follow her up the hill. Some of his folk trailed behind, though others were already breaking away to get to their slaughtering work. Frithugeard and Beowulf stopped before the open doors of the hall, and she nodded slightly to him.

"Hail to you alfs and idises, and kindly wights who dwell here," Beowulf said, his tongue thick as though he had drunk too much mead. "Be welcome, and bidden within, while you come to bring weal and drive out woe. Hail to Thunar and Hamdeall, warder of the holy steads and watcher at the Ase Garth's gates: welcome here aye. By Hammer and Horn, may you bless this door that no ill may pass within. Hail to Woden and his wind riding host. I bid you here in friendship, bringing blessing to land and hall, doing harm to none."

Frithugeard's lips curved slightly, and a little colour pinked her rounded cheeks again, as if in relief. She sprinkled the door posts and the frame above, and they passed into the hall, weaving about the fires burning on the freshly swept and strewn floor to the high seat.

"Hail to you, Frea Ing and Frowe," Beowulf went on more steadily. "Bless you my rule here with frith and joy, fair weather and good harvests. Boar riders, lord of Alfhame and Lady of Folcwong, bairns of wealthy Nerthus I hail you and bid you here." Frithugeard sprinkled the high seat and the two pillars beside it, and they moved about the hall, flinging a fine spray of blood over the walls, roof, and floors, and flicking a few drops to hiss into each of the fires.

When their round of the hall was done, they went out again, halting once more by the large flat stone standing to the right of the door posts. Frithugeard reddened the stone and gestured that Beowulf should put the bowl there upon it.

"So let our holy offering stand this night, greeting to gods and ghosts," Frithugeard said.

She clasped Beowulf's fingers in her own small hands, her skin chill and sticky with cooling blood. It seemed to him for a moment that he could see the flame shining over the wooden blessing bowl as if it were a huge tallow lamp, lighting the way through the Otherworld to whatever wights should wish to follow its beacon fire. The blessing bull was already split open, its liver, heart, kidneys, and lights in wooden pails and its bowels carefully tied off and spilled out upon the clean wet grass. He had eaten well that summer: his fat filled several buckets, which the thralls were hauling away to cut up for rendering. Four men were at work on the harder task of skinning the bull. Beowulf watched for a moment, but there was no place for him to step in to help.

"Cut off the head, and take it up to the hall beside the blessing bowl," Frithugeard whispered to him.

Beowulf took a small axe from one of the butchers. He needed only three strokes to slice the bull's head cleanly free beneath the wound his hammer had made in the skull. The rain had washed away the blood around the gaping hole in the bone, but the bull's dark eyes bulged almost out of its head as though the strength of Beowulf's blow had driven them from their sockets. Carefully Beowulf propped the bull's head up on the stone by the door posts. The black horn that had pierced Osric was clean of blood as well, dripping gray rainwater, but he could not bring himself to touch it.

He would pay the weregeld to Osric's wife Ælfhild that night, as if he himself had slain the man for Beowulf could not help feeling as though his warrior had died in his stead, though the bull had already turned when he gored the doomed man. And I hardly knew him well enough to grieve for him, though he was one of mine, Beowulf thought sadly. This, at least, shall not happen again. Beowulf went among the groups of slaughterers, helping where he could stunning cattle and swine with his hammer, grasping a large ram firmly by his horns, lifting the heavy cauldrons of simmering water to pour a slow stream over the hides of pigs so that their scalded bristles could be scraped from them, or carrying the heavy gutted bodies into storehouses where they could be hung or cut up and plunged into tubs of thick salt brine.

The rain fell hard and steadily all day, but no one spoke ill of it: it washed loose hairs and dirt from the meat, and there were hardly any flies to gather to the blood. Still, Osric's death had put the folk of Hroesnabeorh into an unhappy mood, so that there was no singing and little speech as they worked; and the feeling of an unseen watcher staring at him with grim eyes grew stronger and stronger in Beowulf's mind throughout the day. At last the gray sky began to darken swiftly.

The butchers gathered their knives and axes and saws, heaving the last carcases and skins into the storehouses, and went to their houses where they could scrub hands and faces before changing into their feast clothing. When Beowulf opened the door to his own house, he found that the fire had gone out again, and there was a dank chill in the air. Grumbling, he unbuckled his belt and slid the leather loop that held his oval fire lighting stone free, then crouched down to stab sparks from it into the tinder from his pouch. Beowulf did not hear any sound: it was a change in the air that warned him that he was no longer alone, as though the cold had drawn suddenly in. He let the smoldering tinder drop to the hearth stone, moving his hand beneath his cloak to the Saame knife at his belt.

"Who are you?" He asked softly, lifting his head and looking about himself very slowly, as though not to startle a wild beast. He could see no other shape in the darkened hut, and no answer came to him.

"Who are you?" Beowulf asked again. "Why are you here?"

Still there was no answer; and abruptly he felt that he was alone again. Quickly he scooped up the tinder, then dropped it again with a slight grunt of pain as the coal burned his hand. He added dry bark shavings one by one, blowing upon them until a little flame curled up. When his fire was burning well, Beowulf rose and began to search his house he was not sure for what; some sign, perhaps, that might show what manner of wight it was who followed him.

There was nothing amiss or out of place not so much as a clump of earth or a smear of black ash and yet he knew that there had been another in the house with him. He dressed swiftly and uneasily, putting on his best finery the deep blue over tunic with red and gold embroidery and the red woolen trousers that the women of Hrethel's household had made for him, clasped at the throat with a gold eagle brooch; his glowing amber pendant about his neck and gold rings upon his arms; a headband woven of silk and gold threads to hold back the long damp waves of his hair; and over it all, his bearskin cloak.

Beowulf had gotten a new chest for the remnants of his father's hoard; now he weighed out gold and silver rings carefully in his hands to set Osric's were geld. The fires blazed along the floor in Beowulf's hall, iron cauldrons bubbling over the flames and pieces of meat sizzling on their spits, and the air was rich with the smells of fresh meat and bread and malty ale. Beowulf's mouth began to water at once, and he could tell that the scents of feasting had put his folk into a brighter mood; the long room buzzed with speech, and now and again he heard the sound of laughter.

The taste of fresh pork was sweet as honey cakes in his mouth, the liver and blood sausage rich as any butter pastries. Beowulf ate hugely, filling his belly for what seemed like the first time in months. He had to remind himself sternly to stop lest he be sick from the sudden gorging on meat that always happened to a few men at Winter nights, but it would be shameful for a drighten. The eating went on until late, and there was little left when the thralls carried the tables away at last. Beowulf was pleasantly warmed by the strong ale, and felt more at ease than he had yet done in Hroesnabeorh yet there was one sorrowful duty left for him that night. Rising to his feet, Beowulf shouted for quiet. Slowly the hall stilled, the thanes and their wives staring up at their drighten.

"Is Ælfhild here?" He called, looking through the shadows. Beowulf could not bring her face at once to mind, but he thought he remembered a short slim woman with a green feast headdress. "I would give her a full geld for the death of her man, for that he fell beside me in making holy offering, and was slain by my own bull."

No one answered for a few moments. Then a woman's voice said timidly, "She keeps watch alone in her own house, by her husband's body. She shall not come here tonight."

"Then I shall go to her, for it is not well that she be alone in her sorrow," Beowulf answered.

The strong wind whipped the flame of Beowulf's torch out before him; the rain hissed loudly in its fire, but was not strong enough to quench the flare of the sap rich pinewood. Icy gusts tossed his cloak from side to side, blowing so hard that a smaller man might have been hard pressed to keep his footing beneath their battering attack, and the frozen raindrops numbed his nose and cheeks. The storm's rushing roared in Beowulf's ears, and he shuddered from more than cold. He had bidden Woden's host to ride to his hall and he did not doubt that they had heard. Beowulf made his way through the settlement to Osric's house. He could see a gleam of light through the smoke hole: Ælfhild was most likely inside, although he wondered why no one had stayed with her but that, he thought, was not too strange for Hroesnabeorh, where the folk were less bound by ties of kin and friendship than at other halls. He knocked on the door. No answer came.

"Ælfhild?" Beowulf called. "Ælfhild, are you within? It is I, your drighten I would speak with you."

Still there was no answer. Beowulf stood there, not sure whether to knock again or to leave her be: if she did not wish to see another in her mourning, what right had he to trouble her?

Then the door cracked open, and Beowulf caught the gleam of a light eye looking up at him. Glancing in above Ælfhild's head, he saw Osric laid out on the bed as if he were arrayed for a battle with athelings, with helm and sword and a big silver arm ring glistening over the sleeve of his byrnie.

"What do you want?" The woman asked, her voice tight as though her throat were swollen with tears.

"I have come to tell you that I mourn Osric's death, for he was a brave man and a strong warrior. And I would give you the geld for his slaying, since it was my offering bull that felled him. Will you let me in?"

Ælfhild looked back towards her husband's body, then at Beowulf again, her mouth drawn tight in the shadow of her hood.

"I shall not let you in, for I fear the wrath of the alfs and Woden: enough ill has come upon me at this blessing. But if you wish to make a gift to your thane for his faring, then that is well enough." She reached out her hand like a farmer's wife who had just traded a basket of eggs for a copper ring.

Beowulf set the heavy pouch into her palm. Ælfhild's light eyes widened as she felt the weight of it, but she said nothing, only closed the door. Bewildered, Beowulf turned back towards his hall. He had hardly awaited joyous greetings from a woman whose husband had met his death doing Beowulf's bidding, but it seemed scant thanks for him to be thus turned away from her door when he had come with weighty geld rings. Still, Ælfhild was sorrowing greatly, and Beowulf had seen for himself how such mourning could turn the mind.

Beowulf's bearskin cloak kept him dry and warm enough, but the icy mud and pools of frost edged rainwater had soaked through his shoes and leggings by the time he came back into the hall, and its fire lit warmth caressed his frozen face with welcome. Head still spinning and eyes dazed by the darkness and torchlight outside, he had almost reached his high seat before he saw the dark shape sitting in it. For a moment Beowulf could only stand and stare for it seemed to him that he was looking upon his father as he had last seen him, the deep gash in Ecgtheow's throat crusted with blood and his mouth still fixed in the berserk's snarl. But Ecgtheow's blue eyes burned with the lightless pale flame of howe fire flaring about stones of fathomless blackness, and he leaned forward as his dead gaze fixed upon his son.

"Father," Beowulf whispered. "Why have you come back this night? Did I not see you fittingly burned and buried; have I not made the Winter nights offerings as I ought, even to the God of the Hanged and his troop?"

Ecgtheow's snarling mouth did not move, but Beowulf heard his father's deep voice echoing from it, as though the old berserk were speaking from the bottom of a stone lined well.

"Here shall never heir sit
holding land and gold right
till battle oak has bettered
bale across the whale road.
Geld that never gold pays,
gift of bane spear lifted,
bairn of Grim's storm's bear, be
bound to pay for mound yew,
bound to this by mound yew!"

Then Ecgtheow was gone, but it seemed to Beowulf that his shadow still lay over the bear carved high seat, as though his father had left his dark fell behind. He raised his hand to touch the seat, but his arm fell cold to his side and he yawned, suddenly overcome with a great sleepiness. No one seemed to see him as he hastened back through the hall, seizing another torch to light his way back to his own house, and stumbled to his bed. It seemed to Beowulf that he stood in a hall between two fires. Shadows hid its high arched gables, but bright woven hangings adorned the walls, though the figures moved and twined as he looked at them: the only steady shape was a white clad rider upon a golden horse with ruddy hooves. The floor was strewn with green birch twigs and the pale blossoms of meadowsweet, tapestry mottled with the darker leaves and tendrils of seaweed.

The flames on Beowulf's right flared up from a tangled heap of gold rings and chains, but those on his left burned from a glimmering pile of amber.

"You can have me, if you will win me," said a woman's voice to his left. He looked over the amber fire to see Heofonglowe standing there, but she was clad as she had never been in her father's underwater hall, wearing a gown of deep blue as if she were in mourning.

"You can have me, if you will win me," a higher voice echoed to his right.

At first Beowulf thought the woman who gazed at him over the gold fed flames was Hygd, and a soft cry burst from him as he looked into her violet eyes, seeing her fair hair tumbling loose over her white clad shoulders and the mass of amber necklaces glowing about her neck but then her eyes shimmered to green flecked gray, her hair shining ruddy, and he saw that he was looking at Yrse, clad not in white linen, but in a byrnie like a warrior's, with her many layered gold collar upon her breast.

"What must I do?" Beowulf asked, though he did not know to which of them he was speaking.

"Give me another to mourn, and end my weeping when you come to me," said Heofonglowe.

"Strike down my brother's foe, and end the weeping within the hall of his kin," said Yrse's rough voice but no, she was not Yrse, but indeed Hygd, fair as Beowulf saw her in his thoughts whenever he could not keep his mind from turning to her.

Then the two women spoke together: "Choose between us now, that she whom you will have shall ride above you to ward your battles or wait if you will; but the day will come when you must make your choice.

Beowulf glanced back and forth between the two maids, shining and dark clad. He could not speak or move: it seemed to him that fetters bound his body like ice locking a stream. But already the lights were fading, the shapes of the two women dimming...He awoke thrashing against the blankets that wound his limbs. Someone was knocking on the door, and Frithugeard was calling,

"Beowulf? Beowulf, are you within?"

Beowulf arose with a deep shuddering breath and went to open the door. Though the rain still fell, the clouded sky was bright enough for him to see that dawn was well past. He had slept long but that was of little matter. Frithugeard's white headdress was askew, the pins at the shoulders of her moss red overdress crooked, and her face was crumpled in distress.

"What is amiss?" he asked.

"Ælfhild Beowulf, she hanged herself at dawn. I went to see what could be done for Osric, and found the door of their house open, and Ælfhild hanging from the roof tree, her body still warm. I would not have let her sit the night alone, if only I could have guessed..."

Beowulf patted her on the shoulder, but he could feel his own face twisting with the pang shooting through him. He must have been the last to see Ælfhild alive how long had she thought about faring with her husband? Had she not let Beowulf in because the rope was already dangling from the beam; had she sat there all night staring at the body of her man and the hempen twist above, before she raised the strength to put her head through the noose? Yet even that was better than his other nagging fear for Ælfhild had said that she feared the wrath of Woden and the alfs. The dead had walked that first night of winter: had they taken their own offering, even as the gods had that day? That Beowulf did not believe, for even Ecgtheow had not seemed to come to him in anger, but only to tell him, what?

"Are there any of her kin here, or does anyone know where we may send word to them?"

"Neither Osric nor Ælfhild ever spoke of their kin," said Frithugeard, gathering herself. "It is so with many of the folk of this burg, as you know they are likeliest to have left something behind that they wanted unknown."

"Then, if you will, call the thralls to work and see to it that the two of them are burnt with their goods. I think that Ælfhild meant that they should not go as beggars on their last faring, and the geld I gave for her husband is yet hers to keep."

"That is well done," Frithugeard answered.

Beowulf hastily put on clothes that were better fitted to the slaughtering and went to help his folk as he had done the day before. But the work could not ease his heavy heart at the thought of Ælfhild's death, nor draw his mind from the stave Ecgtheow had spoken to him the words that had made it clear that Beowulf would not sit in his father's high seat until he had fulfilled the ghost's bidding. He turned the lines over in his mind: bale across the whale road…Geld that never gold pays, gift of bane spear lifted… Then, suddenly, Ecgtheow's meaning burst upon him like a wild boar crashing from the rustling undergrowth.

Beowulf's father had said often enough that he owed his life to Hrothgar for the shelter the Dane king had given him; who but his son was left to pay that geld? This thought twined in sharply with the other, harsh as a rough edged iron fetter chafing against a gold ring…Beowulf had failed so far in his rule of Hroesnabeorh: Ælfhild's death seemed to him the last proof of it. He knew that he could not bring himself to sit in the high seat there again until he had done something that would change matters between himself and his folk, something that would show him worthy of trust as Ecgtheow's son in their eyes. Sweartwulf was bent over the carcass of a sheep, skinning it with the practiced ease of a hunter. Beowulf crouched down beside him.

"My friend," he said, "I have something to ask of you, and you are the only man in this hall to whom I can give this trust."

"Ask it, and it is yours," Sweartwulf answered at once.

"I must go to Heorot, for I would seek out Grendel, as my father wished to do for many years in payment of his life geld."

"And you need men to come with you!" Sweartwulf said joyfully. "I will gladly follow you on that faring, for it is a bare back that has no brother to ward it."

Beowulf sighed. "I would wish to have no one with me more than you, but there is another task for which I need you. Because I must leave this hall for a time perhaps forever, if my wyrd is risted so and because I have no bride nor kinsman to keep it for me, I would put it into the hands of a man who is my friend, whom I can trust to hold troth with me, both while I am gone and if I come back. Will you hold my father's stead for me?"

A glum shadow dropped over the half Finn's face. "I would sooner go by your side to fight, for I think it will be a battle worthy of singing when you meet Grendel. Yet I see your need. And in truth, there is no other here to whom I would trust it, save Frithugeard; and the men of Hroesnabeorh need a rougher hand than hers to keep them in line. Yes, I will hold this stead for you, and be glad to give it back when you come home."

It was no more than two days later when Beowulf rode out of Hroesnabeorh's gates with fifteen men behind him. Hondscioh was among them, for Beowulf did not trust him to stay in the burg where he had already spread his mutterings and, though it might be foolish, he hoped that this faring would give him another chance to win the surly thane's trust. The others were chosen from among Hroesnabeorh's best fighters and those men who, Sweartwulf said, could be relied on to do their utmost for Beowulf if matters went ill.

Their riding was slowed by the mud on the roads, but Beowulf and his men found good welcome where ever they stopped for the night, with plenty of fresh meat and ale. As they neared the Swertings' burg, Beowulf felt his heart turning over with memories the hall's high roof peak white with snow, as he had seen it first; the market field where he had walked with Hygd; and the road that led down to Whales' Ness, down to the waves.

If Ran's daughter wishes to avenge herself on me, she will not find it hard, for the seas are growing rough now, Beowulf thought grimly. But he could not flee from the ocean all his life; and there was no way to reach Heorot, save over the water. As they came to the Hrethlings' eastern gate, Beowulf blew three blasts on his father's horn, though the gate was open Hygelac had no one to fear. By the time he and his men were riding in, Hygelac himself stood there to meet them, heedless of the rain soaking his long golden hair.

"Berki!" The Geat king cried in delight. "It is good to see you here again. How are matters with you?"

"Well enough," Beowulf answered. He paused a moment, wondering if he should wait to tell his thoughts to his friend until Hygelac had given him welcome. But he had nothing to gain from delaying. "Yet there is one thing that my father left undone, where I must now take his part. For years he longed to try his might against Grendel in Heorot, for the sake of Hrothgar's kindness to him; but he could not leave his march hall. Now the Swedes are bound to us in oaths of frith, and thus I would go in Ecgtheow's stead."

Hygelac's jaw dropped; under his beard and the first lines creasing his summer tanned face, Beowulf could see the astonished look of the boy he had first come to know.

"I would not have guessed you to seek out such deeds," Hygelac said slowly. "And yet it is true enough..." He shook his head. "I cannot say yes or no yet: we shall have more speech over this tonight. But come in, my kinsman, and be welcome here with all your thanes."

As at Hroesnabeorh, Hygelac's folk had finished their Winter nights slaughtering some days ago, but many of them were still busy at the tasks that remained, scraping skins and rendering the last of the fat and such work. Hygd walked among them in white linen and dark red wool, seeing to it that the work was done rightly Beowulf almost did not know her at first, for her bright hair was covered with a red hood; her babe Hildegeard was in her arms, swathed in white wool against the cold rain, and her belly was swelling already with a second child. But then she turned to look at him, her violet eyes huge and dark beneath the low clouds, and the air rushed from Beowulf's lungs as though she had struck him hard in the pit of his stomach. Not turning her gaze away for a heartbeat, Hygd left the big kettle she had been staring into and walked steadily over to him.

"Greetings and welcome, Berki," she said.

Beowulf stammered something, he did not know what, and let Hygd and Hygelac lead him up to the hall, where Hygd filled the gold bound aurochs horn and brought it to him. It was not ale within, but sweet strong mead, so that Berki had to drink slowly lest his head begin to spin from it. When Beowulf and all his men had drunk from the welcome horn, Hygd settled herself beside her husband and unwrapped the thick soft wool from her child's head. Beowulf could see a glitter of fine golden hair, and eyes that were darkening to Hygd's own violet. Though he had seen little enough of babies, he could tell that Hildegeard was small and fine featured.

"She will be as fair as her mother," Beowulf said thickly.

She could have been mine, should have been. Carefully he reached over to touch her with one fingertip, and a small hand closed about his finger, clinging tight to him. He could not help smiling at the babe, though it felt as though his chest were cracking like an ill made clay pot in the fire.

"Aye, and we have another on the way," Hygelac answered. "And all the signs show that this one is like to be a boy, so the Swertings' aeht tree is putting out strong branches yet."

"May it always be so!" Said Beowulf. He had almost forgotten that after Hygelac, he was the last of Hrethel's kinsmen but Hygelac's words had reminded him of it sharply, and Hroesnabeorh had taught Beowulf how little he wished to rule a greater land.

It was not until late that evening, when everyone had eaten and drunk their fill and most folk had long since left the hall to sleep, that Beowulf found himself telling Hygelac how matters stood at Hroesnabeorh. He spoke of how he had been asked not to make the Midsummer's offering, of the little trust he had won, and of the deaths of Osric and Ælfhild. Beowulf did not complain about Hondscioh, since he did not want to draw Hygelac into the matter; but the Geat king had already seen how leery the men of the Swertings' burg had looked at Beowulf since he came back from his long faring, and could guess easily enough what tales might be spoken of him.

The only things that Beowulf did not even hint at were those he had seen on the first Winter nights eve for those were matters too close to share with even Hygelac, and Beowulf remembered how greedy his friend had been for wonders before he became king. Hygelac would not understand either the sorrow or the fear of seeing Ecgtheow's ghost... nor would it be well to tell him that one of the dream women had taken Hygd's shape.

"I fear that I have not done well at Hroesnabeorh," Beowulf said.

"Perhaps better than Ecgtheow would have done in times of frith. Have there been any slayings within your hall?"

"None save Osric."

"When Ecgtheow was drighten there, if six months went by without a battle, he was sure to lose one or two of his men to their foes within the hall, and there were fights with knives at almost every feast. Eofor told me that living in Hroesnabeorh was like sharing his bed with a host of bears in their first summer hunger. You have done well enough in keeping that band of half outlaws from slaying each other; if they do not love you, at least they have enough awe of you to let you rein them in, and sometimes that is the best a ruler can manage. Yet...who have you left to hold the hall while you are gone?"

"Sweartwulf Half Finn, who is a doughty fighter, and the best wrestler within Hroesnabeorh."

"It has never been your way to speak well enough of yourself," Hygelac mused, his blue eyes staring seriously into Beowulf's. "You must learn better than that, if you are to go among strangers: the Danes are proud folk, and word strong, given much to talk of their own deeds. If you do not match them in speech, they will think little of you.

For my sake, as well as yours, you must be ready to tell of your might and that of your kin."

"I have never learned to boast, but I will do my best," Beowulf agreed though he could not have sworn that the thought of wrangling with words did not daunt him more than that of wrestling with Grendel.

"That is well. If you do not come back from Heorot, then, would you wish Hroesnabeorh to go to him, or is there another to whom you would give it?"

"I would see Sweartwulf hold it, for that he and his wife Frithugeard have ever been true friends to me and Frithugeard has been the gudhija there for some time, and done all the things that a hall frowe should do."

Then Beowulf understood what Hygelac had said.

Tentatively, as though testing early winter ice underfoot, he said, "So you will give me leave to go, without saying that I am forsworn in my oaths to you?"

"How could I do otherwise? I gave you Hroesnabeorh, for that it was your father's holding and I could think of no other man who could rule it, but that has been little joy to you. You can hardly yield your place as hall drighten to become a simple thane again, even in my own war band. Yet if you overcome Grendel, it will no longer be men fleeing outlawry who come to Hroesnabeorh, but the best of men who seek renown by your side; and those who remain of your father's band will know the great honor they have, that you are their drighten."

Hygelac rested his short bearded chin in his hand, staring at the bed of glowing coals where a few tiny flames still writhed up. Then he looked back up at Beowulf, and when he spoke, his high voice was almost that of the boy he had once been.

"Berki, my friend, I will not give you rede to go, for I love you too dearly to wish to hear of your death. I would rather ask you to stay here, if you truly would not go back to Hroesnabeorh, and dwell here in honor among those of your kin who yet live. I was a child when my sister Hildebere died; ill wyrd dropped Herebeald, sorrow felled my father, and Haethcyn was slain by sword how then may I bear losing you, last of my kinsmen and dearest to my soul?" Hygelac took Beowulf's hand in both of his. His fingers seeming small as those of a boy's in gripping a grown man.

"I hope that you shall not lose me in this," Beowulf said hoarsely. "But I have a geld to pay, as needful of deed as if Ecgtheow lay unavenged in the earth: should I hold back from it, I would be no sturdy branch of our clan tree, but a wound gaping in its trunk as a gateway to rot. I know, better than I can tell you, how my might may measure against that of eoten kin."

Hygelac's next words were almost too soft for Beowulf to make out.

"And if there were one single deed that would bring my own father joy even now that he lies in his howe I would not hold my hand back from it a moment, though I knew I would fall in the doing." Hygelac gave Beowulf's hand a last squeeze before he loosed his grasp: his eyes shone water bright, but he smiled bravely. "If any man now living can fell Grendel, I am sure that you are he. And I would never turn you back from what you truly will to do. I shall give you a good ship, with skilled steersmen and sailors, to bear you safely to Heorot, and you shall go with all the blessings we can send."

"I thank you," Beowulf said. His voice was rough with tears, and he found that he had to dash fire dazzled water from his eyes and swallow hard before he could go on. "Should I slay Grendel, I will see to it that none forget my beloved king and friend, who has trusted always in me when others thought ill."

Hygelac laughed. "I wish only that I could fare with you and stand beside you when you meet the night troll! That will be a sight to see like standing beside Sigifrith the Walsing when he went against the dragon. If only," he added more softly, "one of my brothers were still alive! Then nothing could stop me from going to Heorot."

"It is no little burden to be a ruler," Beowulf agreed. "But you have already done great deeds, that day when Ongentheow was slain at Ravenwood, and will doubtless do many more before your wyrd is full dread."

They talked a while longer, Hygelac telling Beowulf all that he knew and had heard about the Scyldings and the great folk of their hall before the Geat king rose and said,

"How long do you wish to stay here before you fare to Heorot? I can have your ship readied within a day, but it may be wise to wait for the weather to lighten."

"It may lighten, or it may grow worse," Beowulf said. "Unless a stronger storm blows up, I would leave as soon as I can not because I do not wish to while here with you, but Heorot has suffered long, and now that my hand is turned towards easing them, I would not wait longer." And I would not see my father's ghost before my eyes again, nor hear his troublesome staves in my skull.

"That is well said, and so it shall be. Come now, your old house is readied for you, and there is much to be done tomorrow if you would fare soon."

Beowulf could think of no more to say, but he put his arms carefully around his friend's shoulders, and the two of them hugged as though their embrace could speak all the words silent in their hearts.

VIII

Heavy clouds hung gray over the barrows of the Scyldings, but a gleam of sunlight broke through over the sea, lighting the rain that hissed into the waves like a shower of silver spears. Wealhtheow had left her house at dawn, as soon as the sky was light enough for safety. Though her feet were cold and wet and her woolen hood dripping water down her face, she stood with one palm upon the tall gray stone, staring out over the ocean. This is Hrethric's twelfth winter, she thought. One more year, and he will be a man. Then folk will look to him to prove himself, whether or not he be worthy to rule the Danes ah, dear gods, why does my son have more to face than the spears and swords of his foes, a challenge that no living man can meet? Wealhtheow knew that if Hrethric went against Grendel, he would be slain.

But if he did not dare to stand up against the troll, none of those men who had stayed with Hrothgar from old troth and because the Scylding's luck was proof against Grendel's claws would follow him however brave Hrethric might be in Woden's sharp edged weather, he would be known only as the one who had not dared to meet the Heorot troll. Nor could those under kings who had sworn their oaths to Hrothgar and paid his scot every year be trusted to rest quietly under Hrethric's hand, if the youth failed to undertake an atheling heir's duty to his father by lifting sword against Hrothgar's foe.

Is it not hard enough for a boy to become not only a man, but a king, without it being laid upon him that he must be a hero from the Walsung tales as well? If their aeht god had been Woden, Wealhtheow might have understood this orlog better, for Woden smithed his steel roughly, and did not scruple to break his swords that they might be forged to greater might but Frea Ing was not so harsh with men: he did not hack down the oak sapling that a stronger tree might grow from its stump. Wealhtheow thought of how kindly Wihbrand had dealt with her at God Home in Frea Ing's name, and a little warmth filled her eyes against the cold rain.

Do not give up hope, the gudhe had said, and she had tried to keep those words with her, wrapping them about her heart like a hard fulled mantle to dull the bite of swords even as it warmed. But Wealtheow no longer knew what to hope for: no one within Heorot, and no man in the world, had the name of such a hero as could meet Grendel in battle, and not all the offerings and runes of God Home could shift the troll. Yet her fore seeing had shadowed something that glinted just beyond her reach, like a glimmer of light on the sea's misty horizon: but there was nothing she could do about it. Except, what if Heorot stood no longer? Wealhtheow wondered suddenly. A woman could wield a firebrand as well as a man: a burning torch did not care whether the hand that held it was white and soft, or calloused and scarred from sword play.

She could not hope to burn Grendel within, but if she crept out at the first light of dawn, when the troll was stalking back to his lair, and set the roof shingles ablaze...A memory rose from the well of years in Wealhtheow's mind: Heorot as she had first seen it, the glow of coals shimmering all through the fresh straw on the floor, rising in a sea of flame to devour the high carved pillars and gilded antlers. If I dared to set foot outside early enough, there would be none who could say that it was not done by Grendel in careless play.

Then the gate between the Middle Garth and the worlds beyond would be closed, and our cursed night guest would find no home. And perhaps that was Heorot's wyrd from the beginning. That would be best, Wealhtheow told herself. She walked back to the hall, the wind whipping the wet hem of her dress about her cold legs. By the time she stepped over Heorot's threshold, the Scylding queen was shivering, but though she was grateful for the warmth of the long fires that the thralls were stoking into fresh flames, she could not bring herself to go too close to the burning trenches.

It seemed to her that she was looking upon Heorot again as she had when Hrothgar had first borne her in, marveling at the cunningly carved tales of Geofe and Scyld upon the beams, the wonder of gold laid over wood in the firelight and the rich deep glints of garnets. Hrothgar's high seat wrought with gilded sheaves, her own with the heads and twining horns of oxen... But there Grendel could never come, for the high seat held the strength of the Scyldings, proof against him in spite of all his hate and might. Its wood would not be proof against flames, though. If Heorot burned, so would Hrothgar's throne and what luck could he then pass on to his sons? I cannot do it, Wealhtheow thought in despair. What is filthied may be cleansed; what is broken may be made whole but what is burnt is gone forever from the world where it flamed. If it is Heorot's wyrd to burn someday, it shall not be my hand that sets it alight.

"You rose early, my wife," said Hrothgar as he walked towards her. "But everyone else has eaten their morning meal: where have you been so long?"

"I was going about the smokehouses and drying houses to see to the meat," Wealhtheow lied. "It spoils easily in such weather." She was not sure why she told Hrothgar that: guilt, perhaps, for what she had just been thinking.

Hrothgar took her hand. His skin felt chill and loose, the strength in his grip no more than a shadow, but Wealhtheow clasped his fingers lovingly.

"You are a good queen," Hrothgar said in approval. "Though the summer was good, the cold has come on so suddenly that I think it is likely to be a long winter."

"As the gods send it," Wealhtheow replied, but she could not help her shudder at the thought: the heavier and darker the clouds hung, the longer Grendel would be abroad by dawn and dusk and the long nights of winter were his time of greatest might and fierceness.

"Well, the slaughter work is done at last, so we shall have quiet and rest for a time. Now I had it in mind to order a keg of ale brought in, and tell Eanmund to attend us with his harp, that our folk might spend the day in merriment within the hall."

"That would be well, for they have surely earned it." Wealhtheow tried to sound cheerful at the thought, but it was not easy: where but Heorot must feasts be held by daylight?

Yet that was better than no feasting at all, which was the other choice when those who had worked hard at butchering and rending and salting must hasten to their houses as soon as sunset ended the day's tasks.

"Where are our children?"

"Hrethric and Hromund are outside with Æschere and a few of the other men, training at sword work. I have not seen Freawaru since early this morning but do not fear, the Sun was already well up, or I would not have let her wander alone," Hrothgar added hastily.

"Do not fear," Freawaru's high voice echoed behind her parents. "I was in the woods, but I did not go far, and Godric was with me. I was gathering mushrooms see?" She held up a woven birch bark basket, heaped high with the gilled orange trumpet mushrooms. "I would have liked to bring back some fly toadstools, for that their caps are so bright and red, but Godric told me I was never to touch them."

She smiled brightly up at her mother. There were a few twigs and brown leaf scraps in the tangle of long fair hair falling back over the maiden's shoulders Wealhtheow's hair had once been so bright, though it had darkened to honey brown as she grew older. Though Freawaru had dressed in plain gray wool to go out in the woods, the gold arm ring that Ingeld had sent as a token of their betrothal sparkled on her arm, its little filigreed knobs sparkling bright as coals in the light of the hall fires. The ring was really too large and heavy for a girl of ten winters, but Freawaru wore it always, as a sign of her pride that she was betrothed and very nearly a grown woman.

"Godric is a wise man, for there is a deadly bale in such toadstools, in spite of their bright red hoods," Wealhtheow told her daughter. Though her voice was as stern as she could make it, she could not help smiling down at Freawaru. "Yet you have done well, and those are fine mushrooms. If you take them to Guthrun now, she shall cook them into something nice for the afternoon meal. Then come back here and I shall comb your hair before putting you into a better dress, for you look like a little wood wife."

Freawaru reached behind herself, touching her back curiously, then rubbing at the base of her spine.

"I cannot be a wood wife, since my back is not hollow and I have no tail see?" She turned about so that her mother could look at her back. Wealhtheow gave her a light swat on the rump.

"Go on, now."

Freawaru grinned at Wealhtheow again, then hurried off. Hrothgar was laughing softly.

"Perhaps it is as well that Ingeld has not met his bride yet," he said. "Freawaru will surely keep his mind from growing too lazy: even her brothers cannot always keep up with her."

"She is a good girl, and will make a fine queen when she is older," Wealhtheow answered.

And if Ingeld lives to wed her, then at least one of my children shall be free of Heorot, whatever betides. Even while the men and women of Heorot sat at their daylight feast, their hands were not idle: the women spun and stitched, and many of the men whittled at spoons and bowls between draughts of ale. When they were not pouring out drink, Wealhtheow and Freawaru sat with the end of a large tapestry over their laps, carefully embroidering the figures.

The tapestry told the tale of Scyld Scefing but the queen and her daughter had begun their embroidery with his last ship faring, since gold thread could not always be gotten, and Wealhtheow had wanted to stitch in the heaps of treasure that the Danes had piled about their ruler before some other use for the thin strands of gold could be found.

So they had started with Scyld's death, and worked backwards through his wedding to Geofe who stood in her ox drawn cart with Scyld lifting a great ring up to her and his battle victories. Now they had reached the final panel, the arrival of the holy hero from the sea as a babe, lying on his shield boat with a pale sheaf of silken wheat beside him. Freawaru's delicate fingers stitched and pulled the thread as swiftly and neatly as her mother's, her silk slipping smoothly through the tapestry. After a little time she looked up at Wealhtheow.

"Mother," she said clearly, "will Scyld Scefing ever come back?"

"It is unknown of knowledge," Wealthow answered, her words coming slow from her mouth, "where Scyld went when he was set adrift from these shores. Men cannot say truly neither hall counselors nor heroes under the heavens who gathered him in at last. Nor is it often that those who fare from the Middle Garth come back to it, though some may be born again. And kin soul and luck are given to children when they are named and lifted up by their father, so in a way Scyld Scefing lives with us while the Scylding line lives."

Freawaru's brows drew in, a single straight line appearing between them. "Yet Eanmund says that the gods sent our aeht father when there was great need in the land. Why has he not come again to save us from Grendel?"

Pride and sorrow wrenched at each other like two strong arms entwined in Wealhtheow's heart. Neither Hrethric nor Hromund, now shouting happily as they wrestled with the half wolf puppies behind Hrothgar's high seat, had ever asked such questions. But though Freawaru already had the wisdom to ask, Wealhtheow did not yet have the wisdom to answer.

"I wish I knew," the Scylding queen said to her daughter. "If we knew the roots of this wyrd we thole, then we might better guess whether Scyld shall come again, or whether there will be an end to Grendel's night rule or whether, in time, we shall have to leave Heorot to him by day as well as by dark. But in three winters more, you shall be wedded to Ingeld, and then you shall dwell in a hall where there is nothing to fear by night, and sunset marks the beginning of feasting instead of its end."

Freawaru lifted her hand, brushing soft little fingers against her mother's cheek. "I know that, Mother. But that is a very long time from now and when I am gone, you and Father and Hrothulf and my brothers shall still be here."

"So we shall," Wealhtheow said heavily. Yet a shadow of foreboding still hung over her thoughts. If Hrothgar lost his eldest son to Grendel, she thought that he would lose the last of his life strength as well and Hrethric would be old enough to name as a man in a year. She knew she could not have sworn an oath that there would be any of the Scylding aeht still dwelling in Heorot by the time Freawaru and Ingeld fulfilled their betrothal pledge, and she bent her head low as she began to stitch the red rim of the shield edge curving above little Scyld's head so that her daughter could not see the look on her face. "And if you sew quickly and carefully, it may be that we shall make the last stitches on this tapestry before sunset, and see it hung up on the wall tomorrow."

"That will be fair to look on!" Freawaru answered, her voice bright again. "Maybe when it is done, Scyld will see it and come back to us, as I have been bidding him come with every stitch I take."

Wealhtheow's face twisted into a rueful smile. She did not think it likely but if Freawaru's tapestry work failed to bring the hero back over the waters, then at least the maiden would have done no worse than had Wealhtheow or Unferth or Hrothgar, or any of the others who had poured out their hearts and offerings to the gods for help. Grendel's mother sat sewing in their underwater hall, the little bone needle in her hand flashing white through the tight woven wool. The shapes forming out of the misty gray cloth beneath her stitching were those of two wrestlers: a red bearded man, mighty and fire eyed, being slowly forced to one knee by a withered old woman the god Thunar in the hall of Outgarth Loke, wrestling with the crone Old Age, the one foe he could not overcome.

The wool of the cloud haired eoten sheep shone sleek as silk, dyed with bright dwarf hues; though her slim fingers were tipped with talons, Grendel's mother stitched more swiftly than any earthly maid, making stitches smaller and finer than any daughter of Ash and Elm could sew, for she had been at such craft work before Wieland the Smith first forged iron for the men of the North. Grendel himself was carving writhing sea wyrms upon a panel of walrus ivory to match the others lying beside his chair: those he would have bound with gold to make a casket for Heofonglowe, and he would bring it to her with a heavy gold arm ring inside as token of his love for her.

"So another winter begins," Grendel's mother mused, setting down her needle and taking a sip of the mead in her berg crystal goblet. "Tell me, my son, are you any closer to your goal than you were last winter?"

"Hrothgar's son is another year closer to manhood," Grendel answered. "Next year the time will come when he must fight or yield to me."

His mother nodded, her blue eyes half closing as she looked into the flames mirrored in the still dark pool.

"Aye, Hrothgar's grip weakens day by day, and there is none with both strength and right to hold what he must let fall."

"And the sooner, the better!" Said Grendel fiercely. "I am tired of circling like a lone spekheawer waiting for a great whale to weaken enough to be torn. Hrothgar could never have beaten me in fight, even had you made no shirt to ward me but he sits and withers, doing good neither to me nor to his own folk. Once he was a worthy foe, and now he is no more than a stone in the pathway that can do naught but hinder, so that it shames me to struggle with him, yet it would be a greater shame if I gave up my vengeance now."

"And," Grendel's mother remarked, "you thought that winning your hall in a great battle would make you look well in Heofonglowe's eyes, but there is little to sing about in years of haunting a hall where none dare to fight you, but which you cannot take."

"That is so," admitted Grendel.

His mother smiled, the points of her teeth glinting beneath her fine marked lips. With a single claw tip, she touched the wizened black shape crushing Thunar down onto one knee.

"Few men see clearly the deeds of Old Age, yet she always fights for the eoten kind. Among the gods, Edunnan battles against her with the might of her golden apples, but there is none who can strive thus for the children of Ash and Elm."

"And so I am to wait for the black crone to finish Hrothgar off for me?"

"Why not, when you have already broken his heart?"

But Grendel knew, better than his mother, that Hrothgar was not wholly broken. He had seen his foe growing less steady on his feet when Hrothgar walked from hall to house in the graying twilight, marked the lines that bit into his face like rough chisel marks yet if Hrothgar's soul had wholly given way, then Grendel could have claimed his high seat. Why was the Scylding so stubborn, clinging to his hall even when he would no longer wage battle for it? If Grendel had won little but frustration from Heorot, Hrothgar had won nothing but a long dying and that saddened Grendel: it was no end that he would have wished on his foe, but there was no way to halt it save for Grendel to give way himself.

"I suppose there is little choice in the matter for me," Grendel admitted ungraciously. "Yet soon his eldest son will be of a man's age, and then I shall have the battle I have been waiting for, and end this shameful lingering."

His mother did not answer. She took the end of her long chestnut plait in her hands, fingers tracing the thick strands of gold glinting braid as though she were following the threads of a woven band through warp and weft. The tiny lines upon her fine boned face smoothed as her eyelids dropped, so that, in the firelight, Grendel might almost have been looking upon a fair maid of his own years.

"Grendel, my son," she said, her voice pouring slow from her throat like a stream of blood darkened honey.

"Do not wish so quickly for battle, for battle shall come to you. Though the Norns be born of Eoten Home, they deal even handed with the gods and the bairns of Yma and the children of Ash and Elm alike, and their runes are no kinder for their kin than for the thurses' foes. Even now I see a bear rising from the sea, and though he share in our aeht, he shakes the bane spear against you: it is often the way for blood to war against itself, for were not even the gods born of an eoten maid?"

A bear rising from the sea, Grendel felt his scaled lips pulling back into a mirthless grin: thus Heofonglowe had spoken of the man who betrayed her. Her sea bear.

"Let him come," Grendel said. "For I think that I have been waiting to meet him. But tell me, Mother is he born to be my bane, or is it I who shall rend him?"

Grendel's mother sat for what seemed to Grendel a long time, her fingers tracing the woven patterns of her braid. When she spoke again, her voice was very low, her words echoing like the far off beating of waves at the end of a sea cave.

"That is unknown of knowledge. The Norns have foretold only that two shall fight, and one shall win and he who slays the other shall have the right to Heorot's seat, if he will take it."

"Then that is gladness indeed!" Said Grendel, fierce joy bubbling up in his heart like steam bursting from an underwater crevasse. "Runes of my death would be an ill foreboding, but a sure victory is scarce worthy of song. When shall the sea bear come?"

His mother did not answer. After a while, she leaned back in her chair with a sigh, reaching for her rime goblet and drinking the dark mead off in one gulp. As the strong brew sank down her throat, the gray under cast faded from her skin and her blue eyes brightened a little.

"I can tell you no more," she said. "Still I warn you: be wary. For you have never yet met any in the Middle Garth who can match your strength; but I think that it will not be long before you come upon the one who is like to you."

"I await him eagerly," Grendel replied.

For he would have his chance to pay his rival back for Heofonglowe's sorrow; he would have a battle that would be fair geld for all the nights of sitting alone in Heorot, staring angrily at the high seat that he could not touch and, if he won, then his battle would be ended and his part of Yma's blood avenged on the Middle Garth. All or naught in a single fight: after the long sluggish war with Hrothgar, Grendel could have asked for nothing better. By sunrise of his second day with Hygelac, Beowulf's boat was moored to a large boulder that jutted up from the water beneath the cliffs of Whale's Ness, rocking gently in the swells. Though the sky was gray, rain drifting down across the white edged waves, the red sail rose bright above the ship, and gold glinted from the carvings that writhed along the ringed prow. On the beach, Beowulf turned to embrace Hygelac in farewell.

"My luck go with you," Hygelac said. He had to bend the arm ring he pulled off: the coils that went thrice around Hygelac's arm barely overlapped once upon Beowulf's. "I shall await your homecoming."

Hygd lifted the farewell horn to Beowulf's lips. "Hale go you, hale stay you, hale come home again," she breathed, her violet eyes deep with tears. Beowulf's throat choked so that he could scarcely swallow the burning mead, but he took as great a draught as he could.

"I shall not shame your trust in me," Beowulf said. "And I shall be glad of my homecoming here when my fight is over." He turned to his men, who stood holding their spears and shields, bright armor and helms cradled in wool wrapped bundles in their arms. "Come, the Sun is rising. We have a long wave road to fare over before we come to Heorot, but the wind is blowing towards Sealand."

First of all of them, Beowulf strode into the surf, the well known cold strength of the waves catching him about the knees. For a moment he felt a great longing to fling himself forward, to plunge swimming into the water and leave the doom his father had laid on him behind him but he was not yet ready to turn from the world of men forever. He waded out to the ship: it rocked hard as he heaved himself on board, but it was a well made and keenly balanced vessel. The others followed him with froth splashing about their legs, Hondscioh coming last of all: the gloved thane glanced back once or twice, as if he were wondering if there were some way to get out of this faring. Beowulf helped each of his men on board, lifting them lightly over the side.

"Shall we cast off now?" Asked the steersman, looking squint eyed up into Beowulf's face as the thanes moved to stow their war gear carefully under the hull where it would be safe from spray and splashing bilge.

"Aye."

The steersman gave a sharp whistle, and his crew settled down to their oars. Lithely balanced against the boat's rise and fall and sway, he leaned out to untie the rope that held them to the jutting sea rock. The hard oar blades dug into the water, turning the ship; then the wind caught the sail, lifting the stout bound wooden vessel forward, Beowulf stood by the prow, watching in wonder as its sharp edge clove a straight furrow of foam through the gray water.

For all his swimming, he had never sailed: he could feel the strength of swells and currents beneath his feet as surely as if he were stroking through the waves himself and yet he was skimming above that realm like a tern swooping swift through the spray, the wet wind blowing his cloak hard against his back and whipping hair and beard against his cheeks, stinging with the blowing salt foam.

Perhaps it was more like riding a horse at a hard gallop than flying or swimming, for the boat seemed to live and move to its own rhythm, rising and falling much like a horse's back; and, like an unskilled rider clinging to a steed's mane, whenever Beowulf would move, he had to brace himself lightly against the ship's wooden side to keep from being flung from his feet. And it seemed to him that he could feel the fragility of the planks beneath him, that the smooth planed wood was a very little thing to withstand the might that heaved and tossed it forward like a frail walled shell over the waves.

We are in the hands of Ran's daughters now, Beowulf thought. But even as he shuddered, his hand went to the smoothness of the amber pendant knotted tight about his throat. Behind him, Beowulf heard the racking coughs of someone retching hard. He looked back to see Adhalberht clinging hard to the boat's edge. The thane's long face was a sickly shade of sallow green beneath his ruddy beard; Beowulf made his way carefully back to him, but Adhalberht lifted a hand weakly to wave him away.

"This will pass in a little while," Adhalberht moaned. "It is always so when I get on a ship, Thunar help me!" He bent over the side again, and Beowulf left him alone, though the crewmen, leaning cheerfully back from their oars, were calling out helpful words.

"Go on, get it all up give the fish something to eat!" "Aye, we'll have fatty salt pork later; that'll settle your stomach for sure." "If you see something round and brown, bite hard and swallow, because that's your arsehole coming up!"

Beowulf looked sternly at the men who had spoken, meeting their gazes one by one.

"Leave him be," he ordered. "You would not speak so freely if you were on land, and he wearing byrnie and helm." The sailors flushed and turned their eyes away from him in turn: Beowulf did not know if they would think the worse of him for it, but he had suffered enough taunts to know the sting of carelessly flicked words. Beowulf turned back to the prow.

"A fair wind," the steersman Gudhere, that was his name said to Beowulf, balancing lightly on the balls of his feet. He was a small man, but square bodied, with a shock of fair hair tangled above a broad weather tanned face. "If it holds, we'll make Sealand's shores in a couple of days, see if we don't."

"And if not?"

Gudhere shrugged. "Who knows, then? I was cast off course once and near shipwrecked; had to put to land in Frisia, and we were three weeks patching broken staves the Frisians asked twice the cost of everything we needed too, since we were strangers and another two waiting for weather that was fit to sail in. There's no guessing Eagor's moods, and it's been a long time since I met a Finn who could sell me a knot string of winds."

Beowulf thought fleetingly of Sweartwulf, but no: his friend had said that he knew little of the naaeijte lore. Gudhere squinted up at the sky, sniffing the rain damp wind.

"Still, it looks as though this will keep up for a while, though the weather can be chancy this time of year. Don't bother yourself about it. Now, why don't you give your man a cup of ale to settle him before he casts up his bowels together with his breakfast?"

The ship skimmed bird swift over the waves, its red sail hoar flecked with foam. Freed from the burden of rowing, the crew raised their voices in rough song, and some of Beowulf's men joined in on the choruses. Those who had appetite ate at mid morning and mid evening; though the food was only salt pork and hard baked bread, Hygelac had sent good ale to wash it down with, and the cold sea air had raised a great hunger in Beowulf. Caught up in the plunging dance of the boat over the water, Beowulf could hardly think on where they were going or what lay before him.

It was enough to hear the sea mews crying about the mast, to see the dark heads of seals rising from the water to stare at the ship with curious brown eyes and the sleek gray backs of sea swine arching and leaping through the waves, sometimes coming up to the ship and raising their blunt pointed snouts into the air as they breathed out little puffs of spray from their blowholes, sometimes swimming in a line ahead of the prow as if to guide the vessel on to land: he would have been no less joyful had the faring had no known end.

They drove on through the night. Though no stars glimmered through the clouds, Gudhere swore that he knew the way to Sealand as well as any land drighten might know the road to his own hall. Dawn grayed cold and wet, and Beowulf and his men awoke stiff from sleeping on the oar benches, stretching their aching muscles as the older thanes cursed the dampness that had crept into their bones and the sailors laughed at them. It was well into the day before Gudhere pointed to the bank of clouds lying over the sea.

"There is land ahead, and by this set hour Thunar be my witness I believe it should be Sealand, and not too far from Hrothgar's hall at that, if our luck is with us."

Peering ahead as the curve prowed craft sailed nearer, Beowulf could see pale cliffs and sheer crags as the wide sea headlands took shape from the mists. Gudhere pointed to the shore where two barrows rose grassy with a tall pillar of gray stone between them, his cracked lips creasing in a smile.

"Did I not tell you? Those are the howes of the Scyldings: now the sound is crossed, and the faring ended."

The Geats drew in as close as they could, until the keel of their ship scraped the sand. Gudhere ordered his men to toss the anchor over.

"You can wade ashore easily from here," he said.

Beowulf picked up his war gear and heaved himself over the side. The water came no higher than halfway up his thighs, save when a swell rose to wet him to the waist. His thanes followed quickly to land, and he heard several of them murmuring their thanks to Thunar and Nerthus that the crossing had gone so well. As soon as the Geats stood on the wave smoothed sand, they unwrapped their armor, byrnies jingling as the men hastily tossed them over their heads and belted their swords on again, then buckled on their helms and took up their gleaming shields and spears.

"Halt!" A man's low voice called from above.

Beowulf looked upwards, to the top of one of the low cliffs that flanked the beach. An armed man on a black maned dun horse was riding down towards them, his stout spear upraised. Swithhelm, the most hot tempered of Beowulf's band, reached for his sword at once, but Beowulf stilled the red haired thane with a lift of his hand.

"If this is Hrothgar's man, he will soon know that we have come in frith," Beowulf said quietly. "Make no move that he could take ill! I shall speak to him."

The Dane stopped on the sandy path, just out of spear cast range. His helm was ridged with gold, a swan's wide beaked head coming down to the nose guard, and it glittered with squares of pressed silver. His square cheeks and strong chin were clean shaven; he could be little older than Beowulf, and was both short and thin, his byrnie hanging from his shoulders as if from a branch lopped pine trunk; but his gray eyes shone bright and stern through the helm's guard rings and he spoke with well measured words, such as were fit for an atheling to use in parleying with armed strangers.

"Who are you, having war gear and wearing byrnies, who have thus brought the high ship over the water road, hither over the sea? I have been set here a while to hold the sea watch, so that no loathed foe with ship hosts might do harm in the land of the Danes. No shield bearers have come here more openly: surely the war wagers have not given you words of leave, nor are you known to have kinsmen's bidding. Never have I seen a mightier man, an earl upon the earth, than that one of yours, a fighter in battle harness: the worth of his armor shows he is no one's underling, unless his unmatched looks lie. Now I shall know of your kin before you fare further from here as spies in the Dane lands: you sea farers, hear my single thought. Haste is best to the wise: from whence do you come?"

For a moment Beowulf's tongue froze. He could hardly keep from looking around himself for Sweartwulf or Frithugeard, for Hygelac or perhaps one of the missing Swertings, he did not know whom. Beowulf had learned to speak before his own folk in Hroesnabeorh, but he had never stood as a leader before strangers. *But I am the ablest here, and the leader of my war band,* he reminded himself strongly. Then his word hoard unlocked, and Beowulf was able to speak in answer, replying in the same measured way as the youth had used to address him.

"We are warriors of the Geat folk, and hyrd thanes of Hygelac. My father was known among your folk, an atheling leader who hight Ecgtheow. He passed many winters before he went on his way, old in years; he will surely be remembered among well learned and wise men upon the wide earth. We seek your lord, the son of Healfdene, warder of his tribe, with kind hearts: be our good guide!"

Beowulf drew a deep breath, pressing his palms against his thighs so hard to keep them from shaking that he could feel the iron rings of his byrnie biting into his skin. Now it was time to speak the words that he could not call back, his last chance to turn from the road he had chosen.

"We have a great and mighty errand to the Dane Frea: what I think should not be hidden! You know if it is as we have truly heard it to be said: that among the Scyldings, some foe I know not what shadowed, showing his hate by deeds, awes in the dark night by terror and unknown nith, shame and corpse fall. With wide hearted soul, I may bring rede to Hrothgar as to how he, wise and good, may overcome his foe, if matters shall ever turn back for him, help coming for the baleful harm and his care whelming be cooled, if ever afterwards he suffer and thole sore need, while the best of halls stands in its high stead."

There, Father! Thought Beowulf. I have heard that drows cannot cross running water; but in your howe across the swan road, do you hear my words? Do you know that I stand now to repay your old life geld? The Dane's mouth had dropped open slightly, but he shut it again hard, staring at the Geat. It seemed to Beowulf that there was something about the young man that reminded him of someone unsettlingly so: he could not think who it might be, but he would have sworn an oath that he had met the coast warder's kindred somewhere before.

"A sea watcher, wise warrior, shall know how to choose among words and works, if they are well thought on. I hear that this war band is friendly to the Scylding frea. Go forth, bearing weapons and battle weeds: I shall show the way, and tell my young thanes to guard your boat against all foes, and hold the fresh tarred ship on the sand with honor, until the ring prowed craft brings the beloved man to the Weders' march. The gods grant that he may come whole from the battle storm!"

The Geats marched on behind him, leaving their ship anchored at the beach. The coast warder led them along a sandy path worn through the long dry grass. Beowulf could not help glancing back at his men, for they made a fine show with their golden boar crests standing high above their helms' battle masks, the sign of Frea Ing's warding in fight. As they came to the palisade, the young Dane called out for the gates to be opened. Beowulf looked up at Heorot in awe: it was the finest dwelling he had ever seen on earth, long and high, its roof adorned with gilding that gleamed bright even through the misty rain as if to shed light on all the lands about it. Their guide turned his dun stallion about, his silvered bridle pieces flashing.

"Now I must leave you: may the all ruling god hold you sound and hale with favour staves! But I shall go back to the sea, to keep my watch against wrathful hosts."

And to make sure, Beowulf thought, that there are no more ships lurking behind us, in case my fair words were meant as a trap. He was not sure that he wholly liked this young atheling, but he could see the wisdom in his doings Haethcyn would have done the same, and might have questioned such a troop longer before bringing it to his father's hall. Beowulf and his men followed the path through the settlement, their byrnies shimmering and jingling as they walked. When they stood before Heorot's carven and gilded door posts, Beowulf let his shield slide from his arm, propping the painted linden round and his spear up against the door.

"We should not go thus armed into the hall of our friends," he said to his thanes. "Set down your shields and spears, all of you."

Not one of the warriors so much as grumbled: Hroesnabeorh's men knew as well as Beowulf did, or better, how they would take it if strangers strode into their hall with shields and weapons ready and should matters suddenly turn to ill, they still had good swords by their sides. The door opened, and an older man whose black beard and hair were streaked with gray came out to meet the Geats. He wore no byrnie, but the gilded hilt of his sword and silver eagle mounts adorning his belt, as well as the heavy set of his muscles, marked him as a warrior of good kin.

He looked the strangers up and down, dark eyes quickly weighing the worth of their war gear and guessing at their fighting measure.

"From whence do you fare, with adorned shields, gray battle sarks, mask helms, and heap of army shafts?" The Dane asked. "I am Wulfgar of the Wendels, Hrothgar's messenger and thane. Never have I seen strangers coming so boldly with many men." He peered up into Beowulf's face, as if the least flicker of an eyelash would tell him the Geat's thoughts; then he nodded in satisfaction. "I think that you are here for mighty deeds, rather than as wretched exiles, and have sought Hrothgar out of greatness of heart."

Having spoken once, it was easier for Beowulf to do it again.

"We are Hygelac's board friends: Beowulf is my name. I will tell my errand to the son of Healfdene, that wide famed ruler who is your lord, if that good man will grant that we may greet him."

Wulfgar answered, "I will tell the Scylding frea, friend of the Danes and breaker of rings, what you ask me to, and quickly make known to you the answer that good man gives me."

The Wendel closed the door, but it was not long before he came back to them.

"My sig drighten, the ruler of the East Danes, told me to say that he knows your atheling kin, and welcomes the hardy souled ones from over the sea swells. Now you may enter in your war weeds, under host masks, to see Hrothgar; but let the battle boards and slaying shafts rest here."

Heorot within was even finer than Heorot without, a blaze of fires leaping back bright from gold, the gilded stags' antlers at the gables gleaming like high tined flames. As well as the torches along the walls, the hall was lit by bowl lamps standing tall on twisted iron stems, their burning filling the air with the sweetness of beeswax. Every pillar and beam was carved and gilded, a maze of swirling figures and lines that almost dizzied Beowulf to look upon, and here and there he saw the deep red gleam of smooth garnets set into the gold burnished wood. Behind the high seats hung a long tapestry.

Its embroidered panels showed a child floating to the sea strand upon a shield with a sheaf of wheat beside him; the babe grown to a man, his sword bright in battle; the man wedded to a woman who stood tall in an ox drawn cart; and, at last, in old age, lying in a ship with gold sewn treasures heaped about him and a golden battle flag flying above his head. Beowulf drew a deep breath, trying to stay steady upon his feet.

It seemed to him if he were standing on a single planked bridge above a great maelstrom; he could see the hall's brightness burning like a torch in the darkness through the open gate between the worlds. It is little wonder that one of Yma's kin could walk openly here, Beowulf thought, dazed: this is too like a hall of God Home to be bound wholly to the Middle Garth. In the middle of all Heorot's light, the two high seats at the end of the fires shone more brightly than the rest, the gilded shapes of sheaves and oxen burning like sunlight off still waters. Beowulf walked steadily forward beneath Hrothgar's roof, halting when he stood by the hearth before the thrones.

"Hail to you, Hrothgar!" Beowulf said. "I am Hygelac's kinsman and thane." He would have stopped there, but he remembered what Hygelac had said to him about speaking well of himself before the Danes. "I have done many deeds in my youth. The matter of Grendel became known to me in my kin lands: seafarers said that this hall, finest of dwellings, stood empty and not enjoyed by any warriors as soon as evening light was hulled under heaven's brightness. Then my friends, blessed and wise carles, said that I should seek you out, folk ruler Hrothgar, for that they knew my main strength. I bound the eoten kin, and in the water slew nicors by night, hard pressed though I was: they wrought hate towards Weather Geats, and sought out woe..." Beowulf did not look back at the thanes behind him. Of course none of them had said such things, or had known before about his battle with the sea wights, and he guessed that they were hanging on his words as curiously as the listening Danes. But they would not gainsay him before the Dane king and he could hardly tell Hrothgar what had truly driven him to come to grips with Grendel. "Now I shall battle Grendel, one alone against the dreadful thurse."

Beowulf drew breath, and in that moment he looked clearly upon Hrothgar. The Dane king was a very old man, withered and white haired, with the sunken look of a strong man whose life was being slowly gnawed away by a rotting crab in his entrails. Only a faint gleam of hope lit Hrothgar's faded blue eyes as Beowulf spoke, and Beowulf could see the king's drinking horn shaking in his hand, as though the weight of the draught were too much for him to bear. A gray haired man with a long plaited beard sat before Hrothgar on a three legged stool, a deep blue cloak wrapped about his rangy shoulders. His gray black eyes did not flicker away or blink, his stare baleful as an adder on cold stone; Beowulf did not meet his gaze, lest his tongue freeze with nervousness again.

The woman beside Hrothgar his queen Wealhtheow, she must be was younger than her husband, but her eyes and forehead were lined with care, and though a headdress of purple silk covered her coiled plaits, Beowulf could see the first tiny gray hairs dulling her honey brown eyebrows like a scattering of ash. But the fair haired girl child who sat in a small chair by the Danish queen was wriggling in her seat as if eager to speak, little hands plucking excitedly at her pale blue dress as she stared openly at the big Geat. Beowulf thought for a moment on how it must have been for this child, growing up in Grendel's shadow; and thought, I wish that I could have come earlier to this hall.

"Now I bid of you, lord of the bright Danes, Scylding ruler, this one boon do not forbid me, folk frea, now that I am come so far! That I, alone with my atheling company, may cleanse Heorot."

Beowulf steeled himself for his next words, but he had thought long on them: he clearly remembered Hygelac asking What manner of wight is this Grendel? How does he fight? The peddler Guthlaf answering, He bears no weapons save his strength, claws and teeth, but he needs no more why should he, when he can tear a man's head from his shoulders as easily as you might pull off a sparrow's, and none can harm him in turn?

No blade forged by men could harm Grendel. There was only one way to do battle with a wight who bore no weapons and could be scathed by none. Though Beowulf's choice might seem over daring to others, it was not rashness or bravery that guided him, but wisdom, and trust in two friends: within the Middle Garth, Sweartwulf; beyond its bonds, Frea Ing who gave up his sword to win his eoten bride, but slew her brother with his bare hands when there was need of it.

"I have also heard that this dreadful one, for his overweening pride, wrecks nothing of weapons. That Hygelac, my drighten, may be of blithe mood to me, I therefore shun to bear sword or gold rimmed shield at my side: but I shall fight the foe with my grip, and battle for life, loathed against loathing. There shall he believe in the Drighten's deeming, when death takes him! I ween that his will, if he is allowed to wield it, is to fearlessly eat the Geats in this battle hall, as he has often done with mighty and great men." Beowulf smiled ruefully, for he knew, in truth, that his winning was not sure. "Now you need not hide my head in any grave, for he will have me, adorned with blood, if death takes me. Going alone, he bears the bloody slain away to hide, eating them ruthlessly in his march lair: nor need you long worry about caring for my body. If battle takes me, send to Hygelac that fine battle garment which wards my breast, best of corslets: that was left to me by Haethcyn, work as good as Weland's. Wyrd guides as she shall!"

The Dane queen's long hands clasped each other tightly, her lower lip pale as if she were biting it inside, and the young girl's eyes were very round. Hrothgar's worn old face showed no change at Beowulf's words, but he leaned forward, as if afraid that his aging voice lacked the strength to carry far enough.

"My friend Beowulf, you sought us out for deeds done before, and for favor staves. Your father started the greatest of feuds: he was the hand bane of Heatholaf the Wylfing: then, for fear of war, his Waegmunding kin could not keep him. Then he sought the South Dane folk, the honor Scyldings, over the rolling waves, when I first ruled the Danish people and held this wide realm in my youth, the hoard burg of heroes. Then Halga died, my older brother, Healfdene's bairn unliving he was better than I! Afterwards I settled that fierce feud, sent old treasures to the Wylfings over the water ridges: he swore oaths to me." Hrothgar's wrinkled hand clenched tight on the smooth dark curve of his drinking horn; the muscles of his forearm tightened under the loose skin, and his white beard bristled.

For a moment Beowulf seemed to see the man that Hrothgar had been, a doughty warrior unbent by years. Then the Dane king's broad shoulders slumped again, the lines of tiredness curving down over his face like branches bowed under the weight of heavy snows.

"It is sorrowful to me," he went on, "to speak my soul to any warrior, how Grendel has harmed me in Heorot with his hate thoughts, carrying out his sudden nith. My war band and battle host have waned: Wyrd swept them away in Grendel's horror. May the gods thwart the deeds of that mad scather!"

A deep sigh gusted through Hrothgar's white beard, the fleeting brightness gone from his eyes as he looked out over Heorot as though he were gazing at a well known sight of sorrow.

"Full often brave men boasted over their ale cups, drinking beer, that they would bide in the beer hall, awaiting Grendel's battle with terrible edges. Then in the morning, this mead hall, the host's burg, was adorned with blood when day lighted, all the bench planks sprayed with gore, and the hall blood clotted I had less of my dear troth band, they whom death had taken from me."

Hrothgar was silent for a little while, and Beowulf did not know what to say. He had already sworn to go against Grendel what more could he offer the old man, who had suffered such pain for twelve years within the hall he had raised in such fair hope? But at last the Dane king's gaze cleared, and he met Beowulf's eyes again.

"Sit now to symbol, and unseal your thoughts to the sig mighty warriors, as your soul whets you."

Benches were brought up for Beowulf and his men, and food swiftly carried in sizzling roasts and thick sausages, white wheaten bread, and stewed leeks dripping with fermented butter, their translucent green and yellow leaves mingled with the faded orange brown of chopped trumpet mushrooms. Beowulf saw Hrothgar frown and lean over to his wife. She, in turn, spoke to one of the bondsmaids, and the girl hurried off to come back with two boys whom she sat down on the bench beside Hrothgar's high seat. Beowulf clearly heard her say,

"Stay there and be good: there are great matters taking place, and the sons of kings should not be playing at such times."

Wealhtheow rose with a goblet and pitcher of Southern glass, their brightness adorned by milky cloud trails swirled through the clear crystal over the deep purple red of the drink within. But before she could pour any greeting draught, or any of the Geats could take a bite of the food that had been set before them, the man sitting on the stool by Hrothgar's feet stood up and faced Beowulf, pale lips pulled back to show his teeth. He was very tall, the top of his head only a finger width below Beowulf's chin; his stance was straight and angry as a bane spear. Beowulf's gut tightened: Hygelac had warned him of this man, Hrothgar's thule Unferth a sharp tongued strife stirrer, who stood to challenge everyone coming to Heorot with cruel words.

"Are you that Beowulf," Unferth said loudly and clearly, his deep harsh voice sounding through the hall so that all could hear it above their speech, "who struggled with Breca on the wide sea, to see out of rashness which of you could swim better, and for foolish boasting risked your lives in deep water? No man, neither loved nor loathed, could turn you from this sorrowful thing, when you two thrashed out on the sound.

There Eagor's stream enfolded you dreadfully, you beat the mighty mere road with your hands, gliding over spear sedge with the surging tide, wintry water whelming. In the water's grip you toiled seven nights: he overcame you on the sound, for he had more strength. Then in the morning time he came up on the Heathoreamas' holm, from whence he sought his own kin lands and beloved folk, the land of the Brondings that fair frith burg where he owned folk and burg and rings. The son of Beanstan truly settled his boasting with you! Now, though you may have done in grim battle and war storm, I ween that it shall go worse with you if you dare to bide here night long for Grendel."

The anger mounted within Beowulf like a storm swept tide rising up the base of a cliff, its churning waters threatening to whelm his thoughts. It was a great struggle to hold himself calm in the face of Unferth's mocking words. But, in truth, Beowulf could not say whether his rage stemmed from Unferth, or from his memories of Breca, or from what he knew he had lost in that foolish boys' striving: unknowing, Unferth had hit his mark through the mist as surely as if Woden had guided his aim. But if I give way now, I will show myself unworthy to meet Grendel, Beowulf reminded himself. He forced his hands to hang loosely at his side, calmed his face to a faintly smiling mask.

"Well, my friend Unferth drunken on beer, you have spoken a great deal about Breca. I shall tell you the truth: for I had more sea strength in struggling on the waves than any other man. We two had said, being boys and boastful and we were both young that we should risk our lives out above the spear sedge: and that we carried out. We had naked swords hard in our hands when we thrashed out on the sound; we thought to ward ourselves against whale fish. He could not float far away on the flood waves from me, swiftly on the swells; and I would not leave him. Then we were together on the sea for five nights, until the flood drove us apart welling waters and coldest weather, misty night and northern wind whipped us battle hard, and the waves were rough. The brave mood of the sea fish was roused; my hard hand locked armor gave me help. The scathe foe dragged me down; he had me fast and grim in his grip. It was given to me that I pierced the dreadful one with my battle blade; the war storm took the mighty mere beast by my hand. Thus the loathsome wights attacked me: I paid them back with my dear sword, as was fitting. They had no joy, those man slaying foes, in taking me to sit about at symbol on the sea floor; but in the morning they lay on the shore with great sword dealt wounds. Since then the loathed ones have hindered no seafarers on the high water ways."

It might have been the smoke in the hall that stung Beowulf's eyes then. He did not dare to blink, lest the water should drop from his lids, but went on with what he could tell to men.

"Light came in the east, the bright alf lamp. The billows lessened, and I could see the windy wall of the headland. Wyrd often spares an unfey atheling, if his bravery holds firm! Yet it was given to me, that I slew nine nicors with my sword. I have never heard of a harder fight under heaven's arch, nor of a more hard pressed man in the water's stream. Though weary, I came far through the foes' grasp. The sea bore me up after my faring, welling waves casting me to the Finns' land. I have never heard that you were in such sorrow straits or terrible battle. Breca never did such in battle play, nor did either of you carry out deeds so bravely with adorned swords though I do not boast of it."

The corner of Unferth's sharp mouth was still turned up, and it seemed to Beowulf that he could see black bale still twisting in the thule's thoughts. He had not wished to speak of the other thing Hygelac had told him about Unferth, for it was such a thing as to give the most grievous pain to the guilty hearer; and yet Beowulf knew that if he did not silence Hrothgar's man now, he would have no words of answer left to Unferth's flyting. I am sorry, Unferth, Beowulf thought. But he who gives harsh speech should know well how to bear it. Still, he lowered his voice so that none but Unferth and those who sat nearest could hear him: it was not well to speak loudly of a man's shame before his folk, though they all knew it.

"But you were bane to your brothers, closest kinsmen. For that you shall dread the wyrd of a warg in Hell's realm, though your wit may serve you. I say this truly to you, son of Ecglaf: never should Grendel have carried out so many grim deeds and awful hate against your prince, or shame in Heorot, if your soul were so brave in battle as you say it to be yourself. But he has found no hindrance to his feud, no dire edge storm from your people, yet rather dread among the Sig Scyldings. He takes tribute, and honors none of the Danish folk, but lusts rule him: he strikes and destroys, weens to have no struggle from the Spear Danes. But I, with the Geats, strong and brave, shall now offer battle. Let those who dare go bravely in the mead hall after morning light tomorrow, when the sun shines from the south on the children of men!"

Hrothgar smiled wearily; but Beowulf could see his blue eyes warming, as though the long cold coals of hope and trust were kindling slowly in the Danish king's battered heart. Wealhtheow stepped forward with her goblet, gold glittering from her arm rings and the great filigreed collar over her breast as she gave the first cup to her husband. "Now, Hrothgar Scylding, may you be joyful at this hall feasting!" She said. Hrothgar drank deeply from the shining goblet, only a few drops escaping his mouth to leave a faded madder stain down the corner of his hoarfrost beard. Pitcher in hand, the Danish queen went about the hall, pouring drink for all those gathered there. Among the Geats, it was usually the way to greet the guests first, but Beowulf knew that save for Unferth's words he would not be treated other than with honor in the Scyldings' hall: if Wealhtheow gave him his draught last, it was because that was the custom among the Danes. When Wealhtheow came back to the high table, she filled a glass goblet that was the match of the one she had given Hrothgar, the glint of her rings shining from the smooth sides of the drink darkened crystal as she lifted it up to Beowulf.

"Hail to you, Beowulf son of Ecgtheow! You are welcome here in Heorot for your father's sake, and twice welcome for your own; for that you have come to set your strength against Grendel, no one could be more welcome here.

I give thanks to Frige and the Frowe, Frea Ing and all the gods, that at last my hopes have been fulfilled a hero to help in our troubles, a warder in whom we may trust."

Beowulf took the goblet carefully from Wealhtheow's hand and drank it off. The drink within was not southern wine, as he had thought from the color, but rather a beer brewed from honey and heath berries, very sweet and strong as the starkest mead.

"I had that in my soul when I stood on the wave, and set the sea boat with my warrior band, that I would work the will of your folk by any means, or else be battle slain in the foe's fast set grip. I shall carry forth atheling deeds of bravery, or bide my ending day in this mead hall!" He vowed firmly.

Wealhtheow smiled as a cheer went up from the Danes at Beowulf's oath, the little atheling maiden's piercing shriek carrying over the rest. The queen poured the greeting goblet full of the precious drink again.

"May the gods look well on what you have sworn, and the Norns answer your bravery with sig staves," Wealhtheow said, her words quiet, but heart felt. "We have suffered long: it is meet that now, as in early days, a hero should come over the whale road to aid the bairns of Scyld Scefing."

Wealhtheow stared at Beowulf for a moment, as if she would say more but could not bring the words up from the well of her breast, and her blue gray eyes seemed to darken as she looked at him. Beowulf wondered what she was thinking: if the Danes had heard of his swimming match with Breca and, as they must have, of the deaths of the Hrethlings and Ongentheow's fall what other tales had they heard of Beowulf himself? Unferth, he was sure, had been about to speak further flytings against him; what doubt shadowed Wealhtheow's gaze? And would he have been greeted so gladly, if the Scyldings were not so sunken in wanhope that they must put their trust in whoever they could? The thought made Beowulf ashamed, and he looked away from Wealhtheow's gaze.

"Shall I ready guest houses for yourself and your men?"

"There is no need, for we will sleep the night here. If you can have blankets brought to us against the cold, that will do well enough."

"I shall do that gladly," Wealhtheow replied. Though she hid it well, Beowulf thought he could hear a faint tremor in her voice fear for me? Or of me? He sought for something else to speak of.

"Your children are very fair," he said lamely.

Wealhtheow smiled. "Yes. The boys are Hrethric, who is the elder, and Hromund; the girl is Freawaru, already betrothed to Ingeld the Heathobard."

"It is well when blood strife can be ended by a frith weaver," Beowulf murmured, looking over at Freawaru again.

The great gold ring had slipped down her slender arm, its filigree casting a myriad of red glints whenever it moved.

Then, suddenly, he was overcome by a seeing that blazed through his eyes, searing into his brain: an old warrior shouting at the young gold decked atheling who stood beside Freawaru, swords scattering blood and torches scattering sparks, and Heorot burning around the bodies. But as for Hrothgar's sons, their young faces seemed misted by the smoke, and the larger chair that stood empty beside the king's high seat overshadowed them both. *I have truly come too late: there will be few years of happiness left in Heorot, even should I slay Grendel this night. But perhaps a little is better than nothing.* Beowulf lifted the goblet to his lips once more, swallowing hard to drive back his foreboding, and said,

"I have heard that Halga's son Hrothulf also dwells in this hall, but his seat is empty."

"I think you have already met Hrothulf, unless he is slacker than I ween him to be. He has taken the coast watch this day, and should have greeted you when your ship sailed in."

Beowulf nodded, easier in his mind. A simple thane would hardly have made the choice to bring a band of armed strangers to Heorot by himself and now he knew who the young man had reminded him of.

"He has something of his mother about him," Beowulf remarked.

Wealtheow raised her eyebrows. "You have met Yrse? But of course; you were one of Haethcyn's fellows on his faring to Uppsala. What manner of woman is she?"

Beowulf turned over the words in his hoard for a little time before he spoke: it would not do to seem to be slighting Yrse in the Scyldings' hall.

"She is a woman of great might, and wise in many things. Nor is it to be wondered at that she has been a king's bride twice."

Wealhtheow, too, paused as if considering what to say in reply.

"I have heard much of her wisdom. It is said that Halga was drawn to such women; his daughter Scyld..." She shut her mouth tightly, as if to cut off the word thread before it could spin farther from her lips.

"Yrse suggested to me that I might do well to ask for Scyld in marriage," Beowulf said carefully, for he could not help but wonder what the Swede queen had sought for him.

Wealhtheow frowned. "Halga named Scyld as his daughter and a true Scylding when she was brought to him, and she is fostered with atheling kin. Yet, I should not give you such rede." Then she smiled brightly, a look that mirrored her daughter's youth. "If Freawaru were not sworn to Ingeld, she would be asking for your hand even now, I think. She is already quite taken with you."

Beowulf did not know how to answer that, nor could he guess whether Wealhtheow spoke in jest or in earnest. But it were best to take the matter lightly, so he answered,

"I have no fear of meeting Grendel's grip, but to be wedded with a young maid of such strong will would be enough to daunt any man. Surely Ingeld is braver than I!"

Wealhtheow laughed, and Beowulf's fleeting worry eased: he had guessed aright, after all, and no ill will with either Scyldings or Heathobards would come of his speech. Beowulf and his men drank sparingly that day, though the men of Heorot drained their horns often. Hrothgar's poet sang for them, lifting his voice clearly above the thrumming of his harp; there was more laughing than Beowulf had thought to hear in the troll haunted hall, though the laughter seemed to be edged with glass brittle nervousness they hope desperately for me to win, but dare not trust in their hopes until the deed is done, Beowulf thought.

Some men boasted of battle deeds in the past: almost all of Hrothgar's thanes, Beowulf marked, were of an age to have fought by his side years before Grendel came; and when his eyes had grown used to the gold glitter and flames and shadows, the Geat saw that the hall was more than half empty. But that was hardly to be wondered at: rather, it was a sign of Hrothgar's luck and his greatness as a folk ruler that so many had stayed with him through the dark years of Grendel's night guesting, and the lands he ruled were so wide that, for all his troubles, the Dane king's wealth did not seem to have waned.

Inside Heorot, there was no way to tell the time save by watching the pale beeswax melt to pool golden in the iron lamp cups; but as the afternoon wore on, Beowulf marked how folk would shift uneasily in their seats before they rose to step outside for a few moments. At last the door opened from without, and the young coast warder Hrothulf, still wearing his gold ridged helm and holding his stout spear came in, walking up to the high seat. His keen gray eyes spared Beowulf a sharp glance before he spoke to Hrothgar.

"The sun is sinking westward, and the night mists are rising; it seemed to me as I rode from the coast that I could see shadow helmed shapes gliding pale through the fog. I think it is time for those who do not mean to face Grendel this night to go to their beds."

Hrothgar rose from his high seat, turning to Beowulf. "Since I could lift hand and shield, I never trusted any other man before to ward the mighty dwelling of the Danes. Have now and hold the most blessed house, mindful of fame; make known main deeds of daring, and watch against the wrathful foe. No wish of yours will be lacking, if you can carry out that work of bravery!"

Hrothgar and his folk left the hall swiftly then, the gray hounds running behind them as if they, too, feared to stay where Grendel would tread; but Hrothulf lingered a few moments. Beowulf unbuckled his helmet, bending over to let his byrnie slither from his shoulders, and took off his sword belt as well.

"Hold well for me, if you will, this battle gear," Beowulf said to the young man. "I would know that it is in the keeping of a trusty atheling."

Hrothulf almost staggered beneath the weight of Beowulf's mail shirt, but he nodded, bearing it up.

"Save that I am told that you asked to watch alone with your men, I should stay here with you as you do battle with Grendel. It will be long before such a sight is seen in the Middle Garth again."

"I think that you shall see your share and more of strange things, and have it in your turn to win a hero's name," Beowulf said without thought.

Hrothulf stared fiercely up at him, and it was nearly Beowulf's turn to stagger back. Though the short lean Dane was as a child beside Beowulf, there was a great strength in his gaze.

"How do you know such things?"

"I do not know," Beowulf mumbled, for the sureness of his speech had, as always before, dropped away from him. "But it is time for you to go now: night is nearly upon us, and I do not think that Grendel will hold back too long from such a feast as seems to be spread out for him here."

"We shall speak more in the morning, if you are still alive," Hrothulf replied.

The Geats spread out the blankets Wealhtheow had brought for them soft and bright dyed wool, hemmed with card woven bands in shining colors: she had spared nothing for her guests, though one way or another, the good coverlets were likely to be stained with blood before dawn. They settled themselves in the clean straw among the benches, Beowulf closest to the door. Wigstan banked the fires and blew out the lamps, so that Heorot was hidden in darkness, with only a few coals glimmering like little red eyes in the fire trenches. Someone in the darkness, Beowulf could not tell who, though he guessed from the words it might be Hondscioh said,

"I wonder who will hold Hroesnabeorh when tidings of us come back to Hygelac?"

"I mean to bear those tidings back myself," Beowulf answered sharply. "I do not count my fighting skill, nor my battle works, less than Grendel does his: for that, I shall not bear sword against him to spill out his life, though I might. But he does not know how to wield blade against me, nor split my shield though his nith works are widely known. Yet we two shall meet tonight, if he dares to seek me out in weaponless battle. And let the wise god, the holy drighten, deem fame on either hand as he thinks meetest! Now let us seem to sleep, that we may catch the murder thurse unawares."

There were no more murmurs after that. One by one the Geatish thanes seemed to settle themselves, breathing loudly as if they were sinking into sleep. Beowulf let his limbs ease as well, his lungs drawing in slow draughts of air. Grendel would come, he was sure of it. Grendel glided through the mists over the moorland, his heart filled with joy and eagerness. At last! He thought. At last! The wyrms of his mere had writhed fiercely in green fire all day, sending ripples through the dark pool on the hall floor; they felt the stirrings of the one who had come over the sea to meet him. Now the half waned Moon seemed to race through the scudding gray clouds above, casting a fitful light through the drifting fog; Grendel strode beneath the storm clouds, ready to do battle.

He did not bear his sword, for he needed none. He had always assailed Hrothgar's hall with his naked strength before, and he would not have it said that he had taken up a weapon in fear of this new foe. The scattered moon gleams paled the gold adorning Heorot's roof to silver, a faint glimmer through the mist. This night, the door was barred and bound fast against Grendel, but iron was no proof against eoten strength. He had only to strike it once with his fist, and the timbers burst asunder with a terrible rending sound.

The darkness within meant nothing to Grendel: he could see the bodies of the men stretched out upon the straw, wrapped in fine blankets as if they were corpses already. Despite the roar of the door's bursting, Grendel heard the strangers breathing in deep sleep, and a new anger kindled in him: he knew that his mother, fearing for him yet, must have sung her seith chants to whelm their souls to stillness, so that they would not be able to stand against him. Yet if the one who waited for Grendel was as strong as he ought to be, perhaps he would be able to withstand her workings, but none stood to call challenge to him. In all the hall, there was only the sluggish sound of snoring and the rustling of straw beneath his own feet: it seemed to him that he stood alone as he had ever been within Heorot.

Wrathfully, Grendel bent to seize upon the first sleeping warrior, catching him up to slit his entrails with talons and bite through his shoulder joints, drinking the hot spray of blood before he set to devouring the man in great gulps. Yet the meal only seemed to whet both his hunger and his rage: he had been cheated of winning his revenge, cheated of the chance to crush the Scyldings' hopes of keeping Heorot in an open struggle. There was no doubt which of the men was the one that Grendel had been meant to meet. He was bigger than any child of Ash and Elm that Grendel had ever seen, his huge muscles smoothed, like those of many water eotens, by a seal's blanket of fat; and even in sleep, his jaw was grimly set beneath the golden brown curls of his beard. But the troll wife's spell had overcome him, as it had his thanes.

How could Heofonglowe have loved one so weak? Grendel thought, looking down at his rival. I shall wipe out her shame in his blood; I shall soothe her hurt with his heart. This man would pay full geld for his lack of soul strength: instead of doing battle fairly with him as men of like might, Grendel would rend and devour him as if he were no more than any other dweller in the Middle Garth. Beowulf had heard his men's breathing suddenly shift from feigned rest to true deep sleep; a cloud had seemed to drift over his own eyelids, but he gripped hard at his own arm until he could feel wet trickles running from under his fingernails, the pain shocking him back into wakefulness and he knew now that the troll was drawing near.

He could not help starting when Heorot's door burst asunder, but he forced his tightened limbs back into a sleep like sprawl, closing his eyes until he could see only through the tiniest lash barred slit. Lying thus, he saw the dark shadow shape gliding into the hall, the pale eyes burning lightless as howe flames. Though neither moon nor fire lit Heorot, it seemed to Beowulf that he could see clearly; he forced his breathing to evenness, waiting for Grendel to come to him. To Beowulf's horror, the thurse paused, lifting his head and looking about as though he awaited something then his taloned hand swooped downward, hooking one of the sleeping men off the floor.

Beowulf could not see who Grendel had taken, but he heard the ghastly sound of entrails flopping to the earth and bones snapping through beneath the shadow walker's teeth. It was already too late to save the man in Grendel's grip, but Beowulf steeled himself to spring up if his foe should turn to another next. Grendel halted a moment, looking down at Beowulf. It seemed to Beowulf then that the eoten's scaled face was more like a man's than he had thought; for he could see not only Grendel's grimace of thwarted rage, but also his scorn and something else behind them, something that might have been bitterness or disappointment. Then Grendel's claw darted dark towards Beowulf; but Beowulf was ready, jerking his hand up from beneath the thurse's grip and around to fasten his fingers tightly upon Grendel's wrist and lean all his weight upon the locked arm. Grendel snarled in sudden pain and shock.

Never in the Middle Garth, nor in any corner of the earth, had he felt a harder hand grip; Ran's sharks had fastened teeth in him before, but their mighty jaws had not clenched him so firmly, nor torn at him so fiercely. Yet his rage was still greater than his pain; with a vicious heave of his arm, though it tore at his own sinews, he heaved his foe to his feet, hurling him hard against one of the hall pillars so that the hollow boom resounded through the hall. Heofonglowe, I shall slay him yet for you! Grendel tried to wrench himself away, but the bear man stepped forward, tightening his hand yet harder; Grendel could not break his grasp, nor turn to strike him, save by wheeling in wide circles about the arm that his foe held locked straight and hard as an iron bar.

Through the battle flood bursting in his brain, Beowulf knew dimly that he had never felt such might, a match for his own or more. He held fast to Grendel's wrist; his finger joints were cracking with the strength of his grip, but he knew that, should the thurse slip his hold, Grendel's claws would tear his flesh like flimsy linen. Beowulf barely felt the shock of his body hammering against hard wood as they reeled about; slamming each other into Heorot's walls and great pillars, the mead benches giving way beneath them with rending cracks like the timbers of a ship storm cast upon jagged rocks.

Only the pale flames of Grendel's eyes lit the battered beams and planks; it seemed to Beowulf that they fought no longer in the Middle Garth, nor in a hall of men, but that they struggled beneath drowning dark water. Then a swelling scream arose from Grendel's throat, like a dreadful eoten song, so deafeningly loud that it seemed to shake roof and walls and earth beneath their feet. Yet it seemed to Beowulf that he could hear the words beneath the howling sound; and that Grendel cried out in despair, Yma, my grandfather! Heofonglowe, beloved!

Though Beowulf's own sinews seemed to be bursting, his bones hot glaives of pain through arms and shoulders, he wrenched Grendel's arm the harder in his own fury and despair as he heard that cry: for the thurse's unknowing words proved at last their kinship, that Beowulf had sought so hard to struggle against. Yet he would not, could not, let go his hold: he clung with all that was in him. Swords flashed around them, edges bouncing harmless as raindrops from Grendel's hide Beowulf's men had awakened at last. But Beowulf had no thought for them: there was nothing to feel save the cold scaled arm beneath his hands, nothing to see but the fallow glimmer of his foe's eyes, searing into his own at last.

The bear man's eyes shone like lightless blue flames over a howe in Grendel's sight; the pain in his shoulder burned in a scream through his whole body. No man, he thought, but eoten kin as my mother warned me. Grendel tried to laugh, but only a wordless wail tore out of his mouth as he flung himself backwards with the last of his strength. He hardly felt his hide tearing open: only the brutal flare of agony shrieking from his shoulder. Then he stumbled to the side, suddenly free of the dreadful hold. A splatter of blackness burned across his eyes as he backed up; he blinked his sight clear, looking down unbelievingly. His right arm was gone, dark blood jetting from his shoulder.

That stream washed away all his thoughts of vengeance, of anger, of Heofonglowe...Grendel clasped his left hand to his shoulder to stanch the blood fountain, turned and ran out through Heorot's shattered door. Above, the Moon whirled silver through the clouds that fled across his face, whelming Grendel's sight with waves of light and darkness. He stumbled through the thin veils of fog, blindly following the long known track across the moorland, his clawed feet splashing through black peat pools and sucking mud. Home, he thought, Mother. Mother will help me. Twice Grendel fell, crawling as best he could with his one hand clenched tightly to his rent shoulder, until he came to solid ground where he could push himself to his feet again. He was staggering now, weaving light headed from side to side in the swirling mist; but ahead he could see the white spume of the waterfall tumbling from the crags, and the glow of the wyrms writhing in the night mere. With a last burst of strength, he ran forward, and stumbled again, falling full length at the water's edge.

The ground struck his hand from his shoulder; though Grendel fumbled through the spurting blood, he could not make his talons grip the wound again. But at least the Scyldings did not overcome me, Grendel thought. At least the sons of Ash and Elm did not slay me. Though my bane be a man of the Middle Garth, he is also one of Yma's kin: perhaps that is some small winning for us. A wave of dizziness arose, drowning that thought, and it seemed to Grendel that he was dying; but then his eyes cleared a little.

"Heofenglowe," Grendel whispered, as if Ran's daughter could hear him. "I fought for you." He could almost see the cool whiteness of her breasts, the greenish gleam of her long hair, but she was fading from his thoughts.

With a last great effort he lifted his head up: a silver shimmer of moonlight on the black lake, the scaled ripple of a mere wyrm rising.

"Mother," murmured Grendel. His head slumped again, and the dark waters rose around him.

Beowulf stood panting, his head down like that of a horse ridden near to heart bursting. The weight of the scaly arm seemed too much for him to lift now, but his fingers were still cramped about it and he could not loose them; the bloody end dragged on the ground. The murmurs of his men rose and fell about him like the lapping of waves, and then little lamp flames sprang up where one of the Geats had blown a banked coal to kindle the wicks again.

"Before all the gods," Adhalberht murmured, his voice hushed. "Look!"

Beowulf saw the eyes of his thanes shining beneath the gold glimmers of their helm crests, all staring at his gruesome burden.

"He tore it off with main strength," someone else whispered. "Has ever there been such a hero born in the Middle Garth?"

"Hail to Beowulf!" Whooped Oslaf. "Beowulf, Grendel's bane!"

Then the men all crowded about Beowulf, shouting and pounding his bruised shoulders until he wanted to cry out in pain. Thoughts were crawling slowly back to his fogged mind, there was something he had to see to.

"Give me one of those lamps," Beowulf said hoarsely had he, too, been crying out in the battle?

He braced his foot against Grendel's dismembered shoulder joint, pushing the thick arm out of his grip. Still claw handed and numb fingered, he took the twisted iron stem from Aethelstan, holding the bowl lamp up and looking at the faces about him as he tried to call up all the names of those who had come with him there was nothing left of the dead man to be recognised. Adhalberht, Oslaf, Aethelstan; Gudhmund and Godwine, Merewalh and Sicga and Eanbald, Hlothere, Berhtfrith, Swithhelm, Wihtgar, Oswald, Beorhtric.

"Hondscioh."

Beowulf looked about for a bench to sit on before his knees gave way, but the boards were all shattered, tossed wildly about the room. Instead, he leaned his back on a hall pillar, paying no mind to the splinters pricking into him.

"Hondscioh is dead," Beowulf said. "Grendel seized first upon him. We shall find nothing of his body, and his grave is that greedy troll's belly but at least he was avenged on his death night, as not many can say."

"How is it that we heard nothing?" Beorhtric asked, and then, angrily. "How is it that we slept here, when we awaited the night slayer's coming upon us? Believe me, my drighten, there is not one of us that has ever slacked on watch before! There must have been some troll craft upon us." The others nodded and muttered in agreement.

"Aye, I am sure of it," Beowulf told him. "I, too, felt sleep coming on me, so that I must tear my flesh with my nails to hold awake." He held up his arm, where a little dried blood showed faintly against the darkening bruises.

"That's it," Gudhmund said wisely. "My grandmother always told me that drawing blood was a sure way to break a troll's spell but what of Hondscioh? Did he fight well?"

Beowulf wished for their sakes, as some had been Hondscioh's friends, that he could lie and say that the dead thane had battled bravely against his slayer. But he could tell from the sad half hope in Gudhmund's voice that he would not be believed.

"Grendel took him in his spelled sleep, so that he had no chance to show his battle mood. Yet Hondscioh was a strong thane, and came bravely to Heorot with us, knowing that it might well be his death faring."

Helmed heads nodded. Beowulf had no doubt that not a man there did not know how little love there had been between Hondscioh and his drighten, yet the words he had spoken were true, so far as they went. What none of the thanes might know was how the guilt for Hondscioh's death was already stabbing at Beowulf. Beowulf had ordered him to come, yes, but he thought the root of the matter was the way in which he had beaten Hondscioh at wrestling, so that the man must mutter about troll kin behind Beowulf's back, and yet could not show himself unwilling when the time came for him to dare Grendel. Could I have done better? Beowulf wondered. If I had, would he live yet or would Grendel only have chosen another to die in his stead? Wyrd works as she will, he reminded himself. And no one can know what might have been.

"Did the good Scylding queen leave any of her strong beer with us?" Merewalh wondered. "I think our drighten must be thirsty after such a night's work."

After a little searching, someone found the keg in a corner by great good luck, it was still whole, bung seated firmly and tap unbroken. Oslaf shouldered Swithhelm aside, filling his own horn and bearing it over.

"You're a cursed ugly hall frowe," Swithhelm accused Oslaf as he gave the horn to Beowulf.

The thanes all broke into raucous laughter, holding their bellies and wiping tears of merriment from their eyes, as if they had heard nothing funnier than that faint jest in their lives. Beowulf felt the laugh about to burst from his own throat, but he held it back; he was afraid that if he started he would not be able to stop. The strong beer soothed him, though, easing his shaking limbs and dulling the swelling ache of his body.

"What of it, Beowulf?" Adhalberht asked. "Should we go to tell Hrothgar that Grendel is dead, and hail out the folk of Heorot to feast it?"

Beowulf looked down at the torn off limb, a black lump lying on the floor like a long trail of iron slag. It seemed to him as though all of his feelings had drained away like a tide ebbing down the beach, leaving only numb relief behind. At that moment, he did not know, nor care, what they should do, but Gudhmund spoke for him.

"Why not let the Danes find out in the morning? I think they ween to see our bodies shredded on the floor: they will be taken a little aback when they see us whole, and Grendel's arm hanging up in the hall."

The Geats took that up gleefully, bearing the lamps about to look for a place to mount the thurse's limb. At last they made a sling out of the blankets that had been worst bloodied and rent, hanging Grendel's arm from the roof beam above Hrothgar's high seat.

"Now, I think, we can sleep safely here," Beowulf said. "And it were well if we slept now, for we can await much ale being poured out for us tomorrow night."

Stiffly Beowulf laid himself down on the floor. As well as wrenching his shoulders, he had strained his right leg badly at the hip joint. His ribs hurt with every breath he took, and he knew that his body must be a mass of bruises: beneath tunic and breeches, he would be blue black as a drow by morning. Yet, almost before Beowulf could gather the straw into a pillow for his head and wrap the blanket about his body, he felt himself slipping into sleep. A bolt of pain shot through Beowulf's shoulder: one of his men was lightly shaking him awake.

"My drighten, dawn is almost upon us," Adhalberht said. "The Danes will be here soon to see what you have wrought."

Beowulf struggled to wakefulness, every sinew in his body groaning as he pushed himself up to sit. His hair was a tangled mass, full of splinters and straw; he raked swollen fingers painfully through it, but it took him several tries to undo the buckles of his belt pouch, and he could not hold his comb with strength enough to straighten the mess.

"Let me do that for you," offered Merewalh. "It is always hardest to comb one's own hair."

Surprised, but grateful, Beowulf gave the comb to his thane. Merewalh's wiry fingers swiftly picked out the pieces of debris, easing the elk horn teeth through the thick mats.

"Now you look as a drighten ought," the Geatish warrior said, a small smile touching his lips beneath his neat fair beard. "Otherwise the Danes would not have been able to tell who had won the struggle."

Merewalh's words still flicked Beowulf hard on his bruises, but the friendly tone in the thane's voice soothed the worst of the sting: Merewalh had truly meant no more than a jest. Swithhelm looked out through the broken hall door.

"Where are the Danes? The sky is light are they sleeping late?"

Sicga grinned. "They must be waiting for full sun up, to be sure that Grendel has gone back to his lair." His gray eyes flickered up to the arm that hung in its makeshift sling above Hrothgar's high seat. "Good, it is still here. I thought that the troll flesh might melt away at dawn, and we would have nothing to show Hrothgar for his broken hall."

"That's alfs you're thinking of, or ghosts," Gudhmund told him. "Alf gifts become dried leaves or such in the morning, and ghost flesh melts; trolls turn to stone, but the sunlight has to touch them."

"I suppose you got that from your grandmother as well?" Sicga said. "What else did you?"

Beowulf looked sternly at him, and Sicga left the rest of his words in his mouth. But the thane had spoken rightly the first time: it was not until true sunlight showed through Heorot's shattered portal that the Geats heard uncertain footsteps outside. The first to look through the broken hall door was Hrothulf. Beowulf almost laughed to see the young atheling's tight calm shatter as he took in the sight of the Geats standing alive beneath the grisly dark troll arm that hung from the roof beam: Hrothulf's blue eyes widened, his mouth dropping open as though he were an untaught farm boy gaping for the first time at Heorot's splendor. Then he turned and ran. The Geats heard his footfalls beating away, and the faint shout behind the hall.

"Hrothgar! Hrothgar, arise and come!"

It was not long before the Danish king, ringed by stout thanes, appeared before the staved in door, together with Wealhtheow followed by her troop of women. Hrothgar moved shakily, wrinkled face pale and eyes red as though he had not slept that night, but the look of joy that spread over his face glowed warm in Beowulf's heart, so that the Geat thought, Whatever sorrows may come after, this deed has been worth the doing. Hrothgar stepped into his hall, stopping before his high seat to stare up at Grendel's arm the black scaled hide tight over bulging muscles, the talons, long and keen as knives with a cruel hook at the end of each, and the tattered flesh and white bone, crusted with black blood, where the limb had ripped away from the body. The old man stood speechless, and Beowulf saw the tears rolling down from Hrothgar's sore eyes.

"For this sight," Hrothgar said, his voice deep and shaking, "let us thank the all ruling Frea! I suffered many ill deeds and sorrows from Grendel: the god works wonder after wonder, the warder of the world. It was not long since I weened, though searching far and wide, that no help would ever turn to me when, blood painted, the most blessed of houses stood drenched in battle gore. There was wide pressed woe for all wise folk: they never weened that they could ever ward the folk's land work against loathed ones, ill wights and trolls. Now a warrior, through drighten's might, has carried out the deed that all of us earlier might not do through wisdom. Yes, the maid who kindled that man of warrior kind might say, if she yet lived, that she was loved by the All Measurer in that childbearing!"

Hrothgar turned to Beowulf, embracing him hard: though the wrinkled skin was beginning to hang in folds over the muscles, there was still good strength in the old man's arms, so that Beowulf had to bite his tongue to keep from crying out at the touch on his swollen bruises.

"Now, Beowulf, best of warriors, I will call you my son, loved in my soul: hold this new sib! Nothing that I have to rule will be lacking for you in this new friendship. I often gave rewards to lesser men, hoard worth to lower warriors, less able in battle. You yourself have carried out these deeds, for which your fame shall live through the ages of men. May the All Ruler ever give you geld of good, as he has done now!"

Tears prickled at Beowulf's own eyes like little splinters. Ecgtheow had never embraced or spoken to him so: it seemed to him that Hrothgar's fatherly welcome had melted that ice which had fettered his heart, like the summer warming a long frozen mountain stream to new flowing. He did not know how to shape a son's words of love, so he spoke instead of his deed, as though Ecgtheow could hear as well as Hrothgar.

"Greatly blessed, we fought and carried out that deed work, daring venture against an unknown foe. I would rather that you could see him himself, the foe slain in the treasure hall. I thought to bind him on his slain bed with hard fetters, that he should lie with life fading under my hand grip, but his body was gone: I could not hinder his going when the measuring god willed it not I was not strong enough to hold him, for he was too mighty in fleeing. Yet he left his hand in life warding, his spoor remaining, arm and shoulder. There will be no comfort for the warriors' foe, nor shall the loathly spoiler live long afflicted by his own deeds, grasped and bound in a nith grip by pain's baleful bonds. There, outlawed for ill, shall he abide by a mickle doom, as the Norns shall predict it for him."

Beowulf fell silent, choked with feeling. Wealhtheow was weeping openly now, tears falling as hard for joy as if she were mourning the death of an old friend.

Her hand clutched tight on her mother's, Freawaru was stretching up onto her toes to look at the grisly battle trophy, her eyes shining as she cried out, "Did I not tell you, Mother? Did I not say that he would come back to save us as soon as the tapestry was done?" Then she pulled her hand loose, running over to Beowulf. "Bend down so I can kiss you," the small maiden ordered.

Flushed with embarrassment, Beowulf bent over, receiving the light brush of Freawaru's lips against his bearded cheek. Her pride reminded him more than a little of Hygd's at the same age; he pushed from his thoughts the memory of yesterday's fiery foreseeing.

"I know who you are," said Freawaru, looking straight into Beowulf's face. "Even if you won't say so, I made the tapestry for you Mother helped, of course and you came."

Mystified, Beowulf straightened up, but Freawaru had said all that she meant to say, and hurried back to her mother's side. The Danes were gathering all around, staring up at Grendel's arm and murmuring.

"Talons like steel," one man remarked, and Wulfgar pulled the neck of his tunic down to show a withered white scar twisting over his collarbone.

"Aye, when Hrothgar first stood to fight Grendel, before we knew that no blade could scathe him, he caught me with the tip of one claw had I been a little closer, he would have ripped my heart from my body. But no one could have struck so with iron, to take off the troll's bloody battle arm as Beowulf has torn it with his main strength."

Hrothgar sat down in his high seat, giving orders to his men as Wealhtheow swept about with the women. Quickly the women saw to taking away the torn and bloodied blankets, bondsmaids cleaning away the stained straw, while men carried out the benches that could be fixed and broke up the ones ruined beyond repair for the fires, bringing in whole benches for Beowulf and his companions to sit on. The daylight showed the damage to Heorot more clearly: cracked carvings, splinted pillars, broken planks only the roof was wholly sound. They breakfasted there in the hall, on fine bread and thick sausages and honeycakes baked with blackberries and crab apples. After his night's struggle, it would have taken more than Grendel's blood clotted arm hanging above the table to dull Beowulf's appetite; even his memory of the troll sucking Hondscioh's entrails in through his teeth was not enough to spoil his meal. When they had eaten, Hrothgar rose.

"Wulfgar, I would have you send riders out through the land, that all folk may know that Heorot is free at last. Beowulf, I mean to feast you as is fitting, but there is much work to be done in this hall before nightfall before it is ready to host high favored and atheling guests," the Dane king added, a dazed smile spreading through his white beard, as though he were just now realizing that Heorot truly could hold feasts after sundown again.

"Hrothulf, let you show these brave warriors how the Scyldings and their thanes rejoice, with games and horse riding and hawking, wrestling and singing and whatever may delight men of kingly kin."

They spent that day outside. The night clouds had passed, and the Sun shone clear in the cold air, the sky's blue pale as winter ice. Beowulf's bruised bones ached too deeply for him to take part in the horse racing, and he had not forgotten how Hrime and Feola had run past his skill to hold them when he urged them on too fast, but the Danes set him on the best steed in Hrothgar's stables a stallion, but so well trained and well tempered that he answered swiftly to the least touch of Beowulf's reins, as willing as if he knew his rider's thoughts and thus mounted, Beowulf rode along the path to the moors with the others at a gentle tölt, marking Grendel's wandering footprints.

Hrothgar's horses were fine beasts indeed, with large eyes and manes braided with silk thread over sturdy, proudly arched necks, their winter coats just thickening into soft shaggy pelts. Though most of them were not as large and heavy as the Hrethlings' steeds, they moved like swiftly trotting flames. Hrothgar seemed to favor spotted horses: not only the usual dapple gray, but also gleaming fallow red spangled with gold and deep brown dappled with rich black. Hygelac would delight in such steeds, Beowulf thought: I wish that he were here now!

Some of the Danish athelings had hawks on their wrists, fair fledged falcons, that they would launch whenever they saw a hare's ears pricking up above the fields' brown stubble. Beowulf watched in awe as the birds plummeted upon their prey: it seemed to him that the rush of wind in his ears, the dry rustling leaves and the brightness of the gold and silver upon the arms and bridle mounts of the men who rode with him were keener than he had ever known them, and the soreness of his body was little to the delight of blood rushing through his veins, the wholeness and movement of his limbs. After the battle at Ravenwood, Beowulf had been too caught up in the doings of men mourning for his father, settling Hygelac's new kingship and the frith with the Swedes, facing the knowledge that he must become drighten at Hroesnabeorh to joy simply in being alive.

Now no worries pressed upon him, nor any foreboding of ill: he had only to sit back upon the high arched saddle with the fallow dappled steed moving smoothly beneath him, and feel himself eased by the sense that he had won friendship at last. They stopped in the early afternoon to eat, and again the best food was brought out sausages scented with caraway, rich earthy tasting mushrooms stewed in butter, and firm white cheeses, with good ale flavored with bog myrtle to wash them down. As the thanes ate, Hrothgar's poet brought out his harp, and after a little plinking and twisting of his tuning pegs, he began to sing. To Beowulf's wonder, the first words the poet sang were of Beowulf's own coming to Heorot.

"They glided over wave swell,wind lifted them on,
 foam throated ship flew like a bird,
 and by the set time of second day,
 the ring staved prow had rushed to goal,
 that the seafarers saw the land,
  shore cliffs fair, steep rising bergs..."
Beowulf listened in awe: just so it had been, though he could not have
shaped the words to tell of it. And the poet knew only what he had heard
from Beowulf's rough spoken thanes; how, then, could his song so easily
take wing from the plain facts of sailing across from Geatland to Sealand?
Yet the singer went on, telling the tale as it had been.
"Then came from moor, under mist hills,
 Grendel stridinggods' wrath on him,
 the man scathe meant among men's kin
 some to snare in shining hall."
The blood rushed dizzyingly to Beowulf's head: he could feel himself
reddening and paling by turns as the poet sang of his battle. He knew that
this song would be echoed in an hundred halls, among the Frisians and the
Swedes and the Saxon tribes who had gone to win new land from Artorius
in Britain, from Godhagastir's dwelling in the far North to the court of
Theoderic in the South. I have won fame that shall last while the world
stands, he thought, and be known when all those who mocked me are but
a growing of mold in their howes. After Beowulf had risen to receive the
resounding hails of the Danes and his Geatish followers, and had another
horn of ale pressed into his hand, the poet told other tales: the story of
Sigimund the Walsing and his son Sinfjotli, that had frightened Beowulf so
as a child, and the deeds of Sigifrith the Dragon Slayer.
"...For Sigifrith sprang
 after death day a doom not little!
Since battle hard man was bane to the wyrm,
 the hoard's watcher. Under hoary stone
 the atheling bairn all alone, dared
 the deed of bravery..."
Yet another wyrm lives. The thought went through Beowulf like a small
amber spark: he had not turned his mind to Ansuwulf's tale since the battle
at Ravenwood, but he had not forgotten the hoarfrost eyes gleaming over
the hoard, nor the berserk's shadowed warning.
"...he was blessed that blade pierced through
 the bright adorned wyrm in wall it stood,
 drighten fair iron. The dragon fell.
 The awe full ruler had wrought the deed,
 thus he had right to rings and hoard,
 choosing for self. Sea boat he loaded,
 bore to ship's bosom bright treasures all,
 the Walsing's offspring. The wyrm had melted."

After they ate, there were wrestling and foot races and stone casting, just as at the Midsummer gathering by Whales' Ness. Some of the Danes had tracked Grendel all the way to his mere: coming back to their fellows now, they spoke of how the troll's footprints showed his weariness and his overcoming death.

"The water welled with blood, the waves rising hard to mingle with the hot gore and battle drops," said one of the trackers, a gray haired, quiet man named Æschere. "Grendel laid down his life there in his fen lair: I think that Hell took him."

A bathhouse by the shore had been readied, and Beowulf gladly settled himself in the heat, casting a few ladles of water on the stones. He sighed as the steam rose up, settling into his sore muscles; soon the sweat ran freely down his body, washing away the last bloodstains and softening the hard clotted scrapes on his limbs. The other men looked in awe at the swollen bruises purpling most of Beowulf's skin, but said little.

In truth, the battering he had taken hurt worse than a clean edge bite, yet bruises were not such a thing as a man should take any thought with though Beowulf would have been grateful for a bucket full of the bone set ointment old Amma had often smeared on him after the other boys had beaten him about with wooden swords. But at least the heat of the bathhouse soothed his sore sinews, loosening muscles that had stiffened painfully while he sat to watch the Geats and Danes test their strength on each other. And for all the cruel stinging of the salt in his scrapes, it eased Beowulf yet further to plunge into the ocean's cold water, beating his limbs hard against the waves though he was careful not to swim too far from shore, lest the currents that lifted him up suddenly drag him once more into the depths of Ran's realm.

As sunset drew nearer, Beowulf marked how the Danes would glance fearfully towards the reddening sky and then catch themselves, and laugh: night would be dreadful here no longer. Yet they still crowded closer to their houses as the evening mists began to rise pale from sea and fen, for though Grendel was slain, it would be some time before his memory no longer crept through the fog. Two iron bowled lamps burned by Heorot's door posts, their long twisted spikes thrust deep into the earth. But the hastily repaired door stood open, fires burning bright all through the hall.

Tapestries had been brought out to hide the worst of the battering on the walls and pillars, their woven colors adding new richness to the gilded carvings, and painted shields hung between them. Hrothulf led the Geats up to their place beside the high seats; Beowulf was brought to sit by the seats of Hrothgar's sons, and Wealhtheow and Freawaru poured out sweet golden mead for their guests. Word of Grendel's death had spread quickly: Beowulf guessed that everyone who dwelt within a day's ride of Heorot had come to gape at the night thurse's arm and share their land frea's gladness. When the thanes and guests were all seated, Hrothgar rose to his feet.

The voice that had cracked with age last night sounded strong and pure through the hall this evening as he called out,

"Now let us bless the gods for their help; let us hail Geofe, goddess of this island, and Scyld Scefing my line father, for their stead is cleansed once more, and the bale from beyond the Middle Garth's walls is slain. Hail to Wodan, who deems life and death in battle, and to Tiw All Meter; hail to Thunar, who wards Godhame as Beowulf has warded Heorot, with mighty struggles against the kin of thurses. Hail to Frea Ing and the Frowe, and to Frige bright: may there be frith and good harvest here now, joy and evening lights burning in this hall, where once there was but cooling blood and Grendel's laughter. You holy ones, gods and alfs, who left Heorot once: now I bid you back with greetings of friendship!"

The Dane king lifted his horn, and all the folk within the hall drank with him. It seemed to Beowulf that a wind stirred the lamp lights, shaking the little flames where they floated mirrored on the golden pools of melting beeswax, but he did not know what that breath betided though the fires burned yet: it was no token of death. Women in dresses of shining white linen filled the horns once more, Wealhtheow and Freawaru pouring at the high table.

Wealhtheow wore a sky blue overdress adorned with card weaving in black silk and white silver, a girdle of gilded plates and garnet set brooches; but all her finery paled beneath the huge collar of gold rings and filigreed figures that rested on her shoulder bones and dipped low over her breast. Yrse had worn such a collar, but it had not been nearly so large or fine: this was a treasure such as might adorn the tree shape of Frige or the Frowe at one of the great hofs. Beowulf could not help being reminded of the mass of amber that Hygd had worn about her neck at their betrothal and of the shining necklaces his bright dream woman had borne.

"Now I call you all to hail Beowulf, Ecgtheow's bairn!" Hrothgar shouted. A great cheer rose up, so that the roof beams seemed to tremble as they had shaken from Grendel's cry; the Danish king had to wait for the noise to die down before he went on. "I am well repaid and more for the day I took in Ecgtheow, coming to me wretched and alone, the Wylfings shaking the bane spear at him across the sea. Then he gave me a gray hound to guard my hall; now, though that brave man lies in his howe, his son has come here as a mightier warder and carried out such a deed as no other man in the Middle Garth might do. Hail to Beowulf, Grendel's bane!"

The tapestries shook and the torch flames bent from the roar of voices; and it seemed to Beowulf that those men who had come with him some of them men who had once been unwilling to see him make their Midsummer's blessing were shouting loudest of all. Unferth, too, lifted up his voice from his stool at Hrothgar's feet, as much gladness on his grim face as on anyone's: it was well with Beowulf, that the thule seemed to bear him no ill will for his harsh words upon their first meeting.

"There is no gift we can give you that will be fair geld for Heorot's freedom, nor, though the coffers of Danish gold were deep and full as those Nerthus owns, could we ever pour out enough to repay you fittingly for what you have done. Yet I would offer you what I can in token of our thanks. Hrethric and Hromund?"

Hrothgar's elder son came forth, bearing a green battle flag embroidered in gold, with a gold boar's head mounted at the top: it showed a shield with two sheaves of wheat crossed beneath it, and it was hemmed with a band of red silk and gold thread woven into holy signs of warding, shield knots and hook crosses shining brightly from the flag's edge. The younger boy carried a helmet crested with a shining wire wound ridge, its sides bright with silver pressed images of warriors wearing boar helms such as those borne by the Geats, and a green shield from which a ring of gilded eagles and boars and fish glimmered brightly. Beowulf opened his mouth to speak, but Hrothgar was calling out again, his voice louder and more piercing.

"Æschere!"

The gray haired thane stepped in through the hall door, reins in his hands. He led in four pairs of matched horses, dappled bay and dappled fallow: Beowulf recognized the mighty steed he had ridden earlier that day, his saddle shining with chip carved mounts, dark garnets and glowing amber and bright polished rounds of berg crystal catching the firelight. Æschere patted the fallow dappled stallion on the neck, saying,

"This was the high battle seat of the king, when the son of Healfdene would dare in sword play never did he fail in wide known battle when the slain fell!"

Smiling, Hrothgar gestured to the battle adornments and the steeds.

"These treasures are yours, and whatever more you should ask. Wield them well, my Beowulf, and have joy of them!"

"I thank you, Hrothgar of the Scyldings, mighty folk king of the Danes. Your gifts gladden me so that I could ask for no more; and yet I was glad enough to have slain Heorot's foe, for my father's sake and for yours."

Next Hrothgar gave treasure to the Geats who had come with Beowulf, rich rings and good swords and spear blades inlaid with silver. When the last man had received his gifts, Hrothgar turned to Beowulf again.

"I would give you geld as well for that thane of yours whom Grendel murdered as he would have done with others, had not the wise gods and Wyrd and your own brave mood stood against him. The Measurer rules all of the kin of men, as she did in this: therefore it is always best to have forethought: much shall be bided, both loved and loathed, if you enjoy this world long in days of striving."

"That is so. And it is kind of you to offer this geld yet Hondscioh had no kin that any man in my hall knew of, nor was he wedded. If you give it, I know not to whom it should be given."

"To you, as his drighten: for you have lost a trusted man."

Beowulf let Hrothgar give him the freely measured rings, for there was no telling him of what had lain behind Hondscioh's coming and little was left of Ecgtheow's hoard: it might be that someday Hondscioh's death would help to buy food or stuffs for the folk of Hroesnabeorh in need, and so be turned to some good. After the gift giving, Hrothgar's poet sang again while they ate and drank, telling the tale of Finn and Hengest the troth and frith sworn between Jutes and Frisians after their battle, the sorrow of Finn's queen Hildeburh at her slain Jutish kinsmen, and Hengest's whiling the winter in his former foe's hall, until at last he raised men and mood again, slaying Finn and carrying home both Frisian treasures and Hildeburh. Though to the Danes it was a joyful song of their kinsmen's triumph, Beowulf found sorrow in it: the words called back the battle at Ravenwood and the following frith too closely.

"Then they pledged trust on the two sides,
fast frith swearings Finn to Hengest,
asked for oaths undisputed the deeds,
that he to the war torn wisely deemed,
holding honors that of heroes none
by words or works would whet on strife..."

Too, the poet sang as one who had seen many bodies of men eaten by fires, and did not hold back from telling of it so as to bring the sight cruelly clear.

"Hildeburh bade on Hnaef's death pyre
her own son be hoisted up
his body to burn on bale fire there
by uncle's shoulder. The idis mourned...
Wended to sky the slain flames greatest,
howled as a howe mound. Heads then melted,
wound gashes burst,blood sprang out of them,
bodies' grievous harms..."

Beowulf was glad enough when the song was done and a horn of mead stilled the poet's voice for a time, so that the gathered folk could talk again. Drink was poured out, mead and strong fruit beer, ale and southern wine; laughter and merriment mounted to the rafters. After a little while, Wealhtheow rose, bearing her glass goblet to Hrothgar, who sat talking with Hrothulf and Unferth. Though the queen's voice was low, Beowulf could make her words out clearly.

"I bring you this cup, my dear drighten, giver of treasures. Be joyful in this hall, gold friend of warriors, and speak loving words to the Geats, as one should do. Be glad of the Geats, mindful of gifts which you have from near and far."

Unferth's eyes narrowed, and Hrothgar looked curiously at his wife, for her words were measured as if she spoke before many folk, though only those closest could hear them.

"Someone said to me that you would have this battle warrior as son. Heorot, this bright ring hall, is cleansed: enjoy many rewards while you may, and leave to your sons folk and realm when you shall go forth to see what is measured for you. I know that kindly Hrothulf will hold these youths with favor, if you, friend of the Scyldings, leave the world before he does; I ween that he will repay our sons with good, if he minds all that we two, by love and by honors, did for his favor earlier in his childhood."

Beowulf looked at the glimmering of the lamp flames in the golden depths of his mead, hoping that none of the Scyldings could tell that he had been listening to them. It troubled him that Wealhtheow could think that he would take the Danish realm from Hrothgar's sons, even should the old king truly wish to give it over into his hands: if, after Hrothgar's death, a grown man were needed to steer the Danes, Beowulf had no doubt that Hrothulf was well able to fill his uncle's seat.

Yet another man in Beowulf's place, having slain Grendel and been greeted as a son by Hrothgar. Beowulf pushed the thought away, gulping down a swallow of mead to wash its taste from his mouth. He was not such a man: and that was what mattered now though he could not know with true sureness whether it was through honor or through the knowledge that he had failed as the drighten of Hroesnabeorh. Though men shouted his name and hailed him as a hero now, slaying Grendel would make him no better at steering a hall, let alone a realm.

When Beowulf looked up, Wealhtheow was standing before him with the glass cup in her hand, the southern wine pooled deep red as a great garnet within. He tried not to start guiltily; though the Danish queen smiled at him, it seemed to him that he could see the anxiousness in her blue gray eyes.

"I bring you this cup in dear friendship, Beowulf Ecgtheow's bairn, slayer of Grendel," Wealtheow said. "We shall ever be grateful to you for your deed here, that has given this hall of the Middle Garth back to men, and freed us from the fear of cruel night death." She gave Beowulf the goblet, and beckoned to Freawaru, whose slender arms were heavily weighted past the elbows with rings of twisted gold; behind her came another woman bearing a cloak of marten fur and a long sark of ruddy silk.

Then the queen reached behind her neck, unfastening the clasps of her great collar so that it swung open on cunningly hidden hinges, and lifted the heavy gold work up to Beowulf.

"Enjoy these rings, dear Beowulf, young man among warriors; make use of this garment, and thrive in these folk treasures. Be known for your strength and give kind rede to these youths," she added, gesturing at her sons. "I shall repay you for it. You have fared so that you shall ever be renowned, far and near, as the sea is ringed by wind garth and cliffs. Atheling, be blessed while you live! I have strewed you fittingly with treasures: be kind to my sons in your deeds, joy holding. Here every earl is true to the other, mild of mood, and good willing to the man drighten the thanes are as one, the folk all ready; the host of warriors for whom I pour drink do as I bid."

Beowulf carefully took the collar from Wealhtheow's hands; it was a wonder that a woman's shoulders could bear its weight through a long feast. His heart swelled with feeling for her, for as her speech came to an end, he could hear the shaking of her voice, and see the look in her eyes shift from anxiousness to something nearer the terrified fury of a mother hare seeing the plough near the burrow where her naked kits curled. Alone of those in the hall, Beowulf understood, Wealhtheow's heart had not been eased by Grendel's death: the thurse's fall had only torn away the overhanging dread of death from her underlying fears, like tearing away a crusted scab to show the bright bleeding wound beneath.

Beowulf would gladly have gone forth to battle a warlike man or another troll for Wealhtheow, but the cruelest thing in her terror was that it stemmed not from any foe, but from her friends terror that Hrothgar would choose to give his realm to a proven man rather than a pair of untried boys; terror that Hrothulf would seek to seize a higher place than that of cousin to the king; and that Beowulf would hold Hrothgar to the word given when the old man had greeted him as a son. Beowulf had not listened to the Scyldings' replies when Wealhtheow brought them her pleading with the frith cup; but at least he could try to ease her for his part.

Thus he answered, "As Hrothgar showed friendship to my father, so I will show the same to his sons, whenever I may. Should they ever seek aid from the Geats' land, I shall give it, gladly standing by the young Scylding rulers.

Open handed queen, I shall bear your treasures with honor, proud to hold such signs of love from the Scyldings' atheling idis. There shall ever be trust and favor staves risted between us." Beowulf bent his neck, that Wealhtheow might fasten the many layered ring on him. But it had been made for a woman: Beowulf's neck was too thick for the collar to close easily about it, and its rim pressed painfully into his shoulder muscles. Instead, he set it on the table before him, letting Freawaru lower her arms so that the rows of gold rings slid over her small hands into a jingling heap, and put one on each of his own wrists before he drank off the cup of wine Wealhtheow had brought him.

Though the southern drink was sharp after the sweet mead, Beowulf could taste the fullness of its fruit, and it seemed to him that the warmth he felt from the draught was mirrored in Wealhtheow's face. The queen found her seat again, and the feasting went on. In time Hrothgar and Wealtheow rose to leave the hall, their children going with them. Most of those who dwelt in the houses around Heorot left as well though some stayed within, as if to simply joy in the understanding of the hall's new safety and those who would sleep there that night began to spread out blankets, finding their places on benches and floor. The evening's drinking had soothed Beowulf's aches and strained muscles, but he was growing sleepy as well, He would have been glad enough to bed down in the straw, but Unferth came to him as he was looking for the blanket that he had left rolled by the wall.

"Guest houses have been readied for you and your men," the thule said. "Grendel is dead, and you have proved your hardiness: you need not sleep in the hall this night."

Weary and sore, Beowulf could not tell if there was any mockery in Unferth's harsh voice. He only nodded, saying,

"We thank you for that."

Unferth led the Geats out. The guest house he showed to Beowulf was warm from a cheerfully burning small fire. A pitcher of ale stood on a table by the bed, together with a bronze bowl of fresh water and a linen washcloth. The bed was soft, covered in fine woven linen and neatly stitched blankets of wool and furs. Beowulf took off his sword belt, hanging it over a carven bedpost, and crawled in: though he had to curl himself tightly so that his feet did not thrust against the wooden foot of the bed's frame, it was easy for him to sleep. Grendel's mother waited outside the wooden palisade until she could hear no more footsteps moving about; then she crept in through the gate, standing in shadow for a while longer until the sounds of snoring began to grate on her ears.

She no longer wept: she had shed all her tears the night before, when she swam up through the mere to find her son's body lying at the water's edge, the light of his eyes quenched and the blood clotting slowly on his torn shoulder. She had carried Grendel down in her arms, as she had borne him when he was but a babe. Though it rent her heart almost past bearing to see her son's swift movement halted, to hear the silence of her stone hall without his brave voice ringing from the walls and worse yet, to think of the long years of stillness ahead, of dwelling in her cave with but her memories of Grendel as mournful comfort she had laid him out upon his bed, dressing him carefully in a soft blue sark with long sleeves to hide his missing arm and adorning him with ornaments of gold and gemstones, the finest work of the dwarves in elder days.

And she had wept bitterly over him; in her anguish, she had cried out as if he were still alive, "My son, my son! You were so strong, so brave, the best of eoten kind born. Why could you not have been content with what you had, with the treasures heaped in our hall, and the wide ring of the sea for your hunting and delight? Cursed be that poet who egged you on to vengeance feud; cursed be the daughter of Ran whose white limbs would not hold you back from your strife!"

Grendel did not answer. Though his mother had lovingly smoothed the twistings of pain from his features and closed his eyes as if lulling him to sleep, the frozen mask of death lay heavy upon his face, and his heart no longer beat with hers, as it had since those days in ages past when she had borne him beneath her girdle. For a long age she had tended Grendel, bringing back fish and deer until he grew large enough to hunt, then spinning and weaving such clothes as he needed, brewing ale and honey mead for his delight, seeing to it that he learned swordplay and song and the tales of their forebears back to Yma.

"Did I fail you in anything, my son?" She had whispered. "How did it come to pass, that you lie here dead, and I yet live?"

Then, when her last burning tears had dried from her cheeks, her anger had settled to a cold stone at the core of the endless aching of her loss. There was no man of their kindred who might avenge Grendel, for his father was long gone. That mighty eoten had been an evening's delight beneath the water, but since she first felt the child quickening in her womb, she had cared for nothing but him for watching him grow clever and strong and bold in the circling years, laughing as he grasped at the glowing trails of the water wyrms and heedless of their snapping teeth. Now all that care was gone for naught, her love and toil laid out still and cold upon his bed. His arm was gone: had the men of Heorot kept it to hang up with their stags' antlers, gloating over Grendel's pain and death?

"Yet where there is no man to lift the bane spear, a woman's hands may wreak revenge," she had whispered to herself. Had not even her kinswoman Scatha clad herself in mail and gone to the garth of the gods, to demand were geld or war for her slain father's sake?

Thus Grendel's mother had put on a dress of deep blue, for her mourning and her killing mood; she had wrought it long ago, with spells much like those she had spun and woven into Grendel's tunic, that would keep any edge of man forged iron from harming her. Though she knew little of swordplay, she had her talons and her teeth, which would serve her well enough against men of the Middle Garth if they tried to hinder her. And when she found her son's slayer among them, she well knew how to wield her broad sax: even stout eoten men had quailed from that weapon in her youth. Though she had no heart to sing the sleep seith she had put upon the men the night before it had failed where it was most needed, anyway it was not too much longer before Grendel's mother knew that all of those within Heorot had sunk to sleep.

She paid no heed to stealth as she strode in. The darkness of the hall offered her eyes no merciful clouding: she could see the glow over Hrothgar's high seat clearly and above it, her son's arm hung in a clumsy sling of blankets, like a head brought back by the hunter to be shown off for a day and then cast into the midden heap. Angrily she sprang over bodies and benches, her taloned feet coming down hard on the soft bodies beneath. Those she trod on shrieked; the others were leaping up, scrabbling in the dark for their sword belts and pawing shields down from the walls. A torch flared at the end of the hall; the cold edge of a sword ripped through her sleeve, stroking harmlessly across her wrist. Blades flashed in the shadows of the torch's wildly wavering light, shields clashing as if the men were battling each other.

Grendel's mother whipped her head about, looking for the one who had slain her son, but she could see him nowhere. One man stood between her and Grendel's arm; she raked out, and a bright arc of blood drops sprayed across a wall tapestry. She had to stretch high to tear down her son's limb, the knotted blankets parting like strands of seaweed beneath her strength. Still the men crowded about her, swords slashing to rend her linen dress to tatters. Clutching Grendel's arm to her breast with one hand, she struck about herself to clear her path. Each blow of her arm shattered a shield, knocking its holders sprawling; some men, wiser or less brave, had caught up spears now, thrusting at her from beyond her reach as she made her way to the door. About to spring out, Grendel's mother halted for a heartbeat. These folk had called forth and guested her son's bane: they should pay some little part of his geld.

A spear drove at her face; as if in a dance, she turned to let it past, grasping the shaft behind the head and yanking suddenly at it. The man who had struck stumbled forward, and she snatched him up, running out into the night. Beowulf woke at daybreak, rising slowly and painfully from his bed. His cramped sleep had stiffened his bruises and strained sinews so that they were worse than before, and he felt himself moving like a very old man as he washed his face and buckled his sword belt about his waist. His head ached a little from the strong drink of Hrothgar's hall, but he knew that would pass quickly enough when he had some food in his belly. When he stepped out, Beowulf saw his thanes also straggling out of the houses where they had slept.

Adhalberht's face was near as green as it had been on shipboard, Swithhelm's freckles stood out against his pale skin like splotches of ale on white wool, and Sicga was rubbing his temples. It was clear to see that none of the Geats had failed to do their best by Hrothgar's hospitality; and though Beowulf had drunk no less than any of his warriors, they lacked the bulk that let him pour down every strong draught offered with no worse than a slightly sore head to show for it. Hroesnabeorh's drighten greeted each of his thanes in turn, waiting until they were all together and had straightened up into something like a troop of men before leading them into Heorot.

Hrothgar, Wealhtheow, Hrothulf, and Unferth were sitting in their places already, though the children were not with them: their faces, too, had the pallor of long feasting. Beowulf walked up to them, trying to keep his stiffness from showing in his movements.

"Greetings, fro and frowe of the Scyldings!" He said. "Did the night grant you good rest?"

The Danish king's eyelids and mouth drooped in sorrow at his words, and a stricken look came over Wealhtheow's face. Struck by sudden worry, Beowulf looked up and saw in horror that Grendel's arm was no longer there, the makeshift slings that had held it hanging in tatters from the roof beams.

"Ask you not after gladness," said Hrothgar heavily. "Sorrow is renewed for the Danish folk. Æschere the elder brother of Yrmenlaf, my rune counselor and my rede bearer, is dead. He was my shoulder companion when we warded our heads in warfare, when battle boars clashed on foot. So should an earl be, an atheling ever good: so Æschere was! A restless slaughter ghast was his hand bane in Heorot: I know where the dire one proudly drew his corpse in full contentment afterwards. She wreaked that feud, for that you slew Grendel violently last night with your hard grasp, since he had too long lessened my folk. He fell guilty in battle; and now another comes, a mighty man scathe, who will avenge her kinsman, coming from afar to return feud or so think many of my thanes, greeting after open handed treasure giver in hard heart sorrow. That hand lies still, that gladly carried out each of your wishes!"

"She?" Beowulf asked, dread thudding hard in his heart. Grendel had cried out Heofonglowe's name in his pain what had passed with the eoten maid after Beowulf left her?

If she had loved Grendel, if she had come to Heorot to avenge him. Give me another to mourn, and end my weeping when you come to me… Beowulf knew that he could never plunge his sword between the white breasts he had stroked in love, yet after slaying Grendel, he could not leave Heorot to another eoten's wrath. Am I to be her geld, for Heorot's sake? The thought both lured and anguished him, as though his heart's hope drew him up the length of a sword. Hrothgar looked at Wealhtheow, then at Unferth. The thule tugged at the narrow plait of his gray beard, his dark eyes closing to slits; but Wealhtheow put her hand upon her husbands. Hrothgar sighed, shifting in his high seat as though the carven wood pressed hurtfully into his aged back. His words came slowly, weighted with shame, as if he were giving up at last a dreadful heart burden to Beowulf's hearing.

"I have heard the land dwellers, my own folk and rede givers in the hall say this before: that they have seen two such great march stalkers holding the moor, ghasts from else whither. One of those was, as they say most surely, like to an idis; the other ill shaped one treading the wretch path was like a man in shape, but greater than any other man. In early days earth dwellers named him Grendel: they knew no father for him, nor if any such dire ghasts were begotten before. They guard a land of wolf hills, windy headlands, and wild fens. There a fell stream falls down under misty heights, a flood beneath the earth. It is not far by mile marches to where that mere stands: over it hang rime frosted bergs, and fast rooted worts over helm the water. There a fearful wonder may be seen by night, fire on the flood.

No man among the bairns of men lives who is so wise that he knows its depths. Even the heath stalking, strong horned stag, fleeing from afar when harried by hounds, would seek the tree holt: he would first give up his life before he willingly hid his head there it is no safe stead! Spume rises up to the sky from that tossing water when the wind stirs hateful weather, until the air drizzles and the heavens weep."

Hrothgar reached forward, clasping Beowulf's hands in one of his own with a drowning tight grip and staring pleadingly up into the Geat's face.

"Now, again, we can find rede in you alone," he whispered. "You know not the lair, that wild place; there you may find that Wyrd burdened wight seek, if you dare. I shall reward you well with wealth, old treasures, as I did before, twist wound gold, if you come away."

Wealhtheow said nothing, but her cloud blue eyes were wide in her pale face, and now and again her glance would flicker to her sons' empty seats. Beowulf could guess what was in the Danish queen's mind: if Hrethric or Hromund had been murdered, would Wealhtheow's heart not yearn for bane blood to slake the burning ache of her mourning? And yet, having slain Heorot's first night terror, they could not let a second take its place: such a feud could only be ended when Grendel's avenger was dead herself.

"No geld is needed between us, for deeds of love are on both sides," Beowulf answered. "Do not sorrow, wise warrior! Better for each that he avenge his friend than that he mourn too greatly. Each of us shall bide to the end in the life of the world, wreak as he may for fair deeming before death: that shall be best afterwards for the lifeless host warrior. Arise, realm's warder, and let us fare at once to scry out the goings of Grendel's kinswoman! I swear it to you: no helming may get her safely away, neither in the earth's embrace, nor in the berg woods, nor in the sea's depths, go where she will! But thole this day whatever woe you must, as I ween you shall."

The men put on their byrnies, and steeds were saddled for them. Beowulf rode the fallow dappled stallion with braided mane that Hrothgar had given him the night before, his saddle rim and bridle flashing bright as sword edges in the sunlight, as though he were a great over king going to guest with another. Beowulf's Geats and a small troop of Danes rode behind Beowulf and Hrothgar. Unferth was there as well, mounted on a dapple gray. The spear in his hand was carved with runes and the shapes of battle birds, all stained red black with blood; Beowulf did not look upon it too long.

The tracks of Grendel's mother were easy to follow, smaller and narrower than Grendel's, but larger than a man's, with the tell tale prints of claws like a wolf's. Splatters of dried blood marked the trail, as if the riders were following a hunt wounded beast. Her spoor led through the woodland, out onto a wet moor overgrown with brown rushes. Even though the day was clear, a light mist hung over the fenland, dimming the Sun's light with chill dankness. The riders traced the tracks of the thurse idis up through steepening stone paths that rose more and more narrowly.

Few of the Danes seemed to have ever passed that way; it was Hrothgar who led them on until at last they came out above the scraggly trees leaning out from a low cliff face where a spume clouded stream tumbled down to froth into the seething black water below. Someone behind Beowulf gasped, and Beowulf heard a faint sound gasp from Hygelac's lips, like stale air hissing out of the lungs of a corpse lifted from its resting place. Beowulf followed the Danish king's gaze, and gulped himself. There on the fell, the gray haired head of Æschere rested propped up on a stone. The thane's mouth gaped as though he were still trying to shriek, but the birds had already been at him.

Æschere's eyesockets gleamed hollow, and watery blood dribbled down his cheeks like tears, wetting his black sodden beard. Below, the dark pool seemed to boil like an iron cauldron, and it seemed to Beowulf that he saw streaks of red gore welling up in the flood. Hrothgar's teeth ground together; then, with a single swift movement, he unslung the war horn from his chest, lifting it to his frost bearded lips and letting fly a loud clear blast that shook the last withered leaves hanging on the twisted tree branches. The riders dismounted, still staring down into the frothing mere. As Beowulf's eyes grew used to the dark rise and fall of the water, he saw that there were things moving in it: wyrm kin of some sort, strange sea drakes sounding, and such nicors as might lie cast up upon headland hills, wyrms and wild beasts watching sorrowful morn tide farings on the sail road.

Hearing the battle horn's song again, the writhing water snakes dropped below suddenly. One of the Danes pressed bow and arrow into Beowulf's hands, as though the man thought the Geat meant to shoot the sea wights. Beowulf had never had luck with a bow, for the staves broke under his strength; but he drew the string lightly back and loosed towards the water. To Beowulf's wonder as much as anyone's, one of the smaller sea drakes rose, pierced through the belly, with the gray fletching standing out clearly against its black hide. It struggled to swim, legs thrashing as though it would flee to the ocean. Whooping and waving barbed boar spears, several of the Danes ran down the narrow fell path, leaning over the water and stabbing towards the wyrm until, as it dived downwards again, a blade pierced and hooked it. It was still struggling sluggishly when they drew it out of the heaving waves, but several more spear thrusts stilled it.

The Geats and the rest of the Danes picked their way more carefully down the stone strewn path, looking at the wyrm in wonder. Its hide was black and scaly as Grendel's; its body was long and snakelike, but its clawed legs were short, and its long snout narrowed sharply as a hunting arrow. Though the sea drake's black eyes were glazed in death, its toothy jaws still moved slightly, opening and closing as if its body still held a faint hope of rending its attackers. Beowulf felt the buckle of his helm to be sure it was strapped tightly, settling his byrnie about his shoulders and touching the hilt of his sword.

"Beowulf," Unferth's harsh voice rasped. "I would have you take this."

The thule had unbuckled his own sword belt, slipping the sheath from it. Beowulf opened his mouth to turn down the offer, for he trusted well enough in his own blade, but Unferth was still speaking.

"This sword is called Hrunting. It is an old heirloom: its edge is iron etched with bale twigs and hardened in heart blood. Never has it weakened in battle for any man who gripped its hilt, nor for he who dared dreadful ventures, faring in army steads; nor is this the first time that it should do brave deeds. And if your own blade be not wrought with great cunning and mighty runes, then it were better that you should take Hrunting, for it may better bite upon the hide of the eoten wife."

"I thank you for that," Beowulf replied, taking off his belt and sliding his own sword free to put Hrunting in its place. "Be sure that I shall wield it well, and bring no shame to him who lent it to me!" He turned to Hrothgar again.

The Danish king was gazing up at him anxiously, with a look that Beowulf knew: though deeper and more filled with dread, it was close kin to the look that came over Sweartwulf's face when he watched Hraefn take a stumbling step proud, yet afraid that his son would fall.

"Now I set my foot to the doing," said Beowulf staunchly; but when he went on, his voice was more gentle for the old man's sake. "Think you now, well famed heir of Healfdene, wise ruler and gold friend of warriors, on what we two have spoken of together: that if I should lose my life for your sake, you were in a father's place to me, the forth gone. Be you a guardian to my young thanes, my hand fellows, if battle takes me; and send on to Hygelac those treasures you gave me, dear Hrothgar. Then may the Geats' drighten, Hrethel's son, know when he stares on those golden smith works that I found a good friend, a breaker of rings fit for warriors' company, while I might enjoy them. And let Unferth have the old treasure, the well adorned and hard edged battle sword: I shall work my doom with Hrunting, or death shall take me!"

Carefully Beowulf folded Hrothgar's shoulders in his embrace. Then, before he could delay or think longer on what he was undertaking, he turned, drawing Hrunting and breathing swift and deep until his head began to swim. Lungs filled to their uttermost depths, Beowulf took three steps and plunged into the seething black water, letting the weight of his byrnie drag him down like a plummeting hawk. Underneath the mere, Beowulf could see nothing.

At every moment he awaited the clamp of toothed jaws upon his body, and kept Unferth's sword moving about himself; but though cold scales, slick over awesome muscles, brushed against him, no fangs assailed him. Still he sank swiftly, until the breath began to burst in his lungs, precious bubbles trickling one by one out of his mouth like southern coins dropping through nerveless fingers. *I was a fool; I shall die here*, Beowulf thought, his heart hammering in his ears. *The mere idis has only to wait for me to drown, and she will be fully avenged for her son why did I not bide my time, to meet her on dry land?*

Though utter darkness cloaked his eyes, Beowulf was beginning to see lightless snowflakes bursting bright red over his sight, his pulse beating hard against his temples and his lungs straining against his ribs in their mindless struggle to draw breath against his will. Then the hands fastened upon him, claws probing at his body: Beowulf could only thank dead Haethcyn, who had ordered that his mail shirt be made thicker than that of other men, that the talons did not slit it open. He was sinking more swiftly now, drawn down as whoever had grasped him the she warg of the depths, it must be she dived towards the mere's hidden roots.

Other things were battering him; jaws tightened about body and limbs, and he heard the water dulled crack of iron links breaking, but yet his byrnie warded him. The breath burst from Beowulf's lungs as his holder flung him sharply down, then swiftly up. He gasped and choked but he was breathing air, rolling over a stone floor beneath a vaulted roof; and beyond him, he saw a fire burning, casting bright light over the hall. Panting desperately, he pushed himself to his feet, tightening his shaking hand on Hrunting's hilt as he faced the black pool from which he had been cast. A woman rose from the pool, water streaming from her long damp darkened hair over her sodden dress.

Beowulf stared at her, his limbs fettered by shock. Save that she was his own height, she might have been any atheling frowe of middle years slim built, though strong shouldered, the youthful beauty of her face whetted down keen and fine by the years like a knife blade worn thin by many sharpenings. Her blue black overdress was pinned at the shoulders with gold mask brooches; on one side of her linked plate girdle, a sphere of silver mounted crystal nestled in the bowl of a silver spoon, and a gold bound knife hung from the other side.

But it was the look on her face that truly halted him: more than murderous fury, it was dreadful anguish and rending sorrow, as though a mortal wound gnawed at her heart; and the rims of her eyes were swollen red from weeping. I slew her son, Beowulf thought, stricken suddenly with guilt. Why should she not? Then Beowulf saw the long keen claws that tipped the mere wife's fingers. Her lips drew back to show pointed teeth, and her blue eyes suddenly flared a baleful cold green that froze Beowulf's bowels within him. He thought of Æschere's head lying eyeless upon the stone, and his will kindled again. She warg of the depths; the words hummed through Beowulf's head as he stepped towards her, swinging Hrunting in a hard stroke at her head. The swords blade rang on her skull like a battle cry, and Grendel's mother grunted softly under the blow; but Hrunting's edge had, after all, failed Beowulf in his need. He did not think more on it, but cast the sword down, knowing that he must trust again in his hand grip's main strength.

Slowed by his long air thirst and the soreness of his battle with her son, Beowulf was not quick enough to fasten his grip on the mere wife's wrist, though she could not dodge his hold and claw him at the same time. But he grasped her shoulder with one hand, digging his fingers in hard and pinning her free arm with the other hand as he forced her towards the floor. Grendel's mother twisted her arm loose again, bending her knees and pushing suddenly forward with her legs. Stunned by the rush of her strength, Beowulf found himself toppling backwards, and was barely able to break his fall well enough to keep his head from striking the stone. The thurse woman leapt upon him, drawing her broad knife and slamming it down at his chest.

Beowulf felt the bruising hard blow as a shock of agony through his battered body; the thick iron byrnie links shrieked as they sprang asunder but the point had not pierced. Beowulf thrust himself up with all his might, heaving to unseat Grendel's mother and rolling out from beneath her in her heartbeat of unbalance. Backing up, he glanced desperately about himself: now she was armed and he was not, and he knew that a second knife stroke would pass easily through the shattered rent in his mail shirt.

Then, between the tapestries and flame glimmering berg crystals, Beowulf saw the great sword hanging on the wall, held there by thin silver chains. Wild with battle grimness, he tore it roughly from the sheath: knowing his death upon him, he angrily launched his life's last blow at the mere wife's wiry neck. The eoten blade broke through her spine's bone rings, slicing through her flesh. Grendel's mother dropped to the floor, her half severed head rolling to the side as dark blood bubbled from her open windpipe.

It seemed to Beowulf that he saw the green bale fire fading from her blue eyes; her lips moved as if she would speak, and though the battle blood was still pounding hot in his head, and he knew that he should strike at the eoten woman again and again until he was sure there was no life left in her body he knelt down beside her to see if he could hear her last words. But no sound came from her lips, and her eyes were already glazing in death. Sighing, Beowulf stood. He remembered then that troll work had put his men to sleep: if Grendel's mother had cast that spell, it were best to finish beheading her, that she never walk again. A single cut did that. The battle over, Beowulf stood and shook. Had there been any more of Grendel's kin in the stone hall, he should have died then: he had no more strength to lift sword or ward himself. But save for the dead, he was alone. After a time, Beowulf gathered himself enough to look around in wonder.

The tapestries on the walls shimmered with bright colour, their stitching so fine that the shapes might almost have been painted onto the woven cloth. The glinting berg crystals he had glimpsed in the battle were clear stone goblets, carved in rainbow catching facets, and a keg of whalebone stood beneath them. There were two great chairs of bone and ivory by the fire, every finger width of their surface carved with coiling and gripping figures done in tiny detail that stood out to the smallest beast's eye pupil. Beside one of the chairs was a basket of soft shining gray wool and a spindle wound with hair thin thread, and by the other was a stack of walrus ivory panels the size of Beowulf's palm, carved by the same craft skilled hand and keen eye that had adorned the chairs though the uppermost plate was only half finished.

The style of the writhing wyrms reminded Beowulf of something; after a moment of thought, he realized that they had been made much in the likeness of the great thrones of Eagor and Ran. Chests stood against the walls, and farther back in the hall, there were two great beds: their arching posts seemed to be ivory tusks, but the beasts from which the tusks had come were greater by far than any walrus of which Beowulf had ever heard, for their broad bases rested on the ground and their tips curled above his head. Silken embroidery sheened the coverlets and on one of the beds lay Grendel, dressed as an atheling, in a deep blue sark from which gold rings and brooches gleamed ruddy rich.

His mother had put his arm carefully back against his shoulder and smoothed the lines of struggle from his face, as any woman might do for a battle slain son. Lying thus, the thurse looked unsettlingly like a man, save for his size and his dark scaled hide. Though Beowulf felt oddly ashamed of the deed, as though he were ransacking a house where he had broken in without right, he lifted each of the chest lids and looked within. Some of them were filled with garments, so cunningly sewn that even when Beowulf stared closely, he could hardly see the seams; others held tools of all sorts, chisels and knives, spindle whorls and loom pieces.

The four largest chests were full of treasures: the well known twists of gold arm rings; brooches set with strange red jewels that glimmered with six armed stars when the firelight struck them; glistening gems of clear white and blue, green and gold; ropes of rough bog darkened amber, leaf shaped bronze daggers with gold wound hilts. There seemed no end to the riches of the eotens. But Beowulf had come as a slayer, and would not leave as a robber: best, he thought, to let Grendel and his mother keep what they had owned.

He did, though, take down one of the rainbow scattering rime chalices, opening the tap of the whalebone keg beneath it. The drink that ran in was a dark red gold, and Beowulf could smell the honey and the strength of it even at arm's length. He was about to drink when he remembered Ansuwulf's words about the wyrm: it is a wight of the worlds beyond, and such things are too strong for the sunlit lands of the children of Ash and Elm to bear. Pulling a hair from his beard, Beowulf lowered it slowly into the crystal goblet. At once the hair singed and sizzled, leaving a small nasty smell in the air.

Very careful not to spill a drop of the eoten draught on his skin, Beowulf put the full rime chalice back where it had been. He picked up Hrunting, sheathing it carefully, then looked again at the sword that had slain Grendel's mother. That, at least, he could take with him: he had wielded it as a war weapon, and felt that he had earned the right to it. Before steeling himself to begin the hard climb to the pool's surface, Beowulf finally lifted the mere wife's body, carrying her over to her own bed. He brought her head over as well, wiping the blood from her face and straightening her hair as best he could drying, it was a rich chestnut color with glints of gold, such as any earthly maid might be proud of.

That done, he looked one more time at Grendel's body. There was something he disliked about it, and not only the manlike shape of the face. Grendel had been dead for two nights, and yet there was no sign of death upon him; and when Beowulf cautiously touched the shoulder beneath the sark, he found that the thurse's mother had carefully sewed the arm back on. And who more likely to walk as a drow than a murderous eoten, who had already been a night haunter in the same stead for twelve years past?

Beowulf hefted the heavy eoten sword it took him two hands to wield it lining up the edge carefully across Grendel's throat, then raising it above his head and bringing it down with all the strength in his back and shoulders. The sword thunked through the thurse's neck, biting deep through coverlet and feather bed, not stopping until it cracked the ivory frame beneath. Then, to Beowulf's wonder, where the thurse's blood had blackened the eoten sword's blade, the metal began to sag and flow, its wyrm weave of light and dark metal running and dripping like ice when Frea Ing unloosed fetters of frost at winter's end, unwinding the frozen wave bonds. Beowulf set the sword down carefully, watching the wave patterns melt, the rippled steel fading into nothingness.

At last nothing was left of the eoten weapon but its gem adorned pommel and hilt. Beowulf waited a little longer to be sure that the gold would not flow away as the iron had, then picked it up, and grasped Grendel's head firmly as well, as final proof of what he had done. There was no more for him to do in Grendel's hall; if the gods let his strength hold long enough for him to swim to the surface in his mail, and the water wyrms did not chew his bones on the way, his deed would be full wrought. The sinking had been bad enough: swimming up was thrice as hard, for the air hoard in his lungs had to fuel the strength of Beowulf's arms and shoulders against the weight of his body and byrnie.

Though Grendel's head also hampered his arms, at least it seemed to float slowly upwards, so that it was no more hindrance than help. The red stars burst over Beowulf's blackened sight again, followed by brightening scatters of white; twice, in his dreadful dizziness, it seemed to him that he had lost his way and was swimming downwards instead of up. With each upwards stroke, try as he might to hold the air in his lungs, a soft grunt of straining broke free of Beowulf's mouth in a little bubble. He could feel the iron dragging on him as heavily as the mere wife's grip. Yet none of the sea drakes neared him, so that he could well have gone without the byrnie: a grim jest of Wyrd, that his breast warding mail might yet be his death.

The lights flashing in Beowulf's eyes grew brighter and brighter, until at last one great burst filled all his sight. Though his arms still flailed above his head, he could no longer feel the water beneath his hands. Now I am dying, Beowulf thought with the last of his awareness as he began to sink and then the water splashed into his face again as he dipped downwards, and he realized that he had broken the surface. Something prodded his side so that he cried out, choking and sputtering on the water rushing into his mouth.

But his hand grabbed tightly, fingers closing on smooth wood: the shaft of a spear. The men hastened to pull Beowulf to shore, dragging him out as he hacked and spat and shivered. Adhalberht unbuckled his helm to free his throat; Eanmund and Sicga lifted his ring broken byrnie off him. Though he had managed to cling to the eoten sword's hilt, somewhere on the way up, Beowulf had let go of Grendel's head. When he looked into the mere again, Beowulf saw his grisly trophy bobbing dark on the sinking swells. He did not need to speak, only pointed: his thanes understood, thrusting their spears out again to bring the thurse's head in to shore like the body of a slain whale. Only then did Beowulf mark that there was no one to be seen at the water's edge save the Geats.

"Where are the Danes?" He asked when his teeth stopped chattering. "Did they wish so little to know whether I had won or lost?"

"Look at the Sun," answered Gudhmund. "You were down there, maybe, longer than you think."

Beowulf blinked: the Sun was no more than a glowing rim of red in the west, hazed by the soft rising mist, while darkness spread slowly up the eastern sky.

"What happened?"

"Everyone thought you were dead," Swithhelm said bluntly.

"We waited and waited, and then the waters suddenly boiled up with blood, and we were sure that you would not come back to us. The Scyldings left at the ninth hour; even Hrothgar left, though he was tearing his beard in sorrow. We only stayed here because we could not bear to come back to the hall and we thought that perhaps some scrap of you might float up, that we could take it home and put it in a howe to bring luck to Hroesnabeorh."

For all the grimness of the red haired thane's words, Beowulf smiled: this was far from his lonely warg wandering at Midsummer, that he be bidden into the land after death. The waves of the black mere had settled now: only the fell stream's falling froth stirred its smooth surface. The sea drakes had all sunken, and again Beowulf remembered something Ansuwulf had said of the wyrm by Whale's Ness: long it sleeps, and stirs only when great things ripple in the Well of Wyrd.

"Take Grendel's head on your spears," he said. "We shall bear our quarry back to Heorot before the Danes have drunken too deeply of my death arvel."

When Beowulf stepped over Heorot's threshold, he saw that as he had guessed the hall was already hung with the deep blue of mourning, and the frea and frowe of the Scyldings wore the same hue. Hrothgar's head was sunken on his chest, so that the king did not see him at first; but Hrothulf's eyes lighted from across the hall. Wealhtheow let out a small stifled shriek, echoed closely by Freawaru's squeal of joy.

Beowulf gestured to the four men bearing Grendel's head, and the Geats all followed him in, marching proudly to stand before the high seats. The hall speech all fell still, save for Hrethric and Hromund, who poked each other and pointed at Beowulf's bloody trophy, murmuring in excitement. Hrothgar's mouth opened; for speech or shock, Beowulf could not tell, but the Geat spoke first.

"Hail, son of Healfdene, ruler of the Scyldings! Gladly have we brought you a sig sign to look upon! I had no soft time of it, clinging to life in battle under the water, struggling hard in that daring work."

Then, as every man and woman in Heorot leaned forward to hear his words, Beowulf told how he had taken the eoten sword from the wall to slay the mere wife, and how the blade had burned away under the bale of Grendel's blood. At last he held up the great golden hilt for all to see, the firelight flashing from red and clear gems as he turned it about before giving it to Hrothgar. The Danish king peered closely at the hilt for a short time.

"This is a great wonder, written here in rune staves. Graven in the gold is the tale of that first of all fights, when Woden and his brothers slew Yma; it tells of how the flood of the old eoten's wound streams overcame all of his children save two, the sea flowing new from Yma's body to drive the thurse kind afar. Thus the staves were set on this hilt, risted for him for whom the sword was worked, the iron blade, wrought hilt, and wyrm adornments first forged."

Hrothgar rose to his feet. "Now one can tell you one who carries forth truth and right among the folk, minding all that is far gone, the old inheritance warder that this earl was born best of all! Be your fame rowned upon wide ways, my friend Beowulf, and among every folk. All that you had to rule, you achieved with mood strong wisdom. As I offered before, as we two spoke, I shall fulfill our friendship. You shall be an easing to your folk in long times yet to come, and a help to heroes most unlike to Heremod, who though he began well, was whelmed by pride and brought ill to his folk, and suffered sorely from slow sorrow in his long struggle."

Then Hrothgar's smile faded as he looked towards the seat that Æschere had held, his gaze flickering towards Grendel's spear mounted head like a snake's tongue tasting the air for danger. He spoke more soberly now; though his voice was still clear and strong, a rueful tang of sorrow muted it.

"It is a wonder how the mighty gods share out wisdom and earth and earlship among the kindreds of men, they who rule all. They may let the mood thoughts of a man of famed kindred wander, grant him the joys of earth in his homestead, and leadership of a warding burg for heroes; let him so rule his part of the world, a wide realm, so that in his unwisdom he may never think on the end. Yet then overweening waxes and writhes within him while his warder, the watcher of the soul, sleeps. That sleep is too fast. Then beneath his helm, a bitter arrow strikes his heart he cannot shelter himself from the strange biddings of his warg ghast, and what he held for long seems too little to him. Niggardly and angry souled, caring not for fame, he gives out no adorned rings, the gifts of the gods to him forgotten and neglected. It often comes to pass when ending staves are risted that the short lived body fails, falls fey: another brave one deals out the unmourned man's treasures, the earl's heirlooms, fearless and uncaring."

Hrothgar took Beowulf's hands in his, the old man's watery eyes gazing up into Beowulf's face.

"Shelter yourself against bale scorn, beloved Beowulf, best of warriors, and choose everlasting redes for yourself. Do not give in to over proud mood, well known champion! Your main strength is famed for a while now, but it may be soon that illness or edge shall hinder your might or fire's grip, or flood's whelming, or the bite of a blade, or a spear's flight, or awful age or eyes' brightness may fade and fail: it may be suddenly, leader of warriors, that death overcomes you. I have ruled the Ring Danes beneath the heavens for an hundred seasons, and by battle cut off many lands throughout the Middle Garth with spear and edge, until I could tell of no one under the skies who sought cause against me. And lo, my turning back came in my own father lands, after joy, when Grendel rose up, striding into what was mine: I bore that guesting with much heart care. Be thanks to the All Measurer, the everlasting drighten, that I came living through, that after old strife my eyes may stare on that battle bloodied head!

Go now to your seat; delight in symbol joy, battle proven man. We shall hold a great many treasures together in the morning."

Beowulf did not miss Wealhtheow's worried glance at her husband before the Danish queen bore her greeting goblet of fruit beer to him. Yet Wealtheow's smile was real enough, as was the tired relief that lit her blue gray eyes like dawn rising behind pale clouds.

"Thanks be to Frea Ing that you live yet!" She said. "There was great sorrow in this hall when Hrothgar told us of the blood on the nicors' mere. You are lucky in your shield fellows, who would hear no word of leaving you, however dire matters seemed."

"I am, indeed," Beowulf agreed solemnly. "But how could I have broken Freawaru's heart by not coming back to bid her farewell?"

Wealhtheow laughed, the sudden bright giggle of a maid. Beowulf realized that she could not be more than ten or twelve winters older than himself: it was only the cares of queenship in Heorot that had hulled her youth beneath graying hairs and aching dignity. Though the feast that night was joyful, it ended far sooner than the last one, for which Beowulf was grateful.

His limbs were beginning to tremble with tiredness, his eyelids drooping, and each small sip of sweet fruit beer seemed to push him farther down into the sinking pit of sleep, so that his eyes were closing even as he made his way to the guest house. Beowulf awoke at dawn to the sound of ravens croaking blithely on the roof.

Again his body was cramping from sleeping in the small bed, but when he had risen and stretched his limbs, he felt far better than he had the day before, though all his bruises were coming to their full brilliance, lurid purples and greens and blues spread over his skin as though he had been playing like a child among dye vats. The sky was brightening swiftly outside, many folk already hurrying over the paths through the settlement. Beowulf hastened to catch up to Unferth: he was already carrying Hrunting.

"I thank you for the loan of this famed weapon, my friend," he said, holding out the sheathed blade across his palms. "No man's sword could have served me more strongly."

Unferth gave him an unfathomable look from beneath hooded eyelids, unfastening his sword belt to slide Beowulf's weapon off and put Hrunting back in its place. "You are a strong souled man, not to speak of the blade's faults," the thule said.

"It has none that I could see, save that the eoten kind were so warded that only their own sword could slay them and you may think it well that it was not Hrunting's metal which melted in the mere troll's blood."

Unferth stared at him a little longer, then slowly nodded. "It may be so. Still, I wish that I could have been of more help to you."

"I am sorry for the words that I spoke to you upon our meeting," added Beowulf in a rush before the thule could turn away from him. "I did not mean for there to be ill will between us."

"There is none. When a man is challenged, whether with weapons or words, there is no blame in it that he wards himself as strongly as he may. Now hasten to the hall, if you will, for it shall gladden Hrothgar to look upon you. And before you fare home, you might do well to ask Wealhtheow for ointment for your bruises, for the wind tossed sea after Winter nights is no place to be wincing in pain whenever you bump into something."

The corner of Unferth's mouth quirked almost into a smile, and he walked on, leaving Beowulf to gape after him. Though it was early in the day, Hrothgar and Wealhtheow sat in their places. Beowulf had to gather his nerves tightly for what he meant to say: he knew that Hrothgar would have him stay until the Danish king's bones were laid in a third howe by the gray shore stone, or at least over the winter; but Beowulf knew that he should not bide in Heorot too much longer, while Hygelac twisted his fingers and looked out from the shore in hopes of seeing his old friend again. Thus, after he had greeted king and queen and spoken with them through the morning meal, trading a few cheerful words with Freawaru, Hromund, and Hrethric Hrothulf had gone back to his place as coast warder Beowulf drew a deep breath and said,

"Now we sea farers from afar would say that we are eager to seek Hygelac. We were treated fittingly, all our wishes attended to, and you dealt well with us. If I may do anything on earth to earn more of your heart love, drighten of warriors, more battle works than I have yet wrought. I am ready at once. If I should hear of it across the ocean's ring, that those bordering you threaten dreadfully, as at times your foes did, I shall bring a thousand thanes, heroes to help you. I know that though he be young, Hygelac Geats' drighten and folk guardian will uphold me in words and works, that I may well honor you and bear my spear shaft to help you; aid to kinsman, where there is need of men. And if the ruler's bairn Hrethric resolves to come to the Geats' hall, he may find many friends there: far known friendship is well sought by him who thinks for himself."

Beowulf grinned encouragingly at Hrethric, seated quietly beside his father. The boy seemed to be a strong atheling bairn, broad shouldered and tall for his age, with sun bleached summer streaks shining almost white in his honey gold hair and a gilded dagger by his side. He sat proudly, straightening his back as Beowulf looked at him; and if he cared more for playing with his brother and Hrothgar's wolf gray hounds than listening to the long speeches of king and warrior well, what atheling of his age did not?

Yet Beowulf understood why Wealhtheow was so fearful for her sons' rights, and why Hrothgar seemed less than sure of the boys he had bred. Though it might be unfair to liken them to a youth of several years older, Beowulf saw in Hrethric and Hromund nothing of the quick cleverness and daring that had marked Hygelac in Beowulf's eyes from the time the two Geats had first met. If he had not known the Danish boys' aeht, he would never, not by sight or by any deeper sense, have taken the Scylding scions for the sons of a king, as Freawaru was in every way the daughter of a great queen.

But Wealhtheow's lips curved in a grateful smile at Beowulf's words, and the disappointment that had drifted across Hrothgar's face like a scattering of snow when Beowulf spoke of his wish to fare home had melted. The king replied strongly,

"The wise drighten sent that word speech to you: I have never heard a warrior sound wiser so young. You are strong in main, and deep in soul, wise in word speaking! I ween that if it goes thus that spear or grim wild battle take Hrethel's heirs, illness or iron the life of your folk guardian, and you have lived through it, that the Sea Geats shall find no better man to choose as any king, hoard warder of heroes if you wish to hold a great realm. Your clear thoughts seem better the longer I hear them, dear Beowulf. You have guided what the folks shall do, Geats and Spear Danes as sibs together: causes of strife, foe like scorn, that dragged out before, rest now. While I wield this wise realm, there shall be treasures held together, many other good greetings over the gannet's bath; ring necked ships shall bring gifts and love tokens over the sea. I know that folk, fast set with foe as with friend, altogether blameless in the old wise."

Hrothgar clapped his hands sharply together, and four thralls heaved a great oaken chest from the floor and carried it over, setting it down at Beowulf's feet.

"Now, my Beowulf, I promised you twisted gold and gifts, and well have you earned them. Though your vow spoke only of Grendel, and that was a mighty enough deed for any, you did not shrink from facing the she warg of the depths. It is my shame that my trust in your might was not great enough, so that I was not there to greet you when you came whole from the waters again: for that, too, I would repay you."

The Danish king rose and lifted the chest's lid himself. Gold glittered ruddy within, rings and chains twining like a nest of fiery wyrms. A smaller box inside held a pitcher and two horn shaped vessels of sea green southern glass swirled about with strands of yellow and blue, carefully packed in wool lest they be jostled in carrying. There were several swords: the iron hilts of some were inlaid with intricate designs of silver and gold, and the finest of them, its blade rippled with light and dark layers as if Beowulf looked down at it through clear wind stirred waters, had a hilt that seemed wholly made of gold, ornamented with swirling beast patterns.

Four stoppered bottles of bright red clay were packed as carefully as the glassware Beowulf guessed that they held southern wine. Folded in the chest was a length of glistening red silk, and at the bottom was an embroidered tapestry, the gleam of gold thread from its uppermost fold letting Beowulf guess that it was the tapestry of Scyld Scefing that had hung in Heorot when first he came there. He was soon proved right: he spoke words of praise for each gift, and when he reached the figured hanging,

Freawaru bounced to her feet, saying, "That is my present for you. And one of Mother's, too, of course. We made it just for you, because I knew you were coming."

Beowulf smiled wholeheartedly at the maiden. While he could not have likened himself to Scyld Scefing, sent over the waters from Godhame and wedded to the land goddess Geofe, still he could admit it without embarrassment now he had truly saved the Danes in their deepest need, and it did not seem too boastful to him to think that Freawaru might have foreseen his guesting at Heorot in some wise. When Beowulf was done admiring his gifts, Hrethric and Hromund got up together, poking each other nervously and giggling before Hrethric spoke.

"We have something for you too, just from us," Hrethric said.

His voice cracked in the middle of his speech, breaking into a sudden low boom, then rising to a maidenly squeak. The two boys giggled wildly again, almost falling about each other, and Hrothgar and Wealhtheow just barely managed to quell their own laughter. Beowulf waited patiently: he remembered, all too clearly, the shame of his voice cords dropping low and splintering high. Hrethric punched his brother lightly in the ribs.

"Where is it?" He whispered.

"You get it," Hromund hissed back.

"No, you."

Hromund ducked behind his father's high seat, coming out with a large covered basket that dripped at one corner. Beowulf heard a high whine from inside, and knew at once what the boys were giving him, but he opened it anyway. A gray puppy, so small that Beowulf could almost have held it on the broad palm of his hand, stood up on its hind legs and scrabbled at the basket as if trying to tip it over. The little hound's ears pricked up eagerly, and its furry tail was curled tight over its back. Its brown eyes were keen and bright as the eyes of a wolf.

"She's Wulfa's great, great granddaughter, and we call her Wulfa as well," Hrethric piped in a sudden rush, as if that news would make all things known. The dog barked in answer, but Beowulf was no wiser than before.

"Maybe he doesn't know who Wulfa was," Freawaru said clearly. "Wulfa was the hound your father gave to our father. Her father was a wolf, and her line are the best of all hunting dogs. We breed them in carefully every other hound age so we don't lose the wolf blood or make them too wild. They are as true as hounds can be, and once you have won their love, you are the heart and soul of their world forever."

Beowulf petted the top of the puppy's head gently with one finger. She wriggled and wagged her tail frantically, almost knocking her basket over.

"Good pup, good girl, little she wolf," Beowulf said to her; and to the boys, "I thank you, young warriors, for this atheling hound. I shall think of you whenever she and I go through the woods of Geatland, and if Frea Ing and the Frowe bless her with children, it may be that someday your bairns and mine shall trade hounds of this line again."

Beowulf stayed and talked with the Scyldings for some time more, but he knew that the sun was riding swiftly up the sky, and the Geats could not hope for as helpful a wind on their homeward faring as they had enjoyed when bound for Heorot.

At last he rose to his feet, beckoning to his thanes.

"Now the time has truly come for me to fare onward. May all the gods and goddesses bless you, beloved ones of the Scylding aeht, holding all of you hale and glad through the days of your life. Good are the treasures you have gifted me with, but better by far is your friendship; and if ever any of you need my aid, may I always be able to help you as well as I did in these nights past."

Hrothgar stretched up to hug Beowulf about the neck, kissing his cheek. Tears rushed down the old king's face, sinking into his white beard like rain into long dry earth. It seemed to Beowulf that he could hear Hrothgar's thoughts as clearly as if the Scylding spoke aloud: I am aged, near to my home faring: I think that we shall never see each other again, when the brave souled ones meet for speech. Beowulf is so dear to me, though I have known him but these few days, that I cannot forbear my breast whelming: the soul bonds are fast on my heart, burning in my blood, knowing that now we must fare our own roads. And for himself, Beowulf felt that he was leaving a father more loving than Ecgtheow, a parting near in sadness to that day when Hrethel turned away from all his living kin. Though he let no tears fall, Beowulf could not speak lest a sob choke him. Wealtheow did not embrace Beowulf, but she quietly poured him a last cup of mead, blessing the draught with all her good wishes for a safe faring and a glad homecoming. But Freawaru did not hold herself back: she hugged Beowulf tightly around one leg, since she could reach no higher, and demanded,

"You shall come back. Shan't you?"

Beowulf coughed his throat clear, answering, "If the gods so will it; for it would be great gladness of mood to me, to see Heorot and my dear friends within once more."

Then Beowulf trod across the grassy ground to where his steeds were saddled. Hrothgar had lent him a wain to bear his goods down to the ship he would have given it gladly, if Beowulf could have gotten it on the boat and steeds so that all of the Geatish thanes could ride to the coast.

"That is a good king!" Said Swithhelm, turning his new ringed arm about to see the gold flash in the sunlight. "I have never heard of anyone so open handed: may all drightens be of his measure!"

"Aye, and they would, if all thanes were like our Beowulf," Adhalberht replied proudly. "But Heorot is a worthy sight, and I am well glad that I set eyes on it. I do not think I shall see its like again until I feast in Waelhall, nor ever look on a drighten with as much wealth to give away as Hrothgar poured out, unless Gundahari and Hagan took Sigifrith's hoard to the green worlds of the gods with them."

The other thanes likewise had nothing but words of praise for Hrothgar. Beowulf voiced his own, often enough, and little Wulfa barked happily from her basket in the wagon whenever she heard him speak, as if she knew her man already. As the Geats rode along the sandy trail down to the barrows, Hrothulf turned from his post on the sea cliff, the sunlight gleaming gold from his helm ridge as he cantered easily down to meet them.

"Farewell, Beowulf," he called. "Farewell, Sicga, Gudmund, Adhalberht..." Though he had spoken little, Hrothulf had learned each of the Geats' names and faces; and Beowulf could not help thinking again that Halga's son would have made a better Scylding king than his cousins, if Wyrd had made it so. "I think you shall be greatly welcome among the Weather Geats, when they see you on the ship in your bright battle hames."

Gudhere lowered a broad plank from the ship, and Hrothulf dismounted to help lead the horses on one by one. The steeds stood trembling and snorting, but calmed when Gudhmund ran a hand down their necks and whispered something in each laid back ear in turn.

"What was that?" Mearewalh asked.

"Something my grandmother told me," Gudhmund said, smiling secretively, but he would say no more of his craft.

When everything had been borne on board except the chest of treasures, Hrothulf offered his arm, and Beowulf clasped his wiry wrist firmly, meeting the stark might of the Scylding's helm shadowed gray eyes without flinching.

"I hope that we shall see each other again," Beowulf said. He had not spoken of Yrse among the Danes save that once to Wealhtheow, not being sure of how they held her. But now it seemed fitting, and he added, "I spent some time with your mother this year. I believe she would be glad of the man you are becoming."

Hrothulf looked sharply up at Beowulf. It seemed to the Geat that, behind the fierce eagerness of the young man's gaze, he could see the shadow of a child weeping, forsaken. Beowulf's mind echoed back to Ecgtheow, and he felt a moment of sorrowful kinship with Hrothulf, aching like linen sliding rough over a wound.

"Was she well?" Hrothulf asked cooly.

"She seemed very well indeed. You may have heard that we stole her away from Upsala, and that is true: but you have my word that we treated her with all honors fitting to a queen and atheling idis, as best we could while fleeing through the woods. And for the most part, as she suffered no ill from me, she repaid me with good."

"I shall fare to Upsala to guest with my mother someday," Hrothulf stated. "Or perhaps, now that Ongentheow is dead and Grendel no longer threatens, the time may come when she fares south to Sealand but I ween that is less likely."

There was a sureness in the Scylding's strong baritone voice that took Beowulf aback: he wondered if he himself sounded like that when he spoke of what should come to be. He had never heard anything said of Scyld's mother, and little of Yrse's save for the ill she had done to Halga; but it seemed to Beowulf that a strand of strangeness ran strongly through all the bairns of Hrothgar's elder brother. So thinking, Beowulf found that words were pouring from his mouth again without his will.

"If you fare to Upsala, you shall need a good sword, and a strong shoulder companion by your side to wield it."

Moving as if in a dream, his body hardly guided by his will, Beowulf unlocked the chest that Hrothgar had given him, reaching down to pull out the gold hilted sword.

"Take this blade: use it well while it is in your hands, and gift it only to one who is worthy of it though his worth may not be seen until he grasps the glittering hilt, his gold hidden beneath grimy rags."

Hrothulf took the gold gripped weapon, staring down at it in wonder. "This is a fair gift, and I thank you. I shall not forget what you have said. Now fare you well, Beowulf. Should we never meet again, you have already risted a good stave into my Wyrd."

The young Scylding turned before Beowulf could speak again, vaulting easily up to the back of his black maned dun. Though the blunted silver spikes of Hrothulf's heel spurs brushed the horse's sides as lightly as a breath of wind, the steed sprang at once into a canter, plunging up the sandy trail to the sea cliff's low crest.

Beowulf stood there between sea and green earth for a few moments, looking at the twin barrows of Beaw and Healfdene, with the gray stone pillar rising tall between them like a hoar frosted beacon, a sign to seafarers from afar. A strange twist of longing turned over in his breast, though he could not have said what he felt himself yearning towards, nor why. Yet he had slain Grendel, and freed Heorot from the eoten kin: that was enough. Beowulf squatted down, lifting the chest carefully to one shoulder. The gangplank creaked and groaned beneath his weight, bowing alarmingly, but it held fast.

"Cast off?" Gudhere asked.

"Cast off," Beowulf echoed firmly.

The anchor was drawn up, and the crewmen went over the sides, putting their shoulders to the ship and plodding hard until their craft broke free of the sand, the waves lifting her on. Back to Hygelac, back to Geatland, back to whatever deeming should await Grendel's Bane.

IX

The sail billowed like a white sea garment from the mast of Beowulf's ship; a mane of white spray curled away from the long neck of its ring coiled prow. More used to sailing than he had been when he set forth, Beowulf did not worry at the sounds of the planks creaking under the driving wind and wave, the long staves moving easily as the sinews of a running horse. Pale streamers of clouds skimmed over the sky, as though the tall mast clove the air into foam above as the keel clove it below. For a few hours the puppy Hrothgar's sons had given to Beowulf had hidden shaking beneath his cloak; now she lay happily in his arms, her pointed black nose sniffing the sea air and her thick furred tail curled over her back. She seemed a strong and fine houndlet, but there was something about her that disquieted him, an echo of memory like the flavor of an herb in mead that he had not tasted for many years had thought to give Berki a puppy of that line.

Ecgtheow's voice seemed to rumble in the back of his skull words from the day his father had brought him to Hrethel's hall, when Ecgtheow still seemed to have hope, and love, for his son. Berki had never been given that puppy; now a shudder slithered quick as a grass snake down the back of his spine. My father's forgiveness, at last? Beowulf wondered, stroking the little hound's silk soft ear points as she wagged her curled tail. Yet he could not forget the grim gleam of the howe fire in Ecgtheow's eyes as the dead man spoke from his high seat: it seemed past believing, that the old berserk's cold grasp should have loosened to give his son that gift from beyond the grave. Or is it only that Wyrd coils on herself like a wyrm in the Well's depths, that the father's gift come back thus to his son when the old geld is paid?

Beowulf touched the long oval of amber at his throat, the golden sea stone warm between the cool points of silver that tipped it the gift Ran's daughter had given back to him when he forsook her; it seemed that the pattern of giving and returning mazed his mind as staring at the coiling patterns of beasts twining over wood or graven metal for long would maze the eye. The ship sped swiftly on, unhindered by any foul wind or false current. Smooth as the journey to Sealand had been, the faring back to the burg of the Geats was faster yet: it was mid morning of the second day when Beowulf saw the ruddy crag of Whale's Ness jutting into the sea, and the winter sunlight gleaming bright as ice from the helm of the watcher upon the cliff. Osric came up to Beowulf with a gold bound blowing horn one of Hrothgar's gifts in his hand.

"Will you hail him, that Hygelac may make ready his hall to receive us?" The thane asked, grinning up at Beowulf. Beowulf took the horn from his man, lifting its mouthpiece to his lips. The low note boomed out across the sea like the singing of a whale; the watcher's spear point lifted, then lowered, and he raised his hand in friendship for even so far away, he could not help but notice that the horn blower over topped the men about him by a head and a hand span.

By the time Beowulf's ship had rounded Whale's Ness, a band of men stood on the snow dusted beach to welcome them, calling distance blurred greetings. Beowulf blinked in bewilderment: for a moment, the memory choked him like a salty mouthful of seawater, his tormentors standing there, shouting taunts of cowardice after him as he swam where they could not follow, but now he was drawing towards them, not away, and their hands were raised in welcome, with banners shining where sticks and rocks had been uplifted.

I could not have dreamed this: how has it come to pass? The tide was out; Beowulf's ship drove in towards the beach until its keel grated against the sand. At once men ran into the water with anchor hawsers to tie her firmly, splashing shivering out again as quickly as they could, and the steersman Gudhere directed that the planks be lowered. Gudhmund led the horses off as he had led them on, whispering in their ears to calm them; Beowulf heard the soft gasps at the steeds' beauty and that of the rich gold mounted trappings they bore, while his thanes, their gilded helms and gold arm rings shining ruddy in the sunlight, carried off the chests that held Hrothgar's other gifts to their drighten. Eofor and Ansuwulf stood waiting on the beach.

Eofor was thickly wrapped in a fur lined cloak, its red hood hiding his ruddy hair; but Ansuwulf, as always, was bare footed with no more to warm him against the freezing winter sunlight than the wolf pelt hanging over his shoulders. The berserk's sharp nose tilted as if to catch Beowulf's scent; then the two brothers stepped forward together.

"Hail, Beowulf!" Ansuwulf said. "I see that you come sig blessed no, say no more of it now, for Hygelac waits your coming in his hall, and it would weary you too greatly to tell such a tale twice. Come, then, and gladden the heart of your kinsman, that was so heavy in his breast until now!"

They climbed up the slope towards the Swertings' hall, Beowulf's men following behind him and his little hound trotting close to his feet. None of Hygelac's men pressed too close; but Beowulf could see the awe in their wide eyes as they stared up at him, not daring to speak. The winter dry grass, dusted with a scattering of snow, glittered keenly about the sunlit path; the wind was sharpening, and though only a high faint veil of cloud misted the blue sky, it seemed to Beowulf that he could smell more snow on the wind. As they entered the Swertings' garth, Gudhmund would have turned aside with the string of horses, but Beowulf gestured to him to follow.

Inside Hygelac's hall, though it was full daylight, the fires all roared high, and tallow flames flickered from the black bowl lamps that stood on twisted spikes driven into the earthen floor, like iron flowers from Eoten Home. Fresh straw covered the floor, and the tables gleamed as though they had just been rubbed with beeswax; pitchers of mead stood ready, covered with shining cloths of white linen to keep out flies and dust. Hygelac and Hygd were seated in their high seats: Hygelac sat straight backed and bright eyed, though it seemed to Beowulf that he could almost see his kinsman's eagerness crackling like tiny lightning sparks through his loose cloud of golden hair, but Hygd's green over gown flowed softly from the curve of her burdened belly to the floor, and a look of wonder shimmered over her delicate face, as though Beowulf were looking at her through clear water.

The gold bound aurochs horn lay on the table before her; slowly she rose, pouring it full of golden mead from her silver pitcher, and trod around to lift it to Beowulf. For a moment their hands touched on the smooth polished curve, her fingers small and frail as a brush of warm spiderweb, and Beowulf looked down into her violet eyes. My fame came too late, he thought bitterly. He knew every strand and fire gleaming pendant of amber about her neck: Hygd was wearing all the gifts he had given her at each Midsummer's Thing, the almost tokens of betrothal his plump hands had put into hers. If only.

"Welcome, Berki, and thrice welcome," Hygd said to him, her voice trembling and her eyes darkening like a cloud about to drop its weight of rain. "There were few days sadder in this hall than the one when you left us; there have been none gladder than this your homecoming. By this draught I bear you, may there ever be such joy between you and us here!"

Tongue tied, Beowulf lifted the horn: large as it was, he drained it in a single great draught, unwilling to let the least drop of Hygd's sweet blessing escape him. Only then could he find the words to answer her:

"Hail to you, fair bride of the Swertings, and to my dear kinsman Hygelac!"

Hygelac grinned down at him, white teeth flashing in his golden beard. "As my frowe says, you are thrice welcome here: sister son, oath brother, and true friend whom I had feared I should never see in the Middle Garth again. Sit down, you who have come safe from strife, and tell me: what befell you on the way, beloved Berki, when you fared forth over salt water to seek battle in Heorot? Did you better well known Hrothgar's wide famed woes?" The young king leaned forward, his blue eyes fixing on Beowulf in earnest and his voice dropping. "I was long whelmed by sorrow and care of mood, for I had no hope in my dear kinsman's journey; I had begged you not to meet that murderous guest, but let the South Danes themselves battle with Grendel. Thanks be to the gods that I see you well now!"

"That meeting is not secret, Hygelac, my drighten what happened on that field between myself and Grendel, where he had wrought so many sorrowful things for the Sig Scyldings. I avenged all of it. First I came to that ring hall to greet Hrothgar; Halfdan's famous kinsman set me with his own sons when he knew my thoughts. And the folks' peace bond, that well known queen, passed through the hall, urging the youths onward; sometimes Hrothgar's daughter, whom I heard the men on the benches name Freawaru, brought the ale pitcher to the earls."

Hygd raised a white fair eyebrow, an inquiring look on her face, and Beowulf thought of what else he had heard of Freawaru; it would be good for the king and queen of the Geats to know how the alliances would lie.

"She, young and gold adorned, is promised to the glad son of Frodha, Ingeld; the friend of the Scyldings and realm's warder had set that before, and counts that good rede, that he deal with slaughter feuds and settle causes by means of that wife. Yet..." A
s Beowulf spoke, it seemed to him that his tongue were growing numb as if he had set it to a deadly fronded leaf of Tiw's Helm; the faces of Hygd and Hygelac blurred in his sight, and the words spilled out from his mouth as though his soul were an over filled pitcher.

"The folk ruler of the Heathobards, and the thanes of that folk, may think it ill when he treads the boards with that fair one Danish youths weened worthy of high praise, the hard, ring adorned blades which once the Heathobards wielded gleaming at their sides until they were led to destruction at shield play, themselves and their battle mates."

It seemed to Beowulf now that he could see the figure looming in the hall a grim eoten tall man, gray bearded and grievously scarred with the marks of many blades, his eyes gleaming like bitter spear tips lifted in anger, and Woden's iron pointed shaft standing cold as ice in his battered hand. Starchath, Beowulf thought, but he would not speak the name aloud, no more than a mountain herder would speak a troll's name after dusk.

Starchath was a storm crow, bound to the Middle Garth by only the thinnest threads, and his coming betided only ill: it had not been said in Frodha's favor that the old warrior had been one of his most trusted rede givers.

"Then the old ash warrior, who remembers all, shall speak over beer when he sees the rings, grim of thought: 'My friend, can you recognize the blade which your father bore to battle beneath his war mask, when the Danes, the Scyldings, slew him in his last fight? Now some bairn of his bane goes decked out and rejoicing through the hall, boasting of the murder and bearing that treasure which you should hold by right.' Many times he reminds him with sore words, until that time comes when the fair one's thane for his father's guilt falls from the blade's bite, bedecked with blood, and his foe flees the land. Then the oaths of earls shall be broken on both sides; slaughter hate shall well up in Ingeld, and his love for his wife shall cool in his seething sorrow. Hence I do not count the dealings of Heathobards and Danes trothful: a friendship unfast."

His own words no longer sounded in his ears; Beowulf fell silent, his heart a weighty ache within his ribs. He knew that he had spoken truth, and already he grieved; he had not wished to foresee such ill for the queenly little Freawaru, who had greeted him with such gladness and trust. Have her kin not suffered enough, that she must go to a sorrowful wedding? He wondered. And he wondered as well Starchath came of eoten blood: was this doom in some way vengeance for Grendel, some last echo of the feud between the blood of Yma and the blood of the gods? Or was the hand of strife stirring Woden in the matter, who would not suffer frith to last too long?

"That is sad news," Hygd murmured, her pale brows drawing together.

Hygelac nodded. "The Heathobards will bear watching: I had heard before that Ingeld is rash of mood." Then he smiled again. "But you have better to tell us, my Berki. What of your battle with Grendel: how did it come to pass, that you slew a foe upon whom no iron would bite?"

Beowulf returned his kinsman's smile, for Hygelac's brightness, as often before, was already lifting his own heart, and the gloom of his fore speech tattered like sea mist before a strong wind as its sureness thankfully, this once faded from him.

"Aye, I shall speak further of Grendel..."

He told Hygelac and Hygd all that had come to pass: of Hondscioh's death, of how he had grappled with the water thurse within the hall, of how Grendel's mother had come to avenge her son, and how he had sought her out beneath her dark tarn. Hygelac listened wide eyed, his lips half parted in wonder; Beowulf could see the muscles straining over his king's wiry shoulders, as though Hygelac mirrored his kinsman's striving in his mind. He would have been there with me, if he could: his heart still hungers for great deeds, Beowulf thought, and did not know why the thought troubled him so. Hygd's delicate face paled as Beowulf spoke; perhaps she could see his perils clearly as she heard of them, made real at last after the long days of wondering.

Only a few things Beowulf did not speak of: he did not mention his flyting with Unferth, for the thule's rude greeting brought no good fame to Hrothgar's hall, and he could not bring himself to tell of how Grendel's mother had laid her son out on his bed, clothed like an atheling for his death faring, but turned instead to praising Hrothgar.

"Thus the folk king lived his thews: I lost nothing of the gifts offered, but he gave me treasures which I would bring to you, my king, for I have few kinsmen left save you."

Beowulf gestured to Osric and Adalberht, who brought forth the gifts Beowulf had chosen for Hygelac: the Scylding battle standard, boar's head shining gold above the shield and sheaf embroidered cloth; the helm glistening with pressed plates of silver showing armed men between its gilded bindings, a fine linked gray byrnie scoured to shimmering brightness, and a long gold hilted sword wrought in layered steel, so that even in the hall's light, the wavering lines of light and dark metal gleamed as it moved like tiny wyrms writhing up and down its length.

"Hrothgar gave me this battle garb; the wise leader spoke some words, that I should tell of the gifts. They were first owned by his elder brother, Heregar the king; the Scyldings' leader had it a long while; yet he would not leave the breast warder to his own son Hereward, dear though he was. Enjoy all well!"

Before Hygelac could open his mouth in thanks, Beowulf waved to Gudhmund, who stood at the hall's open door with his string of horses, and the thane led in the four fallow dappled steeds the best of those Hrothgar had given, as was fitting for a gift to a king. Their gilded bridle mounts scattered bright sparks of light as they lifted their heads and tossed their manes, polished hooves pawing at the fresh straw on the hall's floor.

"These, too, I would give to you, as you once gave me strong steeds to bear my weight when I rode to Upsala. My mother's brother and my oath brother, hardy in battle, so may we ever keep trust together." Lastly, Beowulf gestured red haired Swithhelm forward, opening the chest in his thane's arms and lifting out the heavy collar of ringed and figure wrought gold that Wealhtheow had given him.

"Hygd," he said, looking up into her violet eyes. "The good queen Wealhtheow, open handed atheling woman, gave me this. But it is too fine to be hidden beneath a man's beard; rather, it were better to adorn the Swertings' gem with it as she deserves. Wear it in joy, necklace Frowe, when you pour drink for the athelings at feast…" Remember that I love you, Beowulf thought: but those words he could not speak aloud, and his tongue failed him. But Hygd took the great collar in her hands, tears gleaming in her eyes as she gazed at the tiny filigreed masks and animals between the coils of wire wrapped gold.

"Your safe home coming would have been gift enough for us," she murmured. "Berki, whatever we have offered you. You have given us more in turn: I am whelmed beyond speech." Her tears brimmed, spilling over from the great dark pools of her eyes, and she did not bother to whisk them away.

Hygelac drew himself up, sitting straight and golden, and called out, "Now bring me my father's sword! Aye, fair are the gifts you have brought from Hrothgar's hall, but greater still is the gift of fame you have brought to the line of the Swertings, that shall not fade while the worlds stand. Berki, you swore your oath to me at your father's holding, and well you kept it as drighten of Hroesnabeorh. Now I would not take your udal lands from you, but rather I would offer you more, my kinsman. Those lands and halls that were given to me once as Hrethel's son, I now bestow upon you; I would not be so far parted from you as we were, but have you dwell close by, in the honor which is twice yours, by blood and by deed."

Ansuwulf set Hrethel's ring hilted sword in the Geat king's hands, and Beowulf put his own hands over Hygelac's, swearing his troth once more. The hall rang with cheers as he took his place beside his king, and Hygd rose to refill his horn. The relief he felt, understanding at last what Hygelac's words would mean to him, was so vast it was almost numbing: he would not have to go back to Hroesnabeorh, where though men would speak well instead of ill of him now he would be set apart more than ever by his deed, and he would never again have to sit in the high seat that would still and always, even if Ecgtheow rested in his death at last, be chilled for him by the touch of his father's ghost. Bread and cheese were brought in, fresh roasted sausages with clear droplets of fat dripping from their brown skins and sizzling black blood sausages. Beowulf's puppy barked and stood on her hind legs with her forepaws braced against his shin, looking up hopefully, and he laughed and passed down a piece of meat for her to growl over and tear at.

"That has the look of one of your father's hounds," Hygelac said. "How did you come by it? I had thought that the line had died out."

"Hrothgar had a bitch of that breeding as my father's gift, and the Scyldings kept the wolf blood carefully. She was given me by Hrethric and Hromund."

"An atheling gift from a pair of princes," Hygelac approved. "Tell me, what do you think of the young Scyldings? Do they show the soul of their own line yet?"

Beowulf frowned. This, too, he had carefully avoided speaking of: how Hrothgar had all but offered him rulership over the Danes, how Wealhtheow had run about anxiously like a mother bird luring the hunter away from her nest with one eye upon Beowulf himself, and the other, it seemed, upon Hrothulf, who showed every sign of kingly birth that his cousins lacked. After all Hrothgar had lavished upon him, and all Wealhtheow's praise and fair greetings, it seemed a betrayal to speak his doubt about the young Scyldings; yet Hygelac would have to deal with the Danes whatever came to pass, and Beowulf could not leave his king unknowing.

"They are yet very young," Beowulf answered. "And Hrothulf is of a man's years, with, I think, great strength within him, though he is thin as a tree branch and small of growth. I fear that it is not only from the Heathobards that the Scyldings shall know strife in times to come, for it is in my mind that Hrothulf inherited more from his mother than slender bones and gray eyes."

Hygelac sighed. "And if that should come to pass. What oaths..?"

"I swore that I should ever be friend and helper to Hrothgar's sons, and if they call on me for aid, then I shall give it. Yet I do not think Wyrd has so shown it that I shall ever strive against Hrothulf."

They sat in silence a moment, until Hygd's clear voice broke in, "Berki, do you know yet what your will for Hroesnabeorh is?"

"I left it in the hands of my friend Sweartwulf, for he is a strong and trusty man, and his wife Frithugeard is wise. If they will hold it, I can think of none better to ward our march against the Swedes, and their son Hraefn after them. But as for me, it may be that I shall find more joy close by to the hall of my kin."

"I hope it is so!" Hygelac said heartily. "Now, tell me more of Grendel if only I had been there beside you!"

The longing in his voice was keen as a spear tip, and again Beowulf thought of the boy he had first met, gazing at the cloud tattered winter sky in hopes of seeing the shape of the war boding mound ghost darkening the stars. But maybe it would be enough for Hygelac to have heard Beowulf's tale, lifting him out of the daily round of his duties as king and drighten; maybe that would calm the Geat king's fierce young heart, so that he would not long to dare needless danger for himself, or bring it upon his folk.

The feast for Beowulf's homecoming lasted nine days; though Winter nights was not long past, Hygelac and Hygd led another blessing in the holy grove, and it fell to Beowulf to wield the stunning hammer that the great boar the best of Hygelac's herd be dropped without pain or fear. Hygelac cut the boar's throat, and Hygd caught the red flow in a rime bright silver bowl, casting the hot blood about the ring of athelings and thanes with a juniper twig, while Wulfa, at Beowulf's side, looked up and licked her chops hopefully.

The sprinkles fell warm as tears upon Beowulf's face; when the queen emptied her bowl upon the holy white stone, steam rose from the blood as if its brightness were true fire, melting through the thin crust of ice and snow to warm the boulder beneath. A life in thanks for my life, Frea Ing, my friend, Beowulf murmured. If there was ever any breach between us, for that I aided in breaking your holy frith in Upsala, it is paid for and healed in full now: I freed your kinsman's hall. But he did not look up at the great yew tree where the ice shrouded tatter of rotten rope hung: if he were quits with Ecgtheow as he surely must now be he needed not, nor wished, any word from the dead man to seal the bargain.

The doors of the Swertings' hall were wide open to all comers, and as the news of Beowulf's deed spread, there were many who wandered by to share in the Geat king's ale and stare in wonder at the man who had done what no other man within the Middle Garth's ring might do. Among them, to Beowulf's little surprise, was Guthlaf the Peddler, his battered and broken nosed face freshly marred by the shiny pink patch of a scar where a finger's length of skin and beard had been sliced from his left cheek.

"Wyrd works in strange ways, does she not?" The ugly trader said to Beowulf when Hygd had greeted him, wiping the froth from his beard and drinking deeply again. "If the years do not lie to my mind, it was I who first brought word of Grendel in Heorot to the Swertings' hall; I remember then that you carried a full keg of mead which would have weighted a grown man, though you were but seven winters old, and I knew that there was great might in you. But though I knew the strength of the Waegmunding line well, I had thought that it would be your father, not yourself, who went to meet Grendel at last. Still, many a man has looked at a young cub and not guessed the great bear that it would become. And you still wear the amber you bought from me then: that was a good bargain for you. Though I see that the other pieces you had of me later adorn the throat of the Geat queen beneath her collar and that, men say, you gifted to her as well. If you mean to do as well by your own hall frowe, now, I have a few rare pieces of amber and gold left; though much of my stock was sold this summer, these are treasures meant for the highest of athelings..."

I gifted amber to but one other, and she and I are sundered, Beowulf thought. He did not know what showed on his face, but Guthlaf paled suddenly, drawing back, and a wave of sickness washed through Beowulf at the other man's look of fear.

"Forgive me if I misspoke!" The peddler gibbered.

Beowulf shook his head, breathing deeply as if it would ease the tight bands of his ribs from crushing in around his heart. "Nay, I mean no ill towards you," he said as gently as he could.

"I have no hall frowe as yet; I think your treasures were better shown to Hygelac and Hygd, for they will glean more joy of the Welsh grain than I." Think on that, if you meant to bring word back to Othere that there was aught amiss within the Swertings' household. "But now you will have a better tale to tell all those who host you in your wanderings than was the news of Grendel which you gave us those years ago, if you will listen..." And bring the tale to the Swedes, that they remember it if the thought of oath breaking should ever cross Onela's mind. Though I shall dwell here while I may, if there is slaughter around Hroesnabeorh again, it will be Grendel's Bane who comes to collect the were gild for it but far better still if knowledge of my strength serves to hold the Inglings back, and keep the frith between us whole.

Sweartwulf and Frithugeard came to the feasting as well; little Hraefn was toddling now, and gleefully rolled on a lynx skin rug with Hygelac's daughter Hildegeard, pulling at Wulfa's tail and ears until she ran away.

"You will not be rolling in the furs with young maidens under their parents' eyes for too many more years," Sweartwulf said sternly to his son as Hygd and Hygelac laughed. "Best to enjoy it while you can."

The half Finn and his wife were downcast to hear that Beowulf would not come back as drighten of Hroesnabeorh, but could not deny that Beowulf's place now was in the Geat king's hall.

"Yet we shall come to see you as often as we may," Frithugeard promised.

"Aye, and we shall hold your father's stead safe for you," added Sweartwulf. "While we live, you may be sure of that."

"I have never doubted it for a heartbeat, my true friends," Beowulf replied, folding both of them into his embrace. "Rule Hroesnabeorh as you will, and may you ever have joy of it."

The winter passed quietly, deep in snow and darkness, though it seemed to Beowulf that more guests came to the Swertings' hall at Yule time than he remembered, bronze bridle rangles ringing endlessly through the icy air. Hygd's belly swelled and ripened beneath the thick furs of bear and lynx, though as the end of her term neared, her face began to look drawn and gaunt, her violet eyes shining huge from the dark flesh pooled in their sockets. Though Beowulf knew it was not a man's part to think on such things, at last he found the courage to approach Wynefrith as she walked to the storehouses and ask her,

"Is Hygd well?"

The king's mother paused, considering as the snowflakes settled white upon the thick red wool of her hood, melting slowly beneath her breath from the shiny brown beaver fur that lined it. "Bearing is often hard for small built women," Wynefrith replied at last. "Yet she is having an easier time of it now than when she carried Hildegeard, for all it is said that sons are a greater burden to a woman than daughters. And last summer was a rich one: Hygd does not lack for food, which is the worst ill a bearing woman may thole in winter. You have no more need to fear for her than for any woman in childbirth: what becomes of her then shall be as Wyrd has said it, even as is the case for any man going into battle."

Little as he liked it, Beowulf had to be content with that. Hygd's son was born towards the end of the winter, when, though the days were swiftly lengthening, the cold gripped hardest: he and Hygelac sat in the hall with their mead beakers all that night, the honey drink flowing chill from the silver pitcher in spite of the fires that burned about them, until the hall door opened to the ice pale light of dawn and Wynefrith came in.

"What news?" Hygelac asked, the slurring dropping from his voice beneath its sharp urgency. "How fares my wife?"

"Hygd is well, though worn from labor. And my son, you have a son!"

Hygelac sprang to his feet, Beowulf not far behind him. "I will see him now!"

"You will not," Wynefrith answered firmly. "Be sure, your son is strong and healthy: if no unforeseen ill befalls him, he shall live and thrive. But mother and child are resting, and you should be as well: often, however hard the struggle, it is worse to wait than to do."

After nine days, when it was sure that the child would live and be strong, Hygelac sprinkled his son's head with water in the holy grove, and gave him the name Heardred. The infant wailed fiercely as the icy drops touched him, thrashing in his soft lambskin blanket, and Hygelac laughed.

"There is a warrior soul in the bairn!" He said. "Surely the Swertings' aeht will grow and thrive, with such a strong branch new sprung from it."

The Geat king glanced up at Beowulf as though he were waiting for his kinsman to speak. But for once, no words came unbidden to Beowulf's tongue, no foresight glimmered before his eyes: he might as well have been staring at a wall of dry laid stones, and he did not know if that were some kindness of Wyrd, or what. Still, Heardred grew swiftly; before the end of his fourth summer, his small hands were eager for the hilts of the little wooden blades his father and Beowulf carved for him, and where his older sister Hildegeard already spun fine bright threads for embroidery with her tiny spindle, hardly ever lumping or breaking the wool, Heardred went about with a kitchen knife thrust through his belt like a sword.

He sought to ride Beowulf's wolf dog now a fierce huntress in her prime and the mother of several litters of puppies like a horse; but wild as Wulfa was with elk and deer, when Heardred climbed up on her back and pulled at her ears, she merely sat down quietly and closed her eyes to keep his fingers out of them, thumping her thick curly tail on the ground. At five summers, Beowulf and Hygelac set Heardred up on Feola's back: the golden gelding's manners had only grown more placid with age, and he was content to walk slowly around the meadow, ignoring the beating of the boy's heels against his plump sides.

As for Beowulf though sometimes a longing that he could not ignore came over him in the night, a longing that he could not still except by going down to Whales' Ness and plunging naked into the waves, matching his strength against the sea until the water cold numbed his hands and feet and his great limbs shook with tiredness, he never spoke of it with Hygd: he would not shatter the bonds that held their family together. And, in truth, it often seemed to Beowulf almost as if Heardred were his own son: for the most part, he was content. He mourned when he heard of Hrothgar's death, but not over much, for the Scylding king had been old; and as the tale was told, he had died content in the freedom of his hall. Then more sorrowful news came up from the south: the fore speaking that had come unwillingly to Beowulf's lips when he spoke of Freawaru's wedding had come to pass.

Starchath had come back to Ingeld's hall, as Beowulf had foreseen, and egged his old friend's son to bloodshed: there was feud between the Heathobards and the Scyldings; Heorot burned, and Hrothgar's youngest son Hromund was slain. Yet the Scyldings answered that with strong swords, and did not need to call for aid, and for a time all was quiet again. Othere held to his vow as those years passed. Now and again, a rumour came to the Swertings that there might be trouble, but no fire ever sprang up along the march halls' roofs in the night, nor was the clashing of swords and booming of shields heard where the realm of the Swedes met the realm of the Geats. Heardred was in his ninth summer when Guthlaf the Peddler brought Hygelac the news that Yrse had married Onela, brother of the king of the Swedes' realm.

"How can that be?" Hygelac asked, amazed. "Is she not far too old? She must have passed forty five winters by now, if not fifty and surely Onela could have any atheling maiden whom he desired."

"Yrse was barely past maidenhood when she wedded King Ongentheow, and Onela is older than she," Guthlaf reminded him. "The Scyldings have always been long lived, if battle does not take them, and Yrse has changed little to look upon since she came to Ongentheow's hall. She is still fair, and said to be wiser than ever. Still, it was a wonder to some that she chose Onela, for Othere's son Eadgils has often sat with her in the evenings, and it is said also that Eadgils is a great one for making blessings and other such things as are done in the hallows of Upsala."

Though Beowulf kept his face calm, he shuddered deep within, thinking of the time he had spent with Yrse. He could not help but wonder whether her soul had brightened or darkened with age: he could see her now, veiled by the smoke thickening within the hof's carven walls, ringed about by god shapes of wood and hallowed stones all gleaming with the deep red blood of offerings. Yrse had been near enough a wight of the Otherworld when he had seen her last: would wrapping herself in Upsala's might have brought her closer to the Middle Garth, or drawn her away from it?

But there was nothing he could do, or should do, regarding her: he had turned down her offer, and they had both known that was the end of matters between them. And he remembered his father's words from years ago: Whether Ongentheow loves her or keeps her chained like a snapping bitch, the luck of the Inglings is in their queens. Onela might well ween to take the rule of the Swedes when his brother was dead; later, Beowulf would speak to Hygelac of that. That summer passed, and another: Heardred outstripped his sister in growth for the first time, the crown of his golden head two finger widths above hers by the time the two of them stood solemnly in the ring to watch their father slaughter the first bull at Winter nights.

Eofor, as Hygelac had guessed those years ago when Hildegeard was new born and Ongentheow newly slain, had taken a woman closer to his own age to replace his dead wife; the next year, his son Ingemund stood before the gods and Hygelac's folk to avow his betrothal to the king's daughter in a high voice. Though they would not be wedded for some years yet, Hildegeard made it clear that she was well pleased in the matter. She was much like Hygd had been in her childhood, delicate and fair, but with a strong will hidden behind her pretty face and sweet words, like a little flower growing despite the cold in the highest meadows of the mountains along the North Way; and as Beowulf watched her take Ingemund's small square hand in her own, even as the lump swelled to choke in his throat, he thought, "Though I wish I had been your father, I am glad that my loss did not keep you from being born. That winter passed, and then another: as in the years before, only Sweartwulf dared to struggle against Beowulf in the wrestling at the summer tide Thing. It was a hard fought battle, for Beowulf's skill would never match the half Finn's, but if he once fixed his grip firmly, Sweartwulf's chances were lost, since they had always agreed neither to break bones nor strike wounding blows with fists. This year Sweartwulf was able to slip Beowulf's grasp and trip him up; but afterwards, as they went for ale," he said, "Had you tightened your arms on me harder, I should not have escaped."

"Aye, but who would I have to wrestle with me if I broke your ribs, my friend?" Beowulf said, smiling, and Sweartwulf laughed back.

"True enough, and if we had been fighting in such a manner, you would still be looking for your nuts among the bushes, for you did not guard your crotch as well as you might have during our second pass. You must take heed of that, for most men in your grip will think it their last hope, to knee you in the balls and get away."

"I shall remember," Beowulf replied. "Still..." We have been in frith long, and, if Frea Ing is kind, it shall stay so, he was about to say, but the words caught like a fish bone in his throat. Instead he said, "Perhaps I am growing slow, for that there is none save you who will wrestle with me, while you have every man in Hroesnabeorh who is brave enough to teach your skills to. But at least while you are here, I think you will be glad enough to help me remember what I learned from you."

"Indeed so!" The half Finn said, grinning broadly. "Ah, Beowulf, why do you never come to Hroesnabeorh, when we have come to visit you so often?"

Beowulf opened his mouth to answer with some jest, but he knew that he could not. Now it had been a full twelve winters since he had slain Grendel time, he felt, in a way that he could not name, for Ecgtheow's ghost to lie full still at last. Now, for the first time, he told his friend why he had not dared return to his father's hall. Sweartwulf listened quietly, all the mirth gone from his blunt featured face, and he nodded slowly when Beowulf was done.

"Now I wonder no more," he breathed. "Aye, there were those who cursed themselves, and thought you left because they had treated you ill; those good thanes who went with you swore that it was but your longing to be with your kin once more in the hall where you grew to manhood. Frithugeard said that there was something more to it, and I see now that she was the closest: she said she had seen a shadow of Woden's cloak yet shielding Hroesnabeorh, from all the years when Ecgtheow made his offerings there, and she thought you would never be full easy in a stead which had so long been given to your father's god. Yet even she did not think that the old man had walked after death..."

"His message was for me alone," Beowulf said swiftly, for he could see the dark worry creeping into Sweartwulf's face like cold mist rising from Lake Wener on a winter's evening. "If no other has seen him, there is nothing to fear now drink up, my friend. The boys' wrestling shall begin soon, and I look forward to seeing Hraefn tumble the other lads."

"Even Heardred?" Sweartwulf asked slyly.

"Even a king's son," Beowulf smiled, "must learn that he cannot always overcome all foes by himself. Best that Heardred learn that now, before he makes such a fool of himself as Breca did once for he is already well skilled in many things, and very much proud of his skill. But no man can always be the winner in all contests."

"True enough. Well, let us fill our horns again and go."

The rowan berries turned to orange, then bright red, hanging like sprays of coals among the fronds of green leaves; Hygelac came out to cut the first sheaf of harvest, and his folk hastened to get the grain in before the weather turned wintry, for already the wind was blowing cooler.

Their haste was none too swift, for the first drops of chill rain were scattering over the shorn brown fields when the Last Sheaf fell to Ansuwulf's scythe. The aging berserk looked up with a swift grin as the icy drops struck his bare white shoulders he had worn nothing more than loose blue trousers to the harvest work and he waved away the maidens who jostled each other towards the sheaf and giggled. "The beggar should carry his own bag," Ansuwulf said to them.

"This year none of you need fear giving birth before you are wedded: let me have the cord, and I shall bind the Sheaf myself."

Her hand shaking, Hildegeard took the threefold cord of red, white, and black from her mother, holding it out to the berserk almost as if she feared to touch him. Ansuwulf looked her in the eye, and his sharp weathered face showed a gentleness Beowulf had seldom seen upon it, as though an old dog wolf had turned from snarling at his foe to nuzzling his cub.

"Wyrd speaks, and Woden wills," he murmured, so softly that Beowulf was not sure whether he heard the words spoken, or whether they sounded only inside his skull. "Do not weep for the fallen, for it is Grim's right to harvest the grain he has sown: be cheerful, whatever befalls." Hygd brought forward the stake to mount the Last Sheaf on, and Ansuwulf rammed it into the ground, tying the bundle of golden grain tight to it.

"Well, Hygelac," Ansuwulf said. "Will you give the blessing, or leave it to me?"

Give it yourself, my king! Beowulf urged silently, the ache of stooping and bending in his back chilling to numb stiffness with fear. If there is death to come, I will meet it without flinching but I would not so gladly bid Woden's spear to fly over us!

"The beggar should carry his own bag, as you have said," Hygelac answered gravely. "What you have cut, you shall give: may the offering be enough."

Beowulf sighed in relief, but thought, He knows, too.

"So be it," said Ansuwulf. He raised his hands, looking up to the cloud washed sky, and called out,

"Grim's fair barley grown high,
Grain fall 'neath his raining,
Steed gray, in this stead here,
Sate, and end your waiting.
Reaping for seeds ripened
Rising in new guises,
Fields fair thus yield up,
Fruitful, next years' shoots bright.
Fields fair shall yield up,
Fruitful, next years' shoots bright."

Beowulf shuddered as Ansuwulf spoke his last lines a second time: that was not done by living men, but only by the dead. The rain was falling harder now as the women came forward to lay their garland of blue cornflowers and white days' eyes about the Sheath, the water pouring in cold rivulets off Ansuwulf's bare shoulders, though he took little notice of it, laughing as he bowed his gray head for Hygd to crown him with a wreath of red rowan berries and black elderberries twined into gold leafed birch twigs. The lamps were lit in the Swertings' hall already, tongues of yellow flame flickering from the black iron bowls on their high twisted stems, and the walls were hung with garlands of bright birch and dark pine.

Fresh loaves of bread and bowls of stewed mushrooms steamed on the tables, and ale froth brimmed high in the pitchers; the long fire trenches burned bright, flames leaping in a dance of light and shadow to warm the weary harvesters. Wynefrith and Gerhild, who had stayed in to ready the feast, sat at the board near the high seat but they were not alone: a tall cloaked figure sat beside them, his face hidden in the shadow of a dark hood.

Beowulf stopped dead, as though a knife of ice had pierced his heart: there was something familiar about the man, something that struck him with a sureness of dread, as though the first warning drum of Ansuwulf's words outside were now answered by a louder one. The stranger rose, casting back his hood. A shock ran through Beowulf, as though he had fallen unready into icy water. He knew that narrow, grim featured face, the long plaited gray beard and the keen deep gray eyes that shone raven black in the dimness of the firelit hall.

"Unferth!" Beowulf said, moving forward without thinking, though it should have been Hygelac's part to greet the guest first. "What brings you to guest in the Swertings' hall?"

"Do you remember, Beowulf, the words that you spoke in Heorot before it was burnt?" The thule's harsh deep voice replied. "You swore that you would ever be a friend to the sons of Hrothgar, and come to their aid at need. Now Hromund is slain by Ingeld's hand, but Hrethric still lives or did when I last saw him and the young Scylding king is sore pressed, for his folk rise against him, and at their head is his cousin Hrothulf. Therefore did Wealhtheow send me, to see if you had not forgotten the friendship between Waegmunding and Scylding, or would forsake the sons of Hrothgar, who was as a father to you for a while."

Beowulf's chest heaved, his heart clenching within him. But he stared down into the old thule's eyes, and answered,

"I have not forgotten the words I spoke. I shall go with you to make them good, and as many men with me as Hygelac will allow; but if my kinsman will send none of his thanes, then I shall follow you alone as need be."

"Indeed, you shall not go alone!" Hygelac's high voice rang out. "What my sister son and oath brother swore, I shall stand behind, and all my thanes as well, to prove the word of the Geats. Harvest is done: if it be time now for a redder harvest, and the mead of wolves and ravens poured out on the battlefield instead of sweet honey mead in the hall, then we all stand ready to that feast, for we have idled too long on the ale benches while our swords over slept in their sheaths. Heardred, ride swiftly to Gudhere the Steersman. Tell him to ready four ships, and we shall fare out as soon as we may: fifty men shall stay to guard my hall, but all the rest of us shall go."

"Shall I sail with you, Father?" Heardred asked fiercely. "I am near a man's age now, and skilled with sword and shield: let me but stand beside you in this battle, and I swear I shall bear myself as bravely as any man there."

Hygelac shook his head. "You yet lack a year or two before I set helm on your head and sword in your hand. Yet do not be shamed by the tasks I set you now. In my boyhood I, too, did a man's part in battle as a swift riding messenger; live up to that now, and, as I did, you shall follow it with the winning of wars."

"So be it, Father!" Heardred said, and ran light footed from the hall.

Tired as they were from the struggle to bring the harvest in before the storm, yet Hygelac's men labored mightily to ready the ships for the sailing to Sealand as swiftly as could be done. Still, it was two days before the thanes of Hygelac's war band were ready to wade out into the gray waves to board their vessels, and Beowulf could not miss the grimness that drew Unferth's face tight whenever he looked at the shadows shrinking and lengthening along the ground, as though every heartbeat of time drew Hrethric's doom nearer.

"Swiftly done," the thule said as the men heaved the last bundles of food and armor into the small boats ferrying provisions and gear out to the larger ships. "Yet I fear that we may already be too late."

"Why did you not come before this?" Beowulf asked him.

Unferth ground the butt of his carven spear into the sand, looking past Beowulf at the ships rocking gently upon the waves.

"Hrethric forbade me, for..." He was silent a moment; the shouting of the men loading the boats, and the mewing of the seagulls circling above, hardly seemed to disturb that stillness. "His mood is over high in many ways. He remembers that you came once to save the Danes when our strength could not win our freedom; he would not be remembered only as a beggar to a stronger man. Hrethric was not the best of kings. But Wealhtheow asked me at the last to forget words spoken in fear and anger by a youth whose kingdom seemed to be slipping through his grasp, and to save her son. And so I am here, though I fear I may have come too late for Hrethric."

They stood in silence as Hygelac's thanes said farewell to their wives and children, splashing by twos and threes into the waves. At last Hygelac, Beowulf, and Unferth were the only warriors left on the beach.

"Farewell, my sons," said Wynefrith, lifting the gold rimmed aurochs horn to Hygelac and Beowulf in turn. The draught within was a plum mead, its sweetness sliding smooth and rich down Beowulf's throat. "Go well, and fare well, and come you well home and Hygelac, for all our sakes, be wise rather than rash!"

"Mother, I have passed well over thirty winters," Hygelac said with a small laugh. "I am not the boy I was."

"Remember that if your bravery should tempt you to needless battle," Wynefrith replied quietly. "And you, Berki look after him."

"With all my strength," Beowulf vowed.

Hygd unfastened the great golden collar from her throat.

"My husband, I would that you wear this on your faring: may my luck be in it for you!" She swung the many ringed necklace open on its cunning hinges, fastening it again beneath Hygelac's short golden beard, and kissed him, then turned to Beowulf. "Berki, troth full bear you have given us more than we can ever give you. I can only trust in you once again. Come home safe!"

"If I may, I shall." Beowulf bent down to her, and her kiss brushed over his lips, so soft that he barely felt it, like a warm touch of breeze passing by his mouth. His eyes filled, and he was afraid to speak; but then the children were making their goodbyes, and Beowulf embraced each of them gently in turn before he and Hygelac followed Unferth into the cold water.

Though it was earlier in the year than it had been when Beowulf went to challenge Grendel, the crossing to Sealand was rougher, the white maned waves slapping the Geatish ships about harshly. Once Hygelac essayed a joke about Ran's daughters, but Beowulf shook his head sternly.

"This is no time to speak of them," he told his kinsman. "Later, perhaps, when we are safe on land..."

"If you say so, Berki," Hygelac answered. "I meant no ill by it; but I shall trust your rede, for you look as though this means much to you."

It was near four days before the tall stone between the barrows showed through the scudding sea mist and light showers of rain. Straining his eyes to pierce the grayness, Beowulf saw that the grassy howes seemed to have grown like mushrooms in the damp cool of summer's end: where two had stood, five small hillocks now rose green about the holy stone. Beside him, Unferth sighed deeply, his cloaked shoulders drooping like the wings of a dying raven.

"There is Hrothgar's mound, and there is Hromund's. Beside them sleeps another king of Scylding blood. My heart tells me that we have come too late; but let us turn in to shore nonetheless. I have been wrong before."

Across the water, Beowulf heard the far off sound of a signal horn blowing: it would not be a single rider that met the Geat ships this time, with battle just past and the red war shields hanging at the vessels' sides. Though it dulled the sheen of helms and byrnies, the mist did not hide the sight of the columns of men wending through the low dunes to array themselves on the beach, and as the ships drew closer, Beowulf saw the lines of bowmen with their arrows nocked and the man on horseback who rode out before the army, a short slim warrior on a black maned dun, even as Beowulf had seen him before.

"Hail to the Geats, who once came as friends!" Hrothulf's clear baritone sounded over the waves. "Now you bear the red shields of war: for whose sake do you mean to do battle, when the Scyldings have struggled one against the other?"

Beowulf looked at Hygelac, who nodded to him and called back, his voice ringing high above Hrothulf's.

"We have come to aid King Hrethric, as my sister son and oath brother swore: ever was there friendship between Hrothgar and the Waegmundings, and Hrothgar's son shall not be forsaken by us now!"

"That is spoken well and bravely. Let no man think ill of it, that you sought thus to hold to Beowulf's word: there was love well given on both sides between Hrothgar and Grendel's Bane. Yet you have come too late, for Hrethric lies in his mound. Though kin of mine, he was an ill king, who brought no good to the folk he ruled, and angered many at last to turn on him: thus I fought him, and though I had tended him as a child, thus I slew him as a man. I have paid were gild in full to his mother Wealhtheow, all that she would ask of me: I would have given her far more for a king's blood! If you have more cause for vengeance, speak it now, and I shall meet any of you man to man, or host to host if you will not fight me alone. Else accept that it is done, and come to shore as my guests share in my cousin's arvel, since you can do no more for his sake."

Hygelac glanced at Beowulf. "This is your matter: do you wish to do battle with Hrothulf? Whatever your will, I shall stand beside you."

Beowulf knew that, as Hrothulf had said, he could do no more for Hrethric: with Hrothgar and Hromund dead as well, now there was only Wealhtheow to whom he owed his aid.

"Hrothulf!" He called. "I shall come to shore, for I trust you; but I would that you send for Wealhtheow. I shall ask her will in the matter, and whatever she would of me, that shall I do."

"It shall be done." Hrothgar turned, speaking to one of his men, who ran over the beach as fleetly as a hare, and Beowulf heaved himself over the side and into the cold water, wading through the icy currents that tugged at him like hungry arms.

If any of Grendel's kin...no, that battle is long done. Steadfastly turning his mind away from Heofonglowe, he made his way to shore, climbing up onto the beach. Though Hrothulf was mounted and he afoot, Beowulf had not far to look up into the Scylding's eyes. Hrothulf's squared jaw was firmly set, the bones of his sharp planed cheeks standing out more strongly than they had twelve years ago; small lines marked the corners of his light filled eyes, and his thick straight brows drew together as he considered the man who stood before him.

"I would say that it is good to see you again," Hrothulf said at last, "but I do not know yet whether that is true or not, though I hope that it shall be."

"Matters have gone worse with the Scylding aeht than I hoped when I feasted in Heorot," Beowulf replied. "As for what must come of it that we shall see."

It was but a little time when Wealhtheow rode down to them upon a gray mare. The Scylding queen's hair was coiled up beneath a dark blue hood, but Beowulf could see that her fair eyebrows were almost wholly silvered now; deep lines scored her forehead, and the crumpled skin about her eyes was white as birch bark, as though she had wept all the blood from her face.

"You came more swiftly than I thought, Beowulf," Wealhtheow said quietly. "I should have put more hope in you, but my son's own pride betrayed him."

"I wish that I could have aided you better. Yet now I would ask: is there aught I can do? If you would have vengeance, I will do my best to gain it for you."

Wealhtheow lowered her gaze and shook her head slowly, as though the burden of its weight was too much for her shoulders to bear.

"My husband is dead, both my sons slain and my daughter is wedded to a man who hates all her kin. What should I do with vengeance, when I know too well how Hrethric brought his own end on himself? Now Hrothulf is building a new hall where Heorot stood, though no gilded stags' antlers shall be mounted at its gables, lest they draw down a like doom; it may be that Yrse's child shall bring a new dawn after this darkness. But let your men turn the red shields round and come to shore: the Geats and Scyldings have been friends too long now for me to wish bloodshed between them, for all that has befallen."

The hall Hrethric had built after Heorot's burning a little way from the old building's stead, as though he had feared that some ill Wyrd might yet linger in Heorot's foundations seemed small and poor against Beowulf's memories of Hrothgar's hall; though the day was darkening swiftly and only the first timbers of Hrothulf's new building had gone up, Beowulf could see that it would be a better successor to Heorot. There was barely room for Danes and Geats together within the hall that had been Hrethric's; but for all that, the fire burned brightly, and there was plenty of food and drink for both Hrothulf's men and his guests.

The new Scylding king himself did not seem to rejoice greatly in his place: Beowulf guessed that it weighed greatly upon him, to have slain his cousin. Yet when Hrothulf spoke of the troubles besetting his kingdom of outlaws gathering strength in the woods, of lesser drightens that had feuded and torn at each other and done as they pleased since first Grendel began to walk at Heorot, of laws unmade or forgotten his jaw clenched and his eyes gleamed with slow burning fire. Few of Hrothgar's old thanes and rede givers still sat at the Scyldings' board; most of them had died fighting the Heathobards, or else fallen in this last strife, while the younger Danish warriors stirred restlessly when Hrothulf began to talk of laws and settling matters within the kingdom.

"Let us go south and raid the Franks!" One large man, whose fair hair was braided into dozens of plaits with gold and silver finger rings woven into their ends, shouted loudly. "That will bring more wealth than any scot laid upon under kings in this island!"

A few others cried agreement, but Hrothulf shook his head. His voice was quiet, but Beowulf marked how the men stilled as he spoke, like a pack of hounds hearing their master's words of command that is a true king! He thought unwillingly.

"Who would run to cast the bane spear at his neighbor while his own house is burning?" Hrothulf asked. "Aye, warriors' blood may kindle for a second battle as soon as the first is done. But our land has been hard battered over these years: if we should fare, weakened by war as we are already, out against a strong foe, who will be left to defend our coasts when the wolves come to rend what is left of Sealand? You have a mother and a sister, Oshelm: if we all sail down the Rhine, can they lift swords to ward themselves against Saxon pirates? Or against any outlaw band creeping out of the woods while the king's thanes are far from home? We shall make our own realm strong: then none can stand against us!"

Beowulf hardly heard the cheering for Hrothulf's words, for he was watching Hygelac. A slow smile crossed the Geat king's face, and it seemed to Beowulf that something was growing in his kinsman's mind, though he did not dare to ask what in front of Hrothulf and all his folk. But he has given Hrothulf frith now: I know that Hygelac would not strike at a host in his weakness, nor break the words he spoke. The next morning, to Beowulf's surprise, Hygelac ordered that they make ready to leave.

"You have guested us well, King Hrothulf," the Geat king said to the Scylding, "but I can see that you have much to do, and we would not burden you in your work. One thing only I ask: will you give your man Oshelm leave to come with us."

Hrothulf stared piercingly up into Hygelac's face, and it seemed to Beowulf that there was more than he could read in the small man's intense gaze.

"If that is your wish, I shall not stand in your way. May the gods bless you in your faring, and your fighting."

Beowulf would have stayed to hear more, but out of the corner of his eye, he saw Wealhtheow and Unferth standing together, and walked over to bid them farewell. To his surprise, Unferth carried a heavy pack, and Wealhtheow a smaller one.

"Are you coming with us, then?" He asked.

Wealhtheow shook her head.

"I am claiming the were gild I asked of Hrothulf for my son. A small boat, that will bear me to God Home once more for I found healing there once, and hope. Now the only hope left to me is that of healing; but I think that I shall be welcomed on those shores once more, and mayhap have something other than mourning to fill my days, in time. Unferth is coming with me..."

"Aye," the thule said quietly. "My king is dead, but I will not leave my queen: we have borne too much together to be parted now and I, too, have a place to fill on that hallowed holm. I do not think you and I shall see each other again, Beowulf. I should say fare well, but my foresight fails me: yours is not an easy wyrd to ken. Still, I think there is much that lies before you, but as for me, my tale within the Middle Garth's ring is done."

Wealtheow lifted Beowulf's hand in both of her own, her small cold fingers pressing it tightly. Then she let go, and the queen and her man walked away without another word down the beach, to where a little boat was drawn up on the sand. Unferth let his pack down; Wealhtheow got in and took up the oars, and Unferth pushed it out until the waves lifted it, then climbed in himself.

Perhaps it was a trick of the morning mist; but Beowulf found his eyes watering until he had to blink, and when he looked back, it seemed to him that they were no longer there. Beowulf went back to Hygelac and Hrothulf.

"Fare well, Beowulf," Hrothulf said, his thin lips tightening into a smile. "I wish that I could ask you to stay with me, but I think your king has need of you. May I be able to gather such heroes to me in times to come!"

"You shall have no lack of mighty men to aid and ward you," Beowulf replied without thinking. "Be sure, that the heroes of Hrothulf's band shall be well worth remembering; you shall not think that you are scanted in any way because I am not with you." For it seemed to him that he could see the shadow of a great bear standing behind Hrothulf; and the glitter of a golden hilt, and swords burning in the light of a great fire...Then, as always, the vision was gone, the sureness of his words whispering away from his tongue like ashes whisked softly off on the breeze.

"That is hard to believe. But may your words prove true!"

The Geats were barely out of sight of land when Hygelac called, "Turn the shields about once more! We came forth for battle: is there any man here who would not seek it out, but go home with shield unmarred and unbloodied sword?"

"No!" The Geatish warriors thundered, drumming their heels on the deck. Beowulf had half awaited this: even to him, though he would rather have gone home in frith, it seemed almost craven to have readied themselves so for battle and then gone away so mildly.

"Then let us go and find foes who are worthy of us! Now I have heard that the Franks are doughty men, and rich: there will be drink for our blades, food for the wolves, and gold scattered freely among us when we have brought red slaughter to them. Gudhere, turn our ringed prow towards the mouth of the Rhine: along that river where Sigifrith slew the dragon, we shall find more treasure yet, and war fame enough for all."

The Geatish thanes cheered, catching up shields to drum their swords against until the echo of the booming shivered through all the timbers of Hygelac's ship; as the king's words were shouted to the three vessels flanking his own, the cry went up about them, startling the gulls to veer away in their flight.

"Why are you so quiet, Beowulf?" Hygelac asked under the shouting. "Do you think this ill?"

"No. No, fighting men cannot be kept in frith too long, and I think you could not hold your thanes back now if you wished to. Say, rather, that I still grieve for Hrothgar, whose fears for his sons were not unfounded, and for Wealhtheow, who has now suffered all the sorrows that a woman may know: may she find the healing she seeks at God Home!"

"She was a true atheling frowe, queenly and open handed," Hygelac agreed, the wild excitement of his call to battle drained from his face. "Even in her sorrows, I could see that all you said of her was not enough, and it is not without good cause that you think of her now. But it is also in my mind that the Danes will be better served by Hrothulf's rule than by Hrethric's: there is both strength and wisdom in that man, for though he be brother's son rather than king's son, he is the true keeper of the Scylding soul." Hygelac drew in a deep breath of spray damp air, looking out over the sea, and for a moment some black thought seemed to cross his mind, clear behind his fair face as a wash of dark wine pouring down into a beaker of transparent glass. Then he shook himself, his mouth curving into the familiar smile. "Come with me now, for I would have your thoughts as I speak to Hrothulf's thane Oshelm. He has traveled widely in the Frankish realms, for which reason he urged the Dane king last night to strike against them. He will be our guide to the towns and the men that we find there, and you shall give us rede as we speak of each of them for I know you have learned a little of war craft in these years of frith."

"It may be," said Beowulf.

In truth, he had learned as much as he could from Hygelac, trained in strategies since boyhood, and from the older warriors. For there had been no doubt in his mind that, when war came to the Geats again, he would find himself ruling a flank of their army for the sake of his fame and close kinship to the king; and he had vowed to himself that he would not cast away the lives of men who trusted him from lack of knowledge, or anything else that he could help. Though the gloomy clouds did not lift, an endless fine sprinkle of rain slicking the boards of the ships, the weather grew no worse; the wind freshened as the Geatish fleet neared the mouth of the Rhine, bearing them in past the great flats of rustling reeds. Arrows of geese honked mournfully overhead, black above the gray sky; sometimes when the Geats stopped to camp, they would stir a sleeping flock to rise up in alarm with a great gabbling like the baying of a pack of hounds. They passed by the small Frisian fishing villages without stopping, for, though some of the thanes suggested that it would be easy to take slaves there, Hygelac laughed scornfully.

"What fame should we win in cutting down men armed with fish spears? One of these villages might yield a whole silver ring, if it were rich among its kind. If thralls are there for the taking when we strike, well enough but gold is easier to carry and does not ask for feeding, nor must it be bound to keep it from stabbing its masters in their sleep. When we reach the lands of the Haetware, there will be battle and booty enough for all."

The Geats sailed on until they came to a tree shaded cove, where alders stretched their dark roots down to the muddy shallows and their brown leaves whispered dry above. There, after a few words with Oshelm, Hygelac gave the word to pull in.

"There is a great burg of the Haetware less than half a night's march from here: Oshelm knows the road. Berki, I know that you have the strength to break down any gate, unless it be of eoten crafted stone. It may be that they have more men than we, but we shall take them by surprise and we are a king and his chosen war band, the best fighters in all Geatland: if we strike boldly and without faltering, the battle shall go to us.

Eat a good meal this even tide, and ready torches, for though the way to the Haetweres' burg is smooth, the Moon still hides under his cloudy cloak."

In spite of his king's words, however, Beowulf found that he had little appetite for the dried bread and herring and hard smoked cheese the Geats had brought for their faring. The Haetwere had done the Geats no harm; it sat ill with him to break down their gate at night in hopes of catching them in their sleep it was too close, perhaps, to his memories of Heorot, of the hall door bursting asunder beneath Grendel's strength, and there was a dark foreboding upon him. After a little time he rose and walked over to Ansuwulf, who sat calmly chewing a leathery strip of fish into softness.

"You are troubled of mood," the old berserk said, looking up at Beowulf. "I remember a bear who wanted only to be left alone with his sweet honey, and would not rouse to fighting rage, however often the wolves nipped at him. Has Grendel's Bane still learned no taste for battle?"

Beowulf squatted down. "Not when it is needless," he said, very softly so that no other might overhear and lose heart. "Yes, I understand why it is not: if Hygelac did not lead his men to fight now, they would drift off, one by one, to find a drighten of bolder mood, and then there would be none left to defend the Geats when need to fight truly came. But still, I did not hope for this."

Ansuwulf considered the hard round of bread in his hand, then dipped its edge into the small beer in his horn to soften it.

"My teeth are not what they were," he murmured. Then, louder, he said, "Well, gather your mood as you consider this. If you do not fight with all your strength, Hygelac shall surely die this night, for it is no easy undertaking he has chosen. If the Haetwere are not your foes now, they shall very soon be so: the bear had best rouse himself before the spearmen have ringed him all about!"

The march, as Hygelac had promised, was smooth enough; the torches cast wavering circles of ruddy light onto the churned mud of the road, fading off into blackness over the stubble of the shorn fields. Clouded as the sky was, the Moon was near full behind it; and so they saw the great log palisade ringing the Haetweres' burg dark against the grayness, the tops of the taller buildings looming up like whales' backs through the fog. A light kindled behind the wooden wall, then another, and Beowulf heard the first shouts and sounds of running feet.

"Loose!" Hygelac commanded the archers, and the arrows sang through the air, a half seen shimmer of blackness arching over the palisade. A few screams rose where they landed, and Hygelac shouted, "Forward! Forward behind Berki!"

Shields over their heads to catch any returning arrow fire, the Geats ran forward. Beowulf did not stop when he came to the gate, but hit it with his shoulder, his full weight and strength behind it. It cracked and shuddered beneath his blow, but did not give: he set his feet hard against the ground, pushing with all the might of his legs and back, and the Haetweres' gate gave way.

Beowulf barely twisted in time to avoid the spears stabbing at him; one shrieked off his helmet with an ear rending screech, and another lodged tight in the iron ringed sleeve of his byrnie. He drew his sword, hacking fiercely about him and shouting,

"Hygelac! Hygelac and the Geats!"

Torchlight swung and wheeled wildly; several times, he felt his blade thunk into flesh, or heard the sound of wood and metal breaking beneath his blows, but he could spare no time to see what wounds he had dealt: it was all he could do to block the ceaseless flurry of strokes coming in from two sides at once, striking out only when he could and shouting until he was hoarse, listening for the answering cries that would tell him whether it was a friend or a foe beside him at least none of Hygelac's men would mistake him for a Frank, even in the dark burg lit only by wavering flames in the hands of men who were running and fighting.

Thrusting spears stabbed around his shield from behind, clearing his way. Hygelac's high voice called, "Berki, to me! Onwards!" Beowulf stumbled over the bodies to his king, locking shields and pressing forward. It was a bitter battle, but Hygelac had spoken truly: even though the Haetwere were fighting in their own settlement and their own homes, they had gotten little chance to ready themselves; and between the houses, their numbers counted for far less than they would have in the open: it was the skill of the Geat king's picked men that won the day. By the time the first gray streaks of dawn were brightening the sky, the Haetwere fighting men were all dead Hygelac had slain their drighten, a great red haired man with a gilded helm and gold hilted sword, himself and those who still lived, women and children, thralls and those few men too feeble to lift even a knife to defend themselves, stood in a shivering mass in the middle of the blood dripping hall.

They shrank back from Beowulf as if he were a troll in truth: the sight sickened his heart, but he made no sign of it, and seeing how the Haetwere captives feared him, Hygelac said, "Berki, do you stand guard over these while the rest of us see to our wounded and make sure of what we have won. They shall not defy you, I think." Beowulf liked that little but in the light of the rekindled lamps, he could see that some of the women already bore the marks of ravishment, ripped gowns and bruised and bloodied faces: at least, while he guarded them, he could be sure to spare them further pain.

The Geats had not won the night without loss: Beowulf could hear the moans and screams of the wounded outside, like ghosts wailing in the winter winds, and some of Hygelac's men were already carrying in the bodies of their fallen among them, he marked, the Danish thane who had been their guide; Beowulf wondered if some hidden foreknowledge had egged him on to urge the raid that would be his doom, Wyrd twisting on herself like a carven wyrm? Though Beowulf had been full sure that Ansuwulf would be among the dead, the old berserk lay across one piece of a splintered bench, his bare chest rising and falling deeply in the exhausted sleep that followed his wod fits, and, streaked with blood as Ansuwulf was, Beowulf could see no sign of a wound upon him. But old as he is, he will be lucky to live through another berserk fight.

I should not let him get chilled. Beowulf pulled down one of the woven wall hangings: it was spattered with blood, and a sword stroke had torn a great hole down the middle, but it would serve to keep the berserk warm while he slept off his madness. As he carried the tapestry over to Ansuwulf, one of the captives began shrieking at him. Her words were hard to understand, but when Beowulf listened carefully, he could make out that she was saying something like,

"You! Troll! Don't touch that! My mother...six months' work..." Beowulf folded the hanging carefully over the berserk's body, then he did not know why; perhaps it was only the shocked daze after battle, that could make the littlest things seem of great meaning said slowly to her, speaking as clearly as he could, "The tapestry is already ruined, and my friend needs warmth."

The woman stopped screaming abruptly, staring at Beowulf as if she had not thought that he could have human speech. Even though one side of her face was already darkening with a swollen bruise, her long pale hair hanging in wild blood streaked tangles, Beowulf could tell that she was fair, and the torn garment that she clutched about herself with queenly dignity was red linen trimmed with bright bands of woven silk the daughter of the Haetwere drighten, perhaps, or one of his kinswomen.

"You speak almost like a man," she said, and for a moment Beowulf saw the wonder in her blue eyes. Then her battered face hardened again, her mouth twisting as she spat out, "And no doubt you gloat like a man, as well, and take your pleasure of the defeated like one. Well, troll, you and your masters shall have little time to enjoy your night raid. For Theudebert, son of King Theuderic, is not far: he was coming to guest with the Haetwere this slaughter tide, and he shall be quickly on your heels. Then, whatever manner of eoton or ghast you be, your strength will not save you with Theudebert is the Frankish champion Daghrefn, who has never yet been bested in any trial of strength or skill; the mightiest warriors of the Merovingians travel with him, and when he calls all the hosts of the Haetwere and Frisians to him, he shall overcome you as a pack of hounds overcomes a roe fawn. Then shall you, accursed of God, be paid the geld you have earned this night!"

The other women were grabbing at her, whispering and shushing urgently, and suddenly she hid her face in her hands and Beowulf realized that, in her anger, she had betrayed the Haetwere captives' hope of rescue. He raised his voice, bellowing for Hygelac and trying not to look at how the women and children cringed away from his shout with signs of warding. It was not long before Hygelac hurried into the hall again; not with his usual light footed gait, for the night of fighting had worn on him as much as any, but still moving briskly, and with new gold rings gleaming fresh over his blood stiffening sleeves.

"What is it, Berki?"

Beowulf told him what the girl had said as swiftly as he could. Hygelac shook his head.

"An ill turning, well, we did not come to meet the full host of the Franks in open battle. We shall take all we can carry, and those captives who are fit enough to hasten beside us; there are plenty of good horses here to aid us in bearing our wounded and our booty, and that is well, for Oshelm spoke truly when he said the folk of this land were rich. Now hurry, Berki, for we shall need your strength!"

Tired as they were, the Geats made good haste back to their ships: the plunder was rich enough that few men were disgruntled at leaving off their guzzling at the casks of Frankish wine and ale. Those captives who could not march, Hygelac left lightly bound with a knife to free themselves, saying,

"What should these wretches do against us? Theudebert's host can track us clearly enough, so it matters little what they tell him: and if they cannot march, they can hardly fight, but there is no fame to be won by cutting the throats of such downed sheep."

The rest had their hands hobbled, and were driven along at swords point, though the girl who had spoken to Beowulf did not silence her curses until her voice was worn to a ragged whisper. Before the Geats left the burg, they heaped the bodies of their fallen in the Haetwere drighten's hall and set it aflame, the fire roaring up beneath a great streaming banner of black smoke. The first day's sailing downriver was slower than the Geats had hoped, for though the current was with them, the wind blew hard against them.

By the second day, they saw the sails of four great ships on the Rhine behind them, driving on fast: Theudebert had wasted no time in taking to the water and his troops were fresh, whereas more than half the Geats had at least some minor wound and all save those few who had stayed back to guard the ships were still worn from marching and fighting. The Frankish vessels gained ground slowly, but steadily; Hygelac paced the deck, the wind blowing his fair hair in straggles about his face as he stared back at them, and his voice was hoarse and eyes sunken from sleeplessness when at last, a day and a half from the mouth of the Rhine, he called his chief warriors and rede givers to him.

"It was an ill chance that brought us here at this time, just when Theudebert had come north. But such things no man may guess, nor struggle against, and nothing is left to us but to meet what Wyrd has predicted as best we may. Now they have four ships, as do we, but they are strong and fresh, whereas we have lost men in fighting; we have wearied our arms at the oars, but they, I believe, have thralls to row them. Yet if we can draw off the best part of their strength, our ships may yet escape theirs, and most of us see Geatland again. This I suggest: that whoever will, shall come ashore with me, and raise my banner high. They cannot let us go, and must therefore weaken themselves to chase us on land, while if once our ships can make the open sea, that part of our host can escape them."

"I shall go to land," said Ansuwulf at once. "But you, my king you have a duty to your folk: you cannot cast your life away like this."

Hygelac shook his head, smiling sadly. "You said yourself, old wolf, that the beggar should carry his own bag. The choice to come here was mine: I shall ask no man to pay my scot for me. If I do not come home, then Berki may steer the kingdom until young Heardred has come to a man's years…"

"I shall not be parted from you!" Beowulf broke in. "I am oath brother and sister son to you: I shall stand beside you with all my strength. Did you not save my life, and that of all those with me, in Ravenswood when it seemed beyond hope that we should live out another day? So there is no telling what the morrow may bring, but whatever betide, Hygelac, I shall stand beside you with all my strength."

"I am glad to have you. Well, then, Hildegeard is betrothed to Eofor's son Ingemund: Eofor is a wise man, and strong, and if neither Berki nor I comes home again, he will be a good rede giver to Heardred, and aid Hygd in her rule until my son's age has ripened. But now I would hear who else would come with me unless it be that any of you here has a wiser plan by which we may win the day, or at least some part of our lives."

In the end, threescore men chose to go with Hygelac. Agilar, Herebrand, and Widuhund three of Beowulf's worst old tormentors, though their fellow Thunarstan had died at Ravenswood were among them. Now Beowulf's heart caught within him as he saw them step forward to pledge themselves to fight and die by their king, for though they had all passed thirty winters, their features hardened by age and marked off or blurred by men's beards, he could see the high spirited boys they had been and no worse than that: I would not have guessed then that they and I would make an end with shields locked to ward each other. But they had seemed to fear Beowulf since he came back from his long swim, and in those years, he had never spoken to them, nor they to him. Now he stepped forward, patting Agilar on the shoulder. The curly haired man just kept himself from flinching, but his eyes were wide as he looked up into Beowulf's face, his skin pale beneath the spattering of freckles that still marked his broad cheeks above his tangle of brown beard.

"I remember that you cheered for me when I set off in the water with Breca," Beowulf said quietly. "As for the years before we were children then, and children may wound without knowing, or take hurt when laughter is meant. I bear no grudge against you for a child's harsh words: if we must fall together, I would die as shield brothers."

After a moment, Agilar clasped Beowulf's wrist hard.

"I am ashamed of the deeds of my youth. It is well for me, and for all of us, that you are more high minded than we are but I shall be proud to fight beside the better man, and fall by you, if that be my Wyrd, in warding our king."

Beowulf nodded, giving Agilar's wrist a last squeeze, and turned to exchange like words with Herebrand and Widuhund. Herebrand tried to smile, but Widuhund's voice choked in his throat, and Beowulf could see the water standing in the sharp featured redhead's eyes.

"Come, be of better cheer, my friend," he said as lightly as he could. "We have life, and strength, and keen swords: who is to say that we shall not win through, if our hearts do not fail us? Iron shall bite easily enough on the Franks, and if there be fewer of us, then the greater shall our fame be when we have overcome them."

"Aye, that is so!" Hygelac whooped. "And a cunning array is worth thrice the number of men: this night in the darkness we shall take to the shore, and by day we shall be ready to greet our guests."

By evening, the Geats' luck seemed to be turning, for a mist was settling in, so that the Frankish ships could see them no longer. Small boats carried the chosen half hundred to shore; Hygelac took the standard that had stood proudly upon his own vessel, so that when the mist faded at dawn, Theudebert would know that the Geatish ruler had eluded him. At last the Geats stood all together on the Rhine's marshy bank, their armor chill with dankness, listening to the splash of the last rowboat's oars through the mist. Someone had brought a few coals in a firebox from the ship, and Beowulf heard the fumbling and blowing as he tried to light a torch; at last the resin soaked knot of pine caught, casting a small circle of yellow light through the fog.

"What now?" Ansuwulf asked. "Shall we stumble through the marshes and hope not to fall in, or have you some better plan in mind, my king?"

In the torchlight, Beowulf saw Hygelac smile.

"I did not choose this place by chance. As we sailed in, Oshelm told me that there was an island very near in the marshes where the fisher folk go in time of danger the water is shallow enough that only their little mud boats can reach it, but, save for two narrow fords, too deep and treacherous bottomed to wade; and it is a long way across, so that archers are of less use attacking than they might be, but defenders can shoot at those crossing the ford. We can hold such a place well: we only need to stay on this track until we come to the house of any of the fishers, and they, in turn, can guide us to their holm."

For the first time in days, Beowulf felt a stirring of true hope, and he could tell by the murmurs of the other Geatish warriors that their hearts, too, were lifting.

"Then let us go!" Ansuwulf said, and they began to march.

It was slow going, for the Geats had but a few torches between them, and the track was so boggy and muddy that it could hardly be told from the marsh about them in the darkness. But after a time, they came to a small hut, and Hygelac strode forward and knocked loudly on the door.

"Who's there?" Shouted a man's voice from within, the words blurred by sleep and a strong Frisian accent.

"Wayfarers who need guidance," Hygelac replied. "Come forth to aid us, and you shall have a gold arm ring as your reward."

Beowulf heard the low sound of urgent speech from within, but could make out no words; the fisherman was talking with his wife. At last he saw a faint ruddy light kindling within the narrow window slit, and the man's voice again,

"How d' I know I can trust ye?"

"Because I am the king of the Geats, and my word is good. And because there are sixty of us, and full armed: if we wished you ill, we could fire the reed thatch over your head and spear you as you ran out. But I swear to you that if you aid us, you and yours will come to no harm, and be paid in gold for your help, as I said before."

More urgent mutterings; then the door opened a crack. "Lemme see th'gold first."

Without argument, Hygelac stripped one of the coils of gold wire from his arm and handed it through. After a moment, the door opened all the way and the fisher two pronged spear in one hand, torch in the other came out. He was a small man, gnarled, his head covered with a muddy tangle of hair and beard; his weather seamed face peered dubiously up at the Geats.

"What d'ye want from me?"

"We have heard that there is a holm in the middle of a lake near here, where a few men may hold against a stronger foe. Take us there."

The fisher chewed at his mouth and mumbled to himself, finally drawling,

"Well, that be a place of our folk alone it's a risk to me if I show ye where to find it, a great risk…"

"You have been paid well, and overpaid," Hygelac said, and Beowulf could hear the first edge of anger in his voice, as though the Geat king were carefully drawing a dagger an inch from its sheath. "Yet when you have seen us safely to its shores, I shall give you a second ring to match the first."

"And how d'I know ye won't just cut my throat when ye have what y'want?" The fisherman persisted.

Widuhund made an angry movement towards the little man, as though to take him by the throat, but Hygelac gestured him back.

"Nay, I have vowed you safety if you show us what we need: let that be enough, for if you will not give the help we need, then there are others by here who may and why should I let you live, when you have taken my gold already, and yet hold back from giving aid? But trust the vow of a king, and you shall find it worthy of trust, for I have never yet broken my word."

The fisherman's head hung, and he scuffled his shoes through the mud with little sucking sounds.

"All right, then. Come ye along, and I'll show ye th' way."

The Geats followed their guide through ankle deep muck and murmuring reeds for a long time: without stars or moon, but only the pale rings of torchlight to guide them, Beowulf was not sure how far they had gone. But at last he heard the soft ripples of lake water lapping against the shore, and their guide halted.

"Here's th' wide ford; th' narrow one's th' other side o' th' island. Now are ye done with me?"

"No," said Hygelac firmly. "You shall cross with us, and stay with us until we are all safe on the holm."

The fisherman pulled on his beard, his head down again. "Mayhap I wan't so sure o' th' sign. Over this way, just a few steps."

The ford was rocky underfoot, not the mud Beowulf had thought to feel: he wondered if the Frisians had built it up themselves. Hygelac kept a firm hold on their guide's collar as they crossed, lest he try to slip away. But with his own life at sake, he led them true. Beowulf wondered what would have happened if they had tried to cross at the first point the fisherman had showed them. Rocks for a little way, perhaps, then floundering in sinking mud. He shivered. Behind them someone cried out softly in disgust, and another asked,

"What was that?"

"Something slimy it touched me."

"An eel, most likely," Hygelac said, his voice calm and steady. "I doubt there is anything in this lake more to be feared than we ourselves."

A few men laughed; Beowulf did not, but he felt better for his king's jest. At last they climbed out onto the island, shivering and dripping. Beowulf was soaked to halfway up his thighs, but the shorter men were in worse state.

"I'll leave ye now, an I may," their guide said quickly.

"Not until we have made sure of this stead," Hygelac replied.

Taking a torch, he made the fisherman walk the length and breadth of the island, showing him where the narrow ford that only two men could cross abreast began, and assuring himself that there was no other hidden crossing point. At last the king and the fisherman came back to the rest of the warriors.

"I'll have that ring of ye now," their guide said, a touch more sureness in his thick voice.

"Better to give him his geld at sword's point, after he tried to play us false," Ansuwulf advised coldly. "He will sell us to the Franks when they come, you know."

But Hygelac shook his head, the mist darkened strands of gold about his face shimmering in the torchlight.

"They can find us easily enough in any case: we could not have hidden our trail. And I gave my word: why should I break it now?" He pulled a second ring from his arm. "Take this, though you earned it ill, and a king's rede with it. If you would keep your life, do not be so free with the Franks as you were with us, for they will need your aid far less than we did."

Their guide grabbed the ring from Hygelac's hand and splashed into the water again, his torch glowing fuzzy and pale as an err light through the mist until they could no longer see it.

"All of you held your cloaks up to keep them dry?...Good. I think our foes shall have no chance of finding us until well past dawn: let us eat a little, then sleep close for warmth, for we shall need all our strength on the morrow."

Beowulf awoke stiff, sore, and cold, but feeling a little more rested. The mist hanging over the island shone pearl pale in the dawn; he heard the soft splashing of fish in the lake, and a little farther off, the plaintive cry of a water bird. Hygelac was already up, pacing off the island and muttering to himself.

The Hrethlings' gold ring standard was planted firmly in the middle of the holm, fog beading on the gilded metal: Beowulf wondered how long it would be before the Franks realized that the Geatish king was no longer with his ships, and came looking for him. Hygelac smiled cheerfully at Beowulf, as though they were back in the Swertings' hall.

"A good morn to you, kinsman," he said, handing Beowulf a strip of dried fish.

Beowulf took it eagerly, for his belly was rumbling with hunger: there was little enough to it, but the strong salty taste that flooded his mouth and the act of chewing at least made him feel as though he were eating.

"Come with me, and let us see how best to array our forces. Oshelm the gods guest him well gave me good rede when he spoke of this place. Four men may cross abreast at the wider ford, as we did, but no more than two at the narrower one. I fear that this damp has done our bowstrings no good, but it will be no help to those of our foes either, and they will have further to shoot..."

Beowulf himself, they decided, with Ansuwulf and Widuhund and Herebrand beside him, would stand to block the wider ford, for the strongest push would come there. For the narrow ford, Hygelac and Beowulf chose a pair of sturdy shield men, Thunarfinn and Sigemund: both young warriors were short, but strong, and a row of taller men behind them with thrusting spears could slay as they would if the Franks tried to cross at that point.

"And though they were too young to fight at Ravenwood, I have watched them at training: neither will yield an inch of ground while he lives nor take it as anything but honor that we set them where they will be among the first of our men to fall," Hygelac murmured softly to Beowulf. Indeed, Sigemund fair haired and more lightly built than his stocky comrade, but with shoulder muscles that bulged against the links of his byrnie grinned widely when he was shown where they would stand, while dark haired Thunarfinn nodded in glad assent.

"Be sure, we shall not fail you while we live," Thunarfinn said, and Hygelac patted his shoulder.

"I know that I may trust in you."

At last all the Geatish troops were drawn up as Hygelac wished, and
then their waiting began. A crisp chill wind rose at midmorning, whisking
away the last tatters of thinning mist; the Sun's light shone brightly from
the waters of the lake that surrounded them, tinging the brown reeds
with a hint of gilding. The Geats mostly sat in their places, talking quietly,
though every so often a man would rise and walk around a bit to keep from
stiffening in the cold.

Around noontime, a couple of men in small boats rowed out from shore;
they must have taken notice of the war band encamped on their island,
but gave no sign of it, quietly hauling up their eel traps and collecting their
slithering harvest. Chewing their way bread and fish, the Geats began
to wonder if Theudebert would turn aside from pursuing the ships. The
thought that Beowulf did not speak, but that was chewing at his mind, was
simply that the Franks would do their best to destroy the Geatish vessels
first, then seek out the fugitives on land at their leisure.

They would have little hope of catching us then, if they thought we had
fled from fear, Beowulf thought. Yet if they knew that we were bait to lure
them away would they not be fools to take it? Or are we the fools, to have
offered our king thus? If we had put Hygelac on the swiftest vessel to save
him, while the rest of our ships turned to fight. Hygelac would not have
fled for his own safety, however Beowulf and the rest of his rede givers
might have urged him; but if the Franks waited too long, Wyrd being kind,
it might turn out that he was better off on land than at sea after all. After a
time, Beowulf's thoughts turned to Hygd and her children, Hildegeard and
Heardred. Frea Ing, at least you gave me some easing of the eoton frowe's
curse, he thought. A great longing came over him, to hear Heardred's clear
young voice once more, piping,

"Beowulf! Beowulf, I speared a ring on the ground from my saddle at a
full canter today. Come and watch, I'll do it again for you!"

Or Hildegeard, her little face very serious as she lifted up the aurochs
horn of greeting and spoke to her older cousin as she would someday to
guests in the Geat king's hall,

"Hail and welcome, Beowulf Grendel's Bane! Honor our hall, if you will,
by drinking the greeting draught Hygelac's daughter bears." Had they been
born of his own seed, the two young Swertings might have been taller,
less graceful, though surely no child of Hygd's body could ever be clumsy,
perhaps Heardred's hair would have been brown and curly instead of fine
straight gold; but could they have been so much different if they were
Beowulf's own? And could he love them any more dearly?

"Are you thinking of the children?" Hygelac asked from his easy sprawl
beside Beowulf.

"How did you know?"

"There is a look you have when you are with them loving, but somehow
fierce, as though you would battle an hundred wights like Grendel to keep
them safe."

"I would, indeed."

Hygelac chewed on his lower lip a moment. "Berki, this may hardly be the time to speak of it, but the thought has been in my mind for some time. Will you not think of taking a wife when we come home? You have passed thirty winters now, and there is no maid in the Northlands who would not be glad to dwell with you."

Troubled, Beowulf was silent. He could not tell Hygelac that there would be no woman for him in the Middle Garth, save Hygd, for he knew what his kinsman would say: If I fall in this battle, you must swear to me that you will take her to wife. And less than that could he speak of Heofonglowe's curse, of the fear of what would befall if he dared to seek joy in a living woman's arms.

At last he said only, "I have thought on it, and shall think more."

"Indeed. Perhaps," Hygelac said with a ghost of his old merriment shadowing his face, "it is only that you do not know what you have missed all these years. Will you at least swear to me, then, that if you live through this battle you will find a woman to lie with afterwards? Even the best of men, I have heard said, needs some easing of his body if he is not to go mad, and if that is so, you are long overdue."

Beowulf's ears warmed beneath his helm: he knew that no man save Hygelac would have dared speak to him so and any other man, he might have picked up and shaken until his teeth rattled in his head. But he had never raised hand to Hygelac save in play or training, and never seen the glimmer of fear in his kinsman's eyes that he saw in the gazes of others whenever he showed the least sign of anger; and that he would not change least of all now, when neither of them might live to round Whales' Ness again.

"Swear it to me," Hygelac said, and Beowulf blinked at his friend's sudden stubbornness. "Truly, I worry for you, Beowulf, and if…"

"Well enough," Beowulf growled, for he found that he could not bear to hear Hygelac speaking of his own death. "I swear it." And if, some part of his mind whispered, I can do what I ought, then I will know. Know that Heofonglowe's curse did not truly bite on me, or if it did, that it was only Hygd that she barred from me, that I may still take a wife and carry on my line. I have heard that a man may love a second wife as deeply as a first, though the loves be as different as cheese and honey cakes.

Hygelac laughed and clapped him on the shoulder. "Good! And for my part, I swear that if I live, I shall spare no trouble to find you the fanciest frithle in Geat land, to make up for all the chances you never took."

The western sky was just beginning to turn pink with sunset, the evening mist rising cool from the lake, when Beowulf heard the distant roo roo of a great horn. At once the Geats were on their feet, taking up their places.

"I thought they'd never come," said Hygelac, laughing. "Well, my men: shall we give these late guests the welcome that is most fitting for them?"

"Aye!" The Geats roared, clashing swords against shields until a startled flock of geese flew up from the reeds, their barking honks and rushing wings so loud there might have been another host shouting with the Northern war band.

It was not long until the first of the Franks came out of the tall marsh grasses lining the far shore of the lake by the wider ford; Beowulf saw him lift the horn to his lips and blow again, its harsh note carrying easily over the water. Behind the warders of the ford, the archers strung their bows, cursing the dampness that had crept in even through the oiled leather wrappings. The Geatish bowstrings, as Hygelac had guessed, were not the only ones that had suffered; though a flight of arrows swarmed up like long bodied black hornets from the lake's shore, they fell far short, hissing softly into the water.

The Frankish horn blew once more, and another answered from the other side; Beowulf glanced quickly behind, and saw the armed men gathering before the narrow ford as well. The Franks must have spent most of the day creeping into their places, and Beowulf could not help sparing a second's grudging admiration for Theudebert, who had marked so quickly that Hygelac was gone and guessed at once where he must have fled. Across the water, a golden bull's head gleamed as standard: beneath it stood two men who drew Beowulf's eye. The long dark hair of one flowed out beneath his helm, falling almost to his knees; his byrnie and helmet were gilded, shining mist dulled red in the evening light.

The man beside him was taller little more than half a head under Beowulf's own height, with a short gold embroidered cloak falling from his massive shoulders, and he spun the heavy axe in his right hand as easily as if it had been a child's willow wand. Theudebert and Dagochramn, Beowulf thought: if we can overcome those two, then the battle will be ours!

The Merovingian leader spoke; the horn sounded again, and the first line of Franks waded grimly into the water, shields high. When he judged them close enough, Hygelac said, "Loose," and the Geatish archers shot. Most of the arrows splashed harmlessly into the lake or thunked into the Frankish shields, but a few men cried out, clutching at limbs or toppling down into the water.

We can hold them! Beowulf thought with a wild surge of hope. Then he heard the splashing of oars, and his heart sank within him. All around the shores of the lake, the little boats were nosing out of the reeds: Theudebert had wasted no time in gathering the Frisian fishermen to his aid. Still, each boat could carry no more than one or two men, and they would be hard put to fend off blows as they climbed out and tried to gain the shore. Hygelac was already shouting orders, reforming his troops to deal with this new threat even as the Franks pushed on across the fords. Beowulf waited, the bone hilt of his sword suddenly sweat slick against his palm. The Franks in the water paused a moment, as if gathering themselves, then suddenly rushed up the rocky slope, the ones behind pushing those before them on.

A thrusting spear snaked down past Beowulf's shoulder; he saw the look of gaping surprise on the face of the thin, clean shaven Frank rushing him just as the spear tip bit in through his mouth and he fell. Slowed by their dead, the Frankish charge lost its strength: the first shield slamming into his hardly so much as moved Beowulf's arm. He struck, hammering a helmet in with a spray of sparks and red droplets; struck again, shearing through chain mail, his sword bit deep into a shoulder bone, and he wrenched it free as the wounded Frank dropped to his knees, blade falling from his stricken hand.

The next man, pushing past his hurt comrade, was wiser, his axe blurring down towards Beowulf's calf; Beowulf just managed to block it with his sword, ramming the edge of his own shield into the Frankish warrior's face to knock him into the deep water at the side of the ford, where he sank, face down. He could not glance around to see if the men behind him were holding against the assault from the small boats, only trust in their strength to guard his back; but he could hear the singing of arrows and throwing spears through the shouting and clashing of weapons and shields. Some of the Franks were shouting,

"Theudebert!" Or "Merovech!"; Others cried, "On, Haetwere!" Or "Adalwulf!" Merovingians, Haetwere, and Frisians together, the thought flashed through Beowulf's mind as chips flew from his booming shield and he twisted and struck again and again. *No wonder they have such a weight of numbers, yet we still hold, and Hygelac stands yet.*

At last the Frankish horn sounded from the shore of the lake again, and the men still on the ford drew back hastily with their shields over their heads against the Geatish arrows and casting spears. *Have we won?* Beowulf thought, breathing hard as he let his shield drop down by his side. *Are we too hard a shell for these gulls to crack?* He laid his sword down carefully, pushing his helm back and wiping the stinging sweat from his eyes, then glanced about.

Hygelac had stayed back, shouting men forward to replace the wounded: he was still unscathed, though sweat dripped from the edges of his helmet. Thunarfinn and Sigemund were still holding their ford; across the island, Beowulf could not tell whether the blood on their byrnies came from their own wounds or those of others. Beside him, Agilar raised his thrusting spear in brave acknowledgment of Beowulf's glance, but Widuhund sprawled limp by the edge of the ford, his helm gone and bright red hair darkened with clotted blood. Ansuwulf paced wildly by the shore, chewing at the froth darkened leather rim of his shield. As Beowulf watched, he raised his face to the skies with a horrible howl, his body twisting as though he fought against himself to keep from turning his berserk wod on his own comrades, then dropped to his knees, beating his sword wildly against the ground.

Beowulf had to look away quickly once, in the northern woods, he had seen a fox in the last throes of the howling wod, body drawn into twisting convulsions and froth spewing from its mouth, and it was hard not to believe that Ansuwulf suffered the same agony now. It will kill him, Beowulf thought. Thank you, Frea Ing, that you do not give such cruel gifts!

The mist was thickening, so that Beowulf could barely see Theudebert's gold bull's head standard; the two men beneath it, the long haired Merovingian and his big champion, seemed to be talking, but they were too far away for Beowulf to hear even the murmur of their voices. Go away, go away! he thought. We are too much for you here: you cannot take us, and night shall fall soon. Go away! At last, though, Dagochramn lifted his shield and waded out into the ford, stopping in the middle.

"Ye Geats!" He shouted. The Frank's guttural accent was so thick that Beowulf had to strain to make out every word, though Dagochramn was speaking very slowly. "Is one of ye brave enough to do fight with me, alone? Chlochilaich, Geat king will you take my challenge? Or the big wosel beside you, is he man, that he will fight me?"

Hygelac came forward, his standard bearer behind him. Before he could speak, Beowulf grabbed his arm.

"Hygelac, let me fight him for you," he urged. "My king, my kinsman, I beg you and when have I ever begged you for anything? If you fall in this combat we shall all lose our hearts, but should I fall, it will only spur your men to fight the harder to ward you."

Hygelac shook his head, his blue eyes bright beneath the ring pieces of his helm and his mouth grinning under the gilded beast head that tipped its nasal.

"No, Berki. You have won your fame already; now it is my turn to do single battle for folk and honor. Dagochramn is no Grendel: do not grudge him to me, oath brother! You are tired from fighting, whereas I am fresh and I am king: this is my duty."

The gleeful look on his face was not that of a man taking up a burden; it was the look of the wild youth Beowulf had known before sorrow whelmed the house of Hrethel and Hygelac had to think on taking the throne. Before Beowulf could speak further, Hygelac turned and shouted,

"Come ashore, Dagochramn! I myself, Hygelac Hrethling, of the Swerting line, shall do battle with you. And when you fall before my sword, you shall have this one joy: to know that your blood has been shed by the blade of a king!" He brandished his blade at the Frankish champion. Beowulf could not guess how much Dagochramn had understood, but the Geat king's gesture could not be mistaken: Dagochramn lowered his shield and waded forward, and Hygelac gestured at his men to clear the way.

"Hygelac," Beowulf said softly. "Ward yourself well, and fight well and may luck and all the gods be with you, and idises of weal above your head."

Hygelac smiled. "Now matters shall be as Wyrd shapes them. If I fall, my friend and kinsman, lead my men well, and take good care of Hygd and the children when you come back to our hall." And with that, he turned to face Dagochramn as the big Frank climbed dripping from the lake.

For all his size, Dagochramn was as fast as Beowulf had feared: his axe blurred, cracking hard against Hygelac's shield, and Beowulf saw the splinters of linden wood white as bone against the red paint as Hygelac twisted to deflect the follow up stroke to his head. Beowulf's hand cramped about his sword as he watched Hygelac fighting for his life; he could not force his numb fingers to unclench. Several times, Hygelac's sword rang from Dagochramn's helm or grated along his byrnie, but hard pressed as he was, constantly forced to dodge back, to turn aside the deadly strokes of the Frank's great axe without meeting the other's strength full on, the Geat king's blows lacked the might to cave in the metal head plates or cleave through the riveted links and the flesh beneath.

One quick thrust scored Dagochramn's axe wrist beneath the byrnie's sleeve, so that blood scattered from the Frankish champion's arm with every stroke, but it hardly seemed to slow the big man at all, and each blow that Hygelac's shield stopped took a toll on the linden wood; the warding board was no longer round and brightly painted, but a jagged mess of broken planks.

Dagochramn bore in suddenly, pressing his own shield against Hygelac's mangled one with all his weight behind it. Hygelac stabbed desperately up at the Frank's face; Dagochramn jerked his head aside, so that the blow which might have caught him beneath the chin or blinded him only scored a bloody track up the edge of his short bearded jaw, slicing his helmet strap and lifting the helm from his head. But Hygelac was unguarded in that moment of daring, and Dagochramn's axe came down, shattering the rivets that held the plates of his helmet together and breaking through, bright blood and gray matter flying up in a fan of droplets like spray from the sharp prow of a plunging ship

"No!" Beowulf wailed.

Without thought, he flung himself forward, forgetting the sword in his hand and the battered shield strapped to his arm. His head swam with madness and despair: he did not bother to strike at Dagochramn, but grasped him tight in both arms, as though he could crush away the sight that burned at his mind, the sight of Hygelac's body dropping limp with the Frank's axe still stuck fast in his sundered head. Dagochramn squirmed, trying to butt Beowulf in the face or knee him in the crotch, but Beowulf held him too hard, the riveted links of his mail screaming against each other. Beowulf could feel the crackling of bones beneath his arms, the softer crushing of things giving way within the Frank's body.

Dagochramn's eyes swelled from his purpled face, his mouth opening and tongue sticking stiffly out as blood spurted from his nose and throat; a gush of something hot and sticky tumbled over Beowulf's legs as he squeezed harder, loosing all the main strength he had kept reined back since his battle with Grendel, and his damn Dagochramn had gone limp in his grasp, but still he kept crushing, tighter and tighter, until something struck him hard in the back.

"Beowulf!" Agilar was shouting. "Gods curse you, he's dead and they're coming drop him and ward yourself, you fat ox!"

The stinging words from his childhood pierced Beowulf's madness as perhaps nothing else could. He unclenched his arms, letting Dagochramn's crushed corpse drop into the heap of its own ruptured bowels, and Agilar shoved a sword into his empty hand. It was just in time: the Franks were coming up the underwater slope, axe and swordsmen in front and spears leveled behind them, and Beowulf blocked the first spear thrust to his face more by good luck than any skill. But the rage within him still was not sated: he fought in red madness, not caring or counting where his blows landed, striking and striking again until he could taste nothing but blood in his mouth, see nothing about him but the wounded and dying to every side.

"Behind you!" Someone shrieked, and Beowulf whirled to meet the new threat, sidestepping so that he could fight with his back to the water, the Franks had overrun the island at last, but he did not care, there were more of them to kill, to wipe out the sight of Hygelac's brains bursting from his head.

Yet at last there was no one near him; the holm was strewn with shattered bodies, and only at the far side was there still fighting, a small man with a thrusting spear, gray fair hair streaming from his helmetless head in a half loosed braid, twisting and turning and striking again and again at the Franks that surrounded him as he howled wordlessly at them. Beowulf broke into a lumbering run, though each breath screamed through his chest, but his foot caught in something and he went down. He pushed himself up, cursing his clumsiness, in time to see one of the Frankish blades cleaving deep into the berserk's hamstring. Ansuwulf went down to his knees, but he still brandished his spear; they circled him cautiously, as if he were a wod howling wolf in truth, and when they rushed him together again, he fell with his spear through the body of another foemen.

Beowulf ran towards them, ready to keep fighting, but one of the Franks barked a sharp command, and his foes scattered, leaping into the little boats moored about them and pushing off into the darkening mist, leaving him alone on the shore with the dead.

"Cowards!" He roared, tears streaming down to wet his blood caked face again. "Come and fight me are you not men?" But the Franks made no answer, rowing swiftly away until even the splashing of their oars faded into the fog.

Beowulf dropped to his knees, beating feebly at the ground with his fists. The might of his battle rage was gone, leaving him so weak that the shattered shield piece still hanging from his arm by a single strap might have been a plate of thick iron weighted by a man size boulder; it took all the strength his trembling fingers could muster to push it from his arm, and then he slumped down in despair. By the time he could stand again, pushing himself to his feet with the help of a broken spear shaft, the cold gray mist had thickened over the island so that he could not see to its other side. In the last dim light, Beowulf walked the holm, hoping against knowledge that he would find a comrade not too wounded to heal.

But the Franks had stabbed the wounded Geats where they lay, even as they ferried away their own fallen. More of the battle was coming back to Beowulf now, how they had fled from him where ever he stood, shouting words he did not know, but could guess the sense of for they had feared him with more than human terror. And he, still slow and clumsy on land, had lumbered after them, but could not stop them, nor force them to stand and fight, nor save any of his friends. Beowulf wept again, but no tears came to his eyes, only bitter dry sobs like the retching of an empty stomach. Thunarfinn and Sigemund had fallen together at the narrow ford, mud from many trampling feet mingled with the blood on their broken byrnies they must have died in the great Frankish push after Beowulf had killed Dagochramn. Agilar's throat gaped open, blood matted in his curly brown beard and his blue eyes staring lightlessly up.

"Who would have thought that one day your words of mocking would save my life?" Beowulf said wonderingly to him. "You were a better friend than I could have guessed, if only we had gotten the time to learn it." Herebrand lay face down, speared from behind when the Franks overran the island.

Though Beowulf searched, he could not find the gold ringed Hrethling standard: the Franks must have taken it with them as a battle prize. Sickened by the realization of how he had slain the Frankish champion, Beowulf could not bring himself to look at the mess where Dagochramn's mangled corpse had lain, but he knelt beside Hygelac's body as the last of the light faded. Below the ruin of helm and skull, Hygelac's face was quiet in death, the growing darkness smoothing the last lines of kingship's burden from it, so that it seemed to Beowulf he was looking at the boy he had known long ago, his friend when he had no other.

He tried to close Hygelac's dulled eyes, but the lids had hardened already, and Beowulf had no heavy southern coins to lay upon them. Shivering beneath his blood stiff cloak, Beowulf found himself bending forward, with no more strength in him to stand against the night. He laid his head upon Hygelac's body, as if he were still listening for a heartbeat, and, pillowed thus on his dear drighten's breast, let the darkness take him. Beowulf awoke to clear skies, the mid morning Sun shining brightly upon him. His bones ached like an old man's, every muscle in his body strained and sore.

Beneath him, Hygelac's body was stiff as wood, his limbs drawn up as though he had tried to curl up against the night's cold; with the last of the morning mist gone, nothing veiled the bodies of the fallen Geats from Beowulf's sight save the water blurring in his eyes, and the black ravens waddling among the dead. Painfully he heaved himself to his feet, walking over to the edge of the lake to ease his swollen bladder. It was a wonder that the Frisian fishermen, at least had not come back already to loot the bodies they could have slit Beowulf's throat easily in his sleep.

Kneeling down to scoop up a handful of water for his parched throat, Beowulf recoiled in horror from the distorted shape he saw there a shaggy water eoten, caked with mud and dark blood, its great bulging arms reaching up for him. A moment more, and his mouth pulled into something like a rueful smile. He had seen nothing but his own reflection; but now he understood why neither Franks nor Frisians had been eager to come back to the slaughter holm. One by one, Beowulf chased the ravens off and gathered the bodies of his fallen comrades, carrying them in his arms like sleeping children and laying them out around Hygelac.

The Franks had been in too much haste to take the great gold collar from the Geat king's throat, so that it still shone where Hygd had set it, bright in the sunlight. Beowulf reached down to unhook it, thinking that at least he could bear that treasure back, but his numb fingers fumbled at the catch and could not loose it. It is too much like robbing the dead, Beowulf thought: he, if no other, would leave Hygelac spoiled. There were no stones on the island with which he could pile a cairn, but the water was deep, with sinking mud below, and Beowulf thought that the full weight of iron war harness would keep the dead from rising again.

"Forgive me, my friends," he said softly. "I cannot bury you, or burn you, as I should. But in the lake's depths, no wolves will tear your corpses, and no unworthy hands will strip away your gold for their own pleasure: you shall rest in all frith, and may Nerthus keep you well, you who fought so mightily and died without fear."

When all the Geatish bodies had been sunk, Beowulf waded into the water again. He had walked back to the Swertings' hall once, a longer way than this, it would not be easy, to find winter passage from Frisia to Geat land, but he knew that he must get home.

X

Beowulf's journey through the Frisian marshes was a hard one harder, in many ways, than his long walk back from the lands of the Finns. Whereas the small farmers and herders of the Northern mountains had been willing, after a time, to take in a trollish guest, the Frisians feared the fen wights more than the Northerners feared those who dwell among their crags. Most of the time they ran and barred their doors, and would not open them for all his soothing words; after the first time the men of a little village rushed at him all together with their fishing spears, an attack which he was barely able to escape, he skirted human settlements carefully. Luckily, he had thought to take the last of the Geats' provisions, which, carefully rationed, were just enough to keep life in his body.

He might have tried to steal a goose or duck from the gabbling pens by the fisher huts, but though he had flint and steel, his tinder was damp through and would not light, nor did he know how he might make more in this unfamiliar land. The marshes were dangerous enough by themselves: on his second day, Beowulf floundered into sucking mud that stripped his shoes from his feet and might have claimed his life if he had been a few steps further into the bog. By the time he reached the shore of the North Sea, Beowulf's byrnie and clothes hung loosely on him, and he had to bend the gold rings that Hygelac had given him more tightly to keep them from slipping from his arms.

He was shivering constantly, unable to warm himself either by walking or wrapping himself closely in his filthy cloak, and he craved the taste of honey as greatly as if he had been swimming for hours in the winter sea, a craving that sang painfully through his veins. Beowulf turned westward along the beach, trying to think of what he might do. He had eaten his last strip of dried fish yesterday, and had no way of getting more food. If Hygelac's ships had gotten free, there was little hope that they would still be sailing along these shores: by now, they would surely have realized that their king and all those who had landed with him were dead, and turned their prows northwards towards Whales' Ness.

"Yet I must get home," Beowulf said to himself. "Hygelac told me, I swore to him..." Rain was beginning to fall again, a cold steady rain blowing on the cutting sea wind that iced the byrnie beneath Beowulf's cloak, the chill of his helm seeping even through the padding that should have warmed his skull. He lowered his head and kept walking.

Cold as he was, Beowulf did not stop to rest at nightfall: he feared that if he lay down now, he would never arise. The clouds were breaking in the wind, the thin ice silver crescent of the Moon shining out and dimming as they scudded across the sky. And then ahead of him in one of the fleeting glimmers of moonlight, Beowulf saw the cluster of houses by the shore, with the little fishing boats already pulled up on the beach and roped to their mooring stakes. I am near the end of my strength, Beowulf told himself. Another day or two in this damp and cold, without food, and there will be nothing left for me but to lie down and die.

Then the stubborn spark of pride rekindled in his breast, a faint coal of warmth: he had not faltered in the water with Breca, nor had he given up hope of life when Grendel's mother had him down in her hall. He would have to gain what he needed from the folk in this settlement, and if they would not aid by choice, he would take what he must, and leave a gold arm ring as geld enough.

There was only one house with a faint glimmer of light showing through the oiled leather of a window pane, and Beowulf made his way towards that one. It was on the edge of the settlement, a little away from the others, and he wondered if it might be the hut of some wise carle or crone, such a one might be less likely to turn him away than other folk. Then, as he drew close to the door, Beowulf heard a woman's giggle, and a man's laughter.

"Ready for one more so quickly, dear?" The woman said. "You can if you want...but I won't give it to you free again."

"Nor will Inge believe I've been so long tying up the boat," the deeper voice answered. "A kiss for luck, then, and I'll see you again when I can manage it."

Beowulf hastily crept round the side of the house as the door opened and the man made his way out, humming cheerfully to himself. For a moment he was taken aback: it was the last thing he had thought of, to ask help of a frithle. But then the thought worked slowly through his chilled brain: who better for a stranger to go to than a woman who sold her body? She, it might be, would look at the gold in his hand before screaming for help, and she would be sure to have a warm bed. Beowulf loosened one of his arm rings and slipped it off, waiting until the woman's last customer had disappeared into his own house. Then he came round and knocked on the door.

"My, it's a busy evening," the woman said to herself, not without satisfaction. "Ah well, when the days are shorter, men have more strength left in them by nightfall. Come in!" She called cheerfully.

Beowulf opened the door and stepped in, his hand with the gold ring held out before him so that it would be the first thing she saw. He almost wept as the warmth of her firelight embraced him, even as his body convulsed in a spasm of shivering. The woman drew a deep breath, staring at him. In the firelight, she looked quite young, long brown hair tumbling down about her round, pink cheeked face. She wore only a pale shift over her sturdy broad hipped body, though a gray woolen overdress hung from her hand, as though she had just been about to finish clothing herself. The smoky air in the hut was rich with the smell of fish and leeks rising from the kettle bubbling above the fire in the middle of the room, and a half eaten round of brown bread rested on an iron griddle in the hearth.

"Well, well," she said softly, hazel eyes blinking up at him. "Who or what are you?"

"I am Beowulf the Geat," Beowulf answered thickly through the hunger water filling his mouth. He swallowed hard, trying to keep himself from reaching at once for her bread. "I seek lodging for the night, and food. I will pay you with this," he added.

The frithle took the gold ring from his hand, turning it over in her little plump fingers, then setting a tooth to it. She raised a curved eyebrow at the dent.

"For that, you could buy this village and everything in it, and have enough left over to swive me every day for half a year. What brings you here, so shabby and yet so open handed?"

"Food first," Beowulf said.

The woman hastened to cut a thick slice of bread, spreading it with butter from a little crock, and ladled up a steaming portion of stew into a wooden bowl for him. By the time she had filled a horn with ale, Beowulf had already finished off the bread and burned his mouth on the stew; she buttered another slice for him, and he ate until his shrunken stomach could hold no more. At last, when his raging hunger was stilled and the warmth had soaked into his chilled body so that his shivering had dimmed to a little shudder now and again, he said,

"You have guested me well, and now I shall tell you how I am come here. I was in a battle to the south of here, by the Rhine. My king was slain there, and all my friends and shoulder companions. I only lived, though I avenged my drighten's death on the one who felled him, and sought with all my might to fall beside him: my foes feared me, and they fled. Then I wandered alone through the marshes, shunned and driven away whenever I came to the dwellings of men. Yet I am no fen ghast, but as human as any other, and that can I prove to you on my body." Beowulf drew the long knife that Paanja the Finn had given him, scratching his mud caked arm with the tip so that a line of red droplets welled up.

The woman sighed. "Indeed, I have never heard that water wights bled like men. But some of your tale has come before you, and I fear that the news I must give you is sad. If you are of that Northern band that burned the Haetwere hall, then the Merovingian chased your ships north to the sea, and there they were broken and defeated." She paused, lookin brightly up at him. "You must have been the slayer of the Frankish Dagochramn. As the tale came to us, when Dagochramn had killed Chl...Chlochil...ach, I cannot say the name as I heard it; Franks all speak as if they had stones in their mouths..."

"Hygelac," Beowulf said.

"Yes, Hygelac! That sounds more like a proper name. Anyway, we heard that a great shaggy wight rose from the waters when Hygelac had fallen, to crush Dagochramn to death in his arms, and set terror among the Franks which little enough does: they are bold men and overweening in their pride, who think they rule Frisia, though we marsh frogs obey nothing save the laws Fosita and the gods gave us from holy holm in the earliest days. But I see that you are a man in truth. And if you give me your name truly, you must be he who slew Grendel in Heorot: small wonder that your hand grip should prove too strong for a living hero to bear! As for me, I am but Radegund the frithle, who comforts sailors when they pass by here, and fishermen when the tongues of their wives have grown too sharp and there is no honey left in the pot at home. Now come: take off those fouled garments and we shall set them outside, for their stench is too much for my little house, and I shall wash you and find you something better to wear."

Reluctantly, Beowulf took off his helm. It was all rusted, save where the silver press adornments and gilding were smeared with mud; when he bent over to let his byrnie slide from his shoulders at last, he had to work it and break the rust away from the weakened links. After weeks of wear, his tunic had to be soaked loose from his body in places; his trousers as well, and Radegund drew in a horrified breath when she looked at his feet.

"Those will have to be cleaned, and the poison drained from them, at once dear Frowe, how could you walk on them like that?"

In truth, it was only now that the feeling was coming back to Beowulf's feet a bone deep aching, shot through with sudden bolts of pain as he shifted his weight on the bench.

"I know that you are a brave man," the frithle said soothingly. "Try not to cry out, for I must hurt you now: but this must be done, if the rot is not to take your feet from you. You may trust me in this, for I live by other skills than those of the bed linens."

Beowulf did not watch what Radegund was doing: it was bad enough to feel the keen strokes of flaying agony, and smell the sudden foulness as pus gushed from his swollen feet into the little stone bowl the frithle held. Radegund muttered to herself as she worked; after a time rough cloth scratched painfully over his feet, and then she rose with the stinking bowl in her hand.

"I am going to wash this, and wet your bandages in the sea. Be sure that putting them on will hurt worse for a little time than if you had trodden barefoot into Gundahari's adder pit, but it is the only way to keep the wound clean we marsh dwellers must know such things."

When Radegund came back with the clean bowl and dribbled seawater into the open wounds on Beowulf's feet, he realized that she had told no more than the truth: he grated his teeth against the burning agony, wrestling his legs to stillness under her hands by main strength of will, and let her wrap his feet carefully in the wet bandages.

"Another horn of ale for you, my dear," she said, filling the horn and putting it in Beowulf's hand as she spoke.

He drank gratefully; his feet hurt so badly that he was hardly aware that he was naked in a woman's house. Radegund dampened more cloths and began to wash him carefully, like a mother hound cleaning her puppies. And when the old caked blood and grime had all been loosened from his body and wiped away, and the mellow ale had dulled the pain of his feet to a low throbbing, Beowulf felt his leek beginning to swell under her touch.

"A big man in many ways," Radegund said, looking up at him from under her eyelashes as her hands caressed him. "I think you are recovering from your hardships already."

Beowulf groaned softly when she let go of him, but it was only to pull her shift over her head. The frithle's round breasts sagged slightly, and the curve of her belly was marked with faint pale cracks like scars, the firelight had flattered her face into girlishness, for she was older than he by some years, he thought now, but her naked body was soft and yielding next to his. For a fleeting moment, Beowulf thought of Hygd, and his strength sank; but then he remembered the oath he had given to Hygelac, though it had been half in jest and half to soothe his kinsman's mind.

Hygelac, my kinsman, do you know that I am keeping my vow? Beowulf wondered as Radegund reached for him again, taking one of his hands and sighing as she cupped it around her brown nippled breast. He stroked her carefully he had not felt such silkiness of skin since his time with Heofonglowe. Yet Ran's daughter had been cold to his touch, but Radegund's skin was warm as a fur laid by the fire; and when Beowulf kissed her, he could feel the heat within her. After a little time, Radegund took Beowulf by the hand and led him over to her bed.

"Lie down, for you are tired yet, and I think you would crush me if you lay atop me," she told him.

Beowulf did as she said, and the frithle climbed astride him. He cried out as she lowered herself slowly onto him: the feeling of her hot wetness clenching about his leek was almost too much to bear. And then, for the first time since he had left the Frisians' holm, he forgot about Hygelac's death, forgot the sight of his friends' torn corpses stiff in the morning sunlight: there was only Radegund enfolding and embracing him, the urgent need driving his hips upward as he held her tight to him, and the rising wave within him too strong to name pleasure, after being stemmed for so long; overwhelming his mind as he thrust and thrust again, until at last the cry tore out from his very soul as his whole body spasmed in release. Beowulf lay panting with Radegund slumped over him, lights bursting inside his eyelids and his heart hammering in his ears. He did not know when he came back to himself enough to know that something was wrong, to hear the faint, pitiful wheeze of her breathing, or feel the hot wet drops falling from her mouth to mingle with the sweat slicking his chest.

"Frea Ing," he whispered. "Frowe." Then, the shout rising to rip the very sinews of his throat as Radegund gave a single broken backed twitch atop him and the last breath hissed from her crushed lungs, "No!"

He tore himself free of her limp body, falling to the floor. "I curse you, Heofonglowe," Beowulf whispered, the words scraping harshly through his throat. "You brought her death, when she should have gotten only good of me I should have known, should have guessed, but…ah, no, no!"

Beowulf drew himself up into a ball, rocking with the agony of guilt too great to find any outlet.

"I should have died on the holm with Hygelac. I am as they named me, accursed, a ghast of ill…ah, gods, why do I still live?"

Moving mindlessly, he rose, pulling his filthy clothes and rusted byrnie back over his head. With jerky steps, he made his way out of Radegund's hut, scarcely feeling the throb of his feet as he walked over the sand and down to the waves beating upon the beach, stepping into the moonlight pale foam, flinging himself forward into the water when it had reached his waist. Weakened as he was then, the seal fat stripped from his body by his wandering in the Frisian marshes, he should have sunk beneath the weight of his mail, but there was more strength left in Beowulf's body than he knew.

He swam, hammering at the sea with each arm stroke as though he could venge himself on Ran's daughter thus; and the water that might have taken him when he meant to live yielded beneath the furious desperation that meant to spend the last of his might in death. Dawn came, pale streaks of pink brightening the east, and Beowulf was still swimming, though his chest heaved like a bellows and his muscles shrieked with each stroke: he welcomed the pain, driving himself harder in hopes of forgetfulness. Soon it will be at an end, he said to himself within the faint flicker of awareness left to him. Soon…

"Hai!" A deep voice shouted. "Helm, over here: there's a man drowning!"

Beowulf hardly noticed the boat closing on him; but when the end of rope struck him in the face, his hands closed on it reflexively.

"Heave!" The same voice shouted from the deck. "Thunar and Ing, he's heavy!"

Beowulf found himself being hauled up like a fish on a gaff, and then rough hands were helping him over the side of the ship. He had no strength left to stand; he fell sprawling on the deck, the light fading in and out of his eyes as the sailors' words pulsed in his ears.

"Swimming in a byrnie? What manner of man? You fool, a water eoton wouldn't, clothes off and get him wrapped in something dry, his mouth's blue..." Beowulf closed his eyes and sank into the darkness

When he woke, Beowulf found that he had been picked up by a Scanian trader, blown off course and then kept in harbor by storms earlier in the month.

"And lucky you are," the vessel's steersman, one Hadubrand, said to him. "There's few ships at sea this time of year. How did you come to be swimming in your byrnie, anyway? Was it a wreck?"

Beowulf said nothing, and after a little while Hadubrand decided that his mind must have been addled by the wreck. But he was friendly enough, saying,

"Well, when you're able, you can work a little for your passage: even if you don't know boats and your gear says you've spent all your life as a warrior you're strong enough to be worth three men at hauling and bailing. But don't think on that yet! Eat, and rest, and get well: gods know, if Ran ever plays that same trick on me, I'll hope that other sailors will look after me as I've done for you, and may Wyrd hear that!"

Still, when they came to harbor in Scania, Beowulf broke the last of his gold arm rings for Hadubrand. The steersman was slow to take it, and at last insisted in fitting Beowulf out with such clothes as could be found to fit him, heavy winter cloaks of tufted wool, and dried meat and way bread for a long journey for no ships were sailing to Geatland, and Beowulf was determined that he should not tarry a second time in coming home. Hadubrand helped him to find a horse that would bear his weight, a sturdy, quiet, black gelding. Thus mounted, with the rust cleaned at last from his byrnie though he had lost his helm in the water though Beowulf's way home was long, and often he had to dismount and break the way for his steed through high snowdrifts, he had little trouble in finding lodgings on most nights, and at last he rounded the well known turn in the path to see the ice glittering from the high peak of the Swertings' hall roof in the pale winter sunlight. Beowulf reined his steed in, staring up at the hall.

Now he must choose: to go on, or to turn away. He had wondered before if he had brought ill luck to the house of Hrethel now all dead, save for Heardred and Hildegeard. But he could feel no shadow about himself, no sense of ill foreboding; the roof ice shone gladly, as though to welcome him home, and though Hygelac was slain, Beowulf still had his son to guard and guide. He tightened his knees, and the black gelding walked on. Beowulf did not know the man who stepped forward to meet him at the gate around the Swertings' burg: swathed in lynx and wolf furs against the cold, it could have been any of Hygelac's warriors. But the guard looked up at him, and almost dropped his spear in surprise.

"Beowulf!" He blurted. "It cannot, how can you have come home? Tell me, were the tales false? Does the king live as well?"

Beowulf heard the wild hope springing in the young man's voice, and sighed.

"No. Hygelac lies near the Rhine where he fell: I alone live, of all those who were with him. But I do live, though it has been a long and weary way back. How stand matters with Heardred, and with Hygd?"

"The queen rules yet for her son, but come, she will be glad to know that you are here." He shouted for another man to take Beowulf's horse, and led Beowulf up to the hall, proud as a young running hound with his first hare in his mouth.

Hygd sat by Hygelac's empty high seat, talking with Eofor. Ongentheow's slayer had aged, Beowulf thought, since the news of his brother's death had come to him: the red brown hair and beard had grown all gray now, his heavy features deeply creased. But, though Hygd was drawn with sorrow, her skin pale against the blue black linen of her overdress and white under shift, and her flaxen hair bound up tightly and covered by a dark linen headdress, her loveliness had not lessened, only fined in her mourning. And when she looked up, and saw who stood on the threshold, the light of unbelieving joy in her face speared keenly through Beowulf's heart, so that he would have wept if he had any tears left in him.

"Berki!" Hygd cried, and ran, skirts and cloak flying, to embrace him, as she had never done while Hygelac lived.

Beowulf let her cling to him, encircling her in his arms almost without touching her. Her nearness, her womanly scent, pricked painfully at his eyes, and he cursed Ran's daughter once more.

"Berki, the gods be thanked, you live! I should have known that mere men, however many, could not be your death..." Then she asked the question Beowulf had known he would hear: "What of Hygelac? Is he with you?"

Beowulf answered as he had before, his voice heavy with the sadness that yet knew no easing, "He lies near the Rhine where he fell. I could not save him, for he would do single battle with the Frank Dagochramn for his honor's sake, but I avenged him. Nor did I fly from the field, but the Franks shrank from me: so I, alone, was left alive."

"O, Berki," Hygd murmured, turning her face against his chest. "I had so hoped through these years of joy that our sorrows might be over at last. But I am glad to see you alive once more when I had mourned you, and now that you are home, I feel truly safe again. Come, sit down: I think Hildegeard has already filled the welcome horn for you."

As Beowulf crossed the threshold, Wulfa sprang up from the straw, barking and wagging her tail wildly as she ran to him. Beowulf bent and stroked her head before he let Hygd take him by the hand and lead him up to his old place by the high seat where Hygelac would never sit again; his loss panged worse within Beowulf's ribs than before, for here, in the well known stead, it seemed as though Hygelac had only stepped out for a little time, as if, in a moment, Beowulf would hear his light footfalls and laughing voice as he hastened in with snow melting in his golden hair and beard.

"Welcome, kinsman," Hildegeard said as Beowulf sat down.

This was her thirteenth winter: now, having been parted from her a little time, Beowulf could see that she was becoming a well grown woman. Hygelac's daughter was taller than her mother, and a little more sturdy of build, her hair rich golden instead of flaxen and her eyes more blue than violet, but she moved with the same grace as Hygd, and her delicate features and heart shaped face might almost have been pressed from the same bronze matrix as the older woman's.

"Know that we are glad to see you home, when all hope had been lost: kind idises watched over you, and brought you here again in the Geats' need!"

Beowulf took the gold bound aurochs horn from Hildegeard's hands and drank, the sweet mead running warm down his throat. "What need is this?" He asked. "Have the Swedes broken their oath of frith, now that Hygelac is fallen?"

Hygd sighed, sitting in her own place and looking across Hygelac's empty seat to Beowulf.

"Not yet. Othere, I think, will hold to his oath...but the Geats must have a leader who is a grown man, and wise. I had not thought to speak of this so soon, but I shall hide nothing from you. Eofor and I had just been speaking on this matter: if you had not come back, I should have asked him to take the throne in my own son's stead." Beowulf could hear the pain in Hygd's voice, but her violet gaze was steady: he knew that she had not made her choice lightly, nor without love for Heardred.

"And now?" He asked, half afraid to hear what she would say.

"Now...You were sister son to Hygelac, and have the best right to his seat. Berki, I know that Hygelac would have wanted this: marry me, and take the kingship of the Geats, and tend to all your beloved kinsman left behind." She unfastened the pins that held the blue black linen over her thick coils of pale hair, uncovering her head like a maiden or a widow ready to wed again and looking up into his eyes.

Beowulf bit his lip until the blood started. Scattered images fluttered before his eyes like moths: the Midsummer dancers at Hroesnabeorh, their backs turned to him...the dark mound ghost, his hood shadowed face white as a skull as he spoke the staves of doom...Hondscioh dying in the dark beneath Grendel's talons, little Sigemund's grin as Beowulf said to him,

"You and Thunarfinn shall lock shields and hold the Franks at the narrow ford," though he must have known it would be his death, and Radegund's white body lying naked and misshapen on her bed, ribs crushed in tight to her shattered spine.

"I will not be king," he said. "I shall give Heardred rede as best I may, and lead his host in battle if war come before he reaches a man's age, but Hygelac's son shall rule in the Swertings' hall. But as for wedding you..." Hygd's hand went to the amber apple that hung about her neck, a single gleam of gold against the blue black dress of mourning.

Forgive me, Hygd, Beowulf thought, that I cannot tell you why I will not wed you. But that shame and sorrow is too great for me to speak: I know that I should break again beneath its weight, if I tried to shape it into words.

"Forgive me, Hygd," he said aloud. "I love you still, as I always shall. But if I wedded you now, I should be king in truth, whether I would or not and I would not steal by stealth what I will not take openly. The high seat belongs to Heardred: you are the king's mother, and I cousin, rede giver, warder; highest among the Geats' hall thanes, mayhap, but no more."

Beowulf reached out over the empty high seat, taking Hygd's hand. She closed her fingers about his, her lips trembling into what might have been a smile. Beowulf had thought to see tears, but her eyes were dry: Hygd too, perhaps, had emptied her wells of weeping now.

"Ah, Berki," she said. "It is no shame to Hygelac's memory if I tell you now how I have always loved you, my first betrothed. You are right in this, for now, but maybe, when Heardred has come to his full years, we shall speak of it again."

She clung to his hand a moment longer, then sat upright and pinned her headdress back into place; if it sat a little askew on her head, Beowulf thought that none but himself would mark it.

"Eofor, where is the king?"

The gray old thane had watched them with little change on his stolid face, but now he looked greatly relieved. Beowulf knew that Ongentheow's slayer had not hoped for the kingship of the Geats, for he had ever been content to do his king's bidding, nor had he ever sought to bring the power to his hand that he might have had as father by marriage to Hygelac's daughter.

"Frowe, I believe that the king is out riding with the other young athelings. Shall I send for him to come in?"

"At once," Hygd said, and Eofor rose and left. She did not speak for a few moments, but when Beowulf began to tell her of what had befallen him, she closed her hand tightly on his.

"No, Berki. I can see how this sorrows you: such a tale need be told only once. Ah, if only Ansuwulf were here, to make a song of Hygelac's fall, but he was old for a berserk, and I think that he, at least, welcomed the chance to die in battle as befits Woden's chosen. But the hall has been quiet since he left: I have let the news go out, that we should welcome another poet, yet none has come, though there are still a few thanes who can play the harp and gladden us with song at feast, as much as may be."

Beowulf nodded. "And how stand matters with Heardred? You spoke of him as king, yet..."

Hygd frowned, the faint straight line between her golden brows deepening.

"So he is, since you have come back, and will uphold his claim. Though we drank Hygelac's death arvel and, for the second time, yours " she smiled ruefully, one side of her mouth quirking upwards, "Heardred did not take his father's high seat then, for none of Hygelac's thanes whom he left behind were ready to have a boy as king, even with Eofor to support him. Wynefrith and I could not but agree with them, that the realm of the Weather Geats needed a strong and tried hand at its rudder. But surely the Frowe speeded your steps towards us, for I should have wedded Eofor and made him king on the last night of Yule if you had not come so timely, though my heart were a second time sundered by it."

"Wyrd is often harsh to women," murmured Beowulf. In Hygd's quiet dignity, it seemed to him that he could see a shadow of Wealhtheow, holding herself straight as she spoke her farewell, though Wealhtheow had been worn and aged by her long sorrows and Hygd but seemed the fairer for what she had suffered, like gold coming the brighter from the smelting kiln.

"And to men," Hygd answered. "Yet..."

The words died unspoken in her throat, for the hall door was opening before Eofor and Heardred. Hygelac's son seemed to have grown even in those three months that Beowulf had been gone, his shoulders broader than Beowulf remembered; his golden hair was pulled back in a single braid, lending the planes and angles of his young face a new sharpness. He moved lightly, as Hygelac had, yet even in his twelfth winter, his tread seemed to carry a little more weight than his father's: Heardred had not been reared as a third son, who might go and fight where he would, but as one who would be king, if he lived; and of late, he had born the strain of unknowing whether he might hold the Geats' rule, or whether it would pass to his sister's line.

When Heardred saw Beowulf, his face burst into a grin of joy, and he ran forward with all his fragile young self possession forgotten. Beowulf rose from his seat, catching the boy gently in his arms and lifting him up, for a moment, as if he were only Hygelac's beloved child, and not the disputed heir to a kingdom.

"Beowulf!" Heardred cried. "Father told me that if he did not come back, you surely would. Blessed be the gods and goddesses who guided your path home!"

Beowulf set him down, swallowing hard past the lump in his throat. Had Hygelac, then, guessed that this would be his last faring? If his kinsman had spoken so to Beowulf, matters might have turned out differently.

"Aye, I am home," he answered. "And I am your true thane, if you will have me, my king: for I would see you in your father's high seat as is your right."

Unsureness shimmered across Heardred's keen featured face like ripples across the water of a clear pool, and his eyes flickered towards his mother. Hygd nodded.

"Aye, my son. All the wearisome burdens I spoke to you of, that Eofor would have lifted from your shoulders they must come to you, but Eofor will still aid you until you are strong enough to bear them alone, as will Beowulf."

Heardred looked at Beowulf and Eofor, then at his mother, and his sister who stood silent and watching behind her.

"I know not whether to be gladdened or grieved by these tidings," he said at last. "For you have told me much of the sorrows of kingship, and little of its joys: my father lately met his death as a king, offering himself as bait to the foe in order to save his men, and so, perhaps, must I someday do. Yet the Hrethlings' high seat is my own by right, and if I turned away from whatever I must bear to sit upon it, I should be no son of Hygelac."

It nearly broke Beowulf's heart again to hear such words spoken in a boy's voice that had not deepened yet, but, he told himself, I should have awaited no less from the son of Hygelac and Hygd, who began to learn king craft from his grandmother when other children learn silly songs about foxes and berry gathering. Hygd rose to her feet as well.

"Then, my son, let us send out word to all the drightens of the Geats, and bid those who are able hasten to this hall. It lacks three nights yet of Yule's first day, and I would see you take your father's seat before all the folk when the hallowed boar is led round."

Heardred nodded resolutely. "Eofor, call to me those men who are the swiftest riders, that I may send them forth." He looked up at Beowulf, suddenly unsure. "By far the greater part of my father's war band is gone. How shall I call more men to my side? Surely I cannot order my drightens to send me their thanes, as if I were a herdsman buying more cattle?"

"Gaining men to serve in a king's band is no hard task," Beowulf assured him. "Older thanes will stay with their drightens, but there are always young men who would gladly dwell in a king's hall and fight for him, though it cost them their lives…It will be harder to choose those of highest worth from those who would throng to your mead benches."

"But I have you to aid me, and you, Eofor. So be it, then. Let it be known that I seek strong warriors, and I shall trust in you two to help me choose among them." Heardred's voice did not waver a moment, nor did his deep blue gaze, and Beowulf thought, The child I left has become a man: already he is more a king than I could have been!

Over the next days, Beowulf learned what more had passed while he made his way home from the Frisian holm. Othere still held to his vows of frith with the Geats: he had turned his gaze southwards instead, hoping to strike at Hrothulf before the Scylding king had tightened his grip on the land hearing that, Beowulf wondered if Hrothulf's refusal to listen to his thanes' eagerness to raid had held some foresightedness. Two small battles had been fought, one on Sealand and one in Scania, before the winter weather brought an end to seafaring in war ships. There was no guessing whether there would be further war between Inglings and Scyldings after the early summer planting was done.

Though there had been no clear winner, most thought that Hrothulf had held the upper hand: the Scylding had fought, and been aided by a band of berserks wild and rough men, such as Ecgtheow and Ansuwulf had been before age tamed them; it was not always spoken to Hrothulf's good fame that he had called such cruel warriors to his side, but there was no doubt that his plans had carried through the better for them. It was said of Yrse that she sat spinning in Upsala, and seated herself every day beneath the great yew that spread its branches over the hallowed well before the Inglings' hof.

One tale had it that she had told her men that she would aid neither husband nor son if they were fool enough to fight for no good cause; but others claimed that, though far from the battlefields in body, she had been seen walking among the dead at night, urging them to rise and fight again, and that it had been her words that stirred the first strife between her husband's brother and Hrothulf. Beowulf did not know which story he believed. In his mind, he could see either taking place easily enough, but perhaps there was something about Yrse that blinded his senses, for no feeling of foresight came to him in either case save that he was sure she sat and span between well and tree.

News of great interest had also come from further parts: word had
spread through the Jutes and Saxons that the British warlord Artorius,
who had dealt so harshly with the Saxons who had fled to that island for
long years, had fallen late that summer. The winter weather had already
gnawed harshly at the lands south of the North Sea, the waters rising
to swamp their fields and turn the raised terpen mounds where their
houses were built into islands among the waves; now, in spite of the risk
of seafaring so late in the year, a number of clans were packing up, bag,
baggage, and goats, and sailing to Britain in hopes of better lands.

Beyond that, there was little true news, though the Hrethlings' new
poet, Hlewabrandar from Halogaland, had many songs that the Geats had
not heard before. Though his harsh northern accent sometimes made his
speech hard to understand, his singing was wondrously clear, and when his
strong fingers stroked the harp strings to coax forth the song of Hygelac's
fall, it seemed that even the hounds in the straw piles beneath the tables
lifted their heads from gnawing their bones to listen. He told Beowulf that
Godhagastir, who had just taken rule when Beowulf came back from his
winter with the Finns, was king in Halogaland yet.

As for the Merak Sabme themselves, "Alas," the poet said, a rueful grin
on his rugged face as he tossed a stray lock of thick brown hair back from
his forehead, "I cannot tell one Finn from another: those flat swarthy faces
all look the same to me. I had little to do with them, in any case, for they
know no songs in our tongue, and hardly any news worth hearing."

Beowulf sighed, but quietly, for he knew that it was the way of the Merak
Sabme to keep their worthwhile knowledge for themselves and their
friends.

"Well, Paanja is likely dead by now, for that was some fourteen winters
past, though I would not wager as much as single silver finger ring on the
matter, for he was as tough as dried reindeer hide, and a naaejtie as well."

At that, Hlewabrandar raised a heavy eyebrow, but said nothing more,
though he looked askance at the long Finn knife in its reindeer horn sheath
that always hung from Beowulf's belt; and Beowulf thought it best to
speak on other matters. Though there was some muttering and grumbling,
neither thane nor drighten dared gainsay Beowulf's support of Heardred
as king of the Geats: most thought that Beowulf and Hygd would rule in
any case. It was said several times over the ale cup that Beowulf feared to
dare the gods as Hrothulf Scylding had done by slaying his own kin for
the rulership of the Danes; but it was said approvingly, for such strange
troubles as dogged the Scylding line were best heard between the hall fires
and far from where Heorot had stood.

So Heardred sat in his father's high seat on the first night of Yule, and swore his vows of kingship on ring and sword and hallowed boar; and Beowulf was first to give his oath to the Weather Geats' new ruler. Hlewabrandar had made songs of Hygelac's fall, and Heardred's thanes raised their horn to drink to his daring, though it had cost the Geats dear: they named their dead friends, and poured out ale to the ghosts as they spoke of the slain men's deeds. Sweartwulf and Frithugeard came to rejoice that Beowulf lived yet, and, to Beowulf's surprise, Breca made the faring down from the Brondings' lands, for his father Beanstan was dead.

Though Beowulf greeted Hygd's brother with friendly words, Breca only jerked his sharp bearded chin and grunted: Beowulf could see it in his face, that he still bore the grievous shame of having claimed his rival's death and been proven wrong. The Bronding drighten was almost as sharp with his sister Beowulf could only guess what words had passed between them those years ago but he swore his oath to Heardred with as ringing a voice as any man there, and prickly as Breca was, Beowulf felt no falseness in him.

The winter passed, the ice locking its grip as the days lengthened and then loosing it again. With the first thaws came more news: tales that Hrothulf had been readying ships and men all winter, as had Othere, and rumors that this or that drighten in Scania had chosen to throw in his lot with the Swedes rather than the Danes. At Beowulf's rede, Heardred took in all the skilled warriors who came to him: but most of them were young men, little tried in battle, so that those older thanes who had stayed to guard the Hrethlings' hall had much work to do in training them.

Beowulf gave thanks to the gods that Whales' Ness was so far from the marches where the Inglings' lands met those of the Geats, for otherwise, weakened as the Hrethlings were by the loss of so many hardened fighters, the temptation for Othere to forget his oath upon Sweogris, or think that a vow he had sworn to Hygelac need not hold to Hygelac's son, might have been too much for the Swede's troth to bear. But there were many lesser halls between Swedes and Geats, and strong warriors who well knew the weight of blows within them, so Beowulf did not fear overmuch, even though he urged Heardred to build up his war band's strength as quickly as he might.

The goat willows budded, and the birches put out their green leaves; the last patches of snow in the woods gave way to mud, and it was not long until the oxen began to trudge the fields, with maidens and young men scattering handfuls of golden grain over the brown furrows. Wulfa dropped her summer litter, four sturdy little houndlets that mewed and squirmed over each other in the corner of the hall which she had made her own, and Heardred made the first summer offering in the holy grove on a brightly sunlit day, the little birch leaves and unfurling spears of ash leaves dappling his golden hair with shadows as he waited for Beowulf's hammer to drop on the head of the red coated ox that stood chewing quietly at the young shoots of grass pricking out around the base of the white stone.

Frea Ing, Beowulf thought, grant us some time of frith yet. You bring the springing grain to ripeness before it is harvested; you ward the apple blossom from the withering frost. Folk warder, ward Heardred now, and when the Grim One reaps his barley this year, let it be far from here! A soft breeze stirred the leaves overhead. Even as Beowulf brought the hammer down on the ox's horned skull, he hardly felt the blow landing; and when Heardred's knife opened the great vessel in the stunned beast's throat and the torrent of blood gushed bright into the wide wooden bowl that Hygd held up in both hands, he felt as though a water gate had been opened in his own heart, warm joy flowing through him with the stream of the offering's life.

When the ox had lain down, its dark eyes dull and its hooves no longer jerking with the last twitches of death, Heardred lifted his knife and cut a birch twig, dipping the pale green leaflings into the bowl of thickening blood and casting the drops about in blessing. As the first of them struck the holy stone, shining like red Frowe beetles against its whiteness, a shock went through Beowulf's body, and he drew breath deeply, bracing himself as if to draw up the earth's strength against his sudden faintness. Frea Ing was here: he had heard Beowulf's silent cry and accepted the offering: the Geats would have frith, for a time. Hrothulf and Othere watched each other that year like two tom lynxes circling in the woods: ready for battle, perhaps eager, but each wary of the other.

The rumors of battles to come were endless, but always proved unfounded; small raids took place along the coasts, but those war sparks fell on wet leaves and Beowulf gave thanks to Frea Ing, who, perhaps, worked now to still the swords of his sons and kinsmen. In most ways, matters between Beowulf and the Hrethlings were much as they had been while Hygelac lived, save that there was less laughter in the hall by Whales' Ness, while Heardred was careful to keep himself to both a man's work and, when he had time to delight himself, a man's games, rather than sporting with the other boys as he had done before his father's death.

Hygd and Beowulf often sat together while the lamps burned down: most often, they talked of matters of the kingdom, but sometimes they found themselves speaking of simpler things. Ever, whether they spoke of supplies and alliances and the tidings that came to them or whether their speech turned to lighter matters, Beowulf looked at Hygd across the high seat, and wished with all that was in him that he dared do more than lift her hand in his as carefully as if it were the thinnest beaker of Southern glass. Another winter passed, and another, and a third. The feud between Scylding and Ingling seemed to have died down, though matters still rested uneasily in Scania.

Hrothulf had strengthened his place by wedding his half sister Scyld to Hereweard, an under king of more distant kin to the Scylding bloodline, whose seat was on the hallowed holm Wodenswih. It was also said that his war band was championed now by a one eyed man called Swaefdaeg, who had matched the Scylding's berserks in bravery and deed, challenging them in their places until Hrothulf spoke to calm his warriors. Hildegeard was wedded to Eofor's son Ingemund, and settled herself gladly as his frowe; Beowulf and Hygd marked between themselves with some laughter that Ingemund, though he was like to prove as good a warrior as his father on the field, hardly dared speak a word without turning to Hildegeard first.

Wynefrith had begun the search for a fitting wife for Heardred the year before, but none of the Geat drightens had a daughter of the right age, and no other maidens of whom the king's grandmother had heard had yet suited her. The fifth winter of Heardred's kingship had softened into planting time; the fields were ploughed and sown, and Beowulf and Heardred were walking along the road and looking over the seas of furrowed brown mud that would soon, if the gods did not turn against them, sprout green with another year's grain, when they heard the hooves pounding wildly down the road, and saw the rider bearing down on them. At once Beowulf drew his sword and stepped before Heardred to shield him, but his king touched his shoulder.

"Soft, Beowulf, he is reining in already."

Indeed, the dun horse was slowing, though mud still sprayed beneath his hooves. The rider pulled up not three paces from Beowulf and Heardred, his sweat dark steed blowing foam and rolling its eyes wildly. Beneath the eye rings and long nasal of his helm, Beowulf at last recognized Adalberht's long face, though the thane's ruddy beard was disheveled and caked with mud, and mud stained his byrnie as though he had fallen from his steed at least once in his haste.

"Hail, Beowulf!" Adalberht gasped. "And hail, Heardred Geat king! The gods sent that I find you here, for I have tidings that you must know. Mighty Othere fell to the claws of the eagle, beneath the weapons of the Danes; the battle bird, borne from afar, trod him with bloody feet at Wendel. Onela took the ring Sweogris from the arm of his brother's corpse, and Othere was buried in a howe at Wendel where he fell it is said by some that men who are deep sighted have seen him there yet, sitting upon the mound in the hame of a crow. Hrothulf spoke with Onela on the matter of that hoard which had belonged to his father Halga, which the kings of Upsala had kept to themselves for long, and Onela answered him with fair words, saying that there should be a good reckoning between them. Yet Eanmund and Eadgils rose to challenge Onela's right to rule the Swede realm, and there was further slaughter. The sons of Othere fled across the wide waters of Lake Weter: they wait now in Hroesnabeorh for your word, Heardred king, to know whether you shall shelter and aid them for the sake of the frith your father swore with theirs, or whether they must fly further, seeking other alliance to win their kingdom."

Heardred drew a deep breath, standing very still, and Beowulf thought he could see a faint tremor on the young king's lips. Though Hygelac's son had borne himself well as Geat ruler, far better than might have been awaited from a youth of his age, this was a choice that the most seasoned of leaders could not have dealt with lightly.

"How long ago did the sons of Othere come to Hroesnabeorh?" Heardred asked.

"Scarce three days past, my king. My trusty Sweartmane fell beneath me as I rode to bring you the news: had his strength held, I should have reached you at dawn."

"You have done well and bravely," the young king told Adalberht. "Your message is given; mount down, lest you slay this second steed who has borne you with such might, and come along to the hall. I know already what I am minded to do in this matter, but only a fool would embark on such a course without asking rede of those who are wise. Now tell me more. How many men came with Eanmund and Eadgils, and what do they know, or guess, of the troth of the Swedish under kings and great drightens?"

Adalberht shook his head, gathering the reins and leading his shaky legged horse coaxingly along.

"For the latter part, I know nothing. Sweartwulf sent me as soon as Othere's sons had told their tale. But the band that came with them is small, not more than twenty men, and not one of them without some wound on his body. Many more, I guess, died to bring Eanmund and Eadgils safe to the shores of Lake Weter."

Heardred nodded thoughtfully, fingering the little tuft of golden beard just sprouting on his chin. Though Wynefrith and Hygd saw to it that their king was dressed in the finest linens and softest wools, with silk woven trim on his tunics, their clever sewing could not quite hide the face that Heardred's hands and feet were still boyishly large for his limbs, nor could the severe cut of his gold embroidered hood make his face any older than its sixteen winters; but his frown creased his forehead and shadowed the edges of his mouth like a foreseeing of age.

"What of Hrothulf? Has the Scylding pressed his attack?"

"He withdrew from the field when Othere had fallen: they say that seemed victory enough for him."

Heardred asked no further for the moment, but walked in silence beside the two thanes, and Beowulf did not press him for his thoughts. He had learned that Heardred would listen until he was ready to speak, and say nothing before then, however anxiously he might be asked. At the door of the hall, Heardred gave the order to call Hygd, Wynefrith, and Eofor; no others, save himself, Beowulf, and Adalberht should be allowed within until he gave the word. The lamps and fires were kindled as if it were still a dark day in winter, for there was little light to see by when the hall doors were shut against Sun and fresh air. When the king's rede givers were gathered, Heardred said to Adalberht,

"Now tell your news again."

Eofor drew in his breath in a soft whistle when the thane's tale was done, and Wynefrith frowned, the lines on her face wrinkling into deep crags in the shadows of the flames. It was she who spoke first, and though her voice was beginning to tremble and creak with age, they all listened carefully.

"My grandson," the old queen said, "what are the sons of Othere to you? The oath sworn at Ravenwood was between Othere and Hygelac: they did not swear for their kin, nor did they vow to do more than each leave the other in frith. You owe them nothing, and there is nothing to be gained from flinging the Geats into the Inglings' strife: since the days of King Wisbyre, the hate of brother for brother has ever shadowed that house. My rede is that you leave them to it."

Heardred looked steadily at his grandmother, then turned his deep blue gaze on Beowulf.

"You met Onela by Ravenwood. His brother was a true and trusty man, who upheld the oath he gave to my father while he lived: what manner of man holds rule over the Swedes now?"

Beowulf's breath hissed out through his teeth in a deep sigh. "Othere was a true and trusty man, indeed. But when we met on the field of slaughter after the battle was done, I was glad in my heart that it was he, and not his brother, who would take Sweogris from Hygelac's hands before his folk. Onela is an adder in the hame of a man: I do not know how the shadow came into the Ingling line."

"Ah, Berki," Hygd murmured. "You have ever been too swift to believe that Frea Ing gives only frith and joy, and to forget that he is also king of the mound and the wyrm, Hygelac spoke to me, as well, of how he mistrusted Onela: he would not have Othere's brother in our hall as frith bond after the battle, though Othere offered it himself. If Othere's sons are of their father's kind, it would be worth much to us to have one of them in the Inglings' high seat if the price for setting him there is not the ruin of our own land."

Eofor nodded his graying head. "I must agree. But we are still not what we were when Hygelac lived, before the finest of our warriors fell to the Franks. My king, the choice must be your own."

Heardred stared off into the fire shadowed hall for a few moments.

"I have heard your redes, and they are well spoken. Now you shall hear my words. It is ill that kin should turn on kin, or that a man's brother should steal the seat of his son, if that son be grown and fit to rule a realm," he added, and though there was no haste in his words, it seemed to Beowulf that he sought to reassure his rede givers that he bore them no ill will for having been ready to set him aside for a seasoned leader. "And Othere upheld his oath not only to my father, but to myself after, though the words of his vow did not bind him to it. Further, we have dwelt in frith beside the Swedes these many years, where once there had been struggle and slaughter. Now I am willing to take up sword, if in a battle or two we may keep that which my father won; and for that sake, and because it seems to me that Eanmund and Eadgils have the right of it in this matter, I shall lead the Geatish host in battle to restore Sweogris to Othere's sons. If there be grounds for holding back from this course more pressing than those I have named, then say so now: else I shall call you two, Eofor and Beowulf, to rouse our men at once, that we may ride for Hroesnabeorh."

Though Heardred did not raise his voice as he spoke, a shiver ran through Beowulf's bones: he was ready, almost eager, to put on his weighty war gear again, to look out at the world through the iron eye rings of a helm and feel the hilt of his sword nestling into his palm. A vague sadness shadowed his thoughts, but he paid it little heed: Hygd's son was become a man, in truth, and Beowulf could do no more for him now than give rede to him when asked, and fight for him when needed, as he had for Hygelac. Having made his choice, Heardred moved as swiftly as his father had in coming to the battle of Ravenwood when all seemed lost.

His fastest messengers galloped away from his hall, their steeds' bridles ringing and manes flying, to muster the Geatish host; in a day and a half, the king's war band was ready to ride for Hroesnabeorh. Feola, who had borne Beowulf so steadfastly to Upsala before, was too old to carry his weight so far at speed now; instead, Beowulf rode a young roan gelding named Aelefeax, the son of one of the dapple bays Hrothgar had given him, whose ruddy pelt shone in the sunlight like iron warming in the forge. Beowulf was a better horseman now than he had been in his youth, so that Aelefeax mostly followed his commands and he did not need to fear too greatly that he would lose his seat when the fore guard of the host broke into a canter.

The silvered stud rivets and gilded strap mounts of the Geatish battle bridles glittered in the sun; whenever Heardred's black stallion lifted his head, the eagle heads that tipped the side bars of his bit flashed gold and garnet fire, and gilded beast shapes gleamed from the wide red disc of his shield, writhing around the silver scoured iron boss. Another golden ring standard had been made to take the place of that lost with Hygelac, but Beowulf had turned down the offer of bearing it on the way he had not thought he could carry the standard pole and handle his horse at the same time so young Ingemund held it instead, sitting proud in the saddle as he rode beside his king.

Hlewabrandar sang as they rode, his strong high voice ringing over the jingling of the bronze bridle rangles, and though Beowulf had asked the gods for frith, he felt his blood surging within him, the great round of his shield light upon his arm and his thick linked byrnie no heavier than a cloak over his shoulders. I have passed thirty five winters, he thought: what must this be like for the young?

By the time Heardred's host reached Hroesnabeorh, it had swollen to three times its number as the war bands of the Geat ruler's drightens and under kings flowed into it. Hroesnabeorh stood ready for war, its gates barred. As Heardred rode up to the wooden palisade and winded his father's horn sounding the same low pure note that had sung out hope for the beleaguered Geats in Hroesnabeorh seventeen years before Beowulf realized that he had been holding his breath, and let it out in a great gusty sigh.

"Come not back again, Ecgtheow," he murmured quietly. "Your time is done."

Hlewabrandar raised a heavy dark eyebrow at him, but Beowulf shook his head, and the poet said nothing. An answering horn, its sound lower and rougher than Heardred's, called from behind Hroesnabeorh's walls, and the gates swung open. Beowulf and Ingemund flanked Heardred as they rode in at the head of their army. Things had changed greatly in Hroesnabeorh since Sweartwulf and Frithugeard had taken rule those many years ago.

The great hall and the houses around it were neatly shingled or thatched; though the burg might still be small when matched against the Hrethlings' garth, now everything Beowulf could see looked tidy and well kept. Sweartwulf and his wife waited before the hall's door posts to welcome their guests: though Sweartwulf might have grown heavier over the years, and a few strands of white streaked Frithugeard's shining dark hair, they still looked hale and well. Beside them stood their son Hraefn, wearing a helm that had been scoured to blinding brightness, with a new forged byrnie shimmering over his broad shoulders.

"Hail, my king!" Sweartwulf called. "Hail, Beowulf! Your messenger reached us three days ago, but we have been ready for battle since the sons of Othere came to us. Now come into my hall, for Eanmund and Eadgils are waiting there, and we have much to speak on."

As Heardred and his companions walked up the hill, Frithugeard came down to greet them, horn in one hand and pitcher in the other.

"Well come are you here, as always," she said. "Hail Heardred, Geat king! You have grown to match your father's measure: may you be sig blessed as he was before this stead."

"May there be might in your words!" Heardred answered, drinking from the horn.

Frithugeard filled the vessel again and lifted it up to Beowulf.

"I am ever glad to greet you, my old friend: I would gladly have seen you come back to your father's hall before this, though the greater seat you hold is the more fitting for you. But while you are here, let us share that gladness that we knew together while you bided with us!"

The horn's curve was smooth in Beowulf's grip, warmed by Frithugeard's hands and Heardred's touch.

"You have ruled better here than I could have, though I would that we could have guested more often with one another since I left. May the gods ever bless you, and may the dealings of these days bring you no ill."

The ale in Frithugeard's horn was richer than Beowulf remembered from his time at Hroesnabeorh, spiced with the pleasant faint bitterness of rowan berries and a touch of mugwort. Frithugeard greeted the other guests with Heardred as was fitting, and they stepped between the door posts into the hall. It was warm inside, the long hall fires burning brightly with iron kettles hanging over them. Fresh straw gleamed on the floor, and heaps of firewood were stacked neatly along the walls: the carven bears that wrestled along the planks of the high seat shone as if they had lately been rubbed with beeswax.

The smells of smoke and clean straw and meat boiling over the fires prickled at the insides of Beowulf's nostrils, bringing tears to his eyes: he had not forgotten the grimy nest Hroesnabeorh had been when his father ruled there, better than an outlaw band's hideaway only in size. Sweartwulf's thanes appeared very different than the Waegmunding's had, as well: many of the grim ruffians that Beowulf had known were no longer there, gone to fighting or sickness or age, and though most of the half Finn's men were scarred and hard of face, they bore byrnies and helms that did not look so much as though they had been scavenged piecemeal from the losers in a battle. I did well to trust in him, Beowulf thought, and then, And the long frith with the Swedes has made life easier here, when men can tend field and herd without their byrnies on and swords to hand. Twelve men sat on the benches next to the high seat.

Most of them, as Adalberht had said, bore the marks of late given wounds on their bodies, with bandages still wrapped about them or fresh scars glaring shiny and red from their faces and limbs; a couple showed no clear signs of injury, but sat painfully, one with arms crossed tightly over his belly and one holding his shoulders with a stiffness which hinted at a deep slash or broken bone hidden beneath the red wool of his tunic. Beowulf knew the sons of Othere at once, as he would have known them even had the helms on the bench beside them not been crested with gold wyrms and their sword pommels glittered with gilding on silver. Like all the Inglings, Eanmund and Eadgils were rangy of build and long faced, with light brown hair and ruddy beards.

One of them wore his long hair and beard in a myriad of tiny braids, with little beads of gold and gemstones knotted into them; the other had his hair tied up in a simple warrior's knot, his beard trimmed into a point that jutted stiffly forward from his chin. Both their byrnies had been lately mended, patches of new made links shining from the dull older iron weave like a wyrm's mottling in the sun. The sons of Othere rose as Heardred and his men neared them. Neither seemed taken aback in the least by the Geat king's youth, though the one with the braids looked at Beowulf for a long time, green blue eyes seemingly taking in every detail as if he were considering a horse to buy.

The hairs of Beowulf's arms and legs prickled up under that scrutiny, as though a cold wind were running over his body, and abruptly he was certain that this one must be Eadgils, the younger of Othere's bairns. Warily he nodded to the Ingling, and Eadgils raised a narrow eyebrow in answer; but it was Eanmund who spoke first.

"Greetings to you, Heardred, Geat king. Welcome are you, friend in our need!...for I think you would not have come with your host if you did not mean to aid us, as our men are spent and it would take but little strength to cast us back to our uncle."

"That is so," Heardred replied gravely. "Indeed, I do mean to aid you if you are willing to swear oaths to me that you shall give help in my need when I call on you, and never raise hand or allow Swedish hand to be raised against the Geats or any of the folk who name me as their king, but that there shall be friendship between us, and our sons, while our realms stand. This I would have you swear on the bristles of an offering boar here, before we set out to battle, and again on Sweogris when it has been taken from Onela's arm."

Eanmund looked at Eadgils, who nodded slightly, the beads in his long brown braidlets clinking.

"That is a little geld to ask, for one who would set a kingdom in our hands," the elder Ingling said. "We shall give it gladly and freely; but why do you not look for more?"

"Though I have but few winters, they are enough for me to have learned the worth of friendship, of oaths kept and aid freely given." Heardred looked at Beowulf, just long enough to be sure that everyone within earshot had seen, and Beowulf silently cheered him: however great the Inglings' need, or however willing they were to swear to the oath Heardred asked, it was well to remind them what strength stood at his back.

"That is well," Eadgils said.

His voice was very deep, but muted to softness, like the echo of surf booming into a distant sea cave, and another shudder ran up Beowulf's spine as he spoke. However he bears himself with sword in hand, this is a man of might, Beowulf thought. It were best to be wary of him. Heardred and his men seated themselves on the benches by the sons of Othere, and Sweartwulf settled into his bear carved high seat, with Hraefn beside him.

The boy the man, Beowulf reminded himself: Hraefn was two winters older than Heardred leaned forward keenly, hanging on every word the Geat king spoke. Beowulf could imagine how this was for him, for if Onela fought, and he would, it would be the first great battle for those of Hraefn's years, with the Geatish forces led, not by an old man, but by one who was close to Hraefn himself.

Time for the young to take their place, Beowulf thought. It came to Hygelac and I more harshly than we wished: may it be easier for Heardred and Hraefn! Frithugeard and her hall women poured out more ale, and the thralls brought in fresh baked bread, rounds of hard cheese spiced with fennel, and lengths of thick dried sausages, the good fat leaving glistening trails along Beowulf's knife when he sliced off a piece for himself.

As they ate and drank, Eanmund told the Geats more of the battle in which Othere had fallen, and of how he and Eadgils had gotten free, though at great cost.

"Our uncle had planned this for some time, we think," Eanmund said, his light voice bitter as wormwood laced ale. "Yet our father was ever too trusting in him: he listened to Onela's words of how the battle array should be drawn up, and would not hear of anything but that he himself be in the fore as Onela must have known he would, the gods curse him!"

"Aye," Eadgils murmured under his breath, his deep voice rumbling like a far off tremble in the earth. "They shall, indeed."

"Hrothulf withdrew when he saw that our father had fallen," Eanmund went on. "The hosts were too nearly matched, and the Scylding had gained sig enough to sate him with Othere's death. Onela took the ring from our father's arm, and held it up, and named himself king of the Swedes. Then we came together to challenge him, but he had gathered all those men he trusted most to himself for the battle, while the best of our father's men had fallen beside him we had led the right flank," he added hastily, as if to answer any charge of cowardice before it was spoken, "and Onela the left, while Othere was in the forefront of the host...So he had many beside him, and we had few; and Sweogris had come to his arm, which many others took as a sign. He ordered that we be taken or slain, but we fought our way out and gained our horses in time to flee: we rode through the woods with Onela's men after us, so that we could not stop to tend our wounded when they fell, but must leave them where they lay. And with the help of the gods and all good idises, we came to the shores of Lake Weter, and took a boat, and crossed to Hroesnabeorh, you know the rest."

"What word has come of Onela since?" Heardred asked quietly, his eyes meeting Sweartwulf's. "Is he gathering his men, or has he sent any messengers to us, asking that we give his brother's sons back to him?"

"Nothing yet," Sweartwulf answered. "I have a few men who are woods crafty and stealthy creeping through the march lands, and others who are skilled with boats sailing Lake Weter: those who have brought word back to me say nothing about warriors gathering near to us."

"That will not be Onela's way," Eadgils rumbled. "We may be sure that he is readying his host to fight but we will see nothing of them until he chooses himself to call us to battle, or unless we press him to it."

Heardred thought a moment, his deep blue eyes gazing past the Swedes as he considered matters.

Then he said, "If it is his way to gather his strength and lurk until the moment he chooses, then let us not give him time to lay a trap for us. As soon as we have sworn our oaths of friendship and frith, I shall send a messenger to Onela, bidding him to battle, and with such words as he cannot let pass if he would be thought a man. By Ravenwood we had sig once, and Sweogris came to Othere's hand; by Ravenwood, if Woden so rules the fight, we shall have sig again, and Sweogris come to Othere's sons."

Eadgils' eyelids lowered, slitting his glance, and he murmured, "That is wisely reded. Aye, let it be so."

Eanmund nodded. "Aye. And, if you will, Sweartwulf, let a boar be brought for the offering now, for my thought tells me that the more swiftly this is done, the better matters shall go for us."

Sweartwulf and Frithugeard led them down to the foot of the hill where the Midsummer tree would stand on the longest day, while Hraefn hastened to bring the boar. A huge bristly beast with glittering tushes, it took four men to drag him to the stead where he would be given to the gods, throwing his great weight against the ropes that tied him. But Heardred stepped forward with no sign of unease, stooping to place his hand upon the boar's thrashing back, and spoke his oath in a clear voice that carried easily throughout the folk ringed to witness, Geat and Swede together. Eanmund swore after him, as did Eadgils, but when Sweartwulf came forward with the stunning hammer, Eadgils held up a heavy ringed hand to stop him.

"No: I have the skill to do this myself." He drew the long knife at his side, its dark stained wooden hilt nestling easily into his palm, and crouched down beside the boar, striking just above the breastbone with a ripping twist that came out under the animal's chin in a gout of blood.

Frithugeard was barely in time to catch the thick red spurt in her blessing bowl; the boar thrashed once and twisted, then went suddenly limp, his cloven hooves twitching as his heart pumped out the last blood in his veins through the great gaping wound. Beowulf thought that he had never seen a swine die so quickly, for Frea Ing's beast held hard to life but he had heard that Eadgils was a great giver of offerings in Upsala. Dribbles of blood ran dark over the edge of the brimming bowl in Frithugeard's hands as she lifted it high, but Eadgils was still crouched beside the body of the boar.

Had Beowulf been standing a little to the side, he would not have seen what the Ingling was doing: Eadgils had taken a small clay jar from the blood smeared pouch on his belt, and was stroking at the red lips of the wound to press more blood into the little vessel before he plugged it with a round of wax and tucked it neatly back into the square leather purse.

Though Beowulf did not speak, nor did Eadgils look around, Beowulf was suddenly sure that the Swede knew he had been seen and had not thought he would be, though the offering had been given before all the folk. Beowulf did not say anything about Eadgils' strange deed that evening: he was not sure what he could say, and there were many other things to talk about, battle arrays and loyalties and what might be awaited from Onela when the messenger Heardred had sent reached Upsala.

He and Heardred shared a guest house not only from friendship, though those were the only words spoken on the matter, but because Beowulf could guess his king's mind easily enough: though it was ill to think on, Eanmund and Eadgils could, if they chose, seek to buy their way back into their uncle's realm with the Geat king's death. To set a guard would be as if to name the Inglings oathbreakers but the bravest man would think twice about trying to take Heardred with Beowulf sleeping beside him. The Geat king and his kinsman were among the last to bid a good night to their hosts and go to bed. When they had closed the door behind them, Heardred bent over, casting his byrnie from his shoulders into a jingling heap with a sigh of relief.

"That is a weary burden to bear while talking!" he said, straightening and stretching his arms up until his fingers brushed the thatch. "Well, Beowulf you have said little all day: what has been in your mind?"

Beowulf stepped under the roof pole, the only part of the house where he could stand comfortably upright. "I have said little because my redes were little needed. You have grown into a king of whom your father, and his father before him, would be proud. But as for what is in my mind, I am uneasy."

"About what?" Heardred asked, settling himself cross legged on one of the beds that had been borne in for them.

With his feet tucked up under himself and his chin resting on his hands, he looked younger than his age; and the low firelight blurred the faint differences between his face and Hygelac's, so that Beowulf had the odd feeling that he was speaking to the boy who had befriended him so long ago the only one who would listen to his words: and that freed him to speak all that in his mind.

"Did you see what Eadgils did while Frithugeard sprinkled the blessing blood?"

Heardred's fair brow furrowed in thought. "He stood quietly with his brother, I thought. I saw nothing strange."

"I saw him press some more blood from the boar into a little vessel and stopper it: I think it is no mere tale, that he is skilled in the strange crafts which some are said to work at Upsala. And I find myself wary of him."

Heardred looked up angrily from beneath his brows.

"Do you think he will break his oath to me?"

Beowulf shook his head. "I think, I think that he is too wise to break an oath sworn thus, for he must know that the wights with whom he deals, and all the gods, look with unfriendly eyes on oath breakers. And you chose that vow well, so that it would be hard for Eadgils to work you ill while holding to the words he spoke. Still, I do not trust him. At the very least, he will seek his own good first and I should like to know what he means to do with that blood."

"As should I," Heardred said grimly. "Beowulf, you have had more dealings with uncanny wights than any man I know, and I trust your rede in this, as in all things. Can you tell me what I have to fear?"

Beowulf closed his eyes, the low flames in the ring hearth at his feet swirling ruddy patterns behind the lids.

It seemed to him that he could hear a far off thrumming, like the echo of a deep voice raised in song; that something dark fluttered about the edges of his awareness like a cloak caught and lifted by the wind; but he could see no more, and the words of foreboding did not spring to his tongue.

"No," he said at last, the word cracking into a yawn.

Heardred yawned himself, as if in answer. "Well, we have ridden long, and spoken long, today, and Frithugeard brews a strong ale, though I drank as sparingly as I could without flyting her guest friendliness. We shall think more on this tomorrow. Good night, Beowulf." Heardred yawned once more, stripping his tunic over his head and crawling beneath the blankets.

In but a few moments, Beowulf heard the young man's breath deepening towards sleep, even as he yawned again and again himself. It seemed to him that a cloud was drifting across his eyelids, so that if he did not get into bed at once, byrnie and all, he would fall asleep where he stood. The faint jolt of memory was not enough to awaken him; but Beowulf remembered the heaviness of sleep stealing over him in Heorot. Then, with the fear of Grendel urging him to wakefulness, he had driven his nails into his flesh till he bled; now, vaguely moved by he knew not what, he drew the long knife Paanja had given him and scratched the point across his arm. A faint line of pain, a few tiny droplets of blood welling up beneath the ginger hairs pelting his skin, and suddenly Beowulf was awake and clear headed, listening to the faint deep whisper of a song being sung somewhere within the garth. He did not try to wake Heardred: he was sure that the young king was better off where he was, safe within the house where Frithugeard's blessing of greeting warded him as a hallowed guest. But Beowulf crept out as stealthily as he could, despite his clumsy size and clinking byrnie.

No one stirred within Hroesnabeorh: the half full Moon shone whitely down upon the settlement, casting the shadows of hall and houses starkly on the ground. Beowulf did not need to go down to the gates to know that he would find the guards slumped against the wooden logs of the palisade, sleeping as deeply as Heardred in his bed; the low whisper of song seemed to coil through the garth like a great wyrm, its cold breeze stirring the hairs along Beowulf's neck. Walking towards it was like walking with the wind in his face, its strength growing with each step he took, until he had to lower his head and thrust hard with his legs at every pace: a weaker man could not have withstood it. At last Beowulf came to the guest house where Eadgils had gone some time before. The door was open to the night wind: the Ingling's voice boomed from within, true and fair to hear, though so low that it seemed to shake the ground beneath Beowulf's feet.

"The roots run deep rown under worlds,
the wyrm winds deep to wound the tree's rind.
White falls the dew down to the well,
the runes run deep rown under worlds.
The roots run deep rown under worlds,
the shuttle runs and shapes in darkness,
And yet I call the kin of might,
the runes run deep rown under worlds.
The roots run deep rown under worlds,
and rise the wights to ruling song craft,
the whispering kinat whither gates,
the runes run deep rown under worlds..."

Every hair on his body tingling like a hot needle, Beowulf looked within. Eadgils crouched by the hearth: writhing steam poured up from a small kettle that hung from an iron tripod over the fire, curtaining his face, but the braids of his hair and beard had all been loosed, a wild dark cloud that shone with tiny red sparks swirling about his head as he swayed and sang with his mouth and nose gaping wide. The Ingling wore nothing save a hairy belt around his narrow waist, a pair of dark gloves on his hands, and a pouch on a thong about his neck. His ropy muscles twisted like wyrms writhing over his bones, and Beowulf could see that Frea Ing had not scanted his sons, for Eadgils' half full leek and seed sack dangled and bobbed between his splayed thighs with every movement.

Spread out on the earthen floor before him was a thick tunic of tufted wool such as a man might wear beneath his byrnie to keep a blow from driving the iron links into his flesh, and other things were scattered about it: the clay jar in which Eadgils had caught the offering boar's blood; a string of entrails surely also from the boar woven into an odd eye drawing pattern; a milky wisp of shed snake skin; several hazelnuts; and a number of bones of different sizes and shapes. Eadgils was looking straight at Beowulf now, even as the chant still rolled from his gaping mouth; yet Beowulf knew with strange certainty that the Ingling did not see him, or anything else on the Middle Garth. Looking into Eadgils' eyes was like looking into a lamp after the flame had blown out: a gleaming pool of molten wax cupped without light in iron, clear, but with nothing behind it save blackness. Yet, even as Beowulf thought that he was unseen, Eadgils raised one gloved hand, tracing a run of sharp angles in the air between himself and Beowulf.

"The roots run deep rown under worlds,
let eoten kin leave me unharmed now!
Wend you from here the ways to home,
the runes run deep rown under worlds..."

It seemed to Beowulf that something thrust against him at those words, a strength greater than he had felt in the Middle Garth, though less than Grendel's grip. He stood fast, staring at Eadgils. Even now, he felt no threat, save the danger that always came when the ways between worlds stood open; but he waited, ready to rush in if need be, yet wary of breaking the Ingling's might for there was no telling what ill wights might be freed, or ill luck unleashed, if Eadgils lost hold of his seith spell now. Still staring at Beowulf, Eadgils reached sideways, unhooking the chains that held his seething kettle and lifting it off the fire.

He sang,
"The roots run deep rown under worlds,
the kettle heaved from high flames seething,
and open stand all ways of might,
the runes run deep rown under worlds..."

The Ingling cast something into the fire. A cloud of steam billowed out, hiding him for a moment. Even where he stood, Beowulf felt the faint prickling of heat over his body, and as the steam faded, he realized that Eadgils was no longer alone within the house. The sweat shone ruddy on the Ingling's skin, running over his naked body like drops of molten gold: Eadgils had turned his gaze upward, looking blindly at the emptiness where something stood: though Beowulf could not see it, he could sense the shifting of the air. Eadgils lifted the clay vessel of offering blood, shaking it until the clotted mass slid out to plop into the coals with a fierce hiss of scorch stinking steam. His lips moved, though no sound came out; then he picked up one of the bones, tapping a swift rhythm over the wool tufted tunic before him without dropping his empty water colored eyes from the wight he had called to him.

The wet lump of clotted blood was still hissing, its steam swirling oddly; Beowulf could almost see the shadow within it, something like the twisted shape of a man, or perhaps a man whose movements blurred his dark outline against the pale cloud coils. Though Beowulf disliked this work, he could feel that no trace of it was reaching outside the guest house; he knew, as if Eadgils had told him, that even the sleep that had fallen on Hroesnabeorh had not been meant for ill, but was only what came to pass when those without the lore to withstand it heard such singing. The offering blood charred down, its hissing growing ever fainter; and when the last steam had wisped up from the tiny blackened mass, Beowulf knew that the wight was gone. Eadgils stabbed the sharp end of his bone down at the tunic; it bounced back from the thick woven white wool as though he had struck at a piece of oak, and his teeth glinted through his wild beard in a smile of triumph even as he took up his song again.

"The roots run deep rown under worlds,
let all wights wend their ways to home steads,
in frith shall fare, in frith shall go,
the runes run deep rown under worlds..."

Again it seemed to Beowulf that something was pushing at him, but he stood fast, waiting until Eadgils' chant spiraled down to a note almost beneath his hearing, drawing all the whirling might into that deep well of sound, and from there to stillness. The Yngling slumped forward, head hanging low, and his breathing rasped heavily from his lungs, as though he had just come from the battlefield without rest. His wild hair lay sweat slicked against his skull now, and rivulets of sweat ran down over his shoulders. After a few moments, he sat up on his heels, stripped off his gloves, and reached for the horn that stood propped on the bench behind him, draining it in a single draught. Only then did he look up to see Beowulf still standing at the door.

"You," he croaked. "I should have known. You may as well come in." Eadgils stood up, grimacing as he stretched his back out.

He picked up a piece of folded linen from the bench, shaking it out, and began to wipe himself off.

"What were you doing?" Beowulf asked.

Eadgils glared at him. "Did you not learn enough by spying on me?"

"No."

The Ingling sighed. "If you must know, then Yrse would not weave for me when I went into battle with Hrothulf. Hence, I must work my own spells of warding against the bite of iron edges and what right have you to look at me so for it? Each man wards himself as best he may in battle, whether by strength, or speed, or skill, or wit; what of it, if one has more crafts than another? Nor do you need to speak to me of fairness in the fight, you who crushed Dagochramn with more than a man's strength. I think you have a thicker hide than other wights yourself: you have been in several battles now, and not always on the side that won, but how many scars do you bear?"

Beowulf thought, then closed his mouth. He bore scars, yes the white patch on his leg where the nicor's teeth had torn his flesh in the sea; the marks of Heofonglowe's clawed fingers on his shoulders, and the fading lines on his feet where Radegund's healing knife had scored him to drain the marsh poisons.

But the only injury he had taken through all the fighting around Ravenwood had been when he fell off his horse; no edge had scathed him in the battle with the Franks, though all around him had died. He had never thought on it, save to thank luck and the gods for bringing him through safe and not even that in Frisia, when he would have fallen beside Hygelac; yet he knew that, for all his strength, he was not nearly as skilled a fighter as many who were scarred on every limb.

"Haethcyn ordered my byrnie made thicker than most, for that I have the strength to carry it," Beowulf said, but he could hear the unsureness in his voice. "That has saved me from many wounds, and no other thing."

Eadgils shook his head. "Iron can scathe my hide as easily as any other man's," Beowulf told him. He drew his Finn knife, scratching the point across his arm once more until a few drops of blood welled up. "You see?"

The Ingling looked at the weapon, the bears and petaled stars traced in red upon the white reindeer horn of hilt and sheath, and raised an eyebrow, his thin lips curling into a faint smile in the tangled nest of his beard.

"Believe as you will: I do not doubt that blade can pierce your skin. But do not scorn me until you know what you yourself are!"

"I am a man!" Beowulf said angrily. "I am no seith worker, to weave spells in a woman's stead."

The Ingling only smiled again, his green blue gaze steady.

"Yrse spoke to me of you," he said, and it seemed to Beowulf that something rustled in the deep hoarseness of Eadgils' tired voice something he had heard earlier in the day, though not marked. *He thought ill of me before he came here not because Yrse belittled me, but because she spoke too well?*

For she would have wedded me once, had I been willing, and Guthlaf the Peddler said that she sat often with Eadgils in the evening, was that some cause of the hate between Onela and his nephew?

"What did she say?"

"Chiefly, that you are stronger than you are wise." But Eadgils' eyes wavered as he said that, and Beowulf knew that though his words might be true, he was lying when he claimed Yrse had said it. "But any man might have guessed that. In truth, she thinks little on you."

"I see." The longer he stood and spoke with the Yngling, the more Beowulf felt his tongue beginning to curdle, as if he had sipped at milk going bad. And he could see that Eadgils was utterly worn, his voice croaking in his throat: there would be no more spells sung that night. "Well, you will surely want to sleep after your work, and I shall surely rise early tomorrow, for I do not doubt that my king shall have need of me. A quiet night to you, such as there is left of it."

Heardred was still sleeping when Beowulf came back in, nor did the king stir when the older man shrugged off the weight of his byrnie and fumbled his way to his bed in the darkness. Beowulf lay awake for a time, listening to Heardred's soft even breaths had he slept so quietly when he was young? On shipboard where king and thanes bunked together, Hygelac had claimed that Beowulf snored like a bear with a snout full of wasps. As he grew older, Beowulf found that sleep came a little less easily to him. Perhaps it was because he had more cares to weight him.

"Waken, Beowulf!" Heardred was saying.

Beowulf opened his eyes groggily, the blur of sleep over them clearing slowly to his king's clean featured face. Heardred had pulled on a fresh tunic, of deep green wool embroidered with silver designs about the neck, but his golden hair was flat from sleep on the one side and stuck up in little pieces on the other.

"Onela's messenger is at the gate, and I would have you there when we speak with him."

Beowulf rolled out of bed, straightening his rumpled tunic and bending down to tie on his shoes. He heaved his byrnie up, letting it slither down over his shoulders, and Heardred did the same. Then the two of them belted their swords on, set helms on their heads, and picked up their shields: Onela's man should see that the Geats were ready for war. Sweartwulf and thirty of his men, all armed and armored, stood by the gate; Eanmund was there as well, and Eadgils with his hair and beard all neatly braided up again, although only six of their thanes were by them Beowulf thought that the worst wounded of the Swedes might not be able to rise from their beds that day, though they had made a brave show to greet the Geat king. Heardred nodded to Sweartwulf.

"You are sure that he comes alone?"

"Aye."

"Let him in."

The gate bar creaked back; the gates swung open. The man who rode in was big enough for his chestnut horse to seem like a half grown foal beneath him, though it was a well made steed.

Long wavy brown hair flowed down his back, but his beard was trimmed close to his jaw. His bright blue eyes scanned the crowd of warriors about him; then he deliberately lifted his helm from his head and laughed.

"I thank you for this honor," Onela's thane said in a raspy baritone. "Truly, I must be well famed, that such a band is gathered to make sure it is safe to let me in!"

Some of the thanes smiled ruefully; others stiffened, hands going to the hilts of their swords. But Beowulf could give little thought to his words: looking on the Swede's face, he gasped as if the man had struck him hard beneath the breastbone. He knew that strong straight nose, that square jaw and broad forehead he had last seen that face fixed in the berserk's death snarl, pale in the darkness with howe fires flaring in the blue eyes. Yet here, living. Beowulf caught his breath painfully. Now that the first shock had faded, he could see the differences from Ecgtheow: the cheekbones a little more flared, the jaw more narrow, marked out strongly by the neat line of a short beard instead of the old berserk's huge mat. Yet the likeness was still shocking, so much that Beowulf almost failed to see how dumbstruck Onela's man was, staring at him.

"My kinsman," the Swede murmured, as if to himself. "Well met, Beowulf Waegmunding I think. I am Wihstan, grandson to Ecgtheow's brother Wiglaf."

Beowulf opened his mouth, then closed it. Ecgtheow had spoken seldom of the Swedish kin who had cast him out, and then only to curse their names. But, though he was my father, I knew him well enough not to be sure they were wrong to want such a strife maker far from their stronghold. At last he managed to choke out,

"Well met, Wihstan Waegmunding."

Beowulf's cousin grinned broadly, as if he were pleased to have put his famed kinsman in such a state. Looking more closely, Beowulf could see that Wihstan, for all his size, could be little older than Heardred sixteen or eighteen winters, perhaps. He wondered that Onela had sent such a young and brash man to treat with the Geats, and at once knew why: the Swede king guessed that Beowulf would not slay his own kin out of hand and, almost surely, believed that Beowulf was the true leader of the Weather Geats. The men stepped aside to let Frithugeard through. Her rounded face was calm as she lifted the greeting horn up to Wihstan.

"As you come alone and in frith, be welcome here, kinsman of our friend, in this burg that the Waegmundings held for long."

Wihstan gazed down at her, but did not take the horn. "You do me honor, kind frowe," he said, the mockery gone from his rough voice. "Yet it were better if you heard my words before offering me such welcome. Onela, rightful king of the Swedes, has sent me to bid the Geats to send back his brother's wayward sons. If you will do that, then the frith between Geat and Swede shall stay unbroken, and Onela shall send you worthy gifts of thanks. But if you will shelter these men, whom our king has named wargs and outcasts, then war shall roar around Hroesnabeorh again.

Eagle and raven shall drink deep of the red mead poured out from the breaches in Geatish heart casks, and Woden's gray hounds shall sate themselves on the leavings from the fires of Walhall. These are the words of the bearer of Sweogris: Heardred, king of the Geats, how shall you answer?"

Heardred's gold tufted chin was set firmly as he looked up at the Waegmunding, and his eyes were clear and fierce as he replied,

"I have heard that in earlier days, Ongentheow told the Geats that the sword edge should mow some of them, and some should hang on the gallow tree for the joy of the black fowl, but none should come alive from the holt of the corpse greedy birds. Yet before sunset the next day, it was Ongentheow himself who lay on the blood wet ground, while the Geats rejoiced: it was my father who wrought that! I have already sent word to Onela that Hygelac's son is willing to show him that the Hrethlings' line has not lessened in might, if he dares to meet me on the field before Ravenwood, for as surely as Onela turned against his brother's sons, so shall the god of his line turn against him."

Wihstan clapped his hands slowly together.

"Well spoken, king of the Geats," he said. "Indeed, I met your messenger on the road here he had ridden swiftly. I halted him on his way, though I did him no harm: he waits in Osfrith's hall now, that the rash words he bore not rouse our king to anger before he has heard your own reply."

"And who are you to speak of rash words, Wihstan Waegmunding?" Eanmund broke in suddenly, his high voice sharp with anger. "How often has your tongue brought you to the edge of battle? But you should rein it in now, for you stand before mightier men than yourself, and they have no reason to love you, but only to be wrathful with the message you bring and the manner in which you speak it."

Wihstan shook his head, still smiling. "If you stand before me on the battlefield, Eanmund, you shall have your chance to deal with my tongue though I do not think I shall stick it out where swords are hewing, as it is no easy thing to fit a byrnie to."

In spite of Eanmund's glare, several men laughed, and Heardred was biting his lip as if to keep his own laughter in. Beowulf realized then that he liked his young Swedish kinsman very much and yet, he reminded himself starkly, he and I are like to meet on the battlefield in some days: where shall this liking be then?

"Now I have said what I was sent to say," Wihstan went on. "And, good frowe, if you do not wish to give me the welcome draught now that I have spoken of foeship with your king and folk, there is no shame in that: I shall ride back as I came."

Frithugeard lifted the horn again. "Though you may lift sword against us in days to come, yet this day you are our guest; and you shall bear our king's words back to Onela as surely as you bore his to Heardred. I say again: be welcome here, Wihstan, in the burg that the Waegmundings held until Beowulf gave it over to my husband. And if you will, mount down from your steed's back and let him rest and drink, and come yourself to the hall of Hrocsnabeorh, where we shall give you food and ale as befits an atheling guesting with his kin."

Wihstan took the horn from Frithugeard's hands and drank deeply. Wiping froth from his neat brown mustache, he dismounted, and Sweartwulf waved one of his men forward to take the reins of his horse. Beowulf marked that his kinsman was less than a head shorter than he himself, with the same broad build: the Waegmunding blood ran strong. Wihstan was staring openly up at him, clearly thinking much the same.

"Well," the Swede remarked after a moment, "I see the soil in the Geats' land is richer than that of ours."

Beowulf did not know how to answer that, but Heardred said,

"My father's sister Hildebere died in bearing her son, yet I am told that she was a woman of some strength, and tall for our line."

Wihstan glanced down at the Geatish king: though Heardred, like Hrethel and Hygelac, had grown to middle height, he might have been a boy of eleven winters between the two Waegmundings.

"Indeed," he murmured. "Sad, that she did not live to learn of her son's great fame."

Eanmund was walking away, his feet striking the ground angrily, but Eadgils stood in his place, and Beowulf much disliked the way he was gazing at Wihstan. He guessed that there had been ill feelings between Othere's sons and the young Waegmunding for some time but Eanmund had spoken of how Onela's plans had been long in the laying, and how Othere's brother had slowly turned the Swedish warriors, one by one, to his own side. Still, Eadgils did not speak roughly as his brother had, but said only,

"Wihstan, do you bring me any word from Yrse?"

Beowulf saw a glimmer of surprise pass over his cousin's face as Wihstan turned towards the Ingling.

"As it chances yes. She bids me say that she will not seek to come here and weave frith, as she has already guested with the Geats once, and the feather stuffed pillows of her high seat are easier on her bones than the jolting of a saddle."

At those words, Eadgils' thin lips curled slightly, and Beowulf wondered what message was hidden there that he did not know how to hear. Wihstan went on,

"Yet if matters go ill for you, and you live nonetheless, you are to remember what you and she had spoken of before. She said nothing more to me, for I would not vow not to tell Onela of it how could I, when I did not know what she would say?"

"Still, I thank you for the message." Beowulf could hear the faint sneer in Eadgils' rumbling voice, and he thought that Wihstan knew it as well.

"How could I fail to bear word from so good a wife to her wedding kinsman?" the Swede asked mildly. Eadgils' lips tightened: Beowulf thought that he had, indeed, been right when he guessed that there had been some hidden strife between Eadgils and Onela over Onela's bride, and was briefly glad that he had not been the one to take Yrse for his own. *Save that I shall never be able to take a wife while I live.*

It was easy enough for Beowulf to push that thought away as they walked up the hill. It was harder to keep it in his mind that soon he would be at war with his laughing young kinsman, and that Onela would likely be wise enough to send Wihstan against him if he could, both as Beowulf's nearest match for size and strength, and in hopes that his hand would be slow to raise against his own blood, even on the battlefield.

As they sat to eat, Wihstan proved more charming yet, though he was able to turn aside most of Heardred's questions about Onela with wit and skill. Still, it was clear that he was delighted and a little awed to be holding speech with his cousin Grendel's Bane, while Beowulf found himself asking more and more about his Swedish kin: it seemed to him, who had known Ecgtheow alone of his father's family, that he had at last come within sight of his homeland after a lifetime in exile. Once Wihstan made some scathing remark about Hrothulf's berserk band, and without thinking, Beowulf said,

"Are you not a berserk yourself?" for he had thought from words his father had said that Woden's gift ran strong in the Waegmunding line.

"Hardly," Wihstan chuckled. "Ale makes me friendly, not fight minded, and I have better things to chew than a leather shield rim." He bit noisily into a piece of Frithugeard's fennel cheese to prove his point. "So far as I know, your father was the only berserk among our kin. Ah, the stories my grandfather used to tell about him!" Wihstan shook his head. "When I was a child, I used to play at being Ecgtheow. Then?"

"And then?" Beowulf prompted, darkly fascinated.

"And then all the other boys got tired of me saying that I had killed them all, and got together to give me a good pounding and unlike old Ecgtheow, I didn't have the sense to run away to Sealand before they could catch me. And that was the end of that game."

Beowulf laughed aloud, and Wihstan grinned brightly at him.

"So you can laugh! I had begun to wonder, and to think that mayhap it was the duty of a hero to be grim, with never a jest or smile to turn his thoughts aside from slaying monsters and champions."

Beowulf's mouth twisted in a rueful smile. "It is only that I am slow of speech, and by the time I have thought of an answer to a joke, many more words have already been spoken by those quicker witted than I."

"Yet I heard that you were swift enough to answer Unferth when he challenged you at Hrothgar's hall, as few men might," Wihstan countered. Beowulf blinked: he had hoped that the harsh words between himself and Hrothgar's thule would have been long forgotten with the years, even though the Scylding's poet had already begun putting his deeds into verse before he slew Grendel's mother.

"What I said then was hardly worthy of memory," Beowulf replied. "And Unferth repaid me later with more kindness than I had earned of him."

"Aye, he lent you his sword Hrunting though he himself did not dare strife under the waters, or to do brave deeds; he earned no deeming there, nor works of fame." Wihstan's blue eyes shone brightly as he spoke, his strong featured face alive with excitement of course, the youth would have heard most readily those tales that set his own kinsman highest.

Beowulf thought of Unferth as he had briefly known him worn, like all Hrothgar's folk, by the twelve years of Grendel's hauntings and the knowledge that all his own strivings had failed to keep his drighten safe and shook his head. "Unferth served Hrothgar well, and had tried in his time to stand against Grendel: but it was not his wyrd to slay the water eotens, nor be slain by them. Let no man deem him the less for it! My struggle with the march treader was short, yet the Danes tholed sorrow and loss for twelve years, and held out beyond their strength. As I grow older," he added softly, thinking of Wealhtheow standing gray haired and sorrowful on the beach, with Unferth steadfastly dark beside her,

"I am less sure of which deed was the greater: the night's swift slaying, or the long years' holding beyond hope."

Wihstan looked puzzled at this: Beowulf guessed that his young cousin had never seen such lasting sorrow as he had seen in Heorot and hoped, with all his heart, that he never would. But Wihstan's next words surprised him.

"That is spoken like a man who has mourned greatly himself," the Waegmunding murmured. "And I shall remember it: I am not always as light minded as I seem. What became of Unferth in the end? Did he fall fighting the Heathobards, or when Hrothulf took the kingship of the Scyldings?"

"No. He took ship to God Home with Wealhtheow. I doubt that his god will grant him rest there, for that is not Woden's way, nor was it Unferth's," Beowulf added. "Yet I hope with all my heart that he found what he sought, if that he could after Hrothgar's death. He was greatly true to his drighten, and to Wealhtheow after."

When the meal was through, Wihstan rose, giving thanks to Frithugeard and Sweartwulf, and bidding farewell warmly to Heardred and Beowulf.

"No doubt the next time I see you shall be over a shield's rim," he said smiling. "Yet if I fall, I shall count it an honor to have been cut down by you and if I should slay you instead, then I do not doubt that my fame shall live forever. Be well, my kinsman, and you, king of the Geats, until we meet again." His chestnut horse, looking the livelier for food and rest, had been brought out again; Wihstan mounted up, and, with a cheerful wave, rode out of Hroesnabeorh.

As the gates closed behind him, the oaken log bar sliding back into place, Beowulf sighed.

"Aye," Heardred said quietly beside him. "It is better when one does not like the foe, is it not? Still, I do not doubt that Onela sent Wihstan to us in hopes of shaking our sureness: and for that gift alone, I find it easier to hate the usurper."

XI

The Sun's light flashed from the helms and byrnies of the Geatish host, brightening their painted war shields to the red of fresh spilled blood. Across the field, the army of the Swedes glittered like a great bright wyrm, glints sparkling from war gear whenever a man shifted his weight. Beowulf was already sweating in his byrnie, his hair wet beneath his helm padding, though the mild summer breeze cooled his face. Though the birds had taken flight from the woods behind the Geats in a noisy flock when first their host came marching up the road, a single eagle soared high overhead, his wide wings black as a raven's against the pale blue bowl of the sky. The pale grass of early summer had already been trodden into mud by the scores of feet, only a few patches still struggling up here and there: by the end of the day, Beowulf knew, no green shoot would still stand on the field save by the greatest good luck. Beowulf stood to Heardred's right, with Ingemund bearing the Hrethling's ring standard on the Geat king's shield side.

Eofor had finally owned, though unwillingly, that his years were too many for him to stand in the vanguard beside his king: he led the rear guard, with a horn slung over his byrnied chest so that, if there were need, he could blow the calls to send the Geatish host charging forward or to draw them back. Eanmund and Eadgils were with Heardred, as well, and those few of their thanes who were hale enough to lift sword; and Sweartwulf and Hraefn stood staunchly beside Beowulf. On the other side of the field, the golden Ingling boar reared high in the middle of the Swedish host. Though many men were arrayed before Onela, Beowulf could just see the glimmer of the usurper's gold helm crest but Wihstan was easy to spot, for the Waegmunding stood in the front rank, and was nearly a head taller than most of the men around him.

Three deep horn blasts sounded from the Swedish side, shivering through the mild summer air. Beowulf lifted his shield, locking it tightly against those of Heardred and Sweartwulf as the Swedish host began to move, swaying and flowing like a glittering river breaking its banks. The front line surged forward, shaping itself into a point like a great arrow or like the snout of a boar: the swine array, meant for breaking shield walls. Wihstan jogged at its head, his steps quickening as the first flight of Geatish arrows arched high from behind Beowulf's head, hailing down among the Swedes. A second shrieking of arrows wailed through the air in answer, though the two armies were still too far parted for them to do much harm. Beowulf saw the black length of one streaking towards Heardred's face, but before he could move, Heardred had thrown up his shield with all his strength: the arrow clanged off the iron center boss, knocked ten paces back by the strength of Heardred's blow.

"Well done!" Beowulf cheered his king, and Heardred spared him a swift grin as he shifted his shield back into place, bracing behind it as the next flight fell about them like deadly hail. Beowulf heard the thud of arrowheads sinking into flesh, the sharp cries of pain, but he could not turn to see who had fallen: the swine array was running now with their line pressing forward behind them, casting spears as they came, even as some of the Geats in the front row threw their own javelins at the swift nearing foe.

"Woden have you all!" Someone shouted: Beowulf could not tell whether it was Swede or Geat.

A spear grazed Beowulf's helm, but the blow was glancing: he blinked and paid it no more heed. He saw one Swede stumble and go down, then another, but the men behind them moved swiftly in to take their places. Wiglaf's shield slammed into Beowulf's, rocking him back on his heels; but he did not move a step from his stead. Beowulf struck downwards at his kinsman: Wiglaf did not try to meet his blow, but twisted to turn it aside, even as the man behind him thrust a spear at Beowulf's face. Beowulf ducked, hearing the point grate over the ridged cap of his helm as he struck out blindly and his sword bit deep into a shield's wood.

He wrenched it free, and saw that the Swedish line was shifting as the swine array, its single blow failed, broke apart: Wiglaf was already out of sword reach to his left, beating down hard against Heardred's shield as Ingemund tried to thrust at the Waegmunding with his sword and ward himself from the man before him with the standard pole. Beowulf stepped forward, throwing his own shield hard to the left in front of Heardred to knock Wiglaf off balance. A sword blow took him in the side as the Swede stumbled, and he heard the heavy wrought links of his byrnie break, but felt no edge bite. Then Beowulf was fighting for two, trying as best he could to ward his king without getting killed himself. Hygelac had fallen beside him: his son would not!

The sword Hrothgar had given him, Halfdan's brand Naegling, was harder forged than the one that had broken in his hand at Ravenwood: though shield edges crumbled beneath his blows, byrnie links spattering out like bright water where he struck, this blade withstood the strength that wielded it, hewing through spear shafts and arms alike. Blood sprayed over his face again and again; Beowulf spat his mouth clear of the hot taste, blinking burning salt from his eyes. His shield was hewn down to iron boss and grip, but he could still strike with it; nose guards and faces crumpling beneath his iron weighted fist blows. Then he heard the horn call from behind, two short sharp blasts followed by a long one. That was the signal to draw back: Beowulf thrust forward to make the man in front of him leap back, disengaging. Across the field, another note sounded: the Swedes had been pressing, but now they, too, began to break off the fight and pull back. Beowulf glanced behind him where his shield had sheltered Heardred, and did not see his king, though the ring standard had not dropped.

Ingemund was on his knees, hugging the pole one armed to him his sword arm dangled broken and his face pale with pain, the scattered dark beard hairs standing out on his skin like caraway seeds sprinkled over white dough. Beowulf hurried over to him lest any retreating Swede should think to take this easy victory, standing to ward the youth even as his eyes flickered frantically over the field for Heardred. Wiglaf still stood, though stained with blood; an armored body hung over his shoulder as he walked back towards the Swedish lines.

Beowulf's heart caught in his breast as he saw the gilded helm on the flopping head, the red gaping throat above but then he marked the dead man's jutting brown beard: it was Eanmund whom Wiglaf bore back to Onela, not his own king. Beowulf reached down, helping Ingemund up as gently as he could, though a gasp of pain hissed out through the young man's clenched teeth.

"Can you walk?" He asked, his own voice throbbing faint in his ears after the booming and shrieking din of battle?

"Aye," Ingemund gasped, but when he trod down with his right foot, his leg went from under him. He bit back a scream as Beowulf caught him, lifting him with an arm about his waist to carry him thus from the field. "No, leave me. Go to Heardred I saw him fall behind you, there towards the end when the Swedish spearmen closed from both sides..."

Beowulf did not remember that, but Headred had been slightly behind him, and most of the battle had already faded to a red blur in his mind Half dazed from shock, it took him a few heartbeats to realize what Ingemund had said. Then he let the youth down, leaping over the rent bodies as he ran back to where he had been. All around him, men stirred and moaned; a few still screamed, but more lay silent with their blood soaking into the battle churned earth.

"Heardred!" Beowulf shouted. "Heardred!" His hands were shaking so badly that he could hardly hold his sword.

Unwilling to sheathe it with the blood on it, he thrust it naked through his belt, desperately scanning the fallen. But Frea Ing be praised he saw no gilded helmet on the earth; there was a fair haired man who had lost his helm, but without turning the shattered body over to see the face, Beowulf knew from the size of the thick shoulders that it was not Heardred. Often a foot will slip in fight: Ingemund must have seen him stumble, and thought him dead. When Beowulf looked back, someone else was helping Ingemund back to where the Geats had gathered around Eofor, and he hastened on, looking over the living as he had looked over the dead. Eadgils stood beside the commander of the Geatish rear guard, his byrnie shining with blood; but by his easy stance, the spell the Ingling had laid on his tunic must have warded him as he had hoped.

Beowulf's own side was bruised under the breach in his byrnie, and his head ached someone must have struck his helm in the fight yet he bore no other wounds, and those small hurts did not hamper him as he hurried to Eofor, glancing wildly about for Heardred. But Eofor shook his head as Beowulf ran up to him, his craggy, gray bearded face grim.

"Our king has fallen."

Only then did Beowulf look down at the ground, to see Heardred laid upon someone's dark blue cloak. His byrnie was all broken about the wide hole in his left side, clotted blood gluing the loose hanging links to the tattered flesh, red meat with darker and paler bits churned into it, shining inside; the stink of opened entrails rose in a wave from the corpse. A broad headed spear, Beowulf thought dimly, twisted hard in the wound: they knew whom they faced. Though Beowulf had warded him well before and to the right, he had not been able to shield the young king from his death blow: Wyrd alone ruled in the thick of slaughter.

Beowulf knelt down beside Heardred, gently folding the edges of the cloak up over his body. Heardred's dark blue eyes stared unseeing at the sky, wide in surprise, and there was mud on his nose and in the golden tuft of his beard. Through the blinding numbness of his grief, Beowulf hoped that the young Hrethling had died at once, and not writhed on the ground in pain while Beowulf fought on, unknowing.

"Our king has fallen," Eofor said again. "And now, Beowulf, you must take the rule of the Geats, for there is no other left of Hrethel's line."

"But I..." Beowulf started, and fell silent again. He was Hrethel's daughter's son: many had said before that he had as much right to the high seat as Heardred, though he would not hear it. Eofor was too old to rule, and Ingemund, though he had borne himself bravely on the field, was no king. Yet I have failed a beloved drighten twice: how can I ward a realm, when I could not even ward one man?

A hand touched his shoulder: it was Sweartwulf, standing askew to favour his left leg, and with his byrnie streaked with blood, but still with strength in his grip.

"You shielded Heardred from death more times than I could count, there in the thick of the fight. Yet no man may shield another forever when his death day is come: none may scratch out what the Norns have risted, and Woden chooses as he will. You are my drighten, and my king: will you say now that you are not?"

"You steered the realm well as Heardred grew to manhood," Eofor added. "There is not a man here but trusts in you to steer it now."

Beowulf looked at the men about him, glancing from face to face. Battered and bloody, many wound pale beneath their helms yet the same hope glimmered from all their eyes, a trust that wrung at Beowulf's heart, for that he knew himself unworthy. And there, amid the stinks of the battlefield and the cries of those death wounded who still writhed on the earth, he thought of the dappling of sunlight through the green leaves on Hygd's flaxen hair.

He remembered how she had looked up at him, and the vision of her violet eyes wide in her fair delicate face was like a single pure bell note shivering through the moans and blood about him; and it seemed to him that he heard again the words she had spoken to him when he asked why she had chosen him. It seemed to me that a shadow came over Hygelac, and I thought that his luck flared high now, but it would be quicker than I thought to burn out. And I looked at you, and it seemed to me that I could see a steady flame burning within you, that would grow with the years and cast its light over all the land...dark trolls and thurses howled and threatened outside the edges of that light, but within it all was safe.

"Then so it must be," said Beowulf. "I shall take the kingship of the Geats."

He looked across the field to the Swedes. They were not gathering into array yet; he saw Onela's helm, still bright and unbloodied, below the boar standard, and Wiglaf beside him. This fight had not been so well reded as the Geats had hoped: matched hosts on an open field made for a slaughter, and if there were a clear winner, it would be but by chance, while Onela was too canny to come to the forefront of his host, knowing that it was chiefly his own death the Geats sought. Beowulf stole a glance at Eadgils, who stood silently watching him; he could not read the Ingling's thoughts on his sweat streaked face. Finally he turned back to his own men.

"Who will bear my words to Onela?" Beowulf asked.

"I shall, my king!" Hraefn said eagerly.

Sweartwulf's son had come off well in the fight, though he had been beset as thickly as any of them. There was a small dent in his helmet, and a few holes in his byrnie; a great bruise was swelling red along his scant bearded jaw, but none of his wounds looked worse than scratches, and his Finn slanted blue eyes were still bright. Little wonder, that Sweartwulf's bairn should prove a champion, Beowulf thought dully.

"That is bravely done. Well, then: say to Onela that we are evenly matched, and have scathed each other sore. Let him be content with what he has won, for now; but as for us, we shall go back to the land of the Geats, and Eadgils with us; and we shall see what befalls after."

"No!" Eadgils said fiercely, stepping before Beowulf. "My brother is dead, as is your king, and Onela lives. Should we not take our vengeance now, while we have him close to hand?"

Beowulf stared into the Ingling's blue green eyes, and at last it was Eadgils' gaze that dropped.

"A thrall takes his vengeance at once," Beowulf said. "A coward, never. But I will not cast my men to slaughter in order to win you a kingdom, when it is likely that the field can be held but by the last man standing." When, he thought, you may be bold, for your spell craft wards your hide, while all those you would have die for your sake have no such shielding "You shall be our guest, if you will, and safe within the land of the Geats for as long as you choose to bide with us and in time, we shall take this matter up again."

Eadgils nodded. "I see," he said, his deep voice thudding like club blows on the earth. "Now that the kingship has fallen to your hand at last, you see no need to fight further. You are no better than Onela."

Beowulf clenched his hands into fists half a heartbeat before they closed crushingly on the Ingling's body, breathing so swiftly with anger that he could barely speak.

His nails drove into his palms, his byrnie bit hard into his swelling shoulders: Eadgils' shirt might ward the Ingling against blow of blade, but it would be no help against Beowulf's handgrip. And that Eadgils' spell craft had kept him whole, while Heardred lay on the ground before them Beowulf had not felt that red rage since he crushed Dagochramn's body in his arms; it seemed to him wholly Eadgils' fault that Heardred was dead. And yet, through the bloody mist that clouded his sight, Beowulf could see how his own men drew back from him, the sudden fear flashing across Eofor's aged face and the startled wariness even on Sweartwulf's blunt features. I am a man, Beowulf reminded himself, and none of Grendel's kin. Heardred made his choice to fight as man and king: if I must take his place as the Geats' ruler, I may bear myself no worse than he.

"Be glad," Beowulf grated, "that I offered you guest right before those words were spoken. But perhaps it were better if you found some dwelling place other than the Swertings' burg for a time. Hraefn, go: bear Onela my words as I spoke them."

Hraefn strode off, and Beowulf turned back to the Ingling. Eadgils' face was white beneath the streaks of grimy sweat and spatters of blood, like ice on a winter battlefield, and the beads in his braided hair and beard rattled, even as he drew himself up proudly. But he was not the coward Beowulf had thought him: he had not stepped back a single pace, though all the others about him had drawn away, and still he spoke without flinching.

"If you would keep your word of safety to me, though you will not hold by Heardred's wish to strike down Onela, grant me a score of men to go with me. Then I shall leave your sight this very day: you are right in saying that were best for both of us."

Beowulf gave him a curt nod. "Wait here until we have heard what your uncle has to say. If he will take the terms I give, you may choose your men, and go."

After a time, Hraefn returned. "Onela says that he will abide by what you offer, for now. He says, let there be truce between us while we tend the wounded, gather the dead, and withdraw to our own lands."

Beowulf forced himself to smile at the young man, though his lips were chill as if he had been lying with his face in the snow. "Well done, my thane."

Heardred was burned with the rest of the fallen, not far from the great mound where Haethcyn's ashes lay with the rest of the dead from his own battle. If it had been winter, Beowulf might have tried to take him home to the howes of his kin, but he could not bear the thought of what a long journey in the warm summer weather would do to the body: the bloat and stink and flies were already well begun by the time enough firewood had been gathered and stacked to burn the fallen.

Beowulf sent word of what had happened ahead to Hygd he would have waited to tell her himself, but he knew it was kinder not to let her languish in hope and unsureness, or to give Onela the chance to send a messenger of his own to stir strife and sorrow among the Geats. Eadgils was gone where, Beowulf did not yet know, and guessed that he would not until the thanes that he had sent as the Ingling's warders came back to him.

Hlewabrandar had lived through the battle; he could not play the harp just yet, for he had taken a wound to the muscle of his shoulder and his arm was still bandaged tightly, but his high voice rang clear and pure above the crackling of the bale fire, drawing the minds of the living away from the sounds of sizzling and bursting, and the dark shapes shifting and drawing up their limbs within the greedy flames. By count of the slain, even when those who died of their wounds in the next two days were added in, the fight had not been so costly; but even had Heardred fallen alone among the Geats, that would have been a price greater than Beowulf would have chosen to pay, though they had slain Onela and every man who stood by him.

Yet Wihstan lives. That was some small easing to Beowulf's heart. Even if his kinsman was Onela's trusted thane, and though they had striven to cut each other down on the slaughter field, he was glad that Wihstan's ready laugh had not been stilled: there was little enough of laughter in the world. The fair weather held while the Geats rode home. Beowulf had given Heardred's stallion to Ingemund for his bravery in clinging to the Hrethlings' standard: the youth was, after all, a worthy husband for Hildegeard, though he would not be able to manage the high blooded horse until his broken arm had knitted and the deep slash in his thigh no longer broke open and bled when he put any strain on the leg. Though the worst wounded were still back at Hroesnabeorh under Frithugeard's care, it was a slow and weary way back to the Geat king's burg.

Even when men spoke of their deeds on the field, their voices seemed
muted and their eyes downcast: though the Geats had not quite been
beaten, they had lost far more than had their foes for a war that would have
won them little, at best. The Sun shone fair and hot on Beowulf's helm
at the head of the Geatish war band as he rode through the gates of the
Hrethlings' burg beneath a dazzlingly blue sky. Lush summer grass grew
about the trampled pathways and clearings between the houses now, and
Aelefeax pulled against the reins, his ruddy neck gleaming in the bright
morning light: had Beowulf not been mindful that the eyes of his war band
were on him, he should have let the horse drop his head to eat, for that the
gelding had borne his great weight without faltering or complaint all these
last days and it would have lengthened, if only a little, the time before he
had to look Hygd in the face and let her ask him of her son's death.

The thralls and bondsmaidens were bearing heavy pails of milk from the
byres to the cook houses: the cheese making would be going full strength
in this month when the grass grew thickest and the cows could be milked
thrice a day. The smaller children were bringing in handfuls of herbs from
the woods to flavor the cheese; one little boy dressed only in a grubby
brown tunic, his plump legs and hands all smeared with mud, proudly
carried a huge hwanna stalk that was nearly his own height.

A nanny goat, her udders hugely swollen, stood on the roof of the nearest
dwelling, chewing on the thick rosettes of house leeks sprouting from
the thatch and staring at the war band with an utter lack of caring in the
square pupils of her eyes. Farther down, the tame king boar who walked
about the hall at the oath swearing every Yule grunted softly in pleasure
as he scratched his dark bristly sides against the rough barked logs of the
palisade. Though his sons and daughters would have their lives spilled out
for the gods, and be spit roasted whole for great feasts or chopped up for
sausages with their fine cut flesh stuffed into their own entrails, Frea Ing's
holy boar had nothing to fear from men.

In some burgs, it was the way to send the oath boar to the gods at Yule,
bearing the year's vows upon his back; here, there was no one in the burg
who did not bring him a turnip or a handful of greens for luck at need,
and he had grown so used to being scratched and fed and cosseted that
even the children did not fear to pet him. Beowulf thought of how the boar
had snuffled hopefully in the straw at Heardred's feet at Yule as the young
Geat king had sworn his first vows to care for land and folk, and looked
away from him quickly, blinking back the water in his eyes and swallowing
painfully past the hard lump in his throat. As the war band rode in, one of
the bondsmaids put down her pails and ran up to the cook house. It was
only a few moments before Hygd came out, walking with careful haste. She
wore a simple blue black gown over a white shift, and Beowulf could see
the pale spots where milk had splashed onto it: like Wynefrith, Hygd had
never scorned to see to the hall's needs herself.

Though she had worn her hair bound up beneath the linen head covering of a wedded woman since her son had taken the kingship, as though to say that she would not marry again, now it flowed down her back, the shimmering flaxen curtain dropping past her knees. The blow of that sight struck Beowulf like a spear thrust to his heart. Now it was both his deepest desire, and his duty, to wed Hygd and yet his first promise to her had been to keep her safe, and least of all would he risk her death within his own grip. Wynefrith and Hildegeard followed Hygd. With another stab of pain, Beowulf marked how gray and bent the old queen was. While he had dwelt in the burg, he had not seen her aging day by day, but now she was in her seventieth summer: she moved as though a careless step might shatter her wasted bones, and her back was curving as though her sinews tightened its bow year by year.

Hildegeard's rich golden hair was hidden by a dark cloth for she, too, wore deep blue after her brother and she looked less a twin to Hygd than she had before, for her belly and breasts pressed hard against the plain dark linen of her gown: with a start, Beowulf realized that she must be bearing a child. But she is too young! He thought, before remembering that Hildegeard was a year older than Heardred had been, and in her eighteenth summer now. Hygd nodded to Hildegeard, who, not hampered too greatly yet by the swelling of her womb, hastened to the hall; but she herself came forward to greet the riders. Beowulf swung himself off his horse's back, walking towards her; Hygd reached out to take his hands in hers. With the bright sunlight shining full on her upturned face. Beowulf could see the thin lines at the corners of her violet eyes, like spiderweb cracks spreading out from a hole in a clay pot, and the creases beginning to fold into the fine skin of her brow; yet she was fairer to him than ever before, for he knew the sorrows that had left their marks on her face.

"O, Berki," Hygd said. "Now you are the only one left to me…" Suddenly she cast herself tight against him, crushing her face into his byrnie beneath his chest and holding him with all her frail strength.

Her shoulders shook with great sobs, and Beowulf held her gently as she wept, stroking her soft hair with his fingertips as he had so often longed to do. The scents of fresh milk and cheese and crushed hwanna stalks rose from her dress, her own clean sweetness beneath it, she was warm and delicate as a tiny bird in his embrace, her heart fluttering against him like small wings.

"Hygd, beloved," he murmured. "Hygd…" Even in sorrow, her touch stirred him: it was only by main strength of will that he kept his arms from tightening about her.

At last she lifted her tear streaked face, staring up at him. "Forgive me, that I have no better welcome for you. I did not know when, and the cows will not wait on their milking, whatever betides among men…" A choking laugh broke through her tears, and she held him tighter.

"It is welcome enough to see you," Beowulf assured her. "Ah, Hygd, I am sorry...I stood beside him with my shield over him, but I could not ward him from all sides; I stood before him and to his right, but the spear took him from the left..."

Hygd leaned her head against him. "My son, my dear son...I know that you did all you could, for you loved him as dearly as I..."

Beowulf was only dimly aware of Eofor leading the other thanes away to where Hildegeard waited with the horn of greeting, speaking those words of welcome that were fitting for warriors home after a battle. It seemed to him that sorrow and joy twisted in his heart like striving wyrms: he had lost Heardred, and Hygelac before him, but Hygd was in his arms at last, and he did not know which it was that shook his body and stabbed his eyes with fiery tears. It was Hygd who first came to herself. She wiped the tears from her face, the wetness golden against the pale sleeve of her under shift, and straightened her dress.

"What now, Berki?" She asked. "I heard that you had taken the rule of the war band, for the Geatish thanes would have no other than you. Will you take the high seat as well, now that there is no other who can hold it?"

"I will," Beowulf said sadly.

"And myself with it? O, Berki, I know that I am growing old, that I cannot vow as surely as I might have once that my body will bring forth living heirs. Yet I have loved you so long, and I do not think I can bear it any more, to be near you and yet without you..."

Beowulf closed his eyes in pain. "I love you, Hygd, as I have for so long. Twenty nine summers since first we met at the thing. Twenty one since our betrothal, O, I would with all my heart that I could wed you, but I cannot!"

"Why?" Hygd demanded, pulling away from him he let her go, though he thought he must snap his own arm bones with the strain. "What is it now what is wrong with you? If I am too old, if you want heirs to take the high seat after you, then you may take a frithle to be sure of it. Many kings have second wives, and third, and that is never spoken ill of them."

"That is not it," Beowulf said gently. "You are fairer than in your youth: I want no other woman, and would gladly see the Geats' realm go to the bairns of Hildegeard and Ingemund when I am laid in my howe. But..." Even now, his mind twisted and turned to free itself of what he must say. If there were some way to be sure of Hygd's safety, if he could be bound, perhaps, that he not grasp her with all his strength in the throes of love. The Hrethlings' smith Eadwald was no dwarf, to make such a ribbon as that which had bound the Wolf for the gods, and Beowulf did not trust any iron to hold him could not, if Hygd's life would be the price for guessing wrongly: no earthly iron could have fettered Grendel.

"What is it, then? You have never lain with any woman, you call Frea Ing your friend, are you, then, more like to those men who dance for him in the great hofs? Is that why you scorn me now because you would rather have lain with Hygelac?" Hygd's face was white with wrath, her little fists clenched tightly by her side. Beowulf gasped in pain: neither the nicors' teeth, nor the mere wife's talons, nor the agony of his own sinews straining to bursting point as he strove to hold his grip on Grendel, had rent him like this woman's words. If a man had spoken to him so, there would have been blood on the summer grass already: but this was Hygd, whom he must ward even from himself.

"That is not so," Beowulf whispered, his voice coming strained from his swollen throat. "I have lain with a woman within the Middle Garth's ring, but though I owed her only good, for she took me in and warmed and fed me when I was close to death, yet she died at my hands. I crushed her to death in my embrace, unknowing what I did: I could not hold back my strength as I loosed my seed. She was larger than you, Hygd, and sturdier, a frithle who was used to whatever men could give. How, then, should I take you as wife when, since I first saw you, I have wanted only to keep you safe?"

Hygd stared at him unbelievingly. For a dreadful moment, Beowulf saw the anger in her wide dark eyes giving way to fear of him, as he had hoped he would never see on her face. Then she stepped forward, flinging her arms about him again.

"Berki, my bear," she cried. "That you have borne this so long, and never spoken of it o, my beloved!"

They wept together then: Beowulf did not care if any other saw them, or thought his tears unmanly. But at last the heaving sobs quieted, and Hygd shuddered and sniffled.

"If I may not be your bride," she said sadly, "then you must be wedded to the Frowe when you take the high seat this Midsummer, that the lands of the Geats not fall barren. I shall stand in her place by the holy white stone, and pour out the bridal ale for her for myself, I should gladly go to her halls in your embrace, if that were the price of having your love at last, but I would not leave you with that sorrow. I shall give you to her, because I must. And perhaps, in time, she shall repay that gift, and you and I be as we should have been."

Sweartwulf and Frithugeard did not come to the Geats' Thing that year: with the Swedish frith broken, it was not well for the drighten of Hroesnabeorh to leave his hall. But Hraefn came in their stead, and as Beowulf stood watching the wrestling, the young man walked boldly up to him and said,

"My king, will you try a fall with me?"

Beowulf looked down at Hraefn in surprise. Sweartwulf's son was no taller than his father, and his shoulders had not yet thickened to his sire's strength. But he stood straight, his deep gold hair clubbed back into a short braid at the nape of his neck and his Finn slanted blue eyes meeting Beowulf's gaze brightly.

"You need not fear to harm me," Hraefn told him, a smile quirking the corner of his lip beneath his sparse brown mustache. "My father has taught me most of what he knows, and he said that I am ready to try my skill against you this year."

Still Beowulf balked; but seeing that, Hraefn added,

"My father also said that if you were unwilling to measure yourself against me, I should say that you were growing older, and likely no match for a young man's swiftness." He grinned, and Beowulf laughed with him.

"Well, I shall try a fall with you, and do my best not to break your bones," Beowulf replied. "If you should bring me down, have a care that you are not beneath me when I fall!"

An eager murmur buzzed around those who stood watching the wrestlers as Beowulf and Hraefn stepped into the clearing.

"Who is that boy? Must be a champion already, else the king would never, this gold finger ring against your sax that..."

Hraefn flexed his arms, the muscles cording sharply beneath the sleeves of his yellow tunic.

"What are you waiting for?" He asked. "Come on!"

Beowulf knew better than to rush Sweartwulf's son: that would only end with him flying through the air to land on his back. The two men circled each other warily Hraefn was not such a fool as to close, but waited for Beowulf to reach for him, dodging beneath the king's arm and whirling even as he grabbed and twisted. But Beowulf was ready for that trick as well, while, though Sweartwulf must have told his son everything he knew about wrestling with Beowulf, it was not the same as feeling bones too broad for a man's hand to grip easily and the strength that had torn Grendel's arm from his shoulder.

Beowulf wrenched himself free of the hold that would have brought another man's arm to the snapping point: in that heartbeat of Hraefn's surprise, he could have picked the youth up like a child and set him down on the earth. Hraefn had been brave to challenge him, and it would be unkind to end the match too quickly: let the youth have a chance to show his mettle to the gathered folk! Beowulf nearly paid for that kindness in the next pass. Only long experience with Sweartwulf let him keep on his feet when Hraefn drove his kneecap upwards against the back of Beowulf's own knee, yanking backwards with all his weight at the same time.

But Beowulf heeded the burden little; he could not keep his knee from buckling, but he turned the movement into a forward lunge, pulling Hraefn off his feet. Now Beowulf could swing the young man's body around, dropping him to the ground and holding his shoulders pinned. Hraefn thrashed a moment, then lay back, nodding to Beowulf.

"The bout is yours, my king," Hraefn said ruefully, and Beowulf let him up. "Perhaps I am not yet ready to take my father's place."

Beowulf clapped him lightly on the shoulder.

"No, you did well. Though you lost this time, Sweartwulf has no cause to be ashamed of you. It may be that you shall put me on my back next year. Come, let us go find some ale: wrestling in the sun is thirsty work."

As they walked, Beowulf marked that Hraefn was looking about the crowd eagerly.

"Are you seeking someone?" He asked.

Hraefn started, a flush spreading slowly over his broad cheekbones.

"I met a maiden here last year Ealhburg, the daughter of Ealhere. I had hoped she would be there when I challenged you, but I have not seen her here yet."

"I can tell you that she is here, for I greeted Ealhere and his family yesterday," Beowulf assured him. "If she is close to your height and slim built, with red gold hair that she wears knotted at her neck with the length of it falling down her back, then I can also tell you that she is not yet wedded to another."

Hraefn's grin stretched his rounded cheeks, his slanted eyes crinkling tightly with delight.

"That is the best of news for me!" Then he grew sober again. "Tell me, my king...since my father is not here to speak of my deeds in battle, nor my mother to talk of dowries and portions, will you help me to bring my case before Ealhburg's family?"

"I will, and gladly," Beowulf answered. "And I think I can say that our queen will turn her hand to it as well. Be sure, you shall not lack for help in this, if it is what you wish!"

In truth, he was more than glad to turn his mind to the matter of Hraefn's wooing for it was something to think about beyond what would come that night. The day wore on, the Sun slowly lowering in the south: and at last Beowulf had to go his house to array himself for his wedding Wynefrith had offered him the chamber behind the great hall where the kings before him had slept, but Beowulf could not bring himself to stay there, for he still remembered Hrethel turning his face to the wall and giving himself over to his sorrow death.

Though Wynefrith's fingers were swollen and knobbed at the joints now, she would suffer none other to fasten the gold filigree clasp buttons holding his red linen over sleeves closed along the length of his arm and edging his trouser cuffs, nor to gird him with the new belt glittering with gilded silver mounts pressed, like those about the edge of the helm Heardred had given him in place of his lost one, with the figures of bears. Beowulf hung his Finnish knife from a silver ring mounted on the belt; but his sword was slung on a baldric strap likewise adorned with gilded mounts that ran across his body and over his left shoulder.

His broad arms were thickly wound with coils of gold between the buttons, for that night he would be dealing out rings to his thanes; more gold glittered from his fingers, and, though he little liked the feeling of the smooth end knobs pressing at his throat, Beowulf let Wynefrith bend a torc of thick twisted gold wire out to set it about his neck. The old queen combed his thick brown hair and trimmed his beard as if he were, in truth, her son going to his wedding. Lastly, she unfastened the gilded buckles of his square leather belt purse and set nine hazelnuts inside. "Luck and fruitfulness for you, and for the land!" Wynefrith said, looking with age bleared eyes into Beowulf's face.

"Though I shall go to my husband before long, I shall be glad at this last feast, for I know that you shall rule our folk well. If I were not waiting for this, I should have fared on before."

Beowulf bent to kiss her forehead, the wrinkled skin spiderweb soft beneath his lips.

"You have ever been a mother to me, and dear to my heart. When you guest with Frige in Fen Hall tomorrow eve, and she asks you of your deeds, say this to her. Though you wrought mightily all your life for your folk and kin, and held fast through the worst of sorrow and toil, the greatest of your deeds was this: that through your teachings, year on year, a boy who had been outcast and alone learned how to be a king."

As often before, Beowulf's words had come without his will: he stilled his tongue, shocked that he had spoken Wynefrith's death so soon, but the old woman smiled up at him.

"I shall tell her that no, do not grieve, dear grandson! My sons and my husband have fared before me, and Hygd has long since grown to a queen's work. I am needed here no longer. Be glad this night, that my last feast not be spoilt with tears. Then tomorrow, you may open Hrethel's mound, and lay me in my wedding bed again."

Beowulf nodded, and Wynefrith reached up to pat his cheek as if he were still a boy. She stepped back a pace, looking thoughtfully at him.

"You look well, indeed, but there is still something lacking, ah, my thoughts are weak with age! Yes, that is it."

Her swollen fingers clawed at the buckles of her own belt pouch Beowulf wanted to help her, but he would not shame her so and at last she got it open and pulled out a band of woven green and blue silk, figured with shield knots in fine gold wire.

"Sit down so I can reach your head," she ordered. Beowulf sat, and she brushed his thick wavy hair back from his face, tying the band about his head to keep it in place. "You look very fine, my grandson," she said, satisfied. "Hygd told me that the green would bring out the color of your eyes, and she was quite right. Come along, now: your folk will be gathered in the hall, and you should not make them wait too long."

The blue mourning hangings had been taken down: the Hrethlings' hall was decked with bright tapestries again, garlands of green leaves and flowers hanging upon the walls. The floors had been strewn with fresh straw that morning, and pitchers of drink stood on the tables, shielded from bees and flies with draperies of white linen. All the folk were dressed in their finest clothes, but Beowulf's gaze went to Hygd alone. She was garbed as a bride, her face veiled with sheer white silk; about her neck, she wore all the amber he had ever given her, from the lightest gold to the deepest cherry red.

Her shift was golden as ripe wheat, but her overdress, pinned at the shoulders by bridge brooches of gold set with blood dark garnets, was the light green of new springing birch leaves. The girdle about her waist gleamed likewise with gold and garnets, and its clasp was the figure of a cat set with flat cut pieces of garnet held in gold. Over the white silk that hid her shimmering hair, Hygd wore a crown of thick twisted gold wires with pale yellow cowslips and blue flax blossoms woven about it, and her arms, like Beowulf's, were all ringed with gold coils.

Hildegeard stood beside her, holding the silver pitcher and the Hrethlings' greeting horn: Hygelac's daughter was dressed all in red, adorned almost as richly with gold as her mother. Hygd stepped forward into the long streak of Midsummer's eve sunlight that poured through the hall's door like darkening honey, and Beowulf caught his breath as his gaze met hers. Above the veil, her violet eyes seemed to pierce into his as if his whole heart had suddenly been opened to her; it seemed to him that he stood naked and yearning before her, and that she was ready to take him to herself.

"Beowulf," she said. "The wedding feast is readied; the guests come forth to witness. Now come with me to the hallowed stone, that we may swear our oaths."

Hygd took him by the hand, and though her touch was light, it seemed to Beowulf that a strength greater than his own held him. He went with her willingly, his friends and thanes and all the folk trooping along behind. The Sun was lowering over the sea, staining the clear blue sky with streaks of ruddy gold fire fading to the pink of dog roses towards the heavens' bowl; a warm breeze rustled through his hair, rich with the scents of earth and springing grass and unfolding blossoms.

They followed the path through the trees; a startled wood dove sprang up cooing, its gray wings clapping through the leaves, and farther away, a cuckoo called and called, more times than Beowulf could count. Behind them, Eofor led the offering swine, the finest of the sons that the Hrethlings' king boar had sired last year. He did not balk, but trotted along gladly, snuffling and grunting after the bowl of mead mixed mash that Ingemund held to lure him. When they reached the blessing grove, Hygd let go of Beowulf's hand, walking by herself to the white stone. She turned to face the folk as they arrayed themselves about the clearing, head and hands uplifted.

"Let the gods hear it; let the goddesses hear it! Let all of Hamdeall's kin, high and low, come to witness! Here in this hallowed stead, here by the holy stone, a king shall be wedded, and given to his land Gather, ye wise ones, gather, ye wights, come here over wide wilderness ways!"

The hairs prickled up along Beowulf's spine: in the deepening twilight, it seemed to him that he could see the hidden shapes moving amid the trees, drawing near to the holy grove, and the very air seemed to thrum and sparkle with might. Hygd's eyes glistened wide above her veil, fathomless as dark wells, and the mass of amber upon her breast seemed to cast a golden shimmer upwards, so that she might have been wearing the many layered collar that had sunk with Hygelac again.

"I come to my wedding, in this holy stead," she murmured, her soft voice echoing and rustling throughout the grove. "I come as Sugu, I come as Geofe, I come as Harwine; to my sea bear, I come as Meredeall, gleaming upon the waves. I am the rider of Hildeswin, the driver of cats, and my tears are the fire of the sea. Thrice whelmed in fire, and thrice brought forth; I walk among the fallen, and no wound can withstand my might. The leek grows shining, deep in the earth I lift it forth to my joy, and bright waters spring from under berg. Now come to me, my shield bear, my leek of battle: come to me, Beowulf, if you would offer as you have said."

Beowulf's knees trembled beneath his weight as he stepped forward. Though Hygd's head did not reach his chest, it seemed to him that her eyes met his as though they were of like height, and about their violet depths, her birch fair face flared with golden flames.

"Frowe," he said, the words springing forth from him like waters flowing up from a mountain's roots, "I would offer you all that you would have of me, and give myself to you, for the land of the Geats and because I love you, fairest of all idises."

She took his hands in hers, and it seemed to Beowulf that he felt the fire flowing between them, so fierce that it must burn him to ashes, and yet sweet beyond all measure, so that he held her fast, and all the strength of his hand grip was not too much for her might.

"Then you shall be my husband, in your living and your dying, and frea of the fruitful land, by your seed and bone and blood Beowulf, king of the Geats."

Taking the brimming horn from Hildegeard's shaking hands, she lifted it up.

"Ale I bring you, blessing rich, with rowning might and runes of joy. You shall drink the dear draught, and all gods aid you! The wisdom drink of our wedding."

Beowulf drank. It seemed to him that he could taste earth and hot blood and honey in the ale's strength, the sweetness of malted grain one with the green of springing shoots, and its warmth roared through his body like the whelming waves of battle and love at once.

"Salmon fisher, honey eater, mighty folk warder," she crooned, her words strangely well known to Beowulf, though he had not heard them before. "You have grown strong, and glad am I that you are come to me again, though your way has been long, and cold with sorrow dew. But your sorrows shall be at end for a time: after the storm comes sun."

She clasped him to her, and lifted her veil to kiss him. Then Beowulf saw, as he had known before, that it was not Hygd who stood before him as bride. Though her features were the same, they glowed like molten gold, so brightly that all his strength could barely withstand the sight of her. Almost, his awe whelmed him so that he could neither move nor speak: but he had sworn to give himself, and if he fell beneath her might, then so it must be. And so he leaned forward, meeting her lips with his own.

It seemed to Beowulf then that something burst within him, like the spasm of his seed bursting forth, but an hundred times greater, so that he swayed and staggered and nearly fell, blinking his dazzled eyes until he could see again. Hygd was staring up at him, a dazed look on her face, and she lifted one hand wonderingly, as if she did not know how she had come here. But Ingemund and Eofor led the offering boar before the stone, and Beowulf drew his long Finn knife, crouching down beside the beast where he munched happily on his sweet mash.

"Will you give yourself?" Beowulf whispered to the boar. The boar looked up from his bowl, his dark eyes meeting Beowulf's gaze.

It seemed to Beowulf that he stood in two steads at once that he looked at himself, and spoke to himself, and that, when he struck, he would plunge the blade into his own breast. He heard a woman's voice, faint and far off, like the waves echoing down by Whales' Ness: Slow is your boar to tread the god ways. Frowe, you have your lover on his slain faring. Yet he was willing: and with that, he knew that the king boar's son was ready. The hot blood gushed out over Beowulf's hands as Hygd stooped down with the blessing bowl; the boar's shining black gaze never left his, not until the bright eyes dulled into death, and, though his bristly legs still thrashed, Beowulf knew that the life was gone. When that day comes, he thought, and stood to bless his folk.

Torches burned ahead of them in the blue Midsummer twilight as the procession wound its way back through the woods to the Hrethlings' hall; the high singing of the women wove among the deeper voices of the men like the flames flickering through the dark tree shadows. Within the hall, all the lamps were lighted, flaring clear yellow in their iron bowls, and the fires leapt high along the floor. Beowulf and Hygd walked between the burning trenches, up to the Geat king's high seat. It seemed to Beowulf that he could see a ring of brightness about the wooden throne where Hrethel and Hygelac and Heardred had sat, that the twining beasts carved upon it twisted and writhed like shapes half seen from the corner of the eye, hissing in low voices of warning. Yet if he did not have the right, there was no other: and his bride had named him king of the Geats. The wood of the high seat seemed to spark and thrum beneath Beowulf's touch, welcoming him. He seated himself there and a great cheer went up, roaring in his ears, as all the folk in that hall lifted horn or cup.

"Hail Beowulf, king of the Geats!" Eofor shouted, even as Hlewabrandar's higher voice vied with his, "Hail Beowulf Grendel's Bane, our king!"

The Midsummer feast lasted long past the time when late twilight had brightened into early dawn again. Beowulf sat in his high seat, dealing out gold rings; Hlewabrandar sang of his deeds, and of the deeds of those who had gone before him, and Hygd walked about the hall to pour out ale for all those gathered there, drightens and thanes and sturdy carles alike, greeting each man and his kin by name. The Sun was shining brightly down by the time Beowulf finally made his unsteady way from the hall unsteady somewhat from ale, for he had drunk deeply, but more shaken to the bone by what had passed in the holy grove. Hygd had been able to slip away earlier, but the new king could not leave until it was down to the last few men still holding vigil over the dregs of the ale pitchers. Beowulf hardly remembered closing the door of his house, or taking off his finery and folding it over the bench before he dropped gratefully onto his bed. But it seemed to him then that he dreamed, and knew he dreamed, though his eyes were still open, staring at the carven length of the roof beam as the straw of the thatch faded into fog and wisped away into blue sky.

He heard the gentle splashing and gurgling of a stream behind him, and he was no longer lying upon his bed, but stretched out upon the green grass, the Sun shining warm upon his naked body. The shadow that fell over him then was warmer than the Sun, and he blinked upwards to look upon the woman. As in the hallowed grove, she was like Hygd to look on, and yet not like: though her delicate features and deep violet eyes were Hygd's, she was Beowulf's own height, or near enough, and her knee length flaxen hair flared out about her body in a halo of shining white flame.

She was clad only in a gold collar like the one Wealhtheow had worn, its layered rings so finely wrought that Beowulf's eyes could not trace all the tiny beasts and masks and twists of wire, and a girdle of gold with a single great round garnet on its clasp, the sunlight burning like a coal from its clear red depths. Her pale breasts swayed like cupped flowers in the breeze as she came towards him, her nipples firm and dark as wild strawberries; she moved to kneel beside him with the lissome grace of a young birch tree.

"My beloved bear," she murmured, her soft voice thrumming through the earth beneath him. "My shining folk warder. You need not fear: I joy in your strength." She ran her hands over Beowulf's body, stroking the soft pelt of curly hair on his chest, caressing slow circles down to his full standing manhood, then leaning down over him so that her nipple brushed his mouth.

He suckled at the hot tight wrinkled sweetness, and it seemed to him that drops of fragrant honey mead trickled into his mouth, and that he heard her purring with delight like a great cat. She lowered herself, sliding over his body so that, for a moment, her full sleek length lay against him and her shining hair curtained them both; then, laughing, she jumped to her feet.

"Come and catch me, my bear!" She cried, running a few steps and stopping to look back at him.

Beowulf pushed himself up more awkwardly, hastening after her. Her white rump glimmered through her streaming pale hair as she scampered merrily along, and every now and again she would halt and turn, waiting for him to come closer before she ran on. She leapt the stream like a doe; Beowulf waded through after her, the clear water running cool and fresh about his calves, and she ran on among the trees, a glimmering shape in the green shadows of the woodland. Then she paused a little too long; Beowulf leapt forward, catching her and bearing her down onto the soft moss beneath him.

She smiled up at him, all the world's delight in her violet eyes, and opened her thighs, arching her back. The soft curls between her legs teased at the head of his leek; then he thrust into her, sheathing himself fully in her silken heat.

"Yes, my bear!" She cried. "Take me, give yourself to me I am yours, you are mine!" She held him tight, arms and legs wrapped about him, as he drove into her harder and harder, each thrust sending a shock of fiery pleasure through him. Her mouth found his, her hot tongue writhing about his own so that they cried their joy into each others' breath. When at last his seed burst free, it seemed that he felt his body shatter like a stone heated beyond its strength to bear, sinews and bones flying asunder in a single wild spasm of joy.

Beowulf was still shuddering when he opened his eyes to the daylight seeping in through the smoke hole of his house, little tremors quivering through the muscles of his thighs and arms. The memory was already beginning to fade: he did not try to seize it again, for he knew that what he had borne outside the Middle Garth's ring was too much for his earthly flesh even for his: it would burn through him like the scorching eoten mead Grendel's mother had brewed, and if the Frowe had not burst his living heart in his breast, it was because she would have him still lifting his shield as her folk warder. A knock sounded on his door. Beowulf rose quickly, dressing himself with shaking fingers, and went to answer. Hildegeard stood there, her blue eyes swollen rimmed and her face wet with tears.

"O, Beowulf," she said. "Forgive me for waking you but our grandmother is dead. I went to bring her the brew of herbs she drinks every morning to ease the pains of her hands and feet, and she was sitting on the bed with her back propped against the board, still dressed in her feast day finery, with her needle case and her antler squares for band weaving and her skeins of silk all laid out in her lap...She looked glad, and I spoke to her, but she said nothing, and then I touched her hand, and she was cold. Beowulf, what shall we do now?"

Beowulf patted Hildegeard's shoulder. "We shall have Hrethel's mound opened, and bear her to her husband as she wished to go, arrayed as a queen, with the tools for all those crafts in which she joyed in life. And this night we shall drink her arvel, and speak of what she was in life. But Wynefrith herself shall be guesting with Frige. And you were not dreaming, nor did your eyes deceive you, when it seemed to you that she was glad."

Hildegeard looked up, and Beowulf saw the glimmerings of awe in her fair young face. "That must be as you say, for it is known to all that you are wise," she murmured. "I shall see to gathering her goods, then, for I helped her in everything that she had not the strength or clear eyesight to manage this last year, and I know what she would have with her."

"That is well done," Beowulf assured her. "Have you told Hygd yet?"

"No. I thought to come to you first..."

"I shall bear her the news, then, while you go about your work."

Hildegeard stood up on her toes, reaching up to hug him about the neck. "Thank you," she whispered. She hurried back to the hall a little awkwardly, for the babe growing in her womb was just beginning to unbalance her and Beowulf watched her for a moment, thinking on that.

After Hygelac's death, Hygd had gone back to the house they had shared when first wedded. Beowulf was still a few paces from it when the door opened and Hygd stepped out, pale and blinking in the sunlight.

"Berki!" She said. "I dreamed..." She stopped, flushing and blinking again. "I do not remember what I dreamed," she said, dropping her voice. "But it seemed to me that it was a fair dream, and that you were with me."

"Aye," Beowulf said gently. "I, too, dreamed, though I remember little. Yet there is another matter before us now."

Hygd met his eyes, and he saw the sorrow settling over her face, as though she already knew what he would say.

"Wynefrith?" She asked.

Beowulf nodded. "I had awaited this, though not so soon: I had hoped that she would live to see Hildegeard's bairn born."

Beowulf told her what Hildegeard had said, and she closed her eyes for a moment.

"That is as fair to hear as any death tidings may be. Well, I shall see to readying her arvel, while you call your men to open Hrethel's mound. There is much that must be done, for the burial of a queen."

The harvest was rich that year, better than anyone could remember; the golden grain reached the roofs of the storehouses, and every clay pot that did not overflow with frothing wort was filled to the brim with peas or beans or dried berries from the sweet abundance the woods offered. It was a fine summer for the bees as well: there was honey enough for three years' mead and baking, and so much left over that even the thrall bairns might suck the golden sweetness from a comb's wax when their day's work was done when Hraefn and Ealhburg were wedded at the next Midsummer, Beowulf thought, there would be enough mead at their marriage feast to give the bridegroom strength for siring a whole litter of sons at once.

The sea's fruitfulness matched the land, for the herrings shoaled right up to the shore by Whales' Ness, so that the strand was covered above the tide line by drying racks hung heavy with fish. As at the Hroesnabeorh harvest those years ago, it was Beowulf, reaping ahead of his men with a sickle forged to his own size and strength, who cut the Last Sheaf. But Hygd pushed the giggling maidens aside, coming forward gladly to bind it with a band of woven linen threaded through three yellow apples she could claim that right, for though she was no maid, her head was still uncovered. She was not clad as a queen for the harvest work, but wore a plain gown of gray wool, its back and sides dark with sweat under the Sun's warmth, and bits of straw and husk stuck out of her braid, brown against the pale flaxen hair.

Hygd's delicate face was pink with Sun and heat: save that, even in her simple garb, she held herself so proudly, she might have been any farm carle's daughter coming merry to the end of the harvest. Beowulf's heart swelled as he saw her gather the fallen stalks skillfully into the curve of her arm and wrap the band nine times about them, binding the Sheaf tightly, with the apples hanging yellow from the brown stalks. Beowulf raised the Last Sheaf in both hands, looking up into the sky. A few wispy white clouds feathered across the bright blueness, harbringers of weather to come; but only the softest wind stirred the summery air, cooling the hot work sweat on his face.

"Hail to Frowe and Frea, open handed givers of the field gold!" he called out. "Hlaford, Hlaefdige, fair kin of the Wans richly have you dealt out the store of Nerthus this year, and gladly do we gather it from the breast of the need giving Earth. Now let this pledge stand between us over the winter: though the fields be shorn and white with snow, your steeds shall not go hungry when you fare by the thanes you have fed so well, but the bloody hoofed horse and shining boar shall find this welcome set for them, and know that our love has not lessened, but burns the brighter through cold and dark, through night and waning moon. The harvest is done: we fare to feast, and bid you come, and all our elder kin, to be glad with us at the rim of year turning."

Beowulf mounted the Sheaf upon its wooden stake; then all the women came forward to garland him with blossoms and berries. Hildegeard set a horn of mead in his hand, and he drank deeply as they led him up to the hall like a tamed bear, his folk pressing closely about to touch him for luck. It seemed to him that he felt a bright spark of might flare as each hand touched him, the warmth in his breast kindling answering flames all about him like a torch setting every lamp in the hall alight; and he could not remember having been so joyful in his life. After the grain harvest, everyone turned their hands to gathering apples and plums, nuts and berries: the weather was far too warm for slaughter yet.

Sometimes Beowulf and Hygd wandered into the woods like children with their baskets, and ate as much fruit as they picked, for had there been three times as many folk in the Geat king's burg, they could not have gathered all that spilled over from every bush and tree that year: Froda's mill in the depths might have been ordered to grind out berries in place of sea salt. Other days, Beowulf went alone save for the old gray hound following at his heels, for Hygd had much brewing to do with the abundance of fruit and honey and malt, and the greater the harvest, the more work was needed to keep the grain dry and safe from worm and beetle and mouse. She also had to reckon what was owed them by their many under kings, and, for the most part, it was Hygd who spoke with the thanes who came with the scot wagons, looking at their tallies and listening to the tales they told of how matters went in their drightens' lands; though Beowulf aided her in that, she knew more of that work than he.

Often, as Beowulf passed the place on the forest path where the berserks had taken him, he halted for a few moments, thinking on Ansuwulf and the rest of that wild band. They were all dead now, the last of them fallen in Hygelac's raid, and Heardred had not sought to bid others to come in their place. If there were youths among Beowulf's folk with the bear or wolf fetches that might have been kindled to full battle wod, there was none now to seek them out or guide them to rousing Woden's gift; and Beowulf could not say that this did not make him easier of mind most so at Yule, when the berserk band no longer came roaring into the Hrethlings' hall as in the years before. Though he did not leave Woden out when he made offerings to all the gods, Beowulf was glad not to have the Grim One's eye turned upon his lands.

Perhaps, he thought, the Father of Strife had gotten blood enough to sate him when Hygelac fell; or perhaps it was only that he was willing enough to leave the Geats to the kin of the Wans, for there were plenty of warring drightens and kings elsewhere to fill the Hall of the Slain for him. Such thoughts were passing through Beowulf's mind when Wulfa barked loudly, and he heard the footsteps on the path behind him. Startled, he turned with the berries spilling out of his full basket, like a child caught daydreaming when he should have been working. The man coming towards him was the foremost of the thanes who had gone with Eadgils, a slim built, handsome warrior by the name of Ordheah, who wore his fine red gold hair in an elaborate braid coiled over his right ear. He looked tired, the dark shadows under his blue eyes standing out against his pale skin, but seemed otherwise hale, and Beowulf thought that his fine green tunic with its shining bronze sleeve clasps was new.

"Greetings, Ordheah. Well are you come home!" Beowulf said gladly, for worry about those men he had sent to ward the Ingling had never been too far from his mind. "Are all the men who fared with you still with you?"

"Aye," Ordheah replied. "But I have much to tell you, my king."

Beowulf nodded. "Come to the hall with me, then you look as though you are in need of ale and food after your travels, and I would have Hygd hear your words as well."

The other thanes in Ordheah's band were already in the hall, eating and drinking with the tired hunger and thirst of men who had been long on the way. Hygd was pouring another welcome pitcher full, though Beowulf did not see Hildegeard her birthing time was near, and she often had to sit and rest her swollen feet and aching back. Hygd greeted Ordheah, leading him up to the table before the high seat. Though Beowulf was eager to hear his thane's tidings, he waited until the redhead had most of a horn of ale and a good bowl of stew into him before saying,

"Now, you said that you had much to tell me?"

"Indeed, my king," Ordheah answered, and began his tale.

Eadgils had headed due south after the battle, all the way up to the coast.

"We rode faster than I had thought we would, for he has a way with horses such as I have never seen. He bought a great gray stallion from Aethelweard you remember him, Sweartwulf's southern neighbor?" Beowulf nodded. "No one had ridden that steed before, for he was too wild: Aethelweard had been thinking of giving him to the gods, for he hardly even dared breed from him. Eadgils walked up to him and whispered something in his ear, and the stallion stood there tamely to be saddled and bridled, and answered to the rein as though he had been led on a head collar from his first day out of the womb. Though he was born of kingly kin, Eadgils tended to our steeds every night as well: and I swear that I have never seen horses so eager to run by day, or able to run so long without blowing and frothing."

Beowulf thought of how Yrse had whispered in Hrime's ear when the white mare was close to foundering, but said nothing.

"Anyway, we took ship at the coast, sailing down to Wodenswih. Eadgils seemed sure that he would find a good welcome there, and he did not guess wrongly. For Hereweard is wedded to Scyld, the half sister of Yrse and Hrothulf: she was glad to see her oath kinsman, and hence so was Hereweard."

A warning shiver coiled cold up Beowulf's spine as Ordheah spoke Scyld's name. "Tell me more of her," he said quietly.

The thane's narrow red gold eyebrows drew together as he cast about for words, like a smith picking over his tools for a work that might be beyond his skill.

"You know that she was a by blow of Hrothgar's brother Halga, but her father named her and took her into the Scyldings' aett, and she was fostered in Scania." Beowulf nodded. "It was said of Scyld in Wodenswih though not loudly that her mother was of the alf kin. And that may be so, for though she is near to Hrothulf's age, and that is not far from forty winters, when I first saw her, I did not know that she was hlaefdige in Wodenswih, for I thought her no older than Hildegeard. Scyld is of middle height and fair of face, with gray eyes and hair the color of horse chestnuts. She is very slim, like a girl not yet come to womanhood, yet I saw her knock a big thrall man to the earth with a single blow of her fist when she found him slacking in his work, and her voice is as deep as a man's, though often it rises higher when she sings she is always singing," Ordheah added, "and will sit playing upon the harp for most of a day at a time, as well as any poet I have ever heard. Hereweard loves her dearly, though often she seems cool towards him, and would sometimes go away for days at a time. Some say that she goes to visit her kin in wood and sea, though never where Hereweard might hear it; others whisper that she works seith charms in hiding."

"And what of Hereweard? What manner of man is he?"

"He is tall and strongly built, though growing heavy and gray," Ordheah answered at once. "He is a man who clings long to ill done him: he thinks that Hrothulf did him a great wrong those years ago when the Scylding tricked him into giving his oath as under king do you know that tale? Hereweard and Hrothulf were hunting in the wood, and it chanced somehow that Hereweard came to hold the gold hilted sword Hrothulf wears perhaps to look at the blade, for it is said to be most finely wrought; who can tell? But Hrothulf unbuckled his belt, and then reminded Hereweard of that old custom, that whoever holds a man's sword while he takes his belt off, the sword holder shall be its owner's underling.

Hereweard did not take that too ill then, for the offer of Scyld's hand in marriage came with it. But since then he has brooded and muttered though, to give him his due, he has never sought to break the oath he gave unknowingly."

Beowulf listened to his thane's words carefully, for it seemed to him that he could guess at one thread that might lead through the tangled weave of Wyrd. Hrothulf had been foe to Othere, but seemed to have ended that unfriendship with Onela, though there was no telling whether that frith would last if Onela kept put off the matter of Halga's hoard with fair words too much longer. Yet if Othere's son guested now with a man who thought Hrothulf had wronged him, it might bode ill for the Scylding.

"How stands Scyld in this matter?" Beowulf asked.

"It is hard to know her mind, for she speaks it seldom. But I think that she bears Hrothulf no great love, for that he was fostered in a great king's hall, while she was sent away to learn the arts of a maiden in a smaller holding, for all her father named her a true born Scylding."

Beowulf might have asked further about Scyld and Hereweard, but Hygd leaned forward, her violet eyes dark as wrought iron in the sunlight.

"Tell me of Hereweard's battle strength," she said. "What is his war band like? How many troops can he call to his host, and is he well readied with ships, if he should seek to fare over the whale roads to fight?"

"For a scot king, Hereweard is rich, and his war band is not slack," Ordheah answered. "He is open handed as well he gave us all gifts for bringing Eadgils safe to him so that good men are willing to dwell in his hall and fight for him, however uncanny his frowe may be. I do not know how many troops he can call to his host altogether: though Wodenswih is a fruitful island, and much trade passes through it. It is not large I think one of the reasons he let Hrothulf's trick go without challenge is that he could never have hoped to stand against him."

"So he would not be able to threaten Onela by himself, if he were to take up Eadgils' cause?"

"In a word, frowe: no."

Hygd nodded, her face grave in thought. Whatever was in her mind then, she kept that rune to herself, and said no more on the matter; yet after a time, she rose to walk outside, and asked Beowulf to come with her.

"What do you think of this we have heard?" She asked him when they
had reached the edge of the wood, the yellowing birch leaves casting their
fluttering shadows over her face.

"Of Scyld, that which is uncanny may yet not work ill," Beowulf said
slowly. "But there is little good to be looked for from a man who clings
to his grievances and feeds them within his heart or from a woman who
does likewise. Yet, if Ordheah speaks truly and he is a man of good wit
there is nothing that this alliance can do, either against Hrothulf or against
Onela. And Hrothulf has ruled his lands well: I doubt that it will be easy
for Hereweard and Eadgils to find those who are willing to band together
against him."

"Do you think they will come to us?"

"In a gathering against Hrothulf, it is well enough known that, though
we would have taken sword against him for Hrethric's sake, that cause of
battle was stilled and cannot be awoken again. As for raising a host against
Onela..." Beowulf considered a moment. "Eadgils and I parted with harsh
words, because I would not lead the Geats to slaughter with no clear hope
of winning or gain on the chance that he might be among those few left
standing when we and the Swedes had finished cutting each other down on
the open field. I think it will be some time before he comes to me again for
help."

"If he does, would you give it to him?" Hygd asked, the little straight line
between her brows furrowing deeper.

Beowulf could not guess at her thoughts, but he answered her truthfully.

"That would rest on whether or not I thought we could win at a fair price.
Aye, I would have vengeance for Heardred, and carry out his wishes in the
matter of the sons of Othere; but not if it means leaving the greatest part
of our host strewn on the field as a feast for wolf and raven, with none save
Eadgils to gain from it."

"That is the answer I should have looked for from you," Hygd mused.
"Yet swear this to me, Berki: that if you see the chance to slay Onela and
avenge my son, you will do it, whether it be by your own hand or through
raising the host of the Geats when the time has come!"

Beowulf said nothing. Hygd lifted her hand, touching his chest. "Swear
it!" She ordered. Her face had gone white as frost on birch bark, though her
dark eyes glowed hot as pitch burning in the heart of a bale fire.

Beowulf thought of Heardred fallen, the bloody mass of his churned
innards shifting within the wound where the spear had twisted in him.
Hygd did not have to say, You failed him: perhaps she knew him too well,
and knew when such speech was not needed. Heavy as the words were on
his tongue, he spoke them at last:

"I swear it."

Even as he spoke, he wondered what manner of oaths Scyld might be asking of Eadgils and Hereweard what manner of word Yrse might be sending to her husband's outcast nephew, to her half sister and her marriage kin, or else to her son and brother Hrothulf. Cold are the redes of women, he thought, and shivered despite the late summer warmth. Hildegeard's bairn came a few days later. But though she had shown little signs of hardship while the child swelled in her womb, by the time she had been in labour half a day, her screams could be heard throughout Beowulf's garth. He waited anxiously, whispering his bidding that Frige and the Frowe aid her; perhaps they hearkened to him, for by the next dawn her screaming had stopped and Hygd, pale and drenched in sweat, came to tell him that her daughter still lived, and that Ingemund had a son.

"Yet I fear that this will be Hildegard's last," she said. "We were able to stanch her bleeding, but her womb was grievously torn. Even if she does not begin to bleed again, or die of the fever all kind idises forfend! She will scar within, and it were best for her then if no other child ever took root."

"Still, that is better than I feared when I heard her cries," Beowulf said tiredly. "What of her babe? Is he well?"

"He is not strong," Hygd admitted. "If he grows and thrives in this next little while, then we shall see. Still, it is in my mind that Ingemund will have no easy time of it on the ninth day, when he must choose to take the child in his arms and give it name and aeht soul...or not."

But Ingemund was spared that choice. By evening of the third day, the babe would not suckle, however often its cool little lips were moistened with milk. Even Beowulf took his turn at rocking it that night, though he knew no songs to croon to it; but by morning, the child lay stiffening in Hildegeard's arms. Beowulf wondered uneasily if Wynefrith had some foreboding that her great grandchild would not live long, and had chosen to make her faring before she had to lay yet another beloved body in the earth.

Nameless and soulless Hildegeard's bairn might have been, but if Hygd were right about the injuries her daughter had suffered in the bearing, he had been the last shoot of the Hrethling line save for Beowulf himself, who would never father a child within the Middle Garth. Beowulf went to the woods with Ingemund, holding the small cold body against his chest. Ingemund would have buried his unnamed son alone children who died before the ninth day were not laid in the howe field with rites, as no soul had yet entered their flesh, but laid in shallow graves outside the garths of both the living and the dead but his shattered sword arm had healed badly, so that it would be hard for him to dig a hole between the tree roots. Thus Beowulf laid the little corpse in its swathe of hare fur on a pile of fallen leaves and took the shovel from his cousin's husband.

Beneath his strength and weight, the shovel's blade cleaved easily through the tough roots, and it was not long before a hole deep enough to swallow the child's body yawned at his feet. Ingemund picked the dead infant up, tenderly wrapping a fold of fur over its small grayish face to keep the dirt out of its eyes, and set it into the grave without a word. He had borne his wounds bravely, and never spoke a word of complaint at the clumsiness and pain of his ill mended limb, but now he said quietly,

"Beowulf, should I curse the gods that my son died before I could even name him, when, four days ago, my heart was full of the greatest hope? Should I bless them, that they left me Hildegeard when I seemed like to lose her as well? Or did idises of weal and woe stand by the birthing bed together and strive against one another, so that neither could fully win the field?"

Beowulf looked down at the young man Ingemund's face was already lined from the lasting hurt of his crippled arm, and grimy, for he had not taken the time to wash while he sat watch over his dying son.

There were dark smudges on his broad brow and straight nose, as though he had brushed his hair from his face with soot stained fingers while tending the fires, and his sparse beard grew over his square jaw in ungainly patches of untrimmed brown hair. Beowulf wanted to speak words of comfort to him, but all that came to his tongue was,

"That is unknown of knowledge: few men may guess at more than a word of Wyrd's rowning. Yet Hildegeard sorrows as you do, or more greatly you held the child for but three nights, while she bore him beneath her heart for nine months. I have no way to make good the loss of what might have been, though I gave you all the wide realm of the Geats. I can only offer this rede: that you do your best to soothe her hurt. Perhaps, that you remember this: even the gods cannot always ward their bairns, for I have heard that Frige weeps yet for her son Baldor, whom all her crafts could not save from his Hell faring. It is ill to rail against those who have known the same harms as yourself."

For himself, Beowulf thought that those words would have brought little easing. But Ingemund nodded slowly, as though his king had given him the answer he needed. He said no more while Beowulf shoveled the earth back into the grave, then looked about for rocks large and heavy enough that no boar could snout them aside, nor wolf dig easily under them; but it seemed to Beowulf that he could see the pain on his oath kinsman's face ebbing away, as if Ingemund had drained a horn of strong fruit beer to dull the hurting of a wound. Strange tidings came to Beowulf's hall after Yule. It seemed that there was, indeed, some uncanny wyrd about the site where Heorot had stood, for through the dark Yule nights, another troll wight had risen to threaten the Danes. This one, men said, was like a great winged wyrm, scaled and greedy jawed.

Though it did not dare to assail Hrothulf's hall itself, it wreaked great havoc among herds and flocks, so that no byre or sheep house was left standing, and those thanes who had dared to go out and face it were snapped up by its teeth as swiftly as any kine. Hygd looked anxiously at Beowulf as he heard that tale, looking at the hardy sea man who had made the dangerous winter faring along the Geatish coast in hopes of getting a better price for his southern goods than he would by summer when there were many traders sailing the North Sea. Beowulf thanked the man for his news, and gave him a silver arm ring in addition to what Hygd had paid for his skeins of silk and clay jars of wine; but when Hygd asked at last if he was thinking on faring back to Sealand, he shook his head.

"I have paid my father's geld to Hrothgar; I owe no such geld to Hrothulf. Nor, I think, would he ask my aid in this, when he dwelt so long with a foe that no Dane had the might to overcome. And it is in my mind that there is little wonder if a kinsman's blood should have opened the way to such dark wights not least of all in that stead where Grendel trod for twelve years. Furthermore," he went on, the words spilling from his mouth like grain from a broken jar, "it is in Hrothulf's wyrd to gather his own heroes to him, as I had said to him before, and such men may only be called forth by need.

He shall have his own troll slayer of this in time, and more: and the day will come when, had he known of this, he would be glad that I did not seek to gain more fame than I have already at the price of the Danes' lessening."

Hygd drew in her breath, letting it out in a sigh of relief. "I had not looked for you to speak so, but I am glad of it. You have a folk to steer, and a foe still at Upsala in the north: let Hrothulf ward what he took himself!"

Beowulf blinked at his own speech. For a moment, it seemed to him that he saw the golden hilt of the sword he had given Halga's son at their first parting, and behind it the shadow of a bear, his own shadow? He did not know: but little minded as he had been to give Hrothulf his aid in this matter, he was less willing to do so now, for he had long since learned the worth of the spae words that came to him unbidden. That winter passed, and then a second. Through that time, there was frith in the land of the Geats. The harvests were good, and when blood feuds threatened to flare, Beowulf rode out to speak to the drightens and under kings who shook the bane spear at each other.

Sometimes he thought they gave over from fear of him, which he liked ill, though it was better than open war in his lands. More often, though, it was his words to which they listened, and though there would always be young men who were eager for battle, the most of his folk were ready to think well of a king who was wise and frith minded as well as famed in war. Eadgils still dwelt with Scyld and Hereweard in Wodenswih.

Every few months, the Ingling sent a polite greeting to Beowulf, together with some such gift as high athelings would give one another for friendship the pelt of a white lynx, which Hygd had made into a hood for herself; a lump of amber with two honeybees caught in its clear golden depths; a small flask of the ferocious burnt wine that was said to be brewed by a single tribe in northern Britain. Beowulf sent back to him in kind though he did not fail to mark that most of Eadgils' gifts were such as were more likely to gladden Hygd's heart than his own but as yet, there was no word of anything more. The following summer, the king of the West Geats, one of the many who paid scot to Beowulf, died.

"It would be well for you now if you had no folk and lands to steer," Hygd said laughing. "For I think you could easily fill the West Geats' high seat, you know their way, that it is of a size that would need two men of middling growth to fill, and they will have as king none but a man who can take that seat by himself. By this, I have heard, they hope to get either a ruler who is too fat to rouse himself to needless war, or a king who is so mighty in battle that none can stand against him."

"I am content with my seat here, though it is small for me," Beowulf replied, laughing with her, and they spoke no more of the matter, though they were careful to be sure of getting news of all those men among the West Geats who might be jostling to take that seat.

Scarcely a month later, they heard that a stranger had come out of the woods, and he fit the great throne of the West Geats as if it had been carved for him alone: he bore the strange name of Thura Hound Foot, and was said to have fared down from the mountains north of the Heathoreamas' lands.

"Shall we bid this Hound Foot to come to us for his oath taking?" Hygd asked. "Or shall we go on to guest with him, and see what manner of man he is in his own hall?"

"I should like that better," answered Beowulf. "And the king's seat of the West Geats is but a few days' ride from Hroesnabeorh. It would joy me to see Sweartwulf and Frithugeard again, and to look upon Hraefn's young daughter" for Hraefn had sent word but a few months before that Ealhburg had given birth to a healthy maid child. "Indeed," he added, "I believe that we owe little Bryhthild a tooth fee, for surely she has cut her first tooth by now."

So Beowulf and thirty of his war band saddled their horses, while a fair wain was readied to bear Hygd when she grew tired of sitting her pretty golden mare, and they set off for the shores of Lake Wener. It was a pleasant faring; save for a day or two of light rain, the skies were clear and the road dry beneath their hooves. The elk and deer had thrived greatly in the good weather of the last years, so that the travelers often saw dark high horned shapes grazing shadowy by the road at dawn and dusk, or the little lithe footed roe deer bounding across from field to field in front of them; and when he thought it fitting, Beowulf would command one of his thanes to shoot at the wood cattle so that they might bring the gifts of their hunting to the drightens with whom they guested on the way. It was late in the day, though the Sun was just setting in a warm rose gold light, when Beowulf and his band at last neared the hall of the king of the West Geats.

The gates of Thura's burg stood wide open, and even before Hlewabrandar had managed to tell any of the new king's folk who had come to guest with him, there was a crowd of men ready to take the reins of the horses and bid the visitors up to the hall. Thura's hall was large and well kept, the twilight within brightened with many lamps and rush lights. Several gray hounds lay curled comfortably in the fresh straw, and even beneath their thick fur, Beowulf could see that their sides were plump: he liked that well, for he had often found that a man's measure could be taken by how he treated the beasts and thralls in his care.

The king of the West Geats sat upon his out sized high seat, and he was, indeed, a man of great size and might, with broad shoulders and arms that bulged tightly against the wide sleeves of his madder bright tunic when he moved. A large battle axe, its iron blade adorned with inlaid traceries of gold and silver, hung from his belt. His face was low browed beneath a tangle of thick dark hair, his nose and chin very long; he might have been ugly, save for his engaging smile and the lively gleam of his dark eyes. He was talking with a woman whose black hair was wound about her head in a thick coil under her deep red headscarf and pinned with bright gold: Beowulf guessed that she was his queen, and that guess was proven right when she rose to bear a horn of greeting to the guests.

"Be welcome, wayfarers, to Thura's hall," she said sweetly, lifting the polished ruddy horn to Beowulf. "I think that you are no mere wayfarers, for even were you not garbed as king and queen, no other man could be mistaken for Beowulf Grendel's Bane, while the fairness of Hygd Long Hair is known throughout the land of the Geats. Forgive us, that it was not we who came to you, and know that we joy greatly that you have come to us."

Thura rose to his feet as his wife led Beowulf and Hygd up to his high seat. He was little more than half a head shorter than Beowulf, but there was something odd about the way he stood canted forward a little, and Beowulf could not help glancing down at his strangely shaped shoes. Shoes that seemed to cover feet too short and round for any man. Thura looked up and down at Beowulf, then threw back his head with a bark of laughter.

"It is well for me that you sit a greater throne than this, for it seems to me that you would have more right to it than I," he said. The rough edged sound of his voice gladdened Beowulf, for it reminded him of the speech of those kindly farm folk and herders of the northern mountains, who had gladly shared their goat cheese and coarse husked bread even with the man they thought to be a troll. "If I had been warned of your coming, I should have readied a more fitting welcome but you shall stay some days, so that I may bid my folk to feast and they may witness when I swear my oaths to you?"

"Even so," Beowulf agreed.

Thura bade more drink be fetched, and food the rich flesh of young wild boar stewed with the last year's dried plums and apples, with fresh bread and soft cheese flavored with spear leek, and honey cakes to follow; if his table was any sign of it, the West Geats had not suffered from the loss of their old ruler. Thura and his wife, whose name was Aethelswith, spoke of many things with Beowulf and Hygd, but it was not until the trenchers had been cleared away and the two kingly couples sat each sharing a horn of apple mead together that Beowulf said,

"Will you tell us, Thura, of how you came here from the north ways to take this high seat?"

Thura's shaggy brows lowered, and he looked down at the straw beneath his misshapen shoes, the lamp flames glowering from his dark eyes. But Aethelswith laid a gentle hand on the thick swell of his arm.

"There is no ill for you in that tale, I think," she murmured to her husband. "And Beowulf has a great name for wisdom and it were best if he knew of what kin you were born, and how it is you came to be king here."

A noise of unease rumbled in Thura's throat, but at last he said,

"Very well, I shall tell you. The tale begins some years ago, when the king of my homeland far along the Northern way; a small ruler whose realm was not the half of this I now hold, but nevertheless he bore the name of king wedded with a Finn woman.

She was skilled in spell craft, and had a wandering eye, and our king was aging and cold in bed. So she cast her gaze on the king's son, my father Beorn: aye, I am of atheling blood, though my mother was a carle's daughter! But Beorn would not have her, for his liking had already turned to my mother Bere; but the Finn woman struck him with a wolf skin glove, and his man hame was turned inside out with that of his fetch, and he became a great wild bear. Bere found him, I know not how. She looked into his eyes, and knew the king's son, and came with him to his den: and there she found that he was a man by night, though a bear by day. And he was man enough for her, for her belly was beginning to swell with child when he spoke to her, saying that he had dreamed his death at the hands of the king's huntsmen. He told her that when the hide was flayed from the bear, she should ask for what was under its shoulder, and she wept, but vowed that she would.

Well, it came to pass as Beorn had said; and beneath the shoulder of the bear was the gold ring of the king's son, that should show that her children were true born. Yet the Finn woman had the bear's flesh seethed, and offered it to Bere to eat. The first mouthful she swallowed from fear; the second she spat out, and the third she turned from. And then she went home to her father's house, and bore her bairns, three of us together. The Finn woman's hate was shown forth in us. My eldest brother Frodha was born so large and strong that no one might stand against him, neither bare handed nor at wrestling. Even you, Beowulf, would find him a worthy match: I think you and he are much of a height and breadth but he is an elk from the waist down, loping on hairy legs and pointed hooves.

Men stared at him, and made jests when they thought he could not hear; hence his mood was ever rough and uncertain, so that he slew in anger, when he had meant to do no more than give fair payment for cruel words. Then he had to fare away, but our father had left us more than the Finn woman's curse. There was a chest of goods, hidden in a cave among the berg crags, and with them three weapons: a sax, a battle axe, and a sword. Bere took Elk Frodha up there, and gold and helm and byrnie all slipped from his fingers, so that he could not pick them up. The sax came forth easily to his hand, and when he struck at a stone in anger that so little had been left for him, it cleaved the rock as though it were new cheese."

Thura drank a deep draught from his horn, as if to strengthen himself for the rest of his tale.

"Then Frodha went to the woods, and only my younger brother Berki and I were left. I liked life among the farm folk little better than Frodha had, for they stared and pointed at my feet, and roused me easily to anger. So I thought to follow my elder brother, and my mother took me to the same cave. Some store of the goods my father had left, though it were the lesser part, came to my hand; and though the sword would not move when I strove to pick it up, the axe answered to my touch as though it were shaped for my grasp alone. I went along the woodland paths, and came at last to Frodha where he dwelt in a mountain hut. He lives by hunting and slaying outlaws, and had no small store of booty he had won from them. We had harsh words at first, for he thought me a stranger, but when I lifted my axe, he knew it, and was greatly joyed to see me. It was he who gave me rede to come here, for he is not without foresight, and he wished for me the gladness among men that he could not have himself."

Thura's words struck deeper to Beowulf's heart than the under king could have known: had he not wished so dearly to come home to Hygd, Elk Frodha's lonely life among the crags, as neither man nor eoten, could easily have been Beowulf's own. But there was more in the Hound Foot's tale that drew his mind, and so he asked,

"What of your younger brother Berki?"

Thura's shaggy brows flew up. "That is the name by which your queen calls you, is it not? My little brother was named for our father Beorn, but because he was the smallest of us, he quickly became 'the little bear'. Yet he bears no mark of the Finn woman's curse upon his body perhaps because our mother turned her face away from the third bite of our father's flesh. For that cause, it may be, he is lighter of mood than Frodha or I. I do not know if he dwells with Bere yet, but I think the time shall come when he goes out into the world. The sword that waits for him was the best of our three weapons, and our father left him the greatest store of gold and war gear: if Beorn was fore sighted in his choice, Berki is like to be a hero someday."

Beowulf and Hygd guested with Thura Hound Foot for a week, and, as the under king had promised, he held a great feast, and swore his troth to the king of the Geats. Beowulf gave him a wyrm forged sword with a gold ringed hilt, though, for all its beauty, it was not a weapon to match the axe that Beorn had left his son. The shield he gave with it was rimmed and strengthened with iron heavy, but easy enough for a man of Thura's might to bear; Beowulf had thought on the shields that had been hacked to pieces in his hands, and wondered why he had not had iron fittings put on a battle board for himself before. Though Thura, as he had said himself, could be moody and touchy, he seemed to sense that there was a likeness between himself and Beowulf.

"You remind me even more of my little brother, as if you shared more than a name with him, though you are larger and stronger than he, as well as older and wiser. It gladdens me greatly to have had you by me for this time, and I hope that we shall often feast together in times to come," Thura told Beowulf before the Geat king and his band left. So they parted as the dearest of friends, and Beowulf's heart was easy as he turned Aelefeax's head towards the road that led towards Hroesnabeorh.

Sweartwulf and Frithugeard were even gladder to see their old friend, as were Hraefn and Ealhburg. Their daughter Byrhthild was a fine healthy child, flaxen haired though it was likely to darken to her father's deep gold and with the same Finnish slant to her blue eyes as her father and grandfather showed. Beowulf and Hygd agreed gravely with Frithugeard that Byrhthild would be breaking young men's hearts from Frisia to Halogaland in fourteen years.

The tooth fee they had brought for the small girl was a lump of amber carved into the shape of a cat: Byrhthild laughed with delight at the shining golden thing, and Ealhburg let her daughter hold it, though she took the amber cat from the child's grasp before Bryhthild could get it into her mouth. They spent a pleasant time at Hroesnabeorh, though not so long as they might have wished, for Beowulf knew that he should be back at his own hall for the beginning of harvest. Eofor died not long before Yule. He had been watching the youths with their wooden training swords, shouting advice, for he had been growing harder of hearing in the last years, when he suddenly clutched at his chest, falling into the snow with a surprised look on his face. By the time the boys had dropped their wooden weapons and shields and run to him, he was no longer breathing. Beowulf ordered a great howe raised for him in the grave field, but it was Ingemund who led the burial rites for his father, calling on the gods to bless him and guest him well in their halls.

Always quiet, Hildegeard's husband had grown more thoughtful after the death of his unnamed son, spending a great deal of time with the older men and women of the garth learning the lore of healing and herbs, of stones and holy steads, of the great gods and the wights of wood and stream and sea alike. It was at Eofor's burial that Beowulf realized how much of the blessing work of his hall Ingemund had taken over, as though, knowing that he would never fight again with his crippled arm, the young man had chosen to seek his might and aid his folk in the worlds of the gods. Though Beowulf regretted the pain that had brought Ingemund to that choice, he was glad that, as the old died one by one, he could trust that someone within his garth would remember all the tales that folk should know, and be sure of the right ways of doing things, that the gods and alfs and wights might still look with friendly eyes upon the Geat king's burg for though Beowulf did his best, there was too much work in kingship for him to sit through the long days listening to all that there was to learn of the worlds beyond the Middle Garth.

On the first night of Yule, it was Ingemund who led the procession out through the deep snow to the moonlit barrow field beneath the icy stars, guiding those who would make offerings at the mounds of their forebears and friends. And it was he who, when most of the folk had gone back into the hall, raised the call to Woden, bidding the Wod Host fare over the fields in blessing. Beowulf was relieved at that, for he had not wished to anger the Father of the Slain by failing to greet him, and yet he could not bring himself to hail his father's wild god with a whole heart nor had he been easy at the thought of calling the Drighten of Draugs among the mounds where the barrow rider had once spoken the staves of the Hrethlings' doom; but Ingemund, unflinching, dared what his king would not there, though men said that the Host God had served him cruelly in his one battle.

The winter storms howled in on the third night of Yule, and a few of the drightens and under kings who had come to guest with Beowulf through that holy tide were not able to fare home until some time later than they had planned, though there was no trouble in feeding the rulers and their bands. There was more than plenty of food stocks from a good harvest and the hunting was very rich as well for the weather hampered elk and deer in the wood, while the sturdy great, great grandchildren of Beowulf's gray bitch forged happily through the snow that was chest deep on them.

As if there were a god's special blessing on her, Wulfa still lived, though she was more ancient than any hound Beowulf had ever known, and far past her last hunting days. Beowulf saw that she got a good portion of meat from every kill, and she spent her days dozing happily by the hall fires, her paws twitching with the memory of elk in the woods of summertime past. It was some two months past Yule when the year's first ship belonging to that same brave trader who had first brought Beowulf word of the troll beast at Hrothulf's hall pulled around Whales' Ness, and the sea rime was still thick on his beard and cloak when he gratefully took the greeting horn from Hygd's hands and settled himself by the high seat.

"What tidings do you bring us this year, Aelfred?" Beowulf asked when the seafarer had drunk and warmed himself somewhat.

The trader grinned through cold blistered lips, wiping a drop of sweet honeyed beer from his yellow beard.

"Tidings that I think will gladden your heart. You remember the tales I have told you every year, of the flying wyrm that wrecks the byres about Hrothulf's hall every Yule? Well, the Dane King must no longer thole that woe. A little before Winter nights, a man named Berki came to Sealand he was from the mountains north of the Heathoreamas' lands, and I have heard it said that he is kin to your own Thura Hound Foot. He proved his strength well on his first night in Hrothulf's hall! There was a weakly thrall lad whom everyone called Haett, for he always wore a grubby gray hat on his head; and Hrothulf's berserks made a game of casting bones from their meals at him, so that he went in fear that one day they would kill him in their play. Berki liked that ill: he sat down beside the boy, and when the first large bone was cast, he threw it straight back at the man from whom it came, and knocked him dead on the spot.

Then he did not back down when Hrothulf called him to make the slaying good, but told the Dane King that the man who had cast the bone had earned the return of what he had given, and that it ill befitted warriors to put thralls in such fear. But as geld to the king, he offered to take the dead man's place in Hrothulf's war band, and it was thought that Hrothulf had gotten the better of that bargain. So the Northman began with a name for high mindedness, and that was well. And for his bravery, men began already to name him Beado Berki the little bear of battle, though he might be called little only when set against a man of your own size. Then, when Yule came and all Hrothulf's men crowded into the hall in fear of the winged troll wight, Berki went out with only that same wretched Haett beside him. He has never spoken of what he did that night; but in the morning, he and Haett still stood, and the flying wyrm stood there as well, still as stock or stone. Yet no one dared go too close to it, but Haett said to Hrothulf, 'Give me that gold hilted sword at your belt, and I shall fell the troll or die.'

I saw this myself, that the thrall who had crept and cringed stood straight and brave before the king, and Hrothulf marked it well: he drew his sword and gave it over to Haett, and Haett ran at the beast and stabbed it deeply, so that it fell over. Now it did not bleed, and there was another wound gaping by its heart, so that everyone guessed Berki had felled it before; but Haett was not the poor luckless thing he had been. Hrothulf gave him the gold hilted sword for his own, and a new name after it, for the youth seemed to have gained a new soul that Yule night: now he is called Hiltwine, and stands among the foremost of Hrothulf's heroes."

Use it well while it is in your hands, Beowulf remembered: thus he had spoken to Hrothulf on the strand at their first parting. And gift it only to one who is worthy of it though his worth may not be seen until he grasps the glittering hilt, his gold hidden beneath grimy rags. Hiltwine would be a strong shoulder companion to Hrothulf, and Berki remembered also that he had spoken something of Hrothulf's faring to Upsala, for he had thought that way wound with danger for the young atheling, like a ring of twisted gold with an adder coiling about it, though he had not known why. But Hrothulf slew Othere by Vendel before this is it his wyrd to fare among the Swedes once more? And is it bound in some way with my oath to avenge Heardred? I would be glad to meet this Beado Berki, Berki Beornsson, and to see into what hands that gold hilted sword has come.

"That is well told, Aelfred!" Beowulf said. "You have brought me a gift of a good tale and good tidings, and one gift deserves another."

He drew a thick gold ring from his wrist, giving it to the seafarer, who grinned so widely that a line of blood started from one of the deep cold cracks in his lips as he coiled it about his own arm. The Sun's light brightened, breaking the grip of ice upon the earth, and another year's plowing and planting began; the grain grew high through the summer, and once more, the weather stayed warm until after the harvest was done.

One morning, old Wulfa wandered out of the hall, curling herself in the sunlight; but when Beowulf called to her, she did not lift her head, and when he bent to pet her, he found that she was already cold. He dug her grave himself, laying her in it with a joint of venison, for she had earned death gifting as surely as any man; he built her cairn of stones and mourned her quietly, though not overmuch: she had lived long past a hound's years, and been happy to her end.

Still, Beowulf was long in going to sleep that night without the snuffling of her breath in the straw by his bed, and lay looking into the darkness until lightless bursts of blue brightness began to pattern his blackened sight. Slowly the shimmering shapes drew together into hoarfrost flames flickering sluggishly over twisted gold rings, over the rotten remains of a chest with stamped southern rounds of gold tumbling from the black shards of wood. Something huge shifted in the darkness among the pale howe fires, and he heard the grating of scales upon stone. Beowulf woke. Gray daylight was filtering in through the smoke hole in his roof, and he was drenched with sweat, his linen bedding clammy against his skin.

The weather had turned sharply in the night: sleet hissed against the thatch above his head, and when he pushed the blankets off, the first icy air of winter bit at his body. He was not sure what he had dreamed, but his thought told him that there was some foreboding in it. When he stepped out of his house, he saw that Ingemund stood there waiting for him, wrapped warmly and hooded against the freezing rain. The young gudhe for Beowulf knew of nothing else that Hildegeard's husband could be called had grown thinner in the last year, his blunt cheekbones standing out like ridges of rock in poor earth. Not only had Ingemund's brown beard thickened, but a few strands of hoarfrost grey were already lightening it, as though pain and lore together had aged him beyond his years. His good arm cradled the crippled one across his chest as though the changing weather ached deeply in his ill mended bones, but Beowulf thought something more than that troubled Ingemund's calm face.

"What is amiss?" He asked.

"I dreamed last night, and it seemed to me that it would be well for you to hear of it."

"Tell me."

Ingemund's pale eyes looked beyond Beowulf, as though he were staring still at whatever night seeing had brought him to his king.

"It seemed to me that I rose from my bed in the night, though when I looked back, I could see that my body still lay there. I went from my house, and turned my eyes eastward my sight was long. I saw the two great mounds of Eadwine and Ongentheow at Upsala, where the tree rises above the offering well and the high timbered hof; I saw Lake Wener and Lake Weter, and the ice was already thickening at their banks. And it seemed to me that there was a brightness in the night sky above Lake Wener, and in that brightness, I saw a huge bear walking from the west, and from the east came a mighty wyrm. A woman stood between them, and it seemed that she urged both on to do battle. The wyrm struck at the bear and strove to coil about him, and the bear answered it with blows of his paws..." Ingemund dropped his gaze. "Then Hildegeard woke me, for she said I had been crying out in my sleep and she was afraid. So I did not see which of them ruled the battlefield at the end. But it seemed to me that I had seen the fetches of kings."

"It may well be so," said Beowulf. "I thank you for those tidings, though I do not yet know how I shall answer them."

As the two men stood there in the icy rain, Beowulf heard the sound of a horn blowing from the shore, and lifted his head.

"Ingemund, go to Hildegeard. Unless I am mistaken, that is a battle horn: it looks as though something shall come of your dream, and sooner than we had thought."

Beowulf hastened into his house, arming himself quickly with byrnie and helm and shield, and slinging the war horn that had been Hygelac's over his chest. By the time he came out again, the men of his war band were all gathered by the hall, likewise armed and armored, though with heavy cloaks wrapped about them to keep the worst chill off their ring shirts, and Ordheah was running up from the path to Whales' Ness, his cloak flapping behind him.

"My king, there is a fleet of warships coming in to shore," he panted.

"What colour are the shields at their sides?"

"The shields are white; and it seemed to me, though they were yet far for my sight to make it out, that the prow of the foremost might have been one that I had seen before. If no ill spell craft has deceived my eyes, I think that Hereweard is sailing in to moor beside Whales' Ness, and that he means to bid you to battle beside him."

Beowulf led his troop down to the headland, looking out over the rain lashed waves. As the lithe thane had said, the white shielded warships were driving in to shore, borne swiftly by the harsh wind that swept the ragged dark clouds along the gray sky. The prow of the foremost jutted out sharply, a carven post ending in the ring beaked head of an eagle, and the figure of an eagle gleamed silver from the red banner that flapped wet in the freezing wind above the deck of the foremost.

"That is Hereweard's banner," Ordheah said.

Beowulf could see the folk on the warship's deck now. Though Eadgil's braids were hidden by the deep blue hood shrouding his head, Beowulf knew the Ingling's rangy stance; the man beside him, cloaked in bright red, was tall and heavily built, as Ordheah had described Hereweard. And next to him stood a smaller figure, whose black hooded head came only a little above his shoulder from her slimness beneath the cloak, Beowulf would have thought Scyld a child on the brink of womanhood, save that Ordheah had already told him what she looked like. He lifted his horn, blowing a hail of greeting, and a long note answered him from the ship.

"Byrhtwine, go to the hall and tell Hygd that she must make ready to greet atheling guests: that is Hereweard the king in Wodenswih, with his wife and Eadgils the Ingling beside him. And we must be ready to welcome and feed a large band, for I guess by the size of those ships that Hereweard has brought his whole host with him."

The young thane ran off, and Beowulf turned his gaze back to the warships again, trying to reckon the number of men sailing with the Danish scot king. The lead ship anchored off Whales' Ness, and Hereweard cupped his hands, bellowing to the shore,

"Hail, Beowulf, king of the Geats! We come to you in frith, though we would bid war: will you guest us in your hall?"

For a moment Beowulf felt a strong urge to tell the Dane to turn his ships about and go home. But that would have been unfitting: even had he meant to refuse whatever Hereweard and Eadgils would offer, they had come from afar and the meanest drighten would not have turned such weary guests away. He had sworn revenge for her son to Hygd, and knew that the Dane and the Ingling could have sailed to his lands with their host for no cause other than to lift the bane spear against Onela.

"Come and be welcome!" Beowulf shouted back.

He turned along the path, leading his men down to the strand. Hereweard, Eadgils, and Scyld were in the first little boat bearing the Danes to shore. Scyld stayed seated until the two men had dragged the small craft up onto the beach, stepping out only when she no longer needed fear wetting her skirts though between the sea spray and the icy rain that dripped from the black fur of her hood, Beowulf wondered why she had bothered. Hereweard appeared much as Ordheah had said: his spade shaped beard was altogether gray, and though his rugged face might have been handsome in his youth, now it had the pinched look of a man who had brooded long on old ills, with pursed lips and squinted eyes. But when Beowulf looked down into Scyld's face, he knew that his thane had been ill fitted to describe her.

Her white skin shimmered like sheer silk, as brightly pale as starlight; her large eyes were deep gray, with a flare of amber about the pupils like a fire built in a ring around a hole in ice covered waters. Scyld's features would have been too sharp for beauty, save that they were so finely wrought that there was no other word for them, like the hair splitting edge of a wyrm layered steel sword. When she opened her mouth, Beowulf could hardly believe the sound coming from that small slim body: Scyld's voice, though womanly in tone, was as deep as his own, and though she spoke quietly, he could hear the rumblings of leashed power in her throat. He knew at once that, whether the tales of her being born from an alf woman were true or not, Scyld was no more than halfway a woman of the Middle Garth, and he watched her warily as she said,

"Hail, Beowulf, king of the Geats! It gladdens us greatly to guest with Grendel's slayer: surely you are worthy of the highest fame! But a time of need is on you, though you know it not, and you shall soon find yourself more thankful of our coming than you think now to be."

At her words, Beowulf felt a shudder run through his bowels, as though the deep echoes of her voice were grinding loose the first stones of a great mountain rock slide. He said only,

"Come then, for you have fared far across the waters to me: the wayfarer is often glad of fire and food."

Beowulf led his three allies up to the hall. While he had watched the ships and waited, Hygd had the floor strewn freshly with straw and herbs, and the fires blazed with welcome warmth, though they had not burned long enough to take the not sought for winter chill from the air. The Geat queen came forward with her greeting horn, and Beowulf saw that she was wearing the hood made from the white lynx fur that Eadgils had sent, with the lump of honeybee amber hanging at her throat: there was no doubt in his mind that she, too, knew why the Ingling had come back to the lands of the Geats.

"Welcome are you all, our atheling friends!" Hygd said, though she did not smile. Her small jaw was firmly set, the line of stubbornness deep between her golden brows: there would be no turning aside for Beowulf now. "Drink, and sit with us, for we are eager to hear the tidings you bring."

Hereweard drank, then Scyld, then Eadgils the Ingling's slight frown told Beowulf that he took it ill to be the least of that company, though he said nothing of it. But when the guests had seated themselves, it was he who spoke first.

"It is good to look upon your face again, Beowulf, and to see Hygd at last, whose fairness is famed through the northern lands," Eadgils said. His voice was loud and clear, as though he meant to be sure that everyone in the Geat king's hall could hear it, and its deep rumbling echoes swept through the long building like the first torrents of a wind swift storm. "As Scyld says, we bear tidings that you have much need to hear. Yrse the queen lately sent me word that Onela has been readying himself for war, to march from Upsala when the last harvest is in. He means to fare west and south, over the wide waters of Lake Wener, and strike against you it is in his mind, she says, to harry through the lands of the West Geats and draw you into battle, and he thinks that he can so array his host in those broad and wooded lands as to trap you like a rat when you come to your under king's call."

Beowulf did not ask how that word had come from Upsala to Wodenswih so swiftly: a ship might have brought it in the last of the good sailing weather, but Yrse might have her own means of sending news to both Eadgils and her kinswoman. He only said,

"Though you bring tidings of ill, it is better to know them, and better yet to have help in such a time. I shall call my host, and we shall ride out to meet Onela, that our battle may be in a better stead than whichever one he would choose for us."

Hygd smiled grimly then, though there was no mirth in her burning eyes. "Aye: there are several deaths to avenge on the king of the Swedes. Just as you are come beside your husband, Scyld, I shall fare beside Beowulf with the host, for who should see the geld paid for a son's blood, if not his mother?"

Beowulf opened his mouth to tell her that she should not come to the battle, but Hygd looked fiercely up at him, and he shut it again. Even Yrse had stood with the Inglings' standard in the first fight at Ravenwood: he would not let Hygd come where a stray arrow or sword stroke might cut her down but he could not tell her that she had no right to ride to Heardred's vengeance, and the less so when Scyld sat there by Hereweard's side.

"Aye," Scyld agreed, the soft thunder of her voice shivering through the hard packed earth beneath Beowulf's feet. "Woden has half the slain, but half the Frowe chooses: you and I, Hygd, we have work set to our hands."

Beowulf gave his orders, sending his fastest messengers to his drightens and under kings and most especially to Sweartwulf and Thura Hound Foot. However deep Onela's hate, the Ingling could not have begun calling his men for war until his harvest was done, and that was a little later in the northern reaches of the Swedes' lands than in those of the Geats. The war band Hereweard had brought with him was not so large as Beowulf had thought it would be, but he had made up for that by bringing his horses with him.

Eadgils remarked that there would be need for swift riding, and he had not thought the Geats ready to supply a king's host with good steeds. Less welcome to Beowulf, however was the next thing Eadgils asked.

"This night," the Ingling said, his green blue eyes meeting Beowulf's steadily, "I would have your leave to raise our stools in your howe field, for Scyld and I have much work to do, that matters all fall out as we would have them."

Beowulf remembered how Eadgils had crouched and chanted over his warding tunic, and the sleep that had fallen on Hroesnabeorh: he was loath to have such seith spells worked by his burg, or the dead in the barrow field disturbed. But Hygd was listening carefully, and when Beowulf looked to her, she nodded.

"You have said yourself, Beowulf, that what is uncanny is not always ill," she murmured. "Yet if you have misgivings about this, then ask Ingemund for his rede before you give or deny leave for it."

Ingemund had come to the hall with Hildegeard when it was proven that the war ships did not bear foes, sitting in his usual place by the high seat. Now Beowulf rose and tapped him on the shoulder.

"Come with me, Ingemund, for I would know your thoughts on a matter in which you are wise."

"I am hardly to be named wise," Ingemund answered, but he did not seem ill pleased by his king's words. The two of them went outside. The Sun was setting, her dull light a faint bloody stain on the gray western sky; a gust of wind whipped the sleet into Beowulf's face as he told Ingemund of what he had seen the night before their last battle against Onela. "Now Eadgils would do such a seith work here, and though he asked my leave and would wreak towards our weal, I do not know if we should let him do as he means to."

Ingemund closed his eyes in thought. At last he said, "We have already taken his hand, and Scyld's, in friendship. They are grim wights, but this is grim work, nor is Onela without blame in his deeds: if he had stood bravely to the fore by his brother's side when Othere fell, matters might be otherwise. And though seith charms are wrought most often for ill, yet that craft was brought to the gods by the Frowe. Now my dream becomes clearer to me, for my heart tells me that it is she who rules in this matter: men may lift swords for this battle, but it is women who urge the bloodshed."

A chill of ice like frozen wyrm bale trickled through Beowulf's veins as Ingemund spoke: the young gudhe had not been there when Hygd asked Beowulf to swear vengeance for Heardred, nor had he been close enough to hear the words of Hygd and Scyld in the hall earlier. You have ever been too swift to believe that Frea Ing gives only frith and joy, Hygd had said to him once. Now he was wedded to the Frowe he could not turn away from the knowledge that she was no frith weaver, but the fierce maid who kindled sword as well as leek, and the fire hooded seith singer as well. And how can I love her, if I would turn my face from her craft and will when it seems dark to me?

"So I should give Eadgils leave to wreak as he will?"

"That is your choice. Yet for myself, I would gladly go to the mound field with him, and hold a torch in my withered arm."

A rare bitterness caught on Ingemund's tongue, like a leaf of wormwood stirred into a stew by mistake. Of course, he would still fight against Onela as he can, Beowulf thought, and with that came the brief hopeful thought: Maybe I should leave his rede aside, since he has the grounds of his own hate to twist his thoughts in this matter? But Beowulf knew Ingemund better than that. And more, he knew that he must not let his fear keep him from what he had oathed to the Frowe. Thus not only Ingemund, but Beowulf, bore torches out to the barrow field that night. The firebrands hissed in the sleet, their flames whipping about in the wind.

Two silent men thanes of Hereweard, though Beowulf thought they might more truly be called Scyld's thanes set up the high seith stools on one of the oldest barrows, laying plank on plank and slipping pegs into place with practiced hands so that it was not long before the two carven chairs rose above the black mounds like ship prows surging up from the swell of a dark wave. Scyld and Eadgils had arrayed themselves with care for this working, though, and Beowulf was greatly thankful for this, they were not near naked as Eadgils had been for his rite before. Scyld's slim body was garbed in a dress of red linen, embroidered all over with shining designs in black and white horsehair; her hood and gloves were of lynx fur.

She wore a belt of touch wood, and about her neck was a torc of twisted gold, with large round garnets glowing smooth and dark from the end knobs. Her shoes were pieced together from the close lying fur of the lynx's legs and feet, fastened with toggles of walrus ivory carved into the shape of falcon heads. She made her way over the rough ground with the help of a long stave topped with the skull of a falcon, its wood stained almost black, as though it had been steeped in the blood of many offerings, but polished to a high sheen. Eadgils wore moss red trousers, but his tunic and cloak were black in the torchlight. He was girded with the same hairy belt he had worn for his wreaking at Hroesnabeorh, and a little round copper box hung from it beside his knife. As before, his hair was loosened, the wind whipping his unbraided beard in wet tangles around his face.

He held a small stave in his hand: the torchlight gleamed ruddy from a piece of polished bone or ivory at its base, and a sliver of gray whetstone was set into its tip, bound tight with gold wire. Eadgils lifted Scyld up to her seat, mounting his own easily. Though the darkness cloaked the carvings on the seith stools, a horse's white skull grinned above Eadgils' head, and when Beowulf looked at it from the corner of his eye, it seemed that he could see a flicker of blue light in the black empty eye sockets. Ingemund's face was pale in the torchlight, as though he were having second thoughts about the wisdom of his rede, but he held his firebrand without flinching, even when the sleet laden wind cast the smoke into his face. Eadgils lifted his little stave and began to sing, his deep voice resonating through the soles of Beowulf's feet; it seemed, in the flickering of the wind tossed torches, that the Ingling's high stool shivered with each note of his voice like a tree beneath the storm winds.

"The roots run deep, rown under worlds,
the wyrm wends deep and winds in shadow,
nine worlds below well's waters sink,
the runes run deep, rown under worlds."

On the last line, Scyld lifted her voice with Eadgils'. Together, their singing was an eerie, bone shivering harmony: at first, she followed his tune above in the lesser depths of her throat, but then her voice rose to piercing clearness like a falcon winging high above the earth, her own tune weaving in and out of the Ingling's song; and on the middle staves, Eadgils dropped his voice deeper yet, until Beowulf almost felt rather than heard it.

"The roots run deep, rown under worlds,
 Scathe goddess, fare on skis from berg height!
 Let hail howl from hoary bow,
the runes run deep, rown under worlds."

The cold sharpened as the two seith workers sang, the wind flaying through Beowulf's thick cloak to chill his byrnie as if he were wearing an eoten's coat of rime mail. Ingemund was shivering hard, the light of his torch wavering through the darkness, but he clung to it grimly, though Beowulf could see that he was biting his pale lips.

"The roots run deep, rown under worlds,
the winter kin to Wener ride forth!
Come, Cara, Frosta, cold of breath,
the runes run deep, rown under worlds."

The sleet blew thicker and whiter now; and it seemed to Beowulf that, beyond the pale glimmer of the torchlight through the storm, he could see the whirling shadows of great shapes striding from the north, and hear the shriek of arrows in the wind that moaned over the barrow mounds or was it Scyld's high keening, lifted up almost past his hearing, as Eadgils' bass drone had dropped almost below it? The words of their song were near lost in the eerie wailing; only now and again, straining his ears, could Beowulf make any sense of what they sang.

"The roots run deep, rown under worlds,
let eoton silver lie on lake waves,
horse idis ride on roof of eels,
the runes run deep, rown under worlds."
It seemed to Beowulf that he could feel the blood freezing into tiny dark crystals along his bones like frost thickening on tree branches: the sea's worst cold had never chilled him so. He could not even feel the warmth from his torch flame on his face and hands any longer; it might have been a howe fire burning at the end of a rod of earth chilled gold. Yet deep in his breast glowed a single kernel of warmth, like a red glint of light shining in the heart of a dark garnet, and it seemed to him that it grew stronger as Scyld and Eadgils sang, as though the snow laden wind were blowing up the fire within him.

"The roots run deep, rown under worlds,
Onela rides in easeless wandering,
to Wener's shore his will is bound,
the runes run deep, rown under worlds...
The roots run deep, rown under worlds,
 in Wyrd's Well lie the words of shaping,
up heavens high and earth below,
the runes run deep, rown under worlds..."
Scyld's voice dropped sharply as Eadgils' rose, until the same low note rang from both high seith stools. It cut off suddenly; Scyld slumped forward, and her two silent thanes stepped forward to catch her, lifting her down. Eadgils climbed slowly from his own seat, though it seemed nearly beyond his strength: he clung to it like a sailor to a pitching mast, lowering himself carefully to the ground. Beowulf had no words for either of them, nor did Ingemund; but, leaving one of Scyld's men to deal with the seith seats while the other half carried his queen along, they made their way back to the warmth of the hall. Even when he began to be warm again, Beowulf felt as though the blood had been drained from his body, and he was as chill hungry as if he had been swimming in the winter seas for a full days. He ate ravenously of the honey and fruit cakes that Ingemund had ordered set out for them, and not until there was no more to eat did he finally say,

"What do you await from that work?"

"We shall meet Onela on Lake Wener, and do battle with him upon the ice the ice that he shall not have readied himself for. For Wener is seldom frozen thick enough to bear a man's weight before Yule, and never so close to Winter nights," Eadgils answered hoarsely, drawing his hand back from the empty trencher as though he had not realized that the sweet cakes were all gone.

Beowulf thought on that, and could find nothing amiss with his ally's plan...save that he wished now he had ridden to Upsala before, and challenged the Swede King to meet his strength in single battle like a man. But Onela, who had stood back with his host before him in battle, would never have taken such an offer. The Ingling's skill was in guile if his allies' words were true, Onela was even now doing his best to trap Beowulf as Scyld and Eadgils thought to trap him, though by more earthly means and, if Heardred were to be avenged, only craft could overcome the Swede.

This is no matter of murder by seith work: Onela has both wit and strength to fight with yet; nor will sig in this be given us if we fail in wisdom or war might. The storm had blown past by morning, leaving icy clearness in its wake; a thin scattering of snow glittered over the ground like silver dust from a careless jeweler's filing. The wains were already being loaded for a winter faring, and sledges and ice spikes for the horses' hooves made ready Beowulf's men had looked oddly at him when he ordered those things to be done, but none gainsaid him: knowledge of his foresight had spread quietly among the Geats through the years. Eadgils went among the Geatish horses that stood tied in the garth awaiting their winter shoes, looking carefully at them and running his hands over haunches and down hocks with well practiced skill, but when he reached Aelefeax, Beowulf went over to keep a closer watch on him.

"This is your horse?" Eadgils asked, looking up from where he stooped by the big ruddy gelding's front leg.

"He is," Beowulf answered carefully.

Eadgils lifted a thin eyebrow and straightened up, patting Aelefeax's sturdily rounded shoulder.

"Well, you need a strong steed to bear your weight, and I guess he is better fat than too thin. But when I take my high seat at Upsala, I shall send you a better. This boy is well tempered, but far too tame and drowsy for a king of your might: I guess he has not stretched to a full gallop under saddle more than twice or thrice since you began to ride him."

"Though that gift is offered with a good heart, and I thank you for the offer, a better steed would be wasted on me," Beowulf told the Ingling. "Tame and drowsy Aelefeax may seem to you, but I find him lively, and almost more than my skill can handle if you doubt that, you may ask Yrse what she thought of my riding when we bore her from Upsala."

Eadgils' thin lips curled with amusement, and Beowulf thought that he saw a glimmer of scorn in the Ingling's blue green eyes.

"Best to know when you are over matched, I suppose," Eadgils said, "but let me show you what a fine horse is like."

The Swede's gray stallion was tied a little way from the other horses, tossing his mane and stamping his hooves. Eadgils' steed was huge, his shoulders almost on a level with those of his rider, and the muscles of his haunches rippled like sea swells under his winter thick coat. Beowulf thought that the dapple gray could easily have borne his own weight but he disliked the glitter of the stallion's dark eyes, and he walked wide of his back legs.

"The fool who had owned him meant to slaughter him for the gods, and seethe his flesh for a Winter nights feast," Eadgils said. "Not that he would not have been a mighty gift, but Aethelweard thought only that he could not be ridden and was too wild to breed from: it was he gave him the name Slinger."

He stroked the grays strong arched neck, and the horse nuzzled lovingly at his shoulder, then dropped his head to snuffling at the Ingling's belt pouch as if Eadgils often brought him apples.

"When Onela is downed, there are three things only I would have of him: Sweogris on my arm, Yrse beside me, and Onela's horse Hraefn beneath me ah, the black stallion is the king of Upsala's herd, though it will be some work to keep him and Slinger from slaying each other!" Eadgils went on to tell Beowulf about Onela's stallion for some time, although Beowulf got no more out of it than he had when Hygelac waxed lively about horses: he had been happiest with the plump and lazy Feola, who only ran in the direst need.

After a while, Beowulf was able to free himself from the Ingling by feigning a need to speak with Hygd, who stood overlooking the loading of a wain.

"Careful with that tent, there!" She was saying to one of the thralls. "I won't have cold rain dripping on a warrior's blankets because you tore its covering!" She was already dressed for a long winter faring, muffled thickly in a cloak of lynx skins, with furry gloves on her hands and the white fur of her hood framing her cold pink face.

"It is going swiftly enough," she told Beowulf as he walked up. "I would guess that we shall be ready to leave by dawn tomorrow, if nothing turns amiss."

"That is well," he answered. He sniffed the frosty air. "This would be good slaughtering weather, if we were biding at home to hold the Winter nights offering."

Hygd laughed mirthlessly. "It is good slaughtering weather, and the gods shall not go without their offering long," she said. Then her smile softened, and she laid a furred hand on Beowulf's arm. "It is like you to think of such things first. But there will be time to cut down beasts when we come back, and you know that we would not bide long in frith otherwise."

"Aye," Beowulf said heavily.

Just then, he heard Hildegeard's voice raised sharply, cutting over the clinking of byrnies and horse gear and the speech of the men who worked to ready the Geatish host for riding out.

"I say you shall not go, Ingemund! You have spilled your share of blood, and no man can call you a coward, when you lost the most use of your arm by holding the Hrethlings' standard so bravely. But what would you do in battle now?"

"The same thing I did before!" Ingemund answered his wife hotly, the first time Beowulf had ever heard him lift his voice to her. "I can still hold the standard pole in the crook of my arm, and lift a shield with my left hand: that shall free a man who can swing his sword better than I."

"Beowulf will never give you leave to go into battle thus," Hildegeard argued. "You are needed here who else shall he trust to look after his burg when Hygd is faring with him? And you are worth far more to our king in the holy grove than you are on the slaughter field."

"Let Beowulf be the judge of that!" Ingemund flung back at his wife. "I shall go and ask him now, and if he says that I shall go with him, then there is no more you can do about it."

Beowulf strode over to the couple before they could say any more: whether Ingemund stayed or went, this was no time for hard words between them. They both fell still as they saw him nearing, looking up with the reddened faces of guilty children.

"I need not ask after the cause of your strife, for I think the whole garth has heard it," Beowulf said mildly. "Ingemund, I had indeed thought to give the steering of this burg into your hands while I was gone, for you and Hildegeard between you know well all that must be done, and should I fall in fight, I have no other to whom I might leave all that I hold."

Ingemund's jaw clenched beneath his early graying beard. "My king, I am not so wrecked that I cannot ride to battle with you once more. Why else did you give me Heardred's horse, than that you did not mean for me to sit in the mead hall the rest of my life?"

I had hoped that you would heal, and be whole, Beowulf thought: but he could not speak thus to his crippled thane. Nor did he ask what good Ingemund should be in the midst of sword play, for the young man had already answered that question and not without wisdom. Instead he said,

"And would you leave the holy stone untended, when I am going to a meeting of blades?"

"The standard pole bears the Hrethlings' battle luck," Ingemund argued. "Who is more fit to hold it as we fare to war than I, who have already sprinkled it often with blessing blood and ale? I know how to call its main forth at need, better than any man in your war band."

Beowulf could not gainsay that, either, nor Ingemund's next words:

"Should I not be beside you, when you make the battle offering on the host plain?"

Yet he might still have asked Ingemund to stay behind, but he could see the need shining clear in his thane's flushed face and brightened gaze. Though Ingemund's sword arm was crooked and withered, his soul had not been crippled with it but if Beowulf barred him from the field of fight while he was still young and his heart battle ready, it would be a different matter. Beowulf saw the water swelling in Hildegeard's eyes: she would grieve, and hate him for a time, if Ingemund were cut down, but that was as Wyrd might speak it true, while the harm that would be done if he made Ingemund stay behind when the Geatish host rode out was a much surer thing.

"You should, and you shall," Beowulf said at last. Ingemund stepped forward and embraced him thankfully, but Hildegeard turned and ran off, the white snow dust spraying up beneath her shoes. "I am not sure I have done you any good turn there," Beowulf added ruefully. "Still, you have until dawn tomorrow to better matters with your wife."

"I think I have never gainsaid her will before, and she finds this hard," answered Ingemund, "and there is much else to do we spoke of the standard's luck, and I would bless it before we go, if you will come with me to slay a boar before the hallowed stone. For mighty wights ride with us, but where such might gathers, it may rouse foes that are its match. I would do all I can to be sure that all is done as were best, lest dark idises rise to hinder us at the last and all our strength be set to naught."

Beowulf's war band rode out in the red light of dawn, their bridle rangles ringing brightly through the frosty air. The wains rolled behind the horses; but Hygd sat her golden mare beside Beowulf, her gloved hands light on the reins as the little steed's steps quickened into a smooth pace beneath her. Scyld rode a black maned grey that tossed her head and nickered, and Beowulf marked that she and Eadgils both kept a little apart from the other horses, as though they knew their steeds would kick and bite if they came too close to the rest. As before, the Geatish host swelled with its travels, the under kings and drightens coming to the Geat ruler's call; and when they stopped between halls at night for so many men and wains could not move as swiftly as a small band of riders their campfires glowed in the darkness like an hundred lamps set about a godly dwelling.

The weather stayed clear and cold until they were within two days' ride of Lake Wener: then the gray clouds tumbled across the sky in a great misty rock slide, shedding an ankle deep blanket of snow between noon and nightfall. The ice spikes were set on the horses' feet the next day, and the sledges were unloaded, their runners sliding more swiftly over the snow than the wheels of the wains that had borne them thus far. Beowulf put on the clothes that the Finns had given him those years before, the reindeer hide leggings and cloak of bearskin, and if any of the Geats looked strangely at how their king was dressed, he did not mark it.

When Beowulf looked back at his host, he saw the riders fading to gray shapes in the whirling snowfall, and mist shadows beyond, and no man dared stray too far from the body of the army, lest he be blinded and lost. Scyld sang as they rode, her mood seeming to grow more merry as the weather worsened; and in truth, her songs drew the mind from the numbing cold biting at nose and cheeks, from the stiffening of fingers within gloves and feet within shoes, and the stinging of snow laden wind into eyes.

Hlewabrandar often sang with her, though even the poet's well trained voice seemed like the croaking of a crow against the smooth depths and piercing heights of Scyld's song; but Eadgils held his silence, as if he would not deign to sing for any purpose so simple as lifting the heart. Hygd bore the cold and the soreness of long riding far better than Beowulf had feared or hoped; in a corner of his heart, he had thought that she might give over after a few days, to stay in the warm hall of one of his under kings until the battle was done.

Though her delicate lips cracked and bled from the cold until Ingemund gave her a salve for them, she never spoke a word of complaint; and when the snow fell too fast and thick to melt away from the white fur framing her face, she only set her small jaw the more grimly and stared into the wind as if she could see Heardred's wounded ghost in the swirling whiteness ahead of her. However, when they came at last to the northwestern bank of Lake Wener, setting their camp at evening beside the great flat white stretch of the frozen lake, Hygd made her way into Beowulf's tent, shivering in her furs.

"Berki," she said, "I would share your blankets this night, for the cold is in my bones."

"Gladly," Beowulf answered.

As well as the Finnish clothing, he had brought the blanket of white reindeer hides Paanja had given him: though they shed coarse hairs over everything they touched, no other furs seemed so warm, and there was easily room for Hygd's small body as well as his own beneath them. She did not so much as take off her cloak when she crept beneath the reindeer blanket, but she clung tightly to Beowulf until his warmth began to ease her shaking. Even cold and weary as he was, his leek stirred at her nearness, but he turned so that she should not guess it.

"What now, Berki?" Hygd asked.

"Tomorrow, Thura Hound Foot should meet us with his men: then we shall cross the ice, and trust in the gods that it bear our weight," Beowulf said. "Five days ago, as Sweartwulf's rider told us, Onela's host was rounding the end of Lake Weter, and this snow shall have hindered him far more than it slows us, for he did not come readied as we did. If all goes well, Sweartwulf and Aethelweard and Cyneheard should be marching northward between the lakes, so that we should catch Onela between hammer and anvil."

"It seems to me that this battle array leaves a great deal to luck, and to trusting that our foe will do as we hope he will," Hygd murmured thoughtfully. "Though I was not raised to lead men in war, I have heard enough of thanes' hall speech to wonder if that is wise."

Beowulf bit his lip. He was loath to speak of the seith work Eadgils and Scyld had wreaked; but he did not doubt that Onela would find his steps wandering in the snow until he reached Lake Wener's shore at the spot the Ingling and the Dane woman had chosen. Instead he said,

"If much is left to luck, we have reason to hope that luck will be with us in this. I do not say that you are wrong in your doubts: but I think it is already thus, that Onela and I shall meet above the Wener waters, though I do not know which of us shall hold the icy host field."

"If a woman's might may help to shift the course of battle, then I know the answer to that!" Hygd told him. "Though I may not be as wise as Scyld and I am glad enough of that, for I think the gaining of such wisdom asks a geld I would rather not pay I did not come with you through this early snow and ice only to sit and watch like a maid at the Thing contests. Nor," she added, "will Ingemund stand idle by the standard post, though he never draw his sword. I am glad that you gave him leave to come with us: he did not yield in the fight when Heardred had fallen, and I think such steadfastness will see us yet to sig. It is in my mind that, though a time of stillness has passed since then, that battle was not truly ended at my son's burning, nor shall it be over until Onela's blood steams on the snow."

It was on the tip of Beowulf's tongue to say that he had never weened Hygd to be so cruel of mood. But through the winding depth of years, the memory of another hall idis rose to him: of the rending sorrow on the mere frowe's face, and the eyeless gape of Aeschere's gray head, left bleeding on the stone above her sunken dwelling, and he remembered, too, how a thane in the band of one of his under kings, guesting in his hall, had tried to pick up one of the puppies squirming at Wulfa's teats, and leapt back shaking his bleeding hand and cursing, for the gray hound would not suffer strangers to touch her children.

"I have vowed Heardred's vengeance, and you shall have it if it is within my might to give," Beowulf said to her. Hygd laid her head against his shoulder, and he put his arm over her, though he was careful that it did not weight her too greatly.

By dawn, the snowfall had lightened to a pale sprinkle from the gray sky. Thus Beowulf, standing by one of the cook fires and juggling a hot sausage in his gloved fingers as he waited for it to cool enough to eat, saw the cloaked figure skimming over the knee deep snow, and when one of his men stepped forward to challenge the newcomer, he shouted,

"Hold, I know who is come to us," plowing towards them as swiftly as he could.

"Well met, Beowulf," Sweartwulf said, grinning.

Like Beowulf, he was clad in Finnish reindeer hide leggings, and he also wore a pointed leather cap over his helm; but even without seeing that, Beowulf had been sure that no other man in Geatland would ski like the half Finn.

"Well met, my friend," Beowulf answered. "What brings you to me here? I had thought that your host would be nearly to the northern end of Lake Wener by now."

"And so I am sure they are. I left them to Hraefn the boy knows what he is doing there! I could not leave you to steer your way through this weather by yourself. And besides, I wished to let you know that my scouts say Onela is almost there, and though I have taught them all I could about running on skis, and may not be as swift as I was in my youth, there is still no man in my hall that can match me at speeding over the snow. I was bidden tell you, as well, that the host of Thura Hound Foot is not too far behind, and being from the northern mountains as he is, he well knows how to both travel and fight in such weather. Before the gods, he is a mighty man!" Sweartwulf added. "If there were not such matters to hand, I should have challenged him to a fall or two at wrestling, to see if his skill matches his thews."

"Your tidings are all welcome," Beowulf said. "Have you eaten this day?" He held out the sausage, and Sweartwulf took it from him, biting the end off and chewing noisily.

"I was on my way all night, hoping that I had not lost the path in the darkness though I have a good memory for such thing," the half Finn said around his mouthful of meat. "With your leave, I shall eat and rest: I do not think that the Hound Foot's men shall reach us much before noon, and by then I shall be ready to go on with you."

Though it was hard to tell the Sun's stead behind the heavy drifting clouds, Beowulf guessed that Sweartwulf had spoken truly when he said that Thura Hound Foot would join his host by midday. The king of the West Geats forged through the snow to Beowulf's side; Beowulf could not help marking that he moved more easily through the deep drifts on his pawed feet than most men, but remembering that Thura was touchy on that point, he was careful neither to stare nor to speak of it.

"Here we are, and ready to go forward!" Beowulf's under king shouted when he was still thirty paces from his drighten's side. "Come, Beowulf: why are you lagging here?"

"Waiting for those who are slower than we," Beowulf replied, grinning. He turned to Ingemund. "Mount up, and lift the standard high: it is time for us to dare the Wener's ice. But if the lake's roof does not break beneath my weight, then none of those who ride after me need fear."

"That is true, and I shall ride beside you to make doubly sure of it," Thura said. Then he looked about, blinking as if to shake snow dazzle from his eyes. "Does my sight deceive me, Beowulf, or do you now have women in your host? Or am I fey, and looking upon Woden's maids?"

"You are not fey, nor do your eyes deceive you," answered Beowulf.

"One of those frowes is Scyld, hlaefdige in Wodenswih and sister to Hrothulf Scylding, and the other is my own Hygd for we ride to avenge her son."

"Matters are harsh when women fare to war," said Thura, no longer smiling. "Yet it is not my place to give you rede in such things only to fight beside you: and then you shall see what the axe my father left can do! My little brother has won great fame for himself, as was only to be awaited, but I think I can hew out a few staves of praise for myself now."

As Beowulf rode out onto Lake Wener, his bravery almost failed him. The ice creaked alarmingly beneath Aelefeax's hooves; and looking out at the great stretch of smooth whiteness, its flat snow field fading into gray mist with no end to be seen, Beowulf found it hard to believe that the lake could truly be frozen hard across its width. Yet he had spoken, and Thura Hound Foot rode with him, as he had said, with Ingemund carrying the Hrethlings' golden ring standard on his other side and Hygd sat her golden mare behind him, next to Scyld's black maned gray.

So he urged Aelefeax on: and the ice held. It was a long faring across Lake Wener, and Beowulf knew there was no hope of crossing it before nightfall: they would be lucky to reach the far bank by sunset the next day. The Geats pitched their tents on the lake, driving the pegs deep into the ice and huddling four and five together in a tent for warmth. Thick as the ice seemed, no one dared to light a fire on it, and it was a chilled and tired host that set off at dawn the next day. Yet the way over the frozen roofed water was smooth, the sledges slipping along easily behind the spike shod horses; and Beowulf thought that every man in his host was eager to see something more than whiteness before and behind and about, and gray sky scattering white swirls above.

The bronze rangles had been lifted from the horses, and Scyld had stopped her singing, that they not be heard so quickly from afar; cloaks muffled the jingling of the warriors' byrnies, so that they rode in silence save for the hiss of the sledge runners and the low thudding of the horses' hooves over the snow blanketed ice. Beowulf guessed that it was past mid afternoon when he marked that the grayness at the edge of the lake had darkened: though the snow mist still veiled them, he was looking at black pines and the northeastern shore of Lake Wener. Then he heard the sound of a horn, faint as the cry of a great bird from far away, and what might have been the echo of men shouting.

"Forward!" He cried. "Our friends have found Onela's host: let us go to aid them!" He nudged Aelefeax into a canter, and the muffled beating of hooves behind him rose to a roar as the Geatish host rode swiftly towards the battle.

At first the gray shapes of the men fighting were blurred as the shadows of the long warring dead; but as Beowulf neared the struggle, they resolved in his eyes, the red of shields and tunics standing out bloody through the drifting snow. Eadgils broke off with the right flank, sweeping over the ice in a full gallop, and Hereweard turned to lead his Danes in a wide arc around the other side; Scyld still rode beside him and held his eagle stave aloft, her high falcon shriek carrying clear over the clashing and shouting ahead of them.

The Inglings' boar standard gleamed gold, turning above the rime dulled helmets in the middle of the Swedish host as Onela readied his men to meet the new threat. Hraefn's band, though small, had struck cleverly, pushing the Swedes out onto the ice Beowulf guessed that Hraefn had come upon the foe where he had not awaited them and mounted a fierce attack to briefly daunt them so that he could flee into the trees until help came, as the Geats had done at Ravenwood those years before. Beowulf had trusted in luck...and the Ingling's spell craft, and they had brought him here just in the moment of need. The Geat king needed both hands to manage his reins without bashing Aelefeax with his shield, so he could not blow his horn; but beside him, Thura Hound Foot loosed a deep ringing note on his own battle instrument.

Through the tattered veils of snow, Beowulf saw Eadgils wheel his gray steed in a tight curve before his men but Slinger's hooves skidded on the ice, and the Yngling flew from his back. Beowulf gasped a lung searing breath of cold air at the ill foreboding; yet Eadgils curled in the air, rolling unhurt to his feet, and drew his sword to wave it in the air, shouting the command to dismount and run forward. Beowulf was nearing the rearmost line of the Swedes now, and carefully pulled Aelefeax back and to a halt few men could fight from horseback, and the Geat king would be the last to do so. Swinging himself off his steed, Beowulf called to the warriors behind him as Eadgils had done: only Ingemund stayed mounted, holding the ring standard high.

"Forward!" Beowulf shouted, drawing his own blade and raising his iron bound shield.

Sweartwulf skimmed up to his right the half Finn knew well how to fight on his skis and Thura Hound Foot matched Beowulf's steps to the left, quickening their pace to a run as the blurred faces beneath the helms grew clear in their sight. A throwing spear sang past Beowulf's head; another stuck quivering in his shield, and then they were crashing into the Swedish shield wall. One man went down beneath Beowulf's shield; he hewed at another, hearing the cold brittle iron links of his byrnie break ringingly under his blade, and they were through the shield wall into the next ranks.

Beowulf struck again and again: blood spurted beneath his blows, steaming in the icy air. Then it seemed to him, though he had thought Hygd safe back in the sledges, that he saw her standing in the thick of the fight before him, her long hair streaming out beneath her lynx fur hood; her hands were raised, and she was calling to him, though he could not make out her words through the din of clashing blades and shield boards shattering.

"For Heardred!" He cried back to her as his sword sundered the helm of the man before him in a glistening red spray.

Another Swede stood between them, the tip of his blade flashing out in an adder swift thrust towards Beowulf's face. The rim of his shield just knocked it aside as his answering blow crashed down on his foe's arm; the man reeled away, and Beowulf would have run to set his shield over Hygd, but she was no longer there downed? No, she was calling to him from a little farther away, and now he could hear her shrieking,

"To Onela!"

The Swedish king still sat his tall black horse by his standard stave in the middle of his host, shouting his commands from that high battle seat. Beowulf hacked his way towards him. The glistening boar flickered in and out of his sight, blurred by the blood spattering into his eyes and by glimpses of Hygd's shimmering hair flowing blood streaked over her gold bright byrnie how had she come armored to the field without his knowing? The snow was falling more heavily, swirling the shapes of the men about him into great arching trees, so that he seemed to stand in a wood in the midst of a storm; swords and spears coiled and leapt about him, biting deep through sundered mail shirts, and flames burned hot above the frozen lake, gnawing at the striving tree limbs. Onela looked into Beowulf's face; his helm rim shadowed his green eyes like the edge of a howe door, but Beowulf saw their hoarfrost glimmer, the eyes of the wyrm in its darkness.

"Make the offering!" Hygd's high voice cried, ringing golden through Beowulf's skull. "Send what is mine to me" Beowulf did not know any more which of them she was urging on.

Onela's face twisted, his mouth gaping in a baleful hiss of rage, and he struck outwards, his flickering sword clanging off Beowulf's iron shield rim. Beowulf thrust at the Swede king, but Onela's horse half reared back, and the blade only tore through the leather of his hinder saddle bow in a scattering of golden straw. Onela hewed at Beowulf's helmet; thrown off by the horse's shifting, the blow shrieked over the gilded crest, doing no harm. Yet while the Swede king's arm was up, Beowulf thrust again under it, and as the black steed's fore hooves dropped to pound hard into the ice, he slammed his rider's weight deep onto the sword. Onela twisted, falling from his horse's back, and it seemed to Beowulf that he heard Hygd calling,

"Well struck, my bear!"

Another heartbeat, and the golden boar standard fell across Onela's body: Thura Hound Foot had hewn down the sturdy thanes that had warded the Swedish standard bearer. The fighting was breaking apart into smaller knots of struggling men, veiled by the thick driving snow.

"Onela is fallen!" Thura Hound Foot shouted.

There was no one left near enough for Beowulf to strike at; and, even through the snow and deepening twilight, he could see that the Swedish host was melting like icicles above a bone fire. Trusting in Thura where was Sweartwulf? To ward him from anyone else who might come, Beowulf set his shield down: its wood was woefully hacked and splintered, the gilded bronze mountings broken away, but its iron rim and bindings still held it in one piece. He unslung Hygelac's horn from his neck and blew three long blasts. Man by man, the fighting stilled, Geats and Danes and Swedes disengaging and standing back from each other.

When Beowulf saw Eadgils, the Ingling was on the back of his gray again. The horse picked his way daintily over the heaps of fallen bodies and the wounded moaning in the snow. A long streak of blood marred his cloud dappled flank, as though a throwing spear had grazed him; his wide nostrils flared at the smells of blood and bowels, and several times he tried to shy away from a writhing body, but Eadgils controlled him easily, riding up to Beowulf and looking down at Onela's limp corpse.

"It is time for you to give me Sweogris, I think," the Ingling said. He bore the marks of hard fighting: blood dulled the beads in his braided beard, and broken links gleamed at the edges of several holes in his byrnie, but the tufted wool tunic beneath it, though stained and grimy, was still whole.

"Fetch your ring for yourself," Beowulf answered, his hands shaking as he slung Hygelac's horn about his neck again.

Hygd was nowhere to be seen, neither among the living nor the dead had he truly seen her? The whole battle seemed blurred in his mind, as though he had dreamed it, though the blood gumming his eyelashes and the stink of slaughter were real enough, and the weary fighting ache settling into his stiffening muscles. Eadgils glared at him a moment, but got off his horse, crouching by Onela's body. He stripped off his gloves, fumbling beneath the sleeves of the dead man's byrnie, and tugged, then rose with the thick boar headed ring in his hand and leapt, not onto Slinger's back, but onto Onela's black stallion, holding Sweogris aloft.

"Now I am king over the Swede realm I, Eadgils Ingling, Othere's son!" He shouted, his deep voice thundering across the frozen lake. "Is there any man here who would challenge it?"

The defeated Swedes looked up at him, dumb and resigned as those of beaten oxen not only weary from the battle, Beowulf guessed, but worn from their march through the uncanny early winter. None of them spoke for a moment; then one man called out hoarsely,

"Hail, Eadgils, king of the Swede realm!" Another echoed it, the rest taking up the cry as though they feared Eadgils would see their silence.

Eadgils smiled. "So it is done, Beowulf. You have your vengeance, I my kingdom and Hereweard has what he would. And thus Heardred's oath to me is fulfilled. Now let us swear the frith between us once more, and then see to our folk who are foes no longer; and many of the wounded shall die here on the ice if they are not brought swiftly to some warmth."

Beowulf set his hand on the heavy gold arm ring, and together he and Eadgils spoke the oath of frith, as Hygelac and Othere had before them. Eadgils slipped Sweogris over his wrist and wheeled the black horse with a light touch of heel to side.

"That was a good battle!" Said Hraefn, who had come up without Beowulf seeing him. Then Sweartwulf's son looked about, and his eyes widened in alarm. "Beowulf, where is my father?"

Beowulf tried to think back through the battle. Sweartwulf had broken through the rear shield wall with them, and then he hastened back over the trampled and bloodied snow with Hraefn behind him, looking about anxiously though already he was sure of what he would find. Sweartwulf lay in a pool of blood and ice melt not far from where they had crashed through the Swedish shield wall, the broken shaft of a throwing spear jutting from his chest and red froth bubbling from his mouth. As Beowulf knelt down beside his friend, the half Finn opened his slanted blue eyes.

"Sweartwulf," Beowulf grieved.

Sweartwulf smiled, and Beowulf guessed that he was so near death that he no longer felt the pain of his wound. Beowulf grasped the spear to pull it out of him, but Sweartwulf rolled his head from side to side.

"No...die faster. Not grieve...Woden takes his geld." More blood bubbled from his mouth with each word, and Hraefn stooped to wipe it away with the sleeve of his tunic. "Good boy...led host well...rule Hroesnabeorh. We won?"

"We won," Beowulf assured him. "But o, my friend..."

"Friend...tell Frithugeard...love her." Sweartwulf's eyes widened, and he did not blink at the snowflakes falling into them as he stared at the gray sky. "Riding closer...Beowulf. Take it out."

Beowulf braced himself against the ground, pulling. The narrow blade of the casting spear came out in a gush of blood and pink froth. Sweartwulf thrashed once; then his limbs unlocked, and he lay still.

"Fare well, my father," Hraefn murmured, his voice catching in his throat. Though his beard had thickened in the last years, he still looked very young as he gazed down at his father's corpse, and Beowulf saw the muscles of his jaw tremble as though he were trying not to give way to weeping. "You told me that you would have an offering geld to pay to Woden this day: I would that I had known what you meant!"

"Foresight often comes when men are fey," Beowulf said sadly. "And yet your father was not such a man as to die in the straw."

"No," said Hraefn, and those stark words seemed to strengthen him, for he swallowed hard and drew Sweartwulf's reindeer hide cloak up to cover his face.

"Now you must be drighten in Hroesnabeorh, as your father said," Beowulf told him. "It seems to me that you must have led your part of the host well: I could not have wished for the Swedes to be arrayed other than they were."

Hraefn shook his head, frowning. "I was over eager, and we betrayed ourselves to them too quickly. Had you not come over the ice when you did, we would have had to flee, and trust to the snow to keep them from hunting us out of the trees like a litter of wild piglets."

"Often battles do not go as they are meant to, but you did well to earn yourself the chance to save your men. If you had fled to the wood, that would still have held the main host of Swedes with their backs to Lake Wener, open to our attack."

Hraefn smiled wonderingly, though Beowulf could see the sorrow water still standing in his eyes. "If that is so, then I have no cause for shame. I feared I had failed you, when Aethelweard and Cyneheard thought we were lost."

"Often Wyrd will spare a brave man, if his heart strength hold!" Beowulf replied.

Though all his heart longed to hasten back to Hygd, to see that she was safe and let her know that he had lived through the fight, Beowulf's strength was needed more swiftly for hacking and gathering heavy wood for the fires that would keep some of the wounded alive during the night.

But when the sledges came up over the ice, he set down the log he was bearing and hurried to them. Hygd sat fur swathed in the foremost; as soon as she saw Beowulf, she leapt over the side like a young maiden.

"Thanks be to the gods that you live!" She said, running to him and embracing him without care for the blood that crusted his byrnie and tattered cloak. "I did not know how it would be, to hear the sounds of battle and know that you were in the thick, but yet to be unable to see what befell. O, Berki..." She choked out a sound that might have been a sob, or a laugh.

"I live, and Heardred is avenged," Beowulf assured her.

Hygd coughed to clear her throat, as though remembering her dignity as queen.

"Then all is as well as it may be."

Beowulf held her for a moment, wondering again at what he had seen and heard in the battle. If Hygd had not been with him, and had not known. He thought briefly of what Ingemund had said to him, but there was much to be done yet.

"Are you able to aid?" He asked. "Ingemund is doing his best to tend the wounded, but some of that work needs two good arms."

"Aye, I can help," Hygd said.

Though her face paled at the sight of spilled bowels freezing into the snow and brains crusted icy on the rims of broken helms, she bent at once to deal with those she could aid, and Beowulf went back to doing what he could in building fires and moving the wounded to them. There was no question of trying to get to Oshelm's hall that night, even if he could have guested so many: Swedes and Geats pitched their tents together on the shore of the lake, warming themselves by the great roaring fires that burned through the hosts' camp.

Hygd and Beowulf sat together in one such ring of warmth with Hraefn and Ingemund and Thura Hound Foot. Though there was little to eat save stew made from dried meat and hard bread soggy from freezing and thawing, the stew was hot and welcome, and the hard bread good enough to dip in it. Hygd had seen to it that a cask of her strongest sweet fruit beer had been packed with the food; and the big logs that Beowulf and a few of the strongest men had dragged around the fires did well enough for benches.

"Hail, Beowulf," a raspy baritone said from the darkness outside the fire's broad circle. "Will you welcome a kinsman with a horn of that, even though he fought against your men this day?"

"Wihstan!" Beowulf said joyfully.

He had not seen his cousin during the battle but Onela would, most likely, have had him in the fore when the Swedes closed with Hraefn's band. "Come and be welcome." He stood to give his own drinking horn to Wihstan as the young Waegmunding stepped closer to the fire. The Swede limped slightly, and a bandage lump bulked under his left trouser leg, but the wound seemed to trouble him little. He was carrying his gilded helm by its chin strap; his long curly hair was damp, as though he had at least tried to scrub the blood from it with a handful of snow, and he had washed the smuts of battle from his strong face likewise.

Wihstan tilted his head back, letting the draught run down his throat.

"Ah, that is good!" He said. Beowulf marked that more gold shone on his kinsman's muscular arms than he had seen there before, and as well as the gilded helmet in place of the earlier plain one, Wihstan now bore a ring hilted sword with gold inlaid thickly on its pommel and garnets glittering from its gilded sheath mounts the same sword, if Beowulf was not mistaken, that Eanmund had carried: Onela must have given his nephew's war gear to Eanmund's slayer. "I could have wished a different end to this day, but I am glad that you came through the fighting unharmed dear Thunar, is that a woman by you?"

"This is Hygd, my queen," Beowulf replied. "Hygd, this man is my cousin Wihstan Waegmunding, of that kin from which my father was long sundered."

Hygd looked rather cooly at Wiglaf it would be some time before her heart warmed to any Swede, Beowulf guessed but said,

"Berki's kinsman shall ever be welcome among us."

"That is well to hear," Wiglaf said, grinning. "For it is in my mind to fare west to your hall, and guest with you as long as you will have me. As matters have turned, it seems to me that my life shall be both happier and longer among the Geats than the Swedes."

"Eanmund's slayer..." Hraefn began. "...Oh."

"Just so," Wiglaf replied, his smile gone. "Onela gifted me well for that deed, but I can hardly look for love from Eanmund's brother. Eadgils holds Sweogris, and Yrse shall sit as queen in Upsala yet; and I think I am better following old Ecgtheow's rede and leaving while I still have a life to carry away with me. Luckily, I am not wedded; nor am I eager to find out yet what good my lands can do me when I am buried beneath them. As for any other riches I might have had he is a fool who cannot cast away gold at need. So there is nothing to hold me from going straight home with you."

"I gave you welcome, and most welcome you are!" Beowulf said. "When we first met at Hroesnabeorh, I wished that you might fight beside me rather than against me. The gods have gifted me well, to bring such a kinsman to my home."

XII

When Beowulf stepped out of his tent the next day, the Sun shone mildly on his face, and the ice crystals that had grown thickly on the trees had already melted, water dripping softly from pine needles onto the foot churned mud. A low crackling boomed across the bloodstained field of snow over lake, the sound of ice breaking under its own weight: the Geatish host would not ride back across Lake Wener. Wihstan was waiting for him outside. Though a cold wind still sighed from the frozen lake, Beowulf's cousin had left off his thick fur lined winter cloak, wrapping his broad shoulders in a wide square of herringbone woven red wool flecked with little tufts of gold, and his long unruly brown hair was knotted back from his face.

"You must be glad that you did not wait a day longer to cross the lake!" He said. "If you had been sluggish, you should have gotten a chance to prove that you are still the man who swam from Friesland bearing the armor of thirty slain."

Beowulf clicked his tongue. He had heard that tale before: folk who would girn at believing that a man could take to the sea in his byrnie would say without doubt that he had carried thirty such mail shirts on his back.

"That tale has grown in the telling, as tales often may."

"Well, some do and some do not," Wihstan grinned. "Or was Grendel but a little lizard that crept into Heorot and put the queen into fear that he would run up her skirts?"

Beowulf laughed with his kinsman there were few who would dare to chaff at him so, and Wihstan's jesting left him with the warm feeling of an ale horn drunk in friendship. But he answered soberly,

"I do not know if any poet has the tongue to tell all the tale of Grendel and his dam. There, the minds of men are hard put to stretch even to the truth though I would not have been surprised if he had grown in the story to a whole host of eotens marching from the sea's depth, and Eagor himself at the head of the troop."

"Well, if you would not have that told of you, best hold your tongue now I see your poet coming, and it is too easy to set thoughts in the heads of such men."

Munching on a piece of hard bread, Hlewabrandar joined them, looking out over the lake as another snap of breaking ice echoed across it.

"This is some strange weather, even for Geatland," the poet remarked. "I thought little of the cold I have often seen worse earlier in the year over the mountains of my father's home but this might be winter's end instead of its beginning."

"It seems to me," said Ingemund's quiet voice from behind Beowulf, "that the Wans are well pleased with what they were given yesterday. Half the host to the Frowe, those men that she chose herself and for Frea Ing, maybe, a more fitting ruler to bear Sweogris than the one he had."

Beowulf looked about, but could not see Eadgils anywhere, though Scyld sat by one of the fires with her hooded head bent over the flat board of her harp, plucking and twisting its strings back into tune. He was not sure he liked the thought that the seith working Swede had found favor with his friend god, though he knew how skilled Eadgils was at making offerings, and could not deny the man's might. Yet there was no gainsaying that the weather seemed to be answering the last day's work with weal, though if the warmth held, it would be a slow way back to Whales' Ness over muddy roads.

"How is it with our wounded, Ingemund?" Beowulf asked.

"More of the worst hurt lived through the night than I had hoped," the young gudhe said sadly. Then he lifted his head, looking out across the lake, "and if you wish the bodies of the dead brought to shore before they sink, I think you had best make haste to find men who are willing to risk the ice now! No one has dared to set foot on it this morning, for most were of the mind that water which froze so quickly could melt as fast, and it has been breaking farther out since dawn."

Beowulf followed Ingemund's gaze over the icy battlefield. The corpses lay twisted upon the bloodied and trampled snow like a dark tapestry. Another snap of shattering ice boomed across the lake even as Beowulf thought on the matter, and he found himself speaking before the words had taken shape in his mind.

"Let the lake keep the war offering: it is no shame for the slain to be sunk as a gift to the gods, when they died bravely in fight. Weapons and war gear, battle hardy men: the water's depths shall keep them all. But you, Ingemund, shall lead the blessing for the fallen here by the lake's edge, that none think their kin or friends have been sent unhallowed to the gods' halls."

By the next day, the sun shone brightly off the stretch of open water in the middle of the lake, and the furthest bodies, weighted by their ring mail, were beginning to slip through the spreading cracks. Some men looked warily at the lake, for when the Wener was frozen hard, it should have taken far longer to break free. But more spoke as Ingemund had, and it seemed to Beowulf from what he overheard and what Hlewabrandar told him that the Swedes took it as a good sign for Eadgils' kingship, the ill of the bale words Onela had spread about his brother's son over the last year melting away with the shining ice. More of the wounded died, yet fewer than Beowulf had feared; the others were beginning to heal. The ice broke through the night, crackling like the hewing of an hundred axes; by morning, the dead were all gone, and the lapping wavelets had borne the shards of shattered and rotten ice to pile up on shore like white heaps of twisted bones layered on one another.

Ingemund said that those who had not died yet were likely to live, and could be carried in wain or sledge now, and so the hosts of the Swedes and Geats struck their tents and saddled their steeds. Before the Swedes turned their horses' heads eastward, Eadgils rode up to Beowulf and Hygd, sitting proud on his black stallion's back. He was dressed as a king now, gold clasp buttons flashing from his sleeves and trousers and the slit sides of his red tunic. Sweogris gleamed boldly from his right arm above the elbow, the garnet eyes of the two boar head knobs glistening in the sunlight, and the beads of gold and garnet and berg crystal in his many braided hair and beard glittered with each movement of his head.

"We have fought mightily together," Eadgils said to Beowulf, his deep voice falling heavy on the Geat king's ears. "Nor shall I forget how well the gods looked upon our shield friendship. You shall be welcome in Upsala, should you ever choose to guest with me there. Hygd, it has gladdened my heart to know a queen so fair and wise: may the Frowe's bright tears glimmer long upon your breast!"

"May Frea Ing send you frith and joy in your rule of the Swede realm," Hygd replied. "Should you ever come back to Beowulf's burg, you shall be welcome with us; but may you never be driven there by need and war sakes again." Beowulf remembered that she had ever been of a better mind towards the Ingling than he, but he was content that she should speak fair words to Eadgils for them, as was fitting.

Eadgils reached out to clasp Beowulf's wrist. "Should you ever be minded to mount a better horse than the one you ride now, do not be slow in sending to me. I owe you a great gift, and I am a man who pays his gelds."

"The frith between our folk is gift enough for me," Beowulf answered. "And I have already gotten something else of worth from you: my kinsman Wihstan shall fare home with us, and he is a battle oak to match ten of those who were hewn down."

The corner of Eadgils' mouth twisted, and his eyes narrowed. "So that is where he went," the Swede king muttered Wihstan had been wise, Beowulf thought, to seek out the Geatish camps as soon as he might. Eadgils shrugged his wiry shoulders in a flash of gold. "Well, may you have joy of him. I shall say farewell now, for I have far to ride over muddy roads and a great blessing to make when I am come home to Upsala again and a wedding to ready: Yrse shall soon be my queen."

He turned the black stallion with a twitch of rein and a touch of knee, riding towards the high staved tents of the Danish scot king.

"I would rather that Eadgils rode the rest of the way to Whales' Ness with us, and Hereweard and Scyld left us here," Hygd murmured softly to Beowulf.

"I thought that Scyld was your friend upon the way here," he said, surprised to hear her speak so.

"We had matters on which to speak together. But she is not a woman easy of befriending, and though I treated her with the highest honor, I could tell that she takes it ill that I am queen over the Geats, while her husband is but a scot king to Hrothulf. It is a brave woman who bears her husband's standard to battle, and Scyld's singing is fair to hear," Hygd added, as though she thought she must say something to soften her judgement of the other woman who had ridden with the host. "But I find her hard to like."

"I am very glad that you are not like she." Beowulf bent to kiss Hygd's forehead: such tender gestures had become easy between them, though they would never wed.

Beowulf and Hygd lingered for a time at Hroesnabeorh, though, to their relief, Hereweard and Scyld and their Danes rode ahead, saying that they must reach their ships and sail home before the winter storms roused the sea. They comforted Frithugeard in her grief as best they could, and Hygd, in turn, took some comfort of her own from playing with Byrhthild, who was walking unsteadily on her little plump legs now and could speak a few words the Geatish queen had often been sad of mood since the battle, as though, having achieved her son's vengeance at last, her grief was coming late to her; and she had wept bitterly at the howe in which Heardred was laid.

"When Byrhthild is of an age for fostering, she must come to our hall," Hygd said to Frithugeard and Ealhburg, and both women agreed that this would gladden them.

Ealhburg's belly was already swelling with another child, which she hoped would be a son this time, so that it seemed that Sweartwulf's line would long outlast him.

"But if it is a boy, we shall give him my father's name," Hraefn told them, and Beowulf raised his horn in a silent toast, hoping that Sweartwulf would come again thus to the Middle Garth.

Hygd thought to stay at Hroesnabeorh until Winter nights, but when the weather turned again, cold gray clouds sweeping in from the west to scatter icy rain across the shorn brown fields, Beowulf woke in the night. It seemed to him that he could hear the sound of restless hoof beats from afar, and the echo of a battle horn, and he thought that this was no time for him to linger in the stead where his father's ghost had walked. So the Geats loaded their wains again, and Beowulf bade his friend's family farewell. The Danish scot king and his wife were long gone by the time Beowulf and Hygd came back to their hall; there was a bite of frost in the air, and Beowulf deemed it cold enough to hold the Winter nights slaughter blessing.

As he slit the first bull's throat by the holy white stone, calling upon the Frowe and Frea Ing, the alfs and idises, to receive the offering, a strange chill came over him: once more, it seemed to him that he saw Onela's wyrm glinting eyes, and felt his sword sinking deep into the Swede king's flesh. He wondered how much of his own will had shaped the turnings that brought him to the battle on the ice, and how much might have been crafted it seemed to him then that a glimmering flashed before his eyes, of long fair hair tumbling down over the bone set back of a high stool, and the fiery shadow of a falcon's head masking the face of the woman who sat there by a greater seith than any that Eadgils and Scyld could work.

Frowe, he whispered silently as Ingemund whipped the dark needled blessing twig about, scattering the bull's blood over stone and earth and folk, when that time comes that you would have me as your offering let me pay that geld alone, with none of my folk drawn to die on the field beside me, if there be not need of it! Then there was a time of good frith and joy in the North: the Geats under Beowulf, the Swedes under Eadgils, and the Danes under Hrothulf their fields gleamed fair with golden grain, shining streams of white milk flowed richly from the udders of their cattle, and their swine grew fat in the woods on the acorns that pattered down all about them like brown rain.

Though Beowulf could scarcely believe it, Eadgils sent the news that Yrse's womb had kindled again after her long years of lying fallow there was no one who had not thought that the ill luck of bearing a child to her own father had left the Swedish queen forever barren. But she bore Eadgils a son, whom he named Aistan, and Beowulf and Hygd sent the child a boar carved from amber as a tooth gift. If Eadgils and Scyld meant to work any ill against the Scylding king, no sign of it could be seen. But Hrothulf sent his thanes at times to guest with Beowulf though, to Beowulf's regret, the Scylding kept Beado Berki by his side bringing fair gifts and tidings of what passed in his own realm. Beowulf sent gifts back, and raised a horn to toast the wedding of Hrothulf's daughter Drife to Beado Berki, and his daughter Scure to his thane Swaefdaeg. In spite of their words on the matter of horses, four years after the battle on Lake Wener, Eadgils sent Beowulf a handsome golden stallion at Winter nights.

"He is one of the sons of Onela's horse Hrafn," the craggy faced thane who had come with the horse told Beowulf.

"Our king thought he might be suited for you, for though he is strong and well made, he is too quiet of mood for Eadgils' own riding; and he is young enough that you may train him up as you wish. One thing only our king asks: that if you should breed him with any of the mares from the line that Hrothgar gifted you with, and should find his foals too high of heart for your taste, that you will allow him a chance to send one of us to look them over for buying before letting any other have them."

Beowulf was happy enough to promise that. Though he was doubtful of what Eadgils thought too quiet of mood for himself he had heard two years ago that the Swede king had sent a like friendship gift to the aging Godhagastir of Halogaland, and Godhagastir had fallen off that horse and gotten his death of it those thanes of his own who were skilled horsemen assured him after some trial that the golden stallion was as restful a steed as he could want to ride. Another year turned slowly, as fair as those before. If a little of the gilt of Hygd's knee length hair was wearing down to silver, it did not show against her flaxen white braids, nor could the thickening of Beowulf's limbs and belly be much marked, for, save when he was half starved in his wanderings, his great muscles had always been well padded with fat.

The Geats rejoiced in their good harvest, and when the cattle and swine and sheep were slaughtered at Winter nights, the rendering cauldrons simmered for half a month to melt down enough tallow to keep the lamps of Beowulf's burg burning all through the year. Of the doings of their neighbors to the north and south, the king and queen of the Geats heard nothing until a full month after Winter nights, when a Danish ship sailed in to moor by Whales' Ness. Beowulf and Hygd welcomed Hrothulf's thanes with gladness, giving them hot ale and stew to chase the cold of the driving sleet from their bones.

Though Beowulf wondered that Hrothulf should have sent Swaefdaeg, in whom he trusted so greatly, away from him, he asked nothing, waiting for the Danish thane to tell his tidings.

"I have heard," Swaefdaeg said in his rough mutter not only was he one eyed, a great swath of scarring cutting across the side of his face, but in his warring, he had taken some hurt to his throat, so that his voice rasped and strained like the note of an earth clogged horn "that you are great friends with the Swede king Eadgils."

"We are friends, aye," Beowulf said warily. "At least, I aided him to gain the rule of the Swede realm, and there has ever been frith between us."

"And yet you are not unfriends with Hrothulf, though you thought once to war against him, and at the least do not bear him such love as you did for Hrothgar?"

"That also is true," Beowulf answered. "Yet since Hrethric's death, I have seldom heard ill spoken of Hrothulf, and I have never doubted that he bears the true aeht soul of the Scyldings: all men say that he is a good king."

Swaefdaeg pulled at his grizzled beard, the wide scar across his face twisting his frown into the grimace of a troll. "Then it may be that you will not be glad to hear what I have to say."

"Whether I am glad of it or not, I would hear it," Beowulf told him. "Wisdom may not always bring joy, but lack of wisdom more often brings sorrow."

"I might have looked for such words from you, for you are said to be deep minded," Swaefdaeg grated. "It is thus: Hrothulf sent me to tell you of what came to pass in Uppsala at the end of harvest time, for he remembers you, maybe, with more kindness than you have in your thoughts for him."

Beowulf thought this somewhat unfair, for to the best of his knowledge, he and Hrothulf had dealt with each other for the past years as befitted great drightens who were also friends, though neither of them had gotten a chance to fare to the other's hall. But he said only,

"Tell me, then, what he would wish me to know."

 Swaefdaeg swallowed a mouthful of hot ale to clear his rough throat, and began to speak. Beowulf listened silently, as did Hygd and Ingemund and Wihstan for even Hygd had come to like the light worded Waegmunding, and to bid him often to sit by them at the ale drinking. The heavy sleet hissed over the hall's thatch, and Hildegeard rounded the benches with her pitcher of hot ale. Had Swaefdaeg's tale been of the heroes of early days, of the Walsungs, maybe, or the aeht of Heraware who bore the sword of the Terwingi, it would have been pleasant to hear on such an afternoon; as it was, while the scar faced warrior spoke, Beowulf felt a chill sinking into his bones that neither fire nor cloak could ward away, and the clear burning yellow flames of the lamps did not seem to light the hall as brightly as they had.

"We sat in the hall at the harvest feast," Swaefdaeg began, "and all was joy and mirth. Hrothulf looked over his thanes, all the heroes gathered there; and asked if there was any drighten's band like to his own for fame and strength. Maybe Woden heard him, for Beado Berki answered then some ill wight shaped the words to his tongue! and said that there was but one thing that lessened Hrothulf's fame: that he still had not claimed his father's hoard from Upsala. You will remember that Ongentheow had taken it when he slew Halga, and Othere had refused to give it back, and Onela had slithered about the matter with fair and empty words..."

"Aye, I remember," Beowulf said, and Wihstan nodded gravely.

"So it was that Hrothulf set his mind to it, that he should fare to Uppsala, and bring back that treasure which his father had held. I think that he had long wished to speak with his mother as well, for I know his thoughts often turned to her..." Swaefdaeg coughed as if he had said too much, and drank more ale.

"We did not sail straight there: the seas around the east coast of Sweden are uncertain at this time of year, and Hrothulf mistrusted wind and wave for such a faring." Beowulf thought of Eadgils and Scyld singing up the storm that had frozen Lake Wener out of its season, and it was in his mind that Hrothulf had made a wise choice, but he said nothing. "So we landed some way south of Upsala, and marched through the woods; we seldom came to settlements, nor asked guesting of Eadgils' drightens, for Hrothulf would not give him too much warning of our coming.

In the wood, we came to the house of an old carle, who bade us come in and guest with him that night: he was a tall man and gray bearded, with a broad brimmed hat that he wore pulled low over his face and never took off, and he said his name was Hrani. Poor as his dwelling seemed, there was room for all of us, and no lack of mead; he told us tales until late into the night. But though he had not stinted in building the fires, they went out in the darkness, and it was so cold that the ice of our breath crusted in our beards.

Then in the morning, Hrani gave Hrothulf rede that he should send back that half of his band who had shivered most, for they would not be able to withstand what lay before them, and Hrothulf did so. We fared along the wilderness way, and the track through the trees was clear and well marked, nor did the Sun show us circling: yet as evening fell, Hrani greeted us before the doors of his dwelling again. And then we thought this to be uncanny, but Hrothulf said that he had dealt well with us before, and he himself was not so rude as to turn away from the home of a good host. Again we sat and listened to him: he chanted such poet staves as we had never heard, so that he would have been welcome in the hall of any drighten from Halogaland to Rome.

Yet though he stoked the fires no higher than he had the evening before, they blazed up in the night so that the skin of our faces blistered from the heat, and every man save Hrothulf for he had vowed in his youth never to flee from fire or iron, he said and those few of us who would not stir from his side had to crowd back against the farthest walls. And in the morning, Hrani gave our king a rune of rede again: that he should take with him only those who had not flinched from the heat, else he should surely not ride back from Upsala.

Though those words troubled Hrothulf, yet he did as the old man had said, and so only twelve of us went on with our king to cross over the Furi by the mill at the wolf ford. But the best of us numbered among those twelve, Beado Berki and Hiltwine, and Hrothulf's berserks, and myself, though it is I who says it."

Swaefdaeg drew in a deep rasping breath, letting it out slowly. His single eye stared into the lamp lit shadows of the hall as though he saw yet whatever had come before him in Eadgils' hall. Beowulf waited for the scarred thane to speak, knowing that it would do no good to hurry him.

"Then we came to Upsala. It was much as I remembered I was once one of Onela's thanes, but he repaid me ill for my troth, so that I left his hall for that of Hrothulf though the grass had grown high over Ongentheow's mound and been trodden down again. Eadgils' men took our steeds to the stalls, our hawks to the mews; Hrothulf's hound followed quietly at his heels, and all seemed as it should. Yet there was something uneasy stirring in the air, and I remembered the name that Eadgils had for spell craft even when I was there. I gave rede to Hrothulf that we should all stay helmed, and that none should speak his name, for it seemed likely to me that Eadgils had readied an ill working against him, but the Swede king's might would be lessened if he did not know which of us was the one he meant to strike. Then we came into his hall..."

Swaefdaeg shivered. He lifted his horn as if to drink, but it was empty; Hildegeard came swiftly to fill it again.

"Eadgils' hall was dark within, and smelled of howe mold and rotting bones: only a single lamp burned before his high seat, but it gave little light. It seemed to me that I saw the shadow of a dead thing, but when I struck at it, there was nothing there; yet I seemed to feel the gaze of cold eyes upon me, and spiderwebs clinging about me. Eadgils spoke to us then, and laughed, and bade us come closer. Though it was too dark to make out the shapes embroidered on the wall hangings, we saw them ripple, and Beado Berki called out that we should lock our shields in a ring. Then the Swedish warriors sprang out at us: we cut them down there, until Eadgils shouted at them to halt, and cursed at them, that they had been so rash to attack guests and broken the frith in his hall though they could not have been there but by his will. Still, Eadgils called his thralls to carry away the slain and light the lamps and fires; and then he would greet Hrothulf as a kinsman, but our king was mindful of my rede, and would not come forward from among us. It was I who told Eadgils why we had come; and he offered us drink and feigned to be willing to speak with us, all the while his thralls built the fires higher. At last the flames roared so fiercely that we could no longer see the Swede king: our byrnies seared our tunics, and our breeches began to smolder; and Eadgils said mockingly, 'Is it true that Hrothulf and his berserks fear neither fire nor iron?' Then Hrothulf said, "He fears no fire who leaps high over!"

As he cast his shield upon the burning trench that hemmed us in. The rest of us did the same, drawing our swords; we slew some of his guards, but Eadgils fled us; and when he was gone from the hall, the flames sank down until they were no more than might warm any king's dwelling.

"Only then," Swaefdaeg went on, and Beowulf could see the sweat rolling down the warrior's harsh cut forehead, as though speaking of Eadgils' fires had brought an echo of that heat to his body, like blowing up the last glow from ash banked coals, "did Yrse come to us. Though she had grown older like any woman, with silver in her hair and lines on her forehead, she was still fair but I turned my gaze away from her eyes, for they burned yellow like a wolf's with wrath. Hrothulf asked if she was Yrse the queen, and when she said she was, he lifted his sword torn sleeve. 'Friendship is hard to find,' he said, 'when mother gives son no food and sister will not sew for brother.' Then she came forward to him; and though I think Yrse is the hardest hearted woman that has been born in the Middle Garth since Sigelind gave Sigemund rede to slay her own sons, I saw the tears shining on her cheeks. She drew Hrothulf to her, and told him what she had feared: that her greeting to him had been worked into Eadgils' spells. 'For though I have striven with him these nights past, ever since his wights gave him rede that you were coming,' she said, 'yet he has dealings with many outside the Middle Garth's ring, and even I could not halt all the ill that he had layered for you over the course of these years since Othere was laid in his howe.' Then she had the tables carried in; drink and food were brought for us, and Hrothulf sat and spoke with his mother he had not seen her, I think, since first he came to Heorot as a small child."

Swaefdaeg made an odd strangled sound: it took Beowulf a moment to realize that Hrothulf's thane was laughing through his scarred throat.

"Yet there in Upsala, where we had least looked for it, we found matter for mirth. There was a thrall of Yrse's named Wag, a scrawny little scullion youth; and when he looked on Hrothulf and heard that he was the king, he said in surprise, 'He is Hrothulf Scylding? Why, he is no broader than I as thin as a crook stick!" And we all laughed greatly, for we had drunken well, and hailed our king as Hrothulf Crycc; and that light name has clung to him as no other would. Hrothulf laughed as well, and asked Wag what the scullion boy would give him as a naming gift. Wag stumbled and flushed and said he had nothing, but Hrothulf said, 'Then he who has must give to the other," and took a gold ring from his wrist to put upon Wag's. Wag held his ringed arm out proudly to look upon it, but put the other behind his back.

Hrothulf asked why he did that; Wag said that the gift was so fine that his bare arm must hide itself in shame. And Hrothulf gave him a second ring then that is an open handed king, to deal the Rhine's fire so freely to a man from whom so little can be looked for in return! But Wag took it much to heart, and declared, as if he were a warrior, that if ever Hrothulf were slain, he should avenge him; and we all laughed the more at such bold words coming from such a wretched little wight."

"That was the last of our laughter," Swaefdaeg said, wetting his throat again. "In time Yrse showed us to the guest house: we barred the doors fast and slept in our byrnies, for we thought that Eadgils was not done with us. And in the depths of the night, we heard a battering and grunting at the door. Outside was a boar as big as a horse, and sparks flashed from his tushes and hooves. We stood in the doorway and did battle with him, yet it was the king's hound kin to the gray wolf dogs of this hall, I think who felled him at last. Then we heard the crackle of flames, and knew that Eadgils' men had set our thatch on fire.

We rushed out, and there was hard fighting in that burg yard, but at last there were none left who would stand against us. When morning dawned, Yrse had her men bear out a chest of treasure, and a great auroch horn filled with gold: she gave her son that hoard that Halga had owned, and more beside. Lastly she gave him Eadgils' ring Sweogris, and it was by that, most of all, that we knew how wroth she was with her husband for seeking to slay her son. We rode forth from Upsala as swiftly as we might, but though our king be small of body, his horse was hard burdened: the weight of Hrothulf's inheritance was not light! As we crossed the plains about the Furi, we heard the sound of hooves behind us, and looked to see Eadgils and a band of his men racing after.

Though he be a seith worker and breaker of trust, the greatest nithling of all atheling born men, there is no living rider like Eadgils, and no horses in the Middle Garth to match those he breeds. And he was riding his gray Slinger, the swiftest steed of which I have heard men tell in these days: we thought then that we should leave our bones on the Furi plain. But Hrothulf turned over the horn his mother had given him, and opened the chest on his horse behind him, sowing the gold rings and southern rounds on the earth like grain in the spring. And when the Swedes came to that bright barley, they stopped to gather it, each man for himself. Eadgils rode on, heedless; but as he drew near, Hrothulf held up Sweogris that the Ingling might know it, and threw it down, saying, 'Have this as a gift from your wife's son!' Then Eadgils stooped in the saddle, lifting the ring on the point of his spear; but Hrothulf laughed, and called out, 'Now I have made the highest man of the Swedes' realm grovel like a swine!' Yet with Sweogris in his grip, and his men rooting upon the earth for gold, Eadgils had no mind to chase us further by himself, and we came away from there safely."

"That is a grim tale," Wihstan said. "I am gladder yet that I did not linger in the Swedes' realm after Onela was slain: Eadgils, I think, would have dealt no better with me than with you and I did not have my own band of stout heroes to ward me."

Beowulf was greatly troubled at Swaefdaeg's story as well, but there was little he could say. He had known that Eadgils bore a bane spear for Hrothulf; and now he could easily guess what geld the Swede king had offered Hereweard and Scyld for their aid against Onela: if Hrothulf had died at Upsala, it would not have been long before his sister led her husband to the Scyldings' high seat at Hlaeder.

"It is ill to hear such tidings, indeed," he said at last, "and though Hrothulf slew his father, I cannot say that Eadgils was in the right, to lure and betray his foe in such wise. Let Hrothulf be sure that, if Eadgils is minded to move against him again, he shall not have any help from me in that!"

For I have seen all of the Ingling's seith working that I ever want to see, while I live or after, Beowulf thought, though he could not speak such words aloud, least of all before a man who had lately come out of Eadgils' wight haunted garth. Swaefdaeg's thick shoulders lowered slightly, and Beowulf knew he had guessed rightly in thinking that Hrothulf's thane had come to find out the answer to that question, though Swaefdag did not say so. The Danes lingered some three days before sailing back. Beowulf sent a good store of gifts with them for Hrothulf in thanks for the tidings and thin veiled warning; but also that the Scylding might know by more than words that he would not have a foe in the king of the Geats. Though he was slow to speak of such things, for he would not spread strife where none had stirred before, when Swaefdaeg was about to wade back to his close moored vessel, Beowulf found himself saying,

"Tell Hrothulf that he should look with care upon Wodenswih: I think that an ill wyrd will rise from that lake for him."

Swaefdaeg started; the blood dropped from his swarthy face, the withered scar that cut across it white as a twisted strip of bleached linen.

"I shall tell him," the old warrior whispered roughly. "By your speaking, and from another thing, I think that it is already set."

The winter settled in cold, and Ingemund made the Yule offerings. Another year passed, and another. Then the last tidings of Hrothulf now, to Beowulf's quiet amusement, called Hrothulf Cryc by almost everyone came to Beowulf's hall, as they were told throughout the Northlands. Scyld's hate had waxed full ripe at last; and Hereweard had sailed with his war band to Hlaeder; some said that he had gathered a few of the Scanian jarls to him as well, that he might have the strength to assail Hrothulf's hall. But he had come against Hrothulf in the night: Hiltwine, the bearer of the gold hilted sword, had heard his host and roused the Dane king's men in time to come out and fight, but still Hrothulf's men had the worst of it. The battle had raged throughout the day.

Some said that Beado Berki had fought there in the hame of a great bear, but that Hiltwine had marked that his friend was not in the fight, and gone to bring him forth, waking Beado Berki's man body and calling the bear back. Then matters had gone the worse for Hrothulf: there were tales that Scyld had sent draugs and dark wights against his war band, while it was said that some folk had seen Woden himself, grim in his battle gear, above the host, casting his death spear over the Dane king's men. At last Hrothulf had been felled, and Hereweard had taken the high seat at Hlaeder. As he sat feasting, it was said, he had asked if there was any man of Hrothulf's still living who would take oath to him.

Yet they had all fallen with their king save for Wag, who had gone forth to the battle with a little cookhouse axe in his hand and a kettle over his head in place of a helm, and been knocked senseless, or swept aside as not worth killing. So Wag, Hrothulf's gold rings still gleaming on his arm, had come forward to Hereweard's call, and it was said that Hereweard thought it a good sign, that even this least of Hrothulf's men might swear to him. When Hereweard drew his ring adorned sword, Wag told him that it had always been Hrothulf's way to let his men hold the hilt when swearing, rather than touching the blade.

And Hereweard had given him the sword and Wag had said, 'Here is my oath!' And run it through Hereweard's body: men said now that Hrothulf's avenger had laughed like a hero, fearless, as Hereweard's thanes cut him down. On hearing that tale, Beowulf found his throat too thick to speak. He, too, remembered being thought of no worth, and being the butt of better men's laughter. Though few lived now who could call those days to mind, or had known him as anything but Grendel's Bane and Geat king, for all his strength and luck, he had not been able to do so well for his beloved drightens as had the little scullion boy Wag.

"So the heart of a hero shows itself, even through the least of bodies," Beowulf murmured.

"Wyrd may say thus more often than men know," said Ingemund, who sat close by him.

Eadgils, Beowulf had heard, rejoiced greatly at the news of Hrothulf's death. Thura Hound Foot sent his over king word that he meant to avenge his brother upon Scyld.

"It is seldom fitting that men should seek vengeance upon women," Beowulf said to Thura's messenger who had brought him that word. "Yet, I shall make this known to my thanes, and if any wish to go to that battle, I shall let a ship be fitted out that they may meet Thura on Scania's shore."

It was not long before Beowulf got stranger tidings: many of his folk had seen a misshapen troll wight loping through woods and fields, brandishing a short blade. This wight was more than a shadow or dream, for he had burst into farm houses, threatening harm if he were not given food though the carles whom he had attacked thus seldom found the hearts to stand against him. Beowulf would not have his folk mistreated so.

So he took Wihstan, who was more than glad at the hope to fight a troll as his cousin had, and Ingemund, in case there should be more to the matter than strength could deal with, and the three of them rode after the wight who seemed to have come down through the Heathoreamas' lands and be skirting about towards the foot of Lake Wener: Beowulf already had his guesses as to what he was chasing.

"Aye, he was here but a day ago," said the plump little mistress of the last stead Beowulf and his two friends had been told of. "You see what he did to our door?" The farmhouse's door had been staved in, its timbers shattered by a mighty blow: Beowulf thought of Heorot's hall door at once. "And he took half the cheese I had stored for the winter, and forced me to bake a great sack of bread for him. I thought he would rape me, too, and that would have killed me sure, for he had a leek bigger than anything I have ever seen, but Frige and the Frowe stayed his hand."

"What manner of wight was he?" Beowulf asked.

"He was a troll, as I told you before!" The woman insisted, pulling her linen kerchief straight over her coiled brown braid with a decisive jerk and looking straight up into Beowulf's face.

"Aye, but what manner of troll?"

"Some sort of wood wight, I guess. He was as big as you, my king, though thin as though he had been living hard, and hairy all over. But he had the legs and hooves of an elk."

Beowulf nodded, now sure in his thoughts. He gave the farm wife silver to pay for what had been taken, and somewhat more as geld for her fright, and he and his friends rode on tracking the hoof marks of the elk that ran on two legs. It was two days more before Beowulf saw the one he sought loping across a field, heedlessly trampling through the ripening grain. Though he had wondered at Thura's words about his elder brother for a child could easily be born with misshapen feet, and Beowulf had never seen Thura with his shoes off to judge whether he really had the paws of a hound the farm wife's tale and the tracks had led him closer to believing Thura, and now he saw that his under king had spoken nothing but the truth. Frodha ran halfway bent over, and though the green gold stalks hid the lower part of his legs, Beowulf could see his dark haired haunches and the stilt like bones of his thighs. The sack slung over his shoulder made him look the more troll like, though it was nearly empty Beowulf was glad that he had come with plenty of food in their saddlebags.

"Ho!" Beowulf called, cupping his hands about his mouth. "Frodha! Would you speak with a friend of your brother!"

The elk man halted and straightened, turning to gaze in wonder at Beowulf. In his years as king, Beowulf had almost forgotten how men who did not know him looked on his size: everyone in the Geatish lands, and most beyond, knew that the king of the Geats was large beyond a man's measure. Even across the field, Beowulf could see Frodha's dark eyes widen as he looked at the three of them together. Frodha bent over again, poised as if to flee, and Beowulf feared that they would have to ride him down. Then he turned towards them, leaving a trail of flattened grain behind him.

He stopped some ten or twelve paces from the edge of the field, and straightened his back again he could not walk without leaning forward over his elk haunches, Beowulf guessed. Hefting his sax, Frodha growled,

"Who is it that knows my name and calls himself a friend of my brother, and what does he seek of me?"

"I am called Beowulf," he answered.

He did not speak of his kingship, for if the elk man did not know who he was, he had no wish to put him in fright, and he somehow doubted that Frodha would think the better of him for the seat he held.

"I have fought and feasted at the side of your brother Thura as has Ingemund who is beside me and he spoke of you to me. Now I would bid you to eat with us, for we have ridden long today and are hungry. Our food is poor enough, but we will gladly share it with Thura's kinsman."

Frodha lifted his dark shaggy head, sniffing at the air with wide nostrils as though he could test the truth of Beowulf's words by scent; and maybe he could, just as an elk could scent a man from a very long way off if the wind were blowing right.

"There is food with you, anyway," he grunted. "Show me what you have."

Beowulf had packed their saddlebags carefully: he did not know how much like a man Elk Frodha might be in such matters as eating. So there was plenty of bread, and honey cakes with berries wrapped carefully in bags of waxed leather to keep their stickiness from spilling over; they had brought a good supply of cheese as well, and dried fish and smoked lamb, though Beowulf had been careful not to carry any game with him in case Frodha took that amiss. Wihstan's horse carried two small kegs, one of ale and one of mead. Frodha snuffled deeply as Beowulf showed him all the food they had brought. The long sax wavered in his hand, sunlight flashing from the bright and dark wyrm ripples along its length. His wide lips moved as if he were holding rede with himself, and Beowulf felt that he might be thinking of trying to simply take the food; but something glimmered faintly in his eyes, as though he were remembering, maybe from many years back, how it was that men dealt with each other.

"Good enough," Frodha said at last.

He came forward slowly, thrusting his sax through a loop on his rough tanned leather belt. His face was very long, low and heavy browed; his skin was weather swarthy. His cheekbones stood out in thick arches above sunken cheeks; his ribs stood out as well for he wore no clothing: Beowulf could well see why the farm wife had feared that his lust might turn to her. He reached out a big hand, snatching the round of cheese Beowulf held and biting into it without bothering to scrape its tallow coating off. Ingemund filled a horn with mead for him, and they ate and drank together though, seeing Frodha's hunger, Beowulf, Wihstan and Ingemund ate only of the meat, which the elk man would not touch.

"What brings you down from the northern mountains?" Beowulf asked. "Thura said that you fared seldom among men."

"Seldom? Never!" Frodha roared. "They make the sign of the Hammer against me when I am there, and jape behind my back and then I must fight them to still the laughter, and their bones break like brittle twigs. Save my brothers, I have seen no man save outlaws for more years than I have counted: those wargs, I kill, for I will not thole the things they do." He drained his horn in one huge swallow, holding it out for more mead. "And now I am going to another killing, for I have a brother to avenge my dear youngest brother, who looked altogether like a man, but who alone among whole men never laughed at me."

The elk man picked up the last round of cheese and bit into it, speaking through his noisy chewing.

"When Berki came to me, he told me of how he had avenged our sorrows at last on the Finn wife who brought about our father's death and our curse. I gave him rede to fare to the war band of Hrothulf Scylding, as I had reded Thura to go among the West Geats, for my Wyrd has this easing: many of the wights who fear men will speak with me, and I in turn can see and speak with them when my eyes are open to waking daylight. Yet before he left, I stamped my hoof deep into the stone on the crag where I look out over the mountains, and swore to him that I would look into that print each day. If he died of sickness, mold would sprout on the rock; if he drowned, it would fill with water, but if he were cut down in battle, the stone would gleam with blood. For long no sign came to me, and I was as glad as Wyrd will let me be, knowing that my dear little brother was hale. But then I saw the red sheen upon the rock, and more drops of blood trickling slowly into my hoof spoor: that told me Berki had been slain, and I must go to avenge him. That is all: would you know more, or how?"

"You are not alone, for your brother Thura is also going south to Hlaeder though I would tell you: it is no man whom you must battle with swords, but a woman who raised the host of Wodenswih for Beado Berki's death, and one skilled in seith craft."

Frodha laughed, a shocking harsh sound.

"Thus Wyrd turns on herself! Berki avenged me on the witch woman who wrought havoc upon my life, now I go to avenge him on the one who brought about his death. I thank you for that news, Beowulf, though I should have learned it for myself in due time. And I thank you for the food and drink: but I have far to fare yet, and cannot linger in speech with you."

"One thing more before you go," Beowulf told him sternly. "You have frightened the farm folk all the way from the Heathoreamas' land to here, and taken their food without repayment. That is ill done, and I cannot thole it. Yet I would not see Thura's kinsman fare hungry among the Geats if I can help it. Take this purse: with this you can pay for all you need. If folk fear you, tell them that Beowulf has said that you shall come in frith, and fare in frith, and harm none."

Frodha took the leather bag from Beowulf, weighing it wonderingly. "What manner of wight are you? You are dressed like a man, and those who fare with you are men; but you look very like the berg folk who come to me betimes, and there is that about you which seems kin to them. Are you some great wight of this land, that you care so for its carles and that they ken your might over those who fare from wood and crag?"

"You might say so, if you wished," Beowulf answered. "All good luck go with you, and give my greetings to your brother Thura when you see him."

Since they were not too far from Lake Wener then, Beowulf and his companions decided to ride on to Hroesnabeorh. Frithugeard, Hraefn, and Ealhburg welcomed them with rejoicing, but Byrhthild looked mistrustfully at them over the deep golden plait of hair she had wrapped across her face like a veil. At nine winters, she had grown to be a remarkably pretty young maiden: her pointed chin and Finn slanted blue eyes set above high cheekbones gave her something of an otherworldly look, but that was sweetened by her slightly tip tilted nose and the tiny dimple at the side of her chin.

"Byrhthild, these guests are good friends of ours," Frithugeard scolded mildly. "They are our own good king Beowulf, who gave you the amber cat you carry in your belt pouch as a tooth gift, and his cousin Wihstan Waegmunding, and Ingemund the Gudhe: are they not fine looking men?"

"He is," said Byrhthild, dropping her thick braid and pointing at Wihstan. "But that one " she pointed at Ingemund "is too thin, and the other one is too fat."

Ingemund looked a little shocked, but Beowulf and Wihstan roared with laughter.

"Now that is a maiden after my heart, who sees the truth and is not afraid to speak it!" Wihstan chuckled. "You will be a rede giver worth having when you are grown, Byrhthild and have a handsome husband as well, if you keep your good taste in men."

Hraefn feasted them well for a few days. Sweartwulf's son and Wihstan rode out to hunt by the shores of Lake Wener where the elk and deer came down to drink, the gray hounds descendants of Beowulf's Wulfa running beside their horses with tails curled high. Beowulf would not go with his friends, for no years could wear away the memory of the arrow standing in Herebeald's limp body, and Ingemund would rather sit speaking with Frithugeard about her knowledge of the gods and holy things. So it was easy for Ealhburg to find a time to say to the Geat king,

"Are you and Hygd still minded to take Byrhthild as a fosterling?"

"Very much so," Beowulf replied.

"Then I see no reason why she should not go home with you when you leave here, unless you have some other faring in mind."

Beowulf had not awaited that, but he could think of no reason why he should not do as Ealhburg had suggested.

Byrhthild was able to ride well enough that they would not even need to take a wagon with them, for two pack horses could bear her things easily enough, and she was growing so swiftly that she would need new clothes made for her at Beowulf's hall anyway. So the three were four when they set out from Hroesnabeorh again. Wihstan proved to be the one who most enjoyed riding beside the girl and talking with her, telling her tales and pointing out birds and animals along the way. The charm that had allowed Wihstan to cut a wide swath through all the unmarried women of Beowulf's burg and every settlement for four days' ride around worked just as well on a small maiden as on an older one, so that Byrhthild narrowed her tilted eyes and told Wihstan firmly,

"You had best not think on taking another bride, for when I am grown, I shall wed you, and I mean to be foremost in our house."

Wihstan laughed and tousled her head. "You need not be too hasty to wed," he told her. "I am nine and twenty winters now, and yet there are too many women in the world for me to settle down with any one of them, however fair or wise she be. There are many handsome atheling youths in the world as well: you were best to look at all the stallions for sale at the Thing before you buy one for yourself."

"My mother says when you have found gold, you need not search for silver," Byrhthild replied, and Wihstan laughed again.

"Best not laugh too hard," Beowulf grinned at his cousin. "Byrhthild will be old enough for betrothal, at least, in five or six winters. Sweartwulf's grand daughter has a hard grip: if you are thinking you can escape from her, you had best start packing your gear now."

"I never run too swiftly from a maiden," Wihstan answered. "If I did, I might get away."

When they reached Beowulf's burg, Byrhthild settled in quite happily: if she missed Hroesnabeorh, she never spoke of it. She was glad to follow Hygd and Hildegeard about, learning how to make cheese and malt ale and manage bondservants.

"Byrhthild has a very fine hand with needlework as well," Hygd told Beowulf. "I suppose it comes of being somewhat short sighted though that is little hardship for a girl, if it grows no worse."

"Is she? She seemed to see all the birds Wihstan showed her well enough."

Hygd shook her head, smiling crookedly. "Wihstan could point into the sky and tell her he saw Loca wearing one of the Frowe's dresses and flying by flapping his arms, and Byrhthild would say how happy she was to see it. They will be a good match when she is old enough. She is short of sight."

"Well, since she need never shoot a bow or cast a spear, let alone order a host in battle, I cannot see how that will hinder her," Beowulf said. "I had not even guessed it, nor did Frithugeard say anything about it."

"Frithugeard may not have known: I doubt it showed in a little burg where Byrhthild knew everyone. I should not have known, except that she cannot tell one thrall from another until they get close enough for her to make out their faces clearly."

"That is a small enough thing," Beowulf shrugged. "I do not think it should hamper her in making a good marriage."

Hygd laughed. "No for she is going to marry Wihstan."

"I think you are a little too sure of that."

Hygd only smiled in that way women had when they talked of betrothals, and Beowulf realized that he was out of his depth and had best say no more. It was told later how the war band of Thura Hound Foot took Hlaeder; but it was Elk Frodha who put a bag over Scyld's head, that she do no ill with her last gaze, and battered her to death with his hooves. Of all those who had known her, the only one who seemed to mourn her was Beowulf's poet Hlewabrandar.

"I never heard such singing as Scyld's," he stammered, as if it shamed him to admit it. "The Middle Garth is more silent without her, and the less in fairness."

"I think we shall all manage to thole life without Scyld in the world," Wihstan said dryly, and Beowulf had to agree with him.

Eadgils did not long enjoy his knowledge of Hrothulf's death. That very Winter nights, when he rode his black stallion around the Upsala hof to make his offering to the goddesses and idises, the horse shied at something unseen and stumbled and threw the Ingling. This time, he could not leap up to his feet: his head struck the great ruddy rock by Upsala's holy well, and the brains of the ruler's son blended with stony earth. Beowulf thought of what he had seen and heard when he slew Onela but he also thought of Yrse's wrath at the husband who had sought to wreak her son's death.

Yet, if she still hated Eadgils for what he had tried to do to Hrothulf, that hate did not reach to scorning his body: in keeping with the Inglings' usual custom, she had him burned with his goods and weapons outside the Upsala hof, and raised a third great mound over the ashes of his pyre beside the tall barrows of his grandfather and great grandfather, as is fitting for an offering made at the very stead of the gods, Beowulf thought, though he did not speak those words aloud to anyone. When the howe had been raised, Eadgils' son Aistan mounted up upon it and set Sweogris upon his arm but he was still a child: it would be Yrse who ruled from Upsala for some years yet.

With Hrothulf Scylding dead, and a boy king in Upsala, the worse men grew bold: raiders harried the coasts of Jutland and Sealand, Scania and the Swedes' realm, and there were many men who called themselves sea kings, for they had warships and hosts but no lands some were proud of that title, and said that only he could truly name himself a sea king who never slept under sooty beams and never drank by a hearth corner. The weather worsened: for two years the Saxons on the North Sea's coast ate foxes and crows when they could catch them, and other things that should not be eaten, or starved, and there was great hunger through all the lands, save in the Geats' lands: there, though the rain fell thickly, it did not freeze the sprouting grain nor bring rot to the harvest, and Beowulf's folk still thrived.

In Byrhthild's fifteenth summer, Hygd spoke to Beowulf about their foster daughter's wedding, but when they brought the matter before Wihstan, he said loudly,

"No!"

"Why not?" Hygd asked. "Byrhthild is a fair and skilled maiden, and everything that a man of atheling kin should look for in a wife."

"I have told you before that I have no mind to be wedded," Wihstan insisted. "If I have managed to pass thirty four winters without any one woman setting fetters on me, I think I am well able to say that I like my freedom. I am very happy as your hall thane: I do not want to rule a hall of my own where I must weigh grain and count barrels of ale and worry about having enough to get through to the next harvest. I do not want to own a herd of cattle that I must watch in breeding and milking and slaughtering and carry out to the first summer grazing when the winter has been longer than the hay, and I do not want to be wedded. Most of all, I do not want to be wedded to a stubborn chit of a girl who thinks because I have bespoken her in friendly wise that I will put up with her nagging and overbearing me all my life!" He stood up and stamped out of the hall without another word, leaving Beowulf to gape after him.

"Has some troll stolen Wihstan's wits?" Beowulf asked when he had gathered his thoughts a little. "I do not think I have ever heard him speak so."

Hygd laughed until she was breathless, while Beowulf began to wonder if someone had slipped a red fly toadstool into the hall's ale.

"My Berki," she said at last, "you should know how a man flails when he feels himself sinking under the water for the last time. We may as well start brewing the mead for the wedding feast now."

Wihstan proved himself to be of stouter soul than Hygd had weened. He would not agree to marry Byrhthild that summer, nor the next, nor the next, nor the one after that, no matter what the women did. Byrhthild glared at him across the hall and poured his ale so that it slopped onto his clothes; she let him see her walking about the garth with younger thanes; she smiled at him and spoke sweetly to him and brought him the best portions of food and drink. Wihstan cheerfully paid no mind to her foul looks, spoke well of the young men with whom she went walking, and thanked her for the dainties she laid before him with an air of utter thoughtlessness, until even Hygd was ready to give her foster daughter the rede that there was no hope.

"I shall go home to Hroesnabeorh," Byrhthild said one evening at the ale drinking. "My grandmother is growing older, and I think my mother shall be glad of my help about the garth: there is much to be done, with four younger brothers who are growing close to the age when any proper man should be getting married."

"It is well for folk to think on the needs of their kin," Wihstan answered. "Give Frithugeard and Hraefn and Ealhburg my greetings."

Byrhthild made a noise deep in her throat and flounced angrily from the hall and she did not go back to Hroesnabeorh, though matters went no better between herself and Wihstan than before.

Eadgils' son Aistan grew to manhood, and fathered a son of his own, whom he named Ingware. Aistan kept his father's oath to Beowulf though, in truth, the Swedes had been more than somewhat weakened by their king's youth and the endless raiding along their coast, and could offer little threat to the Geats now. Then the tidings came to Beowulf that one of the sea kings, a man named Salo who claimed kinship to the Inglings, though it was anyone's guess as to whether there were truth in his claim had burned Aistan in his house and taken Sweogris onto his own arm; the Swedes had gathered themselves and there had been a great battle around Sigetun that lasted eleven days, but Salo had won the victory.

Then Beowulf sent out the word to his under kings and drightens that it would be well to ready themselves, for there was no knowing what might come of this. Afterwards, however, he thought that after seeing how easily the rule of the Swedes' realm had passed from kin slaying Ingling to kin slaying Ingling, he should not have been amazed that the Swedes, after their single struggle to cast him down, were almost as willing to take Salo as their leader as they had been to acknowledge Onela or Eadgils. After what Eadgils had tried to do to Hrothulf, Beowulf felt no duty to avenge his son though he hoped for Salo's sake that the sea king knew better than to drink any mead brewed by Yrse, who still sat, old and terrible now, at Upsala.

Beowulf himself had passed his sixtieth winter, though his age sat lightly upon him. He had grown a little heavier, and in changing weather the sinews of his shoulders, that he had nearly torn asunder with his own grip upon Grendel, ached a little; that was all. Hygd's hair was more nearly white than flaxen, and on some days the joints of her fingers swelled so painfully that she could not do needlework, and could barely turn her spindle. Wihstan had forty three winters behind him, but he seemed more handsome than ever, if in a rugged and craggy way, and none of the young women that he courted lightly seemed to mind his age. Therefore it was a great surprise to everyone in Beowulf's hall when, on a bright evening shortly before the Midsummer Thing, Wihstan looked up at Byrhthild as she was filling his drinking horn and said,

"Will you wed me now?"

The pitcher in Byrhthild's hands shattered into an hundred pieces on the floor. She closed her mouth, slapped Wihstan sharply on the cheek, burst into tears, and leapt into his ale dripping lap.

"O, yes!" She said, laughing through her sobs.

"Toast the marriage before they change their minds!" Hlewabrandar shouted, and Beowulf's hall rang with cheers.

In spite of the wagers that one or the other would break the betrothal before Midsummer, Wihstan and Byrhthild were wedded at the Thing. As Wihstan's only kinsman in the Geatish lands, Beowulf stood to speak the tale of Wihstan's deeds in the holy grove before all the witnessing folk, while Frithugeard and Ealhburg and Hygd praised all Byrhthild's womanly skills, and her four younger brothers stood armed and armored to show that there were strong kinsmen who would ward the bride at need.

Though the bride was twenty five winters old now, her face glowed with
such delight that she might have been ten years younger, while Wihstan
shuffled his big feet and looked more ill at ease than Beowulf had ever seen
his glib kinsman before as often and light as the younger Waegmunding's
play with women had been, Beowulf guessed, acknowledging the truth
of his love had come even less easily to him than it had seemed in the ten
years' strife of his lack of courtship.

Ingemund blessed the couple, sprinkling their joined hands with the
blood of the offering ram, and Beowulf had to blink to clear his sight. For a
moment it had seemed to him that he stood, not behind the new husband,
but just in front of the thin gray bearded gudhe in his red sark; and that
Hygd was not on the other side of the white stone, but before him, her little
hands clasped in his and the wedding crown of twisted gold gleaming upon
her flaxen head. Wihstan drew the ring hilted sword that Onela had given
him, offering it hilt first to his bride.

"This sword, old and adorned, was the heirloom of Eanmund's life age,
the son of Othere. I was the bane of the friendless outlaw in battle with
blade's edge; I carried the brown shining helm, the ringed byrnie, the
eotenish sword to my aeht Onela gave his kinsman's battle weeds to me,
and did not speak of foeship, though I had felled his brother's bairn. My
bride, I would that you hold that gear, sword and byrnie, some seasons,
until our son may bear out atheling deeds like his forefathers. By sword
and ring I swear my troth to you, and give to you the keeping of the
Waegmundings' aeht soul."

Byrhthild clasped hands with Wihstan upon the gold ringed hilt, her
Finn tilted blue eyes shining with tears of joy.

"May Frige grant me the might to bring forth a bairn who can wield this
fittingly!" She said. "Wihstan, kin to Beowulf Grendel's Bane, surely there
is no line of living men in the Middle Garth like to the Waegmundings.
Now I swear by this sword that I shall ever uphold the honor of our aeht:
our children shall suckle strength of soul with my milk, and never shall
the sons I bear flee from battle or hang back when the fight is thick about
their shield fellows, nor the wills of my daughters fail, whatever hardships
or grief betide. I am the grand daughter of Sweartwulf, who fought beside
Beowulf in three great battles and who was a match in wrestling even for
Grendel's slayer; I am the daughter of Hraefn, who in his youth led the
host as bravely and wisely as any aethling well used to battle. By sword and
ring I swear my troth to you, and the Waegmundings' aeht soul shall shine
in my keeping, and put forth new branches to blossom in might."

Ingemund lifted the Hrethlings' gold bound aurochs horn in his shaking left hand, steadying it with the skin wrapped bones of his withered right arm. Though the years had worn cruelly on him, his voice was still firm and sure as he said, "Let the gods hear it; let the goddesses hear it; let alfs and idises and all good wights make witness! By ring and sword, Wihstan Wiglaf's son and Byrhthild Hraefn's daughter are sworn and wedded Waer uphold the oaths! And hail to kind Lufen," the gudhe added, a hint of laughter warming his voice, "who gave leave at last to what was gainsaid for so long." A ripple of merriment scattered through the gathered folk; Ingemund waited until it had faded to quiet smiles until he went on. "Frowe and Frea Ing, bring fruitfulness to this wedding; Frige, bless it with your gifts." Ingemund gave the horn to Byrhthild. "Now bear the dear drink to your husband, as you shall do through the days of your life rede giver, house frowe, hlaefdige."

Byrhthild lifted the horn up to Wihstan, saying, "Gladly do I bear you this draught, apple of battle: ale to you ever, and to our aeht!"

"Hail to you, my beloved frowe," Wihstan answered. "House and hold and home you shall rule, keeper of all my keys, and may your runes guide me well in our wedding."

He drank deeply, his voice box bobbing beneath his short trimmed beard, and gave it to Byrhthild, who drank in her turn. As the ale flowed into Byrhthild's mouth, it seemed to Beowulf that he was no longer looking at a woman garbed in green linen and gleaming gold, but at a fair birch tree, her white bark shining pale through her green leaves. At her crown, the tree slowly put forth a branch: at first it seemed too thin to hold any weight, but it grew to a mighty limb on which a golden apple hung.

Then the leaves shook as though a storm wind tore at them, ripping them loose and whirling them away one by one until the birch stood leafless and seeming dead. And the apple dropped from her crown to the earth; Beowulf saw it rotting, the small wyrms creeping and gnawing greedily until the golden fruit was no more than a little heap of mold. One seed put forth a tiny root, and a little leaf, and it sprouted tall beside its mother, blossoming brightly and ripening its apples; and the apple tree's leafy limbs twined with those of the leafless birch, and the birch budded anew.

Beowulf wondered at that as his sight misted and cleared so that he could see Byrhthild and Wihstan again: Wihstan held his wife's hand high, and was leading her through the ring of folk with Ingemund behind them. Hygd gestured to Beowulf, and he quickly fell in behind the gudhe, taking his queen's hand in his own as Hlewabrandar began to sing a wedding song and the other folk joined in. He still did not know what he had seen; but he thought that its boding must be for good, if not without the cost of some sorrow. For all their blessing and love sworn oaths, though, Byrhthild's womb did not kindle easily.

Ealhburg had been as fruitful as any woman might want, with five children living out of six brought into the light of day; but Frithugeard had never been able to bear a child to term after her one son, and though Byrhthild had inherited the Finnish slant eyes and stubborn will of her grandfather, she took after her grandmother in that wise. Several times in the next seven years, Hygd murmured to Beowulf that Byrhthild thought she might be with child; but each time their foster daughter's womb cast out the unshaped blood. Then, at last, Byrhthild's belly began to swell as the grain ripened in the fields. Wihstan gave oxen and swine to Frea Ing and the Frowe and Frige in the holy grove, and his jests grew seldom: it was clear that he thought of little other than his wife and her bearing.

Hygd walked with a stick now, and her hair was all white; but when she unbound it, and it fell to her knees, and though her violet eyes nested in a tangle of creases, her age had not dimmed their deep shine. Beowulf himself was beginning to feel the winters creep into his bones: he slept later in the mornings than he had before, and his knees often ached when they had borne his weight too long. Still, his hand was no lighter than it had ever been when he swung his hammer to stun the cattle at Winter nights; and perhaps because he had never been swift of movement on the land, he did not mark that he had slowed much when he practiced at weapons with his thanes.

The air chilled him more often on rainy days than it had once, but when Beowulf stripped off his clothes and heaved his bulk into the sea, he moved as easily through the waves as he had in his youth, and the coldest winter water did not daunt him any more than it had then. By Yule, Byrhthild was waddling under the ripening weight of her womb, and Ingemund took special care with her: he made sure that she was dressed in red through those twelve dark nights, and that she always carried a few hazelnuts and dried mountain ash berries in her belt purse, as well as a bit of flint and an iron fire striker, to be sure that no ill wights would find her easy to assail. He spent some time with her each evening, murmuring runes of warding and health over her, tracing some staves in ale upon her palms and scratching others upon her nails.

She was not allowed to go to the mound field when the gudhe called out to welcome the Wod Host, though he had led her out to make a blessing to the alfs there earlier in the day. Hildegeard fussed over Wihstan's wife as much as her husband did, pressing the last of the stored apples upon her and making her drink the herb brews that Ingemund had mixed for her. Though Byrhthild would have cast off such close care with rough words before, now she listened to everything that the gudhe and his wife said to her, and Beowulf wondered uneasily if Ingemund had some foreboding or dream of ill which he did not dare to speak aloud lest his words should rist it more deeply into Wyrd. Yet Byrhthild continued hale, save for casting up her food on odd mornings and complaining of the backache and sore feet which, Hygd assured Beowulf, were suffered by all bearing women.

Ingemund's wardings kept her safe through the Yule nights, and her womb swelled through the next month so that she looked as though she were carrying a load of pillows beneath her high wrapped girdle. Then the sickness came to the lands of the Geats. Folk called it the alf fire, for that it was a feverish sickness and seemed to sink more deeply into women than into men; and was worst in young women, especially those who were with child. They were the likeliest to die of it, though most who sickened with it recovered within half a month. Therefore, folk said that the alfs were greedy of wives and bairns for their own.

Beowulf made offerings with all his might, as many as Eadgils had ever made in his days at Uppsala, and asked Frea Ing and the Frowe with his full heart to hold those flames back from his burg; Ingemund likewise made blessings, and charmed and chanted, burying iron knives point outward and tying red bands around the logs of the garth walls to shield those within from the burning shot of the ill willing alfs. But one evening Hildegeard dropped her silver ale pitcher, and when she stooped to pick it up, her hands were shaking too badly to hold it.

Beowulf and Ingemund hastened to her together, and when they got close enough, they could see the sheen of fever sweat beading on her face, ruddy gold in the torchlight. Beowulf carried Hygd's daughter to Ingemund's house: even through their thick winter clothing, he could feel the sick heat of her body. Ingemund set at once to grinding and mixing herbs, chanting softly over his stone mortar and pestle; there was no more Beowulf could do, so he went back to the hall, to find Byrhthild and Wihstan shouting at each other.

"Stay in the house!" Byrhthild railed. "I ache badly enough from sitting as it is if I must stay locked up like a cow in winter, I shall never be able to walk again."

"The fever alfs will find it harder to get to you if you are not walking about in the open where they can see you," Wihstan argued. "You foolish woman, have we not worked hard enough for this child that you do not care if you lose it?"

"How dare you say, we?" Shrieked Byrhthild. "Aye, you worked hard enough to sweat every night for a little longer than the cuckoo sings in summer, but you are not the one who has to carry half your own weight on your belly, or the one who has to leave the hall to piss after every sip of ale. The only mornings I see you casting up your stomach are the mornings after you have been drinking strong mead all night."

In spite of the fear of the sickness that Beowulf knew was on every woman and wedded man in his hall, he saw several of his thanes trying to bite back laughter, and their wives covering their hands with their mouths as their shoulders shook it was held by many that listening to Byrhthild and Wihstan was as good as watching strong men at holmgang.

"A silver finger ring in even wager on her," Hlewabrandar murmured out of the side of his mouth to one of the other thanes, who shook his head and muttered back, "Two for one, or nothing."

"You may do as you please in all other matters!" Wihstan roared. "But in this I shall rule, if I must carry you out of the hall and lock you up by mainstrength."

"How will you lock me up?" Byrhthild taunted him. "I have all our house's keys."

This time, the women did not even bother to try hiding their laughter, and Hlewabrandar's wager friend said low, "I told you it was no even chance."

A flush spread over Wihstan's strong cheekbones, but he grinned ruefully. Bending, he whispered something in Byrhthild's ear. By the time he was done, though she had passed thirty three winters and been married for eight of them, she, too, was flushed, blushing like a maiden.

"O, very well, then," she said, rising awkwardly and letting him take her by the hand and lead her out of the hall.

"It is as well that they are wedded to each other," Hygd said to Beowulf. "Otherwise, I must wonder who would have either of them." But her smile was pale and faint, and something about the worn way she leaned against the back of her seat worried Beowulf.

"My Hygd, are you well?" He asked.

"Well enough. I am a little tired, but that is scarcely to be wondered at in one who has whiled as many winters as I have."

Yet when Beowulf took her hand in his, he might as well have plunged his fingers beneath the gray ash over banked coals. A shock of fear stabbed through him, his heart thudding like a galloping horse's hooves on the planks of his ribs.

"Hygd, you are not well! You must go to your bed at once I shall carry you, if you are too weak to walk."

"I am not," Hygd argued feebly. But when she reached for her stick, her hand waved past it thrice as though she could not gather the strength to both see and grasp it.

Beowulf gathered her up from her chair as easily as he would have picked up a runt puppy, running out of the hall and over the hard packed trail in the moonlit snow to her house. Holding Hygd now made his skin crawl, for he could feel the same heat beating from her body that he had felt from Hildegeard's, and smell the faint foul stink of sickness in the sweat that was beginning to seep from her face. But he cradled her close to his chest nonetheless, as he would have done even had her flesh been rotting, until he was able to set her down in her own bed and pull the blankets up over her. He stoked the fire high, shouting at Hygd's elderly house thrall to be sure there was plenty of wood for it; he dampened a cloth in the bowl of washing water on the table in her bedchamber and wiped the sweat from her face.

"That is better," Hygd sighed. "Ah, Berki, I am so tired...It has been so long..." She closed her eyes, mumbling something Beowulf could not hear.

"I shall come straight back," Beowulf told her anxiously. "I am only going to Ingemund, to see if he has any herbs or such that may help you...he was mixing something up for Hildegeard. You!" He said to the old woman, she was younger than Hygd, he realized, younger than she looked, it was the gray hair and missing teeth made her seem so aged, and his mind was rambling as if he were feverish himself. "You keep a close watch on the queen. Wipe the sweat off her face with this cloth, and be sure that the bedchamber stays warm. If anything happens to her while I am gone, step outside and shout as loudly as you can, and send someone to the house of Ingemund the Gudhe to fetch me, do you understand?"

"I understand," the bondswoman replied.

Beowulf ran across the garth to Ingemund's house, his shoes slipping where the constant treading of feet had packed the snow into rough ice. By the time he reached the gudhe's door, he was panting like a bitch in labour, and his hand shook as he lifted his fist to knock. Ingemund's door shivered with a cracking sound under Beowulf's blow, for he had struck harder than he had meant to. The wood groaned again as Ingemund swung it aside, his thin graybearded face creased even more deeply with worry.

"What is it, Beowulf? Who...?"

"Hygd," Beowulf answered, grim even through his straining bellows breaths.

Ingemund closed his eyes, as though seeking within himself for some hidden store of main strength. Whether he found it or not, he blew his breath out slowly through his mouth.

"I have some left from the brew that I just made for Hildegeard, and she is resting a little easier already. Wait: I shall get it for you."

Ingemund disappeared into his house, coming out with a plain horn in his hands.

"See that she drinks all of this if she can manage it. I shall make more of the herb mix and bring it to you straightaway, and do what I can for her I fear that these two will not be the only ones who fall ill of the alf fire within this garth."

Ingemund chanted his runes over Hygd, and sat for a long time with his palm on her forehead, murmuring something as if to himself. When he rose, his lined face was pinched and pale.

"Though the arrow itself was a little thing, the bale of that shot has lodged deeply in her body," he told Beowulf. "I have done what I might to cleanse her of it, and the herbs I brought should do more, but I cannot take oath on how much. Have her bondswoman brew up more of the mixture, and give her all of that draught she can take. If she grows too much hotter than she is already, bring in a little snow to cool her. Beyond that, there is little you can do save keep her wrapped in her blankets and it may help her simply to have you there: often the heart will pull the ill through when their bodies would fail them."

Hygd opened her eyes again not long after Ingemund had left.

"Breca," she said, her voice high and childlike, "you have stoked the fires too hot again, and your father told you not to do that."

"Breca is not here," Beowulf murmured gently to her. "It is I, Beowulf your Berki. Hush, and rest: all shall be well with you."

Hygd's head tossed. The pins had come out of her hair, and it spread over the pillows in a white tangle like a thick skein of spiderwebs.

"You are lying, Breca!" She cried. "Berki cannot be dead, for I saw that he would live long. And he is more water crafty than you are."

"Breca is not here," Beowulf murmured again. "Breca is dead. For the Bronding's drighten had been slain in a quarrel with his northern neighbor twenty years before, and I am alive, and here."

"Berki cannot be dead, for I saw him," Hygd moaned, "but he was in the arms of another woman get away from him, you water whore! He is my bear, not yours!"

The beads of sickness water shone golden on her forehead and cheeks; the sweat pooling around her eye sockets and the low flickering light melted the lines of age on her face, and the ruddy flames of the house fire gilded her white hair, so that she might almost have been again the maiden to whom Beowulf had been betrothed. A little shiver ran down Beowulf's spine like a driblet of icicle melt at her words: Hygd had never hinted that she had guessed at his time in Heofonglowe's arms. Suddenly Hygd stopped tossing and lay quite still, limbs locked and violet black eyes staring up at the thatch.

"Onela is a wyrm in the hame of a man: the gods deceived Thetsi," she said clearly. "Yet the Inglings all die as offerings to their line father, and it is the Frowe who brings them to their deaths, by means bright or dark as they may come to her hand: the Fearsome wrought seith on Wride. Salo is truly sprung of the Ingling aeht and must likewise fall, though no wedding oaths were spoken to his dam: Wyrd comes out of the well. Yrse bore the golden cup to you in Onela's hall: the wyrm lies in the depths."

Badly frightened, Beowulf hastened to wipe Hygd's face clean, murmuring nothing words in hopes of soothing her. He did not dare to try kneading her muscles in hopes of unknotting them, lest her frail bones snap like dried sticks beneath his hands, but after a time she shuddered and went limp, and her breath came more easily thereafter. At dawn, Hygd lapsed into a fretful sleep, tossing and muttering wordlessly in her sweat stained linens. When Ingemund came back to the house, Beowulf saw that a gray cast underlaid his rumpled white skin, and his eyelids drooped heavily over blood scored eyes.

"The fever alfs ride about our burg, and though I have barred them from our walls, I can do nothing to keep them from shooting their burning shot over. How have matters gone with the queen?"

"She sleeps."

Beowulf did not wish to tell the gudhe of what Hygd had said, but Ingemund asked dully,

"Did she speak any strange words?"

"How did you know of that?"

"The bale brewed for the alf arrows seems to work thus, that those it has scathed most deeply speak words of foreboding in their fever, as though they were half wandered into Alf Home already. I will not lie to you: if Hygd has seen with alf sight of this, it will be a hard thing to bring her back to the Middle Garth. I have heard that these wights hold their deadliest shots for young women with child, for they would win brides, but though Hygd is old, she is yet fair even so."

"Your comfort is cold, Ingemund," Beowulf said.

The gray haired gudhe looked wearily up at him.

"Where there is little hope of sorrow's easing, cold comfort may be the kindest: better to ready for a hard winter than to trust against knowledge that summer shall never end."

Then Beowulf thought more on what Ingemund had said upon coming in. "Who else besides Hildegeard is down with this ill?"

Ingemund named several thanes' wives. "I think Hlewabrandar may be sickening as well, for though he helped me to carry water and lift kettles on and off the fire last night, he was pale and sweating by the end of that work. But...I had hoped I would not have to say this to you until you had rested a little. Wihstan was too late in shutting his wife in safety: Byrhthild burns with fever, as badly as Hygd."

Beowulf thought his tired heart would rip like a piece of worn wool tugged between two hounds. He wanted to go to his foster daughter, and yet he did not dare to leave his queen's side, lest she wake and call to him, he would not let himself think of any worse case. But Ingemund had seen to the sick all night, though his own wife lay burning in her bed, and Beowulf did not want to make matters harder for him, nor to make it easier for the alfs to shoot down their chief foe within the Geat king's garth.

"I know that you are doing all you can," Beowulf said, trying to force reassurance into his wavering voice. "If there is aught in which I may help..."

"Only watch over the queen," Ingemund answered.

Though the winter nights were still long and dark, Beowulf slept no more than a bear in summer over the next two days, just closing his eyes for a few moments now and again as he sat on the bench in Hygd's house with his back slumped against the wall. He left the house only a few times while Ingemund was with Hygd, going to the dwelling of Byrhthild and Ingemund. Byrhthild lay deep in the fiery grip of the alf bale, her head rolling restlessly on her wet pillow and her slanted eyes squinting up at something only she could see.

Beneath the fine worked coverlets of yellow linen better adorned with embroidery than those of any other household, for that she had wrought them for ten winters longer than most maidens had to wait for their weddings the mound of her belly rose like a golden howe above a sunset lit plain, but her arms and legs twitched restlessly under the blankets. Wihstan stood by her bedside, his hands gripping each other as though he would wrap them about the throat of the wight who had scathed his wife so. The bedchamber, like Hygd's, was sweet with the apple wood and herbs that Ingemund had ordered cast upon the fire against the alf bale, while a faint musty scent rose from the hasty stitched pouch of red linen that hung about Byrhthild's neck Beowulf did not think he wished to know what Ingemund had put into those warding bags. Hygd roused often, and would drink like a motherless babe from the pierced tip of the cow horn through which Beowulf fed her the gudhe's herb draught. She seldom seemed to know him: she stared into the fire flickering gloom and spoke to folk who were long dead, or wights unseen wights that even Beowulf, for all his feeling for the uncanny, could not sense any hint of in the bedchamber. It was nearing dawn on the third night of Hygd's sickness when Beowulf, dozing on the bench, heard the queen's trembling voice.

"Berki? Are you still there?"

Beowulf leapt to his feet, crossing to Hygd's bedside in a single stride. "I am here, my Hygd," he assured her, his heart leaping from its weariness in sudden hope. "How is it with you? Are you feeling better?"

"My mind is clear at last. I saw...I cannot recall it now, it is like a dream, but I saw riders hastening over green grass, and they shone fair in the Sun's light; they sang such songs as I have not heard since Scyld parted from us, and...but let that be. Berki, take my hands now."

Berki clasped Hygd's wasted fingers in his own; they felt like twigs lumpy with galls, and they were cold as if the warm blood no longer flowed in her veins.

"It is in my mind," Hygd said weakly, "that soon you must steer the Geat folk alone, for I hear my kinfolk calling to me from across the rushing river. Berki, remember that fire is the bane of trees, but the burgs of the eotens are bound with iron. I know your hand grip has not lessened in might, for that you have aged less swiftly than I; but I think you must keep byrnie and blade close by you, for not all foes will grasp you as Grendel did, nor may you deal with all as you dealt with Dagochramn."

She let her eyelids drop, her breathing softening, then opened them again, her eyes dark wells in the flickering firelight.

"Berki, I love you, and ever have, since you broke Breca's arm when he was trying to haul me about at the Thing. I have only one sorrow from our years together as king and queen: that my womb never swelled with your child. But when I am dead, take the apple of amber you gave me when we first met, and hang it about Byrhthild's neck, and fasten my girdle with the garnet wrought cat clasp above her waist; yet from your arm you shall take that first ring Hygelac gave you, and that you shall slip over her wrist. Will you do this thing for me, Berki?"

"You shall not die so soon," Beowulf argued he would not tell her how close to her own mound Byrhthild lay. But his words rang dull and hollow as knocking on an empty horn, and Hygd did not waste any strength in answering them.

"Though sorrow came before, we have had a fair summertime together, my bear," she whispered. "But the cold wind is beginning to rise, and I must fare back to my kin." Hygd's fingers tightened slightly on Beowulf's hand. She closed her eyes, and sighed, and did not draw another breath in.

Alone in Hygd's bedchamber, with only the fretful sleep breathing of the serving woman from her blankets in the next room and the low crackling of the fire to break the stillness, Beowulf wept for the woman he had loved, alone of all the women of the Middle Garth. He stood there as the fire burned down, until the bed of coals in the hearth could no longer keep the chill from the air. Then, slowly, his fingers numb and clumsy as though he wore heavy mittens, he unfastened the clasp of the little silver chain about Hygd's neck, lifting the amber apple from between her age withered breasts.

He found the girdle she had spoken of, and went on to Wihstan's house. Byrhthild still shifted restlessly in her sleep; Wihstan lay stretched on the bench beside the bed, wrapped in his winter cloak. Their fire had nearly gone out; Beowulf layered a few pieces of wood upon the last flame crumbling bits of log, and bent to do as Hygd had said. Byrhthild did not wake as Beowulf set the apple's chain about her neck, nor even when he carefully worked the gold mounted girdle's clasp beneath her back, fastening it loosely above the swell of her womb. But when he took off the ring Hygelac had given him the skin of his broad upper arm was pale as a cave fish where the gold had lain, he had borne it so long and bent it tighter about her wrist so that it would not slip free too easily, Byrhthild's tilted eyes opened.

"Beowulf!" She said. "I have dreamed many strange things, and I was going to tell you about them, but...ah!" His foster daughter twisted in her bed, pressing her hands against her belly. "Beowulf," she said calmly, "I think it is time now for you to wake my husband, and fetch the women to aid me, for it seems to me that my child shall soon be born."

Beowulf could not help in the birthing: as soon as it was light, he took the strongest of his thanes save only Wihstan, who would not leave his wife's side and went out to the snow covered barrow field, working like an eoten builder to dig the earth and move the stones for Hygd's howe. He had given orders that all be readied for her death faring; that the best blankets and cushions be laid in a wain for her, together with food and drink, a keg of sweet fruit beer and joints of smoked meat, rounds of cheese and fresh baked bread. Iron lamps were gathered to light her way; a brewing kettle was filled with grain, and Hygd's tapestries were lifted down from the walls of her house, for they would soon adorn her new dwelling. Bryhthild's labour lasted until near dawn of the next day. Waiting in the outer chamber of the house, Beowulf and Wihstan heard her shriek the first cry she had made, though the women had said in hushed voices that the bearing was going hard. The next sound they heard was that of a baby's thin wail, then Bryhthild saying loudly,

"Of course I am strong enough to hold my son to my breast!"

Wihstan grinned in relief. "It sounds as though mother and babe are well," he said.

The midwife warned that Wihstan's son was undersized and pale, as though his mother's fever had gnawed at him in the womb, and that they should not rejoice too greatly at his birth though Bryhthild's life was a gift of the gods. But the child suckled strongly, and his grip on his mother's breast did not begin to weaken at once, as had that of Ingemund's nameless babe. Hygd's barrow was full built on the third day, and the horses, golden and bay, drew her from hall to howe field in her wain. She wore all the amber Beowulf had given her about her neck, save only the apple she had left to Bryhthild, and gold glistened on her red dress from the woven trim over her ankles to the fibulas pinning the gown at her neck and shoulders.

Beowulf had said that her long white hair should be let down and brushed out, though she wore a headdress of white silk stitched with gold wire thread and garnet beads; lest the long way to the god halls be cold, he laid her white lynx fur hood by her head and her furred gloves by her hands. In Hygd's wain were skeins of silk and bright dyed linen threads and needles for her tapestry work, shining wool and flax and her favorite spindle with its whorl of green stone. Beowulf sent with her the silver goblets with the lobed leaves and clusters of fruit embossed on their sides, and their matching gold rimmed pitcher, remembering her pride in them; he gave her a conical beaker of blue southern glass as well, and a little keg of wine from the same part of the Rhineland as the glass cup. And at the last, looking on Hygd where she lay among her treasures in her wain, Beowulf ordered that his blanket of white reindeer hides be brought to him.

He shook out a shower of loose hairs onto the snow before he laid it carefully over her body he remembered how the two of them had lain beneath those pelts together on the way to Lake Wener, glad in each others' warmth against the cold of Scyld's storm. As had been the way in the Geat king's garth for many years now, Ingemund spoke the most of the burial rite, but it was Beowulf who cut the throats of the golden and dark horses that had pulled Hygd's wagon to the howe door, their blood dropping over the snow like silky red curtains as they went to their knees, then down. Beowulf dragged horses and wain into the tapestry hung howe himself, and brought the torch to light the lamps that stood on either side of the barrow chamber.

"Fare well, my fair one," Beowulf said softly. "I shall long for you...and someday we shall greet each other once more." He came out and began to heave the great stones into place before Hygd's gate.

In spite of the cold, Beowulf was sweating freely when he came into the hall to lead the drinking of Hygd's arvel. He lifted the gold bound aurochs horn and tried to speak, but the words choked in his throat: he had loved Hygd, but never lain with her; she had but one child still living, and her line ended with Hildegeard. Beowulf's face burned, his head swam and his eyes blurred, and then Wihstan was taking the horn from his hand and holding him up as he swayed.

"The king is ill," someone said, and someone else murmured, "Grief, and the alf fire: I fear it shall go hard with him."

"Come, Beowulf," Wihstan said softly. "I shall help you to bed."

The stars swirled above the moon bright snow in great whorls of pale color, shedding sparks like a pitch spitting torch hurled high into the night. Beowulf tried to speak again, but his tongue was thick, the words stumbling drunkenly from it.

"No, do not strain yourself," Wihstan said. "We are almost there." He led Beowulf into his house, unfastened his king's sword belt and shoes, and eased Beowulf into his bed, drawing the covers up over him. "Ingemund is coming with his herbs, and he shall make you well."

"Not Hygd," Beowulf mumbled, flailing a bit with his blanket bound hands.

But the whirling firelight was humming more loudly in his ears, and he could no longer hear Wihstan's raspy voice, nor see his cousin's strong features through the wheeling streaks of light. It seemed to Beowulf then that it was bright sunlight that dazed his eyes, and when he blinked them clear, he was looking upon a green field where grassy mounds rose. Across the field, he saw the light flashing and glimmering on the gold rings and steed trappings of a band of fair riders, their hair and the manes and tails of their horses flowing pale behind them as they cantered over the little hillocks. He heard their singing on the warm wind, faint and clear.

The deep and high voices together wove a tapestry of sound as brilliant as the finest embroidery work, though Beowulf was too far away to make out the words; but it seemed to him that Hrothulf's sister Scyld would not have been the best singer among them.

He felt himself drawn to run after the bright riders, but he was naked, the Sun's light warm on his shoulders and back, and he felt as though he had just come up from deep water.

"Why do you weep, my bear?" Hygd's voice asked.

Beowulf turned his head, but it was not Hygd who stood there. He had looked just in time to see the flaxen hair deepening to ruddy gold, the violet eyes brightening to the greenish blue of sunlight through the shallows. Though the woman who stood there, naked save for her gold collar and garnet clasped girdle, was so fair that he could hardly bear to look upon her, and his body ached with need of her, she was not Hygd, and the tears stung Beowulf's eyes again.

"No, I am not Hygd," she said, her low sweet voice stroking over Beowulf's skin like a caress of silk. "But betimes I was, for a little while, and you knew me through her: I shone brightly on the shores by Whales' Ness, though I cast my shadow in Upsala. Now that Hygd's wain fares along the dark ways to Folk Plain, I may no longer veil myself in her living hame do you have the strength, my bear, to meet me as I am?"

As she spoke, the flames flared up around her, and Beowulf saw the falcon wings arching high feathered above her head, the shadow of a cruel beak above the golden glow of her face. He looked upon her with awe and wonder, yet he did not reach out to her, for his heart yet ached with his loss.

"Some love but once, and mate for life," the woman said amidst her flames, her voice thrumming with might. "But god kind and eoten kind love no less because we love many: Ran's daughter weeps for you even in the arms of her lovers now, and I weep yet for Wod, wandering far from my embrace." And even as she spoke, Beowulf saw the drops of gold falling from her eyes, as the sea salty tears dropped from his own. "Yet you are king, and though no woman of the Middle Garth shall sit by your high seat, you took me as your queen will you forsake that oath?"

Then Beowulf stepped forward into the flames that licked about her, and he took her in his arms. Her fires burned all through him, and her falcon wings beat about him as her flame hot sheath sank onto his leek; her nipples pressed against his chest like hot coals, and he did not know if it was pain or pleasure that seared all thought from his mind as he thrust up into her. But her water bright gaze held his as he gave himself to her. Her gold tears shining clear as amber through the salt tears that blurred his own sight, and he knew the truth of her love rune. Ingemund was sitting by the side of Beowulf's bed when the Geat king awoke. The gudhe's gray hair stood up in rumpled spikes, as though he had been running salve greasy hands through it, and his beard hung half plaited. When he saw Beowulf's eyes open, he leapt to his feet.

"Thanks be to the gods and all kind wights that you wake!" Ingemund said. "I had begun to fear that you would never look upon the Middle Garth again, but your fever seemed to break late last night, and that gave me hope."

"How long have I been here?" Beowulf asked.

"You lay in the alf fire nine nights," Ingemund told him. "Sometimes you cried out but you did not speak any words that I knew."

Beowulf sat up. He was ravenously hungry, as though his stomach had been devouring itself from the inside; though his limbs were weak and shaky, he felt strangely light and clean.

"What of Wihstan's babe?" He asked. "Did it live?"

"Aye. Wihstan lifted his son in his arms by the hallowed stone three days past, and gave him the name Wiglaf Wiglaf of the Waegmundings."

Beowulf smiled. "That is a good name, and fit for one who shall bear such a sword as Byrhthild keeps for her son. It is well to wake to such tidings: if all joy must pass away at last, sorrow, too, must come to its end."

XIII

Wealhtheow rose well before dawn on the last day before Yule, swinging her feet over the edge of her bed and staring at the fire's low red glow in the blackness while she waited for the pain in her back and knees to ease. As old as she was, it seemed that she needed little sleep: where in her youth, like most folk, she had slumbered long in the cold winter nights and stayed awake for most of summer's brightness, now she was restless in winter's darkness, as though she were holding watch over the hof and its younger folk. In spite of the thick snow outside, her house was warm, for the under gudhijas who tended to her needs always kept her fire well tended. She could hear Aethelgifu's slow breathing, together with that of her babe, in the outer chamber.

The sturdy young woman worked as hard as any of the hof men in the day, carrying logs and heaving big iron cauldrons about, but as the sun began to set, her lynx fetch ran away from her woman hame and she fell into a deep sleep from which none could rouse her. That gift had kept any from wedding her outside God Home, but here, Aethelgifu had found no lack of young gudhes willing to give her Frea Ing's blessing with their bodies. Standing up slowly, Wealtheow dressed herself: she could still do that, though her age thickened fingers fumbled with the pins of her crystal set silver brooches and the silver clasp buttons along the sleeves of her thick woolen overdress.

She girded on the belt that marked her foremost among Frige's gudhijas, with its berg crystal ball nestled in the bowl of a silver spoon dangling on one side and the ring of keys for all the locks in the holy stead hanging on the other, and reached for her winter cloak. Pale blue wool lined with white fox fur, it had been a gift from a woman of Halogaland who had made the long faring down to God Home with her husband in hopes that Frige would end her barrenness the cloak had come later, together with a hood to match it and word that the woman now suckled a son at one breast and a daughter at the other. A small iron lamp stood spiked into the earthen floor by the fire: Wealhtheow tugged it free, lighting the beeswax set wick with a burning twig.

She bore the lamp out in one hand, the other held the staff upon which she must lean now, a pale length of birch wood that she had cut and risted with rune staves herself, rubbing it with fat from the holy offerings to polish it though her hands had been guided carefully through the cunning carvings of twining long necked waterfowl by Aelfric, the most skilled of God Home's wood crafters. The thin pressed gold squares that dangled on linen threads from the top of her staff jingled like the rings of a tiny bridle rangle with each step Wealhtheow took. The stars shone cold and silver above like moonlight sparkling from darkened snow, the thin ice sliver of the new Moon gleaming down upon the stretches of new fallen whiteness between the shadows of the god folks' houses and the glistening rime crusted on shingle and thatch.

Wealhtheow's single lamp flame cast her shadow long and wavering over the blue white snow, and though she was not so gifted with sight as some of the dwellers in God Home, who would tread wide of others to keep from tripping over their fetches, it seemed to her that she could almost see the wings of her swan stretching behind her. Though Grendel had been dead for fifty six winters, Wealhtheow still felt a strange wonder whenever she stepped freely outside at night, as though she had been loosed into a world beyond the burden of the Middle Garth's cares. She walked carefully, her staff coming down hard through the snow: her right hip sent a sharp twinge of pain through her body each time she swung that foot forward, for she had fallen scarce a month ago and been lucky, Thunarbrand the Healer said, not to have shattered her bones such falls were often the bane of old women.

Still, though Wealhtheow knew that it was perilous for her to walk on uncertain footing alone, most especially in night and snow for if she slipped and hurt herself, with no one nearby to aid, she would likely freeze to death before morning she turned her feet towards the path that led out of the gods' garth and on to the barrow field. The hof warder now was the great grandson of that Wihstan who had stood at the gates when Wealhtheow made her first faring to the holy holm with Unferth. His shadow bulked big as an etin's in the light of the torches that burned before the gate pillars, but he stepped aside respectfully when he saw her coming.

He did not speak to her often a gudhe or gudhija would pass him to do something that must be done in silence, both in going out and coming back, and, though she was not set on such a working, she was loath to break the stillness of the night. Though no track marred the fresh fallen snow, Wealhtheow knew well where the paths ran to wood and lake, or down to the town, or across to the barrow plain. It was that third path that she took now, stumping slowly over the shining field. She had not needed the flickering lamp she bore to see her way, for the moonlight on the snow was bright enough for even her old eyes to make out most of the details of her staff carvings. But it felt right to be bearing that flame to the mounds on this night before Yule began, and if it slowed her a little, what of it?

The gods had time to wait for an old woman's lagging footsteps, as did the one she was going to visit. Wealhtheow slowed further as she crossed the little bridge over the frozen stream that sundered the dead among the hof folk from their living comrades: the wood was icy and slippery, and if she were going to fall, it would likely be here. The blows of her staff boomed hollow from the rime slick planks beneath the jingling of the gold plates dangling from its crown, but her shoes only crunched quietly through the thin layer of unmarked snow over the bridge. The aged gudhija could see nothing but herself stirring in God Home's barrow field, and the sole sounds were the ringing of her staff and her footfalls through the crisp snow.

Still, she could feel those who flocked about her, or watched in silence. So close to Yule, the dead were restless in their howes: some would be saddling their steeds to ride forth, while others would be stoking their fires and waiting for the guests that would come to their barrows in the darkest nights of the year. Farther along the field, the western howes were black against the moonlight: no snow would stick there, where Frea Ing's friends were buried. The stone that marked Unferth's mound was almost hidden beneath the snow, only a white capped ridge of gray rising out of a drift on the north side of the burial hill.

But Wealhtheow did not need to read the staves set there to know where she was: she had been coming to her old friend's barrow since he had been laid in it twenty years ago. By the time she reached the top of Unferth's howe, Wealhtheow was breathing hard. She stood for a moment before she brushed the snow off the flat topped stone where she was used to sitting, the cold wetness soaking even through the fur of her gloves. She was not strong enough to drive the spiked end of her lamp into the frozen earth, but she leaned the twisted iron bar against the stone, the beeswax in its cup spilling over in a swift hardening golden stream to dribble down the iron and drop deep into the snow.

"Well, Unferth," Wealhtheow said. "How is it with you?"

No sound answered her, but it seemed to Wealhtheow that she could feel the faint well known rasping along her nerves that told her Unferth was there, and listening that feeling which had long since, when he lived, gone from discomfort to reassurance to something that she had thought she could not live without. The touch of some of the dead in that settlement brought calm and joy when Wealhtheow was in pain or troubled, she had only to go to Wihbrand's barrow to find easing; Frea Ing's friend gave her that help as gladly in death as he had in life. Yet even in summer, Unferth always felt restless and prickly, but he who guested in Wael Hall and lifted his spear in the battles of Woden's hosts should hardly rest quietly when he was at home in his howe.

Wealhtheow had known Unferth long enough, living and dead, to guess when he was glad and when he grew angry. Now his touch was very strong, for he, too, would be saddling up his horse for the Yule riding: it seemed to her that she could almost see him with the blue howe fires gleaming from his helm and the bare white bone of his skull and the keen edge of his spear tip, stroking the neck of the gray stallion that tossed his black mane, eager to tread the wind roads with fire spurting beneath his hooves.

"They say the Geats had a good harvest again this year, though Beowulf's queen died of the alf fire before ploughing season began and he has not taken another bride," Wealhtheow told the thule in his mound.

"No, wait...that was seven years gone. Ah, what manner of news bearer am I, that I cannot remember what has passed when? But Beowulf is still not wedded, and there is no guessing who shall steer the Geats when he is gone, with his cousin Wihstan three years dead now I told you of that when it happened: he fell fighting raiders along the Geatish coast, slaying the leader of a large band, one of those ruffians who call themselves sea kings these days, as if an outlaw were any less an warg on the waves than in the wood. Beowulf has done well to hold his land as he has, with so many wild war bands faring about and that bloody handed Salo rousing the Swedes to raid here and there. But Beowulf is no summer budding shoot any longer. I think this is..." she counted on her fingers, her lips moving as she tried to reckon in her head, "yes, I think it is the thirty ninth winter of his kingship, and only the gods know what will happen to the Geats when he is dead. Wihstan left a son, but that lad is only seven winters old now, and they say he is sickly and short sighted, no king in the making. I wonder if young Wiglaf shall come here in the course of time?" Wealhtheow added thoughtfully. "We get one or two like that every year, atheling bairns who are better fit for learning lore and making offerings than for leading a host. But the gudhe in Beowulf's garth is getting old as well, so more likely Wihstan's son will stay among the Geats to tend their holy stone."

Wealhtheow sighed. "That is all the tidings I can think of. Oh they say Yrse has gotten out of her bed again, though she lay ill for several months after the alf fire struck her down, and everyone thought she would turn her face to the wall and die. I think there are none of the Scylding line who have lived as long as she; and she has a good nine or ten winters more than I. For myself, I am beginning to wonder if she is using the same means as Eadwine the Old to keep herself alive. That would be an ill wreaking and I am told that thralls will not do for it. It must be an atheling's life for an atheling but Yrse was ever said to be a hard hearted woman. Still, she has managed to keep that Salo from slaying her grandson Ingware, and that is something."

Holding tight to her staff, Wealhtheow managed to push herself to her feet.

"Well, I shall come out here with everyone else tomorrow evening when I lead the idises' blessing and bid the alfs to the hof. But I was wakeful this night, and I wanted to talk to you by myself, Aethelgifu is a good girl, but this is her first babe, and she has no more idea yet of how to keep it quiet than she does of how to still a winter wind. Good night, my Unferth, and a good riding to you this Yule."

"Spindle Shanks! Catch!" Eadmer's voice shrilled as he hurled the leather ball at Wiglaf's head.

Wiglaf started, flinging up his hands to knock it away before it hit him in the face, and the other boys laughed. Wiglaf glared around at the blurred faces. They often made mock of him for his short sight and clumsiness, and though he was taller than any of the boys his own age, he was thin as a willow withe, showing no sign that he would grow the great Waegmunding thews of his father or the king.

"The game's ended you lost!" Aldhelm added.

The son of one of Beowulf's under kings, who had come to the Geat king's burg at Yule for fostering, Aldhelm had made himself a leader among the boys in a few days by strength and a quick mind: he was best at all the games, and the first to think of ways they could test their bravery, from teasing the bulls in the fields to hanging by their hands from the little bit of rock that jutted over the cliff at the top of Whales' Ness. Aldhelm licked his finger, holding it up to test the wind and glancing at the sky, his blond hair fluttering back from his face. Everyone said he was the best looking of the boys: of middle height; well made, with sturdy shoulders and legs; his clean features fair as a maiden's but already set in manly fashion. Costly as red dyed linen was, he wore a bright red tunic even at play, and anyone might mark him out from among the other boys at a distance. Wiglaf hated him with all his heart.

"Now I say that it would be a good day to go bird nesting, for the weather is fair and the wind not too strong not too strong for brave hearts to dare, that is. You need not come with us if you don't want to, Spindle Shanks," Aldhelm added, his youthful alto voice wide with generosity. "I think the women are in need of another pair of hands to gather herbs for their cheese making."

"I shall come with you!" Wiglaf answered angrily: no boy over seven winters would let himself be pressed into picking herbs for the cheese if he could help it, and Wiglaf had ten winters now.

Aldhelm shrugged. "Well, if you must, then come by all means. But watch where you put your feet on the cliffs if you can see the footholds or we'll have to carry you to your howe in a bag."

The best spot for birds' nesting was on Eagles' Ness, a little way north of Whales' Ness, where the hill of the huge old barrow mound rose above the sea cliffs: the gray lichen shored stone at the howe's height was large enough that a rope tied about it could have held even the king's great weight, let alone a boy's. The gulls and terns soared below the cliff's rocky edge, their harsh voices rising in a cackling din to the nine youths who looked down with baskets and bags in their hands. To Wiglaf, the waves crashing on the stones below were no more than a dark blur, the wheeling seabirds white streaks through the dizzying emptiness below the gray stone.

"I shall go first," Aldhelm said, and no one challenged him for it.

Working deftly, he looped his coil of rope around the boulder and tied it off. He did not bother to wrap any rope about his body, only took the handle of his straw filled basket in his teeth and began to climb down. Wiglaf watched nervously, standing as close to the cliff as he dared though he was still a long pace away, the ground felt uncertain beneath his feet, as though the cap of grassy turf might suddenly slip off the stones underneath it and tumble over the edge, bearing him along. The wind was stronger here above the strand, so that Wiglaf shivered in his linen tunic, wishing that he had at least worn a light summer cloak.

The seagulls shrieked and dived at the intruder threatening their nests. Wiglaf could not really see what was happening, but he heard Aldhelm's clear alto shouting, "Ha! Missed me, missed me, couldn't hit a stranded whale!" Followed by a squawk and the fair haired boy's cheerful, "Got you!" It was not too long before Aldhelm called, "Haul me up now and careful with the rope, I've got a basket full of eggs."

Eadmer and Bealdwine shouldered Wiglaf casually aside, spitting on their hands before they bent to pull the rope in. Aldhelm's blond hair gleamed in the sunlight as he scrambled over the edge of the cliff with the basket handle in his mouth like a hound trained to fetch bones, Wiglaf thought. Had he been as quick of tongue as the other boy, he might have said something like that, but when he tried to repay mockery with mockery, he always seemed to fumble his words, and even when he repeated his mother's sharp witted words, he came out sounding like a fool.

"Look at that," Aldhelm said in satisfaction. "Fifteen eggs, and not a single crack in any of them. If any one of you can beat that, I shall give him my silver finger ring."

Hereberht got twelve, but no one had made Aldhelm pay the geld for his boast by the time all the boys but Wiglaf had taken their turn at going over the cliff.

"Well, Spindle Shanks," Aldhelm said at last. "Still want to go? You don't have to, you know. I think the rest of us have enough eggs between us to show our worth." He hitched his breeches up at the crotch, and the other boys laughed.

"I will go, and you shall be lucky if you still have that ring by the time we bear our eggs back to the hall," Wiglaf replied grimly.

He took the handle of his own basket in his teeth and crouched down, clenching his hands on the rope and edging towards the cliff. Don't look down, and you won't fear, he told himself. Still, when he felt the emptiness beneath his heels, his muscles froze, and he teetered on the cliff's brink for a long terrible moment.

"Ah, he can't do it," Hereberht said, and the easy contempt in his voice drove Wiglaf to force one bare foot down over the edge.

Then his toes met the welcome ridge of rock, and he was able to stretch out the other foot, bracing it on a jutting craglet as he set hand below hand, lowering himself slowly down. The seabirds were shrieking all about him, flying enraged over their robbed nests. Wiglaf knew that he would have the worst of it in trying to reach eggs that the other boys had not already taken it was seldom that he who went first did not win the egg gathering. Only his longer reach would help him; but his short sight made it the harder for him to guess where the eggs might nestle in their beds of dried grass and moss on the jagged cliff shelves.

Wiglaf was most of the way down the cliff when he spotted the gull waddling warily back and forth on the ledge just out of his reach. She opened her yellow beak, hissing fiercely at him, and for a moment his heart quailed, but he had made his boast to Aldhelm, and this was the first nest he had seen. Toehold by toehold, clinging tightly to the rope, Wiglaf walked himself to the side, towards the gull. The cliff sheered off below her little shelf, but he could brace himself with his feet, and if he let go of the rope with one hand, he could just reach. He leaned over, trying not to think about what would happen if one of his feet slipped from its precarious place, and felt along the rough ledge. Pain stung up Wiglaf's arm as the gull's beak hacked viciously down into his flesh, bringing the tears to his eyes, but he doggedly kept reaching past her until his fingers found the soft crackling dryness of the nest, then the warm smoothness of eggs.

One by one, he brought them carefully to the basket clenched in his aching jaws. Four eggs, their pale blue green speckled with blackish brown splotches, and smeared with his blood, for half a dozen thick red trickles dribbled over his arm and hand from the beak wounds. Only twelve more to find, Wiglaf told himself, gripping tightly to the rope and feeling downward with his left foot. Aldhelm shall laugh out of the other side of his mouth when he must give me his ring! Then Wiglaf's right foot slipped, and he cried out sharply. For a sickening moment he hung free, clinging to the rope and his basket of eggs was tumbling down far below him: he thought that he heard the faint smash of its striking above the deep crashing of the sea on the rocks. His feet found toeholds again at last, though his legs were shaking so badly that he did not dare try to move. The roaring of the surf muffled the laughter from above, but it could not deafen Wiglaf to what Aldhelm was shouting.

"Wiglaf!" He called. "Battle leavings that is a fit name for you, for why should anyone bother to cut you down in a fight? When we fall fighting like heroes, you shall be left alive to pick over the corpses, and no doubt you shall be as clumsy at that as you are at egg gathering. But we shall leave the leavings now: enjoy your climb!"

Wiglaf risked tilting his head back to look up. He could not see over the edge of the cliff rearing above him, but when he angrily shouted,

"Pull me up, and we shall have a reckoning between us for those words!" No answer came to him, nor any reassuring tug of the rope. The young Waegmunding did not know then whether his trembling was from rage or fear, but he had to clutch the rope to his chest to be sure of keeping tight hold of it.

After a few moments, though, he was able to calm himself. They are just trying to frighten me, Wiglaf told himself. They will be back soon, and maybe I shall give them a fright in turn! He thought of Aldhelm trying to tell the king what had happened, when they left Beowulf's only living kinsman in the Geatish lands dangling over Eagles' Ness, and came back to find only an empty rope hanging there, and smiled in spite of his aching shoulders and the burning pain of his bleeding arm. That thought gave Wiglaf the strength to keep climbing down the cliff he knew he would never be able to get up it by himself, so down was his only hope if the other boys were not to find him still clinging like a limpet when they came back.

By the time he reached the rocks at the bottom, the sweat stung in stone grazes all over his arms and legs and face; though his pecked arm had stopped bleeding, it throbbed with a steady painful pulse, and the muscles of his shoulders hurt so badly that he could barely lift his arms. The jagged boulders were wet and slippery beneath his sore feet, though the tide was going out, each wave that boomed white spray up between the rocks striking the beach a little further back than the last. Wiglaf made his way carefully over the big slick stones, working along the foot of the cliff towards the steep path that mounted to the top over a gentler slope.

The anger that had fueled him on his way down had ebbed like the last edge of a wave sucking suddenly back to the ocean, leaving only a bitter rim of froth behind on the sand. He did not know how long it had been since Aldhelm and the others had left, but no one had yet called to him from above, so they had not come back yet. My arms would surely be giving way by now, Wiglaf thought. They left me where I could have died! The shock of that realization bit cold into the Waegmunding's bowels, and he stopped where he was.

"They really did leave me to my death," he said aloud.

The words left Wiglaf breathless: it seemed too much to get his mind around too much for rage, too much for any thought. And he knew he could not tell anyone what had happened without sounding like a whining thrall: after all, he was alive and whole, and the worst wounds of his ordeal were those the gull's beak had left on him and it would be his word alone against that of Aldhelm, of whom the grownups all thought well, and the other boys to back him up. Even if he had died on the cliff, Wiglaf realized in blinding horror, there would not have been much made of it.

All Aldhelm need say was that he had slipped while climbing even grown men were sometimes killed at birds nesting. No one would disbelieve that short sighted Wiglaf had put his foot in the wrong place, or missed his grab at the rope. No one save his mother would even care much, Wiglaf thought. He was old enough to overhear the way the thanes sighed whenever they spoke about Wihstan's son that he had not inherited the Waegmunding strength, nor enough quickness of hand and foot to make up for his lack of thews; that the other boys did not follow his lead, but mocked him, and he could not even defend himself very well with his fists. Only Beowulf had ever spoken up for him: once when Wiglaf was close enough to hear it, the king had reminded his thanes that he himself had been an unpromising child, laughed at for his fatness as Wiglaf was for his skinny frame.

"But I have also heard that at seven winters, you had the strength of a grown man," the old poet Hlewabrandar had said then in one of his rare moments of clear thought though he had not been right in the mind since he had sickened with the alf fire eleven years past and Beowulf had to own that was so.

Tears stung Wiglaf's eyes as he half walked, half crawled over the rocks: it seemed to him that he might as well have let go of the rope when he dangled between heavens and earth, and dashed his brains on the stones below. He was shivering with cold and unhappiness, and his heart thudded like the dropping of a dead thing in his chest. Why should I go back to the hall? He thought. Why should I not just keep walking until I drop from hunger and thirst?

When Wiglaf came at last to a little stretch of sand between the great boulders and the cliff, he stumbled down onto it, his shaking legs giving way beneath him. He fell to his knees, clutching his arms about himself, and wept miserably until his eyes ached and his breath was raw in his throat. Yet he could not keep crying forever, though his tears had brought his heart no easing, and after a time he wiped his eyes and nose on the sleeve of his tunic and stood up.

It was then that Wiglaf saw the dark crack in the cliff, leading behind a rough wall of stone. In his forsaken sorrow, it seemed to draw him like a pool of black water whispering hope of drowning, and his feet bore him slowly towards it. As he walked towards the narrow cliff gate, he rubbed without thought at his aching arm and then stopped, looking at the smear of fresh blood on his hand where he had opened the new crusted scab again.

"Enough of this," Wiglaf said to himself. "If I cannot trust Aldhelm and his friends as shield fellows, then neither can anyone else. And if I am the only one who knows what they are, then I must be there to keep a watch on them."

He turned away from the dark gap behind the rock wall, walking up to the end of the narrow sandy stretch and bracing himself on the foot of Eagles' Ness to climb up on the first boulder. Then Wiglaf was close enough to mark what his short sight had hidden from him before: the end of the rope dangling down to lie half coiled on a big rock somehow in his heart shattered wandering over the beach, he had managed to turn himself around, and come back to where he had begun, under the hoary stone. Wiglaf shook his head and sighed, and started to struggle over the rocks again to where the path mounted up to the top of the cliffs.

"Hey!" Aldhelm called from above. "Did it take you that long just to climb down that little way? How many eggs did you get?"

"The trolls take your eggs, and your leek with them!" Wiglaf shouted back at him, the sea cave beneath the barrow already forgotten.

In the forty eighth summer of Beowulf's kingship, the harvest failed: one hailstorm after another swept over the fields, flattening the green stalks into broken ruin on the ground amid the puddles of melting ice. Still, he made his offerings, and there was plenty of grain and ale that had been put by in the year before, nor was the meat scanty that year, so the Geats did not go as hungry as their neighbors. The next year, the weather stayed ill: it froze hard after planting time, and there was still snow on the ground a month before Midsummer's; and chill rains fell all summer, so that the hay could not dry as it ought in the fields, and those heads of grain that could be reaped were small and ill shaped.

Again, the Geats did not go as hungry as those about them: the sea kings raided not for gold now, but for food, and there was no grain to be bought from Halogaland to Frankland. Then folk began to look at the early falling snow, and to mutter darkly among themselves Beowulf heard that the Swedes, whose snows fell a little earlier and melted a little later than those of the Geats in the best years, were whispering of giving Salo to the gods as they had Domaldar in long years before, that if he were truly of Ingling seed, Frea and Frowe might be sated with his life. It was said that among the Merovingians, rivers had burst their banks and wrecked boats, and that their summer had been as wet and chill as the warm Frankish winters; that two islands in the sea had been wholly burned by fire falling from the sky, and that a pond on another island off the coast of Frankland had turned to blood. Yule was a grim feast that year, for open handed as Beowulf was, all his generosity barely served to wet the throats of his thanes with ale.

Few men came to guest with him, and the snow lay deeper about his hall than Beowulf could ever remember, so that when they went out to the barrow field, he had to forge ahead to break a track through the drifts for his folk to follow. By the time Ingemund had made his call to the Wod Host, he was shaking so hard that he could barely stand, and Beowulf had to half carry him back to the hall.

"It is ill with the alfs," Ingemund said softly to his king when they were back inside. "I think the old mound dweller is stirring strife this night, for I heard the clashing of weapons in the wind."

"Is there aught we can do?" Beowulf asked.

"Make our offerings, and bid the gods look well on us," Ingemund answered.

"Aye, the alfs sing slaughter songs," Hlewabrandar broke in.

The old poet's voice cracked and wavered now, and his left eyelid drooped low over his eye. His wits had wandered somewhat since he fell ill with the alf fire, but he had grown much worse in the last year. His age spotted hands clutched his drinking horn close to his chest, and he uttered a toothless cackle.

"Beowulf, why did you not tell me Scyld was guesting with us again? I heard her singing earlier this eve, the song she sang as we rose to Lake Wener. Oh, I have forgotten the words once more, but there was blood in it, and fire, and the weather of Woden. And I have heard that the Great Winter is on us, that must last three years before the gods go to battle. Winds tear the earth, and wolves harry from land and sea; ice crusts the ale casks in the hall, and axes find homes in flesh surely the age of the world is ending!" Hlewabrandar hunched over his horn, his one good eye looking out warily through a stray lock of thin white hair, and he flinched away when Beowulf reached out to touch his shoulder. Ingemund shook his head slightly.

"There is nothing we can do for him, either, save be kind," he whispered in answer to Beowulf's unspoken question. "In a little time he shall have forgotten this fright, in any case."

A burst of laughter rose from the young thanes who sat further down the hall, and Beowulf glanced over at them. Aldhelm's hands were spread out as if he had just told some jest, and the handsome young man was grinning broadly at his friends.

"There, at least, is one who has not let the thin feasting daunt him," Beowulf said. "He fought well against those Jutish raiders last year, too."

"Aye. As a boy, he had the makings of a fine man, and he is living up to what was awaited of him," Ingemund agreed.

"I have wondered," Beowulf added more quietly, "if I would do well to name him as my heir."

"That is not unworthy of thought," Ingemund murmured back.

His thoughts having turned to that matter, Beowulf could not keep from stealing a painful glance at Wihstan's son Wiglaf. Wiglaf was now in his eighteenth winter, but though Byrhthild had gifted her son with the sword and helm and byrnie his father had left him, Beowulf had been careful that Wiglaf was not among those he called when word came to him that sea kings were ravening along his coast.

The young man had the height of the Waegmundings, but none of their breadth. His gangling body seemed to have been put together clumsily from sticks like a carle's crow scarer, and he was always bumping into benches and knocking things over. He had gotten his mother's short sight together with the Finnish slant of her blue eyes; he shot badly and threw a spear like a girl, and his sword play was awkward at best, with great wild sweeps of his blade and lunging thrusts that often fell far short of the mark. Nor was he liked by the other young men. It wrenched Beowulf's heart to see how his cousin's son sat alone in the best of times, his long face gloomy as he watched Aldhelm laughing with his friends not least, because Wiglaf was often the butt of the jest.

Beowulf would have done something about it if he could, but now he saw the wisdom in those hard words of Ansuwulf's that had set him to weeping long ago: if his king tried to shield Wiglaf from whatever hurt the other youths might give him, it would only be more shame for Wiglaf's part. For years Beowulf had hoped that his lanky kinsman would learn to gather his long limbs easily in sword play or wrestling and end some of the mockery though he remembered that his own early strength had stilled none of the cruel tongues about him, only warned their wielders out of his reach. But at last Beowulf had to admit to himself that Wiglaf was not what he had been, and there was no hope of making a king out of such stuff the alf fire that had racked Byrhthild just before Wiglaf's birth, Beowulf had often thought, must have stolen away the strength that Wihstan's son and Sweartwulf's great grandson should have had.

Now Wiglaf sat slumped unhappily on the bench a little way from the others, turning his drinking horn round and round in his knuckly hands. He had braided his brown hair back from his face, but it was too unruly to stay in the plait, and wisps stuck out from his head like spikes on a dried burr. His tilted blue eyes narrowed as he stared into the horn's depths, judging, perhaps, how much of the precious ale was still left him for the evening. Though he wore a fine tunic of red linen with gold clasp buttons at sleeves and neck as befitted a man of the king's own aeht at a feast, the tunic hung in loose lopsided folds from his bony shoulders, as if it had been slung carelessly over a pole. The ring hilted sword that Eanmund had owned jutted out behind him, hanging from his shoulder baldric; Wiglaf could hardly keep a belt up on his narrow hips even without the weight of a sword to pull it down.

It was not that the young Waegmunding was wholly careless of his looks
he sweated himself clean in the stone bath every couple of days, and even
went to the trouble of scraping his jaw with a keen edge, knowing, perhaps,
how ridiculous his Finn sparse beard would seem if he tried to grow it. But,
as with the matter of raising him to kingship, there was only so much that
could be done with Wiglaf's appearance. He was not ugly of face: though
his high cheekbones and slightly slanted blue eyes touched his looks with
strangeness, Wiglaf's nose was straight and his chin strong. But his brown
hair would obey no rule, and no clothes had ever been made that did not
hang ill fitting from his frame, for all Beowulf had gotten the most skilled
hands among the Geats to shape his kinsman's tunics.

I should name an heir soon, Beowulf thought. His age still sat more
lightly on him than on most men, and his strength had not waned each
year at the Midsummer's Thing, he lifted a stone as weighty as the one he
had heaved up the year before, and cast it as far but the byrnie Haethcyn
had ordered made wide for him had been tight over his belly until these
last months of scanty food, and he could feel himself slowing at sword
play. Each morning, the stiffness of sleep was a little harder to work from
his heavy limbs, and the changing weather ached deep in all his joints,
so that sometimes it hurt even to close his fingers about the hilt of his
sword: sooner or later, some swift blade among the raiders that harried the
coast every summer would make true the words Ansuwulf had spoken to
Beowulf so long ago, warning him that his strength would do him no good
if a faster man had already split his head.

I cannot wait forever in hopes that there is something in Wiglaf to
awaken. Though the winter snow melted in its course, the planting weather
was no better than it had been the year before: hail showered into the new
ploughed furrows like white grain in place of the golden, and after the first
green shoots had thrust up through the earth, snow fell again, hulling the
sprouting fields in unseasonable white. At last Ingemund said to Beowulf,
"If this goes on, we shall truly starve."

Since Yule, Beowulf had been thinking on more than choosing the man
who should sit in the high seat of the Geats after him. So he had half
awaited this, and already reconciled himself to it, when he said,

"Is it time, then, to make the offering of a king's blood?"

Ingemund's eyes widened, and he made a warding sign with his good
hand.

"The gods forfend that should come so soon! No: what I meant is only
that matters have gone beyond my strength to rede. Now it seems to me
that the best we can do is to send to God Home in hopes that they may
have some help to offer us, or wisdom in our need."

"The gifts of God Home do not come cheaply, and their price is often set in something other than twisted rings," Beowulf mused. "Yet I would give every grain of gold in my keeping to see our fields growing high and our storehouses filled again and every drop of blood in my body as well, if it is asked for."

A black thought came to him then, though he turned from it with fear and horror, as he would not have turned even from a draug rising dark from its barrow. For he had heard that such famines often called for atheling blood to end them and he knew that there were many folk in his burg who would rather tie clumsy young Wiglaf upon the holy stone than see the gift of a king who was still strong; the wisdom of that rede could not be gainsaid by any cold counsel. Yet that shall not happen: if such a geld is asked, it is mine alone to pay, Beowulf said firmly to himself. The ship from God Home sailed around Whales' Ness on a gray afternoon, its white sails dulled by the driving rain.

The sea mews cried and yammered in greeting, rising from the cliff in a great cloud as though startled by something below. Beowulf stood on the strand to meet the hof folk, dressed in his finest clothes. Waiting for the little boat to bear its first passengers to shore, the Geat king felt an unease such as he had not felt before any living man or woman for many years. He who had slain Grendel, who had guested with all the tale famed kings of the Northlands in his day and was not counted the least among their number. He did not know how he should speak to the gudhes and gudhijas who were coming to him, or how best to ask their aid for his land.

Two sturdy men in green cloaks and moss red trousers climbed out of the boat when it grounded on the sand, pulling it up past the frothy edge of the rising water. One of them then got back in to carefully lift the old woman swathed in pale blue who still sat in the vessel over the small craft's edge, the other receiving her and setting her down gently on the beach. The helper in the boat put her swan carved staff into her hand, the golden plates that hung on threads all about its crown like offerings on a blessing tree jingling quietly. The ancient gudhija's back was bent with age; she had to tilt her head a long way back to look up into Beowulf's eyes, her heaven blue hood with its white fur lining slipping away from her thin gray hair. Then, though her rain wet face was wrinkled like a fruit so long dried that no one could tell from what tree it had grown, it seemed to Beowulf that he knew that gaze.

"Wealhtheow?" He said wonderingly. "I had not thought that you could yet live!"

"Yrse lives yet, and she is older than I," Wealhtheow answered, her cracking voice soft as the wind rustling through dried leaves. "We have lingered, we women of the Scyldings. You have borne your years better than I. I had awaited a man near as withered as myself, not one who could have lately passed his fiftieth winter."

"My bones feel far older than your words would have them," Beowulf sighed. "But it is good to know that one other lives who remembers Hrothgar and Heorot, that are but names in song to all around me. Come, this is no weather for us to be standing out. Let me help you up the path, and I shall give you what greeting I can when we are inside."

Wealhtheow's arm was twig light on Beowulf's: there was little left of the sturdy woman who had borne Hrothgar three bairns and held the queenship over his haunted hall. Beowulf could not read the rune carved on her staff, for the staves twined in and out among the twisted necks and wings of the carved swans, yet he found the angular lines oddly easing to look at, soothing away his fear and care like a strong draught of ale mixed with sun wort. When Wealhtheow was seated, Byrhthild brought her a blue green glass beaker filled with the last drops of strong fruit beer in the burg, that they had been saving back for such a guest. The old woman sipped at the drink, smiling softly as if the scent of its sweetness brought thoughts of fairer and younger summers to her.

"May blessings be poured out upon this hall, where you give freely of what is left to you!" Wealhtheow said. "I need not ask of your sorrows: your thane told me all. And already I have rede for you. Frea Ing has withdrawn, as is sometimes his way. Yet your luck, Beowulf, is still strong. Thus you must ride about your lands in Frea Ing's wain, bearing blessing where you go: ale to the fields, embraces to the earth, and warding against the eoten stones falling cold from the sky.

Beyond that, my sight would stretch no farther: therefore I undertook this faring myself, though I had not set foot from the hallowed holm since I saw you last, for it is in my mind that you shall need spae speech again before this working is at an end."

Beowulf thought of how she had beseeched him for her sons' sake for all his good will, that had come to nothing. Now Wealhtheow had taken up a wider motherhood, and would bid the gods aid as she had once bidden him: might they be better able to help in her need than he had!

"I thank you, for myself and for all the Geatish folk," Beowulf replied. "It was both brave and kind of you to fare so, though the sea is not gentle to old bones. You are no less worthy a queen now than you were in Heorot, when you ruled over wide lands."

Wealhtheow nodded with quiet sureness a woman of her age, who held the foremost place among the gudhijas of the hof at God Home, needed no false humbleness of speech.

"Ready yourself for your wain riding as swiftly as you may, Beowulf, for you have a long way to go before you come back at last to the Geats' white stone."

Wiglaf stood by the gates of Beowulf's burg, watching as the wain from God Home bore the king out. Beowulf rode in the middle of the procession. His great body was swathed in a golden tunic, red trousers, and spring green cloak, and gold glittered from his sleeve buttons and cloak brooch, the wire woven trim of his tunic and the metal mountings of his belt. The king wore no byrnie, nor any sword; he had even put aside the long Finnish sax that he always wore, for no weapon could be borne on Frea Ing's frith faring.

Though that is little to Beowulf, Wiglaf thought, staring admiringly up at his aged cousin. The king's hair was still as brown and thick as a young man's, held back by a ring of twisted wire, and his brown beard flowed freely over his massive chest men said that Beowulf had eoten blood in his veins, and was long lived thereby. The old Waegmunding's eyes shone green as sunlit water from beneath his shaggy brows; in his hand he held an apple branch in full flower adorned with bright ribbons and the speckled blue shells of gulls' eggs that had been blown out and hung on lengths of thread from the blossoming twigs.

The dark oaken sides of the wain in which Beowulf rode were carved with the twining shapes of long necked horses and curly tusked boars and high horned oxen; and the bristle graven heads of boars jutted forth from its four corners, shining with a thin layer of gold laid over the hard wood. The manes and tails of the golden horses that drew the wain were plaited into many little braids, adorned with jingling bells and with woven silk ribbons of red and gold and green, and their bridle rangles rang, not with rings of bronze, but with figure pressed gold plates like those that hung from the staff of the old gudhija who rode in the wain with Beowulf was she really that Wealhtheow who had been wedded to Hrothgar in early days?

That seemed as strange to hear as if Beowulf had greeted an ancient wanderer as Sigemund the Walsing or Halga Hunding's Bane. The younger women from God Home walked before the wain, their heads hidden with the masks of falcon and wild sow; some of them bore burning lamps, lifting the black fire cups high on their twisted iron stalks, while others carried staves carven into the shapes of spear headed wyrms. By them, barefoot and green clad, danced the gudhes of Frea Ing, their long beribboned hair streaming down their backs as they shook their gilded rangles and beat upon little drums, singing a joyous chant as they swayed and twisted and bent their bodies sinuously. Half of Beowulf's thanes rode behind, though they, too, went without weapon and unarmed for this frith faring, Wiglaf thought somehow that they might find a way to ward their king at need.

Before the wain and that was bitter for Wiglaf to look on! Rode Aldhelm, holding a green banner wrought with golden ring and sheaf high above his shining blond head and smiling with pride in the knowledge of what stead the king must mean to set him, having chosen him to bear the frith standard in this holy faring. All seemed to have begun well, for the rain had passed, leaving mild blue skies behind, and the air was warm with the first breath of summer if it would hold; Wiglaf, like most folk, found that he had lost his trust in good weather over the last two years.

Aldhelm's blue gaze met Wiglaf's, and though his face was not very clear to Wiglaf's sight from where he rode, the Waegmunding thought that his tormentor smiled more widely. Wiglaf did not look away, but he closed his teeth tightly on the inside of his lip: he would not let the other's gloating, or his own hate, ill wish Beowulf's faring in Frea Ing's wain. Yet he ached inwardly Beowulf had not even asked him if he wished to go with them on the long way about the Geats' land.

Had the king not said a few kind words of farewell to Wiglaf before going forward to make his first offering at the white stone, Wiglaf would think Beowulf had forgotten that his kinsman still dwelt in his burg. The wain rolled on in the sunlight; the sounds of song and drum and ringing bells faded slowly as Frea Ing's frith train danced down the road. Wiglaf stood and watched until the procession was a single blur of color against the spreading brown of the sparse sprouted fields and he could no longer hear the music of its going.

"It is not easy to be left behind, is it?" Ingemund said softly behind him.

Wiglaf turned to look down into the old gudhe's face. Ingemund had always been thin, but the scant rations had left him gaunt, his cheekbones jutting out over his hollowed cheeks and the gray waves of his beard like twin wind eaten cliff arches. The right sleeve of his blue tunic fell in loose folds over the gudhe's withered arm, which he held close in to his chest as though it pained him.

"It is not," Wiglaf muttered.

He did not like what he saw in Ingemund's blue eyes: it seemed to him that the old man pitied him, and that grated against his nerves like a rock scraping his bare skin bloody.

"Though it be hard, I would give you rede to hold to your hope," Ingemund told him.

"It seems to me that there is more in this matter than even the woman of God Home can know, and there is no telling what need may give you a chance to find your mettle if you have truly gotten more from your father than shining war gear to show off within the hall when thanes speak over their ale."

Ingemund walked off without another word, leaving Wiglaf no more joyful nor easier in his mind than he had been before. The Moon had been new when the king set off on its faring; now his sharp silver crescent had waxed to a full round, and still the weather around Beowulf's burg held fair. The fields began to sprout green in earnest, and Wiglaf could sense a wary air of hope among thanes and thralls alike, though it was seldom that he could glance about the garth without seeing someone cocking a worried look at the heavens.

Though his spoon was of silver and his bowl was oak carved by a skillful hand with the shapes of twining beasts, there was no more for Wiglaf to eat that night than a scanty helping of leek stew with a bit of smoked swine flesh in it and a little hard bread though he was as well fed as anyone in the hall: even if the weather did not turn again, it would be some time before the new fruitfulness of the land showed on the king's board. Wiglaf sat moodily chasing one of the scraps of meat about with his spoon when a man came hastening in with something large and gleaming in his hand.

"Look at this!" He cried. By the voice, Wiglaf recognized Waerferth one of Beowulf's older thanes, who had stayed behind to ward the king's burg while its ruler was gone. "That thrall Raganwald, the worst I ever bought for all his dreaming when he should be working, and wandering off on wild pathways when there were tasks to hand, he has proven more than his worth now!"

Wiglaf heard the gasps from the others who looked on what Waerferth held, and, half against his will, he got to his feet and moved close enough to see. The thane's calloused hand cupped the bottom of a bowl of pure fine gold, finely shaped and ridged, with a ringed handle that ended in a horse's head. It was a treasure as fine as any that had ever passed through the hands of the Geat king likely in the whole of his fifty years of rule, Wiglaf thought.

"How did this come to you?" Hereberht of an age with Wiglaf, but ever bolder to put himself forward asked.

"Yesterday Raganwald was to muck out a cattle stall, but instead of lifting shovel and bending back, he wandered off again, maybe to chase some alf spoor, I do not know what dreams are in his head. So I cut a birch branch, for I meant to strike him soundly enough that he would put his madness by and settle to work. He got wind of what was in my mind and ran off, and I had more to do than chase after him: with food so scarce, such a thrall is scant loss. I put him from my thoughts and just now, he came knocking on the door of my house with this in his hand, and asked, 'Does this buy me off from the birching?'"

"Where did he get it?" Wiglaf asked. He had never seen workmanship of such a style, though the Geats had traded far and wide all the frith full years of Beowulf's rule.

It seemed to him that there was a strange sheen to the burnished gold, as though a thin film of whale oil lay over the cup, shimmering rainbows in the torchlight when he did not look straight at it.

"He said that he found it down deep in the earth, among the hidden roots of a cave. Some warrior or frowe, maybe fleeing from a foe, must have set it there once, I think," Waerferth added thoughtfully, running his thumb over the smooth curve of the gold, "that it must be very old. I shall keep a close eye on Raganwald hereafter. I would not be amazed at all if he had found other treasures that he is keeping hidden."

For two days, Waerferth's cup was the talk of Beowulf's burg. The thane did not seem to tire of showing it off: he cradled the gold vessel close to his chest, or held it out by the handle so that rings of light glimmered from the ridges around its polished sides. He made Raganwald tell his tale again and again, listening carefully as though he hoped the thrall would let something new slip in one telling. Raganwald was a smallish man, gaunt from hunger as they all were, with thinning silver gray hair. Though Wiglaf had little marked him before, once seen, his face was easy to remember, with a large eagle nose and deep set eyes beneath shaggy silver eyebrows.

Raganwald wore a long stemmed wooden Hammer about his neck, and he had the strong accent of a Saxon from the British shores Waerferth had bought him off a trading ship. He told his story well how he had crept down the cliff path by Eagles' Ness with the surf beating below him, seeking a safe haven from his master's wrath; how he had seen the dark mouth of a sea cave gaping among the rocks, and crept in, seeking to find the depths' roots and, maybe, a place to sleep safe, for he had been awake and shivering outside the garth's walls all the night before. And there, Raganwald said, he had seen the cup gleaming in the darkness, and it was so fair that he thought Waerferth must take it as geld for any wrath he had roused.

"Your thrall is of more worth as a tale spinner than a cleaner of byres," Ingemund said dryly to Waerferth.

"Aye, he often sits thinking up such things, or muttering over verses, when he should be working," Waerferth growled. "But I did not buy him in order that he should tell stories while I hew wood." He stroked the gleaming gold of the horse headed handle. "Still, he has earned the right to sit and think for a little while, I suppose."

On the evening of the third day after Raganwald had brought the cup to his master, Wiglaf had been training with blunted swords all afternoon. Still weighted by his byrnie, with his father's blade slung over his shoulder again, Wiglaf loosed his chin strap and pushed his helm back to wipe the sweat from his dripping forehead.

"You were fighting better this day," his mother told him, handing him a horn of cool water. Wiglaf drank deeply, but did not bother to say anything: he knew how hope and short sight could deceive the eyes.

As Wiglaf lowered the horn, it chanced that he was looking west towards the sea: and the sunset's red light flared up in a blaze of red gold that dazzled his blurry sight. He gasped, his hands flying to his blinded eyes. The brightness blazed behind his lids, flashing in his gaze as he opened them again.

All the hounds in the garth had begun to howl, a bone chilling harmony that sent shivers up Wiglaf's back.

"What was that?" Byrhthild said sharply. "What…is it raiders setting fire to the fields? But…"

Wiglaf hardly heeded his mother, and her next words were lost under the deep roar that rose louder and louder until it seemed to shake the earth beneath his feet. Then he did not know afterwards how those longer sighted than he had borne it he saw the thing of awe and wonder, of might born beyond the Middle Garth. West and a little north, from where the old barrow mound stood on the height of Eagles' Ness, the fiery shape soared upward against the pale flush of the evening sky, bright as red glowing gold flowing molten beneath a jewel caster's bellows. It twined through the sky. It was like a wyrm, but wings bore it aloft; it clawed at the air with shining talons, and when it roared again, Wiglaf saw the flames shooting from its mouth, more eye searingly bright than the heart of any great bale fire.

Like all those around him, Wiglaf stood flat footed on the earth, staring up at the wyrm as it circled above the sea, then arrowed straight towards Beowulf's burg. It flew swift as a falcon, the hot wind of its wings blasting over the garth even as it passed Whales' Ness. Caught between open mouthed awe and bowel loosing terror, Wiglaf did not move until the broad wooden gateposts of the garth flared up under the wyrm's breath like tallow dripping into a fire, and then it was almost too late. Grabbing his mother's arm as she stared at the great glowing shape bearing down on them, Wiglaf flung himself to the side and down, yanking Byrhthild with him. Weighted by his byrnie, he fell hard; the ring pommel of his father's sword ground into his ribs, though he hardly notice. His byrnie scorched hot through the thick felted tunic under it; the wyrm's roar deafened his ears, so that the crackling of flames and the sound of screams seemed faint and far off.

Its lashing tail buffeting the ground below with gusts of forge hot air, the winged wyrm skimmed swiftly over the far wall of the garth. Behind it, the fire was already leaping high from the roof of Beowulf's hall and the palisade to either side of the open gate, black smoke streaming up into the pale sky. Folk were running everywhere like wasps from a sundered nest, men shouting for their weapons and women crying for their children; Wiglaf heard the terrible sound of horses screaming, the fierce drum of hooves battering at stable doors. One woman, hair and clothes afire, rolled and rolled on the ground as she screamed and beat at herself with blackening hands; others, men and women, writhed and moaned on the scorched earth, and a few charred shapes already lay still.

The smell of roasting meat filled the air, horribly hunger rousing, but gratefully, Wiglaf had no time to think on such things. The dragon banked, soaring back towards Beowulf's burg like a great red gold oak leaf floating on the first winter winds. Wiglaf heard its hiss as its long snout opened, fanged jaw dropping in a glowing gape of fire to melt the far side of the palisade in a single brilliant burst and he saw its eyes, clear as berg crystals with blue howe fires burning cold in their shining depths. This time it was Byrhthild who dragged her son away, breaking the dragon's gaze; but Wiglaf could not keep from looking back over his shoulder.

Mad old Hlewabrandar had found a shield and sword somewhere; Wiglaf heard his cracked voice shouting,

"Come on, Ingling! I fear you no more dead than living!"

The wyrm hissed again, and its fire spewed onto the poet from above. With the last memory of his war days, Hlewabrandar held his shield above his head, but it flared and was gone in one swift flash, the burning wood shards showering onto the trodden earth around him and the flames still burned high from his flesh as he staggered blind to the ground and lay twitching silently, his body feeding its own bale fire. Around and around the great wyrm circled, kindling store huts and houses, byres and stables, with each pass, and searing whoever chanced to be beneath its furious path.

Wiglaf's lungs rasped raw with burning smoke, his eyes tearing so painfully that he could hardly see where he was stumbling; it was luck alone that kept him from the dragon's way. At last it leapt high into the air, a writhing golden brand against the deepening blue sky; its last anguished roar drowned the roaring of the fires that burned all through Beowulf's burg, and it soared away.

All that night, Wiglaf struggled bitterly with the rest of those who had lived whole through the dreadful fiery wrecking of the Geat king's garth carrying those who still writhed and moaned beneath oozing red burns away from the blazing buildings, running back and forth to well and stream for water, aiding Ingemund in his search for every scrap of cloth still unburnt to use as bandages, and, more grimly, keeping the flesh hungry hounds and swine away from the mound of charred corpses, though the scent of roasted meat was almost maddening even to the men who kicked and struck at the beasts nosing close to the dead.

Little could be saved from the houses: from the king's high seat to the smallest thrall child's wooden doll, that which the Geats owned had melted into glowing coals and ash. Only iron was not wholly wrecked: though byrnies had glowed red hot and the temper of many weapons was ruined, the sword metal alone had not failed beneath the dragon's breath. As the dawn light strengthened, showing the ruined heaps of black and smoking wood where once hall and houses had stood and the great flat swathes of char across the garth's low grassed earth, Wiglaf straightened wearily, pushing his sweat soaked hair back with a sooty hand.

"Have you any strength left in you?" Ingemund asked hoarsely as he walked up to the young Waegmunding. The gudhe's gray beard was singed black in patches where sparks had caught in it, and an angry red burn the size of a hazelnut marred his wrinkled forehead.

"If something more must be done, I shall try my best," Wiglaf answered, though his bones trembled with tiredness and he felt as though he could not lift so much as a stick of wood.

"Our king must know what has passed here, as soon as may be. You are his kinsman: it is your right to bear these tidings, if you are able to ride."

It seemed to Wiglaf that a new surge of strength flowed into him, humming through his limbs like a swarm of bees. It was the part of a man to be trusted with such news; it was the part of an atheling, of the only kinsman of the king.

He wanted to run straight away to the field where his horse was pastured praise Frea Ing, his steed had not been in the stables when the wyrm came!

"Beowulf must know swiftly," Wiglaf said, though it seemed to him that he tore each word from his heart by the roots. "Hereberht, too, is unscathed, and he is a far better rider than I, with a horse that can outstrip mine easily. I thank you for asking me first, but..."

"Your first thought is for how what should be done can best be brought about. I understand, indeed. I shall send Hereberht."

Byrhthild knelt by a small child whose hair had been seared away, red cracks glistening through the blackened ruin of his face and soft pitiful moans bubbling from the gaping mess where his mouth had been. She closed her tilted blue eyes, tears washing clean streaks down her sooty cheeks, and drew her belt knife. Wiglaf waited until she was done.

"I did not know how badly he was scathed until it grew light," his mother said.

She picked up the little body bloody now, as well as scorched, and they walked together to where the corpses lay heaped upon each other. She looked at the dead for a long time in the growing brightness of the dawn. A few could still be known.

"How is it that the gods have turned against us so?" Byrhthild asked.

Wiglaf could not answer and indeed, she was not looking at him, but gazing eastward where the streaks of pale sunrise yellow seeped through the lightening blue sky.

"Did we not make offerings, and do all that we should? Our king has never done ill to god nor alf nor man the Inglings were far more steeped in blood and shame than he, and yet no such horror has ever risen from beneath the Uppsala howes; nor did the flying troll wight that harried Hrothulf Crycc thus set fire to hall and hold."

The only thing Wiglaf could think of to say was,

"We had best find somewhere to go, and some way to get the wounded under shelter away from here. If the wyrm comes back this night, it will be able to burn us down as easily as slaying a stunned ox."

Byrhthild winced, but the wild look was gone from her eyes. She ran her hands through her disheveled hair, leaving black streaks of soot through its dark gold.

"You are right, my son. Let us speak with Ingemund. If we scatter through the farmhouses, but the wains were burnt with everything else…"

Beowulf rode ahead of the broken frith train, a storm of sorrow and wrath raging within his breast. He wore his byrnie again, his sword hanging at his left side and the sax Paanja had given him at his right the Geats' war gear had traveled, though wrapped and covered so as not to anger the god, in a wain behind the folk of Frea Ing's faring, in case some other should seek to break the frith rite. He had not wanted to believe the tale Hereberht brought but the young man had wholly spent himself to reach his king with all speed.

His ruddy hair and clothes had still been besmirched with soot, stinking of smoke, for he had not halted to wash himself or change his tunic; and looking into Hereberht's hazel eyes, Beowulf had seen that horror he had witnessed, its shadow mirrored back to Beowulf's sight as the youth struggled for a way to put what had happened into words. How did this happen? Beowulf asked himself desperately as his bay gelding paced smoothly along.

What roused the wyrm, after all these years? Ansuwulf had spoken of the old barrow's hidden dweller: Long it sleeps, and stirs only when great things ripple in the well of Wyrd what was turning in that well to trouble the roots of the world? And why had Frea Ing and the Frowe so broken troth with him, that his high seat had melted beneath the wyrm's flame and his folk been burned living outside their homes as no raider band or Swedish host could have done? The warm light of the Sun and mild blue sky seemed a mockery when Beowulf thought on the fiery wrecking of the Geat king's garth: why had the gods offered hope of harvest after long hunger, only to bring forth the wyrm that would sear the grain in the shoot?

"Yet," Beowulf said fiercely to himself, "no man can lift sword to better a bad harvest but I can still fight the wyrm."

Hereberht had spoken of how Hlewabrandar had died, brave even in the wavering leavings of his mind of his shield shattering in the flame that ate through wood and fastened on flesh in one great gout of brightness. The iron of his byrnie had not melted, though the dragon's fire burned hotter than any bale flames. Remember that fire is the bane of trees, but the burgs of the eotens are bound with iron. So Hygd had spoken to him on the shore of her death faring, and Beowulf had thought that she was raving with the alf fire again. He needed no racking of his brains to remember her other words, for he had whispered them to himself in the night over and over again, clinging to them as an orphaned child might cling to a rag doll.

I think you must keep byrnie and blade close by you, for not all foes will grasp you as Grendel did, nor may you deal with all as you dealt with Dagochramn.

"O Hygd, did you guess then what I must face now?" He murmured. "I would that you were beside me still, yet I am glad that you did not have to thole this sorrow at the end of your years."

The folk of Beowulf's burg had scattered to farmsteads all around the ruined stead of the king's garth. Ingemund, and those of Beowulf's thanes who had not died under the wyrm's burning breath, had made their way to the home of one Burgred, a carle who had been wealthy three years ago and, through careful husbanding of his wealth, had suffered less from the bad harvests than most of those around them.

Beowulf and the rest of his war band met his men there, riding into the little garth ringed by Burgred's house and barn, dairy and storage huts. On his arm, to grow used to its weight and movement, Beowulf bore a great shield of iron he had sent a swifter rider ahead of himself, and Beornmod the smith had worked day and night to have that warding round ready for his king. He marked how the warriors standing about the farmer's yard stared at the shield: the eyes of some were wide with wonder, but others smiled, as though they had been sure of what their king would do.

Beowulf dismounted, greeting each of his men and running over in thought the names of those who were not there: no single raider band had taken so great a toll from those best and highest born warriors of the Geats' host as had the wyrm. But that would matter little. Battling a wight from beyond the Middle Garth would not call for a swine array, nor any flanking strikes of a wisely ordered army; he would not seek out the far flier with all his war band, nor with a great host.

"Each of you, tell me all you saw and know of the wyrm," Beowulf said.

One by one, stumbling for words, his men told him what they had seen. Most of them guessed that it was the length of his hall from snout to tail tip; they all agreed that it had swept in as fast as a stooping falcon. A few said that the wyrm's belly had near grazed the ground, but the others swore that it had never come within a spear's length of the earth, and everyone was sure that it had hovered above the burning hall roof when it spat down the fire that had eaten Hlewabrandar.

"Its eyes were ice," Wiglaf said suddenly. "I mean…like berg crystals, and there was a blue light in them. I would have stood staring at them until it burned me down if my mother had not pulled me away," he added, his tilted eyes dropping and cheekbones reddening with shame. Someone made a muffled sound, but Beowulf gave that no mind. "And it hissed just before it flamed," the young Waegmunding added. "When its mouth opened, a noise like fat crackling in the fire."

"Were there any signs before it came?" Beowulf asked, still wondering, as he had for days, what might have stirred it. "Did the earth tremble? Ingemund, did you dream?"

"No, but there is a tale which I think shall answer your question," the gudhe said grimly. "Waerferth, fetch out your thrall, and show the king your cup."

When the stocky thane came back, a small gray haired man in a tattered brown tunic was following him, but Beowulf's eye went at once to what Waerferth held. A bowl of thin beaten gold, fine and well wrought, its handle coiled about with gold wire and tipped with a horse's head, it seemed to Beowulf that he had seen its like before, though he could not say where. Still, it was most fair to see, and Waerferth caressed its smooth sides almost with the proud love of a skilled maker.

"Raganwald, tell your tale," the thane said before Beowulf asked if he could hold the cup.

Beowulf listened to the thrall's accented voice with a growing awareness of foreboding, as Raganwald told of going up into the crevasse of the rocky sea wall.

"...I saw the cup on a stone," the thrall said. Then he fell silent, and Beowulf guessed that there was something hidden in his mind.

"None shall hurt you if you speak the truth now," Beowulf said. "You have my oath on it."

Raganwald met Beowulf's stare, and it seemed that he meant to squirm, but could not turn away from the king's gaze. At last, still looking into Beowulf's eyes, he said,

"I saw the wyrm. The great golden wyrm, coiled in the darkness the cold howe fires danced over all the gold, rings and rondels and well wrought sword hilts. It slept, and I stared at it, for it was fair and terrible beyond bearing." Raganwald's deep set eyes shone with awe as he spoke, and for a moment it seemed to Beowulf that he saw in the gray haired Saxon's soul a yearning that over matched his bravery. "Then I thought that it stirred, and I was seized by fear," the hoard thief confessed sadly. "I caught up the cup, and fled back down the dark passage and out into the light of day. And I brought the cup to my master to buy myself free of the beating he had promised me."

"We have paid a grievous geld for such a small thing," Beowulf murmured. "Yet I cannot say that you are at fault, for I think that this wyrd was shaped before: you were merely the twig of its casting. You shall do one more service, and then have your freedom in payment."

"What is that, my king?" Raganwald asked nervously.

"You shall show me the way to this sea cave below Eagles' Ness, for I alone shall dare the wyrm's bale and if Frea and Frowe uphold me, I shall win vengeance for our fire slain men and flame eaten home."

"Thus speaks Beowulf Grendel's Bane!" Aldhelm declared. "My king, I would go with you, and so would many of your troop." His short golden beard jutted forward bravely beneath the silver inlaid nose piece of his helmet, and his blue eyes shone bright and eager in the battle mask's gilded rings.

"I would go as well," said Hereberht, and the rest of Aldhelm's friends were quick to speak up with him. Beowulf little liked the thought of bringing these youths some of them unblooded, or nearly so into such peril, but he could not deny that the words came from bold hearts. And if Aldhelm is to be king after me, shall not Wyrd spare him? Let Fro and Frowe choose whom they would have, even in the fire.

"At least you shall go to the barrow with me, though I seek the wyrm's inner hall alone," Beowulf told them at last. "The eleven of you may come and that, maybe, will be a band to remember in fame."

At first Beowulf did not notice Wiglaf's mumbling, but after a few moments his kinsman pushed clumsily through the young men who stood proud in the king's regard.

"I would go too," Wiglaf stammered. "As you loved my father, my king, I bid you not deny me this."

Beowulf looked down at the youthful Waegmunding not so far down as at other men: when Wiglaf was not slumped over or hunching his shoulders, he was as tall as his father had been, less than a head shorter than Beowulf himself. For once Wiglaf stood straight backed, his byrnie hanging down from his shoulders and his hand on the sword slung across his body.

His Finn slanted eyes were open wide, and though his mouth trembled as though it had taken all his strength to speak those words, his clean shaven features were set in firm resolution. Beowulf felt an unexpected stab of love for his cousin's son: thin and ungainly as the youth was, at least he would prove himself to the eyes of others as no coward. If all went as Beowulf hoped, though Wiglaf showed his bravery by asking to come with his king, there would be little chance that he would have to near the wyrm.

"Aye," said Beowulf. "Though you are young, I saw war storms in my own youth, and times of battle."

Seven winters old when his father brought him to Hrethel's hall. Beowulf remembered clearly yet how it had been. And he had not forgotten Hrethel's sorrow over Herebeald, nor the red slaughters around Hroesnabeorh.

"I repaid those treasures Hygelac gave me well in battle with lighting sword. So to the end of life age I shall serve my cause, while this sword tholes it. Now shall weapon's edge, hand and hard sword, war over the hoard! I sought battles in youth, and as folk's wise warder I shall seek danger yet. I would not bear sword, weapon to wyrm, if I knew how otherwise I could battle with that wight, grip against grip, as I did with Grendel. But here, I ween to meet war fire's hate, breath and bale for that I have put on board and byrnie. Nor shall I set one foot from the barrow's ward, but we shall find out at its wall what wyrd the Measurer of Men has bestowed on each of us."

Beowulf embraced his older thanes then, and each spoke a few words of luck to him. Last he turned to Ingemund.

"My time for giving you redes is done, I think," said the gudhe. "Will you let me come with you, to bear your sig standard as I did in the days of my youth since Hildegeard is no longer here to say me nay?" He added with the ghost of a sad smile.

"I think not, old friend," Beowulf told him regretfully. "That battle sign bears might into the Middle Garth, but it is no living wight I must face now. Keep it for those sakes it was meant to serve."

Ingemund nodded, and Beowulf knew that he understood. Beowulf, his twelve young thanes, and the thrall Raganwald rode past the wreck of the Geat king's garth. A few bits of the hall were still smoldering, tiny curls of smoke wisping up from the charred ruin. Ingemund had told him that they had finished burning the bodies of the dead outside of what had been the palisade, but Beowulf could not tell which of the great black scorched spots on the grass had been the bone fire heaped by men and which marked the dropping of the dragon's hate.

Looking at the woods beyond where his burg had stood, Beowulf saw that the wyrm had burned there as well, clearings and trails of sooty stumps marking its passage had it dared sear the holy grove and blacken the white stone? Beowulf could not see so far from the road. At the edge of the half burnt wood, they got off their horses, hitching the steeds loosely to tree limbs. Beowulf guessed that the horses could break their halters if they were frightened enough: the wyrm's roar might startle them into flight, and the Geats have a weary walk back if they lived but if all went ill, then at least the good steeds would have a hope of fleeing.

Walking behind Raganwald, Beowulf led the thanes along the cliff track that led up to the old barrow on Eagles' Ness. The tide was coming in, the sunlit waves curling up to crash over the big rocks of the strand in high sprays of foam. The thrall glanced down over the crags only once, his face going even paler. Although a brisk cool sea wind blew over the cliffs, droplets of sweat beaded at the edge of Raganwald's thinning silver hair, and Beowulf could see his legs shaking. Nor was he the only one who marked the thrall's fear; one of the young men behind said softly,

"Not so rashly bold now, are you?"

"Hush," Aldhelm hissed. "We are nearing the barrow."

The wyrm's mound loomed tall and green above the headland, the hoary stone at its crest standing out dark against the blue sky. At Beowulf's silent gesture, the band walked wide of it Beowulf knew that if once his foe gained the air, they would be lost, and he did not wish to warn it that they were there until he was ready to do battle. Now, if Beowulf's hopes held true, the young thanes' part was done save for such witnessing as they might do from the stead where he would have them wait.

"Bide here by the barrow, my byrnied host, warriors in war gear," Beowulf whispered. "You shall see which may best thole his wounds after the battle storm of us two. It is not your part, nor that of any man save I myself, to deal in matching might with this troll. With strength I shall win that gold, or battle shall take your bold frea with life bale!"

Every one of the youths had his hand on his sword, their eyes gleaming with eagerness save for Wiglaf. His face was almost as pale as Raganwald's, and he was staring at Beowulf with a look that might have been either sorrow or fear something in the slight tilt of his blue eyes made his thoughts hard to read. Is it for himself he worries? Beowulf wondered. Or for me? Though the thrall was trembling so hard that he could hardly stand, he led Beowulf down the steep path on the other side of the headland. For the first time in Beowulf's lifetime, though it would be nesting season before too much longer, there were no gulls or terns swooping between the green headland and the deep blue water far below, and no sound of seabirds shrieking.

That little thing the rhythmic crashing of the surf with no harsh high seamews' cries above it seemed somehow as foreboding to Beowulf as all the ruins of his garth. They threaded their way between crags and ledges. When they reached the base of the cliff, Beowulf was breathing hard and Raganwald's legs were not the only ones shaking. I am growing old but there shall be no running in this battle. As the next wave crashed in, a thin stream of water flowed swiftly beneath the great boulders to splash up against the cliff's edge, running out just as fast. Beowulf wondered if he would have to swim to get through to the wyrm's underground stronghold, he would have to go speedily, in any case, if Raganwald was to have a chance to get away before the tide forced him into the barrow as well. The two men made their way over the rocks; though Beowulf tried to keep his shield high, every so often its rim clanged against a stone like an iron bell, and Raganwald would start in terror, looking wildly up from strand to howe mound.

"Here it is," whispered the thrall, pointing down from the rock on which he stood. The sea was already ankle deep over the little stretch of sand; Beowulf splashed down, the cold water soaking into his shoes. "There you see that crack in the cliff wall?"

At first Beowulf did not see it, but Raganwald, now twitching and dancing in his haste to be away, grasped his shoulder and moved him a step sideways. Then Beowulf saw the narrow dark gap between the crags.

"Go!" He said. "You are free now."

Raganwald hastened away, now leaping over the boulders, now half crawling. Though the water was creeping speedily up over his calves, Beowulf waited until the thrall had gained the pathway up before stepping forward. As he waded towards the doorway into the headland, Beowulf's ribs suddenly tightened with heart crushing sadness. Ansuwulf's sorrowful staves echoed in his mind: Battle death took them, greedy life bale bore off each of them…Who are the sword bearers, or polishers of gold goblets adorned, dear drink vessels?

Vanished, that host. Nor may byrnie's rings widely with battle's wielders fare, by heroes' side. No harp sound's joy, the glee wood singing, nor good hawk any flies through hall, nor horse swift running tramples through burg yard. Baleful death so very many sent forth of my kin. It seemed to Beowulf then that those words were his own thoughts. Of all the youths who had played at wooden swords under Ansuwulf's eye, he alone walked the grass where they had run; of Hrethel's kin, there was none living save Beowulf.

Hrethel and Herebeald, Haethcyn, Hygelac and Heardred they were gone, and now no glad voices would ever sound again in the Hrethlings' hall; rain would soak the smoking ruins until the last piece of charred wood fell to mold and rot, and none would know where the Geats' high seat had stood. Hygd's fairness was lost to the earth, with no line of daughters to shadow it forth as Hildegeard had done; Wihstan, too, lay in his howe, his jesting words stilled forever. Beowulf stepped into the darkness beneath the hoary stone, the cold sea lapping about his feet.

He thought that it would be easy to lie down: the barrow was readied, awaiting only his bones. Yet deep within, though all his soul seemed to wither with winter rime, Beowulf felt a tiny kernel of warmth, like a single grain of barley striving to put out shoot and root. The seed sleeps in the mound, he thought, and he did not know whether those words were his own or another's. His heart had held out through the icy waters, and not failed him when he was far from light and air. He took another step in the blackness, and another, and another. It was not long before Beowulf realized that he was no longer splashing through ankle deep seawater: the passage beneath the cliff was turning upward. He drew his sword, holding it warily before him.

Then it seemed to him that he could see the lightless blue glimmer gathering in the darkness over the gold on his sword's guard and the ring upon his wrist, the howe fire beginning to burn. Beowulf climbed further up, the rock carved passageway growing steep beneath his feet. Then, before him, he saw the blue flames writhing and dancing; and though they cast no light, yet he could see the treasures heaped beneath them. King for fifty winters, and king's kinsman before that, Beowulf had never thought that the world could hold so much wrought gold.

He saw cups like the one Raganwald had brought his master, ornamented with delicately stamped patterns; he saw cunningly woven chains looping and twining about each other; heaps of rings piled on rings, arm rings and neck rings that an eoten might have worn, finger rings small enough to fit the least girl child, and every size and shape between thick twisted wires, solid bars bent into circles, cuffs wrought with fine cast adornment, though rust had gnawed the blades of the piled swords and rot had eaten their hilts, the gold still shone bright on their pommels and guards, gleaming from the age crumbling metal of the helms set to watch over the war gear. Beowulf bent forward, thinking to touch the smooth shining gold that lay tumbled before him.

Again, though, the rim of his great shield clanged on the rock, the shuddering echo of that sound ringing all through the gold as though the room were a single bell and in answer, he heard the deep throated hiss of anger. He could not tell where the sound had come from; it seemed to crackle through the air all around him. Gripping sword and shield firmly, Beowulf went on, ready at any minute to crouch behind his own burg of iron. Then he saw the glimmer of light from above: not the hoarfrost gleam of cold howe fire, nor yet the flare of the fire wyrm's breath, but the clean golden brightness of daylight.

The door of the mound was open and Beowulf realized what the crippling sorrow at the cliff's foot had driven from his mind. Only a man could pass through the narrow gateway even a huge man, true; but though the wyrm might be able to slither through tight places, it could not fold its wings close enough to get through that gap. Beowulf hastened up to the howe door, his breathing echoing loud and harsh from the carven stone archways that skimmed the top of his helmet. There was no sound outside if the wyrm had flown, would he surely not hear something? In any case, if it were out, it would have to slither in to get him; if it were in its mound, he had it trapped.

"Wyrm, come forth!" Beowulf bellowed, his voice resounding under the hoary stone. "You burned my burg: will you face me now?"

If Wiglaf had not told him how the fire snake hissed before giving forth its burning breath, Beowulf might have died then. He heard the faint crackling very like fat in a fire, as his kinsman had said and dropped to crouch behind his wide iron round. The wyrm's roar dinned through the earth, shivering Beowulf's shield in his hand, and his eyelids clenched against the burst of brilliance as the blast of flames struck his heavy forged warding.

Fire sprayed around the shield's edges, but none of it touched Beowulf, though the sweat sprang out at once to soak his tunic and he could smell his woolen helm padding scorching in the heat. Opening his eyes again, Beowulf looked around his shield edge, and saw the wyrm. The scales of the mound warder glowed like gold in the heart of a fire, bright enough to sear flashing after lights across Beowulf's eyes.

Its body was long and sinuous, coiling about itself as it slunk forward on low crouching legs; its glimmering wings were folded against its back, and its sharp taloned feet clawed at the stone. The wyrm's glede fiery head, thrice the length of a man's arm, was narrow and long snouted, pointed ears flaring sharply back above the thick skull ridge that shielded its eyes. Its eyes. Wiglaf had spoken of hoarfrost and berg crystal, and the blue fire burning within. Beowulf met the wyrm's eyes, and saw there a world of ice, rime crystals stretching on and on without end, so that he shivered even in the bale fire heat. Yet something shone in those clear orbs: the pale light that Beowulf had seen glints of in Ongentheow's eyes, and Onela's the corpse light glimmering from rot, the barrow light glimmering from gold; the seed of death in all that lived, sprouting the harvest to be laid up in the storehouse of the howe.

Wiglaf had stood frozen in the wyrm's gaze. Beowulf knew it better than that: had he not shared ale with it all his life, even unknowing? When the fire snake's golden head shot forward, bright fangs springing for his face, Beowulf was ready for it. He took the shock of its thrusting weight on his shield, and though it knocked him back a step, he did not lose his footing: he had that gift from Sweartwulf. He struck with his sword, but the wyrm was swift; his blow glanced off the side of its weaving head, doing no true harm.

The dragon's forefoot snaked out beneath Beowulf's shield, clawing for his leg. He was just able to skip back in time, hewing at the foot; this time, the blade bit, scattering drops of burning blood to sink hissing into the stone. Again and again the wyrm attacked; each time, Beowulf fended it off, but only at the cost of a step or two backwards. At last he stood just outside the howe door with the cliff at his back and there, he knew, he must stand at last, for he had vowed not to stir a foot away from that stead.

The earth above it muffled Beowulf's shout and the dragon's answering roar, but Wiglaf felt its deep ringing through the very soles of his feet. Aldhelm stood calmly waiting how could he, when Beowulf battled beneath the gray stone? And the other young men shuffled from foot to foot, their byrnies making little jingling noises, or moved their shield arms up and down to keep the muscles from wearing out with holding the battle boards long in one position. A tongue of flame licked out of the open howe door, and Wiglaf clenched his fists tight on sword hilt and shield grip, trying to drive from his mind the memory of human flesh charring and splitting like a roast spitted too close to the fire, of rib cages bursting under the searing heat to spill out a stream of scorched and stinking entrails. Not Beowulf! He thought.

The sound of a heavy blow ringing off iron echoed harsh through the mound gate; another deep clang followed close on that, and Wiglaf breathed again. He could see Beowulf fighting in his thoughts, standing staunch against claw and tooth, even as the fires played about his blackened shield. From where he stood, Wiglaf could just see the door into the mound. Flames flickered out once more, pale in the sunlight and then Beowulf stumbled a step backwards towards the cliff, recovered, and braced himself.

A strong enough blow, and the wyrm would send him falling to the rocks beneath but Beowulf crouched slightly, mighty legs ready to drive him forward, and held his sword point first as if to spit the fire snake, should it dart at him again. Aldhelm still stood calm, a faint smile on his lips, and something burst within Wiglaf. He remembered, as he had not in years, how the other boys had left him dangling against the cliff at the bird egging. Now they stood in the same stead, but it was Beowulf himself who needed help and no one was stepping forward to give it.

"I remember at the mead drinking, when we swore to our hlaford who gave us rings in the beer hall that we would repay him in battle," Wiglaf shouted angrily at the others, lashing them with his words like sluggard oxen under the plow man's whip. "He chose us, for he thought us good at spear battle, keen helm bearers though our lord thought to do this deed work alone, for that he had done the most famous deeds of any man. Now that day is come when our drighten needs the help of kinsmen and good battle heroes: let us go to him, help the fight leader when heat and grim terror are on him! The gods know that it would be better to me if the flame should wrap my body with that of my gold giver. It seems wrong to me that we should bear shields to our lands unless we fell our kinsman's foe, and ward the Weather Geats' leader we shall have sig together, with sword and helm, byrnie and battle gear, sharing a shield burg."

"He told us to bide here," Aldhelm said.

Wiglaf saw the burning gold talon streaking out: Beowulf braced his heels against the earth to meet it, but rocked back towards the cliff edge as the glede wyrm's foot boomed off his shield. The Waegmunding spat in Aldhelm's handsome face and ran to Beowulf's side. A wisp of smoke seared up from his wooden shield as he locked it behind his king's iron one. The iron was glowing dull red: only the thick leather padding of the grip let Beowulf clutch it still, but the streaming sweat spattered in droplets from his wet dark beard. When the wyrm's head darted forward, heedless of his own safety, Wiglaf swung wildly at one of the ice gleaming eyes, making it weave aside so that its strike glanced less heavily from Beowulf's shield.

"Dear Beowulf," he panted knowing he was babbling, but unable to stop his tongue, even as he hacked downward at the talon swiping towards his leg "may all you said in your years of youth serve you well, that you would never let your fame fail while you lived. Now, staunch souled atheling, known for all your mighty deeds, ward your life! I shall aid you."

The wyrm's hiss crackled around them, the storm of flame bursting after. Wiglaf's shield flared up behind Beowulf's, its heat scorching their faces; Wiglaf dropped grip and red glowing shield boss with a cry of pain. But in the brief heartbeat of the fire's dying, Beowulf stepped forward, bringing his sword down with all his strength on the glede snake's head before it could slip backwards.

"Well struck!" Wiglaf cried: his short sight only saw the edge biting in. But then the wyrm pulled free: its eye ridge was only nocked, and Beowulf's sword was twisted and bent in his hand, as though he had struck too strongly for even that atheling weapon's hard temper to bear. The dragon's long head snapped forward, knocking Beowulf's useless sword aside, and its fangs sank deeply in at the base of his throat beneath beard and gold neck ring, blood spurting bright red through his beard.

Wiglaf dived past the iron shield as it fell, thrusting his own blade up at the dragon's belly.

The point skidded over a coal bright scale, and lodged in the crack between two golden plates: Wiglaf drove the sword in hard with a desperate wrench of hips and back, its edges shearing the scales further apart. Letting go of Beowulf, the wyrm reared back. Wiglaf heard the crackling in its throat, and knew his death but though blood streamed over his beard and byrnie, Beowulf had not fallen. Drawing his Finn sax, he sprang forward as if to embrace the dragon, the long iron knife cleaving through its red glowing hide and deeper through its flesh, until it seemed to Wiglaf's faulty sight that the king's whole arm had sunken into the glede snake's heart.

A torrent of white hot blood hissed from the wyrm's body as Beowulf pulled his knife out. Wiglaf rolled away from its thrashing; but the glow was already fading, the dreadful heat beginning to cool, and in a few heartbeats, the dragon lay wholly still. Beowulf slumped back against the stone archway, each breath burning a more piercing stab of agony out from the tooth wound at the base of his neck. He tried to sheathe his sax, but his fingers were too numb to guide its tip into the slot in the reindeer horn: at last he had to use both hands to get the weapon in its place.

He brushed the singed waves of his beard aside to touched his wound, wincing in agony. The blood seemed to be slowing already the wyrm's fangs could not have pierced one of the great vessels, or he would be dead yet it hurt like nothing so much as a very deep burn, and every heartbeat seemed to spread the throbbing tendrils of pain a little farther from the fang scathe. Leaning his head back seemed to ease the agony a little. Beowulf stared up at the well crafted stone arches just above his face Eotens' work, he thought. He hardly felt it when Wiglaf unbuckled his helm strap, dabbing the blood off as best he could.

I am dying.

Beowulf looked into Wiglaf's tilted blue eyes, and, in spite of the burning ache seeping through his body, he was able to smile, his folk would not, after all, be without a worthy hand to steer them now. Beowulf thought of another flying troll wight, and how he had stayed his hand then, that Hrothulf might find those mighty thanes Wyrd had deemed fittest for him.

"Hailed be need! Though harsh it may seem, it is the help of heroes, for no man may be known to himself until he is proven by hard strife. Tell Ingemund of this, and give him my greetings, and all my folk. Now I would give my son battle weeds, if I had been given any inheritance warder or any heir of my own body remained after me. I held my tribe for fifty winters: there was no folk king by us who dared to greet me with his battle friends, fearsomely threatening. I bid on earth the time shaped for me, and warded my part. I never sought cunning hate, nor swore many unrightful oaths." Beowulf smiled again. It seemed to him now that the pain was fading into warmth, that a faint golden light shimmered around everything in his sight Wiglaf's lean face, the great heap of the wyrm's ruddy dull corpse in the passage, the edges of the mound door against the brightness outside.

Now Beowulf knew that he had kept the oath he had sworn silently on the blessing boar, that first Yule in Hrethel's hall: on this his death day, he might name it fulfilled at last. And he knew that the might of the luck he had won was brought forth in the Middle Garth through the howe gold, that his folk might use it and enjoy it and thrive.

"I may rejoice in this all, though sick with my bane wound: for I know that when life leaves my body, Frea Ing may not blame me for murder bale of kin."

Beowulf lifted a numb hand, laying it on Wiglaf's shoulder he could just feel the heat still in his young kinsman's ring mail, as though he were wearing a thick glove.

"Now go quickly to see the hoard under hoary stone, beloved Wiglaf, now that the wyrm lies sleeping from his sore wound, bereft of his treasure. Be swift, that I may surely see that eldest hoard, and know that gold aeht, gems bright and cunningly wrought: thus I may then go softly, leaving my wealth of treasure, life and lordship, that I long held."

Wiglaf's feet echoed up and down the stone passageway: Beowulf heard the clink of gold on stone, and gold on gold, as the young thane hauled out armload by armload, heaving the treasures with some difficulty over the wyrm's twining body. Precious gems and gold glittered on the ground of the wyrm's den; there were more cups adorned with punched decoration and beast head handles by the men of early days; and many arm rings, cunningly twisted. Wiglaf also brought out a sig banner wrought with gold woven through weft and warp, that had stood high above the hoard, and it seemed to Beowulf that he could see the light shining brightly from it, showing the glede adder's treasure glittering to his sight. But the day outside was darkening in his eyes: he knew that his life tide must ebb swiftly soon, and he could not wait much longer on this faring shore.

"Wiglaf," he said faintly. "Enough: hearken to me. I give all thanks to Frea Ing, and say these words to the glory king and world's lord for I look upon this which I may gather for my folk before my dying day. Now I have bartered my old store of life for the treasure hoard: you must look to the folk's needs, for I may not while here long. Bid the battle known work a howe, bright from my bale fire, on the brine's headland. It shall keep my folk mindful, lifted high on Whales' Ness, that the seafarers may afterwards call it Beowulf's Barrow when the ships drive over the flood from afar in darkening twilight."

Beowulf's fingers would hardly move now, but somehow he was able to get his gold neck ring off, pressing it into Wiglaf's hands.

"Take my gold adorned helmet as well, and my byrnie: use them well! You are the last of our aeht the Waegmundings Wyrd sent forth all my kin to their measuring, athelings in their strength." The weight of breath in his lungs had grown too much to bear: with one last burst of effort, he spoke again. "I shall go after them."

The tide must have come in all the way, Beowulf thought then. Certainly the sea's cold had numbed him from the neck down, and it was easy to slip forward into the water, letting the waves bear him up once more.

Wiglaf caught Beowulf as his king slumped down. Staggering under the old man's weight, the Waegmunding eased his kinsman slowly to the ground beside the half coiled body of the wyrm. Though Beowulf's water green eyes were open, they no longer met Wiglaf's, and the massive chest beneath the thick wrought byrnie was still.

"Beowulf," Wiglaf grieved quietly. "I wish we had spoken together thus before you got your bane wound." He sat by the body for a little time, hoping against hope that he had been mistaken in seeing the Geat king's death; but Beowulf was already beginning to cool.

As Wiglaf waited to be sure of Beowulf's end, his sorrow sharpened slowly to anger, like a dull blade filed keen stroke by stroke. At last he rose to his feet, striding about the mound in wrath. Aldhelm and his ten friends were still milling about there, though they had all laid down their shields, and not one of them would meet Wiglaf's eyes.

"He who speaks truth," Wiglaf snapped, "may say that the drighten of men, who gave you those treasures and war gear in which you stand here, often offered helm and byrnie to those sitting on his ale benches, such as he found finest a folk leader to his thanes. The folk king had no cause to boast of his following! Yet Frea Ing, the world's lord, blessed him with sig, alone with sword edge, as he was able to do great deeds. I might give him little aid in battle to ward his life, but yet I began to help my kinsman above my measure. The deathly hater grew weaker as I struck it with sword, the fire welled with less strength."

He glared at them how dared Aldhelm stand there with not a stain on his fair face beneath the clean gleaming gilt of his helmet, not even a drop of sweat trickling out of the helm padding, when Beowulf's body, bloodied and marred with soot, lay not fifty paces from him? The other young men must have felt something of their own shame, for Hereberht seemed to mumble to himself as his fingers played with the hem of his tunic, and Ecgberht chewed furiously on his lower lip.

"Too few warders," Wihstan said bitterly, "thronged around the folk leader when his time came. Now shall treasure gaining and sword giving, all the atheling joys of your kins, and pleasures all end. From your kinsmen, lacking land right, every man shall turn away after the athelings ask from afar of your doings your worthless deeds. Death is better for any atheling than a shameful life!"

One or two of the young men looked at each other, but the rest were staring at Wiglaf. Then Aldhelm straightened his byrnie in a nervous clinking of links and said,

"Wiglaf, I had hoped to take the high seat after Beowulf. I cannot do that now. You are better fit for it than I."

Wiglaf stared into the eyes of his old tormentor, unbelieving. If he is setting me up for some cruel joke, after what I have suffered and he has not, I shall bid him to holmgang no matter that he is the better fighter by far: having seen Beowulf go to meet the wyrm, how can I ever be anything but brave?

"Aye," Hereberht chimed in. "You dared what none of us would, and your blade lodged in the dragon: what is winning a few bouts at Midsummer, or slaying a sea king, when set against that? But Wiglaf Wyrm Scather must rule the Geats after Beowulf Grendel's Bane."

"Wiglaf Wyrm Scather!" Ecgberht called out, and the other youths took up the cry, as if seeking to make up now for their failure when help was needed beneath hoary stone.

Dizzied, Wiglaf clung to what he knew needed doing. "Hereberht," he said, "you are the best rider among us. Hasten to Whales' Ness, and tell the tale of this day's work to the thanes who wait there for us. Then ride swiftly to Burgred's garth, and have Burgred's wain brought here at once, or Frea Ing's if the hof folk have reached that stead yet. Tell those who are left behind to start cutting pine branches and gathering dry driftwood, for it must be a hot bale fire that chars Beowulf's mighty body to ashes! Others should begin to dig and carry stones for the raising of a howe when the fire shall have burned to end."

Hereberht hastened southward, to where their horses were tied by the ruins of the Geat king's garth. Under Wiglaf's direction, the rest of them heaved and pulled, tugging the wyrm out into the sunlight. Stretched on the green earth, its fire glow faded to a dull ruddy mud color, the dragon looked far smaller than it had when aloft not the length of Beowulf's hall, but only fifty feet long, much of which was neck and tail. Wiglaf directed the other young men in bringing out some part of the wyrm's sunken treasure out into the sunlight beside it, the gold's radiance shining and glittering all about the hoary stone.

The afternoon was wearing well on by the time the wain Frea Ing's wagon, with its jutting gold boars' heads and the ancient Wealhtheow sitting behind the driver with Ingemund rolled slowly up to Eagles' Ness. The thanes who rode beside it stared open mouthed at the sight: the dragon, lying stretched on its side with the two great wounds gaping between its forelegs and where its shoulders narrowed to its neck; and its treasure spread about it. The grass between the wyrm's sprawled legs was almost wholly hidden by rings and chains and cups; brooches set with jewels in a myriad of bright colors; gold cups and bowls crafted by finer hands than those of any smith the Geats knew; rust eaten swords with gold glimmering hilts and helms whose eyepieces and nasals had been gnawed off by time and weather, but from which the gilding still shone fair; and the gold wrought sig standard wavering above it all time had leeched the color from its stuff, and it was brittle and crumbly with age, but the gold work glittered the more brightly from its earth dull weave. Ingemund stepped out of the wain, treading wonderingly around all that lay there to Wiglaf.

"Wiglaf Wyrm Scather," he said his old voice was hoarse, but it carried clearly through the cool sea air. "What is your will for this treasure, and for the body of your kinsman Beowulf?"

"When I showed him the wyrm's hoard, he was still living, wise and with his wits about him. He said many things, the old man in his cares, and sent you greeting. He bade that, in memory of your friend's deeds, you raise the high barrow upon the bale fire stead, mighty and far famed as he was the most worthy warrior among men throughout the wide earth, while he might enjoy the burg treasures. As for the hoard, let us now hasten yet one time to see and seek the cunningly crafted jewels, a wonder under the crag I shall show you the way, that you now see enough of rings and braided gold! Ready the bier, and have it done swiftly. When we come out, we shall carry our frea, the beloved man, where he long must lie in the ruler's keeping."

"What is this of bale fire and barrows?" One of the older thanes asked. "We Geats have never burned our kings: it is only the Inglings who raise mounds over the steads where their rulers were fed to the flames."

"Beowulf wished it," Wiglaf answered sternly.

To his surprise, the man quieted at his voice, but Ingemund spoke into the silence.

"The Frowe chooses her loves in fire thrice she was burned, and she lives aye. Yet Frea Ing dwells fruitful in the mound for the land's sake. So it is with the Inglings; so must it be also with Beowulf."

The howe fires burned no longer, as though they had dwindled and gone out with the last heat in the wyrm's body. But it was easy enough to strike a fire and light a dried branch from the woods, and so Wiglaf led seven of his most trusted warriors underneath the stone archway, past Beowulf who already lay stiff and cold as a heap of rocks. Their murmurs of awe rustled and echoed through the cave there was much Wiglaf and the other young men had not been able to bear out, such as chests of southern coins that were too weighty for one to lift alone.

"This was worthy of a king's life, indeed," Alhwine murmured.

"No," Wiglaf said. "I would not have bartered Beowulf's life for thrice this wealth, no, nor nine times either. The geld that was worthy of a king's life is that the wyrm will no longer come forth to slay his folk in the night."

As they carried out the rest of the treasure, Aldhelm asked Wiglaf, "What do you mean to do with the wyrm?"

Wiglaf looked over the cliff. The tide was beginning to ebb; but the waves still splashed three man heights up its foot.

"Let the sea have it: no one may guess where it shall come to shore."

He bent with the rest of the men, lending his aching back to the struggle to haul the great body that short way to the cliff edge. Like Beowulf, the wyrm had stiffened, and seemed heavy as if its gold and barrow stones still weighted it. But bit by bit, they pushed it over the edge. The wyrm teetered, tipped, and then plummeted down like a broken winged sea eagle, its splash casting a great plume of spray halfway up the crags as the waves enfolded it. For a full day, Wiglaf's thanes gathered driftwood and hewed logs, hitching up the horses to drag the bale fire's fuel to Whales' Ness.

The women and children gathered clay to caulk the chinks in Beowulf's burning mound and dried moss to help it catch quickly. Beowulf himself lay in Frea Ing's wain, the wyrm's treasures heaped all about him. Wiglaf had taken his byrnie and helm, as the old king had wished, but left Beowulf's Finn knife belted around his wide waist. Bryhthild had trimmed the singeing from the Geat king's brown hair and beard and combed them out; and at Beowulf's throat gleamed the long silver capped piece of amber that he had worn for as many years as anyone could remember.

The western sky was beginning to redden over the sea by the time Beowulf's burning house was finished. The high peaked bale pyre was as big as a burial howe: it must be a mighty fire to melt the king and his hoard together. And there was iron as well as gold: helms hung within, battle shields, and bright byrnies, for Beowulf might yet need to ward his land in war. Wiglaf and the seven sturdy men he had chosen to carry the wyrm's hoard up were about to lift Beowulf's body out of Frea Ing's wain to bear it through the wide gate where the last logs had not been placed yet, but old Wealhtheow said,

"No."

"What would you have us do, frowe?" Wiglaf asked her.

Wealhtheow leaned her full weight on her staff, swaying it like a tree in the wind so that the golden plaques hanging from its crown rang sweetly against each other.

"Beowulf must finish Frea Ing's frith faring, for his land's sake. More do I see now; more is shown to me, and I know that thing that was hidden before." Her aged voice had dropped into a soft chant. Standing before her, Wiglaf could see that her wrinkled face was turned up towards the deepening blue of the heavens, and it seemed to him that he saw a white mist drifting over the old woman's bright eyes. "The gold that Beowulf won must fare all to his howe with him. It is too mighty for the Middle Garth; it shall bring but ill to the children of Ash and Elm. Sow Frea Ing's grain in his land again; let the Frowe's tears drop to feed the earth. Half shall burn in the bale fire; half shall lie whole in the howe."

Wiglaf thought of all the byrnies and swords and helms that the least part of the wyrm's wealth could buy. Beowulf had won that gold for the Geats, and wished to look on it in the sunlight before he died how could Wiglaf gainsay that? He opened his mouth, meaning to say that he would give eight parts in nine to Beowulf for his last faring, but that the king had wanted some of the treasure to be dealt out for the sake of his folk. But the words that came out were,

"I would give every grain of gold in my keeping to see our fields growing high and our storehouses filled again."

Wealhtheow's sunken lips curved in a smile. "Hail to the giver!" She said.

Having spoken, Wiglaf could do nothing but order that the horses be hitched up to pull Frea Ing's wain into the high timbered burning house. The wheels groaned beneath the weight of Beowulf's body and the wyrm's hoard, the logs laid across the earth cracking as if the fire already devoured them. The golden stallion and the bay stood still as Wiglaf stepped into the pyre: hardly thinking on what he did, the Waegmunding drew Beowulf's Finnish knife from his belt to make that offering, and then raised the gold worked sig standard from the wyrm's den above the laden wain. The twilight was deepening swiftly when Wiglaf came out.

A band of brightness still shone in the west, but the first stars already glimmered overhead. As Wiglaf's thanes finished stacking driftwood around the wain and the horses' bodies, and heaved the last logs into place, Ingemund struck sparks into kindling, coaxing the flame to burn higher and hotter until he was able to light a long piece of driftwood as a brand. Wiglaf thought that the gudhe would light the bale fire, but Ingemund gave him the makeshift torch instead.

"What do I do?" Wiglaf hissed to Beowulf's old rede giver.

"Speak your farewells," Ingemund whispered back.

The sea wind blew a long plume of smoke from the bone pale twist of driftwood flaring in Wiglaf's grasp. It seemed to him almost as if he were speaking to himself: at least he did not stammer or fumble as he had feared he would.

"Now shall dark smoked fire wax, and the glede eat the battle leader of the folk, he who often dared the iron showers, when he stood staunch against the storm of arrows arching over the shield wall: the shaft did its part, the feathered shaft furthered the point. Yet long the folk king ruled in frith, for none dared shake the bane spear at the Geats while he stood to ward. He lessened sorrows; he wrought mighty deeds, and no hero under heavens stood as strong. May Frea Ing care well for him in Alf Home, and Folk Plain's fair field give welcome!"

Wiglaf bent to thrust the fiery driftwood into the waist high heap of moss and sticks just inside the last gap left in the slanted wall of the burning house. Flames leapt swiftly, running along the twigs; smoke curled up, beginning to drift dark from the lighting gap and the little chinks between the logs and the peak where the tree lengths were lashed together high above his head. The fire caught more and more of the driftwood and dry moss within, and the smoke rose black, the sounds of women's weeping twining about the roaring of the flames within their death oven. Though no wind blew to fan the fire, it crept steadily upwards, flickering through the log ends crossed at the top of the bier house.

There was a brief stink of burning horsehair, then a hissing from beneath the fire's hungry crackling, and the scent of roasting meat. The black smoke was rising more thickly now, streaming into the air to be drunk by the darkening heavens. Beowulf's bale fire burned like a great beacon on the headland throughout the night. If any seafarers were sailing past, Wiglaf thought, it would seem to them that the Geats were trying to signal to some unknown folk across the ocean's wide waves.

Sometimes he heard sounds from within the burning house, the deep thumps of something heated until it burst from within, or the sizzle of something else flaring suddenly into ash among the great heaps of glowing wood inside the high log peak. But though he was not far from the burning of all the scorched bodies the wyrm had left, and for all his short sight had seen too clearly what the log walls around the bale fire hid, Wiglaf steeled himself not to flinch at the noises from the pyre. He listened, instead, to the songs of mourning and the tales of Beowulf's deeds in earlier days, and if the smoke stung his eyes to unmanly tears, there was none to see it through the darkness.

While the wide bed of coals still glowed around the half melted shapes of war gear and scattered drops of gold, the Geats began to haul boulders up to the headland, setting them about Beowulf's burial fire in the oblong of a ship, and laying the other half of the dragon's hoard in glistening heaps within the curving lines of gray stones. It took ten days altogether for the barrow to be raised as high as Wiglaf would have it, that Beowulf's last words be fulfilled. By that time, the stead where the Geat king's garth had been was covered by a burg of tents, for word of Beowulf's dragon slaying and death had gone out through his land, and every drighten or carle who was close enough had come to drink Beowulf's arvel and swear their oaths to Wiglaf.

Wiglaf waited until the Sun was glowing red in the west to blow the horn call that summoned all his folk to Beowulf's barrow. Though its weight hung sore from his shoulders, Wiglaf wore the byrnie that the old king had left him, for all his atheling clothes had been burnt with Beowulf's garth; the Geats no longer had a high seat, but Wiglaf had ordered a stool placed atop Beowulf's mound. Yet Wiglaf's gold bright helm and the ring hilted sword hanging from his baldric were those his father had left him. As he walked up the steep slope of bare earth to the crown of Beowulf's howe, Wiglaf's palms chilled with sweat and he began to tremble. Beneath, the faces of his folk were no more than a blurred pale sea; but it seemed to him that he could feel each gaze upon him like the weight of another thick link in his shirt of heavy ring mail.

His tongue was stickily dry in his mouth, and he did not dare cough to clear the gathering tightness in his throat. Wiglaf reached the top of the mound, looking downwards at the fogged faces some folk he knew, but most of them strangers, as most of his realm were strangers. And yet they would all be ready to swear their oaths and spill out their blood for him, just as he would live, and give his life, for their sakes. Then it seemed to Wiglaf that he felt the might streaming upward from the howe's depths into his own body, like the shining root of a leek in darkness shooting tall green leaves up into the light. He opened his mouth, and the words spilled from him in a bright stream.

"Hail, my folk!" He called. "Beowulf lies in his barrow; but the Waegmunding aeht lives on, and the Geats' folk king has not yet forsaken you!" Wiglaf drew his father's ring sword, holding it high. "By the holy oath ring I swear this, and by the blade that scathed the wyrm below hoary stone: to be first to the field in war, and first to the fields in frith; to rule well reded; to uphold the gods in their hallowed steads, and make blessings to the holy wights; to deem fairly in all my dealings with you, and rule in right and law. So I, Wiglaf Waegmunding, swear it upon Beowulf's barrow: may Frea Ing hear me, may the Frowe hear me, may the all mighty Ase stand witness!"

Wiglaf took a deep breath, and sat upon the mound stool. The folk below broke into a great storm of cheering. Something more was sweeping over the Waegmunding now, fierce and cold as needles of hail driven by winter's first wind. As the words flowed from Wiglaf's mouth again, it seemed to him that he saw the helmets and byrnies gleaming silvery beneath the gold boar standard of the Swedes, as he had heard in songs; the bearded hunger gaunt faces under rich war gear, and the fear shadow of bloodied harrow and burning hall in the eyes of the tall gray haired warrior who wore the boar headed arm ring. Wiglaf heard the hoof beats of a riding host, and the thudding footfalls of a marching host, coming ever closer as wolf and raven sang their grim slaughter song, and he knew the truth of what he said.

"Our folk should ween
that battle's coming be now soon,
when Franks and Frisians the fall of our king
hear from afar. Hard strife passed there!
Nor from the Swedes sibship nor troth
ween I to have: wide known those causes.
Leave sport and joy the spears must be
many, morning cold made to fly,
hefted by hand: no harp may sound,
waking warriors, but wound glad raven,
greedy for death doomed grants much speech,
boasts to the eagle how eating he found
speeding to rend the slain with wolf."

"Let no hall be built for me yet!" Wiglaf went on. "The Swedes gather their host even now, turning their eyes westward; and many foes shall soon be circling around us, when they ween that Beowulf is dead. It is time to set on byrnie and helm, to lift the battle board, to raise the bane spear. Will you follow me, my folk, that the Geats' realm not yet be cast down, though our strongest shield is broken?"

"Aye!" The men's voices roared, a deep wave of sound cresting and breaking over Beowulf's barrow. Someone shouted, "Hail, Wiglaf Wyrm Scather! Hail, host leader of the Geats!" And the others took it up. Old Wealhtheow, her two sturdy young gudhes at either elbow, made her way painfully up the howe to call the blessings of the gods upon Wiglaf and the Geats; and then, one by one, the thanes and drightens who had given their troth to Beowulf climbed up the mound track to swear their oaths anew on Wiglaf's ring sword.

As the vows were sworn, Wiglaf' twelve best riders saddled their horses, setting their finest war trimmings upon the steeds' gleaming necks. The cunningly wrought gold strap mounts burned red in the sunlight from dapple gray and black, bay and roan, dun and white; the bridle rangles rang through the warm summer evening over the swift hoof beats as the horses sped to a full gallop, thundering in tight turns around the high mound of raw earth. The riders' voices swelled over the swift drumbeat of their hooves, keening their sorrow song before the folk. They sang of Beowulf's deeds, from Ravenwood to his wyrm slaying; they sang of his strength in war, but also of his open hands and mighty heart, of oath keeping and trust, and a folk held long in golden frith. There about that howe, the Geats drank Beowulf's arvel, pouring out the last of their hoarded ale, and in the deepening blue twilight they grieved that great king, their matchless folk warder. When the ale had all been drunk and poured on earth, the Geats began to drift back to their tents, following the fire brands that gleamed here and there in the starry darkness.

Wiglaf stayed upon the mound stool, weary and alone in the night, keeping the east watch over his land. The fires among the tents burned down; the voices raised in song fell, one by one, to stillness, and at last all slept save Wiglaf. He watched through the night, until he saw the first gray glimmering of the eastern sky. The dawn light grew, gray brightening to pale blue in the east though the west was yet dark. And then it seemed to Wiglaf that he saw the shapes of two great women nearing Beowulf's barrow.

One strode from the east, the strengthening light behind her. Her fair hair shimmered in a long curtain about her green cloaked body, and it seemed that the red Sun glowed bright from the ringed gold collar at her neck, and dark from the huge garnet of her girdle clasp. The other walked over the waves, her white skin glimmering like foam on the night black waters; the green of water weed tinged her golden hair, and she was all adorned with gleaming amber. The frowe shapes halted, each at one side of Beowulf's howe, and Wiglaf saw their eyes meet. She who had come from the west spoke, her deep voice rolling and crashing in the surf that beat at the headland below.

"Let me claim my sea bear now. He forsook me, but never forgot me: he wears my token yet."

The other's voice was higher, and honey sweet, but Wiglaf heard the fierceness of the falcon's shriek veiled beneath it, and the lynx's snarl.

"Maid of maids, the king of the Geats swore oath to me, on holy harrow and twisted ring. What oaths did he ever swear to you, in your father's sunken hall?"

"My sea bear is kin to my kin, mighty in the waters, with more sea strength than any other wight," the woman from the west argued. "I would not have led him, as you did, on his slain faring, but kept him to joy in my hall."

It seemed to Wiglaf that he saw the gold tears drop from the blue green eyes of the necklaced frowe, glowing gledes falling upon the earth.

"Neither you nor I may shift the drawing of Wyrd: no kin of the gods may withstand it, nor yet the aeht of eotens. But Beowulf lies in my brother's wain, ever his trusted friend, ready to fulfill that frith faring he began."

"My sea bear lies in his ship ring, ready to fare to me," the wave bright woman said. "Ase and alf you have held in your arms: let the eoten kin keep our own!"

Their eyes met over the mound. Wiglaf said nothing, and they did not seem to mark that he sat there, but he could feel their struggle of might, and it seemed to him that sea and fire were evenly matched. And he thought of Beowulf, breathing his last words against the wall beneath hoary stone, bidding his howe be set on the headland, that march between earth and ocean, for the sake of his folk. The tides of strength rose and ebbed; and yet the two women stared at each other. It was she who had come from the east who spoke first, as the burning edge of the Sun rounded the world's rim behind her.

"Aye," she said, "he wished to lie on the edge of the land, with his face turned towards the sea. He loved us both, but neither had all his heart: there was a maid of the Middle Garth who drew him ever back to the green earth, warder against all foes without.

Let him lie among the shining seeds of might as he would, luck to his land; and betimes we shall both come to him in death as we did in life."

The woman from the west nodded, her long green tinged hair flowing about her as though she stood in clear rippling water.

"Let it be so," she said.

They stood there a moment more, then turned and walked away, one eastward towards the rising Sun, one westward over the sea. Wiglaf sat in his stead on the mound, weary to the bone. Soon he must make his way down from the howe's height and go among his folk, gathering them for the battle to come

"Though the bale fire burned red at evening, the Geats' day is not done yet," Wiglaf swore softly to Beowulf. "While I live, kinsman, I shall keep your troth."

Author's Notes, Character Guide, Glossary, and Further Reading

Of all my works to date, Beowulf has been by far the longest in the making. I started preparing for it as an undergraduate at Southern Methodist University in 1989, when I undertook an independent studies project on Beowulf under the enthusiastic guidance of Dr. Bonnie Wheeler. At that time, I was already considering a novelized version of it, but Dr. Stephen Flowers suggested to me that I might be better off to start my literary career as a 'reteller' of Germanic epic with a rendition of the Völsung/Nibelungen story, since that had been revived far more often. Dr. Flowers was right, and I therefore put Beowulf aside and started on Rhinegold, which I completed at SMU under the guidance of C.W. Smith.

Since that beginning, other things have happened which led into the creation of this book as it is. I undertook my doctoral thesis on Woden/Óðinn in the Anglo Saxon, Norse, and Celtic department of Cambridge University, and spent three years working with experts and enthusiasts in the fields of Anglo Saxon and Norse literature (not to mention absorbing and enjoying something of that Oxbridge environment which flavored so much of Professor Tolkien's life).

After that, I was at Uppsala University for a time, living not far from the great mounds attributed to Eadgils, Ongentheow, and Eadwine the Old; I came to know and love the Swedish land, and to learn more about that fascinating dynasty, the Inglings, and the god Freyr, favorite of the Swedes, from whom they were descended. As I had been raised in an urban environment, the chance to live in an agricultural area also gave me a much different understanding of what life was like for my ancestors, an understanding improved when I moved to a country manor in Ireland with sheep, fowl, Icelandic horses, and Norwegian elk hounds.

I went on my first bear hunt, which led me to serious consideration of the nature of bears and the Finnish and Saami bear cult. Meanwhile, I wrote several more books, and continued to grow in my craft as a writer and 'reteller' of heroic legends. I began writing Beowulf in 1997. My previous books have almost all been completed within a year of the start, but I had several other literary projects going on at the time, as well as managing a household and becoming involved in several rather time consuming crafts and organizations. So Beowulf has been the longest in the actual writing time as well as the preparation.

The young man I was in 1989 might have written a Beowulf, but it would not have been this Beowulf, and it would not have been nearly as good. I should, therefore, like to thank Dr. Stephen Flowers one more time for his wise rede, and hope that he finds himself amply repaid by what this book has become. The primary source for this book is, of course, the original Beowulf, often called the oldest English epic though it is set almost entirely in Sweden and Denmark.

There is much debate on the age of the actual poem, with theories ranging from the early seventh century to the early eleventh. Some of the events it describes, however like those of the other great Northern epic Völsunga saga and its German counterpart, Niebelungenlied are surprisingly easy to locate in history, thanks mainly to the chronicler Gregory of Tours, who mentions Hygelac's unsuccessful raid on the Franks, even giving the king's name (Chlochilaich, in the Frankish form), so that there is no doubt of the identification.

Unfortunately, Gregory did not mention the specific year, but it seems to have happened sometime in the neighborhood of 520 reasonably close to the generally assigned date of death for the (possibly) historical Arthur. Using Gregory's description of the natural disasters and anomalies in the 580's as a guide for the end of the book, I have arbitrarily assigned a date at the late end of the plausible range for Hygelac's death. In the lengthy history of Beowulf criticism, the academic interest has swung from a fascination with the politics outlined in the historical excursions, treating the monsters as an unfortunate poetic periphery (cf. The discussion in Tolkien's "The Monsters and the Critics"), to an interest in the two primary episodes of the dragon and Grendel. Literary interest has, in general, completely ignored the complex political world of Migration Age Scandinavia in favor of the monsters.

I felt that, in order to do full justice to Beowulf, it was important to give a complete picture of him both as a man (and a man in a relatively key position during an age of major political expansion, at that) and as a monster slayer. I was also moved by the awareness that the audience for whom Beowulf was originally intended were equally fascinated with the semi historical dealings of the legendary kings who appear in its lines and the semi mythological activities of the hero himself: Alcuin's frustrated cry, "What has Ingeld to do with Christ?" Reflects the passionate love for the tales of the various dynasties who battled around the North Sea in Beowulf's age which lingered long after the conversion of England. Beowulf does not stand by itself as a description of the history of the North in the sixth century. The Migration Age was the chief period of the evolution from clan organization to state in Scandinavia, and the key figures of this age quickly passed into legend. Many of the people in Beowulf also appear in Hrólfs saga kraka, the Scandinavian version of Hrothulf's story ('Hrólfr' is the Old Norse form of 'Hrothulf' see Glossary).

Ynglinga saga, based on the ninth century poem Ynglingatal an account of the deaths and burial places of that tumultuous dynasty also covers some of the people and events mentioned in Beowulf, as do the Danish author Saxo Grammaticus in Gesta Danorum and a few other fragmentary sources. These accounts, distorted by oral tradition and authorial attempts to create coherence, frequently contradict each other (for example: Ynglinga saga has Hrothulf dying during the rule of Eadgils' son, while according to Saxo, Eadgils died of celebrating Hrothulf's death to excess) or give inadvertent misinformation as a result of the author trying to make sense of his received tradition (in Ynglinga saga, Snorri identifies Onela/Ali as being from Uppland in Norway rather than Uppland in Sweden, as the Swedish civil war remembered in Beowulf had been forgotten by Snorri's day, so that he had to rationalize the pieces of information he had as best he could).

In attempting to present a full picture of Beowulf's world and political activities, I have used all these sources, though which version I chose to follow at which time depended very much on what seemed to fit best with the main Beowulf story, the characters as I perceived them, and the effort to create a moderately plausible chronology. I confess to also having been influenced by Poul Anderson's Hrolf Kraki's Saga, a brilliant retelling of Hrólfs saga kraka. Although all the characters in Beowulf are Migration Age Scandinavians, because there is a single primary source for the book and because most readers will only be familiar with the Anglo Saxon name forms for these characters, I stuck to Anglo Saxon for almost all the names, with only a few exceptions (i.e. 'Dagochramn' is Frankish; the northern Norwegian characters 'Godhagastir' and 'Hlewabrandar' have Proto Norse names, suggesting their physical remove from the main body of Northern society).

This presented some difficulty in translating the names which only appear in the Norse sources, particularly the names of gods and other beings, which are often difficult of etymology. In some cases I had to arbitrarily choose one etymological theory and work from that; in other instances, I had to guess. I hope that any real philologers reading this book will forgive these efforts. The Anglo Saxon god names (or reconstructed forms) may also be somewhat confusing at first to those familiar with the native Germanic religion only through the Old Norse sources. For this reason, I have listed the better known Norse names beside the forms I used in the list of characters (below). The masculine a ending for some Anglo Saxon names may also be a trifle disconcerting at first to readers more familiar with either Latin or Old Norse (where the a ending is characteristically feminine). The author of the Old English Beowulf was a Christian, and, though aware that his characters worshiped their native gods, did his best to play this down except in situations where criticism was appropriate (i.e., the effort to ask the gods to help with the Grendel problem).

In attempting an historical setting of the story I have, of course, restored the tremendous importance of religion to Northern life. My interpretation of Beowulf as a Vanic worshiper with a marked wariness towards Woden (Óðinn) is not entirely institutional or artistic. It is based to some degree on Thomas Hill's article "The Confession of Beowulf" (in R.T. Farrell, The Vikings, pp. 165 179), which presents Beowulf as an anti Völsung, anti Óðinnic figure. Scholars and worshipers of the Scandinavian gods may note that Beowulf could just as well have been, and often is read as a Thórr hero: elements of the "Bear's Son" motif which defines the monster slaying episodes of the poem are associated with Thórr, and Beowulf's great physical strength is obviously comparable to that god.

However, Beowulf's love of peace, expressed in his death statement, and preference for fighting bare handed, as well as some elements of the imagery of the poem (the emphasis on water and hidden treasure, for instance, as well as the reference to protective boars on the Geatish helms) match well enough with a Vanic theme. Beowulf's opinions on Woden do not reflect those of the author (who did his doctoral thesis on this god and loves him dearly), but do reflect the views of many people he knows. Christianity was at this time just touching the peripheral fringes of the Scandinavian world, so that the only Christian characters in the book are the Haetware girl and the British Saxon Raganwald, and the main characters are not particularly aware of this.

The entire episode with Ran's daughter is, of course, my own invention, in order to give a fictionally satisfying explanation of why Beowulf never bothered to marry or get heirs (the probable real reason, of course, being that he is a figure of legend rather than being an historical king of the Geats). Grendel's desire to avenge Yma (Ymir) on the descendants of the gods is mere conjecture, but it fits nicely with the repeated theme of blood feud running through all the tales of Beowulf's age. Those who are familiar with the original will notice a great many other such inventions: these I can only excuse as authorial prerogative, and hope that they fit in well enough with the world of the early Norse not to jar the reader unduly. The unceremonious burial of Ingemund's unnamed child is supported in archaeological, as well as literary evidence.

Even allowing for circumstances of preservation (smaller bones rot more easily than larger ones), there is a marked shortage of children's bones in Scandinavian Iron Age and Viking Age cemeteries. According to the sagas, Norse parents got a nine day return period on their children, after which the father had to decide if he was willing to pick it up, name it, and make it a member of his clan, or put it out to be disposed of by the forces of nature. The archaeological material suggests that this was more than a literary exaggeration of a native custom. The major religious centers of the North, according to reports made near the end of the Viking Age and afterwards, were Uppsala and Lejre ('Hlaeder' the Danish kings' seat).

The name of the Danish site Gudme actually means "God Home", and archaeological discoveries there suggest that it was a seat of cult like activity in the Migration Age. Whether the historical God Home resembled my fictional description in any way will probably never be known. The association between homosexuality and the cult of Freyr, particularly in regards to ritual performance, is suggested by Saxo Grammaticus in his remarks about the effeminate activities of the Freyr priests at Uppsala; some have also interpreted Snorri's description of seith craft as "effeminate" for men and suited only to women as being related to a homosexual element in either the Vanic cult or in Nordic trance practices.

The descriptions of the bear cult among the Saami are based on practices common to Saami and Finns (Norse sources use the word "Finn" for both peoples), recorded in the last few centuries, but possibly stretching back to the dawn of prehistory (Inuit bear customs are remarkably similar). In the lack of many early accounts, I have used the more recent descriptions of Saami religion and life, going on the archaeological indications that many elements of worship remained constant among that people for a number of centuries. The usual poetic form in this book is that of Beowulf itself; it is the common early Germanic form, characterized by half lines linked by alliteration.

Some of the characters (the mound ghost, the dead Ecgtheow, Ansuwulfar) use the later skaldic dróttkvætt metre (adapted slightly to suit the English language) and also employ elaborate kennings of a type more typical of the Viking Age, i.e. 'flames of Wind God' = 'flames of Woden' = swords. My only excuse for this anachronism is that they are all inspired by Woden who, as a god, is clearly versed in that poetic form before humans learn it. The 'harps' referred to in both book and original text are similar to the Anglo Saxon lyre, not the better known Celtic harp. The song sung by the spae workers in chapter III is adapted from the 'Summoning Song', written by Tom Jonsson and William Karpen to a traditional Norwegian tune, though I changed the style from modern end rhyme to Germanic alliterative. Eadgils' version is adapted farther from that, though his words fit the original tune more closely.

The general format of the spae ritual is roughly derived from that used by Diana Paxon with her group Hrafnar, which in turn is based largely on the account of the trance seance in Eiríks saga rauða. In general, I have tried to be as faithful as possible to the Old English Beowulf, translating directly from the poem whenever possible. I cut some of the longer speeches, notably Hrothgar's homily and the very lengthy accounts of the early history of Beowulf and the Geats in the final section while grateful that the Beowulf author saw fit to include them, I thought that by that point both the reader and the Geats themselves would already know the stories quite well.

I also transposed some sections such as Hrethel's lament and the "Lay of the Last Survivor" (recited by Ansuwulf in ch. 6) to fulfill narrative requirements differing, in a modern novel, from those of the epic. I used Klaeber's third edition for my original source. I have also introduced elements from other Scandinavian and Anglo Saxon sources where appropriate. Those familiar with the Icelandic sagas, in particular, may recognize these references scattered throughout the book. The careful reader will particularly notice that the female characters appear to play a much more influential role in my Beowulf than in the original, where almost all of them are very marginal. The reason for this is that most poetry dealing with battles and politics as chiefly manifest through war doesn't have many important female characters.

However, the role of women in Germanic society as advisors and social arbitrators was, at least as suggested by the sagas and such para-historical sources as Tacitus, of very considerable importance, and I have attempted to reconstruct this significance in my imaginative description of Iron Age Scandinavian society. Among minor details, both the horses and the dogs known to Beowulf still exist in a very similar form today. The horses are Icelandic horses: short (12 14 hands), but extremely sturdy and enduring: a strong Icelandic in good condition could carry Beowulf without too much difficulty.

They have two additional gaits, the pace and the tölt, both of which are exceptionally smooth and pleasant. The dogs are Norwegian elk hounds, which, as shown by skeletal remains in burials, have not changed substantially from the Stone Age onwards. Remains from Migration Age burials in Sweden show that the domestic cat was already known in Scandinavia at this time (probably via Rome and Britain), but it was not a common animal. The long haired Norwegian Forest Cat was probably a later introduction brought back from the Viking trade to the East.

Migration Age Scandinavian trade was surprisingly extensive. Swedes and Danes in this period had access to silk, wine, and glass, among other products from the south and east. Foreign dyestuffs were also imported: there seems to have been a direct connection between clothing color and social status, with red and (slightly less notable) green being associated with the very highest strata of society. Garnets were the most popular gemstone, and may have had some religious connotations as well. The horse handled gold cups of Uppsala and the dragon's hoard, however, are not recent foreign imports, but date from the Scandinavian Bronze Age (though they may have come from Central Europe originally). An original may be seen in the National Museum in Copenhagen.

We know very little about bare handed fighting in early Scandinavia, but wrestling was a popular pastime, and it is probably safe to assume that techniques such as those used by Sweartwulf and Beowulf were quite well developed. My descriptions are obviously influenced by modern "soft" martial arts, though I am not an expert in any of these styles; however, in consulting with someone who is (Sensei Jesse McCarthy), it was described to me how several such techniques would work for the key episode where Beowulf rips Grendel's arm off. The armed combat in this book has inevitably been influenced by my heavy fighting (reconstructed armor and rattan swords) in the Society for Creative Anachronism.

For those who want to know more about the highly developed craft of sword making in the Iron and Viking Ages, I recommend H.R. Ellis Davidson's The Sword in Anglo Saxon England. For the physical description of Beowulf as overweight, I obviously started from the identification of him as a bear hero. However, his ability to swim long distances in cold water also suggests a generous padding of plumpness. And, as those who follow power lifting or watch the World's Strongest Man competitions know, super heavyweights tend to have a marked amount of body fat, not only from a bulk oriented diet, but because it actually increases raw lifting strength. Although Beowulf is decidedly heavier than the modern male ideal throughout nearly all his life, he is perfectly designed to be what he is.

Character Guide

Here I list the major characters who appear in the literary sources under the names I have used, giving their best known alternate names and sources where those exist, and a brief note as to their identity and roles in the various literary/quasi historical materials.

- Aistan Eysteinn, Ynglinga saga. Son of Eadgils/Aðils.
- Ansuwulf Wulf, Beowulf. The prefix is Primitive Norse, meaning 'god', esp. applied to Óðinn; the form used here is a byname formation after the manner of Úlfr Mostrarskegg, called Thórolfr from his dedication to Thórr. Brother to Eofor.
- Beadu Berki Böðvarr Bjarki, Hrólfs saga kraka et al. This bear hero is a duplicate of Beowulf, assigned in the Scandinavian tradition to the heroic cycle centered around Hrothulf's court.
- Beowulf not otherwise attested due to Böðvarr Bjarki having taken his place in the Scandinavian tradition. The name means "bee wolf", a poetic term for a honey eating bear; I interpreted 'Beowulf' as a by name and assigned him the personal name 'Berki', 'Little Bear', after the Norse Bjarki (the Anglo Saxon form should probably have been
- Berca, but that would have been too easily confused with his recorded swimming competitor Breca).
- Breca son of Beanstan, drighten of the Brondings (one of the Geatish sub tribes). Known only for having a swimming contest with Beowulf. Cara Kári, a personification of the cold winter winds.
- Dagochramn Daeghrefn, Beowulf. Mentioned only in the poem, which describes the Frankish hero's slaying of Hygelac and Beowulf then crushing him to death.
- Eadgils Aðils. The best documented of any of the characters in this cycle, Eadgils appears in all the accounts of sixth century Sweden. His practice of questionable magics is mentioned in Hrólfs saga kraka; his love of horses and horse breeding comes from Ynglinga saga. His portrayal in this book is probably the most sympathetic he has ever gotten from any author, modern or ancient, who made him more than a peripheral figure. Gwyn Jones comments, 'The Athils of Ynglinga saga was a true Swede in his love of fine horses, but the poets and sagamen have not dealt kindly with him: it is a grotesque and baffled mischief maker who squinnies at us from their pages' (A History of the Vikings, p. 39). Having said that, one may suspect that Eadgils/Aðils probably suffered considerably from being under the heroic shadow of Hrothulf/Hrólfr, which puts him in the same class as the much maligned Mordred: historical antagonists to legendary heroes seldom get fair treatment in epic works (or, worse, quasi historical pieces of propaganda).

- Eadwine the Old Aun the Old, Ynglinga saga.
- Eagor Ægir, the giant personification of the sea, husband to Ran, father to the nine waves (Himingleowe and her sisters).
- Ecgtheow Beowulf's father, whose tumultuous career is described in the poem, though the identification of Ecgtheow as a berserk is my own extrapolation.
- Edunnan Iðunn.
- Eofor slayer of Ongentheow. The poem mentions that he is given Hygelac's daughter, but considerations of chronology meant that I actually married her to his son.
- Fosita Forseti; also Fosite. Patron of the Frisians and instrumental in the myth of their law giving, peripheral in the Norse sources.
- Elk Frodha Elk Froði, Hrólfs saga kraka.
- Frea Ing 'Lord Ing'; Freyr. Father of the Ingling dynasty, and possibly of Scyld Scefing; Beowulf's patron god.
- Freawaru daughter of Hrothgar and Wealhtheow, married to Ingeld, who then revives his family's feud against hers.
- Frige Frigg, wife of Woden/Óðinn. Frigg is associated with the female role of the frith weaver or peacemaker, in contrast to Freyja, who is associated with the equally typical female role of strife stirrer.
- Frosta Frosti, a winter etin.
- Frowe Freyja ('frowe' is not Anglo Saxon, but a normalized English form of the Freyja/frau word). A number of the Inglings' frequently bizarre deaths are caused by women who have characteristics in common with Freyja, which has given rise to interpretations involving sacred kingships, sacrificial marriages of king and goddess, etc., all of which I felt free to use in a work of fiction but would be more cautious about in an historical sense. Her characteristic artifact is the Brísingamen, which is either a necklace or a girdle (sources differ), but has been loosely associated with both the huge layered gold collars from Migration Age Sweden and with the many pieces of garnet jewelry from the same time and place. Like Óðinn, she is a collector of the battle dead, and also associated with the Everlasting Battle (she brings the dead back to life every night so they can keep fighting).
- Geofe Gefjön, patron goddess of Sealand; also Gefn, a by name of Freyja.
- Gilpa Gylfi, protagonist of the Gylfaginning section of the Prose Edda.
- Godhagastir Goðgestr, Ynglinga saga. Killed by falling off a horse sent to him by Aðils (Eadgils), according to the saga.
- Grendel got a book of his own by John Gardner, in which he appears as an existential (and rather adolescent) anti hero. I preferred to show him as a typical young Germanic warrior in personality: the difference in mental attitude between gods, giants, and humans is usually not easy to spot in the Norse materials without a strong magnifying glass.

• Grendel's mother as Grendel is a typical young Germanic warrior, so his mother is largely a typical mother of a grown son: her role as advisor and magical protector of her son is seen in the human realm in several sagas. Only her direct physical attempt at revenge for him, in place of shaming a male relative into doing it, is unusual.

• Haethcyn second son of Hrethel, older brother of Hygelac. Takes the rule of the Geats after he has inadvertently killed his elder brother Herebeald and their father has curled up to die; killed by Ongentheow's forces at Ravenwood.

• Halga Helgi, Hrólfs saga kraka, Gesta Danorum. Hrothgar's older brother. Neither lucky nor careful in his loves, Halga managed to produce one child (Hrothulf) with his own bastard daughter Yrse, and one (Scyld) with an alf woman. In Hrólfs saga, he is killed by Aðils (Eadgils) after the latter has married Yrse; the chronology of this book made that unreasonable, and the killing is shifted to Ongentheow.

• Hamdeall the god Heimdallr.

• Harwine Hörn, a by name of Freyja.

• Heofenglowe Old Norse Himinglæfa, one of the daughters of Eagor and Ran.

• Heraware Old Norse Hervör, Hervarar saga ok Heiðreks. The "sword of the Terwingi" is the cursed sword Tyrfingr (associated with the Gothic Terwingi tribe, later taking on their name).

• Hereweard Hjörvarðr, Hrólfs saga kraka. King in Wodenswih (Odense), husband to Hrothulf's sister Scyld. In the poem, Hereweard is the son of

• Hrothgar's brother Heregar, but this would have made him Scyld's first cousin, which seemed problematical since I had already used the incestuous relationship from Hrólfs saga.

• Herebeald eldest son of Hrethel, oldest brother of Hygelac. Killed by his brother Haethcyn in a hunting accident.

• Hiltwine/Haett Hjálti/Höttr. Hrolfs saga kraka. As described here. The coast guard to whom Beowulf gives a gold hilted sword in the original text is never named; identifying him with Hrothulf and making Beowulf the source of the heroic blade which Hiltwine/Hjálti eventually receives is my own invention.

• Hrethel father of Hygelac, maternal uncle to Beowulf. Dies after his second son has killed his eldest.

• Hrethric son of Hrothgar, killed by Hrothulf.

• Hrothgar Hroar, Hrólfs saga kraka. Brother of Halga, husband of Wealhtheow, builder of Heorot, king of the Danes during the period when Grendel's depredations are going on.

• Hrothulf Crycc Hrólfr kraki, Hrólfs saga kraka et al. In Beowulf, he is rather a sinister figure, with the shadow of his semi usurpation of the Danish kingdom from Hrothgar's children hanging over his portrayal in the Heorot scenes. In the Scandinavian versions, he is a relatively unambiguous hero. The degree to which he was honored is shown by the backhanded compliment given by Óláfr the Fat (later sainted for his bloody murders of his countrymen in the name of conversion) in Flateyjarbók: when the disguised Óðinn enquires as to which among the old kings Óláfr would prefer to have been, the christian king replies that he would prefer none of them, since they were heathens but eventually admits to a grudging affection for Hrólfr kraki. A kraki is a pine tree with branches lopped to use as a ladder. Interpretations of what this says about Hrothulf's physique vary Saxo insists that he was very tall, but well built but I chose to follow Poul Anderson in making him both short and thin.

• Hygd wife of Hygelac, mother of Heardred. Some have identified her with the "Weder woman" who mourns Beowulf at the end of the poem, but this seemed to me unbelievable if Beowulf's fifty year reign was to be accepted. Hygd's initial betrothal to Beowulf and her position as Breca's step sister are inventions of my own.

• Hygelac Chlochilaich, Gregory of Tours. His name means "Mind play" or "Spirit play", and his raid on the Franks in the poem gives the impression of having been rather light minded and pointless. Gregory of Tours describes the raid in some detail, including the intervention of Theudebert, the separation of Hygelac and a small band from his ships which were sent on ahead, and the trouncing of the Geats both on land and in the naval battle.

• Loca the god Loki.

• Meredeall Mardöll, a by name of Freyja. Probably 'Sea Gleam'.

• Moon the Moon is always male in Germanic languages and lore ("the Man in the Moon" survives even in English).

• Nerthus one of the gods, identified as "Mother Earth" by Tacitus. A masculine form, Njörðr, exists in Old Norse; Njörðr is the father of Freyr and Freyja by his unnamed sister.

• Onela Ali, Ynglinga saga. Ongentheow's son, Othere's brother. Misidentified as a Norwegian in Snorri's description of the battle with Eadgils on the ice of Lake Wener (Väner); his strife with his brother's sons and his death are described in Beowulf.

• Ongentheow possibly Egill, Ynglinga saga. Gwyn Jones makes the connection between the poetic description of Othere's father being torn by a boar (or bull, as Snorri interprets the stanza from Ynglingatal) and the slaying of Ongentheow by a man named Eofor ('Boar') in Beowulf.

• Othere Óttarr, Ynglinga saga. Son of Ongentheow, father of Eadgils. Called "Vendel Crow" for reasons of mixed explanation (the name also appears for his father); I ignored the Ynglinga saga reason because the malicious insult seemed to me uncharacteristic for Hrothulf (or Hrólfr kraki). Killed and buried in a mound at Vendel, which still bears the traditional name "Ottar's Howe".

• Ran a giantess who seems to personify the sea in its more hostile and greedy aspects. Her daughters are the nine waves, including Himinglaefa (Heofonglowe).

• Salo Sölvi, Ynglinga saga. As described here.

• Scyld Scefing the legendary ancestor of the Scylding dynasty.

• Scyld Halga's daughter Skuld, Hrólfs saga kraka. Hrothulf's half sister, Halga's daughter by an alf woman. Though confusingly similar, the name is not the same as that of Scyld Scefing one is feminine, the other masculine. The feminine means, roughly, 'guilt, debt, sin, or fault'; the masculine is etymologically connected with "shield". The alliance between Scyld Halga's daughter and Eadgils is my own invention, but seemed logical considering their family connection and their mutual hatred for Hrothulf.

• Sibbe Sif, Thórr's wife.

• Sigefrith in the Old English Beowulf, it is Sigemund who slays the dragon. I have kept Sigefrith to link my Beowulf with my other excursions into the heroic world of the Migration Age (Rhinegold, Attila's Treasure).

• Starchath Starkaðr, Gautreks saga, Gesta Danorum.

• Sugu Sýr, a by name of Freyja. 'Sow'.

• Sun the Sun is female in all the Germanic languages and lore.

• Swaefdaeg Svipdagr, Hrolfs saga kraka. One of Hrothulf's foremost thanes.

• Tiw Týr.

• Thrum Thrymr, an etin

• Thunar Thórr.

• Thura Hound Foot Thóri Hound Foot, Hrólfs saga kraka.

• Unferth Hrothgar's thule, a title which has been variously translated as 'orator', 'herald', and even 'jester', but which is identical to the Old Norse þul, a title which seems to indicate a man who is known for wise or possibly supernaturally inspired speech. Óðinn's names include Fimbulþul 'the great thule'; this, and Unferth's role as challenger of the hero, suggested a Wodenic identification. Unferth does not come off very well in the poem; I always suspected that he might have done better with a writer who was not a christian.

• Wealhtheow Hrothgar's wife. A dignified and respected figure in Beowulf, but one who, like Frigg, fails in her efforts to protect her sons by asking for peace pledges. Her retirement to God Home with Unferth is my own invention.

• Wihstan Waegmunding cousin to Beowulf, father of Wiglaf. Mentioned as Eanmund's slayer and receiver of his war gear in the poem. The original Beowulf never explains how Wiglaf ends up as an unblooded member of Beowulf's war band, but it made a great deal of sense to me that the killer of Eanmund wouldn't want to stick around in Sweden after Eanmund's brother became king.

• Wiglaf Waegmunding Beowulf's heir, son of Wihstan. The name, "Battle leaving (in the sense of a leftover, not in the sense of departure), can be interpreted as meaning either a warlike heirloom such as Wiglaf's sword (as Beowulf suggests at the end of chapter XII), or indicating a survivor (as Aldhelm mockingly says in chapter XIII, though his malicious interpretation is not intrinsic to the name). Both are extremely appropriate to Wiglaf.

• Woden Óðinn.

• Wyrd (personified) Old Norse Urðr. The eldest of the Norns; the determiner of fate.

• Yma Ymir, the father of all giants. Killed by Woden and his brothers, who made the world out of his body and the sea from his blood.

• Yrse Yrsa, Hrólfs saga kraka et al. 'Bitch' or 'She Bear'. Halga's bastard daughter by a queen; fostered by peasants; met and fell in love with Halga by chance. Her mother informed her of the situation after she had borne Hrothulf, whereupon she left Halga and married a Swedish king (Aðils/Eadgils in Hrólfs saga, Onela in Beowulf). Ended up as wife of Eadgils not a very happy marriage, particularly after his attempt to murder Hrothulf. The abduction of the Swedish queen is mentioned in Beowulf, though Yrse is not named in that section, and appears in the poem only as the sister of Hrothgar and Halga and the wife of Onela. The reliance of the Ingling kings on the holy queen as one of their sources of a ruler's legitimacy is a fictional extrapolation from the whole holy king/sacred marriage concept (see 'Frowe' above).

GLOSSARY

The language of Anglo Saxon and Norse poetry is incredibly rich, in part due to the extensive poetic vocabulary. Sadly, many of the key words which give the original works such a rich resonance have either been completely lost in modern English or are so archaic as not to be familiar to most readers. In the interest of maintaining the flavor of my sources, I have resurrected or reconstructed a number of them. I apologize to any readers who are disconcerted by this; I can only hope that you will find the reward worth the effort.

- aeht clan, family line
- ale an alcoholic malt beverage, often flavored with herbs, including hops. The word 'alu', found in runic inscriptions of this period and apparently suggesting 'good luck' or possibly 'magical power', is probably related to or identical to the ale word, an interpretation also hinted at by the tremendous importance of ritual/ceremonial drinking in Germanic society.
- alf an elf; Alfhame 'World of the Elves'
- arvel ceremonial drinking as part of a funeral ritual
- atheling a noble
- aurochs wild Northern European cattle, now extinct
- bairn a child
- bale poison
- bale fire funeral pyre
- bane slayer, cause of death
- barrow a burial mound
- beer not the modern hopped malt beverage: a sweet, very strong, fruit drink.
- berg mountain
- berg crystal rock crystal
- burg a fortress; a settlement around a fortress
- berserk a man who goes berserk in battle, becoming impervious to pain, demonstrating hysterical strength, etc. Berserks in the sagas tend to travel about in bands of twelve, and to be generally anti social, aggressive, and offensive.
- bridle rangle a noisy decoration for a horse's tack with several metal rings strung through a longer loop.
- byrnie chainmail shirt
- cachalot sperm whale
- carle a free farmer; also, used in general for a man.
- deem to judge; deeming 'judgement'
- draug a walking corpse
- dree to carry out, fulfill, or suffer usually in the phrase, 'dreeing one's wyrd'.

- drighten a warlord bound by oath to the members of his war band.
- drow see 'draug'
- elk the same animal is called 'moose' in America.
- eoten ON 'jötunn', modern English 'etin'. A giant.
- fetch roughly, the animal form which embodies a human's inner nature.
- fey doomed to die; in a state of irrationality presaging incipient death
- frith fruitful peace
- frea lord
- frowe lady
- frithle concubine/second wife or prostitute
- garth an enclosure
- geld payment
- ghast a nasty spirit
- glede a burning coal
- gudhe priest (Old Norse 'goði')
- gudhija priestess (Old Norse 'gyðja')
- hame skin; also used more widely to describe either a physical or a spiritual form.
- harrow an altar
- hide see 'hame'.
- hlaefdige 'Lady' (the Anglo Saxon origin of the 'lady' word), literally, 'loaf kneader'.
- hlaford 'Lord' (the Anglo Saxon origin of the 'lord' word), literally, 'loaf giver'.
- hof a temple.
- holt a forest
- howe a burial mound
- hwanna angelica
- idis a noble lady; also, a minor goddess much associated with luck of various sorts (I have used this modern reconstructed word instead of the Old Norse dís, which may not be identical to Anglo Saxon ides).
- kine cattle
- march border; march warder "border guardian"
- mead an alcoholic drink brewed from honey, sometimes with herbs or fruit added.
- mere pool
- Middle Garth Old Norse 'Miðgarðr'; the human world.
- nicor a supernatural water creature
- nith hate
- nithling coward/oathbreaker; generally scum
- orlog fate
- rede advice; also 'to rede' to give advice
- rett part of the process of preparing flax, it is left in dew or a stream to break down the fibres

•ring sword a sword with a gold ring attatched to the pommel, often
used for swearing oaths, also a sign of status (in that they were owned
by people of the class of people to whom oaths were sworn).
•rist to carve.
•rown to whisper
•rune a secret, a significant phrase, a verse.
•runestave a letter of the 'alphabet' in which runes are written. In this
period, the Elder Futhark (runic 'alphabet'; the word is taken from the
first six letters) is still being used. Each stave has its own name, and
seems to have been capable of carrying magical connotations related to
that name.

    Fehu: cattle
    Uruaz: aurochs
    Thurisaz: thurse
    Ansuz: god
    Raidho: riding
    Kenaz: torch
    Gebo: gift
    Wunjo: joy
    Hagalaz: hail
    Naudhiz: need
    Isa: ice
    Jera: harvest
    Eihwaz: yew
    Perthro: lot box
    Elhaz: elk
    Sowilo: sun
    Tiwaz: Týr
    Berkano: birch
    Ehwaz: horse
    Mannaz: man
    Laguz: water
    Ingwaz: Fro Ing
    Dagaz: day
    Othala: inherited land

    For those interested in more information about runic magic,
see 'Further Reading' below. Sadly, the most popular books on the
runes range from relatively uninformative to actively promoting
misinformation (such as Ralph Blum's ubiquitous A Book of Runes).
•sark a long tunic
•sax a long fighting knife or short sword, single edged.
•scathe to harm; a scathe an injury.
• poet a bard
•scot a tax
•scot king an under king who pays tax to a superior ruler

• seith a type of consciousness altering magic, usually malicious. An Anglo Saxon word 'ælfsiden' (elf seith) exists, referring to a nightmare or hallucination. I chose to use the normalized English 'seith' rather than 'siden' because of the word's familiarity to readers who are versed in Norse materials and its corresponding resonances of usually malign and perverse magic.
• shanks legs
• shild a debt
• sig victory
• skald a poet
• spae prophecy
• spear leek garlic
• spekheawer killer whale (literally 'fat cleaver')
• stave a staff or stick; also, a significant phrase or a poetic verse.
• stone bath sauna, known to the Norse and Anglo Saxons as well as the Finns
• Sunne wort St. John's Wort
• thane a warrior bound by oath to a drighten (the leader of a war band)
• thole to endure
• thrall a slave
• thule a Woden priest of a particular type characterized by verbal acuity; see 'Unferth'.
• thurse a type of giant.
• Tiw's Helm aconite (wolfsbane)
• tree god wooden idol
• troll a magical creature or thing. Often used more specifically for land wights in wild and rocky areas (the modern Norwegian troll).
• troll craft magic, probably hostile.
• troth oath, pledge, trust, belief
• udal lands inherited lands (as contrasted to bought or given; they frequently had a different legal status, and were certainly more emotionally important).
• ur old ancient
• Wael Hall Valhöll; 'Hall of the Slain'
• wain a wagon
• wand to transport
• wanhope despair
• ween to expect
• wend to travel
• weregild a death payment set by law or personal agreement, which could be honorably accepted in place of taking blood vengeance.
• wight in the most general sense, any being, including humans. More often used for land wights (local spirits) and unspecified supernatural creatures.
• wod madness; the howling wod rabies.

- Wod Host more commonly known as the Wild Hunt, although the related Wild Hunt legends (with a single hunter rather than an army of ghosts) are probably mediaeval in origin, whereas the Wod Host, the dead riders who storm through the air in winter weather, may go back to the earliest days of Germanic religion. Generally, but not necessarily, associated with Woden/Óðinn.
- wort fermenting ale; also, an herb.
- wyrd (non personified) fate, chance, luck.
- wyrm a snake or dragon.

FURTHER READING

Although this is a work of fiction, the historical and spiritual background of Beowulf's world exert a considerable fascination of their own. For those readers who are interested in such things or curious as to the origin of certain elements in this book, I recommend the following. These, of course, represent only a fraction of the materials I actually used in researching Beowulf.

NON FICTION

- Aswynn, Freya. The Leaves of Yggdrasil. Runic magic by a modern magician.
- Bauschatz, Paul. The Well and the Tree.
- Carver, Martin (ed.). The Age of Sutton Hoo.
- Ellis Davidson, H.R. Gods and Myths of Northern Europe
- Flowers, Stephen E. Runes and Magic. An academic text on runic magic in the historical period.
- Grettir's Saga. Grettir's adventures include a doublet of Beowulf's, and much has been written about the similarity between the two although their personalities are complete opposites.
- Gundarsson, KveldúlfR Hagan (ed.). Our Troth (out of print, but mostly available on the Internet via the Ring of Troth). A massive compendium dealing with both historical and modern practice of the native Germanic religion.
- Gundarsson, Kveldulf. Teutonic Magic. (The Three Little Sisters). One of the main sources for the runic magic in this book, although geared towards modern practice rather than academic study.
- Gundarsson, Kveldulf. Teutonic Religion (The Three Little Sisters).
- Hollander, Lee M. Poetic Edda (a verse translation).
- Lehmann, Ruth P.M. Beowulf (a verse translation).
- Sturluson, Snorri. Edda Snorra Sturlusonar (the Prose Edda); Ynglinga saga (in the collected Heimskringla).

- Ramqvist, Per H. Högom: The Excavations 1949 1984 chief source for the descriptions of such mundane things as belt fittings, saddles and tack, and tunic buttons. Other major sources for the physical culture of Beowulf's age were the Sutton Hoo excavation; the Oseberg burial; and the Valsgärde and Vendel excavations.
- Thorsson, Edred. Futhark: A Handbook of Runic Magic (Weiser). An excellent introduction for those interested in the practice of runic magic.
- Tolkien, J.R.R. "The Monsters and the Critics" (recently anthologized by Christopher Tolkien in a collection published under the same name); also, Finn and Hengest.
- Turville Petre, E.O.G. Myth and Religion of the North.
- de Vries, Jan. Altgermanische Religonsgeschichte; Altnordisches etymologisches Wörterbuch; "Contributions to the Study of Othin, especially in his Relationship to Agricultural Practices in Modern Popular Lore" (Folklore Fellowship Communications 94, 1931, pp. 3 79); "Wodan und die Wilde Jagd" (Nachbarn: Jahrbuch für vergleichende Volkskunde, 1963, 31 59).
- Many of the descriptions of life on the land are inspired by my own experiences on my farm. In regards to trying to scrape entrails out to make completely natural sausages: don't. For those intrigued by such homely crafts as cheese making, rendering tallow, etc., I can heartily recommend Carla Emery's The Encyclopedia of Country Living (Seattle: Sasquatch Books, 9th edn.).

FICTION

This is by no means the first effort to deal with Beowulf and his contemporaries in a novel form. Other books related to this topic, directly or peripherally, include:

Anderson, Poul. Hrolf Kraki's Saga. A brilliant translation/interpretation/retelling. Anderson also tries to integrate Beowulf coherently with Hrólfr, but takes the path of least interaction in regards to Beowulf and Dano Swedish politics, which suits better for a book retelling the Norse version.

Crichton, Michael. Eaters of the Dead (retitled The Thirteenth Warrior for the movie). This is a combination of ibn Fadlan's reports on the Rus along the Volga with the Beowulf story, via the invented abduction of ibn Fadlan. A note of caution: the author engages in the medieval literary tradition of citing invented sources to theoretically validate an original work. His notes on the alleged source from which his book is supposed to be translated are a part of his fiction. Having gotten past this, the book is great fun and the movie based on it is absolutely brilliant and surprisingly well researched in its details.

Gardner, John. Grendel. A modern classic in which Grendel is the point of view character.

Godwin, Parke. The Tower of Beowulf.

Niven, Larry, and Steven Barnes. The Legacy of Heorot; Beowulf's Children (confusingly retitled The Dragons of Heorot in a different edition). Science fiction about an isolated colony beset by water monsters. Despite the title and the name "grendels" for the monsters, it really doesn't bear much resemblance to the original.

Tolkien, John Ronald Reuel. The Hobbit. The sequence with Bilbo's theft of the cup and the dragon's subsequent annoyance is, of course, a direct steal from the old hoard of Beowulf.

Vollman, William. The Ice Shirt. Although this is mostly about the Viking explorations of Vinland, it includes a lengthy excursion into Ynglinga saga, which may be of interest to anyone fascinated by the tumultuous dynasty of the Inglings.

Beowulf's gods and goddesses are still worshiped by many people today. The chief American organization dedicated to the study and revival of native Scandinavian religion is the Ring of Troth, which can easily be found through any search on the Internet.

BIOGRAPHY

From his humble beginnings, Gundarsson would make his mark on the world by writing on the most rare and obscure myths breathing new life into them, for a new generation of readers. His fictional works written under Stephan Grundy focused on mythology and history and were met with international success. Along with his fictional works, Gundarsson made a name for himself writing books on Germanic Paganism (also known as heathenry) and Germanic Culture. He is an Elder in the organization The Troth where he has dedicated a majority of his life influencing major changes in the organization, including the development of anti-racist and anti-sexist ideals. He has fought for equality in transgendered communities, as well as fighting for the acceptance of Loki. Gundarsson has shaped heathenry through his numerous academic and fictional works as well as his extensive articles, thesis papers and his creation and sustainment of the lore program within The Troth. His hobbies included wood-working, jewelry making and gardening as well as historical re-enactment. He is currently attending medical school in Ireland supported by his loving wife Melodi where they maintain a local hof called The Tribe of Thor.

The Three Little Sisters

The Three Little Sisters is an indie publisher that puts authors first. We specalize in the strange and unusual. From titles about pagan and heathen spirituality to traditional fiction we bring books to life.

https://the3littlesisters.com